Boston Adventure

Other books by Jean Stafford

The Mountain Lion
The Catherine Wheel
Children Are Bored on Sunday
A Mother in History

Jean Stafford

Boston Adventure

A Harvest/HBJ Book
Harcourt Brace Jovanovich, Publishers
San Diego   New York   London

Library of Congress Cataloging in Publication Data

Stafford, Jean, 1915–
   Boston adventure.

   (A Harvest/HBJ book)
   Reprint. Originally published: New York: Harcourt,
Brace, c1944.
   I. Title.
PS3569.T2B6   1983   813'.54   83-8467
ISBN 0-15-613611-2

Printed in the United States of America

A B C D E F G H I J

For Frank Parker

Book One

Hotel Barstow

One

BECAUSE WE WERE VERY POOR and could not buy another
bed, I used to sleep on a pallet made of old coats and
comforters in the same room with my mother and father.
When I played wishing games or said "Star light, star
bright," my first wish always was that I might have a
room of my own, and the one I imagined was Miss
Pride's at the Hotel Barstow which I sometimes had to
clean when my mother, the chambermaid, was not feeling well. I knew its details so thoroughly that I had only
to say to myself the words "Miss Pride's room" and at
once my feet stood on the tawny rug with its huge faded
peonies, and before me was the window seat covered
with flat, flowered cushions, at one end of which was a
folded afghan, at the other, three big soft pillows on
which cherubs floated amongst blue daisies, holding up
in their dimpled hands a misty picture of a castle. And I
could gaze through the windows which overlooked the
bay. On a clear morning, looking across the green, excited water, littered with dories and lobster-pots and
buoys, I could see Boston and its State House dome,
gleaming like a golden blister.

Often at night, I pretended that I was sleeping in the big brass bed, under the fringed white counterpane, my head upon the inflexible bolster. Turning over, I imagined I could hear the rattling of the loose balls which decorated the foot-rail and which, when I tucked in the sheets, gave the Spartan bed, with its hard mattress and thin blankets, a kind of saucy vitality. Suddenly, as if it were borne on a wind, there came to me the fresh, acrid odor of Miss Pride's costly soap which she kept in a large carton under the bed. She was part owner of a soap factory, I had heard, and so, of course, it cost her nothing.

Some nights, though, my vanities were driven off, and I could not hold in my mind a picture of the room nor could I summon up the rich old lady. For on those nights, I lay terrified at the sound of my parents' quarreling voices. I mocked the deep breathing they expected of me, but the air would not go down into my lungs and was caught like a hiccough in my throat. There was a raw-edged blade of pain straight through my chest to my backbone as though fear had laid back the sheath of my nerves. Anxious for morning, I lay on my back staring at the invisible ceiling or cautiously I turned over on my side, making out the contours of the sagging bed where my mother and father were enormously sprawled out and humped up, hissing their fury at one another. Until I was about ten years old, though, my distress did not continue after their voices had ceased and, exhausted as much by being an audience as they were by being the actors, I would fall asleep at once. It was not until then, the summer of my tenth year, that I learned, in what terms of childhood I cannot remember, that peace was to be desired above all things. The upraised voices, the bitter blasphemies, the profound outcries of hatred carried through the day. If at the end of it there was a silent night, I lay awake for a long time waiting for the storm to break, and in the morning got up fretful for my vigil.

Our poverty was my mother's excuse for perpetuating the old anger. Although she had never been anything but poor, for her life in Russia before she married had been a tale of privation and suffering, still she had dreams of what it was like to be rich and, as she accused him, my father had promised her the finest of goods when he asked her to marry him. And what had she instead, she demanded. A two-room house in a fishermen's village where the sand seeped in the doorways and across the window sills, where the winter winds gained access through the cracks in the walls, and where in the summertime the heat descended from the low beaverboard ceilings in a steady, unmerciful blast. And had she to eat the fowl, the caviar, the strawberries and melons and pears he had promised? Our fare was no better than the poorest peasant's: day-old bread, *pokhlyobka*, side meat, and on great occasions, eggs. And did Shura Korf have a servant girl to go to the wine-cellar and fetch up champagne, Malaga, Rhine wines and Scotch whiskey, vodka and kümmel? Perhaps four times a year my father bought a bottle of corn whiskey from a bootlegger, and in the sordid kitchen they drank it in hot toddies which neither pleased their palates nor elevated their spirits and made them waken the following day with headaches, biliousness, and intermittent vertigo. Where were the yellow dresses, the summerhouse and the island in the lake, the solid silver samovar and the little black dog and the chestnut mare? What a brazen liar he had been! He was not the clever, ambitious man he had said he was when on the boat, caressing her as they leaned against the rail of the third-class deck, he had told her how he would have a great shoe business in the United States, selling only shoes made by hand and of the best leather money could buy. Why, he had declared he would have ten workmen under him! He would have commissions from the millionaires of New York City and Washington and Boston!

But see how it was instead: after ten years he was a nothing, a nobody. He *repaired* boots for the poor fishermen; he did not make them for the millionaires. He had not made a single pair for anyone but her, himself, and me.

My father, his pride lacerated, his shame festering would, at this point, retaliate. He would call on God as witness to his wife's failure to observe the laws of marriage: she did not honor him nor love him nor obey, but had made for herself a stifling little box of a life where she did nothing but slothfully brood and cry because she had no yellow dress. What man on earth would *want* to work for a creature like that?

I remember one of these quarrels especially well, not because it was different from any of the others, but because of what followed it on the next day. It was in September, the week before the Hotel Barstow was to close for the season, and I was awake, sorrowing that Miss Pride would soon go back to Boston and that all winter long I would have nothing to do but go to school. My father had gone off to the Coast Guard house where he often spent the summer evenings, playing checkers and drinking home-brew with the men off duty. I was always glad when he went, for usually it meant that my mother would be asleep by the time he came in. But tonight she was restless and several times she spoke to me, "I can't sleep. Sonia, are you awake, darling?" I did not answer and I heard her turn over, sigh and murmur to herself, "Too hot." It was always either too hot or too cold for her, and not even in the spring or the autumn would she admit that the temperature was pleasant. She would present her perspiring face to my father, or, in December, would hold out her blue hands and say, "You want to kill me!"

For some time I had been living with Miss Pride, first in her room at the Hotel and then in her unknown Boston house and I was either half-asleep or else so preoccupied with my thoughts that I did not hear my father come in and it was only when I heard my mother whisper, "I hate you! Christ God, I hate you!" that I realized he had got into bed and that the close room was full of his breath.

"Let me alone," said my father. "I'm drunk."

But my mother repeated her malediction over and over as if neither he nor she would ever realize its full meaning. After a while, my father howled wearily, "Then go away, for the love of God!" He turned over and the bed springs gave a prolonged creak. My mother, though, knew that he was not asleep, and she began to talk in a monotone, marshaling the injustices she had suffered her whole life long until their perpetrators thronged the room. She began, as was her custom, with the beastliness at hand: "He tells his wife to go away. First he promises her he will be rich and give her a fur cape and French perfume and a hothouse with a gardener to grow white grapes. And then, in a little bit, he tells her to go away out by herself in America where she don't know how to talk or beg. He wants this wife of his to be a beggar! You wish it was winter, don't you, *mein Herr?* So you could send me to the snow without shoes, me and my little girl. Well, sir, wait till the first cold weather and drive us out then. It won't be the first time for me. The child, she knows the words to beg with."

"You speak English," said my father.

She paid no attention. The past was advancing slowly upon her. I knew, because in the quiet I heard her sighing and I heard her rubbing her hands together as she always did when she was thinking of Russia. "It will not be the first time a man drove me into the snow."

"Shura!" implored my father. "Don't tell me again! I will go tomorrow to Boston for work if only you'll go to sleep now."

Heedless of him, she began. Under the night's still heat, her voice flowed like a deep, unbending river as for the millionth time, using the familiar words and images, she recounted the disasters of her childhood. It was a tale so fantastic that not even I, a little girl, could believe it. Yet it was one so horrible that to scoff at it would have been inhuman. In the pauses I listened but could not hear my father's breathing and I knew that he was wide awake, counting off each episode as it fell from her lips and calculating how many more were still to come before the end. As she mourned on, the heat was dispelled and the cold of Moscow's winter streets invaded the bedroom. As clearly as a few minutes before I had seen Miss Pride's afghan and pillows, now I could see nothing but crusted snow, a little cold, yellow sun, and the blue faces of poor people freezing in the gateways and the alleys.

When she was nine or ten years old, her mother died. Her father, who was a tailor and a libertine and a brute, commenced to drink heavily at the funeral dinner and continued to stay drunk for a week. It was in January and it was bitterly cold. The seven children, whom their father and his rioting friends drove away from the stove, kept warm only by hugging one another while the revelers, warm as toast with vodka and the stove heat, poked fun at the shivering little bodies and the chattering teeth and the bright red noses. One day, Constantin Ivanovitch Korf began to malign his dead wife, calling her in one breath a whore and a pious old crone, though she was neither but only a good hard-working creature who had come to the city from the farm and perhaps had died of years of homesickness.

Here came a hiatus in the narrative and I knew that my father, like myself, was mouthing the words that were to follow. She brought out: "The Russians are always homesick people." It was a minute or two before she went on, and in the firm enclosure of the silence, I seemed myself to ail like a Russian and a hot cloud grazed my eyelids.

"There was a yellow-haired German milliner who sat on his lap and pulled at his beard. *Fräulein* Lili, she called herself. I suppose she had no real parents and that was why she had no family names. She would sit there plucking the old goat's beard and call him, 'Constantin, my little bear.' Ah, it was sickening!"

His grief had flown away like a sparrow and he shouted for a song from *Fräulein* Lili. One of the children whimpered, whether from sorrow or shame or cold no one knew, but whatever its cause, the outburst was contagious and directly all the children were sobbing and wailing. You would have thought Constantin Ivanovitch would be too drunk to hear or care. But he flung the woman from his lap and stood up, his feet wide apart, shaking his fist at his sons and daughters. He shouted that he was through with his brats, they could freeze that night for all of him. Then he advanced and together they rose, holding up their little arms as if to thwart the blows from his hairy hands. They turned and made for the door as he followed, slapping their backsides until they were across the threshold. The door was shut. The bolt was drawn. Immediately the milliner began to sing:

> Till with age my hair starts graying,
> Till my locks have ceased to curl,
> Let me live in joy and gladness,
> Let me love a pretty girl!
> Let me live my life in joy and gladness,
> Let me love a pretty girl!

The children scattered, knowing that no one would take them all in together. Whether my mother wandered by herself for hours or for days, she was not sure, she said, for such cold as the cold of Moscow tyrannizes over the light and the dark; the sun is like one poor candle in a vast hall, or else, shining forth with a rowdy blaze, it burns and the kindled snow sears the eye. But at the end of whatever time it was, she was taken into the house of a witch, so-called because of her profession: for a price, she mutilated men who wished to escape military service. She cut off their fingers or their toes or broke the arches of their feet. This Luibka was a dried and wrinkled old prune of a woman with a cackling voice and a bright, shrewd eye and hands which, even in idleness, crooked as though they held a knife.

"*You* would have to come to Luibka, Hermann Marburg," she accused my father. "*You* would be too lazy and cowardly to be a soldier."

"I served my time," he replied dully.

"In Germany, yes, where everything is soft. But you would have come to Luibka in Russia where the food is scarce and the soldiers' boots are no good."

The witch was not a bad woman, my mother insisted, but was only the innocent slave of the wicked men who patronized her. The customers might cuff and kick the little girl who washed the knives and handed up the cloths, but the old woman never raised a finger against her and never spoke so much as a single word of reproof. And still, though she had enough to eat and a dry place to sleep, there came a time when the witch's kindness was not enough to stop my mother's ears to the screams

9

nor to close her eyes to the bloody blades and the anxious hound who sprang from his corner whenever a gobbet of flesh fell to the sawdust-covered floor. She was already a tall girl, about fourteen years old, when she left Luibka; and she was so comely that once she set about it, she had no trouble in finding work. She became a waitress in an officers' tavern. From two o'clock in the afternoon until two in the morning, she brought the gentlemen dinners and tea and suppers with champagne as well as the occasional glass of vodka and Löwenbräu beer, imported from Munich, the specialty of the house.

In many ways, my mother felt she had advanced considerably in the world for she was supplied with a pair of handsome uniforms and she was allowed to feed on delicacies, and her tips, because she was beautiful, were by no means trifling. And yet, with all her good fortune, there were times when she would sooner have been handmaiden to Luibka, for the officers made such impertinent overtures to her that she could scarcely sleep at night for shame. Once, in her second year, a cossack whose advances she had rebuffed slapped her face in a drunken fury and his companions jeered her and to him they cried, *"Touché!"* A few days later, she fell ill of a mysterious fever. She recalled that two old nuns, friends of the landlady of the tavern, came to see her sometimes in the afternoons and stroked her hot forehead with their cold white fingers. When she told them that her sickness had been brought on by a ruffian's spitefulness, they exchanged a glance and, smiling benignly down on her, they said perhaps God would call her to a convent.

All the officers were angry with Shura when she was well and went back to work, and as she served their dinners, they twisted her arms or dug their nails into her hands or stepped on her feet, and she was afraid to cry out lest she be discharged if the master learned how much his clients hated her. Once, as she was going home to her room a few streets away, a soldier followed and pushed her under the wheels of a cab; she was not hurt badly, but her face was cut and her whole body was one great bruise.

In her seventeenth year, she had saved enough money

out of her tips and wages to set forth into the world. It was on the boat which brought her to America that she met my father. A week after they disembarked they were married. How great had been her hopes the day she left Moscow! Her fellow waitresses, clinging to her, sobbing with envy, had sworn that she would be rich. Disentangling herself and mounting the steps to the train she laughed and called to them over her shoulder. "Your turn will come. Come to a picnic on my island, my dears!" And how close to fulfillment had seemed those hopes when the fair-haired German boy, tall, well-dressed, smelling of expensive cologne, had promised her that fine house, that immense wardrobe, those journeys to Paris and to Shanghai and to the Panama Canal. Each night, as the old boat rocked and groaned through stormy water, he shouted his promises over the racket of the wind and the protesting timbers.

"What do I have?" she groaned. "Nothing. No dresses, nothing but slops to eat. Ah, Hermann Marburg, I hate you from the bottom of my soul!"

My father, now that the long, sad tale was done, had had enough. He laughed at her, and that laugh, made up of all the scorn of devils and all the resentment of the damned, made me half sick to death with fright and I was glad for the darkness so that I could not see his genial face askew and scarlet, for the sound could not help corrupting what it issued from.

"Hush!" said my mother. "You'll wake up Sonia."

But he only laughed the harder, gasping and choking as though this glee were a convulsion beyond his control. Then, quieted, in a solemn, even voice, he said, "The child should never have been born."

His words concluded the scene. Worn out, they went to sleep. Over and over, until my eyes closed, I imagined the day on which my parents would die and Miss Pride would come to take me to live at the Hotel, if they died in the summer, or in Boston, if in the winter. Or I watched the waves part and saw a dry path laid for me between the water's furniture and then I stepped forward off the beach and walked across to the first wharf in Boston harbor. I could hear the calm waves washing the rocks and the shore and although my mind was far away, I could hear their undertone, gentle and melancholy, reiterating endlessly my father's words: the child should never have been born.

2

On the following morning, both my parents slept late, and I was on edge, fearful that my mother would not be on time at the Hotel or that a customer would come to my father's cobbling shop at the rear of the house and finding the place closed would leave and not return. My worry made my fingers all impatient thumbs and the fire would not start for me. Through a shimmering veil of tears, particulars of the room, aglow with morning sunshine, were distorted in a dream-like beauty: the stains of the dark blue sink under the window were invisible and it appeared, with the glittering waterdrops that depended from its brassy taps, patinated with green, like some old and precious vessel. The crimson geraniums on the sill above were blurred in a tropical splendor. As the kindling caught, my eyes cleared, winking away the transformation of the sink and seeing once again its preposterous graceful legs and its drainboard bristling with sodden splinters. I counted slowly to sixty before I lifted the stove-lid again to see the progress of the fire, and as I counted, stared at the two pictures which hung one above the other over the table. The lower one was a barnyard scene of russet hens and two majestic roosters avidly pecking at the foot of a pile of manure while beyond them there loomed a red barn from which stared out a thoughtful cow. The higher picture represented two little girls in white dresses and white satin slippers playing with five white puppies under the supervision of the snow-white mother dog.

When the kindling had caught, I dropped in a few lumps of coal, then waited until I had counted two hundred before I closed the damper. I gazed at one object until I had counted fifty and then shifted my eyes to another. We had three hard chairs with imitation leather seats adorned with lions' heads in bas-relief; a bright red step-ladder; a footstool made of a cheese box; a pea-green washstand where stood a pitcher and bowl, discarded by the Hotel Barstow. Long ago, when he had bought the house, my father had put shelves up against one wall which were called "the book shelves" although they contained only a German translation of *Riders of the Purple Sage*, a Bible, my schoolbooks and a very old copy of *Harper's Magazine* in which I had one time read a bewildering advertisement: "Everyone wants a gold tooth. Now you too can have one by sending only ten cents (10¢) for a complete Dento-Kit." The shelves were crowded with pliers, hammers, Mason jars full of bacon grease as old as myself, an empty caviar can which my mother fondled now and again in memory of the day, ages ago, when she had eaten its contents; broken pipes, broken knives, shattered sea-shells, a landing net, a wooden snake, a gauze bag filled with venerable headache pills.

Just as I lifted the stove-lid for the third time, the door to the bedroom burst open and my parents tumbled out, shouting at me to put the kettle on for tea and to run unlock the shop and to run to the Hotel to say Mamma was not well today and I would do for her. These tousled, foolish creatures seemed not the same at all as those hobgoblins who had rollicked and bawled in their temper tantrum the night before. My father, while he rubbed his eyes with one hand, patted my cheek with the other and said, "*Good* morning, *Fraülein*. Look sharp, there. Today is the day we get rich all of a sudden, *ni't wahr?*" My mother did not hear him, for she was running water at the tap for her perfunctory toilet.

My father gave me then a purposeless wink and nodded toward the box of corn flakes on the table. "Esel von Hexensee hasn't eaten his hay yet." This was my favorite joke. Out in the shop, in the dark little room that smelled of pipe smoke and leather, he made up stories, pretending that I was a boy named Fritz or a donkey named Esel von Hexensee, and if I were the latter, he would fit a saddle to my back and two Concord grape baskets for panniers and drive me up the Zugspitz

13

for some droll, pious purpose such as taking hot soup to Fritz who had fainted from the altitude. The games delighted me and when he was tired of playing, I would beg him to go on. "Na," he would say, suddenly sober. "I am stiff from beating that *Dummkopf* Esel," and picking me up like a cat, he would put me out of the shop and bolt the door behind me.

I drank a cup of tea that had not brewed long enough, swallowed a few spoonfuls of corn flakes and ran out of the house towards the road leading to the Hotel. The fishermen were untying their boats and calling greetings to one another. Their wives stood on the doorsteps complaining to their neighbors that it looked like "another scorcher." Mrs. Henderson, who lived next door to us, cried something to me but I did not hear what she said and I ran on, flinging back, with no thought of its meaning, "I know it!"

We did not live far from the Hotel, perhaps no more than a quarter of a mile, but because after the cluster of fishermen's cottages there were no houses at all on either side of the curving white road, it seemed a long and tedious distance. Here there were no shade trees to interrupt the glare of the sand and the dry flowers that straggled half-heartedly along the road were too dwarfed even to cast a shadow. It was a relief to take a turning and then, from a slight rise, to see the big white frame Hotel with its bright flower beds and its verandas where hung baskets of fern and ivy.

The Hotel Barstow was the sort of place which never changes and then, with very age, it falls and the site is used for a new structure. Such a day was impossible to imagine. Anyone who had lived there assumed that the stuffed hoot-owls and the Wilson snipes and the herons would go on forever patiently standing on one leg in hoary moss or placidly sitting on unseen eggs behind their glass cases in the dining-room, that until the end of time the same old ladies, musty-smelling and enfeebled, would be offered cream-of-wheat as the first entrée on the evening menu. Forever, too, the same sort of pert, plump man would stand behind the curved desk in the lobby, fetching down keys and mail and inquiring after his guests' health.

Miss Pride, an early riser, was drilling on the beach, unwithered in spite of the sun which was already very warm. The clerk, Mr. Hagethorn, called from the veranda, "Well, Miss Pride, is it hot enough for you today?"

Unsmilingly she replied, "I observe no change from yesterday. Has the mercury risen?" Even in midsummer, she always wore black broadcloth suits and an olive beaver hat. She apparently suffered neither from the heat nor from the cold, for she did not shiver or perspire, and she was never heard to discuss the temperature.

I slackened my pace in order to hold her in my vision: straight as a gun-barrel, she carried her lengthy shadow up and down the golden sand; or she rested it, squarely facing Boston, looking with her formidable eyes into the very conscience of her care-taker who was probably loafing on the job. I had heard someone say of my mother, "She is beautiful except in one thing, her eyes are too large." I believed, therefore, that Miss Pride was beautiful for hers were very small. They were eyes more like a bird's than any other creature's: that is, such was their intensity and their sharp change of direction (they never wandered, but rather, disconnected their focus from one point of concentration and abruptly fixed it upon the next) that they gave the impression of being flat to the skull or slightly convex, that they had a container more like a plate than a socket. They were "on" her head rather than "in" it. I suppose in her passport they were called "gray" or "hazel," but to me they were "cold gold" and were like the yellow haze that followed sundown when the shine of the sand was gone.

I hesitated a moment in the hope that she might turn and greet me. A sigh, involuntary and profound, ruffled up through my lips and when it had passed, I ran to the back of the Hotel. Without explaining to the head chambermaid that my mother was ill, I snatched a mop and a broom and a dust-cloth from the closet off the kitchen and ran up the backstairs two at a time. For I wanted to repeat the strange experience I had once had of regarding Miss Pride through the windows of her very own bedroom. She was still on the beach when I stole to the central window. Now a few bathers had come for an early dip and Miss Pride was plowing up and down through the sand, fixing them with her clear, indifferent eyes as though, without loss of dignity to herself, her gaze could penetrate them to their very giblets. As I watched her, taking in with admiration each detail of her immaculate attire and her proud carriage, I heard, from the adjoining room, embedded in a yawn, the waking squeal of Mrs. McKenzie, a garrulous and motherly old woman whom I had always disliked. Her room was no pleasure to clean: her bed was strewn with corsets and short-sleeved nightdresses, and on her bedside table, I often found drying apple cores which I removed gingerly, having in my mind an image of her with her sparse hair unpinned sitting up in bed cropping with her large false teeth. Upon the bureau, amongst sticky bottles of vile black syrups and tonics and jars of fetid salve, there lay her bunion plasters and her ropes of brown hair which she sometimes arranged in a lofty cone on top of her head. Usually she was in the room when I entered and she saluted me with disgusting moonshine as "mother's little helper" or asked me if my "beauteous mamma" was sick.

Now in Miss Pride's room, there was never anything amiss. Perhaps once or twice a summer, I found a bottle of imported wine or whiskey on her writing desk; this was the only medicine she took and she took it regularly in small quantities. On the bureau, the china hair receiver did not receive a wisp of hair, and there were neither spots nor foreign objects upon the white linen runner. A hatpin holder, sprouting long, knobbed needles, two cut-glass cologne bottles, and a black glove-box, shaped like a small casket, were reflected in the clear swinging mirror. Though I should have loved to dearly, I had not the courage to investigate the drawers which were always neatly shut, but I was sure that they were in scrupulous order. The other old ladies, almost without exception, allowed the feet of stockings and the straps of camisoles to stream from each gaping tier like so many dispirited banners.

As I watched, Miss Pride ascended the steps that led from the Hotel beach, and I knew that now she would enter the dining-room and, after she had eaten one boiled egg and one slice of toast, she would examine the newspaper over her coffee while all about her, her coevals would be prattling of their sound sleep or their insomnia, depending on how the dinner of the night before had affected them. It seemed to me that Miss Pride looked up and saw me even though my face was hidden by the marquisette curtains and my body was behind the heavy drapery. I backed away from the window and began to run the oiled mop over the edges of the floor which the rug did not cover. While I worked, I heard Mrs. McKenzie thrashing about in the bed and rise finally, stumbling over her shoes, bumping against the furniture and repeating her vociferous yawn. The sound of the bed rolling across the floor, as I pulled it out to make it, roused her to rap on the wall and cry, "Good morning, Mrs. Marburg! I've been a lazybones again today!"

I did not answer. There was something in the tone of her voice, a quality of dampness—as though the words themselves were kisses from unminded lips—which embarrassed me. She called again, "Yoo, hoo, Mrs. Marburg!"

"It's Sonie," I grudgingly gave out.

"Oh. Well. Sonie, I'll be out of my room in three shakes of a lamb's tail and then you can come get me straight."

"Yes, ma'am."

"Get yourself a lemon drop, dear!"

Presently I heard her door open and close and heard her toil down the stairs, one dropsical foot at a time. I now worked rapidly, brushing my cloth over the bed-side table, the writing desk, and the bureau, plumping up the cherub pillows and setting the bolster precisely at the head of the bed. When I had finished, I stood for a few minutes before the mirror and, as I had done many times before, pulled out the stoppers of the bottles and inhaled their clean, alcoholic fragrance. I opened the black box and gazed upon the white silk button gloves, the yellowing white kid and black chamois ones, amongst which were scattered single cuff-links, broken bone buttons, a mysterious, star-shaped brooch and three edible beads. My brief survey finished, I sat down before the desk and though I touched nothing, I took in everything: the brass letter opener with its carved wood scabbard, the matching ink-pot and pen and the dark green blotter in a brown leather holder, the calendar which gave the date, September 7, 1925. A week from today she would leave. All winter she would live in a house I had not seen and could not imagine, a house of which I knew nothing except that it was on the celebrated Beacon Hill, perhaps close by the luminous dome of the State House. My sorrow was reinforced when I saw a stamped letter, addressed in her careful hand to her niece, Miss Hopestill Mather, Camp Pocahontas, Southport, Maine. For, if I could not envisage the house which stole her away from me each autumn, I knew exactly what the little girl looked like who lived with her. Once, the summer before, when she was ten years old and I was nine, she had been brought by a small nervous woman, Mrs. Brooks, her second cousin, to have luncheon at the Hotel. She had been so self-assured, carried her head with such a grown-up dignity that she seemed advanced in her teens. I, who that day had been charged with filling the water glasses, stared from the sideboard at her bright red hair, caught at the left temple by a green ribbon and falling down her back, long and straight, over a white batiste dress, printed with tiny yellow flowers. As I passed by Miss Pride's table on my way to Mrs. Prather, I heard her say, "How absurd, Auntie! You ought to know the counselors are all stupid." And later, when I had returned to my post where, sick with envy of her voice and her cultured language I felt my face color and the pulse in my forehead leap, she signaled me with her white hand, calling, "Waitress! Water, please."

I could linger no more in Miss Pride's room, but cleverly I omitted to put clean towels on the rack beside the washstand in order that I might return after my other work was done, this afternoon when she had gone for a drive.

It was nearly luncheon time when I came into the lobby to dust the albums on the brocade covers of the round tables, and all the old ladies were spryly exercising the rocking chairs on the veranda, having a chat about relatives with diabetes and friends with Bright's Disease, and talking of their own improper pains, their bizarre sensations in the region of the gall-bladder, and their physicians who were either "very understanding" or obscurely "unsatisfactory."

"I love cucumbers," Mrs. Prather was saying, "but they don't love me."

Mrs. McKenzie replied, "I'm the same way with seedy things. They give me heart-burn and of course they clog the colon."

I drew back my hand with horror from the golden callosities of the "worked" cover on the albums for, smooth and round, they resembled human organs as I recalled them from the colored diagrams in my hygiene book.

A voice I did not know well inquired, "Has the Hotel Barstow always had a restricted clientele?"

"No, indeed!" cried Mrs. McKenzie. "About three years ago, a new manager came, a really vulgar person whom I'm perfectly certain was a Jew although his name was Mr. Watkins. And by the time I arrived—I came a little late that year—the Hotel was swarming with uninvestigated guests. I dare say we won't forget Mr. Johnson in a hurry, will we?"

The story of Mr. Johnson, one of the veranda favorites, was retold for the newcomer. From what walk of life he had come was impossible for anyone to tell. But he was no gentleman as a child could see in the first glance at his reversible silk shirts, his diamond tie-pin, his bright orange oxfords and his loud, checked jacket. He teased the old ladies by putting a bottle of bootleg whiskey on his table in the dining-room in imitation of their phials of medicine. "Oh, my hair hurts so," he would say and take a drink. He carried a walking stick, although he was neither a cripple nor a great walker, and the other guests thought it was probably hollow and contained a rapier.

"I've heard of such a thing, you know," said Mrs. McKenzie. "When my poor sister was in Wiesbaden taking the baths for her arthritis which nothing on earth would cure—how much money she spent I couldn't tell you and she must have suffered twenty years—there was a man living in a pension a block away who was proved beyond a shadow of a doubt to have a rapier in his stick."

"But now," pursued the unfamiliar voice, "now your manager is discreet?"

"Oh, Mr. Hagethorn is the soul of caution. He caters solely to those of us who have been coming here for at least twenty years. We call ourselves the Barstow family."

Mr. Hagethorn, pleased with the compliment that had come to his attentive pink ears, bawled in authority, "Sonie, clean up around the ferns there. Don't dawdle." The ferns and several potted palms made a little triangular garden in the far corner of the lobby, and as I made my way towards them, I perceived Miss Pride, sitting erect on a straight chair, half hidden by the foliage. This was her reading hour. Today she held *The Atlantic Monthly* directly in front of her. Her thin lips were set in concentration beneath her short, sharp nose with its contracted nares. She did not look up when I knelt down, three feet away from her and began to brush the fallen fronds into a dust-pan. I kept my eye on her and presently I saw a frown invade her high forehead. I did not know if she had come to a word she did not understand or if she were annoyed with the chatter that came through the screen door. Evidently the old ladies were now scrutinizing the fashionable young people on the beach who had drifted down from the smarter hotels and who were clad in bathing costumes that exposed long, sun-browned legs. "I just don't know," said someone, "I just don't know. Are we advancing? Or are we going back to paganism? I don't say it's immoral to expose the legs to the public eye: I say it's not fastidious. Why, our chambermaid, Mrs. Marburg, has more modesty than those young ladies out there who, you can rest assured, either have come out or will come out at the Chilton Club."

Even at this mention of my mother and although she must have known that I was beside her, Miss Pride did not look at me. Her frown deepened; reluctantly she closed her magazine just as the only male guest of the Hotel, Mr. Brock, slipped quietly through two pots of fern, carrying with him a folding chair which he set down beside hers. What impressed me in that moment was that the frown, which had lasted two or three minutes, showed that she had known of his approach long before I either heard or saw him.

"Good morning! I hope I am not disturbing you at your devotions?" The chuckle following his remark was not returned and Miss Pride only said, "Good morning."

Mr. Brock was a soft-spoken and scholarly old man who, although he had come from New York, called himself "a professional Bostonian." He was a victim of a delusion which he propounded, whenever he had the opportunity, to myself, my mother, the Mexican gardener, Gonzales, to Mr. Hagethorn, to the waitresses. He believed that of all languages, only the English was capable of vulgarity, and he claimed that bad American books were transformed by translation into promising, if not brilliant, prose. He had made a collection of such translations, having E. P. Roe, for example, rendered into French and the Elsie Dinsmore books into Spanish. He had given my father his copy of *Riders of the Purple Sage* and my father, although he was totally indifferent to Mr. Brock's thesis, so thoroughly enjoyed the book for its adventure that the old man danced for joy, sure that this was the proof of the pudding.

Now he produced a leather-bound book from his brief-case and handing it to Miss Pride, said, "I sought you out to show you my latest find. This is *Bob, Son of Battle* in German or *Old Bob, der graue hund von Kenmuir* and it is enchanting. Would you care to read it?"

"No, Mr. Brock, I would not," said Miss Pride sternly. "I do not share your enthusiasm for foreign languages. And as for dog-books I had no use for them in my girlhood and feel quite sure I would find them even less to my taste now that I have passed beyond the age for juvenile literature."

He was not rebuffed. "I admire your linguistic singleness, Miss Pride, since in you I am sure it is the result of strong nationalistic convictions. Alas, we are not all by opinion or antecedents eligible for membership in the English Speaking Union."

"I am not a member of the English Speaking Union," she returned. "But in any case your remark is, to use a foreign phrase, a *non sequitur*."

Mr. Brock, receiving the book which she extended, allowed his disappointment to show briefly in his foolish old face and then, catching sight of me, he cried, "Now here is someone whose father will appreciate the book." In a voice a little lower but not intended to be inaudible to me, he added, "Did you realize that this child's father is an educated man?"

"I believe I haven't had the pleasure of knowing him." Miss Pride took me in, perhaps for the first time since I had been coming to the Hotel, and I felt that in her rapid but comprehensive examination of my face and person she had discerned everything about me, that she knew I had once broken my collarbone, that I did poorly in arithmetic and singing and well in reading, and that brushing my teeth had not yet become habitual with me.

"Yes," Mr. Brock went on, "Hermann Marburg, the Chichester cobbler, is an educated man. A graduate of the *gymnasium* of Würzburg, Germany, and, except for an ineffacable accent which I myself find appealing, has been completely bilingual since the age of eleven, and partially trilingual—his third language, of course, being French—since the age of fifteen."

Miss Pride did not seem impressed but rather than humiliate me, as I assumed, said nothing. "I have had several illuminating conversations with Mr. Marburg, sometimes in German, sometimes in English. I neglected to mention, by the way, that through his wife he has also picked up quite a considerable Russian vocabulary. Now a graduate of a *gymnasium*, Miss Pride, as you are perhaps not aware, is, if anything better educated than a candidate for an American baccalaureate degree. Yet the *gymnasium* is the counterpart of our preparatory school!"

"What do they learn?" inquired Miss Pride, frankly dubious.

"Having been something of a Latinist myself at Mr. Greenough's, naturally I admire Mr. Marburg's firm classical foundation. I must admit his Latin is less literary than ecclesiastical, for he was trained by the Franciscans, but it is, nevertheless, good, sound Latin. In addition he knows history. Oh, he knows his history *well*, Miss Pride! Roman and the French Revolution are his specialties. And then, although he's a modest man, I have no doubt in the world he could put many of our Harvard men to shame in the field of philosophy. Literature he is not so keen on although he did drop the remark that he had at one time been a great admirer of Goethe. Now there is a man who has the perspicacity to see what I mean when I say that in his language *Riders of the Purple Sage* is a superb piece of craftsmanship."

Miss Pride had had enough. She rose and her face, shaded by the wide brim of her hat, represented the pure substance of scorn. "You will forgive me, Mr. Brock, for finding your crotchet fantastic. It is my cantankerous opinion, sir, that you do not believe this nonsense yourself, but that you wish to disguise your appetite for rubbish. Not to put too fine a point on it, how could you, without the aid of some such camouflage, indulge yourself in Elsie Dinsmore at the age of seventy-two?"

Mortally wounded, he gave her a wan smile. "Your wit is all that it is said to be, ma'am."

Less coldly but with the same firmness she went on, "What interests me about this Mr. Marburg is, does he make his shoes well? Does he know *that* craft, Mr. Brock, as well as his Latin?"

"Oh, I have no idea. I never discuss business with him."

Miss Pride was looking at my feet, shod in a pair of white moccasins which my father had made. I was ashamed that they were so dirty and that my socks were ragged. She turned at the announcement of luncheon, but I did not fail to hear her say to Mr. Brock as they crossed the lobby, "I gather that he knows his business and has little of it."

After Audrey, the headwaitress, and I had set the tables for dinner, I went upstairs with Miss Pride's fresh towels. The corridor was quiet, for all the guests were napping. I could hear, through the wall by Miss Pride's bed, the faint popping of air in Mrs. McKenzie's nose as she slept deeply. Immediately I took my post at the windows and in about a quarter of an hour, I saw Miss Pride go down the wooden stairs of the porch, pinching the hand-rail with her gloved fingers. Then she waited on the lawn for her high, black limousine. Once I had seen in it vases for flowers on the sides, hanging like pictures in a house. I believed she had other decorative furnishings in the back seat as, perhaps, a needle-point footstool and a writing board. What if she even had a tea-table and at a suitable hour and place, ordered the car to be stopped and then served herself tea! I would dwell on this enchanting thought sometimes as long as half an hour, seeing with an overwhelming happiness the actual seeds of the strawberry jam.

Here came the car! Slipping round the corner of the Hotel, its long black snout caught the rays of the sun which shot fitfully into my eyes. It stopped and Mac, the chauffeur, stepped out. He was a thin, sharp, silvery young man who, in his gray livery, looked like an up-right rat. He suffered from some strange distemper that caused his feet to swell, but though the valetudinarians of the veranda perpetually foretold Miss Pride's doom when the man while driving should die at the wheel (for they were enough acquainted with his symptoms to know that foot swelling indicated a rheumatic heart for which there was *no cure*), she kept him on and about twice a week was handed into the car by his lean, gray paws which, since they went out and withdrew so quickly, seemed to abhor their contact with the desiccated elbow that they briefly cupped.

"Well, Mac," came her voice, "I trust we are all in order. I must run in to Pinckney Street today."

So that was the name of it: Pinckney Street. I repeated the words to myself and the house where she lived all winter now seemed less strange because it was not merely in Boston but was in a specific street with a specific number of houses. Henceforth my daydreams would not begin with the vague condition, "When I live in Boston with Miss Pride," but with, "When I live on Pinckney Street."

"Oh, but before we go," she said, her foot on the running board, "I want you to take me to the shoemaker here. A Mr. Marburg."

The car drove off and I sank into the chair at the writing desk, faint with a conflict. For the joy I felt in Miss Pride's going to call on my father was scotched by my shame of our shabby shop, my father's untidiness, and my mother's loquacity. Nor did I know whether she was seeking him out as Mr. Brock did, because he was educated, or if she was going to him on business, to have him half-sole her Ground Grippers. If her intention were the latter, now, at this very moment, I must relinquish my ambition to be her young and well-beloved friend.

The letter to her niece was gone from the writing desk and in its place was one addressed to herself and postmarked London. I was less moved by the foreign stamp and the strange, thin paper of the envelope than I was by what next caught my eye: it was my own name, Marburg, written on a memorandum pad together with the legends: "Call Breckenridge at three" and "flue in the upstairs sitting-room." That meant, then, that there was also a *downstairs* sitting-room so that the house was surely big enough to accommodate me as well as Hopestill Mather and Miss Pride. Perhaps even now she was saying to my father that although she realized he was a good man and well educated, she believed he owed it to me to give me a better home which she herself was willing to provide.

While I was meditating, I was interrupted by Mrs.

25

McKenzie. She took very short naps and I heard her suffocated scream. I was afraid she might sense my presence in the room next to hers and summon me to eat a lemon drop or send me to the village to fetch her a bottle of Moxie. I tiptoed out of the room and through the Hotel and then stood in the back yard hesitating. For I could not decide whether to go directly home and present myself in the shop where the interview would probably take place—unless my mother's curiosity were aroused at the sight of the black car and she insisted that they sit in the kitchen—or to go down to the Point and wait there until it should be over, passing the time in watching the sailboats and the barges going out from Boston harbor. But as I debated, I saw two old ladies round the corner of the Hotel with walking sticks and parasols, and I heard one of them say, "It's not far. The view is gorgeous and at this time of day, we'll have the whole Point to ourselves."

In order that my mother might not intercept me, I took the toad on the bay side of the peninsula, approaching the shop from the rear. I stood on tiptoe outside the window and I saw, enveloped in the shadows, Miss Pride seated primly on a stool beside the wheels and shoe stands, while my father knelt, taking the measurements of her right foot. This foot, short and narrow, wore a tan silk stocking with heavy cotton reinforcements at the toe and heel, and I was momentarily shocked at the sight, for I had assumed that every article of her clothing, down to her underwear, would be black.

"I understand that you are a friend of one of my fellow-lodgers, Mr. Brock," she was saying.

"He comes sometimes. He is a scholar, I suppose."

Miss Pride smiled. They were both silent as he removed her other shoe and began to measure the left foot. I wondered what she thought of this large shaggy man who always looked unkempt and would have even if he had fastidiously groomed himself. He was the opposite, in this respect, of my mother who never looked dirty or untidy though she was both, and to a far greater degree than he. He was a tall man and the muscles of his youth had not yet been overlaid by flesh, but, at thirty-three, had begun to sag a little as though they were preparing themselves for a permanent relaxation. His thick, yellow hair looked like a palm thatch and now, as he bent over and it fell forward from his skull, I felt that I could lift up a flap of it and clip it at a single root like the midrib of a leaf. His face was broad and red and its hollows were scooped out cleanly so that, although it was full, the shape of the skeleton was clearly visible. His chin was cleft and his lips, whose usual attitude was one of curving downward, were quiet and contemplative and seemed not to belong to the chilled blue eyes which were those of a decisive man. Today, because of the heat, he was dressed like a boy and when he stood up to get something from the work table which required him to turn in my direction, I saw to my embarrassment that his white, short-sleeved shirt was torn at the shoulder, revealing a segment of skin, browned by the sun on the days he had gone bathing. His hair seemed fairer than usual and at the temples it was almost white.

Miss Pride, who had been leaning over his bent back, withdrew as he stood up, and she said, "I expect a good pair of shoes, Mr. Marburg. Your price is steep, but I have every confidence in German workmanship."

He did not rise to her compliment but gave only the smile which politeness demanded. I fairly danced with impatience in the sand at his unresponsive face and at the impudence which had made him charge her a high price when he should, I thought, have done the work free and presented her as a gift the finest pair of shoes he could make. Ah, if she had come to call on *me*, not my father, how I would have entertained her! I would have made her a pot of tea and run to the village for a lemon and half a dozen jellied doughnuts. And I would have listened carefully to every word she said and nodded my head in constant agreement as she talked.

Although she saw that he was disinclined to talk (he could so easily, with the opening she had given him, explain that he had not always been a poor, shabby man, but that in Germany, he had been of a well-to-do family), she persevered. "You learned your trade in Germany, did you not?"

"Oh, yes!" In his voice, there was an impulsive note which, combined with my sudden apprehension of a half-empty whiskey bottle on the shelf over the door, alarmed me, and I was afraid that he might begin to calendar, not the events of his past life, but its errors. For when he had been drinking, he became neither rebellious nor self-pitying as did my mother, but he brooded, morosely accusing himself of heartless infidelities to the traditions of the Catholic church, of his family, and of his country. My mother believed herself to be persecuted by everyone she had ever known—with the exception of Luibka, myself, and a few neighbor women —but he knew, and was powerless to rectify the fault, that all his torture came from his own flabby will which swung him like a pendulum between apathy and fretful indecision. I could see through the clouded windowpane that he was preoccupied with some tangential thought as he wrote down the specifications of Miss Pride's feet in his notebook, and I was in mortal terror that he was going to tell her how long it had been since his last confession. When he did speak again, it was not in self-accusation, but it was from a point far removed from her question.

He said, "But even so, they don't know good shoes from bad here."

"If by 'here' you mean Chichester," returned Miss Pride, "I'm certain you're right. And while they might know skill when they saw it, these poor fishermen could not pay for it. But I beg to differ with you if by 'here' you mean something larger. Don't you think, Mr. Marburg, that in Boston, *we* know the real thing?"

The light which flickered in my father's face was quickly extinguished. "It's too late for *that*," he said.

"You are an obdurate man, sir. My father used to liken your countrymen to our own Puritans. Therein, he said, lay the greatness of the nation. I must confess Papa and I never saw eye to eye on your 'greatness' for even as a young lady, I was displeased with your romancing and your 'earth-spirit' but I can see that some of you are hard-headed. If you were not, how could you work so cleverly?" She paused, watching my father closely as though she were waiting for a reply or a confirmation, but neither was forthcoming. She went on. "If you came to Boston, you would be out of the doldrums. I recollect the governess to the child of one of my friends. When she came, poor *Fräulein* Ströck, she was timorous and wistful, for she had been for some time in an establishment in the middle west where her gifts—a little too Prussian for my liking—were not appreciated in the least. But she had not been with us, with Boston, that is, for a month before she had blossomed into what she had been born to be, a first-rate disciplinarian. I believe you will find we have our feet on the ground and that we need no divining rods to find our treasures."

My father, no more than I, did not know what to make of her lecture. Had I been inside with them, I would have inquired how many children were under Miss Ströck's charge or why it was that she was too Prussian to please Miss Pride entirely. My disappointment in my father's indifference and in the gesture he made of passing his hand before his face as if he were befogged, was converted into anger as I realized that he did not intend to make any sort of comment at all. Surely he, a grown-up man with an education so proudly advertised by Mr. Brock, could select something out of that subtle speech as a point of departure! How stupid and contrary of him not to ask, at least, if Miss Pride had ever been to Germany. Why, I, a little girl, could do that much!

But Miss Pride, to my astonishment, did not appear annoyed. With a grace which obviated the need for a transition, she said, "If I am pleased with my shoes, I shall want you to make more for me. I shall be anxious to put you in the way of further commissions. Surely you won't refuse."

"No," he said, but there was neither gratitude nor excitement in his voice. "If I am nothing else, I am a workman who does his work."

She stood up. "Now when the shoes are finished, you

may mail them to me at this address." Taking a leather case from her handbag, she extracted a card from it. "I must say there is something about your shop I like. It strikes me as what I spoke of before: the real thing. Nothing is so close to my heart as that, sir: the real thing. And if you had known my father, you would see I came by my passion honestly."

"I hope you will be satisfied with the shoes," said my father. "But you must not expect too much. My hands are not as clever as they used to be. I am, you see, no longer a shoemaker, I am a shoe-fixer."

Miss Pride gave him her hand. "It's time you changed. Good-by."

He stood stupidly in the center of the room and did not open the door for her, did not, indeed, bid her good-by. When she had gone and the motor of her car started up, he sat down on the stool she had just occupied and putting his hands over his face, the fingers so tightly interlocked that their knuckles whitened, he groaned with some profound, enigmatic misery, and I stepped softly away from the window, perplexed that she who could cause me only happiness had caused him only pain. As I went toward the house, I was gradually infected by his terrible sorrow and felt my face grow feverish, recalling his words last night: the child should never have been born.

In the kitchen, I ran my fingers over the cold stove. My mother was sitting in a chair beside the sink and she drew me down to kiss me. "Who do you love, little Sonie girl?" she said, gazing at me with her great black eyes. And while I answered her as she desired me to, my mind was telling me the truth: "Miss Pride, not you, Mamma."

Two

DURING THE TWO YEARS that my father supplied Miss Pride, her niece, and a couple of her friends with shoes, there were frequent conferences on the advisability of buying me a bed. But because the plans were always projected when my parents were drinking a bottle of whiskey and the morning found them oblivious of everything but their malaise, I continued to sleep on my pallet, made a little longer now to accommodate my increased height. Our prosperity was manifested in very little beyond a regular Saturday night pint of liquor. We did have a cerise rayon bedspread, a piebald linoleum for the kitchen floor, an eccentric shower-bath crowded into the minute closet we called the "bathroom," and I had a red coat with an astrakhan collar. But my mother had none of the things she longed for, and if my father, when he was drinking, offered to buy her a yellow dress, she refused, saying sadly that she did not want pretty clothes unless she had an estate with a lake where, on its island, she would be hostess at summer picnics. My father would commend her good sense and tell her, in a foxy whisper, as if for the first time, that he was "laying

31

away a little something" and in a few years his savings would accomplish everything her heart desired.

When there was no whiskey to provide a recess in their old war, they sang two different tunes. My father cried that he was enslaved to Miss Pride whom he had come to detest, for he believed that her patronage of him was an alms-deed. "Four pairs of shoes in one winter for an ugly old woman!" he exploded. "Maybe she sells them at a profit. She can't wear out my shoes so quick!" He was displeased, too, that all his transactions with her were conducted by mail, as if she counted herself too good to come to his shop. When she ordered a new pair of shoes for her niece, she sent a careful drawing of the girl's feet together with the height of the arches. And when the sandals or the moccasins or dancing pumps were delivered, he received a curt note of thanks which was folded around the check. Time and again he declared, "I will make no more for them." But he could never resist new, costly leather and he always took the work.

My mother, on the other hand, deplored his failure to exploit his Boston customers and said, with considerable truth, that if we moved across the bay to the city and opened up a shop there, we would really become rich. Then I could have as many pairs of shoes as Hopestill Mather and she could be driven about in a black car like Miss Pride's. But nothing could avail against my father's indolent pessimism, and he went on living in our poor little village precariously, like someone who, being exposed to the cold, finally quits the struggle to keep awake and sinks into what he knows is his last sleep.

For myself, I was torn between gratitude to Miss Pride for noticing us at all, for affixing her signature to letters to my father—letters bearing her address on Pinckney Street—and the knowledge that her relationship with us would never be anything but commercial. Nevertheless, my reveries of life in Boston persisted, became, indeed, as my experience widened, more specific and in a sense more real than my existence in Chichester. In the wintertime at school, I was known as a daydreamer and often my teacher would hustle me out of Miss Pride's house with a mocking rebuke that made the whole class laugh: "Tell us what is so interesting that you can't remember the capital of Rhode Island, Sonie." At home, depending on the tempers of my parents, I was called "bright" or "stupid" or "silly" or "older than my age." Confined during the day by school-room walls where hung Sir Galahad and "The Stag at Eve," George Washington and President Wilson and Kipling's "If," plied by unanswerable questions, required to sing "I am a little *blue* bird" in reply to the teacher's full, contralto query, "Who is a little *blue* bird?", I would gradually float away, leaving my body behind, still sitting at the stained red desk. As I vanished, I would see the teacher jump to attention, gather her forces and in a moment overtake me, but not before I had slipped into Miss Pride's drawing-room, wearing a brown velvet dress and a yellow bone round comb in my hair.

At night, bound by the narrow walls of our kitchen, I was not always absorbed in my book about girls at boarding school whose clever mothers had sewed for months before their departure, making silk dresses and dark wool jumpers, warm wrappers, innumerable muslin guimpes, had crocheted fascinators and had bought blue merino stockings. Although I envied the fortunate creatures, my own life which I plotted in a variety of patterns was richer. My hair became blond; my name was Antoinette de la Mar. "Soon after Antoinette or Toni, as her chums called her, went to live in the Pride mansion on Pinckney Street, a handsome Harvard student named Andrew Eliot Cabot Lodge fell passionately in love with her. But as she had already decided not to marry anybody, she spurned him with a few kind but firm words. That night he shot himself, but he did not die and she nursed him back to health. She had many suitors but she lived only for Miss Pride who adored her and often had her do a toe-dance for her visitors who were often foreign kings and queens. They would say, 'I say, Antoinette de la Mar has it all over Denishawn. Why, Denishawn could never whirl on one toe that long.' "

My mother, who spent nearly every winter evening

playing Patience (she always cheated, to my indignation, and as other disrespectful children in a fury curse their mothers, I would howl at mine, "You cheat at cards!"), would notice that for an hour I had not turned a page in my book. "Are you asleep, booby?" she would scold. "Are you asleep sitting up like a little cow?"

If my father raised his eyes from *Riders of the Purple Sage,* quaintly called *Das Gesetz der Mormonen,* to join our quarrel, perhaps to accuse me harshly of thinking of boys, my mother would instantly come to my defense and would commence to belabor him with vituperation. When they had finished the skirmish, my father would lift the red felt cozy off the white china coffee pot and drink from a thick cup. He would then return to his book and my mother to her cards as she remarked, "*He* gets the fine pot for his coffee but Shura Korf has to keep her tea in a tin can." Perhaps he would ignore her, or would say, pointing to his chest, "The pot is *mine.* It is a *coffee* pot. Why don't you drink coffee?"

If she were in the mood for it, my mother would burst into tears and weep, "I hate you, ah, God, I hate you!" The real battle would then begin. They would threaten to kill each other or to kill themselves; they would wish damnation to each other's immortal souls; and each would blame the other for behaving badly in front of me. "*Lieber Gott!*" my father would groan, pressing the knuckles of his big red hands into his eyes. "What will become of my baby girl?"

My mother, clasping her hands together as if in prayer, would return, "She is safe with me! I will kill you if you hurt one single hair of her precious head!"

The outburst would be followed by a lamentation on my father's part as my mother sank into a brooding silence. He would draw me close to him and run his fingers through my hair and tell me he was sorry that he had neglected me. Sometimes he apologized because he had not reared me as a Catholic and he would go out to the shop, bringing back a catechism. But we made no progress. Our minds wandered from the questions, mine to Boston or to the last movie I had seen, and his to his boyhood. He would talk for a long time, but to himself.

"Sonie, my patron is Bonaventure, but how I have forgotten him like all the other saints! It is the irony that he should be my saint because he hated idleness. Brother Sebastian, one of the friars who taught us, brought my brother up short and myself a few years later. For we did not like to be shoemakers like our father and our grandfather and our great grandfather. Friedrich would have nothing to do with the trade. He would go to Paris, to the Sorbonne, to study literature, he said, and philosophy. And I, I would go to Berlin to study the law. But Brother Sebastian knew it wasn't in us. He made us not ashamed of shoemaking. He would quote Saint Bonaventure: 'You, Friedrich, and you, Hermann, are amongst those to whom the Lord has given the grace to labor.' I would pray to my saint night and morning, to cure my sloth! It was a monstrous state. *Monstruosum quemdam statum inter contemplativam et activam.* See! It comes back."

In his excitement, he would take both my hands in his and cry, "My Latin is not gone, Sonie! I will teach you. Have we a book? A grammar? Well, then, tomorrow we must buy one."

But by the next day he would have forgotten. The catechism went back to the shop where for the next month it would lie untouched. Saint Bonaventure, Brother Sebastian, and indeed God, would be shelved like the little book. My father's face would resume its mask. While I, glad that I had escaped his instructions, happily pursued Miss de la Mar's career.

In my twelfth year, hardly a night passed from September until November that I was not unhinged from my sleep by my parents' voices. Something, I knew not what, had brewed between them a hotter rancor than ever before. I was propelled by their curses into consciousness and seemed driven into a socket in the dark from which there was no outlet. My bounded brain was as unalterable as a ball and it could neither veer in flight nor proceed to understanding: solid and of one material, terror, it lay in a minute cavern whose walls were fashioned from the rhetoric and the darkness. The daylight, freeing the sounds of boats and trains, the voices of fishermen and children, discovering the diverse landscape and the harmless countenances of my sleeping parents, repealed the fast laws that had held me to a rapt and aboriginal response and gave me the relief of wild tears. As soon as I had dressed, I would run to the porch of the Hotel Barstow as to a shrine and there, all alone and out of earshot of anyone, I cried until I could cry no more and until the reason for my grief had become obscured by the cold and my hunger. Often at this hour, the fog lay on Boston; I would be unable to see the State House dome and unable to visualize Pinckney Street. At last I would get up and start towards school, slowly at first because my legs were cramped, then faster until I was running through the mist. I usually arrived out of breath, a little late. Among the teachers it was a great joke that when I was asked why I had been crying, I would reply, "Oh, no, I wasn't crying. I didn't sleep well last night." They would say, "How imitative children are at this age! Don't you know exactly what has happened? One of her parents often says at breakfast, 'I didn't get a wink of sleep last night' and the child has picked it up."

On a morning in November, when the snow had fallen, I was crouched in a corner of the steps of the veranda, my face muffled in the harsh curls of my astrakhan collar. Today it was not foggy, but my view gave me no pleasure for the sky was leaden and the angry bay was deserted by all the boats. Last night my father had laughed, it must have been for half an hour and then, as if something had broken in him, shattered like a glass, he had begun to sob. I could hear his heavy body trembling on the creaking bed, and the weeping claw at his throat. And because each morning that was the way I cried, I knew his stomach ached and his nose was full. Not a sound came from my mother. In the intervals between the plunges of his agony, I could hear him whisper, *"Verzeihung!"* How far away he seemed! As I peered upward through the darkness at the dim white block which was the bed, I could not feel that the person weeping, as no man should do, was my father. Rather, it was the figure of a nightmare which crudely represented

36

him. And yet I knew I was awake, for nothing was distorted as in a dream. Quaking upon the clattering springs, the figure was like a caged beast that had broken down in its futile struggle to escape. Downwards it plummeted into some unknown and pitch-black chasm of despair, but rose again in a brief respite to breathe that one word, *"Verzeihung!"* Twice, thinking I could stand it no longer, I started up to go to him and to lay my hand on his arm. But I thought then of how I was enraged at such a gesture when I was crying, and I lay back, mouthing the words, "Please don't cry, dear Papa." Why did my mother not comfort him? Once I heard her sigh and thought perhaps that was the prelude to some speech. But she said nothing and my father wept on, for hours it seemed to me.

The snow had begun to fall in the night and by morning it was thick on the ground. My father's face, in a deep sleep, was ashen and his eyelids were distended, the golden lashes stuck together. An arm was curled about his head. The woman who lay beside him, as motionless as he, appeared the soul of innocence as the gray light, filtering through the holes in the green blinds, exposed her white skin and her red lips and the black hair, unpinned and spread like a fan upon the pillow. She lay straight, her arms at her sides, as if she were dead.

This morning I did not and I could not cry. It was as though my father had done all the crying that could be done. Against my will, I continued to review his terrible collapse. What could it mean, I wondered, in a grown man? And would it happen again? Once he had broken the rules of a man's behavior, would he cry as often as I did?

I was startled at the sound of someone's boots on the gravel path at the side of the Hotel and before I could get to my feet, Gonzales, the gardener, was standing before me. He had always frightened me, for no reason that I could discover. He had the mildest of pink mouths under a thin, romantic mustache, and large bovine eyes beneath a low, protuberant brow. I disliked the way in the kitchen, in the summertime, he would steal up on me in his sneakers and put a soft finger on the back of my neck so suddenly that goose-flesh covered me and my heart pranced in surprise.

"What do I see?" he said, laughing, showing his teeth which were so small that the gum was visible above them. "What is the matter with *Señorita* Marburg? You tell Gonzales your troubles, honey."

He sat down on the step and put his arm around me. There was a strong assorted odor about him of something oily and something acrid, of garlic and of bootleg beer. He put his lips close to my ear, lifting up the edge of my tam. "Tell, Gonzales, honey."

Too frightened to move or to cry out, I trembled in his embrace as he continued his unwelcome consolations. "There, there. If you don't watch out your face will freeze that way, sweetheart. Don't you want to tell your Uncle Jesus what's the trouble?"

"Is your name Jesus?" I asked him, my admiration for a moment making me forget both my misery and his rank smell.

He said "Yes," softly, like a lover, and hugged me closer to him. "If I was my own master like your daddy, I would make a lot of Novenas. But me, Jesus, I don't have the time."

In the summer, he always greeted me with some such pious announcement. He would remind me that my father was in a state of mortal sin because he had not been to confession or mass for seven or eight years, and he would ask me if I did not long to be baptized. He himself, with his eight children, received the Blessed Sacrament every morning at the six o'clock service and on Sundays entertained the priest, Father Mulcahy, at breakfast after the eleven o'clock mass. Once he had come to my father's shop, beseeching him to deliver himself up to the mercy of God. His big brown eyes had been full of tears. But my father had only confounded him by saying, "I know my own mind. I am no boy."

I said nothing in reply. He released me, lowered his head, and dangling his hands between his outspread knees, murmured, "Always remember, *Señorita*, that you and your poor father are in my prayers."

"Thank you, Mr. Gonzales," I said and slipped over on the step. "I've got to go to school now."

"Yes!" he cried, slapping his knee. "And I to work must go. I'm afraid to look in the pit. I'm as sure as my name is Jesus Francisco Gonzales that the hydrangeas were frozen last night." He stood up and started down the path, but pausing at the corner of the porch he faced me once more. "How is your mother, sweetheart?" I answered that she was well enough only a little tired, for I was remembering how soundly she slept when I left the house.

The Mexican winked at me. "Tired of carrying the little one?"

"What?"

"I mean your little brother or sister or whichever it is Our Savior intends it to be."

"I don't know . . ." I began, but he cupped his hands round his plump lips and whispered loudly, "Your mother is going to have a baby, *muchacha*."

2

When I came home from school that afternoon, my mother was not in her accustomed place beside the stove, a most surprising fact, for she was a creature of tenacious habit, and had, since I could remember, taken up her place there an hour before sundown to idle over a glass of strong and bitter tea. She would rise, as I entered, and embrace me as if I were an intimate friend for whose visit she had been impatiently waiting, and then, drawing me to a chair beside hers, she would rub my cold hands between hers and say, "Oh, Sonie, how cold you are! Oh, the darling little hands all red!"

Often at this hour, I found neighbor women seated round about her, going over in exhaustive detail the difficulties of maintaining a household when there was no money to pay the high prices of food. I wondered if these women were as gloomy in their own houses as they were in ours, or if my mother's winter melancholy was contagious to them as it was to my father and myself.

Strangely enough, when the heaviness of the bad weather skies had invaded our kitchen, she cast off the dark colors she had worn all summer and stepped forward, as lively as a bird, in a costume like a ballerina's. But her full skirt, the length of a peasant's dress, which was made of black challis and printed with bright pink flowers and fantastic pea-green leaves, her scarlet flannel blouse with tarnished German silver buttons, and her high blue leather boots, laced with tan hide, were not an antidote to her perverse mopes but seemed rather to be the excuse for them. Mrs. Henderson would come in and say, "How gay you look, Mrs. Marburg! Why, I can warm my hands at *you*." But my mother, in a voice bleaker than any winter wind along the beach, would answer, "It is the red that fools you. But look at the boots. Now *they're* the color my hands used to be all day long in Moscow, even in the house, and they were so stiff I couldn't hold so much as a wine glass by its little tiny stem." Sometimes, out of spite, she would then slip her arms into the sleeves of a blue Beacon-cloth bathrobe whose skirt hung to the floor; a high, pointed hood was attached to the back of the neck. It belonged to my father, and the sleeves were so long that the unfilled portions of them flapped like seals' flippers as she gestured with her invisible hands. Had it not been for her face, she would have looked like a monk of some outlandish order.

Softly I opened the door to the bedroom. She was lying there, either asleep or else so deep in thought that she did not hear me on the threshold. The dark green blinds were down, but the light of the sunset, coming through the holes and falling on her immobile face, gave it an even incandescence like that which comes through the hand when it is held up to a bright light. Her body was covered with an army blanket and though the room was cold, one bare white foot dangled over the side of the bed. I could see my breath. The windows did not anywhere quite fit their frames and we had failed to stop up many of the cracks in the walls, either through laziness or through the conviction that it would do no good.

There was only one other article of furniture in the

room besides the bed, a tall combination wardrobe and bureau with a sliver of flawed mirror at the top, in a frame carved with the same ornate roses that decorated the feet. My father, I suppose because it was solid and perhaps reminded him of something at home, admired the *schrank* as he called it, and each spring he spent one entire day polishing it with salt and olive oil. Today, to my surprise, I saw that the two pots of geraniums stood on the top, blocking out the mirror. Their transfer from the sunny kitchen window was stranger to me even than the sight of my mother lying in bed before we had had our supper. Was she, I wondered, going to have the baby now?

Presently I tiptoed out and went to my father's shop. He was not working. He was sitting on the bench before the monkey stove, his head in his hands.

"Papa?"

He did not look up, but he thrust forth his long arm in welcome. "Hello, Sonie girl. Didn't you eat anything yet today?"

"I guess not."

"Why didn't you come home at noon?"

"Oh, I don't know. I guess I wasn't hungry, Papa, I guess I had an apple. What's the matter with Mamma?"

"She's tired maybe." Now he turned his face toward me and I saw that his blue eyes were troubled, but they showed no sign of their storm of last night. He smiled and with two hard fingers that smelled of tallow, he tweaked my nose. "I know what you want, Gretchen von Hexensee, you want to look at the tintypes."

They were not really tintypes, but the word amused him. I fetched the fat album from the high shelf above the window. It lay with his fat little *Messbuch* and a few fine leather-bound volumes of Schiller, Leibnitz, Cicero, Goethe, Mommsen, and Balzac. The books were not worn. Probably my father had never read them. They were mostly gifts from his schoolmates on the day of his commencement from the gymnasium and were inscribed in a bewildering handwriting, the same that I saw on the occasional letter which came to him from Würzburg.

Together we looked at the photographs in which my

relatives genially smiled forth, all with my father's eyes. My grandparents sat side by side on a plush settle with a high, carved back. Their fat arms were intertwined and they stared directly into the camera. Their round faces were frank and innocent and benign, and their sober, old-fashioned clothes—my grandfather wore a long collar with a full ascot, a black coat with wide satin lapels and upon his knees he balanced a gleaming top hat, while my grandmother, with a black lace jabot at her stout old neck, was dressed in a striped jacket with leg-o'-mutton sleeves and a deep pointed bodice which met a black skirt—advertised them as people of respecability. Both of them were dead. One of the letters that had come to my father had been from his brother, Christian, announcing that they had died within half a year of one another.

My favorite picture was one of my cousin Peter taken when he was about five years old. His wide eyes stared at the photographer's incorporeal birdie and his lips were opened in perplexity. He was a bewitching little boy with fair hair, matted in curls tight to his skull; his solid body was encased in leather breeches, a jacket decorated with hearts, and tassled socks. In his hands he ferociously clutched a hat with an improbably long feather.

"Some day, when we are rich," my father said, "we will go to see that boy. Shall we take our Packard car with us and honk outside of Fransiskanerstrasse *zwei und zwanzig?* Or should we not take it and walk from the station as calm as you please?"

I debated for a moment. "Let's take the Packard car," I said.

"I don't know when it would be that we would go."

"If Miss Pride keeps on buying shoes, we'll get rich."

"She only feels sorry for me, and I don't like that. No, in America they don't know a good boot from a bad."

"Then why don't we go to Germany, Pa?"

When he answered, he looked away from me. He moved to the window and stood looking out at the last glow of the sun on Boston. "I would be ashamed," he said. "How am I going to explain to my brothers and friends that I never had my child baptized?"

Whereas it embarrassed me to have Gonzales talk about his sins of omission, it frightened me to hear my father speak of them. Once, at Christmas time, he had made a *crèche* for me, carving out a youthful Mary and the doe-eyed animals and three Teutonic wise-men and the faceless Christ-child with a boyish rapture. I was delighted with it until, once it had been brought from the shop into the house, I saw that my mother had no interest in it and that my father had lost his. It was as if some ungovernable force in her was determined to extinguish every joy her husband might have. In his frustration and furious disappointment, he abruptly seized the platform and dashed it to the floor so that all the figures were broken and the frame was splintered. He stared down at the fragments, his hands hanging loosely at his sides. He said nothing, but in a moment he took his hat from the shelf and went out. Hours later, when he came back, totally drunk, he sat in the kitchen for a long time, laughing his inhuman laugh. In the morning I found him sleeping with his head on the table. For a week thereafter, whenever we were alone together, he invited me to look on him as the most obstinate of all sinners, and while I was not certain what he meant, I would rack my brains for a pretext to escape him, for I was mortally afraid.

He had pressed his cheek against the windowpane and when he spoke, a cloud formed on the glass. "Or how confess it to a priest?" he inquired. "Or anything else?"

There was no sound in the room but the spanking of a live coal against the purple sides of the monkey stove. And my father was motionless, with his eyes and his lips closed. Perhaps he had cried last night out of fear of his sins and the punishment God would deal to him. And what were his sins? He did not tell lies and he did not steal and he was not a murderer. It was true that he spent a good deal of time carousing with the Coast Guards, but so did the fishermen. What, then, had he done that tormented him so, even now when there were no outward signs of it beyond the pallid weariness of his face and the tension of his pose? I would have asked and my lips parted, but something hindered me from intruding upon his mysterious meditations and I said, my voice cracking, "I guess I better go help Mamma."

"*Ja*, you better." He sighed so that his whole lengthy frame shivered, and he turned to me with a willful smile which did not fool me, for the corners of his mouth twitched and would have turned down but for the effort he expended on their upward curve. "Don't you expect me for supper. I have some business." With this, he took down his sheep-lined mackinaw and his hunter's cap, put a pipe and tin of tobacco in his pocket and drew on a pair of mittens.

"Are you going to the Coast Guard?" I asked him.

"Curiosity killed the cat," he said waggishly but, like his smile, his jollity was forced and did not take me in.

"Where are you going, Pa?"

Suddenly irritated, he pushed me towards the door. "Shut up now," he snapped. "Go along to the house and mind your own business."

I watched from the kitchen windows until he had disappeared round the bend of the road, and then I stole out and followed. Over the crusted ruts for a mile I ran, ducking behind cottages and sheds when I feared he might turn around. At this hour the village was usually deserted save for the men going in and out of the pool hall in the splattered window of which a sign futilely proclaimed, "Ladies Invited." I had expected my father to turn in there, but he went on, passed the large, shadowy general store about which, even in winter and when the door was closed, there hung an odor of fish and fishermen and a rich, sweet smell which came either from raisins or chewing tobacco. I glanced across the street at the Bijou where the obfuscated films which wavered before our eyes like dispirited ectoplasm bore no more relationship to entertainment than the lusterless exterior bore to any jewel known to man. It was closed now and the torn sign advertising "Ben Hur" was streaked from melted snow. These, with a few churches, a little library, and a post-office made up our business district. On one side, overlooking the sea, was the Coast Guard house,

44

on the other, overlooking the bay, was a small white hospital, enveloped for a quarter of a mile on all sides by a pall of mortal silence. Midway between the village and the hospital was the school, so newly built that its yellow-brick walls had not yet been relieved by shrubs and ivy. As I lingered in the doorway of the store until my father should be a safe distance ahead of me (he had paused to knock out his pipe), I was visited by a longing to see Marblehead, Salem, and Boston, and I was as weakened by the feeling as though I had seen them and something in the winter evening had made me nostalgic. And then I conceived the stubborn notion that the crisis which my father was passing through would end in a change of residence. Perhaps even now he was headed for the Marblehead bus stop and when he came home, he would have news of a house and a shop to which we would immediately move.

It was with a flush of anger that I saw, in a few minutes, what his destination was: the Catholic church, a small white building with a high green spire. It was called "The Chapel of the Little Flower." I followed him.

My schoolmates had told me, in frightened whispers, that Catholics prayed the dead out of Purgatory, whatever that might be, and I fancied my father kneeling before a High Necromancer, chanting in an unknown language. I had heard that priests were ghosts and since they had no substance, could never marry. Someone said they could change from one thing to another: "They can look like anything they want, like a billy goat if they want." There was something impressive to me in the sight of my father starting out to Mass on Sunday, wearing his suit and his polished boots, and carrying the *Messbuch* with its bright ribbons. Impressive and a little scandalous, even though I knew he never got as far as the church porch, but instead took another road which led to the Coast Guard house where he would spend an hour playing checkers.

A few parishioners were kneeling in the front pews of the darkened chapel, and now and again the door to the confessional swung open; I could hear the wicket slide and presently another penitent entered the box. There was a murmur, caught by a silence, and broken at last by the faint, sibilant Latin of the absolution. Those who had been cleansed slipped into the kneeling benches to say their penance, and as their lips mouthed the words of the prayers, their eyes were fixed upon a shining golden object on the altar: it looked like a child's drawing of the sun, for from the round white center, a thousand rays of gold shot out, glittering in the red light cast by the vigil lamp which swung very gently at the end of a long iron chain. My eyes grew accustomed to the shadows and I saw my father at the altar rail, far to one side, his head buried in his arms. Each time someone emerged from the confessional, I expected him to go in, but he did not stir. It was cold in the church and I shivered, leaned up against the side of the pew, and hugged my knees. It seemed to me a long time that I waited for the terrifying moment when my father would become a part of the esoteric game. At least five people went into the closet with their sins and came out purged of them. The last light of the day perished from the stained glass windows. Now only two people besides my father and myself remained.

Presently, the Irish priest came out, a tall, red-haired young man, round-shouldered and near-sighted, with a face ravaged by boredom and eczema, but not an unpleasant face and in no way similar to my picture which had represented him as lithe and swart, wearing a mustache and pointed beard over which darted bright evil eyes. He passed close by my father as he went into the vestry, but my father, deep in his prayer, did not look up, and only after the door had closed behind the priest did he rise and hasten out, looking straight ahead so that he did not see me. But when the swinging doors had shut upon him, I heard a voice in the vestibule intercept him: "Thank God, man! You've come back by the grace of God! The new one will have a better chance than Sonie." It was Gonzales. There was the sound of a match being struck, and my father replied, "You fool busybody." The outer door opened and banged to, forcing a blast of cold air into the church. Gonzales went down the central aisle, genuflected at the altar, and went to the right where he knelt before a statue of a woman saint in a brown robe who held roses in her hands. He crossed himself and began to pray audibly. I ran from the church appalled, for there was a presence there, not of God nor of angels, but of something human, yet shockingly bodiless, and I felt as I had done the time I had dreamed that I was dead and the only thing left of me was the knowledge, suspended in a ball of solitude, that I was dead.

The house was as it had been when I came in from school. My father was not there and the shop was dark, and my mother, still lying in bed, had not changed her position. I spread a piece of bread with margarine and sprinkled it with sugar and I ate, sitting on the floor by the stove, as in the light from the fire through the isinglass I read a book lent to me by a schoolmate called *Frances and the Irrepressibles at Buena Vista Farm.* The thick pages were glossy and each one bore an actual photograph of a character or a whole group of them together, posing in the costumes they had worn at a mock wedding or at the minstrel show they had ingeniously produced. A child cannot sustain his moods for long, and I, after a few minutes of inattention, became completely absorbed in the adventures of these wealthy, carefree, and urbane children. They were all upright and considerate with the one exception of a rotten little boy named Dickey Doolittle who one had no doubt would come all right in the end under the influence of his companions. They all lived in Wisconsin on a farm where fresh diversions presented themselves every day and where in the neighborhood, chicken thieves, Indian caves, buried treasure, and watermelon patches were to be had for the asking.

The door opened and my father, in an ugly temper, scolded me: "Now you'll go blind. What is the meaning of this, young lady?" When he found that the mantle of the Coleman lamp was burned out, he cursed savagely and ordered me to fetch a new one from the top shelf. As I did so, a pipe clattered to the floor and broke in two. It was one he never used, but he kept it as a curio, for its bowl was porcelain and baked into it was a picture of the cathedral at Worms.

"Now damn you!" he screamed. "Now give me the mantle from your damned butter fingers!"

He slapped me on the side of the head with his open hand and there was a sudden ache in my opposite ear. Then he turned away and as he adjusted the mantle, he growled, "What is the use? They make me come into a dark house and then they break my things. They should go to jail." When the white light flared up, I saw him move the red felt cozy and look at a heap of bits of white china, all that was left of his coffee pot. "*I* didn't do it!" I cried. "I never did!"

"I know it," he said. "Your mother did it. She picked it up and threw it at the stove." Our eyes turned together and saw, beneath the oven door, two or three white glittering splinters amongst the ashes. I could not imagine so violent a gesture in my lazy mother. Her only weapon was her tireless voice. There must have been a quarrel of unprecedented savagery while I was at school, and I was glad that I had not come home at lunch time but instead had eaten an apple and a fig-Newton given to me by the Hendersons.

"Well?" shouted my father. "Well, where is my supper?"

"You said not to expect you, Papa. You said you weren't coming home."

"I did *not*." He spouted like a child and stamped his foot.

My mother did not come out, and my father was angry with me for cutting his bread too thin and burning the bacon, and when I asked him what I should put the coffee into now that the pot was broken, he pounded the table with both his fists so that the cutlery bounced, and then he put his head down until his forehead was in his greasy plate and shouted, "*Confiteor Deo omnipotenti, Beatae Mariae, semper Virgini . . .*" but he could not go on. He rolled over until his face was pointed upward to the ceiling and he wailed, "*Gott! Gott, warum hast Du mich verlassen!*"

"Papa, do you want some cheese?"

"Cheese? Yes, that's the remedy! Give your father a spoonful of cheese and that will get him out of hell!" He took me by both arms and shook me until my dizzied eyes began to hurt. "We're fit for nothing!" His eyes, afire and yet still as cold as ice, looked upon me with such hatred and so terrible a threat that I commenced to cry. My chin lifted and my eyes narrowed and when he shook me again, the tears fell out. I could not stop and though, when he released me, I covered my mouth with my hand, the sound escaped me and the warm tears welled up as freely as water from a drinking fountain. He let me go and stepped back, aghast. Cruelly, yet out of the necessity to justify myself, I sobbed, "I don't care! You cried last night!"

Twice he told me to be quiet and when I could not, being now at the mercy of my gulping, he drove me into a corner of the room, out of the circle of the lamplight and there, beside the dark blue sink, I huddled against the wall, bawling softly as my stopped-up nose bubbled and a faint interior disturbance in my skull made me think my brains were rattling.

He pushed back the dishes and settled down at the table to read, still so distracted that by mistake, he opened *Frances and the Irrepressibles* and for some moments stared stupidly at the pictures of little girls in hair ribbons and white party dresses and high button shoes before he realized, with an outburst of wounded dignity, that this was not *Riders of the Purple Sage*.

Just as he had thought I deliberately broke his pipe, now he thought I had mischievously substituted my book for his, not only to insult him with its childishness but to remind him that he could not read English well and that I could. He strode across the room and plucked me to my feet. "I've had enough of your monkey business." He turned me around and hit me four or five times on the backside. I did not cry out but my tears continued to fall and I felt giddy as the blows stung me through my thin skirt. The action satisfied him and he drew his chair to the fire and began to read. I collapsed once more into my corner, pondering how I could avenge myself.

Probably from his frequent readings of this book, my

father longed to see the west and one time, some years before, when he had made a little extra money carrying trunks at the Hotel, he bought a fine yellow hide and made a pair of cowboy boots which he sometimes wore on Sunday. As he read, I could tell by the pleasure that illuminated his face and caused him now and then to chuckle deeply in his throat, that he was far away from me and that the world in which he rode a pinto cowpony or a roan mare contained no blubbering, angry child nor any sullen, pregnant woman. Once he paused and swung an invisible lariat over his head, leaned forward on his horse's neck as to its flanks he pressed spurs with tied rowels. A little later, he whipped a revolver from his holster and aimed at the empty caviar can. Then, conscious once more of where he was, he kicked the stove in vexation and scratched his head.

As I crouched in my corner, I felt thin drafts of bitter air coming through the cracks in the wall and I thought of the hard, dirty snow outside and of the wind that came across the bay whipping granules of sand into the faces and onto the legs of walkers. I thought of my mother, when she was about my age, being cast out into the brutal night, and it came to me with a shock that that incredible man who dandled the German milliner on his knee was my own grandfather. I tried to imagine him and succeeded only in calling up an image of my father as he might be when he was old. This person I brought into the room and allowed to approach me and to send me away as he had sent away my mother and my aunts and uncles, and I tried to imagine what it would feel like to be exiled from one's own house. I was intent upon my painful fancy; I had closed my eyes and the cold from the window seemed more acute. The vision of my father-grandfather seemed actually to take on flesh and spirit.

A harsh and sudden voice spoke out: "Sonie, get to bed."

I had thought my father had forgotten that I was still in the room; his unexpected command, though its intention was disciplinary rather than unkind, thrilled me as if it were the completion of the scene behind my closed eyelids. For a moment I was not sure whether I had heard him say, "Get to bed," and not what I had expected the grandfather to say, "Get out." Whether it was the confusion in my mind or merely the shock of hearing words after so intense a silence, I do not know, but I burst into fresh tears, so stormily this time it was as though I had been storing them up and had only waited for a trifle to start the avalanche. My baffled father stood up and peered at me in my dark corner. He came towards me uncertainly, but I could not tell whether he was angry or remorseful. "Now, Sonie, now, girl. Come out of your corner." I did not stir.

"Come, *Mädchen*," he wheedled and I knew, because he used that tender word, that he was not cross. Perhaps he regretted his harshness and had realized my inno-cence. Still, I did not move, and he continued to come closer. He crouched down on the floor beside me. "There. There." He followed the dirty meanders of the tears on my cheeks with his forefinger. "Maybe they'll freeze there like icicles, *ni't?* The kids at school will call you a cry baby girl." Grieved at his mistake and not try-ing to make up for it by caresses, as my mother would have done, he had a dignity which I was bound to ad-mire, and at last I smiled at him. "*Jawohl!*" he cried in genuine pleasure and then, in imitation of the friendly rancher of the Saturday night movies, he awkwardly of-fered me his hand and said, "Put 'er there, pardner!"

The cold from the windows laid metallic ribbons across my back. I was sickened to think of my aunts and uncles trudging, whimpering, in the Russian night, and in a glow of relief at my better fortune, I grasped the extended hand. In a meditative way, with his head bowed, my father began to finger my hand, pressing the ball of his into the hollow of my palm, lacing our fingers together, feeling the knuckles.

"Sonie," he said after a time. "What is it you want to do when you grow up?"

I could not tell him that my only ambition was to live with Miss Pride, for I did not want him to know that I preferred her to himself. But I said, "I guess I want to live in Boston."

"Boston? Is that all you want to do? Why, I thought you wanted to be a school teacher at least."

"Oh, no!"

"I guess I haven't done anything right. You should want to be a school teacher, I think. How far are you in your Latin now?"

"We don't start Latin till the eighth grade," I told him and then, because I saw how curiously he looked at me, I added, "I'm in the seventh now."

"It would be a comfort for a man to know what he used to know," he mused. Then, to include me he said with a spurt of good spirits, "I'll tell you what we'll do, Sonie, we'll go west some day to Cheyenne, Wyoming. Wouldn't you like to ride a little wild horse?"

I said I would in much sincerity, but because I was unschooled in both the scenery and the customs of the west, I did not immediately seat myself astride a horse or envisage Cheyenne, but instead, heard Miss Pride say to a friend, as I entered the drawing-room, "*Here* is our cow girl. You know she and her father own several thousand wild roan stallions."

"I could make us some boots." He said that undoubtedly there was a place for a man like him who could make leather things. Cowboys were particular about their clothes, he had heard; that is, not dandified, but but they liked expensive wool shirts and Stetson hats and since they hadn't for the most part any family to support, they could spend all their wages on clothes and *Schnapps.* He dwelt for a long time on their emancipation and prosperity; sometimes, for variety, he called them "the punchers" until I became breathless and pleaded to go at once.

I returned him from his rapture. He looked down at me through the sad gloom. "Well, now, *Mädchen,* when will you be ready to go?"

"Now!" It did not occur to me that we could not go the moment we had agreed on our destination, for, being altogether unacquainted with travel, I was not aware that it cost anything. I supposed, moreover, that if we needed money for our dinner on the train (I already saw myself eating a pork chop and as many bananas as I wanted) he, like Betty Brunson's father, the dentist, could "sell a bond." For this, I believed was the prerogative of a father. Whenever anyone said, "I wish I had a ukulele," or "I wish I had a solid gold barrette," Betty would reply, "Why don't you ask your father to sell a bond? Daddy always does." I had always had the vague idea that my father's bonds would be German and therefore less easily disposed of but that in an emergency he could market them.

"I am thinking," he said with a sigh, "that it might be better if I went on first and got things lined up, you might say, and then sent for you. By that time I would have the corral built and have you a nice little palomino horse. It's a long way out there. You would get sleepy."

"How far?"

"Maybe as far as two thousand miles. I expect it's five days or so on the train. A long, long way, Sonie girl."

"I want to go with you, Papa. Now."

He stiffened and stood up. My mother was standing in the doorway of the bedroom, her shadow so long it fell the length of the room and, making a right angle turn at the juncture, continued up the wall. She was pale and her staring eyes seemed uncommonly large. It seemed to me that they were never so beautiful as when she was angry. The whites of them were immaculate, not marked, as most eyes are, with shabby red tendrils, and the iris was so dark the pupil was nearly invisible, but in the sun or in the lamplight as tonight, an amber ray appeared intermittently in the iris, ending in the profound depths of that rich center. When my parents drank together, my father would gaze into her face and murmur, "Die wunderschönen Augen! Die magischen Augen!" Tonight, in her sickness or in her despair or her fury, whatever it was that had driven her out to us, these eyes seemed, because of their wonderful and awful size, to be holding back their lids with effort.

Her black hair, pouched with white combs into a pompadour, hung to her waist and swung heavily with the movement of her body; it shone like a blue-jay's feathers. She stroked one hand with the other and in the hush we could hear the muted hissing of the skin being rubbed. On her right forearm, I saw that there was a long scratch that had been painted with iodine.

My parents stood as if entranced, each waiting for the other to speak. If only they would now be merciful, embrace, speak softly! How could my mother, so beautiful a woman, create so much unhappiness for us all? For she was beautiful and her beauty was as holy a kind as that of the statue in the church before which Gonzales had been praying. Her rosiness, her clear skin, the sheen of her hair, her calm eyes, made the old ladies at the Hotel Barstow say of her, "She is the image of a saint." The line of her hair on her high forehead was almost straight as though a child, drawing a picture and unable to trace in it the actual irregularities of his model, had simplified, had tidied up. The planes of the face were clean and the silken flesh shrank shallowly beneath the cheekbone and became pallid or golden as the light struck it. She was a tall woman, with a graceful, lethargic carriage. Her hands were her only blemish, for they were always red and scaly with the cleaning powders she used in the summer to clean the bathtubs, and in the winter they were chapped. Her fingers were torn with cracks in the tips or hangnails or cuts from knives or gouges from bedsprings. They were always cold as though too much blood had flowed out of their rents, and I supposed that was why she continually rubbed them.

"It is no use, Shura," my father said at last. His voice was even and formal.

At his words, she bent her head down on her breast. The hair tumbled about her like a veil and at the base of her skull, the scalp was visible between cords of the hair heavily tossed forward. She moaned, "But you must not take Sonia away from me!" She flung back her head again and I saw that not even now was her face distorted by her feelings. Not even her mouth, filter of anger, bitterness, sorrow, became less charming, and the sweetness of its shape, the texture of its dark red flesh seemed to abate her passion, making it something strapped and aimless.

"If I go, I will take nothing but my body and my soul."

"Soul!" She spat on the floor before her bare feet. "Does a man have a soul that cuts his wife?" She held out her scratched arm. "Sonia, look! What do you think of a father like that, eh?"

"Why do you lie before the girl? She knows I never laid my hands on you. Tell her that you broke my china coffee pot and nagged me until I was crazy!"

"I hate you. Ah, I would hate any man that cried tears like a woman."

"And I hate you, Shura, with all my heart. You've ruined everything for me and I've had enough."

For the briefest moment, alarm showed in my mother's face, but then she smiled. "And so have I. If it weren't for Sonia . . ."

"Even for Sonie I've had enough now. From the beginning it is all wrong."

My mother's insistence flagged before the determination in his voice and she could not accuse him of any specific thing, but only said, complacently, "Thank God, she's a little girl. And by the grace of the Holy Ghost, there will be another little girl. I'll call her little Luibka."

"So, Luibka!" He laughed like a lunatic. "So we will call the witch's daughter after the old hell-cat. But what if the little whore in your belly turns out to be little Ivan instead? Little, little, little Russian woman, little God damn you to a little tiny Russian hell!"

"Hush! Before the child!"

His raging voice did not alter in pitch as, wheeling upon me, he commanded, "Pray for yourself, Sonie! Sonie . . ." He faltered and then, calmed, he took my mother's arm. "Put on your shoes, Shura, and come to the shop."

My jaws were sour and my mouth was full of saliva which escaped and wavered on my lips. When they had gone out, I moaned, and still, while my misery did not lessen, I saw myself slipping out of the house and running up the road to the Hotel. I would go through the basement and creep up the dark stairs and through the kitchen, the dining-room, the lobby, up the staircase and through the corridor until I came to the door of Miss Pride's room. I would lie on the window seat with her afghan over me and my head in the plump pillows and there I would go to sleep. Perhaps I would find the furniture covered with ghost-clothes as I had once seen them so dressed in the lobby when I peered through the cracks of the boarding at the window. I would be delighted if the hat-pin holder were covered with a dust-shroud, and if the cherubs were dressed for winter. But I remembered, sadly, that there would be nothing in the room, for before she went away, Miss Pride always locked her belongings in the closet and handed the key to the manager. Well, then, what I must do was go to Mr. Henderson next door and ask him to take me across the bay in his boat. If I came to her, late at night, without a coat, she could not refuse to let me in. "I was expecting you," said Miss Pride to Antoinette de la Mar as the latter sank down on the green velour davenport in the elegant drawing-room, "and so I have some sandwiches and a big pot of cocoa ready for you. Will you take one marshmallow or two?"

I was awakening for a long time, climbing the waves of my sleep and relapsing, dreaming and knowing that I dreamed. A cat had laid five hen's eggs which Betty Brunson advised me to name "Frances Irrepressible." The purr of the mother cat shaped into words, "Sonia, are you awake?" Beside me was my mother's lax, warm body, and through my half-opened eyes, I saw that her scratched arm lay across my chest. I was afraid she might kiss me and I pretended that I was still asleep.

"Sonia?" she inquired again.

The room was dark so that I was not sure it was day until through the thin walls I heard Mr. Henderson's voice. "Sarah!" he called. "*Oh,* Sarah! Bring me the gaff like a good girl," and I knew that he was going out to his lobster-pots. Immediately afterward, the bells of the Catholic church rang eight o'clock and my mother sat up, as though the sound had alarmed her. She tested the temperature of the room by exhaling her breath in little puffs and saw, by the vapor issuing from her mouth, that it was keenly cold. Before she got out of bed, she shivered into her blue wrapper and drew on her stockings. I opened my eyes and asked, "Why am I in the bed, Mamma?"

She smiled. "Because your father went off somewhere last night. We are all alone, darling."

"Did he go in the *storm?*"

She nodded, but her thoughts were not on him. "You lie there till the fire is going," she said. "Maybe you won't go to school today? I'll make you a boiled egg for breakfast!" The prospect of so unusual a festivity brought a dancing light into her eyes, and with a liveliness I had never seen in her before, she moved about the room, stroking the velvety leaves of the geraniums which still stood on the bureau. "He said he was going to put them into the stove because his pot got broken," she said as she took the flowers down. "But I hid them in time."

I lay still after she had left the room, listening to her shaking down the ashes and drawing water for the tea. I remembered, as from a dim former life, that sometime in the night I had staggered, bloated with sleep, upon my mother's arm into the bedroom and I had flung out protesting arms and had muttered, "Leave me be," as she took off my middy blouse and undid the waist from my skirt.

I had never dreamed that the bed was so soft. The blankets and pillows were like loving, hugging arms, and I closed my eyes again, wishing that now I had it all to myself I might stay in it the whole morning. Directly I heard the Hendersons joining the Kadish children on the road to school. "Where's Sonie?" said one of them, and when there was no answer I was certain that they were whispering amongst themselves. Probably the Kadishes had heard the quarrel last night, for our houses were only a few yards apart. But I was not yet wide awake enough to be conscious of shame, and careless of all but this snug bed, I burrowed deeper into the blankets like a hibernating animal and thought of how, presently, I would break my boiled egg over a piece of bread and salt and pepper it while a cup of tea at the side of my plate steamed into my face.

Three

My FATHER HAD TAKEN NOTHING with him: no clothes but those he wore, no tools, not even an extra pipe. Through the years of his absence, I used sometimes to wonder, as I looked at the kitchen shelves or at the traps in his shop, if he had not had time to collect his things together, if he had wanted to be on his way before the violence of his decision capitulated and left him still obliged to go but to go now without the desire; or if he had taken nothing in the intention of beginning anew, as unencumbered as possible, free both of the nuisance of carrying his belongings and of the reminders implicit in them of the life he had left behind.

His empty-handedness struck both my mother and me as evidence that he would come back, for he had a strong sense of possession, obvious from the clutter in his shop. He had brought from Germany four great boxes besides numerous small ones. These had never been opened because, being a poor man and unable to make new acquisitions, he did not want to wear out what he had. He saved everything for a "rainy day" but even when he was deluged with bursting clouds, he never so much as considered unlocking his treasures.

58

After we had had our breakfast, my mother, explaining to me that she was now in the fourth month of her pregnancy (sensing my disapproval she implored me, "Ah, good Christ, Sonia, you be nice to your poor mother!"), sent me to fetch Mrs. Henderson. She was feeling unwell and thought that the neighbor woman would prescribe something soothing to help her over the shock. She did look ill and weary and I was glad to shift the responsibility for her to someone else. Actually, I suppose, she was not in much discomfort, for as soon as Mrs. Henderson came, she brightened up and began to talk and eagerly to drink the tea into which had been poured a little rum. Mrs. Henderson was a large, good-natured woman, prematurely gray. Because of her hair and because she wore bifocal spectacles, I thought she was old, and at first had believed that she was the grandmother, not the mother of the children with whom I played. Plainly, she did not want to hear my mother's account of last evening, the preface to which greeted her the moment she stepped across the threshold. She asked me a great many questions about school, whether I was looking forward to the Christmas pageant, and if I liked Civics this year and if I did not agree that Miss Pickens, my teacher, was the sweetest woman on earth. My mother, who had no interest in my education, nodded her head now and then in bored courtesy until she could bear it no longer and wrested the conversation from us. She began to talk in a passionless monotone of what she called her "condition," and as she spoke of my father's disappearance only in relation to it, I could learn nothing new about what had happened after I fell asleep on the floor. Blushing, I went out to the shop.

For some time, I sat on the work-bench gazing about me at the tools and the bottles of dye and polish and the hides hung along the walls. I intended to open my father's boxes, and it was as though I expected a new world to rise in primeval mist when I had lifted up their lids. For, knowing nothing but charm of Germany, I assumed that their contents would be charming. From my father, I had learned that castles were a natural part of the landscape of his country, that a faëry life as old as the earth whispered and flirted in the enchanted forests, that all families were large, rich and congenial and every Sunday afternoon went walking through the hills until they came to an inn tucked away in the chestnut trees. The father would point his stick and cry, "Listen, what do you say to a piece of cake, you, Hermann, you, Friedrich?" And they would all go in to drink some coffee or perhaps some red wine with a cherry *torte* or a plate of *lebkuchen*. I knew, moreover, that on the façade of my father's house in Würzburg, there were bas-reliefs of kings' heads, bunches of grapes, lyres, and goblets, and that within the house there was a big tile stove and all the sheets were pure linen.

Near-by the nail where the key of rings to the trunks hung, there was another nail from which dangled a black rosary with golden gauds, a present, he had told me, from his Aunt Therese, on the day of his confirmation. As the sheen of the beads caught my eye, I wondered if perhaps this afternoon, wherever he might be, he would go to confession. What would the father in the cubbyhole say to him? Would he tell him to come back to us? I was not sure yet that I wanted him to return. I had no feeling of loss thus far, and I could think only with joy that there would be no more quarrels at night. Perhaps now that he was gone, my mother would change, would emerge from her slovenly wrapper and her lazy ways, and would no longer spend all her time staring at the sea. (It happened that my father, from his windows, and I from Miss Pride's, looked toward Boston, but my mother, looking out the windows of our kitchen, could see only a long white stretch of sand and a few crags far off, and then the endless sea itself. It was an arresting landscape but one whose eternal monotony became maddening in time. But towards the sameness of her prospect, she was altogether indifferent.)

Into my life, moreover, my father's escape introduced a theme of mystery. Already he was, in my mind, an almost mythical figure, belonging to no category I had hitherto known outside the pages of books, for he was not merely a fugitive, he was also particularly my father whom, after a while when I was grown up, I might seek my whole life through, as I had seen daughters do at the Bijou, missing by a few minutes a reunion in a South American cabaret, a Peking tea-house, an English garden party, our gondolas passing one another on the Grand Canal just as the moon was darkened by a cloud.

There were moments, to be sure, when I rebuked him for leaving us stranded with nothing but twenty-four dollars, which my high principled mother had tried, this morning, to put into the stove. But my prayers for our better fortune were today not directed towards him but towards some unknown benefactor. And when, as the day wore on, I began to miss him, I did not wish he were here with us, but wished that I were with him, as he walked along a road, smiling, his fair hair blowing, unconscious of everything but his freedom and the strength of his body.

I took the keys from their nail, pushed aside some cartons and heaps of kindling in front of one of the trunks, found the proper key and opened it. The lid resisted and the hinges faintly screeched. The odor of camphor balls rose strongly. Each article was wrapped separately in heavy brown paper. Everything was unused, but some of the cloth had rotted at the folds from lying there so long, and the paper of the brochures of cobblers' tools was brittle; the *Lederhosen* and the ski boots were stiff. I found cleated shoes, woolen underdrawers, skis, ski poles, ice-skates, embroidered suspenders, hunting knives, and a rucksack. His clothes showed that he was not only a sportsman, but a gentleman as well, for amongst them were a dinner-jacket, a white silk ascot, a top hat, and a walking stick with a gold snake's head.

There were pictures of my grandparents taken at various times in their lives, tinted and contained in heavy gilt frames. Did these old people with their stern eyes and kindly mouths know, before they died, that they had a grandchild in America? Perhaps in the big shop in Würzburg, run now by my uncle Christian, there was a picture of Cousin Sonia tacked up on the wall. I could recall only one picture of myself, taken on an Easter day by Mr. Henderson. Together with his children I had posed, holding a calla lily in my hand like a scepter, and because the sun was in my eyes and I could not close my mouth for I had a cold in the head, my face drooped with stupidity. But I had worn new shoes, made by my father, and stood with one foot thrust forward; they were riding boots and at the tops, my initials, S.M., had been burnt into the leather. Perhaps even if my uncles and my Cousin Peter did not care for my face, they would see by the boots that I was their "kind."

My shoes, and nothing else, had always set me apart from other children, for they were of the finest leather and were most elegantly embellished. As I saw this morning how shabby my boots were, touched the thin spots on the soles that would soon be worn quite through, and remembered that I could no longer wear my summer sandals for my feet had grown too large, I was sorry that Papa had gone away. For if the other children had been surprised at this incongruous note in my raggedness, they had admired it. Even Betty Brunson, the wealthy dentist's daughter, had begged her mother for shoes like mine. And the band of horrid boys who, when I had pigtails, teased me for them and teased me even more when they were cut off and my ugly "bob" was fashioned to the uncompromising lines of a cereal bowl: they, too, had looked with envy on my red-brown boots of this year, laced with rough yellow thongs and equipped on the outside with pockets in which I carried a small, dull hunting knife, salvaged from the kitchen shelves, and an eight-inch celluloid ruler.

I looked again through papa's effects, in the hope of finding some bauble that I had overlooked which would distinguish me as much as my shoes had done. There was nothing but the rosary, and although I was tempted to slip it around my neck, superstition checked me. In my ignorance, I thought its magic properties might operate to my destruction.

The sun was high and the piled snow was melting. I heard the Henderson children coming home for dinner, and I knew it was time for me to leave the shop which I already thought of as my own. I looked back one more time for a treasure, and now, not amongst the things spilled over the sides of the boxes, but on the work table,

I saw a pair of slippers my father had made for Hopestill Mather. They were sandals with a strap up the center, through which passed another strap, fastened at the side with a gold buckle, and they had been dyed green, the color of the first leaves in the spring. One was unfinished: the sole had not been trimmed and jagged spears of thick leather stood out on all sides. But the sole of the other was so smooth and polished that it felt like satin to my cheek. I supposed she would have a green dress, made of taffeta or chiffon, and that in her hair she would wear a green ribbon like the one she had worn at luncheon that day with her aunt. I could see these little slippers dancing across a ballroom and I could smell the child who wore them: she would smell of Miss Pride's soap and of the sharp lily-of-the-valley cologne in the cut-glass bottle. I could see no one else at the party and even her partner was no more than a black mist. But the girl, with her yellow eyes and her white skin, her head flung back so that the bright hair fell far down, was as real as the soft sandals I held in my hands, and I hated her. I took off my boots and my lisle stockings and sat down to try on the finished shoe. It did not fit. My foot was too long and so broad that it would not even go into the vamp although I struggled and pulled until I was sweating. Angrily, I flung it into a corner of the room where, in the smudged shadows, it gleamed like a wet leaf. Her hands would be small too! Half the width, half the length of mine, white as her face, smooth as the sole of the slipper, her hands would be covered with rings and bracelets, set with green jewels. And her room in her aunt's house on Pinckney Street would have a green carpet and pale green walls and a green satin counterpane for the little green bed.

I ruined the slipper with the crude sole. Both straps I cut in two with a pair of heavy shears and I dipped my thumb in machine oil to deface the surface of the kid. I pulled off the buckle with a pair of pliers and I drove a long nail through the heel and into the wood of the work table so that it was pinned there. And then, leaving the contents of my father's boxes in disorder on the floor, I went out, glancing backwards once at Hopestill Mather's absurd shoe.

Mrs. Henderson had prepared a meal for us: a cabbage soup, made according to my mother's instructions, was simmering on the stove and beans were heating in the oven. She had brought a loaf of fresh brown bread, a glass of apple jelly, and a nicely colored pat of margarine. My mother had been asleep and she looked rosy and rested. When I helped her into the kitchen—for she said with entreaty in her eyes, "My condition makes me feel funny"—and put pillows at her back, brought the table near so that she would not have to stir about, I felt a momentary affection and kissed her lightly on the forehead. I told her that I thought we might sell my father's clothes and his ski equipment. Since they were foreign, I believed they would fetch a high price, and I fancied a sign which I would put up over the door of the shop: "Miss Sonia Marburg's Sports Goods Shoppe."

"Sell them? My God, you are talking crazy! He would kill you if you sold any of his trash. Kill you till there'd be nothing left of you."

"But perhaps he's not coming back," I said.

"I'll take another plate of *pokhlyobka*. Mrs. H. is a saint from head to toe." As she dawdled with the spoon, she went on, "He'll come back, you'll see, darling. I won't say when, not knowing where he went, but he'll come back and I know that. And if he finds his wool drawers sold, there's no telling what kind of way he'll kill us. I was saying to Mrs. Henderson that what I think he did was go to Boston to get a gun. For us, you know, sweetheart. And so tonight I am going to keep a lamp on and if they see it go out they'll hurry over to save us."

This transformation of my father into a murderer made me laugh aloud and when I covered up my giggle with a cough, she remembered that he had, she had always suspected, "sores on his lungs" because he coughed so much, and a pity it was he couldn't have kept his hands off me. Though my cough was purely voluntary and though I had never known my father to be ill, the remark distressed me and it was not for years after that

64

that I was completely free of the notion that I had or might develop tuberculosis. She spoke of it from time to time, occasionally giving me garish accounts of his hemorrhages when his face turned blue and his eyes all but dropped from their sockets and blood spilled out from his lips as freely as wine from a bottle.

In vain I tried to convince her that it was only right we should sell the things in the shop. I said he would want us to, that, granted he was a bad man, he was not so bad as to want us to starve. After she had several times repeated in agitated whispers that he would be back that night to shoot us, she fell into her old, familiar placid grief, believed he would never return, and that I, poor, thin child, must make our living. "And the Hotel not open until summertime," she mourned, turning her eyes to the sand, the crags, and the ocean. "And Luibka coming. You must go to your teacher, darling, and tell her what a fix we're in." I asked her if I might have one of the dollars my father had left so that I could buy something at the store for our supper. She did not answer. Her elbow rested on the edge of the blue sink and she stared through the leaves of the geraniums, restored to their proper place.

2

On my way to school for the afternoon session, I thought considerably of my father. If he had left us at a different time of year, I think perhaps I would have been more casual. If it had been spring, the illimitable activities which the warm weather provided would have allowed me to set the catastrophe aside to think about when nothing appealed more strongly to me. For once April had come and my summer sandals were on my feet and my heavy sweater had been laid away with bags of tobacco to keep off the moths, I became a furious engine, liking to pursue, with an imaginary bow and arrow, an imaginary deer whose wild hoofs carried me on a windy chase to the Point and back. In the fresh evenings, I played Run-Sheep-Run with the Henderson children and their cousins from Marblehead. Sometimes, hiding in a pack, feeling the hot breath of my fellows upon my neck and arms as we hunched up together under the shoulder of a rock or under the branches of a spreading bush, I would try to imagine another occupation: "What if I were doing arithmetic at home?" but the question would sink under my intentness and I could not, try as I might, conjure up a picture of myself in any other circumstances.

One spring, a disaster had befallen me. I had a pitiful little cat of which I was fond. It was ridden with fleas that it hunted with its sharp teeth, seizing bits of its hide ferociously enough to draw blood. And its ears were bald with mange which had also thinned the hair of its neck so that pink skin showed through. In its misery, it never purred, but under my petting turned up milky, half-shut eyes in a sort of stupid gratitude. It had been a charming kitten, though, and I hoped through some benevolence of nature it would be restored to its original state. And then, it was killed by Gonzales' bulldog when it still ailed. I saw the dreadful slaughter: the dog's eyes popping as he rent and strangled the creature, spittle mingling with blood, and I heard the cat's single wail of entreaty. Yet, although as a witness I was nauseated, once the cat was underground in a shoe box filled with petunias from Mrs. Henderson's flower boxes, my tears dried, my faintness passed and all that evening, as though nothing had happened, I exuberantly played Kick-the-Can. But then, months later, after the summer was over and the early evenings were too dark and cold for outdoor games, I felt my loss and besought my father to kill the bulldog and, for good measure, Gonzales too. He replied that it was "good riddance." Not only was my only companion for these winter nights gone from me forever, but my bereavement was mocked. My mother, hearing my lamentation, added to my sorrow such a weight of depressing generalizations on death and cruelty that the cat assumed a tragic stature and I thought I should never forget to mourn.

Now it was still winter when my father left, and in the desolation of the beach, I felt the desolation that would fall upon our house. The thought came to me that perhaps he would never walk along this road again and that he was therefore, in a sense, no longer alive, just as on foggy days when I could not see the State House dome, it was as though there were no Boston but that the city had dematerialized in the mist. A little wind, cold and wet with salt water, blew freshly into my face. I stooped to tighten the lace of my boot and as I did so, I felt that I had done this same thing before, but although I troubled my memory, I could not recall the other time. Afterwards and for many years, whenever I thought of my father, I saw him as though I were kneeling in the sand looking up at him on a gray winter day, our hair curling in the wind. Because my hands were cold and the lace was damp, the knot was not easy to tie. As I bent over, the smell of wetted leather came to me. When the odors, as distinct as on the day he left, came back at certain, sudden times throughout the years, with them always came the evasive feeling that every gesture I made and every particular in the landscape had been copied from some earlier day.

The fear that I might be taunted for my father's desertion rose to make me walk more slowly. I hoped to arrive after the others had already gone into the building. But immediately afterward, I quickened my pace at the thought of being stared at if I were tardy. I could hear the cries of children playing in the yard, mingled with the thud of balls being caught by the big boys of the eighth grade, and with the whizz and whine of swings where the younger children were pumping up. Then, when I had reached the gate and poked my head about one of the big cement columns which advertised the name, "Chichester Public School," and the date of erection of the building, and saw my boisterous schoolmates, I was urged forward by the desire to be hailed by them and was held back by the fear that I would not be and that my deficiencies, so mysterious to me and so apparent to them, would be more laughable today than ever. (I was always or nearly always the last to be chosen on a team, and I was convinced that the snub was directed against something less fundamental than simply my awkwardness in catching a ball or my inability to run without falling down on my face.) I expected to be greeted with a volley of catcalls which would proclaim my poor father's delinquency and would not spare my hair-cut. But my advance to the front door, although it was observed, did not disrupt the games.

Betty Brunson, who rarely addressed me, was embracing a young elm tree near the door and swinging round it, her head appearing now on one side, now on another. "Hi, Sonie Marburg, whatcha going to do this aft?"

"Oh, I don't know," I stammered.

"It so happens," she said, "that I happen to be going to New York. My father happens to be buying a car in New York City, New York."

A week ago, or yesterday, her voice would have been supercilious, for she would have been poking fun at me for being poor. But today, through a wonder of wonders to which I had no clue, she was *including* me as if her news and even her father's car were to be shared with me in the casual, communistic spirit that inspires the friendship of children. Heretofore, she had found space in the circle of her father's reflected glory for only two others, Esther and Ruby Beeler who were, strangely enough, even more impoverished than I. They, who had been pale, insipid waifs, bloomed under the patronage, became hearty extroverts with bold grins on their pinched little faces and roses in their cheeks which came, not from an amplified diet, but from happiness at being chosen. My first thought today was that they had offended Betty and that she was replacing them with the first person to come along. Her round face, with bright blue eyes and an obtuse nose, was framed by yellow, marcelled hair and the waves were held in place by tortoise-shell barrettes studded with rubies. She wore a coat of lambskin and a hat to match and from her pocket protruded fur-lined capeskin gloves. Without preamble, she began to relate the events of a "keen" Sunday she had recently spent with her highfaluting relatives in Boston. In the midst of her account, the Beelers came up. The three entwined their arms about one another and swayed round the elm tree with solemn faces as Betty listed the vegetables in the salad and the different designs on the coffee spoons. When she had finished, she said, turning to Ruby first and then to Esther, "We know a secret, don't we, Beelers?"

Her protegées said chorally, "We *sure* do."

Their solemnity reassured me. It was very likely no secret that my father had run away, for the Hendersons and Kadishes would have conferred and brought the tale to school. There was, in the manner of the three girls and in the circumstances of the encounter, evidence that the secret bore a relation to myself and was not in the same category as the new automobile. I assumed that it was something from which I would make either a social or a material gain: I saw myself riding in Dr. Brunson's new car, going to a Valentine party at the Brunsons' house, receiving a box of candy, a charm bracelet, a round comb or a bottle of perfume from Betty, and, finally, achieving the summit of the improbable whose ascent is so easy when we are lifted up by the wings of our dreams, I imagined going to a "slumber party" at the house of Betty's surgeon uncle in Boston. Betty and Betty's life became the Alpha and Omega: I aspired to her small, snobbish sorority that fed on Tootsie Rolls and licorice wands, and whose insignia, provided by her father, was a Roi-Tan cigar label worn on the middle finger of the left hand.

The girls, or, as I now thought of them, "my friends" would not tell me, but continued to repeat in singsong, "We know a secret and we *sure* won't tell," until finally Betty, using her father's language nonchalantly, remarked, "Oh, by the by, old girl, I almost forgot. Pickens wants a word with you." Ruby, who was dazzled by her friend's recherché speech, but not too dazzled to follow with what, in her social stratum, she believed was as debonair, said, "Ain't it the truth." Betty gave me a push, "Well, ta-ta till after school," she said and they retreated, walking backwards, their smiles giving way to brief glares of consternation as they almost lost their balance.

So Pickens (I dropped the "Miss" in my private thoughts, out of respect to Betty Brunson), I surmised, was in on the secret. This I did not relish, for it was to

69

her that my mother had insisted I appeal for help. "Just tell her that your rascal papa left you and your mamma is in a condition. You beg her, Sonie, there's a good girl. You cry and say, 'Oh, Miss Whatyoumaycall it, I am *so* hungry, and we haven't no money, no food, nor fire and not a thing.'" Of course no child could say anything of the kind. I had made up my mind to speak to Miss Pickens about customers for my sporting-goods shop, to make it clearly understood that I was launched already on a commercial enterprise of which the mechanism needed only the turn of a switch—the turn she would execute—to start producing a livelihood for me. In my determined independence, I thought of offering her a commission "per head" for any customer she brought me, a trick of business I had heard of through friends of my mother who paid taxi-drivers for touting rooms which they wished to let in the summer. My offer would demote Miss Pickens automatically from any position of benefactress. She was not a warm-hearted person but she was very sentimental and she viewed all successes as well as all misfortunes through tears which misted her spectacles but seldom acquired enough body to fall.

Miss Pickens was young but she already bore the marks of spinsterhood. Her fine chestnut hair was sparse at the temples and she vainly tried to hide her baldness with an absurd pompadour, bolstered up with a transformation, or, as we preferred, in our beastly way, to call it, a "rat" which sometimes became dislodged and hung spiritlessly down her cheek until she could repair herself in the teachers' rest-room. In her choice of clothes, she seemed to aim deliberately for the most unbecoming; she was perversely fond of chartreuse, mauve, and tan, which influenced and increased her sallowness. And so great was her belief in the ensemble that she wore everything to match exactly, including her stockings and gloves, even if she had to dye them, with the result that she resembled a caterpillar whose cocoon matches the leaf on which it is spun. Her medicine fetish was as persistent as any old lady's at the Hotel. During arithmetic in the morning, she ate a whole cake of yeast; at recess she measured out ten drops of belladonna from a bottled labeled "Poison!" and in the afternoon, stirred up a glass of psyllium seed which, mixed with water, looked like a thin brown mucus and repelled us all. No child had a crush on Miss Pickens, although I had at first been attracted by her cold, cultured voice and her elevated vocabulary which contained such words as "literally" and "intolerable" and "indefatigable," but her mannerisms quickly began to irritate me and I joined mine to the general growl, "Aw, she thinks she's smart." Her tear-clouded, octagonal glasses had given her the reputation of meaning well among the parents, who met all the teachers annually at the P.T.A. clambake. My mother was fond of relating how moved Miss Pickens had been when she told her of the time I broke my collarbone at the age of four by falling off the roof of the shop. "A person would think," my mother said, "that it was her own collarbone or her own child and happening right now instead of eight years ago." But really Miss Pickens' tears were trumped up. When Lottie Cummings' mother died, our teacher was blinded when she first interviewed the child but made no move to comfort her, only made her cry the harder by calling her "My poor, poor little girl." And after that, Lottie, who at the age of thirteen weighed 135 pounds, complained to her that the other children had commenced to tease her again now they felt the interval of mourning was over, but Miss Pickens did not restrain us in any way.

The building was empty save for a few teachers clustered about the radiator far down the corridor. As I opened the heavy storm doors and my nostrils were greeted by the familiar but always new odors of school—varnish, floor oil, felt erasers full of chalk—I experienced the feelings of light-headedness and pleasure I always did after I had been ill and then was well enough to go outdoors again. For it seemed ages ago, not yesterday, that I had entered here. I advanced, hunting signs of change, and found them everywhere: the old freckles on the drinking fountain I had never seen before, the ancient chains on the cloudy transoms, a green, crazed flower-pot which must have stood for fifteen years in the corner of a window sill above the stairs. And there was added to the heavy atmosphere a smell that was new to me, yet one I must have smelled daily for seven years: the smell of wet paper towels that filled the wastebasket beside the drinking fountain. It was so strong that the varnish, oil, and erasers were all but obliterated.

Miss Pickens, who had been humming "Comin' through the Rye" and supplying the percussion by tapping the gauge of the radiator with her long foot encased in a "health shoe," broke off her song and detached herself from the group of teachers to come toward me, her arms extended. I halted, suddenly trembling, like a person armed to defend himself against wild animals, but on meeting one face to face is immediately turned to stone. I quickly went into the seventh-grade room and scurried to my seat, laying my head on the desk, my arms folded on top, with the ostrich's belief that I was perfectly concealed, even though I could see her through an aperture of my intertwined arms, swaying through the aisle, the frolicsome tails of her beige chiffon scarf floating above the inkwells. She sat down in Rosalie Kadish's seat opposite me where there always hung an aura of onions which combined now with the teacher's smell of yeast, sachet, and a slight mildew.

"I understand," she said in her clear, uplifted voice, "that your father literally flew the coop. It was a naughty and intolerable thing to do. But every cloud has a . . . ?"

"Silver lining," I promptly supplied.

"Exactly. For one thing we won't ever drink beer at noon again and be sleepy in our sewing lesson, will we?"

Her sweetness curdled at the allusion. It was true. Whenever my father had the money, he brought home several bottles of beer from an old man who lived behind the Presbyterian church and carried on a paltry bootlegging business. I always begged for a glass, but my father, more through greed than prudence, refused me more than a cupful which he poured into my soup. However, this was enough, having it as I did in the middle of the day when I was already drowsy from the morning in school and the long walk home, and having it in combination with heavy food, to make me thick-witted and often Miss Pickens found me "*li*terally asleep," a state at any time deplorable, but in my case magnified enormously since its cause was immoral, bar-barous, and illegal. "To spoil good soup!" she fretted. Once, after I had committed some monstrous blunder in buttonholing, she called on my father and charged him with rearing me to be a drunkard. My father shrugged his shoulders and pretended not to understand her: "*Bitte, sprechen Sie Deutsch, gnädiges Fräulein?*" he said with a troubled face. She left, defeated and un-friendly, and had thereafter a chillness towards me which accounted, as much as my dreaminess, for my low grade in Deportment.

I said I supposed I would not drink beer again and the prospect saddened me. My teacher then laid a damp hand on mine and said, "There, there, it's hard, poor child, but we mustn't cry," and though she was not, of course, referring to the beer, I decided that my life would be unendurable without it. "We" had had until now no urge to cry, but her words, so mushy and stale and yet so tender and personal, started up a torrent of tears, and each time my inquisitive tongue received a drop, I was reminded, bitterly, of the way my father had put salt in his beer. I suffered her to lay her moist fingers on my head and arms and to come quite close to me in an embrace in which all the unhealthy odors she dispensed rose and eddied about me at the slightest movement on the part of either one of us.

"We must be *brave* and not be a burden to Mother who is bringing a baby into the world just for *us*," and then, to distract me, she said, in a fun-loving way, "I'll tell you what: I'll bet you a dollar to a doughnut it's a boy." When I agreed with a sobbing "Okay," she went on to tell me that as luck would have it, Betty Brunson's mother was also expecting the stork very soon, and she had been saying only the other day how much she would like to find a girl to help with the housework, and Miss Pickens had said to herself, "Why, I know just the girl. My Sonie Marburg is very capable and works at the

Hotel in the summer so she must know how things are done, dishes and so on. I wouldn't be a bit surprised if she wouldn't love to work in the nice shiny new house where her chum Betty lives."

I lifted panic-stricken eyes to my teacher and dropped them at once. The shock had stopped my tears. I could not become a servant in Betty's house when she was about to admit me into her circle! Such a job, possible anywhere else and even attractive (for, in spite of my intention to refuse, I saw what I might gain in the way of petit larceny of sugar lumps and birthday candles and other staples which would never be missed), would cancel all those social engagements which had practically been proposed to me on the school ground just a few minutes ago. It was only after my stammered reply that my mother needed me at home, when Miss Pickens said, "Why, Betty thought it would be lovely. She'll be *so* disappointed," that I realized this was the secret. Everything had been ill-timed, and I, in my uncircumspect cockiness, had been caught in a trap.

Miss Pickens was stubborn and set before me arguments that I could not refute. I saw that the sooner I resigned myself the better, for my commercial pipe-dream could avail me nothing now that the teacher, essential to its working out, was set upon the new plan which, in her surpassing conventionality, she regarded as great good luck for me. She, being comfortably off herself, had no patience with pride in the poor as she often told us, apropos of tales she had read in the newspapers. Nevertheless, urged by desperation, I told her what I had intended to do.

Her befogged eyeglasses glared at me. "I'm surprised at you, Sonia. I didn't think you were a *silly* girl. You've been reading silly books instead of good books, suitable for your age group." ("Age group" was the sort of expression that had once fascinated me. She had learned her "Education" well and had not forgotten it, so that she sprinkled her speech with its vocabulary with a serene disregard for the class or age of her interlocutor. She had baffled Mr. Henderson by telling him that one of his children had no "community urge.") "Nothing, you poor silly child, could be less feasible than a sporting-goods shop in Chichester. There is only one sporting man in town so far as I know, that Dr. Galbraith at the hospital. And he, of course, goes in only for riding equipment. But I have a friend" (by a faint glow that simmered in her face I knew she meant a man friend) "who likes winter sports and if your father's skis are any good, it is quite possible I may be able to arrange a sale for you."

She obviously doubted the quality of my father's paraphernalia, and I said, "They're very expensive."

"Well, we'll see about that part of it. Don't you worry. I'll do my bit for you if you'll be sensible and go work for Mrs. Brunson."

I was gradually persuaded; rather, one self, already installed in the Brunson kitchen and reaching out a hand toward the sugar canister, was persuaded. Miss Pickens was pleased with my change of heart. "And now," she said, rising and plucking me by the shoulder, "now we must get rid of our tears, isn't that right? Hurry along, the bell's about to ring." And she hustled me down the corridor toward the teachers' rest-room. There was a recrudescence of my disappointment and I felt that I could not face Betty again today. I told Miss Pickens I felt a little sick and had a headache, couldn't I please go home?

"Certainly not," she said severely, but then, seeing how woebegone I was, she relented and in a burst of kindliness, even suggested that I wait in the lavatory until the other children had assembled in the classrooms so that I might leave the building without being seen. I was surprised that the teachers' rest-room smelled like ours and had the same gray enameled doors to the toilets. Only on great occasions of illness or accidents were children admitted to the room. Once, in the year before, some privileged little girl told us that as she was recovering from a nose-bleed, she had seen a cigarette butt on the floor, stained with lipstick. We tried to detect signs of guilt in all the teachers' faces, and could not, but the worldly Beelers said, "Oh, piffle, you dumb-bells. They *all* do it, but they flush them down the toilet."

I thought, as I sat on a backless couch, waiting to hear the last column of children march up the stairs and into the classrooms, that if only circumstances had not conspired against us, Betty and I, fast friends, might have taken up smoking.

3

To my mother, my father's desertion was like an eternally renewing spring from which she hourly drew accusations and complaints, and she shared her poisoned, enervating drink with anyone who would partake. Her companions in misery were poor neighbor women who, alternately pitying and envying, welcomed our misfortune as a distraction from their own worries. Mrs. Kadish, a thin, pinched, crotchety woman, the wife of a ferryboat engineer and the mother of six famished children, often came to call. She sat prissily erect, her hands folded tightly in her lap, nodding her long, hard head which was topped by a coil of graying hair. When she was not speaking, she pursed her lips in permanent displeasure, and when she did speak, it was in a high, nasal key, not loud, but like a distant scream.

As I came in one afternoon, she was saying, "I was on my feet at five A.M. this morning and I'm telling you, I've been on the go ever since. It's pick up! Wash up! Sew up! Rinse out! till a person could drop down senseless. You was saying, Mrs. Marburg, that it's hard if the man goes off and leaves the woman, but to my mind it's six of one and half a dozen of the other. If you don't have a grown man around, you don't have to cook so much and do up all them work shirts. Kadish would leave tomorrow and I wouldn't hardly notice only for the little dab of money he brings in."

"He hasn't left you yet, sweetheart," said my mother. "It's not the money. It's the *shame*. My God! You'd think this here wasn't his child not born yet and he went off to punish me. I know *you* don't think so, Mrs. Kadish, darling, nor Mrs. Henderson nor two or three other Chichester ladies, but what about the *other* people?"

Mrs. Kadish did not regard it a likely suspicion though it interested her. "You mean maybe they think you you-know? Oh, no, I don't *think* so. Why, Mrs. Marburg, nobody would say you was that type lady."

My mother began on a new tack: "Well, then, maybe they say *he* was the bad one and went off with one of those women from Marblehead, and maybe that's true, Mrs. Kadish, who knows? I'm no fool and I used to see them last summer wobbling down the beach by the gentlemen's house in dresses no longer than your camisole." The "gentlemen" were the Coast Guards, so known because one of them, five years before, had gone to Harvard.

"You're not telling me news," returned her friend. "But I wouldn't think that a family man like Mr. Marburg would take up with that type."

"Whatever people say—if they blame it on drink or on the other thing or something else besides—it's all a shame. But what can you do with Hermann Marburg? He is a *German,* dear."

Her voice fell upon the word "German" in such a way that the emphasis was ambiguous: either a German was infamous beyond pardon or pitiable beyond hope. Mrs. Kadish, after this statement, perused my face for a time. "German," she intoned. "And you, Mrs. Marburg, what was you saying was your nationality?"

"I am a Russian," said my mother without pride and without deprecation but with a kind of finality which set "Russian" distinctly apart from "German" as though it was perhaps not ultimately the best thing to be but was at least comprehensible. I could have corrected her: Russians, to the children at school, were utterly improbable though all that was known about them was that they had ludicrous names. A favorite sport was to tease me by saying: "Hisky, Sonivitch, have got your geographysky home-workskivitch?" In a way, I was flattered by this, for it had replaced Pig-Latin and was known as Sonie-Latin. On the other hand, Germans were perfectly credible and, because of their reputation for cutting off the hands of sleeping children and of being sired by Kaiser Bill, they enjoyed a certain prestige. Sometimes, the

three or four of us in the lower grades who knew a little
German were bribed to sing, in a secret place, *"Stille
Nacht, Heilige Nacht"* and the eyes of our audience
grew more enraptured with each evil word.

"Rooshun," brooded Mrs. Kadish in her piercing
voice. "So your kid is half Rooshun and half German—
half Hun, as they say. Well, mine are bad enough: half
Jew and half American. But not so bad as that." I felt
a rush of shame which my distaste for her smelly children did not intercept. "But I don't doubt," she added
in the same shrill note of lamentation, "but what she's
a bright little slip."

"Bright!" cried my mother. "She's full of brains as big
as an apple, that little thing is. And helpful, my God!
Well, she's everything in the world you could want, Mrs.
Kadish. Come here, Sonia girl, let me show Mrs. K. how
long your eyelashes are," and she gathered me to her,
pulling my hair as she held up my head for our neighbor's admiration.

"Tchk, tchk," said Mrs. Kadish. "She'll be pretty. She
won't have no trouble getting herself a man, you know
what I mean?"

"There's where you're wrong," replied my mother.
"Not but she couldn't have any man in the world for the
asking even now and only twelve going on thirteen, but
what kind of a mother would I be to let an angel like
her be treated the way my poor self has been?"

"You wait and see," warned Mrs. Kadish. "The time
will come and whoosh! she's gone. But I wouldn't be
thinking so far ahead, Mrs. Marburg. I must say I don't
agree with you that she could get a man right now at
her time of life. To my way of thinking she looks poorly.
My Nathan might take her, along about sixteen or sev-
enteen."

My mother gave a foolish laugh. "Your Nathan! Well,
pardon *me*, Mrs. Kadish, but no thank you. I don't
mean anything by that only I couldn't do without her."
She pressed my head into her breast until I could
scarcely breathe, but I had the strength to pull away
from her and turn aside, my cheeks blazing. I did not
know, indeed, what she would do without me, but I
knew well enough what I would do without her. Right

now, I thought bitterly, I would be *playing* with Betty Brunson instead of being on my way to her house to *work*. I murmured that I must go, that I would be late, for the sun was already going down.

"Poor baby," said my mother, stroking my hand. "She is her mother's staff of life."

"Would you mind telling me, Sonie," said Mrs. Kadish with a wily leer, "just what them Brunsons pay you?"

I told her they gave me three dollars a week. "Well, I'll be!" she exclaimed. "'They're real free, ain't they? If you ask me, that's pure charity or pure show-off, I don't know which. Three dollars! And pretty soft, I expect?"

"Soft!" burst out my mother. "Soft! She slaves herself to the bone!"

Mrs. Kadish's curiosity was not satisfied. "You live high on three dollars a week now, and I'm not saying that isn't dandy, I'd just like to know how you do it. Now, me, I have close to ten a week and I can't hardly make both ends meet."

"We have a golden egg," said my mother proudly. "But we don't touch it only now and then."

"A golden egg?" queried the neighbor. "How's that?"

I was infuriated with my mother. She was talking about our "nest" egg as Miss Pickens had called it, the fifty dollars her friend had paid us for my father's skis, poles, boots, and leather shorts. I had wanted to keep our wealth a secret for I was sure it would be stolen as we had no good hiding place for it. Miss Pickens had advised me to take it to the bank in Marblehead, but I was afraid to go so far alone with that much money on my person, and we had put it between the leaves of my father's Bible, so close to Mrs. Kadish at this very moment that she could stretch out her hand without moving from her chair and take it all.

"You know the teacher, Miss Pickens?" whispered my mother. Her friend nodded, leaning forward. "She brought a man here and he bought all Hermann's trash for fifty dollars."

"No!" Mrs. Kadish's lips curled into a smile of disbelief. "May I inquire what this here trash was?"

I said, quoting the purchaser, a sickly young man who

had resembled Miss Pickens and who had scarcely been able to contain himself at the sight of my father's belongings, "Four pairs of Bavarian skis and poles covered with plaited leather and four pairs of genuine Salzburg *Lederhosen* and galluses to match."

"Galluses?"

"I don't know the English word," I said.

The woman looked at me with respect. "Nathan knows some foreign words, too. Fifty dollars. I'm glad for you, I surely am. No telling what will happen. Sonie might get appendicitis and have to have them out. That fifty dollars would come in handy." She rose to leave and my mother extended her hand, fingers pointing downward as though she expected it to be kissed. "You come again, sweetheart, I'm always here in the afternoon."

"Some pregnant women crave dill pickles," said Mrs. Kadish. "I'll bring along four or five when I come next time. I was always crazy for them myself."

When she had gone I put out my mother's supper for her: a plate of cole slaw, a loaf of rye bread, a dish of Liederkranz, and a casserole of beans that had been heating. She looked with displeasure on the meal. "If only I could have one small cucumber in a dish of sour cream, I wouldn't ask for anything else in the world." We had been through the cucumber argument many times before.

"Oh, Mamma!" I cried. "You *know* they don't have them at this time of year."

But, as always before, she either did not hear or did not believe me. "A cucumber is a little thing to ask. If I could have just *one*, just a small withered one in just a little bit of sour cream, ah, ah, I could bear all the rest!"

She did not move from her chair beside the stove, and knowing that she would only eat when the notion struck her, I went out. But I did not go at once in the direction of the Brunsons' house where I had long since been due. Instead, I ran across to the Kadishes' house where a light was burning. Through the uncurtained window, I could see the children gathered about a round table in the kitchen, each of the six intent upon some project, piling up matches or painting with water colors or cleaning a comb, but not too absorbed to chatter now and then and to dart their black eyes about the table with a controlled ferocity as though they all hated one another but knew that they must stick together. All of them came from the same mold: the same crisp black hair glittered under the lamplight; their faces wore sharp, shrewd expressions, the upper half seeming to be drawn down by the weight of the nose, loosening then below the nostrils into soft lips and little chins.

Nathan, the oldest, a boy of fourteen, sat near the window reading, and as the lamp was directly shining upon him, brightly illuminating his face, I was able to study the birthmark on his cheek. It was probably because of this shocking purple disfigurement that he was so ill-tempered and also so precocious. He was as sensitive as if his mark were a raw sore, continually being rubbed against or hit. It extended from the cheekbone, over the eyelid and the low forehead, to the hairline, appearing the more brilliant because of the dead pallor it interrupted. His lips were pouted in profound misanthropy and he seemed, for all his concentration, to detest his book, for his forehead was drawn into a scowl and his erect body wore an air of unwillingness. I knew by hearsay as well as by the ever meditative look upon his face and by the constant presence of a book under his arm that he was learned. He did not read *The Boy Scouts in Arizona* or the *Motor Boat Boys,* but instead, lives of Napoleon and histories of Rome and the Waverley novels. He had greatly admired my father, and often on Sunday afternoons had come to the door, inviting him to take a walk. My father never refused him, and it was on these expeditions round Chichester that Nathan had learned the foreign words of which his mother was so proud. Tonight it was *Quo Vadis* that he had propped up against a sugar bowl.

I respected his scholarship, but in my lassitude felt no urge to emulate him. I sometimes wished that we were friends so that I might absorb his culture through our association. But I did nothing to make myself commendable to him, nor could I have, for he was a formidable critic of everyone and especially of girls. A foolish girl of his age had once cried out in derision, "Cranberry Kadish is my ideal of a perfect man, like fun!" "Her ideal," said Nathan with a contempt that far surpassed hers, "I suppose she means platonic ideal because I wouldn't touch her with a ten-foot pole." The girl blushed and said, "You know what I *meant*. I meant 'idea.'" But her correction was too late and as she fretted over the failure of her arrow to kill, he regarded her with a triumphant sneer that twitched at his birthmark.

Tonight, made thoughtful by my mother's conversation with his mother, and, restless in my trap, I wished more than ever that Nathan were my "best friend" and that we took walks together in the evening, confiding in one another our sorrows and our ambitions. The desire for his companionship was tantamount to a betrayal of my mother who for so many years and so diligently had schooled me in the treacheries of men, although I believe she assumed that I would marry in spite of her warnings, would profit by none of her precepts, but by my experience would confirm what she had told me. And I, although it was my intention to remain unmarried (more in imitation of Miss Pride than to escape the pitfalls my mother had described to me), had a quite reasonable curiosity to know what were the manifestations of a man's descent from Satan. The marred Jewish boy, at his sullen labors, roused in me a strange new ravening and I all but tapped on the window glass as a sign that he was to come out to speak to me. As quickly, the impulse waned and I turned to go. But as I did so, I resolved hereafter to come each night about this time and take up my brief, secret vigil. I was light-headed as I went on my way and I felt a little sick. Each time his image returned to my mind, my throat thickened and my footsteps faltered. But though it was novel and mysterious, my disquietude made me happy and I began to sing one of my mother's songs:

> Far from where the men were reaping,
> Soon my weary self was sleeping;
> Slept and then waked—oh,
> Slept and then waked.

Thus as I the time was whiling,
Came a fellow, started smiling,
Courting me, too—oh,
Courting me, too.

Long my mother waited, wondered,
Long my sister waited, pondered
Where I might be—oh,
Where I might be.

Night came down upon the stubble.
Women have all kinds of trouble!
Woman's sad lot! Oh,
Woman's sad lot!

My installation in the Brunsons' house had been a disappointment, for I was in many ways farther removed from Betty than before. And so it was that I plucked the sting from my evenings there by silently communing with Nathan Kadish through the lamplit window.

At the Brunsons', as in my own house, the central figure was a pregnant woman, the very blazing personification of indecency, and Betty, quite unlike myself who found my mother daily more distasteful, adored hers increasingly, though I forgave her for she believed that her mother was going to a hospital to buy a baby from the supply kept there in a large ice-chest. The myth had been so fully developed in her mind that she was convinced the child had been specifically planned as a birthday present for her. It could not be a surprise since sometimes babies spoiled and you could never tell when there was to be a shortage. The Beelers, thoroughly sophisticated, left off their vain instructions when she told them sternly not to *dare* say anything nasty about her mother ever again. "But lookit how fat she's getting!" said Esther. "Look here," snapped Betty, "my Uncle Harry told my mother she *had* to get fatter, and if you don't like it, you can go jump in the lake."

The presence of the Beelers in the house was a sharp thorn in my side, for while I was confined to the kitchen, except when my chores took me into other rooms, they roamed at will throughout the house, obstreperous, dirty, and either through preoccupation with their absurd hilarity or through snobbery, they ignored me. I pondered how Betty, with her fastidious ways, could possibly find them preferable to me. They had warts and they did not wash. Yet, while I was paring vegetables, the three of them sat in the parlor playing Old Maid or came into the kitchen to blow soap bubbles or raced about in the upstairs, howling and giggling in some aimless game. I was not ashamed, though, as soon as they left the house. I was pleased to wear a starched white apron over a black sateen uniform when I brought in the soup and then served the dinner. The dark, round table glittered with silver and pink glass. The center-piece was a bunch of crystal grapes on an oblong mirror. The Brunsons always ate by candlelight; the radio played soft "dinner music," "Roses of Picardy," "The Bells of Saint Mary's," and "The Blue Danube." They had elegant table manners, holding their left hands in their laps, breaking bread into small pieces before they buttered it, and making not a sound in their throats as they drank water.

My duties were very slight and Mrs. Kadish's accusation that I was overpaid was quite true. The reason was not, however, that Mrs. Brunson was a spendthrift, but that the cook, Maudie, shocked by my pallor and emaciation, did all my work while she kept me in the pantry eating beef sandwiches and doughnuts, and drinking eggnog. Maudie was not a native of New England, but had come here from Idaho because she had always wanted to see "the spreading chestnut tree and Plymouth rock and that old bridge where they disappointed the British." And so, when her husband was thrown by a "spooked" horse and died of a skull fracture, and her two sons had got married, she set out with her insurance money to see what she called "the old country." She was a horsy, red-cheeked, raw-boned woman, nearly six feet tall. On her day off, she lounged in a one-room house not far from the Brunsons', drinking whiskey and reading magazines called *Lariat, West,* and *Rio Grande Romances.* The combination of the liquor and literature produced in her a virulent home-sickness which was contagious to her cronies—all men— so that her shack rocked with sighs toward evening when the men had gathered after work, as Maudie, in a plaintive, guttural voice, "My whiskey tenor," she called it, told anecdotes of horses, cattle, and bears, for all of whom she was lonesome. "Why don't you go back, Maudie?" the men would ask. "Oh, hell," she would reply, "it wouldn't be the same. My husband's dead and that dear old bench that throwed him is dead, and without them two Idaho'd be an ornery outfit. She was a little strawberry roan by the name of Skylark and she loved him like another horse and he loved her like another human. I often say it's good they went together." She would relapse into a dreamy silence. The men were deeply touched.

During the week she was never sad. She sang a great deal, but she had a very small repertoire. I think she knew only "Home on the Range," "I'll Build a Coffin of Pine," "Holy, Holy, Holy," and the obscene verses of "Frankie and Johnny," and she had only one tune to which she fitted all the words, like square pegs in round holes, as Dr. Brunson said. Finally she was asked to stop. She did, but the moment the kitchen door banged to and she was on her way home, her voice came thundering back to us.

She called onions "engerns" and told me to "pack them spuds to the dudes," and if Mrs. Brunson scolded her, she said with a laugh, "The old heifer's on the prod again." I memorized her expressions and used them in imaginary conversations with men in ten-gallon hats as I rode the range or hog-tied the steers or branded the calves. Under the influence of Maudie's magazines, which I pored over far into the night after my mother had gone to bed, I began to write a story: "On a cold November morning," I wrote with a blue pencil on manila drawing paper, "you might have seen, if you had been on the sharp lookout, a shabbily dressed man standing in a dark doorway on the main street of Boise, Idaho. Over his left hip was a bulge and that was a shiny black single-action Colt .44 meant to kill Buck Johnson, steely blue-eyed foreman of the Lazy S 4 later in the day. The party in the doorway was a tough customer and his name was Scrub Maxwell. The men of Boise, who were every last one of them square-shooters, hated

Scrub's innards, for he was a cattle rustler and a scala-
wag in more ways than one." There followed a series
of unconnected adventures, including stampedes, the
discovery of wolves in the chuck-wagon, the puncturing
of the bellies of "five million head of pure-bred Here-
ford white-face cows and bulls as well as calves, heifers
and steers that had the bloat off Indian paintbrush."
Miss Pickens, to whom I unwisely showed my story, deplored this intellectual climate as much as she had my
postprandial snoozes when my father had given me
beer, and my compositions, all upon the same subject,
that is, the heroism of the young sheriff, Sonny Marburn,
came back marked in a vehement red pencil. And when
I wrote in an examination that "st." was the abbrevia-
tion for "steer" she held me up to the class as an
outrageous example of the idle mind.

Maudie left as soon as the Brunsons had begun their
dessert and I stayed on to serve the coffee and to wash
the dishes. It was strange, rather than embarrassing, to
serve Betty and to find her eyes always elsewhere than
on me, and after dinner to see her hidden behind a magazine in a corner of the sofa while I cleared her parents'
coffee cups away and brought in the ice-water. But later,
when I was washing the dishes, she came into the
kitchen and sat on a high green stool, talking with me,
telling me the plots of movies she had seen, reporting
on her Saturdays in Boston which were filled with visits
to the dentist ("My daddy wouldn't hurt me for the
world," she said, "so I have to go to Dr. Harrison on the
Bay State Road."), with music and dancing lessons, fit-
tings at the dressmaker, excursions to Schrafft's for hot
chocolate with tons of whipped cream, and visits to her
Uncle Harry's house on Beacon Hill. Or she told me
about the decorations in her bedroom, as if I had never
seen them, had not, on Saturday when she was away and
it was my day to clean the upstairs, fondled and pawed
the porcelain shepherdesses that supported the lamps
on her dressing table, their crooks bursting incongruously into parasols. I had gazed, awed, at the glassy
photographs lining the walls, of Bebe Daniels, Clara
Bow, Ramon Navarro, Janet Gaynor, Richard Barthel-

mess, inscribed with grandiloquent scrawls to "Betty."
I had looked through the windows of the doll-house
where a whole family was engaged in ossified enterprises: a baby with a rosy backside lay face down in a
cradle; a fat old grandmother stood in the bathroom, intently studying the tub as if she wanted to make sure
how things looked before she left the house—she wore
a hat and a fur-trimmed coat and carried a folded um-
brella in one hand and a knitting bag in the other. A
mother stood squarely in the center of the kitchen, a
china broom lying flat at her feet; and on the roof, the
father of the establishment was always emerging from
the chimney where he was presumably making repairs;
his legs, up to the waist, were invisible from the top but
could be seen dangling through the ceiling of the dining-room, his heels nearly touching the rare roast beef
(so life-like there were smudges of blood on the platter)
and the golden banana which dwarfed the meat, these
two dishes being the sole fare of the family from the beginning of my acquaintance with them until the end
of it. Two children, a boy and a girl, stood facing each
other at opposite ends of the parlor, doing nothing. I
was charmed by the tiny kitchen stove with a door that
really opened, the delicate round gilt table in the vestibule which showed, through its glass top, a bright blue
butterfly with folded wings resting on a shasta daisy, and
with the perfect little Christmas tree that stood in the
sun parlor, everlastingly green, its bangles and loops of
tinsel and tiny Santas proclaiming that to this happy,
paralyzed family, Christmas was every day.

I liked to look at Betty's collection of tortoise-shell
round combs, her barrettes and her grosgrain hair-rib-
bons, her party dresses with artificial roses at the shoulder, her splendidly equipped writing desk with lavender
and pink note paper, a brand new set of Prang's non-
poisonous water colors, red sealing wax, a gold pen and
pencil engraved with her name, and a soft, white leather-
bound New Testament with many colored place ribbons
given her, it said on the flyleaf, by her loving mother
two years before when she had been an angel in a Sunday School pageant. The inscription impressed me:

"From your loving mother, Mrs. Robert Killigrew Brunson."

Occasionally, when I had washed the dish towels and had swept the kitchen floor, Mrs. Brunson would call out to her daughter, "Go on and make the popcorn if you want to, angel face." I would stay on then sometimes until ten o'clock if the Brunsons, absorbed in magazines, forgot to send Betty to bed, and as we ate the buttery popcorn (made in an electric drum with a wooden handle which one turned round and round) she might digress from her own affairs to talk about people and things that I knew.

Once she said, "I don't know how you stand living next to those awful Kadish simps, chum. Honestly, they're lousy. Cranberry makes me sick to the stomach to look at him. My mother wouldn't let me go with them for anything. Do you want to know something? They're *Jews.*"

I was ashamed of my passion for Nathan and I said in defense, but meekly, "My father was a Catholic."

"Oh, that's different," she soothed me. "Daddy says you don't have to be a Catholic just because your daddy is. I mean, that's silly. I mean, well, after all, I'm not a Mason, am I, just because Daddy is?"

Despite her cordiality, there was a note of reserve in her voice as if my heritage had been discussed and rationalized and not merely accepted. "Anyhow," she went on, "Daddy has some good friends that are Catholics, but he won't have anything to do with a Jew."

A little later, on an evening when the Brunsons were entertaining, I learned how I was regarded in the household. Someone remarked on my extreme youth, and Mrs. Brunson replied, "But she's a jewel even so. You see, she was practically born in the pantry of the Hotel here and was trained before I got her." Dr. Brunson, a rash democrat, said, "She's good company for Betty, too." But his wife snapped irritably, "That's beside the point, Bob."

Betty, in our kitchen conversations, had not a trace of the haughtiness with which she had hitherto behaved towards me at school. At the same time, she gave me clearly to understand that our lives would never run parallel. She was to go to a finishing school and afterwards would come out in Boston at a double début with her cousin Frances Barker, the daughter of Mrs. Brunson's wealthy and successful surgeon brother.

One evening in March, Mrs. Brunson suddenly cried out during the salad course. We all—all but Betty—knew that her labor had begun several weeks before it should have. In their prudish way, her parents had planned to spare Betty any demonstrations like this and had hoped to have her installed in New York with a distant relative. In the tumult of getting Mrs. Brunson off to the hospital, the child was all but ignored, her father only casting instructions over his shoulder to Maudie to stay all night in the house and to me to keep Betty company as long as I could. Yet even in his agitation, he recollected her innocence and shouted loudly from the vestibule that he would telephone from Boston as soon as they had selected a baby. She was perplexed by the abrupt departure and a little annoyed since her mind had been made up to receive the baby after her trip to New York, but far from suspecting that she had been misled, she thought her mother had been informed (presumably by telepathy) that a particularly choice specimen was available and that if she wanted it she must make haste to be the first bidder. This delicacy was hard to understand, for in every other way the Brunsons were extremely common or, as they put it, "broad-minded." I, whose rearing had been far from gentle, had been told that it was unseemly to discuss any adventure remotely connected with the bathroom at the table, but any of the Brunsons might say, without a hint of embarrassment (although, because they always laughed, it was clear that they were somewhat self-conscious), "There isn't any more toilet paper."

Maudie, Betty, and I put up a card table in the parlor and Maudie taught us how to play five-draw, deuces wild. In the midst of the game, she brought us some hot chocolate and said, "Well, boys, let's lay off for five-ten minutes." Betty's mind had not been on the game and she was glad for the recess.

"Maudie," she said, "do you think Mummy is terribly beautiful?"

"Shucks. Of course she is. *You* know that and you're just fishing."

"I want to be just like her when I grow up."

"Don't you worry," said Maudie with a wry smile and a wink to me, "you will be. You're the spittin' image of her now."

"I love her dresses!" cried her daughter in a rhapsody.

Mrs. Brunson dressed flamboyantly, even when she was pregnant, wearing, in the evening, flowered chiffon dresses that trailed the floor behind and barely covered her knees in front and black satin afternoon dresses touched up with rhinestone gimcracks. She always wore high heels. From her rather large, powdered ears depended tarnished bangles. Her blond hair, lighter than Betty's, dipped and rose in hard permanent waves that framed a puffy face with orange lips and an orange circle on either cheekbone, eyebrows like peaked black thread and a beak of pink nose.

Maudie and I agreed that not only was she the handsomest, she was also the best dressed woman in Chichester.

"Mummy has style," said Betty smugly.

"Yeah," replied Maudie with a chuckle. "You mean the way she talks." Betty nodded. Her mother did have a certain style but it was not the kind that prejudiced anyone in her favor. Her everyday language was a mixture of slang and profanity. For years she said "for crying out loud" with an occasional variation, "for crying in the beer," and something that pleased her was "the cat's pajamas." But if she was annoyed with her husband, Maudie, a trades person or myself, she used a fastidious vocabulary and an elegantly sarcastic tone. "My good man, I scarcely mean to imply that *all* your meat is inferior," she said once over the telephone to the butcher, "but the cut you have sent me is *effroyable*," pronouncing the "effroy" to rhyme with "cloy."

Betty, after a moment's silence, inquired of the cook, "Maudie, when you got your boys, did they come right off the cake of ice or were they down on the shelves underneath?"

"Honey, I never got my boys that way. I got 'em like the cows git calves."

The little girl was startled. The Beelers had used dogs for illustration. She had believed that they were insulting her parents and indirectly calling them liars by stating as fact something contradictory to what she had been taught. Now she was disturbed in her ivory tower to find Maudie, an old woman and a mother, addicted to the same heresy. She asked for a fuller explanation.

"Well," Maudie began, "I ain't saying it's the same with everybody. Maybe we just tackle it this here way in Idaho." She talked with an impersonal candor as Betty's lips began to tremble and tears to falter from her eyes. When Maudie finished, "And I think it's a mighty shame you never knew about it before. Why, dearie, my boy Horace went to his first bulling when he was four years old," Betty burst into sobs and buried her face in the woman's bosom. "It spoils everything!" she cried. *"Everything!"*

"Now looky here," said Maudie, "you just quit that favoring yourself. Do you see Sonie Marburg bawling?"

But Betty sobbed on and on until finally she drooped with fatigue and Maudie carried her upstairs to bed.

The telephone did not ring that night, and it was only the next day that we learned what had happened. Dr. Brunson came back to Chichester and, harried, cruelly disappointed, he made no allowances for Betty's innocence, but announced forthrightly that the baby had been stillborn. A week or so later, Mrs. Brunson came home from the hospital and, quarrelsome in her convalescence, she discharged Maudie with the declaration, "This is an upper-class household, my good woman, and here we do not discuss certain facts, or, to put it in plain English, sex." But she was obliged to re-hire her when she could find no other cook. She made neither an explanation nor an apology to Betty; moreover, Dr. Brunson decided at the last moment that he could not take her with him to New York to buy the new automobile, and on her birthday she sat in the kitchen on the high green stool with Maudie and me, blowing out the candles and wistfully beseeching me to share my mother's baby with her.

Four

I HAD GROWN STIFF from kneeling on the floor of the shop, my head pressed against the splintery workbench. My hands were blue with cold for the fire in the monkey stove which I had built earlier had died. I must have been there a very long time. It was still some hours before dawn when my mother had jostled my arm and told me to run for Mrs. Henderson and now, from the looks of the shadows, it must be nearly noon. I had alternated a game of Patience with a prayer all morning long, for Mrs. Henderson, a pious woman, had enjoined me to implore of God my mother's safe delivery, and she must have known my mother very well for she had added that I should pray also that the baby be a girl. Now and then I had made a plea for myself, asking for the fulfillment of the wish I now wished every evening on the first star: "Let me go live on Pinckney Street." From time to time, carried away with speculations on the *décor* of Miss Pride's sitting-room, I quit my devotions and went to the window, pretending that I saw there not the bay but the Charles River and that the ungainly dories were the sculls of Harvard crews whose existence I had learned of through Betty.

Hopestill Mather's slippers were where I had put them on the day my father disappeared: one, soiled now to a greenish gray, sat forlornly in the corner while the other was pinned to the work table. Miss Pride had written about them. I had opened the letter, addressed to "Hermann Marburg, Esq." and read her request that the slippers be sent at once and that my father begin to make her a pair of "stout brown walking shoes." She expressed her surprise that my father was doing his work with less than his usual speed, but went on to say that his tardiness would be of no consequence if only the slippers were delivered on such and such a date. I assumed that on that day, a month before Christmas, Hopestill Mather would be going to a party. Several times I made an attempt to write to Miss Pride, explaining why they would never arrive, but I tore up each letter when I had finished it, and it was only after a second and much sharper note came from Pinckney Street that I at last sent off my apologies: "My father," I wrote, "has gone west and will never come back to Chichester again. He went to Cheyenne, Wyoming, to his cattle ranch. I am sorry about the dancing slippers, but he never finished them before he left and he said for me to tell you that he was sorry. He would have written you himself but at the last minute he had so much business to attend to that he did not have time. Yours truly, Sonia Marburg." A reply came by the return mail: "My dear Sonia: It was very thoughtful of you to write to me. I regret that your father has left Massachusetts. With best wishes, sincerely yours, Lucy Pride."

Even though the envelope had been addressed to me and this was the first letter I had ever received in my life, and even though its author was the one person whom I had never dared dream would write to me, I had been disquieted by it. It was not the brevity that disappointed me so much as it was the finality which was twofold in its implication: it told me that my father would never return (when I had written the word "never" to her, I had only half believed in it) and that now he was gone, she would have no further business with our household. And still, though her meaning was so clear it made my heart ache, so old and habitual were my aspirations that I did not cease to plan my life with her on Pinckney Street. And now, as I was awaiting the birth of my mother's baby, I was so far removed from the present time and Chichester that each moment of delay was a moment of bliss. A sound recalled me: I was still in tatters, the room was the reeking shack, the March wind through the cracks of the walls had set my teeth to clattering. Someone was tapping on the window and I turned.

"Come along, child, open the door!" It was Mrs. Henderson's sister from Marblehead who was visiting in Chichester that day. I unbolted the door and met her greedy face which nosed into mine, seeking my feelings. "Is it a girl?" I asked.

"It's not anything yet, sweetie, but it will be one or the other in a minute and your mother wants you there."

"I'll wait till it happens and then I'll come in," I said.

"No, you come along with me now. She's carrying on bad and wants you near."

Indeed, I could hear her carrying on, and while my feet were wooden, I knew at the same time that something must be done to hush her, and so I followed slowly, deliberately shutting off from my mind what was taking place in the house and instead calculating the number of steps from the shop to the back door. There were thirty-seven. I had never failed to count them when I went to the shop or when I returned and I never failed to forget how many there were.

Mrs. Henderson's sister ran her fingers through my hair as I opened the screen door for her. "How old are you?" she asked me. I told her that I was twelve. "Such pretty hair!" she said, but her face said, "To go through this and only twelve years old!"

The air in the kitchen was solid with heat and even the March cold we brought in with us was immediately absorbed. The stove raged and the ebullient pots danced on the iron lids; roasted and sealed into the atmosphere was the smell of carbolic acid and, I thought, of yeast. Seeking the sources of the odors, I saw in the wide window-ledge, beside the geraniums, a shallow bowl over the sides of which swelled an unbaked loaf of bread, and I wondered vaguely which of the two ladies had left my mother's side to make it.

The house was suddenly quiet. The door to the bedroom was closed, and beyond it I could hear nothing save the rustle of cloth and a splash of water. Mrs. Henderson's sister, her finger upon her lips, motioned me to the door, but I told her, "I'll go if she calls." The woman, who was not at all like her sister but was small and pretty and wore a velvety brown mole on her cheek like a beauty mark, hesitated and asked me if I were hungry. When I said I was not, she suggested that we play "Twenty Questions." I replied that I would rather just sit and wait. She felt then that she had done her duty and, relieved, hurried into the bedroom and its fascinating business.

My mother did not call for me, but now and then in the long hour when the obese and sweating dough held my gaze and my thoughts never came to life but labored futilely, I heard her groan and heard Mrs. Henderson speak kindly to her as she persuaded the child from its hull. Both the ladies had said to me when they arrived separately in the morning that they loved nothing so much as a tiny baby. I thought of Mrs. Brunson who still kept to her bed. Her pudgy fingers were always quarreling in a box of chocolate creams, trying to find one "fit to eat. My Gawd!" Now Betty, who had set her hopes on a baby, must content herself with her father's Packard sedan, with presents he had brought her from New York: a fire-opal ring, an angora cape, a rock garden in a glass sphere. For the least of these, I would have traded my mother's baby.

At last I heard the cry of a child, and I sprang to my feet. Mrs. Henderson was intently slapping the skinny backside of the wailing baby boy who looked like a brick-red fish and nothing human. His black hair did not grow from his skull but lay close like a mat pasted on, and his poor head which seemed all out of shape, curiously dented and noded, lolled over the midwife's wrist as though his neck had been wrung. When he was bathed and oiled and swaddled in a blanket, Mrs. Henderson carried him to the bedside and with a scoop of the blanket, framed the pitiful face from whose crimson mouth issued a ceaseless protest. My mother turned away with a groan. "Oh, take it away! Oh, leave me be!"

The neighbor woman, her kindly mouth half open with anxiety and surprise, whispered to her sister, "Poor dear, she's all worn out. Look, would you, he has his mother's hair and eyes," and she turned her bundle to me. I could see no eyes among the furrows of the ancient, vociferous face. But I pitied the improbable thing and against my will felt drawn toward it and asked if I might see its hands and feet, for I wondered if they, like the useless bud of a nose, had been executed as amateurishly. Indeed, no! Several authors had collaborated on the composition of this creature. The novice hand that had created the nose which possessed only one property common to noses, that is, two large nostrils, had not been the same one which, with so grim and un-Christian a humor, had made the long, prehensile feet with all five toes the same length, flexing and straightening as though a jungle vine to swing on were just outside their reach.

"Somebody's pleased with her little brother, that's not hard to see," said Mrs. Henderson's sister with a giggle as she held out a finger for the gruesome foot to grip. Brother! I felt with this prodigy only the most general fraternity: we breathed and were flesh. And yet, immediately the words were out, a leaven commenced to resolve my wonder into the emotion the women had assumed in me and my pity became protective. Almost as soon as my instinct to mother him matured, there came to me the more complicated feeling of love, so that I longed to hold him myself and to kiss his bawling, cockled face, and to bestow upon him all the tender services that were the right of anything so supremely helpless.

He was, said Mrs. Henderson to her sister, a "puny one," and the sister, feeling his feet and skinny legs, agreed, although she said she had seen punier. My mother, who lay with her eyes closed, scarcely moved her lips when she said, "If it's true he's puny like you say, maybe he won't live forever."

96

The midwife cried, "Oh, perhaps he's a little small, but he's healthy as you please. Just look at these fine hands and feet. Why, he has lovely bones, Mrs. Marburg!" But my mother had no wish to feel her son's well-shaped feet. Her hands curled as though protecting themselves from contact with the baby and only when he was taken from the room did her long, scarred fingers lie straight upon the coverlet.

Thinking she would fall asleep, I started to follow the women into the kitchen, but she called me back, piteously begging me not to leave her, and when I had gone to the bedside, she grasped my hand and would not let it go. From under the lids of her still closed eyes, a few tears seeped out. I was shocked at the sight of them and felt my throat grow thick.

"Come closer," she said softly. "I want to tell you something and I don't want the ladies to hear." I knelt at the side of the bed and she put her lips to my ear. "You're only a little girl," she whispered, "but you're not too little to learn something. Your papa won't come back now because somebody has taken his place. Listen to me: he prayed for a boy!"

"Oh, Mamma!" I cried. "It's just a little baby!"

The poor red parcel wailed in the kitchen and Mrs. Henderson cooed, "There, there. Isn't it a squirmer though!"

"Everybody's a baby once, darling," continued my mother. "That don't mean they don't get cruel by and by. I'm afraid of it, Sonia!"

But there was fear neither in her face nor in her voice as she lay back upon her pillows. I stood up. "Can't I open a window, Mamma?" I asked. "It's hot in here." It was not hot but it was close with a strange odor.

"Yes," she said with a sigh. "Open the window and let me get some air. Even though the sea air is bad for a person. I should live in the mountains."

I drew up the green blind, opened the window, and stood there breathing in the moist cold. The sun was bright as gold on the sand. My mother talked on. "There is nothing here but sand! In the mountains I would have a garden with melons and radishes and cucumbers.

My God, I would have flowers! I love flowers, Sonia girl. Maybe you might buy me some? Fifty cents out of the golden egg wouldn't hurt, would it, to get your mother some *tsvetiki?*"

"I'll get you some," I said. "Maybe when Mr. Henderson goes to Marblehead he can bring them back. Is it violets you want, Mamma?"

"No, it's roses I want. Little yellow ones, Sonie." She stretched out her hands to me but withdrew them as I went to her. "Do you remember what was the name he said for a boy that night he left?"

I did remember. "Ivan."

"Yes, that was it. We'll call him that. Ivan." She pronounced it like a curse in order that without delay the child might shoulder the double burden of her hatred for him and her hatred for his father who had used the name to taunt her.

2

Until the Hotel Barstow opened and Miss Pride had come back and the Brunsons had gone to Provincetown, I was completely absorbed in my brother, and my daydreams of Boston came to me only at intervals. And still, though my love for him was so despotic that I could not imagine loving anyone else so much, I realized, the first time I saw Miss Pride at her regular place in the dining-room, that he had not, after all, won my whole heart. One of the waitresses had cut her finger, and I was sent in with the dessert, a bowl of canned peaches and a thin slice of chocolate cake. Miss Pride had been reading a letter but when I served her, she looked up.

"How d'you do, Sonia? Are you taking your mother's place today?"

"Yes, ma'am. I'll be here in her place all summer."

"Oh, indeed? Does she have other work?"

"No, ma'am. Mamma isn't very well this summer." Her eyes demanded the nature of my mother's illness and I faltered, "She had a baby on the twenty-first of March."

"Mm." Then, as though she had given me as much time as she could spare, she turned again to her letter. I thought I had heard a note of disapproval in her voice and I regretted that I had not said my mother had broken her arm.

A few days later, she came into her room as I was dusting the bureau and, handing me a parcel wrapped in blue tissue paper, said, "I didn't know whether the baby was a boy or a girl, so I brought a little thing that would do for either." She left the room at once, before I had even time to thank her. My hands trembled as I untied the white satin ribbon around the little box. I was sure she had given Ivan a silver spoon. Instead, from a nest of white paper, I lifted out a bright yellow celluloid rattle made in the shape of a gourd. Still pasted to the neck was a sticker giving the name of a Marblehead novelty shop and the price, "15¢." My disappointment lay heavily on my heart until it was lightened by a remark my mother made when she looked at it. "Now that's what I call *lady*like," she said, shaking the rattle for her own amusement. "It shows she don't think we're poor or anyway she don't want us to know that she knows we're poor. If she had given us something useful, I would be mad." Mrs. Brunson, she went on to say, was not ladylike, because she frequently reminded me of my poverty by giving me Betty's outgrown dresses and sweaters. Until now I had not perceived the insult at the core of her generosity and had been only grateful. Mrs. Henderson, who was calling on my mother, eyed the rattle and said nothing. "Isn't that right, Mrs. Henderson?"

"I don't know but what it is, Mrs. Marburg," replied our neighbor in a voice of restraint. "As the saying is, it's not the gift but the spirit in which it is given."

During this summer of my thirteenth year, I was in the dining-room regularly, and because I often served Miss Pride's table and carefully attended whatever she said, I learned a great deal about her. I had been in the habit of thinking that she had come to the Hotel Barstow all her life, but I learned that a long time before she had spent every summer in Europe. Travel had left no mark upon her. When she spoke of France or Italy or Germany or England, it was to condemn the train service and the touts who "sprang out of the ground, especially in the Latin countries, selling everything regurgitated by the ocean and everything exported by the Japanese." She would say, "They hang too many pictures on one wall in the galleries. The Uffizi is a tiresome junkshop." And I could see her marching through Europe without surprise, taken in by nothing.

Occasionally Miss Pride's lawyer, a Mr. Breckenridge, came to luncheon and I heard them talking of taxes and dividends. Once she said, "When you get back to town, I'd be obliged if you'd give Barton a ring and tell him I want to sell my Sears Roebuck. I'm going in for public utilities." I was deeply impressed by her State Street argot, a few phrases of which I had heard Dr. Brunson use to his friends. But Dr. Brunson could never have said, with such casual yet unfeigned interest, "By the way, what did the pound do in the Bourse yesterday?"

Even more than by her familiarity with high finance, I was stirred by her intellectual life. For years without fail, she had set aside two hours of each day, from eleven until one, when she sat erectly in a corner of the lobby reading *The Atlantic Monthly, Harper's Magazine,* and the novels of Trollope, Henry James, Thackeray, and William Dean Howells. When I was enchanted by a book and did not put it down for several hours together or when, in the wintertime at school, I found myself in arithmetic lesson dreaming of being free to read, I was ashamed of my intemperance, remembering Miss Pride. I wondered if she would not be flattered if I dropped an intelligent remark now and again which would reveal that I had read what she had. Consequently I borrowed *The Awkward Age,* by Henry James, from the public library. The title appealed to me for I heard Mrs. Henderson say of her daughter, Sarah, that she was at "the awkward age." After a tormenting evening of poring over the completely unintelligible sentences of the novel, I returned it early in the morning of the next day and I did not try again to read Miss Pride's favorite authors, but contented myself with attracting her attention in more modest ways. I made her a pen-wiper out of the top of a black cotton stocking and delivered it with a bunch of black-eyed Susans. She thanked me graciously. "You are very thoughtful," she said. "I will think of you every time I wipe my pen." Emboldened, I invited her to come see my little brother of whose appearance I was very proud, but she declined. "Some other day, my dear," she said. I never had the courage to ask her again, for I felt that she was not really interested in Ivan. I told her once that he had prickly heat. She shuddered. "Oh, mercy! How dreadful!" It had not seemed dreadful to me, but only uncomfortable for my little brother. Later on I realized that by "dreadful" she had meant "unattractive."

I was pained that summer by an episode in which she figured. Gonzales' little boy, Emmanuel, had clever hands and often painted water colors of flowers and waves and bright blue birds, and this year he had begun to carve things out of soap. One day he came proudly into the kitchen with a little madonna he had made. Everyone marveled at the folds of her gown, the delicacy of her halo, and the perfection of her tiny, snubbed nose. Audrey, the headwaitress, said that the figure must be exhibited in the dining-room to the guests at luncheon. Emmanuel's protests were taken as modesty, and so that day, the little Virgin was passed around from table to table and was universally admired. At last it was placed before Miss Pride who examined it carefully and did not smile; with a frown of annoyance, she lifted it to her nose and sniffed. "This is my soap," she said sharply. A silence fell upon the dining-room and Audrey blushed as Miss Pride handed the figure back and waved her away. Some days later, I heard Mrs. McKenzie tell Mrs. Prather that Gonzales had paid Miss Pride ten cents for the cake of soap his son had stolen from the box under her bed.

The old ladies, with whom Miss Pride never associated, gossiped about her incessantly when she was out of the Hotel, and it was through them that I heard tales of Hopestill Mather, so discrediting that they afforded me the greatest joy. Mrs. McKenzie had heard from the mother of one of Hopestill's schoolmates that she had so hot a temper not one of the mistresses could discipline her, that she deliberately chewed gum in chapel, had spoken of God as "the old boy," and of the Apostles as "the whole gang." Miss Pride, it was said, obviously had no affection for her and only tolerated her in the house during the brief vacations at Christmas and Easter. In the summer, she was sent to camp in Maine.

"I pity the little thing," said Mrs. McKenzie in a low voice. "It can't be a natural life, you know. I've heard that her father wasn't all he should have been. Bad blood shows up, try as you may to conceal it. But fancy the high-spirited child spending her holidays in that gloomy old house on Pinckney Street! As I understand it, she hasn't any other close relatives. The line is dying out, and I do believe our friend is the last of the Prides."

If I were Hopestill Mather, I would never permit my dear aunt to send me away to boarding school. I would prevail upon her to let me go to a day-school in the neighborhood so that I might sit across from her each day at tea and on certain nights have dinner with her. On Sunday I would go, dressed soberly like her, to church. After the service (and I supposed we would sit in her own hired pew) we would walk around the basin of the Charles, no matter what the weather was, and then would lunch together at a long table, being sparing of our helpings.

Occasionally I heard Miss Pride speak of her niece to friends who came to the Hotel. I recollect one conversation I heard when Mrs. Brooks, who had brought Hopestill to the Hotel some years before, had come to spend the night. Miss Pride said, "I sometimes wish I had never seen the child, Josie. Yesterday I had a most unfavorable letter from one of the counselors. She's a born troublemaker, you know. What will she be at twenty? It's not only bravado—one can't begrudge a child a measure of that. It's a deep rebelliousness against everything fitting and proper."

"You exaggerate, Lucy," replied Mrs. Brooks. "You can't get her father out of your mind. Amy says all the girls like her. Isn't that the important thing, after all, at her age?"

"I don't believe Amy said that, Josie," said Miss Pride, peering deeply into her cousin's skull. "Did she now, truly? No, I won't make you answer, for I know what's what. But anyhow, it's not what she does now that worries me, it is what she will do when she has, so to speak, reached the age of discretion. For I am as certain as I am that you are sitting here with me that with her it will be *in*discretion. The counselor wrote me that she had been caught smoking. At fifteen, Josie! And that she had tried to run off from camp in a baker's truck. I won't have you telling me that these are only a child's pranks. There is something loose in her character. Her holiday tantrums are blood-curdling! If she were not a child, she would have apoplexy, I'm quite sure—her face turns as blue as the sky."

Mrs. Brooks stretched out a consoling hand. "Lucy, you will never change. We can't all have your self-control, my dear! Why, Amy, your affectionate Amy Brooks, has her temper too. It's Hope's lovely red hair, as the superstition goes. But don't suppose I don't sympathize with you."

"I must confess her hair endears her to me."

"It should. She looks more like you every year."

As I was removing the plates, Miss Pride said, "By the way, Josie, remind me to show you the pen-wiper this child made for me. Isn't she clever to be a chambermaid and seamstress when she's only thirteen?"

Mrs. Brooks smiled at me and I noticed that her left eye twitched as she did so. "I should say! I expect my Amy and your Hope could learn a great many useful things from her. Is your father a fisherman?"

"Her father is a *fuyard*," said Miss Pride. She explained to me that she had told Mrs. Brooks that my father was a cobbler and added, "You don't know French, do you, Sonie? It's German you know, isn't it?"

"Yes, ma'am. In German it's *Schuhmacher*."

Whether Miss Pride appreciated my pen-wiper or whether she compared me, to my advantage, to her niece, I could not tell, but at any rate, she was increasingly cordial to me that summer. She sent me on errands to her room when she was waiting for Mac or settling down to her reading in the lobby. "Run upstairs and bring me a handkerchief, my dear," she would say, and the "my dear" or "my good child" made me think my case was not an altogether hopeless one. And when she left in September, she gave me a sealing wax kit in token of her approval of the way I made her bed. The wax was rather old and did not go on smoothly and the "S" of the seal was backwards. But I did not care. On the flyleaf of each of my school books I dripped the blood-red taper and impressed my initials in the molten mound. So that just as each time Miss Pride wiped her pen she remembered me, I remembered her whenever I opened a book.

3

My brother Ivan would have granted my mother's wish and died soon after his birth if it had not been for the constant ministrations of Mrs. Henderson, who was both a generous and a sharp-eyed woman. If her attitude had been preponderantly the first when the baby was born, it was the second that for five winters and summers kept her in daily communication with our household. For she was one of those people we call "good." There was in her not the impulse to intrude, but to embrace, not to scatter kindness but to mend with it, and to do so not in the light of this or that principle, but because love was her nature. Mrs. Henderson's reputation was widespread in Chichester and had even reached the Hotel Barstow. Once, in the third summer of Ivan's life, I heard Mrs. Prather saying to a young relative, "I'm far more tolerant of the Catholics than most of my friends, but I can't agree with them that everyone must go through Purgatory—oh, *I* shall, I'm a sinner, but I've known people so pure I'm certain it's the good Lord's intention they should go straight to Heaven."

The girl looked doubtful. "I don't believe you do know such a person—at any rate it can't be anyone I've ever seen in your house."

"No, she has never been in my house. But you know her if you've ever had any sewing or mending done when you've visited here. I mean Mrs. Henderson who lives on this road up about a quarter of a mile."

"Oh, yes, I've been there. But how do you know? Surely you haven't struck up a friendship with her!"

"There was no need. Her goodness is as plain as the nose on your face." And she went on to describe the serene household, equipped with children whose manners imitated their mother's and with a husband who, whatever he might be outside the house, behaved in that atmosphere as commendably as one of his own children.

The girl was still unsatisfied. "You have given me no proof. What has your seamstress *done?*" There was a silence. Mrs. Henderson's advocate could not publish the chief reason for her immediate assumption into Heaven when I was near-by. But when, glancing back at the table from another part of the dining-room where my duties had carried me, I needed not to hear the words issuing so eagerly from her lips: she was, I knew, recounting our "story."

No doubt Mrs. Prather, who was a sentimental woman, exaggerated our benefactress's virtues. Mrs. Henderson was a "natural" and was to be envied and respected as are all people to whom being good seems the easiest part of life. A more sensitive person, one more dedicated to *doing* good, would have had, as I believe she did not, periods of despair at my mother's indifference to her services, Ivan's malicious ingratitude, and my own mercurial humors. She was as patient and dependable as a devoted dog who suffers his master to pull his tail and play all kinds of humiliating tricks on him without once growing angry. If, finding her at our house on my return from school, I saw that her finger was bound up with court plaster, I did not learn from her what the injury was, but rather from Ivan who had done the mischief himself with his sharp little teeth while she was fitting a new suit of clothes on him. And when he planted himself in her path as she was crossing over to our house with a plate of hot food and cried some unpleasantness which he put in the slang he had learned from me and the Kadishes, calling her a "lousy drip" or a "crazy dope" or a "dumb bunny," she only chuckled and with her powerful hands set him aside like a hurdle made of tissue paper.

She dressed my brother in the clothes her own children had outgrown and cut them down, taking great pains to make them fit his puny body properly. In the early years, she had been his faithful nursemaid, had, when she was too busy and I was at work or at school, charged her eldest daughter, Sarah, with his care. Between them they had fed and bathed and aired him and taught him to walk and talk. If they had failed to teach him manners (as my mother accused them—she had long since forgotten that she had any responsibility towards him herself), it was not their fault. They had tried to make him learn to say "thank you" and "please" but since in his own home there was no occasion for such delicacy, they had been unsuccessful.

If Mrs. Henderson deplored my mother's apathy, she never revealed it. Indeed, she treated her much as she did Ivan, receiving with composure the most outrageous insults, the most preposterous complaints with which my mother besieged her. She had once, soon after Ivan was born, made an appeal to her: "It's not my business, Mrs. Marburg, but I was wondering if you couldn't get a place now. There are jobs to be had for the asking in Marblehead and Lynn."

My mother stared uncomprehendingly. "And may I ask what Sonie would do if I was gone all day long and nobody was here to have a piping hot dinner for her?" Mrs. Henderson, who knew that I always prepared our evening meal before I reported at the Brunsons' in the winter and at the Hotel in the summer, sighed. "The child worries me. She don't look strong. I've a good mind to put her on Josephine's tonic."

Even though, since there was a shortage of help, my mother had been offered a slight raise in salary at the Hotel, she steadfastly refused to go back. She spoke of her "disgrace" and said that she could never face respectable people again. "Respectable people" became, in time, all the world but Mrs. Henderson and myself. If another neighbor—Mrs. Kadish or Mrs. Radcliffe whose society she had heretofore enjoyed—came to call, she bolted the door and slipped into the bedroom where she stood trembling until the knocking stopped. But if she were surprised out of a daydream and looked up to find a caller outside the screen door, she put her finger to her lips and motioned towards the bedroom. "Sh! The child, he's sleeping." The visitor, who as likely as not had seen Sarah Henderson sitting with the baby on the beach, put down her offering—a pot of soup or a bowl of pudding—and smiled and went away and finally, wiser after a few more rebuffs, did not come back.

Although my mother had never particularly liked her neighbors and had rarely returned calls, she had always had sufficient relations with the women of Chichester to remain something like them, and had gone abroad enough to realize that the world was larger than her kitchen. Her walks now became shorter. She no longer, in the summer evenings, sat on the little step beside the door, star-gazing and dreaming of Moscow. Nothing would have induced her to go to the village, for she was afraid of being ridiculed. Once, when a Fuller brush man came and offered to give her, without charge, a toothbrush with black bristles, she believed that the whole community, in the person of this representative, was teasing her for not brushing her teeth. Thereafter, when peddlers came, she pretended to be a deaf-mute and gesticulated at them with a look of hopeless regret on her dreamy face. Her voluntary imprisonment gradually became complete, and for four years, after my brother's first birthday, she never crossed the sill of our door, save on a series of winter evenings in the last of those years.

One day, when my brother was about three, Mrs. Henderson came to sit awhile and as she sat, worked at some embroidery for a table runner. It represented a green straw basket from which radiated a bouquet of larkspur and daisies of unlikely colors, these being the satellites to a rose, three times their stature and as big as a plate in diameter. In the void of muslin on all sides of the design, single pansies, petunias, and bachelor's buttons came fortuitously to life under Mrs. Henderson's needle. My mother watched, entranced, and as the neighbor filled in a petunia's corolla, she bent over the work excitedly. "Oh, how magical!" she cried. "Could I ever make those beautiful posies?" Mrs. Henderson assured her that she could, and laying aside her table runner, she took up a piece of plain cloth and gave my mother a lesson in the elementals of fancy-work, demonstrating the "lazy daisy" and the French knot and the feather-stitch. My mother was impatient to try her own hand and when she had finally got a needle threaded and her hoops fitted together, began to copy the stitches. They came out all askew and unrelated; her French knots were rough burls and her draggle-tailed lazy daisies exposed their unkempt framework which should have been on the underside. But she was not in the least disheartened and long after Mrs. Henderson had gone, she continued to practice, admonishing herself, "Ah, Shura, you're clumsy. All thumbs and butter fingers."

The following morning, I found she had got up hours before me, had had her breakfast, and had even washed her dishes and now was back at work on her embroidery. I was sure she would be tired of it by afternoon, but as it turned out, I quite underestimated my mother's patience with herself. From that day onward she stuck to her late calling with the tenacity, the absorption, and the humility of an artist. When I could not buy cloth for her to embellish, she set to work on her own petticoat or on my winter underdrawers or on the kitchen curtains. Once, being without anything at all and having a great urge to execute some oak leaves and acorns, she ripped open one of our pillows, letting the feathers fly where they would, with the result that for weeks we inhaled down. The ticking, when it was re-stuffed, was still so roomy that what feathers I had salvaged assembled at one end or the other but never spread out evenly. She was so proud of the leaves and acorns which were, to be sure, done in remarkable verisimilitude but interested me less than almost any other of her creations, that she made a new pillow cover to protect them which had the same design, and as it turned out well—better, she felt, than the original—it too required a protector, also bearing the same design, and so on, until it appeared that our pillow was to have as many skins as an onion. And no doubt it would have if Mrs. Henderson had not providentially given us for Christmas a very elaborate pillow case, adorned with hollyhocks, which my mother felt was just the thing to cover all her precious acorns. She would gaze at the pillow and say, "You would never guess what's underneath!"

I thought that her activity should be functional and once suggested that we try to sell some of her work. She greeted the proposal with surprise but acquiesced and pulled out from under the bed one of the boxes that had contained skis and was now used as her treasure chest. She could not make a choice: this was the only spray of lilac she had ever made, that was her most successful poplar tree, the dish towel half-covered with a cerise posy had been made in honor of my birthday. She could not part with anything. As our house was becoming overcrowded with her heaps of decorated rags, I at length persuaded her to use the shop as a storeroom, and finding that once the things were out of sight she forgot about them, I advertised them at the Hotel the next summer among the help. Though I realized no money, I sometimes had the luck to exchange a pin-cushion bearing a Russian monogram in cross-stitch for a dozen eggs or a pot-holder in the form of a purple rooster for a pat of butter or a pair of old shoes. Some of her work I still have: a flour sack, smocked in scarlet silk which she gave me one Christmas. She could assign to it no purpose but said she knew I would like "the red." When this poor thing, its banal legend GOLDEN GRAIN showing through the smocking as GLDE RIN, turns up as I straighten my bureau drawers, Chichester's long winters return, sprouting their evergreen leaves and everlasting flowers in the snow and the wind.

After the first rapture of fancy-work had spent itself and she merely burned with a steady, sober flame which only now and again flared forth, as in the case of the oak leaves, she found several supplementary diversions which never lasted but which she undertook when she had nothing to embroider. Thus, on four evenings running one winter, I was commissioned to take dictation from her. I wrote long lists of all manner of things: the names of the guests at the Hotel as far back as she could remember, the nations of the world, kinds of flowers and fruit and fish, the days of the week, and the months of the year. And as she dictated, she drew from memory the designs she had worked in her colored thread, covering page after page of a composition book with likenesses of cosmos and bumblebees. She complained that her memory was bad and she wanted the names of things preserved for her. Even though she could not read my lists, the very paper was reassuring; looking at it, she said, she knew that she had the key to things, even though she could not find the door.

During the same winter that she employed me as amanuensis, she fell one day to musing on the wicker furniture on the Hotel porch, one piece of which, a rocking chair, had been given us by the manager when it had reached a state of total dilapidation. It was quite useless, but Mamma had dressed it up with a cushion and a tidy each saying "Hotel Barstow" which I had lettered for her and which she had filled in with lavender feather-stitching on yellow Indianhead. She inquired of me if the Hotel chairs were ever cleaned and when I told her I doubted it, at least that I had never been told to do anything with them except to move them into the sun or out of it, she was scandalized. Who knew but what that Mrs. McKenzie, who was always nibbling, had lodged an apple core or nutshells between the cushion and the frame? She began to explore the crevices of our rocking chair with a hairpin and brought up a quantity of lint and poked out to the floor a good deal of fine sand.

"There!" she cried triumphantly. "What did I tell you?"

All day she worked at the chair and when I came home from the Brunsons' that evening, I found a shocking monument of dirt on the floor which she had patiently dislodged. She was wearing a coat and a scarf on her head and she told me that she had a little business to attend to, would I accompany her and be so good as to find some candles? Since she was, I saw, bent on going and bent also on not divulging where or why or for how long, I agreed, and took Ivan to Mrs. Henderson's where he directly disrupted the tranquillity of the house with his evil howls, clinging to me as though I were the last familiar spar in that sea of piety and kindness. He bit my leg, at once to declare his ownership and his dependence. One of the little girls, Josephine, offered him a cookie which he threw to the floor in a fury. Unruffled, she picked it up and tried him with a balloon which pleased him slightly. "Now, then, aren't you ashamed of yourself!" I said and shook him by the elbow. But Mrs. Henderson pulled my brother to her and said soothingly, "Now you run along, Sonie. He's my boy for the evening. It wasn't a nice cookie and he had the good sense to see that."

It was a fine, cold night with surfaces that split under our feet and a bare sky furnished only with a few stark stars and an austere moon that pitched, in a thousand elliptical and gouty travesties of itself, amongst the waves and whose light resurrected from the shadows shafts of earth and the roofs of sheds and exposed completely a steep incline to the water which seemed, so regular it was, to have been paved by hand with smooth, round stones. We took the road that led to the Hotel and walked fast because of the cold. My mother, companionably holding me by the hand, walked erect and seemed herself, herself of days so long ago that now they had all but slipped from memory since there was so little in her now out of which to construct her as she had been.

It was the first time in years that we had gone out together and it was this phenomenon, coupled with the vigor of her movement and vivacity of her talk about most trifling matters of the village, and the inexplicable joy in her face, that unburied for me a Christmas Eve when I was four or five years old. My parents took me to a pageant in the Sunday School rooms of the Methodist church on such a night as this. Part of the way I walked between them and part of the way my father carried me, grumbling that I was too heavy. The Christmas tree was as tall as the room and topped by a sugary star, and onto its branches had been grafted incongruous fruits: crimson bulbs and asbestos peaches and tongueless bells, all floured with snow and illumined with a hundred candles whose flames tossed whenever the door opened and closed. The people sang carols, so simple and loud that I could catch all the words, and my father, in a great tuneless voice, roared out the German to the ones he knew. Each child was given a popcorn ball and a glazed apple by a masked and padded Santa Claus. I was terrified, when I received my presents, to see, between his glove and cuff half an inch of black skin! I told Rosalie Kadish the next day and she, after conferring with her brother Nathan, informed me that underneath his fine red suit, Santa Claus was the pastor's Negro chauffeur.

All the way home from the party, my mother and father drowned the sound of the waves with Russian and German songs, interrupting one another and seeming to me, who rested half asleep against my father's shoulder, more talented than birds, for their repertoire was endless and their voices were the loudest I had ever heard. I could scarcely keep my eyes open, but I refused to be tucked into my pallet and sat in the kitchen while they drank spiced wine that simmered on the stove, giving off a fragrant steam from cloves and sticks of cinnamon. A slice of lemon floated in their glasses. My mother blew on her glass to cool it and my father suddenly seized her hand. "I wish we were on the boat again, don't you?" My mother laughed and flirted at him with her black eyes. "Go on!" she said. My father mouthed at her the words "I love you," and then they looked at me and smiled. "The sandman's got a certain party," said Mamma. I stumbled, dizzy with sleep, into the bedroom and swayed as my mother took off my clothes. When I was buried under the comforters and coats, they both knelt down beside me, their arms entwined. The sweet odor of the mulled wine was heavy on their breath. The last thing I recalled was my father turning to kiss my mother on the mouth as though their love had been refreshed by the songs, by the wine, and by the sight of me, their child, going to sleep.

My brother would never have so pleasing a recollection as this. I had tried to amuse him with the games my father played with me, but he was bored with Esel von Hexensee and he detested Fritzie. If I read him a story, he would stamp his foot suddenly, stick his fingers in his ears and scream, "Shut *up!* I hate *Black Beauty!*" On rare occasions, if I brought him a stick of chewing gum or a jaw-breaker, he rewarded me with a pinched, reluctant smile, but an hour later, for no reason, would slip up behind me and give my hair a savage pull. He was so horrid and perverse and unresponsive that I think I should have lost my patience and whipped him if I had not known from experience and from Mrs. Henderson's tactful advice, that if I allowed my mother to see that he tormented me, her hatred would be dangerously magnified. Consequently, I suffered him to pinch and bite and scratch me, laughing if I could.

As I felt my mother's warm hand in mine, I was perplexed by the change that had come over her in the years since that happy Christmas Eve. Tonight, I found her lovable as she had been then, and as I had not found her for a long time. Each time I made a resolve to dedicate myself to loving her and making her happy, I was at once disheartened by the apathy in which I found her or, instead, by the senseless, fussy affection in which she buried me. These wards of mine were incorrigible. In both of them, the rare moments of joy and sanguine temper which I so greatly wished to protract forever, were accidental, and no matter what new order I introduced into our life, it would still be some short-lived genius of disorder that would galvanize them. Thus, for a week together, I might bring a new toy or sack of goodies each day to Ivan, sent by Maudie or Mrs. Brunson, and he would hate them all. Yet he would discover in my coat pocket a Luden's cough drop, fuzzy with lint. His eyes would dance with pleasure as he held it up to the light. "Let me have it, Sonie!" he would plead.

We were approaching the Hotel and my mother quickened her pace until she was nearly running. Reaching the porch, she went up the stairs two at a time. Then she held out her hands to me. "Why, they're not here, Sonie!" she cried. "Not one of them!"

"What aren't here?"

"The chairs, darling, all the dirty wicker chairs!"

"They're inside, in the lobby. They aren't left out during the winter, Mamma, you goose. Why, the rain and snow would ruin them."

"I suppose," she said sadly. "And I had looked forward so much . . . " She was peering through a crack in the boarding of the main door. "I can't see a thing," she said. "I don't believe they're in there." But another survey of the veranda convinced her that they were not outside. "Well, then," she went on, "the only thing to do is go in. A pretty pickle of fish."

I was about to object. My mother's absurd business might, if it were found out, cost me my job. How could we force a way into the Hotel without leaving traces? And would it not be guessed immediately that only crazy Mrs. Marburg would do such a thing, in the dead of winter, when even the most naïve burglar would realize that there would be slim pickings there? But I did not object, because I was curious about the way the Hotel looked, and had many times thought of doing just this myself, in those nights when my father was still with us, and most particularly the night he left. There was in my mother such a buoyancy, even after her first disappointment, that I was affected by it. We set about to find some entrance and at the back discovered a window with loose boards that yielded easily, and when we had rattled the frame awhile, we pushed it up and climbed inside the outer kitchen.

While from the outside, the building appeared impenetrable to light or air, within, drafts and moonlight, admitted through cracks, were everywhere. The old coal range, mammoth under a silvery hood, was lighted with a lackluster glow and it seemed, from the broken pane of its isinglass window and from the rim of its lids and its half-open damper, to expel cold air like needle-fine projectiles as we passed by. In the dining-room, the faithful birds stood obscurely behind their moonlit glass, waiting patiently through the long winter for the diners who, slowly through the years, had come to resemble them. Here was the owl that hung above the table where sat Mrs. Thompson, an obese, bedizened woman who had, in recent summers, abandoned her lorgnette as being both troublesome and ineffectual since she was half blind and vanity could hold out no longer. Now, upon her raptorial nose, she wore tremendous tortoise-shell glasses which, combined with the feathery, touched-up curls that beset her cheeks and the boned neckpiece of tawny lace that upheld her jowls, made her so like the staring owl above her that it would not have seemed altogether odd to hear a duet of solemn hoots proceeding from that corner of the room. And no less like her bird was Mrs. Holman whose table was beneath a blue heron, for she was lengthy and slim and she dressed in faded blue or gray; she swooped her graceful wings downward for the salt cellar or upward to arrest a slipping hairpin, as though she were always about to alight or about to fly off. Mrs. Prather, whose minute head, untidy as a nest, was an impudent joke upon her spreading, pyramidal body, was as ludicrous as her benumbed ptarmigan. Providentially, Miss Pride's table was in the center of the room and there was no feathered cartoon of her above her head.

There in the lobby crouched the chairs, their laps obliterated by diaphanous shrouds of muslin. The covers of the round tables hung to the floor like skirts; I knew that the square humps atop the tables were the photograph albums and the paper weights in whose glass interiors were embedded pictures of a Sequoia redwood through which a man could walk, or a photogenic waterfall beneath an emerald sky, or a burro whose mouth released a balloon to hold the words: "Hee-haw! Howdy, Folks! You're looking at a Rocky Mountain Canary."

Our candles gave a gelid animation to the unshifting moonlight. The glass eyes of an antelope glinted darkly at us from above the desk and the shadow of the newel post on the main stairway swelled upon the wall like a jinn. My mother at once set to work. She uncovered a chair and set two candles on a cherry-wood milking stool, making stands of drippings. Her tools were a paring knife, a hairpin, and an awl from the shop. She was as intent as a surgeon. I watched her for a few minutes until she complained that I made her nervous and as the light was poor enough anyhow, she did not want my shadow interfering. "Run and play, sweetheart," she said. "You've made my hairpin slip through and now it's caught in a crack. Go away, do."

I glanced around, wondering if there had ever been a child who could obey her command, "Run and play," with any joy and frolic through this chilly company of ghosts without a backward glance. I lighted the third candle and proceeded to the stairway. My mother did not look up; she was humming faintly an old tune she had used to sing to me long ago.

Miss Pride's room was utterly bare. Even the mattress had been taken away and the skeleton of the bed rattled tinnily as I crossed the creaking floor. Its rug gone and its windows stripped, its cushions removed from its bare bones, the room was like a fowl plucked clean. There was no aperture in the boarding at the windows big enough for me to look through towards Boston, and in my disappointment, I tore at the wood and filled my fingers with splinters. The gesture was one almost of panic though my feeling had been disproportionate to it, but because my hands were so furious, I abruptly plunged into a welter of introspection, a train of incoherent moods. I had not thus indulged myself for a long time, for the simple reason that I had been too busy balancing my brother's humors to observe any lack in my own equilibrium.

Now, in her appalling summer room, my old longing to live with Miss Pride was revived in so weakening a way that I sank to my knees before the wooden barriers, feeling my face grow warm in spite of the cold and my eyes swell with tears that did not fall but clung to my lids. And when this first pain had gone—like the pain of a lover who visits an old rendezvous without his beloved—I dully recovered myself. The only gain there could possibly have been in this bizarre trip to the Hotel was a return of the joyous feelings I had had in the summer when I looked out these windows. And I had, without fully realizing it, expected an altogether novel sensation in seeing the dark, moon-tracked water from this hiding-place. For, although the years had brought me new and sometimes strong infatuations, knowledge had not abused the dream of my childhood. My perspective of all else might have changed, but Miss Pride and Miss Pride's room had remained unaltered, so that even now, when I was no longer a child, I had often in the summertime been healed of my anxieties over Ivan and Mamma the moment I stepped across the threshold of the room.

But tonight, in this cold nakedness, I was cheated out of my solace for I could not, with my eyes, burn a way to her in Boston. The uproar in me was brought on partly by the discrepancy between the placid vagary that was holding my mother's attention downstairs and my own tempestuous one upstairs, for, although they were equally profitless, mine had a kind of direction, and it seemed consistent with my bad luck that she was happy while I was so miserable, that she could sustain herself indefinitely on follies and unreal pageants and old woes. And my suffering was augmented when I reminded myself that I was nearly eighteen years old and in my last year of high-school and that the unplanned future was like a jumping-off place which I rapidly approached. My classmates talked confidently of college or business school or marriage and in all their talk, there was an implication that whatever they did, they would do it away from Chichester. The farther distant they set their next year's residence, the more unshakeable seemed their resolve so that I believed they would all be in Alabama or Oregon or New York and I alone would remain.

In truth, though, I had an indisposition towards all these careers. When I fumbled in my adolescent semi-sleep for what our teachers called "a way of life," there would come to me the image of Nathan Kadish who, of all the people I had ever known (excepting, of course, Miss Pride), commanded of me a profound respect. I had been in love with him for five years and all that time had carried with me a sharp recollection of the exact moment I had fallen in love, so that whenever I saw him, I could feel myself, a child, rise on tiptoe to look through the lighted window at his birthmark.

He had become, in his graceful, small-boned body and in his right profile, a coldly handsome boy. But because from one side he was beautiful, from the other, with its brilliant smear, he was more hideous even than he had been as a little boy. He had won a scholarship to Boston University where he was studying literature, but he came home for the week-ends and for holidays. Occasionally he came to call on me, late at night after my mother had gone to bed, and he talked to me with a grave, impersonal grandeur of his intellectual accomplishments.

In his Freshman year, in the first flush of rebellion against everything he had heretofore known or longed for, he had been a member of the Communist Party and had always carried with him his membership card with the alias, Stanley Finn. He made it clear to me each time he came to call that he would not have come if he had had anything better to do; our economic system was such that he had no money, he said, to go to Marblehead to get drunk; obviously he could not endure the atmosphere of his house where all aspirations were bent towards the impedimenta of a bourgeois life, the Philco radio sets, the Frigidaires, the upholstered parlor suites. There was nothing in his conversation or in the complete indifference of his countenance to indicate that he in the least enjoyed my companionship. I listened patiently to him, understanding almost nothing of what he said. As he talked, he concealed his birthmark with his long hand. But presently he would forget. His fingers would reach for a cigarette in the pocket of his sporty checked jacket and I could see the exciting monstrosity of his left profile. Feeling that I could no longer listen to his monologue, I would suggest that we drink some coffee, and as I busied myself with the stove and the water, he would continue, unperturbed, to analyze the villainies of liberals, but I would pay no attention. Instead, I would nurse the thrilling, secret glimpse I had had of his peeled cheek. He would be saying, "I'll tell you what. If you ever come to Boston, I'll take you to a meeting of the Party. You may be our type, as a matter of fact, though I can't be sure. The most sensible laborer often turns out to be a solid individualist. Some members of the Party used to be rich; they *know* that bathtubs and evening clothes are decadent. The rest of us have to take it on faith, and of course we do. But witness the perversity of human nature: here I am, a crusader of the Revolution, and do you know that even I sometimes would like to get dressed up in tails and go to the Ritz roof? Of course if that ever did happen, I'd snap out of it in pretty short order. I imagine I wouldn't be able to take their guff and would flash my C.P. card and land up in jail."

In this year, Nathan had withdrawn from the party although he repeatedly told me that he still upheld its principles and had only stopped going to meetings because he had other things to do. Now he fancied himself not as revolutionist but as a literary person of Paris. His resolve had been made shortly after an evening we had spent together in my father's shop. He had asked if he might look at the books there, remembering from his boyhood that some handsome volumes had stood on the shelf above the door. He took down two, bound in red leather and heavily engraved with gold, and he said, "These are what he used to talk about. Your old man, I mean." They were *Wilhelm Meister* and *Werthers Leiden*. After that, whenever he came to see me, his manner was strangely gallant, his voice was softer, and he often used German words, uttering them with surpassing tenderness. He would go to the window and say, *"Ach, der Abendstern!"* Or he would fall into long, melancholy silences and occasionally would leave the house without a word.

Only the last Sunday he had brought me a book to read. It was called *Confessions of a Young Man*. I had not read much of it yet, but its effect on me was already marked, and I was anxious for the next week-end to come so that I might tell Nathan that I understood why it was he wanted to go to Paris. Shivering in the icy room, I thought of the book and wished that I were a young man, queer enough to keep a tame python, clever enough to educate myself at the Nouvelle Athènes where the painters and poets gathered nightly as a learned and bibulous academy. I thought how simple my actions would be if I were a great, confident pagan egoist like

George Moore. Would I not, if I were a young man, leave Chichester and my foolish mother? But I was not fitted for such a life, not only because I was a girl, but because I was an ignoramus. I nearly cried aloud thinking of the sloth of all these past years that had prevented me from reading less than a tenth of what Nathan had read. Here, only two years older than I, he was a storehouse full of books. Even at my own game, he surpassed me, for he spoke and read German with twice my facility. To be educated was the privilege of our class, he had told me. That was the weapon whereby we could conquor the bourgeoisie. I did not know precisely what he meant. Whenever I dwelt upon his words, I could only imagine myself dazzling Miss Pride with my culture; I had no desire to overthrow her, only to make her welcome me.

All plans were as cold as my quaking shoulder-blades. I stood up and stamped awake a sleeping foot. Opening the door, I heard my mother caroling happily at her excavations. I called, "We've got to go now, Mamma. I'm nearly frozen."

"Why, we just got here, silly. I've only begun. Flap your arms."

When I went down, I found that she had finished one chair and was beginning on a magazine rack. She said, "If you'll help me, we'll get through faster. But it's not easy work and you're not used to it, so perhaps you'd better just sit there quiet and watch Mamma." She had, for years, spoken to me as if I were still ten years old. I watched her for a while. She had stopped singing and her lips were parted in concentration. Her eyes sparkled in the candlelight and when she withdrew a long, matted strand of lint she laughed for joy and cried, "Goody!" At last I could hold out no longer and begged for a hairpin. It was good fun and when I, too, extracted a rope of lint, I felt the same brief glow of achievement that I did when I won a game of Patience. But my enthusiasm for the business quickly died and I grumbled that I would leave Mamma alone there if she did not come home at once.

On the way back my mother enumerated the varieties of filth she had brought to light. She planned her schedule for the next night's work. With industry she believed she could finish all the chairs in less than a month. She found me quiet and suspected that I did not care. Very well, I needn't go back. She would go alone if I preferred to stay at home idling with that little black beast of a boy.

Knowing perfectly well how angry she would be if I did not mollify her, I still could not bring myself to speak. For after my fretting in Miss Pride's eviscerated room and after I had become disgusted with the explorations of my hairpin, I had concluded that my predominant feeling towards my mother was boredom. I was surprised because always before I had thought it was a mixture of rebelliousness and loyalty. I was suddenly impervious to her and did not care if she burst into tears and cried for days. I even smiled smugly in my brutal silence.

The pitch of her voice never changed, but its volume increased so that halfway between the Hotel and the Hendersons' house, she was howling abuses, not at me, for as always her madness showed its method, but at my father whose bad treatment had made me lazy, dull-witted, completely insensitive to important things. She railed to the wind for I steadfastly held my tongue. I was closer to my father because her racket had brought back those nights when she had quarreled with him. If I had broken my silence, it would have been to imitate his laugh, provoked by the devil that had taken up permanent residence in her and, anxious for a wider acquaintance, sought admission also to me.

From a little rise, we could see the Christmas tree alight in the village square, a bright triangular scar in the darkened town, and to me, a mockery of that other one, that charming, dressed-up fir whose needles' fragrance lingered still in my memory and seemed even to cling to my mother's hair as she spluttered beside me. She, too, saw the tree and stopped talking, ending a sentence with a smile. She touched my arm. "Now isn't that pretty?" she said. "It would make a nice Kodak picture."

"I was thinking I would get Ivan a Christmas tree, Mamma," I said. "Do you remember the one in the Sunday School rooms a long time ago?"

"That must have been when Hermann Marburg was

still here. He used to pinch your little toes and I would tell him what a terrible thing it was to do but he would never stop."

My anger flared forth. "You mean *you* pinch Ivan's toes!" I cried.

"Sonie, you stop it. I don't know what's come over you. Did you ever *see* me pinch him?"

"Yes! No, oh, I don't know and I don't *care!*" I took her firmly by the elbow. "Look here, you've got to stop being mean to poor little Ivan. Do you hear?"

She did not answer but tried to wrest herself away and looked at me with widened, terrified eyes. "Damn you!" I cried. Because I had never cursed her before and the sensation was intoxicating, I repeated it twice until she, stricken speechless loosed from my grasp, hurried on ahead of me. On the instant I saw her disappear from view I felt released from my responsibility to her and it occurred to me that if she were walking out of my range of vision forever, I would not have the slightest remorse.

Yet my emancipation vanished when I had reached the Henderson house. Ivan, being part and parcel of my duty towards her, required my care, and while it was too late to reform her, he was not yet damned. I must continue as before. Sarah Henderson opened the door for me. In her face, calm had been replaced by solemnity and the gesture she made of extending her hand and laying it upon mine, so gently I knew she meant me to be quiet, made me sense that disaster had befallen someone.

We entered and I saw my brother asleep on the leather sofa. At the first sight of him, I thought I had been mistaken at the door and Sarah had only intended me not to disturb his sleep. But then I saw the signature of agony in the blotches of red on his white cheeks and the blood on his lips, the saliva that bubbled up with each deep, sighing breath. The pose of his body was not like a child's but like an adult person's, drugged or unconscious. Simultaneously, I heard the voice of my heart consenting to the appeal of his collapsed flesh, and heard Mrs. Henderson telling me that he had been "seized" while he was playing. He had been in a temper that I was so slow in coming and had flung himself to the floor and kicked his heels, had been so convulsed in his rage that he was doubled up and frothing at the mouth and muttering all manner of strange things. Finally Mr. Henderson had gone for Dr. Galbraith and the doctor had said the child was epileptic.

"Will it happen again?" I asked Mrs. Henderson.

"Yes! Yes!" cried Sarah, beside herself, unmindful of her manners and of the charity in which she had been schooled by her mother. "You must take him away and never bring him here again! It's too awful!" And she ran from the room weeping. I was unnerved by the change in her and knew that what she had seen must truly have been "too awful" if it had disrupted her serenity.

Mrs. Henderson and I faced each other over the sleeping child. "If he's not excited, he won't have the fits. It's temper brings them on. Don't you mind Sarah."

Mr. Henderson, a small, sandy man, usually as easygoing as his wife, shifted his chair beside the fireplace and said, "Well, *I* mind Sarah and I mind my other children, and God save you, Sonie, but you mustn't let us see this again."

"Hush, Ross," said his wife. "Pity the poor girl and boy."

"I do! I do! Lord knows I do, but I'll do nothing more than that."

He pronounced the ultimatum without rancor, but I knew he would never retract it. He kicked the hearth and commenced to pare an apple. A curl of red skin coiled into the coal scuttle and at last the globe of fruit was naked and white. He quartered it, leaned back, and began to eat, surveying his domain but never once permitting my brother and me to enter his ken. I stared at him with envy. There was a look of satisfaction in his stark, rusty face as though he were in command of his squads once again after an undisciplined excursion. His house, with its long-waisted, uncomfortable chairs, and the sturdy tables, more hewn than built, and the useful gimcracks—the basket for firewood, the cast-iron hearth accessories, a dun-colored cushion or two, a braided rug —the house and his sleeping children were like a standing army at its post, not hostile but prepared for hostilities, on guard at all times against intrusion. At a distance he might pity the enemy but he would fight to the death if they tried to impose their outlandish ways on his world.

He finished the apple and spat into the dying fire. "Well, tomorrow's another day," he said, and as though he shut a book, he closed his face for the night, locking in its changes of expression and its few words. Presently he left the room.

"I'm sorry," I said to Mrs. Henderson. I could think of nothing else.

She put her large arms about me. "There," she said. "You don't pay any attention. You pray, child."

4

For five successive nights my mother went alone to the Hotel and each time stayed past midnight. She did not know until the sixth day what had happened at the Hendersons', for Mr. Henderson and I had carried Ivan home after Mamma was asleep and in the morning, except for a clot of blood on his lip, he appeared normal. But on the sixth day, Sarah Henderson came to bring some bread to us while I was at school. Probably still under the influence of her terror and knowing too little of my mother's aversion to Ivan, she told the whole story and heightened some of the details. She was fascinated in spite of herself and was drawn to us with a morbid curiosity. If we met on the street, she paled and would have turned into the nearest shop to avoid me had she not longed to know the answer to the question she asked me each time, "Has he had another one yet?" Her myopic eyes behind rimless spectacles registered her disappointment when I told her no.

By evening of the day on which my mother first heard of Ivan's affliction, she was convinced that she had seen the fit and she described it to me in such accurate detail that I was half convinced myself. She told me how his face had turned purple and his eyes had started from his head and his voice had sounded strangled. There was a frightening eagerness in her face as she talked and when

Ivan came in from the bedroom, she stretched out her arms to him and said, "Come, sweet baby boy, come, darling, come kiss your mother." Ivan stuck out his tongue and Mamma laughed as if nothing had ever pleased her half so much.

Later that evening I was studying my lessons and she was at work on a stamped bureau runner I had brought her from town in the hope that she would give up her sprees in the Hotel lobby. Ivan was quietly playing on the floor with a toy truck Mrs. Henderson had sent. Absorbed, I was not watching them, though now and again I was aware of them, for I would come to a word in *Macbeth* which I was obliged to look up in the glossary. The interruption caused my mind to slip back into the ordinary world and I looked up, taking in my surroundings with detachment. They constituted, with their other occupants, a prison escapable only through some such occupation as I was just now engaged in. My dog-eared book, bound in maroon cloth, bandaged with adhesive tape where it had been pulled apart by careless hands, was called *Literature and Life*. I had never fathomed the title.

It may have been a sound or it may have been intuition that made me turn and see my two companions hypnotically attached, their gazes joined, their large eyes directly focused and mirrored as though the reflection could burn through to the brain and destroy it, gazes of equal strength, age meaning nothing. Hatred and desperation freighted all the black eyes. But age gained. As I watched, Ivan screamed, throwing back his head which languished on its stem while his live mouth travailed in calling my name, "Sonie! Sonie!" He was purple when I reached him and gripped by a vise I could not pry apart. His teeth were clenched and his fists were clenched and his head, which the second before had been horribly agitated, was turned to one side as though fixed there forever. But before I had really taken in this petrifaction, he was violently released from it and his head, his arms, his eyelids, his legs twitched, and over his busy lips poured blood-stained foam such as I had seen drool from the jaws of the bulldog that had killed my kitten.

"The beast!" shrieked my mother, and in her face and

body, a sympathetic disquiet began, aping his, until she rose from her chair and went to the window where she stood sobbing with her forehead pressed against the glass.

He *was* a beast, the very repository of all bestiality, composed of filth and evil, as though his interior life, in the cavern of that rocking skull, were one of utter nastiness. In a moment, he passed into the third phase of the fit, a coma so profound that I might have thought him dead if I had not seen him like this at the Hendersons'. I carried him to the bedroom and put him on the army cot I had bought for him the year before. While I bathed his face, I heard the sobbing of my mother in the other room, like the sad cries of certain birds or the collision of breakers with the sand. I sat down on the floor beside the little boy, feeling no longer any disgust now that he was relaxed. In a little while my mother came in, bringing another lamp. She had unpinned her hair which rippled to her waist and glowed in the light and upon her face there was, as I saw so often, the beauty of a saint which flowers through the perpetual renewal of mercy.

"My God! What shall we do, Sonia?"

"He'll be all right in the morning," I said.

"Will he do it again?"

"He won't unless . . ." I was on the point of saying, "unless you scare him again," but I changed the syntax to the passive voice, "unless he's scared."

"But he wasn't scared tonight. How could he have been scared?" Her direct, innocent gaze did not prevent me from hearing the guile in her voice.

The next morning, before school, I took Ivan out to the shop on the pretext of giving him a present and I told him that if Mamma ever frightened him, he must run out of the house and either bolt himself into the shop or else walk down the beach and wait for me to come home from school. But he must not go to the Hendersons.'

"She don't scare me," he said sullenly. "*You* scare me, you lousy old girl," and he gave me a kick on the shin that made me wish to thrash him.

My warnings for a long time were useless. He remembered nothing of what had happened before the fit, but only that he fell asleep and awoke, inexplicably sick at the stomach, his lips and tongue sorely bitten. Gradually he began to attach these feelings to me, for I was always the first thing he saw when he came out of his coma, and he developed such a repugnance to me that when he saw me coming home in the afternoon, he hid under the bed, and it was only my gift of candy or a new lead pencil that induced him to come out. Again and again, I begged him to leave my mother when he felt nervous, and at last, after a particularly severe attack when he had emerged from the coma only to repeat the frightful process two or three times, he told me that he remembered something Mamma had done: she had been looking at him although he had his back turned to her, and when he faced her, he was afraid, he did not know why.

Then, instead of me, he began to avoid her, and sometimes he followed me all the way to the Brunsons' like a little dog and sat in the pantry without moving or making a sound until I was ready to go home. Nearly every afternoon I met him on the road, his overcoat buttoned up wrong, his pilot's helmet pulled down so far over his face that he could barely see where he was going. He refused to go to the shop, for he said Mamma came after him and looked in the windows and he could not look away when her eyes were on him.

5

On a Friday afternoon, early in January, a snowstorm came up. The snow fell in swift spirals, floating like gulls into the tree branches in the school-yard. The soft, circling petals smoothed away the harsh outlines of buildings and bony trees and transformed the light in the study hall. By the time school was out, the snow was several inches deep and was still falling. Mrs. Brunson was having a dinner party and had asked that I come to work immediately instead of going home as I usually did to prepare supper for my mother and Ivan. I enjoyed the evenings when the Brunsons entertained: the overheated house, immaculately clean, was redolent with the perfume of cut flowers delivered that morning from Boston, with the smell of roasting beef or turkey, of whiskey, and of cigars. Latterly, much of the management of the dinner parties had fallen to my lot since Maudie had begun to drink more and more and at the same time had lost her ability to hold her liquor. As a consequence, she often forgot essential dishes on the menu and ruined others.

The guests lingered a long time over their drinks. When the Brunsons drank, it was neither in the manner of my father and mother who had been maudlin or gay by turns, nor in the manner of Miss Pride whose indulgence at specified hours was less for pleasure than for the observation of custom. With them, it was a ritual which employed its own argot and its own paraphernalia. They drank whiskey highballs made with ginger-ale, out of glasses decorated on the outside by a horse's head which, on the inside, underwent a sly metamorphosis into a naked woman. At the end of the third drink, Dr. Brunson would say, "Well, I guess this one can't be told in mixed company. No, no, I can't do it." But he was quickly persuaded that the ladies were not so easily embarrassed, that they themselves could tell much worse, and he would tell a story, usually with a medical background. I, passing the canapés, could not understand it, but I could not have been more shocked, for the laughter that exploded at its conclusion was as brazen and knowing as the look on the face of a small boy who has just chalked an obscene expletive on the sidewalk.

Tonight, in addition to drinks beforehand, the guests were served wine at dinner and they dallied at the table an unconscionable time. Maudie had complained early in the evening, "Somebody keeps spiking that grape juice I have to drink to keep my strength up. Why, Momma dear, that there's so all-fired potent, like the feller says, you could float a sledge-hammer on top of it," and she had staggered out of the house the moment the dessert was served. It was after ten o'clock when I got home, and I was surprised to see the light still burning in the kitchen, but more surprised, when I entered, to find my mother idle for the first time since she had taken up fancy-work. She looked up, smiling.

"What kind of soup did they have, darling?"

"Chicken," I said, warming my hands at the stove. "It's cold, Mamma. You've let the fire go nearly out."

"It snowed hard, didn't it? A big deep snow, wasn't it? And did they have a salad?"

"Yes, and chocolate soufflé and two kinds of wine."

"Ah," said my mother. "Ah, how nice! But tell me, Sonia, sweetheart, how *deep* is the snow?"

"It's terribly deep. In some places it was up to my knees and there's a terrible wind."

"It's funny that you came home alone."

"Why? Did you expect someone?"

"Oh, no."

I was taking off my galoshes when she said, "Ivan went to meet you. It was snowing, but he didn't care about that. He only thought about seeing his precious Sonie."

"When did he go?" I cried.

"Oh, a long time ago. Just after the storm began. Here, have a little tea. You look tired."

"Which way did he go?" Though I knew I must find him at once, I could not leave for my amazement at the way she sat there, offering me a cup of tea. What would she be able to say to herself if I found him dead? And I knew, without believing it, that if I did, she would not feel the least necessity of making excuses to anyone, certainly not to herself.

She laughed uncertainly. "I don't know which way he went, but he went fast." And then, reaching out her hand to me she whispered desperately, "Let him go, for God's sake, Sonia, let him go!"

I did not answer but ran out of the house. The snow, which had let up for a little while around dinner time, was falling more thickly than ever and the loud wind drowned my voice as I stumbled down the road toward the village, calling to Ivan. Twice I thought I had found him and when I discovered that what I had seen in the distance was only a rock, I sank down with weariness and grief and would have stayed there but for the image of my brother as he might be suffering that drew me to my feet again. The versatile wind enclosed me in a live, round cloud and the next moment flattened me against a moving wall and then withdrew, leaving me in a noise-less little space where the snow fell gently and straight down. From time to time, I felt warmth slowly return-ing, but it never reached my feet or fingers because the wind halted it again and exploded charges of snow into my face or beleaguered me with unremitting blasts. Sometimes I plunged up to my knees in drifts as soft as pudding. I was trying to go in the direction of the Brun-sons, thinking he might have found his way there, but I could distinguish no landmark to set me right. In a brief lull of the wind, I heard the angry ocean and the next moment slipped and fell into a deep pit which I recog-nized as being a hundred yards from the Coast Guard house. I rested a moment and closed my eyes to the wet snowflakes and then struggled up the steep bank. A sharp stone cut into the palm of my hand and I could feel blood seeping through my rent wool mitten. I called, "Halloo! Halloo!" hoping that one of the Coast Guards would hear me. I went on, bent nearly double against the blast. Now I had lost all sense of direction: when the wind paused, I listened for the ocean but the sound came now from one place, now from another. I did not know whether I was hearing the bay or the sea. I rose up straight to call again and saw through the snow, near-by, a lighted doorway, and I ran on shouting. As I drew closer I saw that the figure framed in the yellow block of light was Mrs. Henderson, shaking out a tablecloth.

"Ivan is lost!" I cried.

"Lord have mercy! Sarah, Ross, Jack, Josephine, get on your overshoes! The little Marburg boy is lost in the snow!"

The three children and the father were ready at once, as if they had been awaiting the alarm, and with no more account of the catastrophe than they had heard through the open door to the dining-room where they had been sitting round the table playing Lotto, they hur-tled out the back door and into the storm while Mrs. Henderson filled a glass with rum and told me to drink it before I went out again.

"You're soaking wet," she scolded me. "You should have come here first." She tied a scarf about her head and went out after the others.

I started after her but halfway to the door shivered with mortal cold and turned back to drink the rum. It had an immediate effect on me. A bone-deep drowsiness made me nod and shake myself. I stared into the dining-room from my place at the kitchen table and saw the scattered Lotto cards, the chairs pushed back, the up-turned ash tray on the floor. The alarm clock in the window sill above the sink, ticking off the minutes of my brother's absence in the furious snow, attracted my eyes and I watched the minute hand creeping so slowly it seemed not to move at all. I closed my eyes, but the measured tick-tock stayed with me. It must have been for the briefest moment that I half fell asleep while I still heard the tinny seconds clicking into the past, and when I opened my eyes again I knew that I had dreamed of being in Miss Pride's drawing-room where I had seen a box of ferns like that in the seventh-grade room at school. I had been alone. I felt I had just come in off the street, for cold enveloped me like a loose cloak. It was the selfishness of my dream that made me leap to my feet and run out the door, but just as I reached the bottom step, I heard voices near and Mr. Henderson came into sight, carrying Ivan's insensible body.

"The poor little duffer," said the man. "He was lying in the pastor's garden."

We kept him there that night, though Sarah and her father protested, sure he would have a fit immediately on regaining consciousness. I said I thought we should have a doctor, but Mrs. Henderson assured me that a doctor could do nothing that she could not do for the time being and that we would call one tomorrow if it were necessary. She made a bed for him on the sofa in the parlor and we sat up all night, for he was feverish and tossed so violently that he would have hurled himself to the floor if we had not been there to hold him back. Mrs. Henderson took up her knitting and worked nimbly at the heel of a sock. The room was unbearably hot and smelled of the camphor-oil on Ivan's chest.

"Why don't you sleep a little, Sonie?" said Mrs. Henderson.

But I refused. I felt I must be vigilant now since I had abandoned him this afternoon. "I love Ivan," I said.

"I know you do," replied the woman. "I'm sure of it." "I couldn't bear it if anything happened to him! Do you believe me, Mrs. Henderson?"

"Indeed I do, Sonie. You mustn't feel bad about staying away this afternoon. He'll be all right, you'll see. Sonie, over there you'll find some magazines. Don't you want to look at them? I think we oughtn't talk too much for fear of waking the little boy."

Toward morning he was more peaceful and his forehead was cool. At sun-up we carried him home. My mother had been waiting up all night for me, and she was melancholy. She said nothing, only stared as we lowered Ivan to his cot.

He improved during the day although he developed a cough that troubled us and when in the afternoon he seemed to be choking with it, Mrs. Henderson sent me to the hospital for Dr. Galbraith. "Be clear with him, Sonie," she said. "It's sometimes hard for the doctor to follow what a person's saying, you know."

It was not because he was stupid but because he was an alcoholic that Dr. Galbraith could not follow. His quick speech, hampered by a hasty stammer, was deceptive. He spoke so rapidly he concealed the degeneration of his mind and appeared to be a man whose energy outdistanced his tongue, whose attention at any moment was subdivided many times, giving to each focus a degree of concentration varying with its importance. Breathless with the long run through the cold, I stood beside the desk in his sterile cell, while the doctor nervously twisted a fountain pen round and round between his plump fingers and interrupted me.

"Just a minute, you must try, you must try to control yourself."

I sensed in his voice an agitation that surpassed my own. And while he kept me there with his trivial questions which he brought out with a great struggle (he even asked my age) he only made me wilder and himself more confused, so that, in the end, when he did come, he was not in the least prepared for what he found. I had identified Ivan as the child he had seen at the Hendersons' and he thought he was being summoned to another epileptic fit. For a moment I was not sure that he would come at all. He sat staring at me, moving his lips. He had a repulsive face, flabby, blotched, and dissolute. The crescents of dark flesh under his eyes were distended and the eyes themselves were bloodshot, filmy, and of a color akin to auburn. His lips, tumid and wet, worked slowly over what his eyes saw as if, once the object were removed, he would still be able to recall it by running his tongue over his lips which had mouthed it and shaped its secret formula. He had had, I had heard, several attacks of jaundice and his skin was permanently stained to so dark a color that it resembled sunburn.

At last he rose with a convulsive jerk. "Will I need my stethoscope?"

Thinking he spoke to me, I said, "Why, I should think so, sir!"

He laughed self-consciously. "I talk to myself. It is the privilege of an old man." And abruptly he pinched my chin between his thumb and forefinger.

Ivan's illness was diagnosed as bronchitis. The doctor prescribed mustard poultices and a benzoin kettle. "Keep him well covered up and put on the mustard as hot as he can stand it. It's not a bad attack and the fever isn't high. Call me if he seems to fail, but he won't, he'll be all right, quite all right."

He left some sleeping powders with us and these we gave Ivan every eight hours so that for several days we kept him asleep save when we woke him to pour a little water or broth down his parched throat. We made a tent of an old sheet and kept a pot of benzoin bubbling on a kerosene stove beside his bed. He was never himself but muttered and groaned and stared at us without recognition. His bright cheeks blazed under my fingers as I tried to stroke away the illness that racked him, hooped his body with a cough and cast it down, gasping.

My mother remained in the kitchen, sleeping on the floor occasionally, but for the most part making feather-stitched pot-holders. As she worked, she sang *Fräulein* Lili's song in a soft but penetrating voice, over and over again until I begged her, bursting into tears, to cease. And when she did not, Mrs. Henderson laid her hand on mine and shook her head.

When I came home at noon and later after school and

then in the evening, I could hear her before I had left
the road to turn into the lane:

> Well they know without my telling
> Where she lives, for whom I long.
> Round their hoofs the snow is swirling.
> Loud the coachman sings his song.
> Round their flying hoofs the snow is swirling.
> Loud the coachman sings his song.

Or, in the night, half asleep but alert to every noise, I
could hear her sorrowing, for she had changed the gay
tune into a dirge:

> Hurry, horses, faster, faster!
> Quick, my flying hawks, away!
> Days and hours like these are golden—
> We must seize them while we may.
> Golden days are these and golden minutes—
> We must seize them while we may.

She never spoke to me. She might look me full in the
face as if she were about to say something. Then, if I
spoke, she drowned out my words with another verse of
her song or, instead, repeated one line again and again
with a passionate monotony:

> Hurry, horses, faster, faster!
> Hurry, horses, faster, faster!
> Hurry, horses, faster, faster!

But my little brother heard nothing. His fever was
coy; each time it went down, Mrs. Henderson and I were
comforted, but only for an hour or so. On the fourth
day, there was no diminishing of it at all. On the contrary, it went steadily higher until it had reached 106
degrees. Mrs. Henderson said he should be taken to the
hospital at once and she called out the window to Sarah
to run to the village and telephone the doctor. It was
late in the afternoon and I had been home from school
for an hour or so. Terrified as I was by the anxious tone
of the woman's voice, I was so weary that when she advised me to go into the kitchen to rest for a few minutes
until the doctor came, I agreed.

My mother, her head bent over her work, was singing

through smiling lips. The sun was going down. The red light glowed on her face and hair with a softness and subtlety that made it seem a property of her own being, an interior light which, passing through the many filters of her body, the tissues, bones, and muscles, was revealed, at its mellowest, upon her skin so that her face did not reflect the sunset but resembled it. Through the window I could see the sky, striped with stratus clouds of pink and deeper shades of pink, separating here and there to disclose a streak or patch of green like pale shoots and leaves amongst flowers.

Each day, I wished to prolong this hour so that I might have time to do in it all the things that were suggested to me. I wished to walk down the road to the Hotel Barstow to see the rows and rows of windows shining like solid blocks of wine-red ice, giving to the old-fashioned, quasi-baroque façade an interest which was lacking at any other time. The whole aspect of the building would be improved, for this was a benevolent kind of light which enriched the shadows with the same ruddy color it infused into the surfaces, but in such a way that there were no abrupt contrasts, only a deepening and reinforcement. It was quite unlike the light earlier in the afternoon which, cold and white, accented the dirtiness of the old paint and brutally discovered all the vulgarity of the building, the whimsical fenestration following the roof line, the tedious repetition of egg-and-dart, the ogees of the veranda, the festoons of roses looped and ribboned over the doors and windows. I should have liked, too, to look at the State House dome from Miss Pride's belvedere and to accompany with my eyes the snail-paced approach of coal-boats to Boston harbor; or to watch, from the topmost of the rocks at the Point, the fearful, reddened water which now in the winter supported few fishing and no sailboats, as if it had devoured them all but still in hunger thrashed many tails and snarled for something more to swallow.

I could not even choose between the sky and my mother's face, and my eyes roamed heavily from one to the other. Her chant, toneless, and yet indescribably sweet, went on:

Till with age my hair starts graying,
Till my locks have ceased to curl,
Let me live in joy and gladness,
Let me love a pretty girl!
Let me live my life in joy and gladness,
Let me love a pretty girl!

I felt that I had all the time in the world. In various versions, I posed myself the question: Is she mad? Can she sing really as carelessly as this when her son is dying? Or is it that the song hides her feelings? Her needle's movement followed the pattern of the rhythm of her voice; at the end of a line or at a rest, she would gracefully and deliberately draw out her green silk thread and let it hang in the air a moment like a sunbeam. I could not tell, afterwards, if it was one or several minutes before I realized that she was silent and had looked up from her fancy-work. She rose and crossed directly to the bedroom door. I followed her.

She went to the cot and said in a whisper, not to me nor to Mrs. Henderson but to herself, "I think he's going to die." She touched the little boy's forehead lightly with her fingertips. A shudder coursed through Ivan's thin body under the bedclothes, and my mother drew back in alarm. His stifled breathing seemed to stop and then began again, a rattling, wheezing inspiration. Forgetful of my duty towards him and even of my love, I could only look on him with horror, but I was impelled to his side where I knelt down, taking his tiny wrist between my fingers. The pulse raced under my untutored touch. His sharp little face was distorted and blue; the red lips hung and the cheeks drew in. I heard someone come to the door and, thinking it was the doctor, turned in relief, but it was only Sarah. "He advised another poultice and he's coming in half an hour."

"Oh, Lord!" cried her mother. "I don't know what to do. His poor little chest is raw where they've been." But, although she was certain that the doctor was wrong, she was obedient to his professional orders, and went to the stove to heat the mat. I followed and opened a new shaker of mustard. The sharp smell stung my nostrils; in this one whiff seemed to be embodied all the others that

I had taken in in these four long days. I lunged heavily against the stove in my sudden fatigue and burned my wrist. Instinctively, I put the hurt place to my tongue and as I did so, my mother called from the bedroom, "Sonia! Hurry! I think he's dead."

As I dropped his hand, thin as a bird's foot, and turned to my mother I thought I saw, passing like a light across her face, a look of pity and regret; but perhaps I only imagined it for immediately she smiled and said, "See how peaceful he is."

Mrs. Henderson covered his face with the sheet and, turning, hid my face from him in an embrace. I could feel her bosom rising and falling tranquilly as she murmured. "There, there, the little fellow's better off now God has taken him. Just you rest a little, pet, and then you go over to my house and stay until I come." But in the other room, while she was comforting me, my mother was admitting Dr. Galbraith and I heard his voice, curiously cleared of its stammer: "What charming work you're holding there, ma'am. I had no idea my little patient's mother was an artist."

"My son is dead."

"Oh, I didn't know! It must have been only a few minutes ago."

"In there," she said. "I was just making a poultice—you see I had everything ready, when suddenly he cried out and I went to him. He died in my arms."

"God bless you."

My mother began to cry softly. "I tried!"

I did not ponder then what she meant. I leaned against Mrs. Henderson and breathed in, with the sweet, herbal odor of the benzoin, still bubbling futilely, the smell of her freshly ironed cotton dress.

"You run along, Sonie. Get Sarah to make you some lemon verbena. It'll rest you."

I did not want to leave her, for I was protected by her kindly, corseted body in its pale blue dress printed with little white flowers. The moment I released myself, I would see Ivan and know that he was dead. I was broken suddenly and I sobbed against the cotton, "Oh, Mrs. Henderson, my wrist hurts where I burned it!"

Five

OVER THE PLACE where Ivan's cot had been and where now there was nothing but a rag rug with four square indentations, the smell of benzoin still hovered faintly. The snow from the storm had melted and a dense fog enveloped Chichester. All day, from early morning, we had heard the solemn foghorns. My mother and I sat silent before the stove in the afternoon. Her face was overcast and I believed that when she had wailed to Dr. Galbraith, "I tried!" she had meant, "I tried to love him." For in the night, sleepless for both of us, she had murmured, "My tears are all gone, Sonie," as though all the springs of her being, save her love for me, had been drained, perhaps long before his birth.

Mr. Greeley, the undertaker, had come to take my brother's body away when I was still at the Hendersons' house. He was a man of dreadful stature and horrifying countenance which consisted of a pair of lifeless eyes set in deep, dark pits, a long nose which had deviated markedly to the left, and a set of long and murky teeth behind a walrus mustache. He relished his profession. His parlors were situated in isolation on the road towards the hospital. The yard behind his sprawling, tacky yellow house was planted with tombstones, for he was a merchant as well as an undertaker and a licensed embalmer. When Mr. Greeley learned that we had no money and that Ivan was to be buried as a pauper, he could not conceal his disapproval from my mother and Mrs. Henderson. "For a child," he reproached them, "I have such a nice choice: one sandstone group of angel, lamb, two doves, another along classical lines in which the lily *motif* is used. My real prize is waiting for a little child, a granite headstone with an all-over design of cast-iron roses." He went on to complain that a child should not be sealed into the ground without the services of either Father Mulcahy or Pastor Ferguson. The grave would be unmarked, he said, and we would never know where my brother lay.

Mrs. Henderson, repeating his words to me, assured me that he was not an unkind man but only tactless in his disappointment at being cheated out of a ceremony. But she deplored his effect upon my mother, who had become almost hysterical, had declared that she would die of shame if she could not buy the cast-iron roses for her son. And she had implored the undertaker to wait a few days before he buried the child, for we would surely be able to find some way to have a decent and proper funeral.

Exhausted, my grief still tightly coiled as the kernel to my shock at seeing him die, I was vexed and said heartlessly to the neighbor woman, "Oh, why *can't* Mamma leave well enough alone!" for I felt that now I could not bear to hear her lamentations, which I knew would be forthcoming if the gravestone had become, as I believed it had, a fixed idea.

Mrs. Henderson replied, "She will forget, Sonie. Never you fear. She's upset, poor thing, but she'll get over it."

"You don't know Mamma," I said irritably.

"Oh, I'm not so sure. Here, you take her this bit of upsidedown cake and see if you can't get her to take a little nourishment."

To my surprise, my mother did not mention the funeral that evening, and in the morning when she spoke of it, I was sufficiently relaxed to feel my loneliness and to think she was right in wanting something better for Ivan than an anonymous grave in a potter's field.

We had been shown great kindness by the townspeople: they had sent us flowers and notes of sympathy and someone had brought a book of funeral hymns. Dr. Brunson, with well-meaning generosity, had personally delivered a bottle of imported brandy and had said bluffly, "I think at times like this you ought to think of the living." My mother had wanted to open the bottle at once but I had dissuaded her. These tokens of commiseration offered us only a spiritual crutch, and there was not one name signed upon the cards that I could call out and ask its owner for the price of a headstone. Not even Gonzales who, although he had neither called on us nor given us flowers, had sent one of his children with a note informing us that he would offer his mass each day that week for the repose of Ivan's soul.

That morning, I had gone to the store for a box of matches. The hush which greeted my entrance and passage between the long, brown counters was more than the ordinary respect paid to the bereft. Accompanied by intense stares and a coloring of cheeks and a withdrawal away from the aisle, it had in it an edge of doubt. And when Mr. Bennett, the store-keeper, said to me, "How is your poor mother?" and without realizing that his question was elliptical and expanded would have been, "How is your poor mother bearing up?" I replied, "Oh, she's awfully well, thank you," a murmur of voices rose behind me. I knew, although I could not catch a word of what they said, that the story of Ivan's illness was known and that this self-appointed jury which convened whenever the population of Chichester was reduced or added to was putting down his death as "peculiar."

Set into the counter there were bins of dried foods and in the glass door of one, I caught the tilted reflection of my face. I saw, to a shame that made me cringe away, that upon my lips there was a light and careless smile! Then, as though to show my judges that my sorrow had not left me so indecently soon, I turned to face them and as I did so, saw Sarah Henderson and her father at the center of a knot of people in the back of the store. Mr. Henderson averted his gaze as I looked in their direction, but Sarah met me coldly with her enlarged, nearsighted eyes. Then Mr. Henderson looked up. Encircled by the marks of sleeplessness, his eyes accused me, I thought, of bringing trouble to his household, and when, in a voice I could not control so that it was cracked and breathless, I said, "Good morning, Mr. Henderson," he did not answer. Later, remembering his silence, as wounding as ice to the bare skin, I told myself I cared nothing for his opinion. But my urgent indifference did not heal me.

A change had come over Sarah Henderson which alarmed her father and herself, and indeed her whole family, and which had begun shortly after Ivan's first fit. Whether the shock of what she had seen that night wakened what had been merely dormant, or whether her strangeness would have come about anyhow, I cannot say. At any rate, she had begun to walk in her sleep, and while she never wandered farther than the back porch, she was in dread lest she should walk down to the sea and be drowned before she could master herself. She had headaches and bad dreams and she was ill-humored. Mrs. Henderson thought new glasses would cure her headaches, and that her bad dreams came from eating indigestible sandwiches and pickles before she went to bed. And if Sarah would take a little more exercise, her disposition would improve. She had been out of school for several years and had never been able to find work; she had no talents, no interests, and no beaux. Mrs. Henderson said, "You're bound to get notions if you're idle."

But Mr. Henderson blamed Ivan. He also blamed his wife who, he thought, in going so often to our house, brought back with her some contagious and powerful virus. At last he saw nothing for it but to move away and had got a job in Maine. He was already making his preparations, and this morning in the store he had piled up several pasteboard cartons. Now I have no doubt that we did not drive him away and that the removal to Maine promised the family far more than they had ever had in Chichester. But my self-consciousness dyed everything to match its own color, and for a long time I believed that I had uprooted Mr. Henderson and had unbalanced Sarah.

The villagers recovered their voices as I stepped away from the counter with my matches. As though by way of apology to me for their silence or to indicate that they had not yet heard the news, they began to talk of things which bore no relation to the death. They commented on the fog and listed its attendant injuries to motorists and mariners, and they prophesied the immediate ruin of the United States under its existing government, exchanged receipts for salt-rising bread, and told jokes involving a judge and a colored man named Rastus. But the lively tone was betrayed by a slackening of pace as I went down the aisle toward the door, feeling the eyes of everyone upon me.

And yet, when I had been at home only a few minutes, the flowers began to arrive and the notes, composed laboriously in an embarrassment that concealed itself behind phrases like "the dear departed" and "passed on to a better world," so that I thought I had misconstrued the silence in the store, for the names of some of the people who had been there were on the cards.

We sat among the sweet carnations and daffodils and roses whose fragrance and chaste petals, some of them made even lovelier by the whorls of steam rising from our teacups, softened the edges of our predicament.

It was my mother who spoke first. "If it was summer, the ladies at the Hotel would get us a nice coffin and a pretty tombstone. Miss Pride would give us the money if it was only summer. Don't you have anything left of the golden egg?"

The golden egg had been used up years ago, but my mother could never believe it and now and again she sought it in my father's Bible, tearing the thin pages in her impatience.

I had thought of Miss Pride, but I had hoped my mother would not. The temptation to send her a letter had been strong until I remembered that often I had heard her talking to her friends of the impertinent requests she received through the mail. A young man who described himself as a "would-be writer," after paying Miss Pride and her deceased father (neither of whom he had ever known) three pages of fulsome compliments, asked her to forward him a Remington typewriter at her earliest convenience. It was his specifying the make of the machine that most appalled her, and she had sent him a lead pencil with the note, "I regret that I cannot supply you with a Remington typewriter and hope that you will instead accept, with my best wishes, this Ticonderoga lead pencil." But, on the other hand, I had heard that she had sent two deserving young men, of good but impoverished families, through Harvard. I thought of how, when I was a little girl, I used to dream of her coming to our house, wearing black silk gloves and carrying a funeral wreath for my dead parents. I said aloud, "I wonder if she *would*."

Pretending that I was going for a walk, I went out of the house, but instead, crossed over to the shop. It was here before Ivan's epilepsy that I had done all my reading and studying, for in the house I could never be free of interruptions. I had made my father's work table into a desk, its principal feature being a German silver inkwell embossed with doves which I had found in one of the boxes. The room was dark from the fog and I lighted a candle by whose unsteady flame I composed my letter to Miss Pride. I stated my case formally, saluting her "Dear Madam" and offering her, in exchange for the fulfillment of my "novel request" my services in the humblest part of her establishment for the rest of my life. I asked her to telegraph her reply. But if she were disinclined to forward me the money, I begged her to forget my importunity and to regard me still as her "obedient servant, Sonia Marburg."

The moment I had dropped the envelope through the brass lips of the box in the post-office, I burned with shame and had I not dreaded the curiosity of the postmaster, would have begged him to return it to me. The text of the letter now seemed at once flippant and turgid. I had been tricked into my pomposity by the corpulent silver inkwell as though its original owner had left his nineteenth-century clichés behind to mingle with the ink.

Dr. Galbraith was fitting the key to his post-box and as he withdrew a packet of mail and glanced through it, he was the object of the scrutiny of the postmaster who, leaning forward against his bars, remarked, "Well, Doc, I sure did fill your box this morning, but I guess it's mostly ads and them journals."

"Oh, yes, yes," said the doctor in his pestered way. "Thank you. It's a very interesting collection," though he was shuffling the envelopes so rapidly that he could not possibly have told where they had come from.

"You been riding a horse, Doc?"

To the doctor's fuscous cheeks arose a blush as he looked down at his clothes and then at the postmaster, who had not been in Chichester long.

"Uh, no, no, as a matter of fact, I haven't."

The doctor's innumerable costumes were all spectacular and meticulously tailored, and they gave him the air of a "sporting gentleman" of a bygone era. One thought of his "cravats," not of his neckties, and remembered their large, loose knots in the French style. He very often wore riding clothes as he did this morning, and it was said that he had once been an excellent horseman, just as it was said that he had once been an insatiable student of literature and had once "performed creditably" on the violin. Now, the only reminders of those talents were his dashing habits, his immense, unhandled library (presided over, I had heard, by busts of Dante, Pericles, Shakespeare, and Vergil under whose staring eyes he drank each night to a point of stupefaction), and the recollection of Mrs. Prather who had heard him play the solo of Dr. Joachim's Hungarian Concerto.

With his russet breeches, which descended over his handsome legs into boots so lustrous and pliant I longed to touch and crush them in my hands, he wore a checked and belted red-brown jacket and a maroon silk ascot, and upon his head, a green hat grizzled with silvery veins and proclaiming its continental origin by a *gans-bart* sportively stuck in the band. It was no wonder that the old ladies at the Hotel Barstow, too old to be the object of his lascivious eyes, found him charming and said he "cut a fine figure." They admired his apparel and said that too often a physician tends to resemble his successor, the mortician. His other suits were of fine materials, all double-breasted and of a cut which did not vary through the years, yet always seemed to be at the peak of fashion. And while the colors and the patterns of the stripes or checks were conservative, the accessory trappings were of the liveliest declensions, being the racing lifeblood of the subdued carcass: neckties (or cravats) of orange silk and crimson wool, printed challis, dotted China silk, pongee, fortified linen, diapered or imprinted with arabesques or stripes or hexagons. His handkerchief and his muffler, if he wore one, matched or complemented the tie as did his socks and the band in his hat. And carrying to its uttermost his nice feeling for detail, he even had alternative spectacles which today, to go with his riding togs, were horn-rimmed, but tomorrow, with blue serge would be rimless octagons, and the next day, if the fancy struck him to dress for dinner and go into Boston, would be a pince-nez with a black ribbon and mother-of-pearl nose pieces.

Dr. Galbraith did not seem to recognize me, though once or twice he looked in my direction as I lingered in the room, studying the announcements of Civil Service examinations and the photographs of coarse, unshaven rascals with prices on their heads for the robbery of banks or the kidnapping of children. I wished to speak with him but hesitated in the presence of the postmaster who was still regarding him with the frankest inquisitiveness.

He was about to leave and I prepared to follow him, but the postmaster, perhaps in the intention of keeping him there a little longer so that he might continue his investigation, bawled, "Doctor, what can a person do for the bloat? Seems like every meal I get all bloated up afterward."

The doctor wheeled about. "What a thing to say," he spluttered, "in front of a lady," and he motioned toward me, "whose brother has just died."

The man gaped stupidly behind his bars. "Well, bless your heart, hasn't she ever heard of the bloat? I'm real sorry to hear the bad news, but I don't see I gave her any reason to be peeved."

"Come, Miss Henderson," said Dr. Galbraith and held the door open, adding, as we passed into the fog, "What the devil is your name?"

"Marburg. The Hendersons live next door to us. Dr. Galbraith, I wonder if Mr. Greeley would let us have another day . . . you know, about my brother. My mother doesn't want him to be buried like a pauper, and I thought if you spoke to him, he might give us some more time so that we can try to find some money."

We were walking so close together that our arms kept brushing and each time I moved away from him, his hand groped out towards me for support.

"Just a minute. I can't seem to think in a fog."

We could see no more than ten feet in any direction, and I felt as if I were suspended in a gaseous sphere, for the blindness of the air made my locomotion seem rotary and almost effortless, and when the doctor softly collided with me, it seemed even more that we were going round and round in a circle, he overstepping the bounds of the outer ring while I, with difficulty, maintained my footing in the inner one.

I repeated my question to him. "Well, I don't know . . ." he said.

Beyond us, we could now and again hear voices and the distant foghorns which only isolated us the more since there could be no proof, until someone entered our shortened range of vision, that the experience was not unique for us, just as it is said that perhaps a tree, falling in a forest, makes no sound if no one hears it.

The doctor stopped me and sighed deeply. "Look here, Miss Martin, I don't believe . . . I'm not certain, but the fact is that when a cor . . . someone is buried in this way it is not . . . well, frankly, it is not embalmed. I . . . no, I regret very much that it really is an impossibility." He clasped my arm tightly with his trembling fingers.

"But we will know by noon tomorrow and it could be embalmed then, couldn't it?"

"I wouldn't worry about that if I were you, my dear. These things are . . . my poor girl, there is no *shame* in being a pauper! But if you should know by noon tomorrow, I dare say something could be arranged. I'll speak to Mr. Greeley."

I thanked him and prepared to take leave. "How is your mother?" he asked me.

"Very well, thank you, though she's terribly upset to think we may not have a funeral."

"Ah, yes, yes, it's too bad. She is an, ah, an admirable woman. What is her name again?"

"Mrs. Marburg."

"Oh, yes. She is very handsome. She isn't an American?"

"No, she's a Russian."

"Fascinating!" he cried. "She looks like a painting I used to be fond of. A madonna, you know, something of that sort, very likely by a Russian painter. Will you give her my regards?"

"Yes, Dr. Galbraith, and thank you for all you've done."

"It's nothing, my dear, nothing at all," and he grasped my arm again before I could escape our hollow ball and get into another where I was alone. When I had gone some yards beyond him, I heard him call, "Morgan, is it, or Martin? What the devil is the name again?" But I did not answer.

My mother was embroidering when I got home. Upon the chest of Ivan's outing-flannel nightshirt, she had made an enormous rose in black cotton and was now sketching a wreath of smaller roses to encircle it.

"The shroud," she explained.

I would have snatched my brother's pitiful nightshirt from her hands, but I knew, by the diligence with which she bent over her work, that if I did, I would be subjected to an endless tirade. I only said, "Listen, Mamma, you mustn't count too much on the funeral."

147

She looked up innocently. "But you promised the cast-iron roses, darling! Why, Sonia, I wouldn't have gone to all this trouble to make the shroud if you hadn't promised me!"

"Mamma . . ." I began, but words were useless. I drew a chair to the fire and sat brooding, my eyes fixed upon the oven door where the word "Enterprise" was elaborately printed in blue. "For God's sake, Miss Pride, help me," I thought. "If she doesn't get the cast-iron roses, what will I do?"

The fog continued into the next day so that when we got up, it was only the clock, not the appearance of the world, that told us it was morning. From six until noon, I waited for the telegram. I was no longer ashamed of my letter. I was conscious of nothing but the hours ascending to their climax, three o'clock, which was the hour Mr. Greeley had told me he would "dispose" of the body. One of the hours dragged by so slowly that each second of it was a lifetime, but the next was swiftly gone. Because, in my impatience for the message, I could not bear my mother's humming and smiling as she patiently filled in those gruesome black roses, I had gone to the shop soon after breakfast where I fidgeted with the playing cards and dreamed over *Ethan Frome*. Each time I heard a voice calling another name, not mine, I bent my head over my desk and closed my eyes in a total blankness of disappointment. Hopestill Mather's time-blackened slippers, which had remained all these years where I had put them on the day my father went away, infuriated me as they had not done in a long while. I would have slashed to ribbons what was left of them if my father's tools had not been rusted beyond use. Now, at this very moment, when grief and terror were consuming me, Hopestill was probably laughing, with her handsome head flung back, her bright mind far from death or poverty. What would she do, I wondered, on a slow, gray day like this? She would still be in bed, under a light green eiderdown. Or perhaps she was having her breakfast on a tray and in a little while would lazily get out of bed for a long, perfumed bath. Why, her allowance for a month would pay for my brother's headstone!

The time was so deliberate that I could fix my attention on nothing save the knocking at our kitchen door and even my desire for what the telegraph boy would bring became vague. My necessity was so pressing that several times I was sure I heard my mother call to me. At last, indeed, I did hear her, and I ran out. As I crossed the yard I heard, like an insistent warning, the long-held note of a foghorn which was answered on the other side of the tongue of land by another, the two echoing and re-echoing. Then they subsided and there was a silence until a still more remote bleat sounded up the coast.

My mother was smiling radiantly and I smiled in response, sure the telegram had arrived. "It's all right, darling," she said. "You sit down and I'll tell you about it."

I glanced round the room for a yellow envelope, but I saw none. I observed that my mother had laid aside Ivan's nightshirt and was now making a basket in cross-stitch on a pot-holder.

"We have been stupid," she said. "Why, Sonie girl, the thing to do is to give our little boy an ocean burial the way the sailors do."

"In the water, do you mean, Mamma?" I cried.

"Yes. It's clean out there, and, oh, so much better than to be buried like a poor person!" She leaned forward eagerly and took my hand, saying in a whisper, "After dark, we can go tonight. No one will see us."

"But we would have to have a boat. Oh, no! No, Mamma, I can't bury little Ivan that way."

She tried to persuade me. Softly and affectionately, she described the dignity of such an act, told me how the bells and the waves would be eternal mourners for the little boy. She said the strange things that grew at the bottom of the sea would be fine flowers for his grave. If we must go out in a boat, would not Mr. Henderson take us? We three would go out, dressed in black, early in the evening. It would be ever so much nicer even than the cast-iron flowers.

Hearing once again the inconsolable moan of the foghorns, I was almost won but I did not speak.

"You run ask Mrs. Henderson," she coaxed, "and then go to the man who took him away. You fix it for me, sweetheart."

Mrs. Henderson had toward the sea the animadversion common to all the wives of Chichester mariners and fishermen. She personified it as a treacherous siren, forever discontent with her partial government over the men and striving with all manner of clever devices like storms and fog, to win full sovereignty over them. Thus, when I told her of my mother's proposal her bland face was disordered with revulsion. She recovered her voice and told me she was very sure so irregular a procedure was quite illegal, but as she was by no means an authority, we would go together to inquire of Mr. Greeley, and we set out through the fog.

It was a little after two when we were admitted to the mortuary parlors by a disheveled and grumpy housekeeper who, having been so long in the society of cadavers, seemed to have lost the use of her voice and addressed to us a solitary grunt, presumably intended as a command to us to follow her. We waited for Mr. Greeley in a small, cold room, immoderately decorated with rubber plants which had grown to a disquieting height, and furnished with seedy leather rocking chairs. Perhaps I only imagined it, but it seemed to me that under the smell of disinfectant that pervaded the house, there was the rank odor of putrefaction, and I whispered to Mrs. Henderson, "Oh, let's go home! I'm frightened!" But the undertaker had entered the room. He greeted us with as warm a smile as his parody of a face could muster and said, "Ah, ah, then you have found a way to get the little boy a headstone. Well, I'm glad, indeed I am. I hope you'll take my jewel, my roses. He will sleep better beneath it."

"No, sir," I said. "We can't have a funeral after all. But there is something else . . . Mrs. Henderson, *you* tell him."

The woman told him my mother's plan, and as she talked he pulled the ends of his mustache, exclaiming softly, "Ridiculous! Fantastic! What on earth!" And when she had finished, he rose to his full, improbable height and declared, "One may not cast a body into the street or into a running stream, or into a hole in the ground, or make any disposition of it that might be regarded as creating a nuisance or be injurious to the health of the community. This is the law, Madam. And 'running stream' can, in this instance, refer to the water of the bay or of the ocean. Do you think that I care to be apprehended by the Boston Harbor Police? Do you think that *you* have the authority to do what you wish with this body?"

I could feel the large and abundant tears crawling down my cheeks at his impressionistic yet graphic picture of my brother's corruption. Seeing my misery, he was gentler when he spoke again and even laid his hairy hand, which wore a Masonic ring, on my jerking shoulder.

"Look here, young lady," he said, "you let me bury him now as I planned and if you get some money some day, we will disinter the body and start all over again. All right?"

I nodded my head, for I could not speak. I heard Mrs. Henderson inquire if she might at least supervise the dressing of the child for whom she had had so great an affection and heard the undertaker refuse. She took me by the elbow and I rose. "God bless him," she said, and as we left the room, Mr. Greeley's voice came to us in a clatter of enthusiasm. "I hope you will be able to get my rose piece! The best of luck to you!"

"You mustn't mind him," said Mrs. Henderson as we started home. "It's his job, and a thankless one."

"Oh, I don't blame him! I only don't want to have to tell Mamma."

"Well, then, we won't tell Mamma," said Mrs. Henderson with a trace of annoyance. "I suppose there's nothing against a white lie to give *you* a little peace of mind, Sonie."

"But she'd want to go to the grave sometime."

"Not if she thought he was buried at sea, dear."

"But she wants to go out in the boat herself, Mrs. Henderson!"

"Oh, we could change her mind with a hot toddy, I

think. You mustn't suppose I don't know your mother," she said grimly. "And since we're going off to Maine directly, I'd like to think I left you without too many worries. Let her come down to the wharf, yes, and let her see you get into the boat with Ross. He'll take you out a little piece and she'll never know the difference. If she wants the poor lad to be down with the seaweed, let her think that's where he is." She was very angry. With an outraged, "I declare!" she fell silent for so long a time that I thought she had not been in earnest. The plan was, I saw, ideal, but I dared not hope it could ever be realized, for I was certain Mr. Henderson would not agree to so romantic an enterprise.

We had reached our cottage before the neighbor woman spoke again. "Sonie, you mustn't ever think I was being harsh with you a while back there. I was out of sorts with your mother for a minute, thinking as I was how you're nothing but a child yourself and put up with all these carryings-on. I'll serve my time for those mean thoughts about poor Mrs. Marburg. I do think it's best to humor her. We'll do what I said now. I'll step across to your place after supper."

That evening, about seven o'clock, my mother and Mrs. Henderson and I were waiting on the bench by the wharf. Although we could not see them, we could hear the dories dip and sway at their sodden moorings. Someone passed behind us and we could hear the hiss of his slicker and dimly we saw his lantern. My mother, wearing her bright winter dress covered with an old, rusty black cape, stood erect beside me. I was surprised to see that she was a little taller than I. Her arm was linked in mine, and through the mist I could see her long fingers on my coat sleeve. Mrs. Henderson stood on the other side of us. None of us spoke, but there was something in my mother's stance and in the way her hand, seemingly relaxed, was firm on my arm, which told me that she was profoundly excited and a stealthy glance at her parted, upward curving lips, informed me that her excitement did not come from grief. My glance, shifting, met Mrs. Henderson, who had likewise been looking at my mother, and it seemed to me that her eyes, behind her faintly glimmering spectacles, would be cold and unforgiving.

"A nice night," said my mother after a time. "Don't you think it's nice, Mrs. Henderson?"

"A little chilly," replied the woman. "I'm worried about you, Mrs. Marburg. I don't think you're dressed warm enough. As soon as he comes, we must hustle back to the house."

"Oh, yes," cried my mother. "Oh, of course we must! Did Sonia tell you what that good man said when he brought the brandy? He said, 'I think at times like these, you ought to think of the living.' "

It was some minutes before we heard Mr. Henderson call out to us. "Ready!" he cried. "Can you see, Sonie? Come straight to the end of the wharf."

I stepped forward, the two women following me until we reached the wharf, which seemed no more than a long, insubstantial shadow. Mrs. Henderson squeezed my hand, and my mother, who had already withdrawn, called, "Dear Sonia! Dear little girl!"

"Mamma!" I cried in an abrupt, inexplicable desperation. "Mamma! Mamma! Where are you?"

"Hush!" said Mrs. Henderson.

"Are you lost?" came Mr. Henderson's imperative voice.

"She's coming, Ross!" returned his wife.

I lingered for a moment at Mrs. Henderson's side. We were both motionless. We heard my mother's feet lightly running over the wet sand, and in a little while, an eerie voice singing in the distance. Then I ran to the end of the wharf, my head down, scuffing my rubber soles to keep from falling on the slippery boards. I went down the ramp to the float where the boat was moored. As Mr. Henderson stretched out his hand to help me, a phrase of my mother's song came swelling towards us on a little wind.

"Mr. Henderson, I'm sorry . . ." I began.

But his calloused hand was full of sympathy and he muttered, "Rich or poor, a person must stand by another person."

The dories softly plopping in the water made a sound sadder even than the horns. "We'll go round the Point and out a bit," said Mr. Henderson. "I like a fog myself." The whirr of the motor prohibited talk, and the fog-horns were all but obliterated save when they were very near. To our right, until we rounded the Point, were the lights of Boston, blurred into one long line which shifted with the movement of the boat. Miss Pride and her niece would be just sitting down to dinner. I could hear Miss Pride say crisply, "I had another of those beastly begging letters today. Do they think we're made of money?"

The water was choppy around the Point and I was filled with a mixture of terror and exultation when I considered that not far from here were the high seas in whose tumultuous bowels lay the bones of the dead and the timbers of shattered ships. The fog was a little lighter. Far away were dimly visible a bunch of lights and I knew that it was the steamer to New York proceeding to the Cape Cod Canal. What worlds there were on this side of Chichester! On the bay side, there was Boston, single and supreme. But here: the furious cemetery, over the residents of which one plowed in a massive ship to Europe; the fabulous New York; and to the west of New York, that variegated land so tediously described in the geography books. I supposed that bizarre as its name was, even Nebraska was real. The feeling and the taste of the spray were unaccountably thrilling, and I, forgetting the absurdity of our errand, wished that we might all night long cut through the water, our motor as loud as gunshot in our ears, and all about us the danger of death. And I knew then why Mr. Henderson had been so amenable to his wife's suggestion: he, I was sure, enjoyed the outing as much as I.

Suspended in my excitement so that for that brief time my life was one dimensional, I could not tell how long it was before Mr. Henderson cried at the top of his voice, "Now, girl, it's time to turn back!" Then I wished my brother's body *were* in the boat. Here, out at sea, I would push it into the water and the waves would move him miles away. The putrid smell, in its thick envelope of formaldehyde, which I had detected in the mortuary, returned to me and I retched as I did whenever I smelled ether. I would rather have Ivan in this vast natural grave than in the unmarked, communal earth where lay the unclaimed bodies washed upon the beaches.

I bent my head in my hands and cried because the child was dead, and I did not look up again until I knew we were going through the narrow shoals at the Point. I could see the sharp, glistening rocks and could hear the gulping of the water against their base. Since I could remember, I had been afraid of this place, for here, in a storm, a fisherman's dory had been dashed against the crags and his two children's bodies had never been found. We entered the dense fog again and made for the wharf. As he shut the motor off, Mr. Henderson said, "Well, Sonie, well, you had your ride."

I said, "Mr. Henderson, I am very grateful. I hope you don't think I'm crazy."

"You? No, I don't think you're crazy, Sonie." He was searching for something in the bottom of the boat. "Look out you don't lose your way in the fog."

"Well," I said. "Good-night, then."

"Good-night." I moved on up the ramp. "Was that your mother singing?"

"I guess so," I said.

"I never heard a thing like that before."

Though his words had perished, I now, as I reached the float, apprehended the note of fear in his voice.

I had just passed the great shadow of the Hotel when I heard footsteps somewhere near me. "Where are you?" cried a man's voice.

"Here!" I called. "Are you lost?"

We approached each other, crying out at intervals, my invisible companion saying he had lost his way. We met then, and I was able to make out the indistinct contours of Nathan Kadish whose voice had been in no way familiar.

"What a hell of a thing," he said angrily. "I can't even find my way home."

"I'll lead you." We took hold of one another's hands and moved forward through the murk, he with his other hand thrust out before him as though he were brushing branches aside.

"I went to see you and your mother told me where you were. Listen, Sonie, I'm sorry."

We groped in silence. I did not know whether to tell him that the journey in the boat had been a ruse to fool my eccentric mother or to allow him to think that I had buried Ivan so that he would not know we were now technically known as paupers.

Suddenly, when our feet told us we had reached the road, he stopped and seized me. His mouth waspishly raged over my face with kisses while he held me in an embrace so disabling I could not breathe or defend myself. "Isn't it queer like this in the fog?" he whispered.

"Let me go, Nathan," I gasped.

"Come back this way. Let's sit on the Hotel porch."

We walked far apart, the fog rearing a barrier between us; we found the path leading to the Hotel, fumbled up to the top step, and sat down side by side.

"I suppose you think it's funny that I picked tonight of all nights to start making love to you. I didn't do it accidentally. I was waiting for a sign and tonight I got it when your mother said that Henderson was taking you out in his boat."

"What kind of a sign was that?" I asked him.

"Oh, that you're deep."

"But it wasn't my idea," I protested, immediately regretting my honesty. "It was Mrs. Henderson's."

"Hell," he brooded. "But you *are* deep. I couldn't be in love with a woman who wasn't. If I could, I would have been in love with your mother for her looks."

I laughed. "In love with Mamma? Why, she's middle-aged!"

"She's thirty-four, as you told me yourself."

"But, Nathan! You're nineteen."

"That doesn't cut any ice. I happen not to be in love with your mother. My interest in women does not lie entirely in their accidents but in their substance, and the substance of your mother appeals to me about as much as the substance of Mrs. Gonzales. However, the point is not that I am not in love with Shura Korf, but that I *could* be if I wanted to. I might add that I at one time conceived a major passion for a woman of forty and discontinued the affair only when she talked of divorcing her husband, a beauty-parlor operator, in order to marry me. And mind you, it was not her age that made such a marriage unappetizing to me. I am, and I acknowledge it without false modesty, extremely precocious and I have known for many years that marriage precludes love."

Recognizing the source of his position, I said, "Oh, I forgot to tell you. I've been reading *Confessions of a Young Man.*"

"By that I assume you mean to imply that I picked up my ideas about matrimony from George Moore," he said with a sneer. "The presentation of your charge is grotesquely naïve. My integrity obliges me to correct you: I am, to be sure, very similar to Moore, but the similarity antedated my reading of the *Confessions.* I have *always* been a citizen of the world, a pagan, an iconoclast, and from time immemorial my motto has been *Ars longa est.*"

"Are you going to be a writer, Nathan?"

"Of course," he replied simply and his voice was surprised that I should ask the question. "I am a satirist."

"What are you going to write? Poetry?"

"I will not choose my form until my soul is ready. My knowledge is vast but inchoate. At the moment, I am collecting experience. That is why I sought you out tonight. You interest me and when I say I love you, I am not using the word in its conventional sense. In a way, the word is almost synonymous with *curious.* I am curious to know what sort of person has emerged from that amazing combination, Hermann Marburg and Shura Korf."

"Have you found out?"

"No, but I have a clue."

I remembered, from long ago, the words of this boy's mother: "So your kid is half Rooshun and half German, half Hun as they say." I said, "Do you think I'm more like Mamma or like my father?"

"I can't tell yet. If you got to be like your father, I'd

157

want you to live with me—for a while at least. He was the most sensitive man I ever knew."

"Did you know my father very well?"

"I know him better now than I did then, of course, because when we used to take those walks together, I didn't know as much as I do now about what had soured him. But looking back, I can see that he was crucified. Why, God! His conscience was hammering the nails in every minute of his life, and because he couldn't reason well—he didn't have much mind, you know—he figured that that eminent monument to filthy lies, the Roman Catholic Church, was right and he was wrong."

"I wonder if he ever went to confession after he left us."

I began to muse upon my father. How immediate before me were his crude bones, refined by the sunburned flesh! How directly did the wintry eyes advance! The face retired, and instead, I saw myself kneeling in the road to tie my boot lace. My loneliness was spatial and atmospheric, implanting in my heart a sadness which had not been there when the fact of his leaving stood alone. And as I saw that figure of myself in the uninhabited landscape where, in the leaden sky, the sun seemed slowly to fade rather than to sink, like a lightglobe with weakening filaments, there came again that disturbing half memory which had eluded me as I knelt down and felt the salty breeze in my face.

"And that is why I love you," Nathan was saying and I realized with a start that I had not been listening to him.

"Why?"

He looked me full in the face. His eyes alone were distinct in the misty darkness. "Which one of them were you thinking about? Your father or Ivan?"

As he spoke, six horns, one after the other, lamented Ivan with a single, prolonged moan. Nathan took my hand as the sound died. "How wonderful it is in the fog," he said, "when you can't see Chichester and you can't see Boston and *ergo*, if you have any gifts, you are, as I said, a citizen of the world."

"I'd rather be a citizen of Boston."

"You're not that stupid." His head hovered over mine, swaying down and withdrawing as if, preoccupied with his thoughts, he had started to kiss me and then had forgotten. "Really, you're not that stupid, Sonie. Don't you know you don't fit into the pattern?"

"I don't know what the pattern is."

"I don't know either, but you don't fit into *any* pattern, not any more than I do."

"Oh, but I'm not intellectual like you, Nathan."

"I should say you're not. Still, that doesn't keep you from being intelligent, does it? For instance, you don't have to know the theology of the Catholic Church to know that your father was persecuted, do you? And you don't have to know psychology to know that your mother is . . . well, to know what your mother is like."

"What did you start to say about her?"

"Nothing." But his arm pressed hard against my shoulders. "Freedom is the first thing you've got to get. Think of the *Confessions*. That was the primary requisite for him, and it's the same thing for us."

I was seduced by the memory of the Parisian apartment and in that moment, when Nathan's proximity lent me strength and when, moreover, Boston was visible only as a line of murky lights, I promised myself that I would have the best, whether that was to be had across the bay or across the ocean. I said to Nathan, "Now I know what you mean."

"Do you?" he cried. "If you do, I'm mad with joy! But you must know independently of me, you see, Sonie."

"Oh, I do. I see it quite apart from you."

And I did, because in that vague but luminous and intricate future, that tree-filled and fragrant garden, I did not see Nathan more clearly than I saw any other of the witty and sensitive and handsome people. What I saw was myself, that activating principle which set my feet upon a boulevard, and simultaneously made me love, sense loss, hear, now in Chichester, a final foghorn, that law or theorem of nature for which the term "Sonia" and its variant "Sonie" had arbitrarily been chosen.

Nathan stood up. "What happens next," he said bitterly, "is that we do what everybody else does. We fall in love and then it goes bad, but that can't be helped. You are in love with me, aren't you?"

"Yes."

He ran down the steps. I could hear his feet quickly crunching the sand as he withdrew into the fog. I sat still a little while. His kisses, like echoes, were repeated on my skin. From the points where his lips had touched, sensation rayed out until my whole face throbbed. But although I felt as brilliantly branded as he was himself, I was aware, not so much of the maturation of my love for him as I was for the achievement of knowledge: the knowledge that my father had deserted me forever and that forever Ivan would be dead.

2

The fog was dispelled on the next day; all traces of the snow were gone save for small pyramidal drifts in the corners of steps and in the crotches of leafless vines on the wall of the Catholic church. And the sun, in the vivid sky, warmed the wind, disclosed again the waves and the broad, shining shingle. It was one of those days that come as a surprise in the middle of winter, like a gift sent on no anniversary, so that the pleasure takes us unaware.

Early in the morning, hunger had awakened me. But as I dressed, my desire for food faded and I felt a little sick, for I remembered, seeing the empty space where Ivan's bed had been, that last evening I had been unfaithful to him by greedily snatching at Nathan's praise and affection. I made myself a cup of tea and as I sat down to drink it, I heard the Kadishes' door slam and through the window saw my lover running, hatless, his shirt tail streaming out behind him, with a book in one hand and a cinnamon roll in the other. He did not seem ludicrous. I half rose to call out to him, but remorse arrested me, and I deliberately looked away, whispering my brother's name as I bent my head: "Oh, Ivan, Ivan, Ivan," but the invocation was futile.

My mother kept to her bed all the morning and in the early afternoon she called me in. At first, when I sat down on the edge of the bed, she only stared at me. In these past months, her eyes had made me uncomfortable; I was afraid when a look from her demanded one directly from me, for it was as if she spun out a thread connecting with me which some vague superstition prevented me from breaking. If I came in from school and found her huddled into the old wrapper, staring at the oven door or gazing out the window, removed in a world as private as sleep, yet obliged by habit to make a transition back to the world that contained my presence, she would carry her stare to my face and, after a time, would see me. "I didn't hear you," she would say, for her senses were confused. Actually, she had heard me, but the sound of the door and of my footsteps were only now related to the sight of me. So now she regarded me for long minutes before she spoke. Her eyes, in another setting, might have made her look perpetually feverish, but because of her high color, they were the domestic and innocent eyes of a healthy animal. And yet there was something added to them; they, like the lines of her face, had been touched up, refined, perhaps by some ancient drop of Oriental blood. It was not hard for me to understand, seeing her this morning, how Nathan could be in love with her.

"He's drowned," she said. "You can't imagine what it looks like when they take it out of the water."

"Hush, Mamma, you go to sleep now."

But she would not be quieted. She gave me a sly smile. "Let me tell you what happened to me once, Sonie. Okay?"

"No! I don't want to hear."

"Please! It's not about Luibka, darling." Knowing that if I did not hear the story now I would be obliged to later, I sat down. She held both my hands tightly and her eyes never left my face.

On a feast day, when the summer was at its hottest, she had gone in the evening with four friends to the river to swim. They had to pass by the cemetery at the Devitschiepol convent where tents had been pitched for the feast and where *kwass* was sold at little pavilions along the paths. Each of the five girls carried a white sheet to wrap herself in when she came out of the water. On the way they had been joking, calling them their shrouds and winding sheets.

A group of Cossacks, a little drunk, were standing beside a booth, listening to a fair-haired Pole who, in a piercing, sorrowful voice, was singing this song:

> They shout the loud alarm,
> My war steeds paw the ground;
> I hear him neigh,
> O, let me go!

One of his companions cried out, "And what does the girl say to that, eh?" And so he sang again:

> Let others rush to death
> Too young and gentle, thou
> Shalt yet watch o'er our cottage home;
> Thou must not pass the Don.

Laughing, the girls went on, and one of them paraphrased the last line of the soldier's song, "Thou must not swim the Moskva." Already they could feel the cool water on their hot, dusty bodies and they hastened on through the crowds into a quiet lane that led to the river bank. One by one, as silently as fish, they slipped under the still, black surface. How good the water felt when they floated on their backs, letting their unbound hair be soaked to the roots! They called to one another: "Isn't it splendid, Dounia?" "Are you cool yet, Varenka?" "Look at Shura! She is going under the water!"

Afterwards, they sat for a while, wrapped up in their sheets, listening to the remote, enchanting voices from behind them in the town. Across the river they could see the fires of night fishermen. A trout leaped like a silver tongue. Someone began to sing the Cossack's song, but all at once broke off and cried, "We're not all here! Shura? Marfa? Dounia? It is Varenka who is missing!"

With the tails of their sheets flying behind them, they ran in their bare feet up and down the grassy bank, calling to their friend, but there was no answer save for the sleepy murmur of the river and the bumbling of the city. They called for half an hour until their throats were sore and then, crying, clutching at one another, they fled back the way they had come. The festival was as lively as ever, and the Polish soldier, drunker than he had been before so that his voice was deeper, slower, and more melancholy, was singing still as if he had never left off:

> Let others rush to death
> Too young and gentle, thou
> Shalt yet watch o'er our cottage home;
> Thou must not pass the Don.

The girls, half naked, their bare legs showing through the folds of their white wrappings, shivered though it was a hot night, ran into the church of the Virgin of Smolensk, and after they had told two nuns of the catastrophe, fell on their knees and prayed.

Days later, the body was found in shallow water and brought in by a boatman. Varenka's companions were summoned to identify the sodden, bloated parody of a human being. Faceless, livid, softened, it was a horrid spectacle. Of all the girls, Varenka had been the gayest. Only two days before, her grandfather, a rich merchant in St. Petersburg, had sent her a pair of Torjeck-leather boots and a blue silk blouse with a thousand tiny pleats. How Dounia, Marfa, Shura, Manetchka prayed for her! And yet, not one of them could remember how she had been when she was one of them, but only how she had lain dead on the counter, swollen like a fat fish, and like the fish, white, shapeless as if the bones themselves had been worn thin by the water and were no stronger than those of a halibut.

"If you had touched her, your finger would have gone in like dough, Sonie. Oh, you can't imagine!"

I was dazed, not by her dreadful story, but by the realization that she had hated Ivan so much that she had tried to make his burial the most loathesome she could conceive. It occurred to me to tell her the truth, but I was afraid of the cunning in her face.

"If I could forget about *him*. But his head keeps floating up at me. Oh, so white and ugly!"

In my astonished face, she laughed! She was laughing not with humor but with joy, like a young girl in love who can find no other expression for her rapture. And then it came to me with a shock that the song she had been singing last night as she went through the fog was the same one she had sung me this morning when she told me the story of Varenka, so that I knew it had all been planned and she had not just now recollected her friend.

I looked upon my mother with sheer fright. It was as if I looked upon naked evil in the person of that woman whose beauty so far surpassed any other I had ever seen that it was almost divine, as if she had come directly from the hand of God, but had, immediately afterwards, been inhabited by a ravenous and indefatigable fiend. Or perhaps she was not alive with wickedness but was dead with it: an empty vessel, or an excellent hull holding a withered fruit. I wondered how deep she was and if my own depths of which Nathan had spoken were the same.

There was a familiar expression in her face which had taken on repose after her fit of laughing, and seeking, at last I redeemed the day Ivan had been born when her strength had rallied to give him a name. I had wondered why she had called him Ivan rather than Hermann since the latter had come to be a generic term of opprobrium to her. It was that her eccentricity, her madness, call it what you would, was shrewd. Hermann would have been too much. I had known that even in her stupor then she had hated my brother and, later throughout his lifetime, I had sometimes wondered why she had not hated him as she carried him before his birth and why she had not hated me. She had not, because she had fortified herself, long, long before, with the conviction that men were all villains and women were their innocent victims.

She had closed her eyes. "Leave me alone now, Sonia," she said wearily. "It is all over."

I stood looking down at her for a moment and I exulted in the trick Mr. Henderson and I had played upon her. Saddening as it was not to know where Ivan was buried, I was consoled by the fact that he lay in the dry ground.

Just as I closed the door behind me, I heard a car stop on the road beside our house, and stepping to the window, I saw that it was Miss Pride's and Mac was handing her out. Rattled as I was, I collected myself sufficiently to realize that it would not do to receive her in the house, for my mother might repeat to her the story of Varenka's death. I went out to meet her. She was carrying a fuchsia-colored cyclamen planted in a little white pot. When she caught sight of me, she said, "My dear, am I too late?" vesting her cold voice with a gentleness I had not heard in it before, and looking at me with a genuine compassion.

"We buried him yesterday," I said.

She took my hand. "I only got your letter this morning and I came immediately."

The word "immediately" made me see her leaving her breakfast half eaten and her mail unopened and not waiting even to cancel her engagements for the day. Had I observed my picture carefully, I would have seen it was full of errors, for it was already afternoon and if she had got my letter in the morning post, she would have had ample time not only to finish her breakfast but her luncheon as well. Neither did it occur to me at once that she was not telling the truth and that she must have got my letter the day before.

"It's very kind of you, ma'am," I said. "But I'm sorry that I troubled you."

"What kind of friend would I be if you weren't free to trouble me?"

Twice as electrifying was this second shock, this designation of herself as my "friend." But strangely, my first reaction was not one of pleasure, but almost of disgust as for a few seconds she stood before me, not as that grand Bostonian to whose slightest favor I had aspired, but as a selfish old woman who, as a sop to her conscience, had brought me a potted plant. It seemed to me that she had aged remarkably since the past summer. Probably no change had taken place in her at all. It is difficult, in a wrinkled face, to compute how many new wrinkles have appeared in a year's time, or to see, in white hair, all the stages of its purification. It was, rather, that I had changed and my altered feelings had turned a spotlight upon the arthritic stiffening of her fingers from which she had removed the white gloves, the desiccation and the yellow hue of her creased skin, the protuberation of her veins, the liverish patches on her wrists, the aridity of her thin lips. But a censor in me checked me before I had disarrayed her features beyond repair, and as from her small, brisk person there emanated the sharp odor of her expensive soap, she recovered her familiar and beloved shape.

She said, "If you're not needed here, won't you drive to Boston with me and have a cup of tea? Mac will have you back in time for dinner."

I told her I must be at the Brunsons' by four o'clock. "Nonsense. No one would make you work today. What Brunson is it?" And when I told her Dr. Brunson's name, she said, "Oh, then he must be the Brunson brother-in-law of Harry Barker. I dare say he's not such an ogre that I can't beard him in his den. I'll just run on and tell him you won't be there while you're getting your things and we'll pick you up afterwards."

It struck me, as I went into the house to get my "things" (a large blue tam and a shabby leather jacket the sight of which, hanging listlessly on a nail behind the kitchen door, made me wish I had not accepted the invitation) that it was odd she had gone to the dentist and not to Mrs. Brunson. I concluded that she was afraid she might be trapped into a conversation with my mistress if she called upon her and such a conversation, entertaining as I conceived it, would cause Miss Pride severe discomfort.

My mother had fallen asleep. I put the cyclamen on the high bureau, predicting as I did so that when Mamma learned where it came from, she would remind me, as she had often done in the past, of Miss Pride's gracious gift of the rattle. (I was not disappointed. That evening when I came home, she was drinking a glass of the dentist's brandy and tenderly cupping one of the blossoms in her hand. "It's just like that man said, a person ought to think of the living. I think that Miss Pride's sweet.")

Warmed by a lap robe as soft as fur and lulled by the steady speed of the automobile, I looked through the windows with careless eyes, not paying the close attention I had always planned, to every feature of the road and the villages through which we drove. And yet I repeated to myself, "At last I am going to Boston," and the wonder of it was reinforced when Miss Pride marveled that in eighteen years I had not been farther away than Salem. Had she known, she said, she would have come to fetch me long ago. Sometime this spring she would come for me and would show me the Public Gardens when the tulips were blooming and the children were riding the swan-boats.

She inquired if I had heard recently from my father and when I told her I had heard nothing since he left, five years before, she shook her head with some unexpressed disapproval and said, "You have been very brave, my dear child."

I could not reply to the compliment and I had no wish to deny it. I said, "Did Dr. Brunson say it was all right?"

"Oh, perfectly. He's a very good-natured man. I was amused to see a placard hanging prominently in his office which read 'Terms Strictly Cash.' He appears to be more prosperous than most men of his profession in small towns."

"He has a practice in Marblehead too," I threw out.

"As a matter of fact, I have met him before and his wife, too, on several occasions. And isn't there a girl about your age? I met them under circumstances which makes it more convenient for me to be unable to place them clearly."

Inspirited by my curiosity, I asked, "Was it here or in Boston that you met them?"

"Why, it was in my own house, Sonia. They came uninvited to my open house on Christmas Eve two or three years running, and each time I was so muddled by the throngs of people, all of whom appear at those affairs more or less familiar, that I said to Dr. Barker, with whom I have a nodding acquaintance, 'One does see such remarkable people in one's own drawing-room on these Christmas Eves of ours. Can you tell me, for instance, who that blond woman is over there by the buffet with the identical daughter? Perhaps they are friends of the accommodator.' And of course, as you've already guessed, the woman was Harry Barker's sister. But what an unconscionable snob the doctor is! He did not enlighten me. He allowed me, each year, to make the same mistake. This past year, someone standing near-by jostled my arm and led me away to inform me of my *faux pas*. I was at first outraged with Dr. Barker for disclaiming any connection with his relatives. It's not the sort of thing one does. But on second thoughts—and on looking for a second time at your employer—I forgave him, but could not resist the temptation to apologize for my mistake. I fear I made the poor man quite miserable. He greets me most perfunctorily on the street now." She smiled at her triumph, effaced the look of amusement, and said, "You are disloyal. You should not have allowed me to tell you that unfortunate story. As penalty, you must now tell me *your* opinion of Chichester's leading citizens."

"Why, they have been very good to me, ma'am."

"You speak the language that befits the grateful servant. But it was my intention today to give you a little vacation from your servitude. I wanted to have a long talk with you about that very charming man, your father, and what you remember of him, and what you think has become of him. And I wanted, even more, to know something about *you*." Placing her hand lightly on my wrist, she said, "I admired your letter. Its restraint, its language gave more pleasure to me than anything that has come in the mails in thirty years."

"Thank you, ma'am."

"Now, Sonia, for the rest of the afternoon, *do* call me not 'ma'am' but 'Miss Pride.' As I was saying—you must forgive me; I am an old woman and apt to shoot off on a tangent at any moment—this is your holiday. I want you not to speak as a servant. I want to know something about you and therefore, I wish you to begin with your opinion of the dentist's family."

I thought for a moment. "They are rather money-minded, I think. And Dr. Barker won't come to their house, although they invite him all the time. It's as though he were ashamed of them. I don't know why he should be unless it's that Mrs. Brunson wears an awful lot of lipstick and she's too fat for her dresses and for the high-heeled shoes she wears."

My companion's face showed nothing. I did not know whether her objective had been the one she had stated to me, or if she had wanted, out of sheer malice, to hear ill spoken of people so far her inferior that I was surprised she even troubled herself with thinking of them. She questioned me not only about the Brunsons' reading habits and their friends and their political and religious opinions, but also about my own, and when she had exhausted my information, said, "Now that I have your *dossier,* let me ask a final question: Would you really come to work for me without any wages?"

"Indeed I would, ma'am."

"Miss Pride, please. You don't think you could do better? You don't think you have any other talents?"

"Oh, no, I have no talents, Miss Pride. I'm very poor in school. I won't be given any honors at commencement."

She smiled. "Nor was I given any honors. But I wasn't thinking of that kind of talent. I mean the talent of character which hasn't much to do with braininess. With brains, yes, but not with braininess. That, you may as well know, I can't abide. It isn't useful to a woman and I'm not altogether sure it's useful to a man. Dr. Philip McAllister is a brainy man and he's not as sensible as he might be. Do you know him?"

I said I did not, that I had only heard his name. He was one of the house physicians at the Chichester hospital.

"He's one of my niece's beaux and a charmer. But brainy, as I say. I suppose you had Dr. Galbraith for the little boy? Between you and me, Sonia, he's a rascal.

He's killed as many patients as he's cured, but then, as I often say to Philip, they all do. I am my own physician. I ventilate my house well and I take a walk every day. As a result, I'm never ill. I don't believe in any of these fads, these vitamins, allergies, neuroses. I am the most old-fashioned woman in Boston."

I told her—because I could think of nothing else to say—that I was never ill, and that I believed I had made up my mind never to be ill when I was a child and was offended by the medicine bottles of the Hotel guests. And then, when she said nothing, I asked her pointlessly if she were coming back this summer. "What made you think I would not? No, *I* don't change."

There was a momentary silence. Twice she parted her lips but thought the better of it. Then she plunged in. "You have read more than I thought you had. Not more than I should have expected you to, but more than I really like. At your age, you should concentrate on manners, my dear, not on ideas. But that can be remedied later. Will you be satisfied with a very simple explanation of why I have fetched you out of Chichester? Can you believe it is no more than that I am interested in human nature and see in you an interesting juxtaposition of class—whatever that absurd term may mean—possible only in a democracy in an advanced stage of decomposition? I mean by that: my family, on my mother's side, was established in this country by an indentured servant whose master settled in Virginia. The descendants of my ancestor, having acquired their freedom, worked north to Massachusetts. In those days, to be sure, such servitude was often little more than a convenient way to get passage to the colonies. A servant had not necessarily been a servant. In the case of my family, I don't know, for the records are full of gaps. But for the sake of argument, let us say that servants' blood runs in my veins. Yet I am, for all practical purposes, a member of the oldest American aristocracy."

Her glittering golden eyes, full on my face, commanded me to keep my mind on what she was saying, and I listened intently, nodding now and again as I did in Plane Geometry class when I did not understand a word of the instructions.

"You're no servant, Sonia. You belong to a class which no longer exists in this country, that is, the artisan class. And since so august a body of society has been demolished you must, so to speak, skip a grade. I may as well tell you that your father is the only specimen of his lamented genus I have ever had the good fortune to know, and it was a bitter day when I heard he had left us. For he left *me* as well as you and your mother, my child. I felt, 'So long as Hermann Marburg makes my shoes, I will be in touch with the reality of the past.' Ah, he did not realize his responsibility!"

As she spoke, she lifted the hem of her long coat. "You see what I wear now. Painful, hideous, expensive, flimsy! And look at your poor feet, those poor feet I used to see when you were a little girl. Then they wore shoes that had been *wrought* with devotion. I hope for your good father that he went back to his family in Würzburg."

"I hope so too, Miss Pride. But he said that night when he left that he was going out west."

"Perhaps you'll meet once again. You must forgive me if I am blunt: he was a fool. He took the indifference— they were poor, how could they help it?—of the fishermen as an index to all Americans towards good leatherwork. He was like the visitor who sees only New York and carries away the impression that the United States is a hodgepodge of skyscrapers and horrible racket. Actually, if he had come to Boston as I begged him to do time and again, he would have prospered."

"I guess so. But he didn't have any energy, you know."

I was thinking of how he would brood on the winter evenings because Saint Bonaventure had failed him or he had failed the saint, he was not sure which. He was not altogether dead, for, corruptible as were his vows to go to Mass, they must have sprung from a recognition of his sloth which, by the creed of his hard-working family as well as by that of the church, was a deadly sin. And the fact that his reaction was overt, even though incompleted, suggested a residue, at least of the talent of remorse. Paradoxically, this very filament of remorse had served as the central thread in a great fabric of mortal sin, for stirring him out of his house on Sunday morning, setting his feet on the road to the chapel, it languished; his contrition melted and, his mind reflecting, his will consenting, he went no further, took the other road leading to the Coast Guard house. But it had not occurred to me until now, hearing Miss Pride praise his talents, remembering how Nathan had admired his sensibilities, that my father was not a man whose misery could be mitigated by a change of environment or an increase of worldly goods or an establishment in a society. He was a robbed man, and the robber of what Miss Pride had esteemed was the very thing Nathan had loved: his sensibility, refined by what influence I could only conjecture. And this sensibility had led him away from the traditions of his religion and his work and neither the one nor the other could stand alone.

"Energy?" queried Miss Pride.

"I don't know how to say it. I only mean that I'm not sure he would have been happy just to thrive in Boston."

"Why, on the contrary, I think he would have. He was, after all, not a very complicated person. I dare say if he had just had his beer and *Wienerschnitzel* and had been able to hold up his head amongst his neighbors, he would have been completely happy."

Although I did not disagree with her, I did not, reflecting on him, think that my father had been so naïve a man, nor had he been so much the conventional comic-strip German. Miss Pride was either forgetting or ignoring my mother who was the author of a good deal of the tumult in him. Quite different, for example, from the rough kindness he showed me in the shop had been the nature I saw in the house when all the mild amusement at our jokes had faded from his face, as if he stepped from the sunlight into the shade, or as if his skin, obedient to the affections of his soul, darkened with his entering into the gloom which enveloped my mother and all she touched. Just as, at other times, in his shop, he would be gazing out the window at the bay and his

heart could not fail to impart to his face some of the joy
he felt in seeing the clean white sails under the blue sky
and on the blue water. The impressions, altered by his
heart into a desire for a life inclusive of such things,
would be altered once again until in his eyes and lips
there would be indications that he was deep in a radiant
dream of being already part of such a life, being free, I
suppose, not only of his duty towards my mother and
me, but free even of the memory of it. How inevitable it
seems that happiness will be the next state we come to
if only we are once rid of our present sorrow! Our troubles seem to have but one axis: we forget that even
though our love were returned, our debts would not
willy-nilly take themselves off; that even though the
headaches which plague us were cured, we should still
suffer from a broken heart. Could my father, who had
cried like a child and sobbed that despairing word,
Verzeihung, be content ever with what Miss Pride imagined for him? His sin of omission, because it seemed imposed upon him by some external evil, angered him, for
he had gone so far in his transgressions against the law
of the church that he could no longer bear his terror of
the consequences and temporarily substituted another
emotion. Just so, the dipsomaniac wrests himself from
the fear of his desire by changing the name of it
to "need," thus to tolerate his destruction as if it were no
fault of his own. It was this reasoning in hallucinations
whose existence he felt obliged to prove to others that
made him say, if I asked him why he had not gone to
church, "Something I can't account for held me back."

Miss Pride was asking me a question. "You're finding
the approach to Boston distasteful, aren't you?"

I quickly looked out. We were going through the
merry slums where wanton cats sprawled full-length on
the sidewalk and dirty, murderous children shot pop-
guns at one another and hideously howled against the
exasperated clang of the trolley-car. Bleak tenements
nudged a pallid sky where Chichester's sun did not shine.
Dark cafés, sunk like black eyes into the walls, advertised
with winking, blood-red lights, "Beer . . . Schlitz . . .
Beer . . . Schlitz." Some distance ahead of us I saw the

white column of the Customs House, and I realized with disappointment that all the way, the State House dome had been invisible, and that, because of the detours we had made, my original impression of it as dwarfing all the other buildings on the mainland, would be altered, would be perhaps forever lost. I asked Miss Pride if we drove past it.

"Oh, you shall see it, never fear. I see you've been properly brought up to respect Boston." Her voice was ironic. "But I'll let you in on a secret—I think the State House is a perfect fright."

She said there was no time today to acquaint me with Boston's points of interest (dashed by her contempt for the State House, I was just as glad) but she would show me the one thing which she had always felt was the jewel of the city. She would not care about the destruction of everything else, the First Church or the Gardens or King's Chapel, if only the Granary Burying Ground were preserved.

We entered its iron-bound precincts and advanced down the central path between the splitting gravestones that tilted backwards toward the austere obelisk of Franklin and the eroded sarcophagi. The several trees of the yard, black-trunked, thickly burled, and leafless now, and the naïve death's-heads, sprouting angels' wings on the decaying wafers of rock, were dextrous accidents, for they, and the wind we heard when the noise of traffic was briefly suspended contrived to give the place an air so formidable and esoteric that I felt death, at his most facetious unsightliness, walking beside me. I understood why she had said this was the heart of the city. Walled on one side by the Atheneum through whose back windows a solitary old Bostonian, withered and hewn, was gravely regarding us, the sparse and lowly graves of the harsh garden testified to the city's conviction of its rightness and its adamant resistance to change.

Miss Pride confessed that she was partial to grave-yards and often spent a full day in the one in Concord where the famous authors were buried, and of which she was particularly fond since it accommodated many of her ancestors. She spoke of others in New Hampshire and in Maine but declared that this small antique plot where we moseyed was her "first love."

"I don't know why it is nowhere but in New England do you find a well-turned cemetery. In France, they're nondescript. There is one other graveyard that took my fancy. When I was a young lady, I one time went to New Orleans and took a side trip to a little town where some sort of pioneers, German, I believe, had been buried. (My ignorance about the rest of this country, my dear, will shock you. I'm like the woman who said she went to Los Angeles by way of Charles River Village.) It was in a grove of oaks, dripping with Spanish moss which made everything most gloomy, most Doré. I found it creepy, I must admit, but it *was* handsome."

I admired the darling of her heart but asked her why she preferred it to all the others, and she said, "Well, in some of them, the newer ones, the horticulture is rather too much and the epitaphs have certainly gone downhill. But the fact is, that the names in the others are second-rate. That is, even Mr. Emerson can't compete with Revere or Otis. Don't misunderstand me. Some of my best friends are named Emerson."

She had sent Mac on and we walked to her house down the street past the State House to which I found myself indifferent. And at the moment I released my long-cherished impression of it, I realized that my desire for Boston had never been so real as it was now as, grimy, tattered, large for my age, I strode beside this clean, tart woman, so certain of her good blood, her wit, her wealth, her position in society (so *au courant* with her ancestral history that she could call a Cabot inferior to a Prescott, like a Howard running down the House of Windsor) that she could appear on the streets of her city in any company without the slightest risk of censure. Earlier, I had told her that I was not properly dressed to go to tea. "Dressed?" she had said. "Do you call me dressed? You may be more formal in Chichester at tea time than we are in Boston, but you look dressed enough to me. The important thing is, are you warm enough?"

"Now, we turn here," she said, "and then we start going down. Our Hill is a real hill. I always say it's really much steeper than the Great Blue Hill." Indeed, with a push, one could go hurtling down the brick-paved sidewalk and never stop, but shoot into the Charles which was visible, far below, as a wedge of chilly blue, crossed now and then by a white sail. Miss Pride, sure-footed as a burro, marched briskly down, and I, joyously regarding her from the corner of my eye, kept as close to the houses as I could in order not to bump clumsily into her. Her house was not far; its front windows faced Louisburg Square and here, as if it were an oasis chosen to delight the eyes of some favored heavenly power, the sun, hidden elsewhere by the city's smoke, shone brilliantly on white doorways and their brass trimmings.

Tea was served to us in the library, a lofty room at the back of the house, chilled and dark. Through the drawn, dark red curtains, the late afternoon light barely penetrated. Miss Pride asked me if I would like to have the lamps turned on and when I replied that I liked the dimness (it was not true; I would have liked to look at everything under a searchlight), she said, "It seemed a little *triste* to me, but you, of course, are feeling a little *triste*." She had thought to have a fire today but it had turned out so warm we would only be uncomfortable— she found the room stuffy as it was. I agreed, although the damp coolness of the place filtered through the layers of my skin and set my bones to dancing.

When she went out for a moment to speak to a servant, I made a tour of the room. The middle sections of the end walls were recessed for twin fireplaces with black marble frames; in either was a bed of solid, tawny ashes, the careful accumulation of years. The hearths were flanked with book shelves reaching to the ceiling and in a far corner, near the windows, stood ladders which might be attached to a track at the baseboard and to an upper shelf so that one might investigate the high books. I was more impressed by these appurtenances than by any other in the room, for they suggested a most serious purpose and I had never dreamed of seeing anything like them in an establishment other than a public library or a shoe store. The outer wall was taken up by two long casements between which stood a Governor Winthrop secretary. On the wall above, a gentleman forthrightly speculated on the tall cabinet opposite him through whose glass doors were visible silver loving cups and brass placques standing upright in a narrow trough. I say "gentleman" because I knew at once that he could have been nothing else. The edges of his gray waistcoat were piped in white and his cutaway, the warm color of a dove's back, was striped with fine silver threads. He was a lean man and in his severe face, age had peeled the flesh almost to the skeleton, but it was evident, in the bright, flat eyes (uncannily perceptive either through the painter's skill or his model's power to project his character into the canvas) that age had not deprived the brain of its faculties; they almost spoke. He was, I knew, some relative of Miss Pride's, and I believed he was her father, for the eyes were exactly like hers and, for the sake of experiment, endowing them with life, I observed that from numerous angles, they, too, seemed to stare suddenly first at one thing and then at another. They did not *follow* me, but waited until I had reached my new destination before they apprehended me again. I was standing near the cabinet when Miss Pride came back into the room. Before me was a small table on which stood a satinwood chess-board and ivory men. Two chairs had been drawn up in readiness for a game and upon a little glass-topped stand, a decanter had been placed with two inhalers.

"Oh, do you play?" asked Miss Pride. I said I did not. "You should learn. It is the best of all games, the greatest test of intelligence. Bridge, I have no use for. My father, whom you see up there above the desk, was the foremost chess-player of Beacon Hill in his time. This room, in a sense, is dedicated to his pastimes. For in addition to being a past-master at chess, he was a great reader, as you can see from the size of his library. And here, in this cabinet, are his yachting trophies. But I have tried to make the place cozy, not too much like a museum, you know, not too much like a mausoleum. After all, we have graveyards to take care of the dead, we needn't keep their ghosts in our houses."

I was curious to know who the chess-game had been set up for, and presently she enlightened me. "I must confess to a degree of vanity over my own game. My friends were corrupted some years ago by that humdrum Oriental importation, Mah Jong, and have never since been able to keep their wits about them at the chess-board. Consequently, for a long time I have had to be satisfied with playing against myself. Occasionally I get wind of a young man at Harvard College who knows a smattering and I do enjoy the combat. But a young man against an old woman is not quite pleasing. They're always anxious to finish the game so that they can start reforming me." The word "reforming" she whispered, drawing out the second syllable with an intentionally comic puckering of her lips that made me laugh and ask her what their mission was.

"My dear," she said, leading me to a fat, short sofa, upholstered in red velour which had faded in some places to a rusty pink, "don't ask me that until I have had a cup of tea." The tea had arrived just then, and I was disappointed to see that the refreshments were only rye bread spread with sweet butter and thin slices of fruit cake to which I had always had an aversion. "Will you have sugar and lemon or sugar and cream?" she asked. I told her I took nothing in my tea and I refused anything to eat. My abstention seemed to please her for she remarked, "Why, you're a perfect guest. I think it's foolish to stuff oneself at tea time on strawberry tarts and all sorts of sandwiches. In some houses it's become a regular meal. I feel we carry our Anglophilia too far sometimes, don't you? Or perhaps you think we don't go far enough?"

I had no idea what she meant. There was nothing patronizing in her voice, nothing in the least supercilious and I concluded that any young lady should be able to specify at once, and with reasons for her choice, the camp to which she belonged on the question of the American imitation of British customs (I was at least, through the help of my reading, able to grasp the meaning of the word). I was tongue-tied, but at length, when I saw her hand poised over the teapot as she waited for my answer and realized that she did not introduce subjects of conversation that one might take or leave, I brought out, "I have never been to England." The faintest of smiles pinched the corners of her eyes, and she changed the subject to literature which I had told her, on the way in, was my principal interest.

I learned that she regarded literature as utilitarian, as essential to good breeding. It was an ingredient of life like religion, and just as one believed in God and invoked Him but trafficked only with the minister, so one believed in Shakespeare but depended on *The Atlantic Monthly*. Instinctively she felt learning was a masculine province, even though she was an advocate of equal rights. She told me how well-read her father had been, how he had been instructed by all these books that lined the walls, whether they were poetry or fiction or history, and she rather raised her voice on "poetry" as though it were remarkable that he had found it useful, and admirable that he had renounced the temptation to enjoy it, had solemnly been "instructed." In the last years of his life, he had taken up Oriental languages and for this she had the deepest respect. "Now the mastery of a language I can understand. It is as thrilling as chess, and it is useful, although poor Papa never benefited from his Japanese as he only learned it when he was too old to travel. But he had the illusion, at least, that he was getting somewhere, don't you see." Hastily, as an afterthought, she added, "My dear, you must not think for a minute I'm like that quixotic Mr. Brock at the Barstow. A foreign language is useful in a foreign country, and I suppose that if one were cast on to a desert island and had nothing to read but a French translation of Mr. Emerson, one would be justified in reading it."

The mission of the young men who played chess with her was, it appeared, to induce her to read modern poetry. She had no patience with these eccentric cubs who had demolished tradition, and she found particularly infuriating certain New Englanders who had seen fit to poke fun at their countrymen. "I see nothing intrinsically humorous in the name, *The Boston Evening Transcript*," she said in temper, "and much as the author of its contumely is respected, I think he writes dog-gerel. I have never quite got his connections clear. All I know of him is that he was born in Saint Louis, even though he really was an Eliot. Times change. In the old days the people we claimed as our literary men were born in Concord or Cambridge." I asked her if she had known Amy Lowell well and she replied. "The less said about Amy Lowell, the better," so that I supposed—because I was sure Miss Pride had the pick of all Boston society—that the two had had a disagreement in which, of course, Miss Pride had been in the right. And later when she said, reverting to an earlier subject, that literary people were often "brainy" and that she did not enjoy brains when she was relaxing at her tea-table ("All things," she said, "in their places."), I decided that Miss Lowell had perhaps never been invited to the house and that their meetings had only taken place in the Atheneum.

Poetry frankly made her uncomfortable. She had not the same aversion to music or painting, perhaps because the media of the composer and the painter were foreign to her and she did not see their creations in the context of their lives. Not so with a poet who laid his very heart at her feet, tracing upon it as upon a contour map, his unbridled passions. Some young person, child of an old friend, had one day come to tea and had brought with him the Holy Sonnets of John Donne, and in spite of her protests, had managed to read one aloud to her. It was a particularly passionate one (Miss Pride, disliking such words as "passionate" said "fantastic") ending with the couplet:

Except you' enthrall me, never shall be free,
Nor ever chaste, except you ravish me.

The same young man had, she understood, taken to writing poems himself, much in the insolent tone of the mocker of *The Boston Evening Transcript*, and had composed some vicious lines on the Granary Burying Ground. The young man's "case" was a mystery to her because he had not only come from a perfectly dignified family and had gone straight to Harvard from Groton and was going into the law, but also because he was directly descended from at least two of the illustrious skeletons in the yard.

I was in love with that young man who had perhaps sat on this very sofa, resplendent in a long coat and trousers of a different cloth and thick-soled shoes and a bean-shave, reading poetry in the accents of Beacon Hill's Olympians. Magnificent creature, that intellectual aristocrat, pausing between crew practice and an evening at the Porcellian Club to exhibit, in an old lady's fusty house, the fullness of his life! I at once hoped that I should one day see him here in all his gentlemanly regalia and that he had been forbidden to come again for his importunity. For equally in love was I with Miss Pride whose small, dour world was governed by one and one only principle, a principle that varied neither in time nor place, a law which forbade riot to follow on the heels of chance: John Donne might once in her house pose as a forward woman, begging, in so many words, to be seduced, but he would not behave so twice. Between those two astronomies, the young man's whose earth was plural, and Miss Pride's whose solitary world was Boston, round which the trifling planets revolved at a respectful distance, I could not choose, for both were true.

We had finished our tea. Miss Pride rose and as she moved about the room turning on the lamps, she said, "Your letter so charmed me. And as I read it—let me say that I was impressed by your calligraphy which has the purity without the flourishes of the Spencerian hand —I said to myself, 'Here is *one* person of the new generation who preserves the ideals of my own. I will, indeed, come to her aid.' I cannot tell you how much it grieves me that I was too late. My little flower, I'm afraid, was hardly a substitute. Yet, without me, you solved your problem, you were not stumped. Oh, you'll be all right! I will say quite candidly that it flatters me to think I have perhaps had some influence on the development of your character. I have, although you have perhaps not been aware of it, been closely observant of you for several years and had thought, from time to time, of making the proposition to you which you set forth in your letter, that is, that you enter my service. But when you wrote me, I knew then that was not the ticket. My dear child, what talents you have! And a chambermaid!"

I had nothing to say in reply, but cast my eyes down at the carpet as she went on, "I was saying to my niece that if she had only kept her eyes and ears open 'as you have done, she would have been a singular young woman. Now I know nothing of your circumstances and little of your capacities, but I shall not lose my interest in you and since I should like to do a little something, in return for the rare pleasure your letter gave me, I have ordered *The Atlantic Monthly* for you and in the next few days will send you a box of books which I am sure you'll find profitable."

"That's very good of you, Miss Pride," I said. "I like to read."

She asked me then if I knew stenography. "What a pity," she said. "I thought they taught you that sort of thing in the public schools. I was about to say that I shall presently be looking for a secretary. The fact is, my dear, which I hope you won't breathe, that I have been thinking of writing my memoirs. Now you'll think me outrageously pretentious. I haven't a scrap of talent, as I'm quite aware, but I feel it my duty to preserve certain things, certain recollections of my father, a most praiseworthy man. But there's no time to tell you about Papa. Perhaps you wouldn't care for that sort of work anyhow."

"Oh, on the contrary," I cried. "I should like nothing better. But of course I could not leave my mother."

"No, I suppose not. One's first duty, after all, is to one's mother, or to one's father, as in my case. Well, we shall see."

The chiming of an unseen clock warned me that I must leave. Miss Pride led the way to the drawing-room to show me her Copley which she had mentioned earlier. As she opened the door, I saw, seated before the fire on a low bench, a girl with long red hair. She did not turn at the sound of the door but said, "Auntie?"

Miss Pride turned to me. "Some other day you shall see the Copley. Good-by." And without shaking hands with me, she disappeared into the drawing-room, closing the door behind her.

The word "drawing-room" had fascinated me for many years. When I first learned that Miss Pride's house was equipped with such a place, I furnished it with an erratic ensemble, elements of which I borrowed from every interior I had known or read about. It contained, among other things, a box of ferns like the one in the sixth-grade room at school. I had at first interpreted the meaning of the word as "a room where people draw pictures"; but this I rejected when I heard the expression "to draw out," and I thought that a drawing-room would be the setting for skillful conversation. When at last I learned that the word had been truncated and was actually "withdrawing," I envisaged a group of ladies cringing through a door as brutal men advanced, much in the manner of "The Rape of the Sabine Women," a brown, stained print of which hung in the classroom of the Latin and French teacher.

Today, seeing my first drawing-room, I was deeply shocked, for in that brief glimpse, I was able to take in everything. It was no larger than the library and because it was well-lighted and the other had been dark, seemed even a little smaller. It was dominated by three large rival "units": a bay window equipped with a long seat and a great many pots of foliage, a grand piano draped with a Spanish shawl, and a fireplace. Amongst, between, around these three behemoths, crouched chairs, to each of which had been assigned a companion, if not a table, at least a footstool or a standing lamp. The impression I got from the threshold was that if one wanted to reach the bay window, for example, he would have to "thread" his way through the furniture as in a crowded restaurant where the only vacant table is at the farthest end from the door.

As for a moment I stood where she had left me, I tried, quite frankly, to hear what was being said beyond the double doors. I caught only one sentence, spoken by the girl: "No, Aunt Lucy, it isn't that *you* depress me, it's the house. Otherwise, I would have dinner in tonight."

I tiptoed across the hall. I did not know what to do. My jacket and tam were nowhere to be seen, and for a terrible moment I thought Miss Pride had forgotten to tell Mac to drive me home and that I should either be obliged to wait until she came out of the drawing-room, displeased to find me still here after she had told me good-by, or that I would have to find my way back to Chichester on foot, through the evil purlieus of the city. Near-by me, I saw a table on which lay a silver plate containing calling cards. The magic names sprang forth from their immaculate plaques in the dim light of the hall: Cabot, Frothingham, Coolidge, Hunnewell, Adams, Hemingway. I could feel the very breath of her eminent callers who dropped, as though it were nothing, their venerable surnames in her vestibule.

A door behind me opened and, startled, I wheeled about, still holding a card that bore the name Apthorp. I thrilled to the recollection of having seen the name in *The Education of Henry Adams* which I had read by mistake for Civics class instead of *The Americanization of Edward Bok*. To be caught thus snooping in the calling cards gave me the same feeling of terror that I had felt in grammar school when I was apprehended in the act of passing or receiving a note, and for a second, being unable to make out who was in the hall with me (for I was so confused that I saw a white apron without realizing it), I was sure that I would be turned out of the house in disgrace. But it was only the servant girl with my things to inform me that Mac was waiting.

3

My mother had been ill for a long time with stubborn influenza, complicated with bronchitis. For two months, with a few brief intervals, she had been stupefied by fever and by the enervating sweats which came on when her temperature fell. Her sleep was disturbed by nightmares and she would call out to me in a terror that did not leave even when I had wakened her or when she had told me her dream and I had talked soothingly to her. The dreams pursued her even in her lucid moments and she would fall to weeping because the room had taken on the appearance of the cave she had seen last night or because, superimposed upon my face, was a word of Russian written in huge black letters, or because the bed was intolerably filthy to her since a few hours ago, two colossal tomcats had relieved themselves there. I suppose her dreams tarried exceptionally long because of the fever which could construct a complete hallucination from the barest materials: a piece of lint on the counterpane could swell and shape itself into the mammoth cats, or, vice versa, the cats of the dream could be reduced to a piece of lint. Her whole life was a fantasy, whether she was awake or asleep. If by chance her mind cleared and the objects about her righted themselves, it was not because she had recovered her senses, but that pain had driven the delusions away. Then she lay gasping, pressing her hand against the place in her chest that ached and burned from her shattering cough, and what she saw then: the bleak features of her impoverished room, my face ashen from the glare of the snow-light, the snow itself outside the uncurtained windows, these things were worse than her imagined tormentors and she would tell me to draw the blinds and light a lamp, do anything to change the scene of her suffering, to divert her for a few minutes at least.

Chief of her nightmares was one in which Ivan appeared to her. Often, when I wakened her, she would mistake me for him. She would shrink away and breathe, "You're dead!" Invariably, after this exclamation, she would be seized with a violent attack of coughing which even her syrup would not soothe. I could hear the tortured rasping of her breath between the barks, and if any ease came at all, she used it up in moaning, "Oh, God! I can't breathe!" It was no doubt only coincidence that made her suffer particularly after dreaming of Ivan, but I believed, half superstitiously, that she was being punished in her own heart. She often spoke of him and of Varenka, and whenever she heard the foghorns, every muscle in her body tensed and between clenched teeth she said, "It is down where *they* are, wrapped in seaweed." Who "they" were she could not or would not tell me. And she thought his hair had grown long and that his nails had pierced through his shroud. "I can see him, Sonie," she mourned. "His little body, swish, swish with the waves, just like Varenka. Oh, Merciful Mother! Oh, *mertvoye ditya!*" The Russian words, "the dead child," were uttered with an elegiac languor, implicit in the syllables themselves.

It was partly because I was sure she would not believe me that I did not tell her where the dead child really was. Even more, though, it was because I took a cruel and perverse pleasure in what I was sure was the remorse of her inner soul. His death seemed newly accomplished each day and gradually, while at first my grief had been intermittent and like a tide had washed over me only at intervals, now it became a constant and a profound pain, reaching to the farthest corners of my heart, delivering an unpredicted blow to every delight, whether or not I had been reminded of him. Flirting, in a band of girls with a company of boys, I abruptly ceased my giggles; the isolated moment silenced the flattering insults. I could smell the strange rankness of Mr. Greeley's waiting room, could see the black roses on the little nightshirt, and I could feel in my temples the vibrations of Mr. Henderson's boat as we passed through the shoals where the water had a sinister, subterranean rhythm. Or I would waken in the night and leap from the bed, thinking he had called out. Confronted by the emptiness, my being screamed at the knowledge that he was dead.

Dr. Galbraith came once or twice a week to see my mother, although I had never summoned him. The excuse he gave me, jocularly as though I had no connection either with her or with Ivan, was that he did not want to lose another patient in our house. He gave her, I thought, too much sympathy, so that as she grew a little stronger, she declared that she was growing weaker, and when for a whole day her temperature was normal, the next day it had soared, by the aid of hot tea, to 103 degrees. Beguiled by the idea that she might have consumption, she told the doctor that her mother and father had both died of it, and she was delighted when he promised that as soon as she was well enough to go to the hospital, x-rays would be taken of her chest. In the beginning, I believed that he was deliberately leading her on and that he hoped to cure her psychotic mind as well as her infected bronchial tubes. Thus, one day when he left her bedroom, after a cursory examination and a long talk, I walked out to his car with him on the pretext of asking him how her chest sounded. But instead I told him of her cunning trick of elevating the mercury in the thermometer by immersing it in her tea. "I don't want Mamma to become a hypochondriac, sir!" I said. "Can't you help me?"

But he missed the point entirely. "The temperature may be absent altogether in a case like this," he said. "It's the sound of the *râles* that tells the story."

"Oh, I don't deny that she's ill," I replied. "But Dr. Galbraith, she shouldn't put the thermometer in her tea!"

"No, she shouldn't." He laughed. "Be sure you don't give her very hot tea or the thermometer will break into smithereens and you'll have to buy a new one. Good-by! I'll drop around in four or five days. In the meantime, just follow my directions."

When even her authentic abnormal temperatures had subsided and her cough had gone almost entirely and by her color and her returning flesh I knew that she was nearly well, the doctor still did not discontinue his visits. He came only in the evenings, and sometimes called for me at the Brunsons' to drive me home, a courtesy that never suited me since he was not the kind of man who could inspire young people to chatter, and if he asked a question, the answer was always too simple, and I would reply in a monosyllable. He would inquire, for instance, if I liked Latin, and because, in his voice, Latin acquired a colossal unimportance, I could say no more than "Yes" or "No," depending on how well I had translated that day. A gluttonous boredom resided in him and its appetite was insatiable. He might look at the full moon whose reflection floated on the dark blue water and he would sigh with a vast ennui. Occasionally, he exhaled the piney odor of gin and at these times he was more animated, but he looked at me so lecherously and his talk tottered so perilously on the brink of obscenity, that I preferred his other mood. "I bet you're the kind of girl that keeps the boys at arm's length, aren't you?" Or, "What do you young people do after the picture show? You don't go home and you don't study. Or do you study nature, that is, *human* nature down at the Point?"

Some people, among them the charitable but mawkish Gonzales, declared that Dr. Galbraith had only taken to drink after his wife's death. But others, like the Hendersons, said he had always "gone pretty heavy on the bottle." He was known to have women just as he was known to be a drunkard, but he took great pains never to be seen in the company of the women and never to be seen drinking. Thus, his depravity, never demonstrated as sordid, was surrounded by an appealing aura and no one identified so dapper a "professional man" with a "drunk" or visualized him with a fancy woman. Through a wonderful stroke of luck for him, the old ladies at the Hotel knew nothing of his reputation as a voluptuary, and if they had been told that his eccentric color came from jaundice which had been brought on by many years of copious, solitary drinking, they would have said confidently, "Oh, you're quite mistaken. He goes every year to Florida and somehow manages to keep his tan twelve months at a time."

My Latin teacher, a scholarly man named Mr. Sylvester, thinking that Dr. Galbraith was a friend of my mother's (for he, like the rest of the village, had heard of these visits, but had not troubled to acquaint himself with my mother's social position so that for all he knew she could have been a well-bred woman who had seen better days) told me that I should value his society since he was a man of rare talents and had written more than a dozen musical compositions, chiefly string quartets. The information had come to Mr. Sylvester in a roundabout way and he could not even recall whether he had heard it from anyone of taste, but he was under the impression that the doctor had been first-rate. "But he gave it up for some reason, and one wonders why," said the teacher. Accordingly, partly to satisfy my curiosity and partly to stave off his discomforting badinage, I told the doctor one night what I had heard.

"Yes, as a matter of fact, I did make up two or three little things. I hadn't thought of them for years. I haven't played my fiddle since my wife died. Who told you about that?"

"Mr. Sylvester, my Latin teacher."

"Apropos of what?"

"Nothing. I suppose he knew you were taking care of Mamma."

"Oh, yes, of course. I suppose you told him your mamma was sick and that I was bringing her prescriptions and what not? Well, will you give my regards to Mr. Stuyvesant and tell him that my music is a dead soldier?" He had stopped his car beside our house and turning his fuddled face away from me, said into the fresh, windy April air, "You have brought up the past to me by what you've just said. When you are my age and can look back as many years as I can, you will remember this evening and say, 'Ah, at last I know what Dr. Galbraith felt.' Miss Moffatt, I had the most beautiful wife in the world. She was French and she was religious. My house is full of sacred objects that she bought in the by-streets of France and Italy. I have a *prie-dieu*. A Spanish crucifix dating from the thirteenth century, set in a tabernacle of Carrara marble. On my desk, a *memento mori*, a small skull carved of bone. I could never replace the least thing." He faced me again. "You forgive an old man his reminiscences, don't you?" He leaned across me to open the door, and as I stepped out, he said under his breath, "The odd thing is I have forgotten every word of French. *Madeleine*, there, I pronounce even *it* the English way."

The wistful note had left his voice and the sorrowing smile his lips by the time we had entered the house. "I'll just have a look-see at my patient," he said heartily.

189

"She is, ah, she's valiantly combatting this pestiferous bug." Because I knew as well as he did that the combat was over and that if she wished she could get up any time and resume a normal life, I looked away from him in embarrassment. He sensed it and said, "The peril of this kind of thing is the relapse, you know. There's the danger of tuberculosis." The last word he said in a whisper, stretching up on tiptoe as if to carry the sound completely out of reach of my mother in the next room.

"Sonia!" came her voice. "Sonia, darling, is the doctor there? I coughed some blood up this afternoon."

Dr. Galbraith's face twisted in a faked consternation.

"I don't believe it," I said sulkily.

"Coming, Mrs. Morgan!" cried the doctor. "Oh, by the way, I forgot the bouquet I brought your mother. It's still in the car. My garden is, so to speak, overflowing, and I thought I would like to share it with someone. I don't know what it will be . . . my man just snipped a few things for me. Would you be so kind as to fetch them?" He went into the bedroom, leaving the door wide open. As I left the house I heard him say, "We'll get the better of those darned old bugs yet and put some roses in your cheeks."

I was out of the house for only a few minutes, but when I came back, I found the door closed although, because the lock was defective, it had fallen slightly ajar. I heard a conversation about my mother's fancy-work. In her convalescence, she had begun to make fir trees, the decorative possibilities of which she had heretofore overlooked, and extraordinary birds which never pleased her. She would say, "I've left out something," and puzzle over the creatures, turning her hoops now to one side and now to another and never seeing that each one of their plump behinds was destitute of tail feathers. But the doctor, blind with infatuation, assured her that they were beautiful, that she was a "regular ornithologist."

"I like to see these homely virtues in a woman," he was saying in a voice that had borrowed some of the nocturnal quality of my mother's. "My own wife was a great hand at dressmaking. I still have some of her gowns in an old trunk in my attic."

"Did she die or did she light out one fine day?" asked my mother.

Shocked by her expression, he did not immediately reply. "She died," he said at last. "It makes one lonely."

"Lonely! After my Hermann went away I used to cry myself to sleep every night of the world. But that was nothing to what it's been like since little Ivan died."

"I know, I know."

"You was saying you have some of your wife's clothes. I wish to God I had some of Hermann's. But my little girl sold them all as soon as he was gone."

"We can't expect children to understand these things." There was a long pause. I had put the flowers in a jar and thought to take them in to Mamma, but as I approached the door, I was urged by a powerful curiosity to know what was taking place in the bedroom, and I crept along the wall to peer between the hinges of the door. The doctor was bent forward, his hands palm upward lying on the counterpane. Their skin was even darker than his face and the nails were a corpse-white. The fingers were short and swollen, the skin stretched so tight it seemed about to split like the skin of a sausage as it is being cooked. These clean, brassy hands played the supernumeraries in the drama of the eyes and lips, and as I watched, they curled into cups as slowly as a flower closes. Then the thumbs moved over the nails of the index fingers with voluptuous deliberation as though the contact with the smooth surface were exquisite. The left hand was raised. The man carried the source of the sensation to his mouth, passed the nail several times over the sensitive area under his lower lip.

My mother's eyes were cast down but her lashes coquettishly flickered. Her fancy-work lay at her side. The doctor wiped his shining lips with a purple handkerchief (This evening he was dressed in a gray suit and his accessories were purple. He smelled, as well, of lavender water) as if he had been eating the face before him and its flavor had been so delicious that in his gorging he had been too enthusiastic to mind his lips. But he was not making love. In a moment, although he whispered it, he said, "Let me listen again to that right lung." I saw him push her nightdress down and explore her breast with his stethoscope, his head bent down so low he seemed to strain not to lay his face on her naked flesh. "Oh, that's so-so," he said with a laugh. "I must keep you here another week," and gazing, deeply stricken, into her eyes, he took her pulse and announced, as if it were a declaration of love, that it was still a little rapid. My mother made no response, but picked up her embroidery hoops across which, this time, was stretched a branch of honeysuckle to which a deformed hummingbird was paying a visit. Dr. Galbraith glanced down and cried, "Charming! How I would like to have some of those things in my house! Would you . . . could I . . . my dear Mrs. Marburg, would you do some table runners for me?"

"Just at present I'm rather busy," said my mother. "But perhaps I could do a few later."

"Excellent! I'm going to New York next week. I'll just pick up some stamped things there."

"My hoops are cracking."

"I'll buy you some new hoops! I'll buy you some ivory ones inlaid with gold. I dare say they have such things?"

"Why, certainly they have," said my mother. "Once I had a pair of solid gold ones with diamonds set in. That was just one of the things Hermann carried off with him." She coughed a little and the doctor bent closer to her.

"What you really need," he said with such terrible excitement that the stethoscope shook in his hand, "is mountain air. Don't you know anyone in the White Mountains or the Adirondacks that could put you up for a few weeks?"

"Ah, doctor, that's just what I've always said! The sea air is bad for me. But no, no, I don't know nobody in the mountains. I'll just die here like the child."

"Yes, yes, well, that's neither here nor there. I have made up my mind that you *must* have mountain air. I will see what I can do—come to think of it, *I* have a friend in the Adirondacks who might very well let me, that is, let you have the use of his cabin. Charming place, set in a grove of fir trees with a lake near-by. The problem, of course, would be finding someone to take care of you."

"Oh, Sonie's a good mother's helper. She's a dreamy girl and goes off a little crazy now and then, but she's a sweet nurse all the same."

"I don't doubt that," said the doctor. Frustrated, unable for a moment to find his way to the fulfillment of his obvious scheme, he swore softly under his breath, apologized, and said he had just remembered an important engagement he had not kept that afternoon. Then he continued, "I don't wish to interfere in the upbringing of your daughter, Mrs. Marburg, but it seems to me that this is a very important time of her life . . . that is, in school. That is to say, from my point of view, it would be actually *dangerous* to take her out of school now, just a few months before commencement. Why, she might not get her diploma! Where would she be then? No, I think you ought to let her finish the year out. I will find you a companion myself."

My mother's eyes shone at the prospect of the mountains. It was the first time, to my knowledge, that she had ever earnestly wished to leave Chichester. I have never known anyone in whom wanderlust was so completely lacking. Perhaps she was incapable of imagining a place in America other than this seaside village, but tonight she was granted second sight. As if she were already listening to the wind through the fir trees, she murmured, "I love the mountains. They don't smell of clams."

"True, true! And not only that but they're healthful. Why, you'll be a new woman in a month or so. I'll just send my friend a telegram. You leave it up to me, Mrs. Marshall, I'll arrange the whole thing."

My mother did not thank him, for, completely egocentric, she was never aware that the betterment of her fortunes initiated in anyone but herself. Yet for his reward, the doctor got a flashing smile of joy which so enlivened her pale face that he could not resist the temptation to touch her and he lifted her hand which still held the hoops and yarn and kissed it. I nearly cried out, for I was not only surprised at the doctor's premature and uncircumspect advances, but I was afraid my mother would be shocked out of her placid daydream of the mountain cabin and would realize what his motives were. But either through greenness or complacency, she did not object to his caress. Barely conscious of it, in fact, she allowed her hand to lie in his until she was urged to go on with her humming-bird.

The doctor rose and as he did so, his greedy eyes suddenly widened with horror as he realized that they had been talking loud enough for me to hear. "I completely forgot! I brought you some flowers. The girl went out to my car to get them . . . it's strange I didn't hear her come in."

"She came in all right," said my mother. "She'll be out there doing her lessons. She wants to be a school teacher, doctor. Won't that be a feather in my cap?"

"It certainly will!" he cried passionately. "She's a fine girl. Now I must be running along. *Au revoir.*"

I slipped back to my place at the table and opened *Literature and Life* at random; the pages fell back at *The Deserted Village.* I pretended to be so engrossed that I did not hear the doctor come up behind me and jumped, startled, when he said, "Well, now that's a coincidence. I was about to tell you that the village of Chichester is soon to be deserted by its gracious citizen, your mother. I have been thinking for some time that she needed mountain air to dry up those little scoundrels in her bronchial tubes, and I've got her consent to send her off to the Adirondacks."

"That's awfully kind of you," I said. "But we have no money even to pay her railroad fare, and I shouldn't like to let her go alone anyhow."

"But she wouldn't be alone. I would . . . that is, I intend to get a companion for her, a sort of nurse person, you know. I'll pick up someone or other in New York."

"But the money . . . we haven't any money at all."

"In questions of life and death, we cannot consider money. I understand that you intend to be a school teacher. Very well, then, when you have your post you can pay back the money I intend to advance you. No!" He raised his hand for silence. "I won't hear any objections. I *owe* this to you. I have few pleasures in life. I am a lonely man, a widower, and where I can spread happiness, I *will*. Let me, I implore you, let me send your mother to the Adirondacks in memory of my wife."

He did not look at me as he spoke but gazed about the room and finally, his eye lighting on Dr. Brunson's brandy, he seized his hat and cried, "I must get on at once. Now, Miss Marburg, I'm not taking 'no' for an answer. I'm going to drive your mother down myself. Doesn't that reassure you? I've got to run on to New York anyhow in a week or so and it will fit in perfectly. Good-by for the present. I'll look in tomorrow."

My mother was delighted with the flowers and buried her face in them. She was still flushed with her thoughts of the mountains and she talked ecstatically. "My stars, darling, imagine it! It was fate that made me start doing the fir trees. Oh, how happy I am! I've been so unhappy! You don't know how unhappy a person can be, baby girl."

"Mamma, don't go away," I said sadly. "I would be so lonesome without you."

"There! She's cross that I'm happy! She doesn't care if her mother dies. Oh, Sonia, I never thought you'd turn against me, I never did!" Tears started to her eyes and she drew up a pathetic cough. "All right, I won't go. I'll just die here. I suppose it was a whole cup of blood that came up this afternoon, but it don't matter." She caught her breath. "Give me the syrup . . . No, no, don't give it to me. I'll just go on and die now."

"Don't talk like that, Mamma," I said. "Wouldn't you like a cup of tea?" But she refused. I sat down on the edge of the bed and pulled her fancy-work toward me. "Oh, what a lovely humming-bird! You're so clever, Mamma."

Pleased, instantly reconciled to me, she caught my hand and kissed it quickly. "Do you like it, darling? What do you say I do some of them around the hem of your voile dress?"

"Well, I don't know . . ."

"No, I don't either. It might make the other little girls jealous. It might hurt their feelings. Oh, you're good, dearie, always thinking of others. You're my baby girl, aren't you?"

"Yes, Mamma. Shall I turn out the lamp now or do you want to work a little longer?"

"I'll work a bit. I'll tell you what, when I get my ivory hoops, I'll make you a blouse with tulips on it!"

As I studied, unable to concentrate, I heard her talking to herself. I thought that perhaps it was the approach of sleep that made her mutterings more and more incoherent. Several times I looked in, but she was wide awake, still multiplying the blossoms of the honeysuckle. At first she talked of the mountains and the fir trees, inquired of herself if she thought the snow would still be on the ground, said, "Yes, it will be a good thing for her. Shura, even as a child, didn't like the smell of fish. She was real unusual about it, Mrs. Henderson." She proceeded then to her work. "It's not as easy as rolling off a log to do a sandpiper, Sonie, darling. Naturally it looks easy as pie to somebody that don't know the first thing about needlework, but all the same I'm willing to make them. Do you want two on each side of the collar or just one? No, the sandpiper is not my favorite bird. Best I like peacocks, next best parrots, third best bluebird. Sandpiper is way down the list, maybe last."

Then she ceased to make sentences and though she did not raise her voice, it became intense as she uttered single nouns or strung together a group of unrelated verbs: "Run and swim and holler." After a moment, "Mrs. Purple Grackle?" she inquired. "No, Mr. Humming-bird. *Mister?* Or *Doctor* Humming-bird?"

I paid little attention to her. Gradually I forgot about the doctor's visit and I read hard at *Ode on Intimations of Immortality,* my next day's assignment. My interpretation of the poem, nevertheless, was influenced by the childish prattle that issued from the bedroom and a part of my mind (the same shallow part that put into my mouth most preposterous errors when I was translating Latin at sight, making me read "In the midst of its boughs and yearly arms spread the opaque elm tree, huge, where sat Sleep vulgarly," for *"In medio ramos annosaque brachia pandit Ulmus opaca, ingens, quam sedem Somnia vulgo"*), obeying the advice of my English teacher to bring literature into my life and vice versa, suggested to me that my mother was returning to her childhood and if her mood lasted, she might go even further and briefly visit her heavenly home.

She talked continuously, then sang a little, then imitated a drunk, "They're flying *all* around thish room. Get thosh boids out of thish room." Something clattered to the floor. "Sonie!" she screamed. "Come quick!" I ran into the bedroom. She had flung off the bedding and was sitting up straight, her hands over her face.

"Mamma!" I scolded her. "Put the covers over you. You'll catch cold again."

"There were birds in here, Sonie!"

"No, no, you only dreamed there were." I put the back of my hand to her cheek. It was blazing. "There, now, you've got yourself worked up into a fever again," I said and put the thermometer into her mouth. Troubled, I wondered if she had actually coughed blood that afternoon. I looked around for signs but saw none. Gently I drew the blankets up about her again but she cast them off, mumbling around the thermometer that I was trying to suffocate her. She did have a fever, higher than it had been since the last acute phase of her illness, but I told her that her temperature was normal. "You're just tired, Mamma. It is a little warm, I guess. Would you like a sleeping powder now?"

"Yes. And you come to bed, do, darling. I know there were birds in here. You keep watch for two hours and then wake me up and I'll keep watch. I don't want them to get tangled up in my hair. They do that! Especially the kind that are part mouse, you know the kind I mean."

"Bats?"

"Yes. I wish I had a nightcap. I know, let me wear the little boy's stocking cap."

I took the little red and white cap out of the bureau drawer. "It won't fit," I said. But she reached out her hand for it and set it on top of her head. She pulled at it but when she had let go, it immediately contracted, skimmed to the top of her head and sat there precariously. But she was satisfied: "It looks like a nightcap, anyway, don't it? It's like not letting a dog know that you're afraid and he won't bite you. I suppose it's the same with bats."

She was still restless and insisted that I sit with her a little while. First the lamp, then the darkness after I had turned it out, harried her and she turned her head this way and that, groaning and sighing until at last she fell asleep and I went to bed on the pallet. Because I was exhausted and slept dreamlessly, I was sure I had only just closed my eyes when a cock's crow and my mother's shriek came simultaneously to my mummified mind and I awoke to the grisly light of early dawn and to my mother, kneeling at my side. She had had a nightmare. She was in the house of the witch who was no longer a woman but a man; a semicircle of people stood round about an ancient hag dressed in black who writhed in death-throes on the floor. The onlookers were solemnly interested but made no move to help the woman who had been poisoned by the witch. My mother was accosted by Ivan, grown into a tall young man, and he said, "That is my mamma. We knew it would happen at the Reds of Easter. When is it your turn?" Suddenly, looking at her hands, she saw that they were covered with a crumbling brown incrustation, green in spots with mold, and the witch, who stood near her, touched her bare foot so that more of the crusty scabs appeared. He touched her at various other places until her whole body was infected; she could not get away from him although he was not holding her; her feet were rooted to the floor. A hideous scream came from the throats of the people who watched. At last, when she was entirely covered with the vile stuff, he seized her by the arms and kissed her lips until the blood streamed from them, soaking her blouse. She saw then that he intended to lift her up and carry her to a couch, set in a vast bowl of water through which swam goldfish with enormous human eyes that devilishly winked at her. In shame and fear she begged to be released, and as he laughed at her protest and lifted her up, she screamed and wakened.

I got up and led her back to bed. She was crying now with horror at the memory of her loathsome skin and yet with relief that it had only been a dream. Her skin was cool and in spite of her tears she looked rested. I would have liked to go back to bed, for my head was throbbing from insufficient sleep and my eyes were hot, but my mother declared that she could not close her eyes again for fear the dream would go on to its dreadful climax. She asked for a lamp and while I was getting her breakfast, she commenced to work again the proboscis of her humming-bird. "Talk to me, Sonie. You know, talk a blue streak so I'll know you're still there."

Sleepy and cross, impatient with her fancies, I talked, with an intended irony which missed its mark, of my stolid mistress, Mrs. Brunson, who slept until ten every morning, never had nightmares, was never ill, and did not depend upon her daughter for her amusement. I did not, it was true, have the slightest respect for her. She was growing stouter as the result of overindulgence in chocolate creams and alcohol and although it never occurred to her to reduce her consumption of either, she had become extremely touchy on the subject of her expanding hips. If someone paid her the compliment, "How well you're looking, Dorothy," she interpreted it as meaning "How fat you're getting," and she would reply testily, "Same to you." I had at no time envied Betty her mother, but this morning, as I waited for the tea to brew, I wished my own mother's silliness were more like hers which did not rouse the household out of sound sleep and did not, even when she was drunk, conceive the notion that birds were flying about her bed. Moreover, Mrs. Brunson's dreams, which she was fond of telling at the dinner table since her best ones came during her afternoon nap, were of the most pedestrian variety, as banal as her speech.

"And Betty writes to her mother once a week from boarding school," I was saying, "and every time says, please send me a white bengaline evening dress or please send me twenty-five dollars to have my picture taken.

199

And Mrs. Brunson just says okay. She's the most unselfish mother I ever knew. Mamma, are you listening?"

"Sure. That Mrs. Brunson must be lazy. Why, I wouldn't feel I was worth my weight in gold if I didn't get up till ten o'clock."

"Do you by any chance mean worth your weight in *salt?*"

"Toot toot toot toot toot! Somebody got out of the wrong side of bed this morning, it seems to me."

I went on with my narrative. The tempo of the Brunsons' lives slowed down as I talked until, by the time the tea was ready, the dentist and his wife had become as inactive and unfeeling as the china family in Betty's doll house.

"I can't wait all day for my breakfast," called my mother.

"It's only five-thirty. The fire won't get hot. Oh, Christmas, Mamma! Why can't you be like *other* people?" I had not intended to be harsh, but I had burned my fingers on the metal teapot as I lifted it from the stove and since I was vexed already, the little injury enraged me. No reply came from the bedroom. When I took in her tray, my mother did not look up but stared at the back of her hands. "In the dream, the bones right there felt like they were broken under the sores. It was awful! I don't know if I can eat anything, thinking about them."

Nevertheless, she lifted the teacup and drank a little. "Listen," she said, "it wasn't Luibka in the dream at all. It was a man, like I said, and he wasn't a stranger either, but for the life of me I can't think who it was. Not your father. Not Gonzales. Not Mr. Kadish. Who in the world was the nasty dog?" She named the men she knew: doddering old Mr. Brock at the Hotel, Mr. Henderson, the Fuller brush man who had given her the black toothbrush, Mr. Greeley, her father, Nathan Kadish. The doctor did not cross her mind.

I thought of going to the hospital after school to tell the doctor that my mother could not see him that evening, and yet I reasoned that I could give him no proper excuse, that I might offend him by appearing to be suspicious of him when perhaps he was only acting out of the goodness of his heart. All day I was anxious. I could feel my forehead wrinkle into a frown that did not come from my diligent following of the text of the *Aeneid* or the *Ode*. I did not hear my name called out in the Algebra class roll and I elicited from my teacher the remark, "I must be having a hallucination. I could swear someone was sitting in Sonie Marburg's seat."

All the day I was thinking the word "insane." In telling my mother that morning of the daily life of the Brunsons, I had recalled a recent conversation between the dentist and Dr. Roberts, the only other physician of the town besides Dr. Galbraith. The doctor had just been reading of new surgery which was now employed in some cases of insanity. "The cure, to my way of thinking, is as bad as the disease. To be sure, they don't take after you with butcher knives and so on, but they become inhuman, have no feelings. The optic thalamus is put out of whack. Tell them somebody died and they'll laugh their heads off. Tell them a rattlesnake is behind their chair and they'll just grin. I'm an old-fashioned man. I believe in the good old-fashioned insane asylum." Mrs. Brunson who, when she had had too much to drink, tried always to ask intelligent questions—perhaps to prove that she could still follow the talk even though she could not hold her fork in her hand and spilled water in her lap as she lifted her glass to her lips—said, "But that would be used only for violent cases, wouldn't it? Not for the people that just say strange things and think they see pink elephants and so on?" The doctor, a man who in all things saw black or white, replied shortly, "I may be wrong, but personally, I think people who see pink elephants—unless they're stuffing you—are insane. We all have our off moments, but I don't think a healthy mind is ever off enough to see a pink elephant."

Had my mother actually seen the birds last night, I asked myself, or was she only teasing me? Perhaps it was the fever that had made her talk so strangely, so much more strangely on reflecting today than it had seemed last night. Moreover, I wondered why she had forgotten the mountain air and the pine trees in the Adirondacks this morning when she had been so enraptured at the thought of them last night. I did not want her to go! I was sure she did not need mountain air—the doctor himself, at the beginning of her illness, had told me that the idea that climate had anything to do with pulmonary diseases was nonsense—and I believed that on the contrary what she needed most, and what she would always need, was my pampering, for she was a very young child. And while I pitied Dr. Galbraith, I was not willing to sacrifice my mother to his loneliness, not even in the memory of his devout French Madeleine. Nor, on the other hand, was I any more willing to sacrifice him, poor gallant goose, to the persecutions to which Mamma had subjected my father.

Briefly I desired to tell Dr. Galbraith how she had literally driven Papa away, and when school was out, I started down the road toward the hospital. But I turned back, realizing what such a revelation would imply. It would be the grossest impertinence on my part to tell him, a physician, and presumably acquainted with mental as well as physical disorders, that my mother was insane. It struck me that perhaps I had been wrong all along, that he had no improper designs on her, that in reality the cabin in the Adirondacks was a sanitarium. I planned to talk with him that night and to beg him not to take her away.

The doctor did not call for me at the Brunsons', and as there were guests at dinner and the cocktail shaker had been refilled so often that I did not begin to serve until nearly eight, I was late in leaving for home. Maudie had gone sometime before, inviting me, as she did almost every night, to drop in "for a snort." For the first time I had been tempted. I was very fond of Maudie, even though she was tiresome, and my spirits never failed to rise in her presence so that even my boredom was curiously exuberant. I did not want to go home; there was something gruesome about the doctor, and I kept thinking of the *memento mori* on his desk in the library where he drank alone, as his servants reported in the village. And I thought of the marble tabernacle for the crucifix. When I visualized the latter, I was simultaneously reminded of the shoals, I cannot possibly say why except that the word "marble" suggested something chilled and ghostly and "tabernacle" made me think of the dark-room at school where the physics teacher developed films and where, because of the structure of the room or its position in the building, the acoustics were peculiar and the sound of feet in the hallway above was like the surge of waves.

I thought perhaps he would not come tonight or that he would have left by the time I got home. Consoled a little, as I passed by Maudie's cottage I was glad I decided not to go to her, for from the open door, brightly lighted with a Coleman lamp, came the sound of her loud, untrue contralto harmonizing with two masculine voices in obscene excerpts from "Frankie and Johnny." The rest of the way home, I reiterated a telepathic message to the doctor, "Go home, Dr. Galbraith, go home."

But his car was beside the house. The kitchen was mobbed with flowers as though a garden had magically been planted there since I had been gone. Branches of lilac drooped over the sides of the blue sink; the table was piled with jonquils and iris; on the chairs, wrapped in wet newspapers, were sprays of syringa, forsythia, and Japanese quince. Old marmalade jars and jelly glasses were filled with lilies-of-the-valley whose little ivory bells trailed down or nestled close to their broad caressing leaves. I stood on the threshold, breathing in the sweet air. A breeze blew through the kitchen window and carried to me the whole essence of the lilac with which it had been charged as it traversed the sink. For a moment, overjoyed with his bountiful gift, I was remorseful that I had been suspicious of the doctor. His flowers showed that our pleasure was his purpose.

From the bedroom, as usual, came the voices. They were laughing tonight over some private joke and I gathered that it had to do with the cabin in the Adirondacks, for I heard the isolated words "lake" and "firewood" and "chipmunks." Evidently they had not heard me for they continued to talk as I walked about the kitchen from one group of flowers to another. Shortly the door opened and the doctor came out.

"Good evening," I said. "How lovely your flowers are!" The doctor grinned obscenely at me and leaned against the table for support. One foot, handsomely shod in a half-boot, moved in an uncertain circle on the linoleum. The bright bronze hands tossed fretfully from their limp junctures as he said thickly and in a masterful imitation of my mother's accent, "I am *so* glad you like them, dear. They are all from my garden and they are *all* for you." His sweet breath came to me in gusts, mingling with the flowers' fragrance. Abruptly, his hands and feet were stilled and he rose to his full height, rocking slightly but apparently in command of himself again. "It's close in the bedroom," he said, still thickly but now without the accent. "I felt a little giddy for a moment. I was just about to examine your mother. It wouldn't do to fold up in the midst of that, would it? Give a patient a bad idea, make her say, 'Physician, heal thyself.' " Suspecting that he had a mission of delicacy in coming away from my mother, I asked him if he would like to wash his hands before he made his examination, and although the door to our "bathroom" was open and revealed only the toilet, its sole article of furniture besides the shower, he thanked me, said that was what he had come out for and went in.

After I had kissed my mother in the dim bedroom—for instead of her lamp, only a single candle burned on the stool at her side—I went to open the window at her request. Just as I turned back into the room, Dr. Galbraith entered and resumed his seat at the side of the bed. I saw that more of his flowers were strewn on the floor and my mother clutched a spray of lilies-of-the-valley in her hand. She had not been working on her embroidery; there were signs of no activity at all, and to my relief, I saw that there were also no signs that the doctor had been drinking here. Beside the window was our clothes closet—a rod across which had been stretched a cretonne curtain—and I stepped back into the large shadow it cast, less out of the desire to spy than out of reluctance to pass the doctor and be required to speak to him again.

"All righty," he said. "We'll just have a look at this clogged-up ventilator and then I'll be running along. Will you just slip your nightie down over your shoulder, please?"

My mother obeyed docilely, gazing the while at her nosegay. "Isn't it sweet," she murmured, "just like little darling bells."

Dr. Galbraith ran his hand over the smooth round of her shoulder and a look of alarm fled over her face as she glanced up at him. Almost shyly he looked away and fumbled at the clasp of his stethoscope case. But he did not complete the business. "Oh, Shura!" he cried. "Let's not pretend any longer!" He slipped his arm under my mother's shoulders and drew her up to him, covering her face with long kisses as his whole body shuddered.

My mother struggled and screamed, her head flung back and her eyes dilating as the stubborn man continued to kiss her neck. "Sonia! God Almighty!" I stepped forward into the weak light but the doctor was oblivious of me. "Darling, forgive me, I frightened you." His forehead glimmered with drops of sweat which he wiped off with the back of his hand. My mother, whimpering, could not take her fascinated eyes from him while he, as if he were paralyzed, hovered over her, afraid to kiss her again, yet afraid to move lest he break the enchantment cast by her unworldly eyes.

I touched him on the shoulder, feeling nothing but the deepest commiseration for him, and he drew back from the bed. But still he could not rise and, relapsing into his violent desire for her, he grasped her stiffened hands as she shrieked again, quivering pitiably like a baffled mole dislodged from his safe tunnel. "The sores!" she howled. "Oh, oh, God! They're all over me!" He stood up, and perceiving that I was beside her and that she was free of him at last, my mother turned away from us and buried her head in the pillows, and there lay murmuring.

"What the devil is she saying?"

"She's talking in Russian. She does that when she's upset."

"My God!" He strode in fury out the door and I followed him. "Well?"

"My mother has always been a little strange, Dr. Galbraith," I said, "ever since my father went away. Even before that I guess." He stood with his arms at the sides of his long gray tweed coat. He was staring bleakly at the barnyard scene above the table. "Dr. Galbraith," I went on, "there is no way I can pay you. I'm very grateful, really."

"I had never considered a fee. A doctor assumes responsibility for a patient without thinking of the money," he said impatiently.

"I'm so sorry about it all, sir! You see, I think my mother is insane."

It was the first time I had said the word aloud and it shocked me almost as much as it did him. He stared at me, absorbing the words after the sound was gone. "Insane?" he repeated. "Why, of course she is insane, but, I must confess, she hides her symptoms well. I swear, Miss Marburg, I had no proof of it until tonight."

"What shall I do?" I asked him, for it was natural for me to appeal to him since he shared my knowledge. His expression changed from disgraced rage to anxiety. "Come to my office tomorrow afternoon," he said, "and we'll discuss it. She shouldn't hear us, you know, in her excitable state. Tomorrow, promptly at four." He hurried out, businesslike, professional, hiding beneath his manner the relief he must have felt in knowing that my mother had not "rejected" him since she was incapable of doing so.

When I had heard his car drive away and I went in to her, I saw the marks of her real madness in her glazed eyes that looked at me without recognition and did not move as I moved but continued to focus in the place I had just quit, and in her rigid pose which broke only when she tore the petals languidly from the doctor's flowers, and in the steady monologue in Russian that ended at last in a fitful sleep. And when, in the morning, there was no change in her and she would not eat, but pushed the tray aside, spilling the tea on the counterpane and watching it spread, I thought there was no hope. "Mamma?" I tested her, but she would not look up. I should perhaps stay with her, I thought, lest she conceive some devilish desire to hurt herself or to wander to the village in her nightdress. But because she was no longer recognizable as my mother, but was only an inhuman parody of her, I was frightened and did not want to remain in the house. A little faint, because I could not eat my breakfast, I took up my schoolbooks, locked the door behind me and started down the road.

It was a fine day; as green as leaves, the water was bifurcated by the yellow spear of the land. Our little white house and the Kadishes' blue one sagged on their shallow foundations, hiding from my backward view the Boston shore-line. Just ahead of me, Father Mulcahy sauntered slowly, reading his breviary. As I passed him, looking sideways into his raw-boned face that years in Chichester had not filled out or sweetened, it occurred to me with a wild, obscene humor that I might ask him to come exorcise my mother. I was so close to him for a moment that I could smell the wine on his mumbling lips and by leaning a little towards him could read, at the top of his book: "Die 28 Apr.—S. Pauli a Cruce." He jerked his head like a rooster and said, "God's warning."

"What? What did you say?"

"I said good morning." He looked curiously at me.

"Oh! Good morning, Father. I thought you said . . ."

And I ran on, strangely exhilarated by the priest's odor, with which the air still seemed saturated, though I knew that was impossible and what I smelled now was the perfume of the lilacs blooming in all the yards.

Six

DR. GALBRAITH was not in his office at four on the next afternoon, and I was told that he was ill. I did not believe it, but felt sure he was avoiding me. Nor was he there on the next day, and the nurse, refusing to tell me when he might be back, suggested that I go to Dr. Roberts. On the fourth day, having resolved that this would be the last time I should inquire for him (I thought the nurse had been given my description with the orders that on no account was I to be admitted to his office) and should then go to the other doctor, I was informed that he had died that morning, a little before noon, of a heart attack. Upon the words "heart attack" the nurse ever so discreetly placed a stress which told me that he had perhaps died of what he said but that its cause was a prolonged debauch.

The nurse behind the circular counter wheeled her swivel chair back into place before her typewriter and began sorting large yellow cards. I wanted to ask her more, but I could not think of a way to frame my questions. To be sure, the doctor's death was no more than coincidence and my mother, who all day long talked tenderly to herself in Russian and one by one ripped the petals from his fading flowers, was no more to blame for it than I, or than this imperturbable woman in the starched white cap. Though I had cared nothing for this stammering dandy and had many times wished him out of the way, I had wished him no harm, "out of the way" having meant only "out of our house." But I was shaken with something simulating the grief I had felt when I dropped my brother's hand, and my knees went weak, as I remembered that I had sometimes pitied the man. I had pictured him in his library, perfectly groomed, as if his loving toilet had been made for some honored guests, though no one ever called on him, and he sat alone, sunk in his jejune thoughts that the whiskey enshrouded. Gossip ran that in this room, the shrine of his dead wife's sacred objects, there was a bar concealed in the paneling —which opened at the pressure of a button, so that in the evenings Dr. Galbraith could dispense with the services of his butler who was allowed to enter the room only in the morning to clear away the evidences of his master's lonesome spree before the parlor-maid came in to clean. I wished to ask the nurse if he had died there. Once he had told me that two malachite urns stood on his mantelpiece and that the draperies were ruby-colored brocade. Perhaps he had chosen as his shroud one of his Scotch tweed suits in which the brown was enriched with red and with it he had worn green socks and a green cravat.

"When is the funeral?" I asked, although I did not really want to know.

"I haven't the least idea," replied the nurse without looking up. "You might ask his housekeeper. All I know is that he is to be cremated."

I felt that if I moved from the counter where I rested my elbows, I would fall in my weakness. An interne who had been watching me absent-mindedly as he whirled a piece of rubber tubing round and round, pocketed his plaything and stepped to my side. Out of a mechanical kindness, he placed his hand on my shoulder and said, "Take it easy." I burst into tears, inexplicable to myself, and stumbled through the sunlit lobby, my legs enfeebled, my mind a blank. The scene detached itself from its aseptic smell and the white entourage of nurses and internes: .its properties receded and I, hurtling up the road, was too alone to measure the degree of my loneliness, for I did not know where to turn for advice.

Yet, on the day following the doctor's funeral in Cambridge, I was receiving counsel from young Dr. McAllister in the same office where I had first seen Dr. Galbraith. That other day, the hygienic glare of gray walls and white wainscoting had combined with the blue shadows of snow-filled trees beyond the windows into a hard, glacial light. The old man's skin had been green as if its natural yellow hue had been mixed with the blue shadows, and his eyes, pillowed by their pendulous sacs, had ambled sensually over me while his addled brain danced in bewilderment. The tall, bony elms of the hospital courtyard had whined and rattled and then, when the wind died, a company of discursive sparrows raised their voices in the hush. The only other sign of animation to be seen from the window was a solitary pigeon promenading over the slate roof of an adjacent ward about whose red chimney wound the steam from two small exhausts.

The new occupant sat before the open windows through which, gentle and billowing, came the May day's limbering breezes and edgeless light. The world beyond was spacious and subtly illuminated; the landscape, perhaps as much as the young doctor's adroit kindness, loosed the strictures of my terror, and after my first ferocious declaration that my mother was insane, I was able to speak without a stutter.

Dr. McAllister was somewhere between twenty-five and thirty; he was spare and angular and erect and his obvious good health recommended him, whereas Dr. Galbraith's diseased complexion and unstrung manner had made him seem, from the very beginning, an uncertain ally. The tone of the young man's voice was restorative, for he was at once casual so that my story seemed automatically less calamitous than I had thought, and authoritative so that I knew I could depend upon him.

I had come to him because I had not wanted to consult Dr. Roberts, who, being a good friend of Dr. Brunson, might, despite his professional ethics, drop a few hints to the dentist. I wished, so far as possible, to keep secret this new excitement of our household. To be sure, everyone in Chichester had said for years that my mother was mad, and the children who had used to come to play up towards our house no longer came. The villagers and the shopkeepers had, after Ivan's death, stopped inquiring about her. But still, they had no proof.

It had not been easy to gain an audience with Dr. McAllister, who was a house-physician and not allowed to have private cases, and so I had written him a note, saying that Miss Pride had asked me to look him up. He had sent back the reply that he would be delighted to meet me at such-and-such an hour on Sunday afternoon at a tea-room in Marblehead. It was the hasty note of a busy man who, aware of his duty towards his friends, parcels out his leisure time with no sign of the irritation he feels that he can keep no part of his life to himself. I would have let the matter rest there had I not, on returning to my mother, found her up and dressed, carrying a basket on her arm with the intention, I was afraid, of going to the village. I had urged her to go back to bed, but my entreaties were futile for she understood nothing but Russian. I had then given her a glass of brandy (she had at least not forgotten brandy) in which I had dissolved one of the sleeping powders left over from her illness. I must say here that this ingenious trick afforded me the only amusement I had in ten days. I could not help smiling, as I pulverized the pill, at the grave necessity that had driven me to practical joking, and when she began to droop, after no more than a quarter of an hour, I laughed outright. I had then locked her in and run back to the hospital where, on a sheet torn from my loose-leaf notebook, I wrote Dr. McAllister that I had an urgent message for him from Miss Pride. A cold, dubious answer came back at once saying that he would see me in his office in a few minutes.

The doctor had been reading. When I came in, he

took off his horn-rimmed spectacles, uncovering eyes which were a blue resembling the flame from certain kinds of wood or oil, a color simultaneously fierce and smoky. In his face there was a union of austerity and simplicity, coming partly from its actual architecture: the defined planes of the jaw and cheek and forehead, the thin lips, the narrow nose, and partly from his expression as he intelligently and nobly appraised me, trying to adjust me to my note.

"You have a message for me?" he said, smiling and motioning me toward a chair. "You must be a friend of Miss Pride's."

"I am, in a way," I said. "But I am really here under false pretenses, for I have no message for you. I had to see you. It's about my mother."

"I don't have a private practice," he said. "Our head, Dr. Galbraith, recently died, as perhaps you know, and his place has not yet been filled. But Dr. Roberts is in town, I'm quite sure." As though to clinch his dismissal, he withdrew his spectacles from the pocket of his white coat and opened them.

"I know that," I said. "But I don't want to go to Dr. Roberts." He waited for me to go on, but I could find no more words, and as I kept my eyes averted from him, seeing the green felt under the glass top of his desk with the harried realization that I had no idea what I was looking at, I knew what his next question was going to be, but as in the dream when our benumbed throats will not let pass a cry for help, I could summon nothing to stave it off, and when he spoke, I heard him as though his voice came from a phonograph record whose revolutions I did not know how to stop: "Look here, I don't know who you are but I don't believe you are Miss Pride's friend. All this mystery doesn't ring true. Are you quite sure it's your mother who is ill? I don't want to sound unkind, but tell me frankly, isn't it instead that you've committed an indiscretion and, to use the common expression, have got yourself knocked up?"

Because I had known that that was the way he would interpret my timidity and my lie about the message, I could not be angry with him for anything but the vulgarity of his phrase, which he had used in the intention of lowering himself to my level, but at the same time had uttered in almost audible quotation marks to assure me that he would have nothing to do with the matter, that I had come to the wrong person for an abortion.

I found my voice and said, "Oh, no, it's not that at all. It's that I think my mother is insane."

"You should have said so at once. Please forgive me, but your coming here was so unusual. Why do you think your mother is insane?"

I told him her history. As I talked, his attentive blue eyes showed me that he was marshaling recollections that my presence and my story disinterred, was giving the skeletons flesh and blood, yet was keeping me, my "case," separate like the solo part of a concerto which is enriched and surrounded by the ritornelle. To ease me, to divert me from the horror of what I told him—for one's sin or sorrow is most intolerable at the moment of confession even when we know that we are soon to be absolved or comforted—he halted me now and again with seemingly inconsequential questions or observations. He had, for example, been to Würsburg and as he spoke of it, pleased that I had caused him to remember the hotel where he had stayed which had formerly been a Franciscan monastery and still preserved an atmosphere of asceticism, he canceled out the distaste and aloofness that had been in his voice when he thought I was pregnant, and without deviating from his purpose as a physician, elevated me to his own plane as at first he had descended to mine. He was, I could tell, profoundly moved by Ivan's death and burial. He said, "Your story *is* a Russian one," and asked me if I had read Dostoievsky. I said I had not, but he led me to the place from which he surveyed the geography of my mother's mind so that I saw her not as my mother, but as a type, as the embodiment of the traits he had read about. We looked together from our vantage point and, lighted by the stories and the novels from whose context he extracted what was applicable to my mother, I saw her, for a little while, as he did.

When I had finished my account and he began to

213

speak, he did not offer me any solution and he said he could not counsel me until he had seen my mother and had judged for himself whether her symptoms corresponded to my report of them. It was easy enough, he said, even for an experienced person to confuse hysteria with insanity, and while he did not say so, he implied that possibly because of my concern over Ivan, my own hysteria had made me exaggerate her eccentricities. "She is perhaps best off at home," he said, "where she can be guarded against excitement. If, that is, she's curable, and the chances are that she is."

"But where else could she be?"

"Perhaps I have misunderstood you." He looked away from me and briefly examined the scene from his window as though he were trying to integrate all its essentials, its colors and its forms, as if he hoped to find there the way to put his words best. "That is, I assumed in your coming to me that you wanted more than a listener. I thought you had been debating whether or not to send her to an asylum."

Chiefly, I suppose, because there was none near Chichester and I had, therefore, no actual impression of the appearance of such an establishment, an asylum had never once occurred to me. My mother's madness had been clearly separated from any other madness. And I said to Dr. McAllister. "Oh, but she isn't violent! She couldn't be put into a strait-jacket."

He laughed. "You're behind the times. We're not going to put your mother into a strait-jacket. Why, mental hospitals are no worse than this these days." He motioned toward the silent corridor. "But we needn't talk about that any more. I'll look around some evening soon, as though I were paying a call on you, and see what's what." He glanced down at the blue card on which he had been making notes, to refresh his memory of my name. "We've covered everything now, haven't we, Miss Marburg? I would like, though, to ask you one more question. Why was it you used Miss Pride's name instead of another? You know, you could have said Dr. Brunson sent you."

"She spoke of you to me. I connected your name with

her and with her niece, for she said you were friends. You see, last February, when my brother died, Miss Pride came to see me and took me into Boston. I had tea with her . . . in the library." I had heard no more from her. She did not come to fetch me to see the Public Gardens, as she had promised, nor had she sent me the box of books although *The Atlantic Monthly* came regularly. Boston had receded a little farther each day until now, the sea again seemed the only road to the State House whose glittering dome had once more recovered its pure shape after my new impressions of it had shuffled off into the past. I had thought my afternoon with Miss Pride was engraved indelibly on my mind, but at last I remembered clearly only the horny black trunks of the trees in the Park Street cemetery, only the names Franklin and Revere, and only the metallic voice of the girl saying "Auntie?"

But the proximity of this man, to whom having tea with Miss Pride was probably the most ordinary occurrence, brought back the objects of our common knowledge: the portrait, the chess-table, the silver platter for the calling cards. And with the objects came my hostess's warm, albeit noncommittal, compliments. On an impulse, I said, "Perhaps you could tell me why she invited me to come to tea?"

"Miss Pride is a very generous woman," he said with the simplicity but lack of conviction with which, in speaking of the people we do not like, we acknowledge their virtues that are good in themselves but can serve no purpose to us. "She is known, I believe," he continued, "as one of the *most* generous women in Boston. Last year, for example, she gave five thousand dollars to the Community Chest."

"I have admired her ever since I can remember," I told him.

"Really? Well, then, perhaps that's one of the reasons she was, as you say, so 'kind' to you. I have never had the honor to be at tea with her alone . . . and never in the library."

I could not grasp his irony. Did he mean that I *had* been singularly honored? Or had she, by shutting me up in the library, merely been taking precautions against my being seen by a chance visitor? I rose to go, dissatisfied with what the doctor had said and liking him a little less for not praising Miss Pride with the passion that I had believed must reside in the breast of anyone who knew her. He came around the desk and I observed that when he walked, his body did not bend in the slightest; his back was as straight, as inflexible as Ivan's had been a few hours after his death.

"You can count on me. But the next time you want to crash a gate, make sure you have the right password. You wouldn't have got in today if I hadn't had an inkling that your 'message' was nothing but a leg-pull."

I knew, by the pink eastern sky showing through the leafy chestnut trees, that it was time for me to be at the Brunsons'. Since my mother had been ill, I had been allowed to come an hour later but had made up for the lost time by working all day on Sunday. Mrs. Brunson was displeased with me, for I had been distracted and had done my work carelessly. Still, she had made a tentative promise to promote me to Maudie's place in the fall. Maudie had by now completely lost control of her appetite for whiskey and twice had watered Dr. Brunson's Vat 69 to his humiliation, on the second occasion, before a guest who, sipping a cocktail made from the expurgated bottle, remarked, "They certainly don't put any teeth in their whiskey any more, do they?"

In spite of knowing that I would get a dressing-down, I dallied along the way. This garden-filled and springtime world through which I moved was perfumed with the closely clustered lilac blossoms in the yards I passed, roofed over by a coral, turquoise, and violet sky. The heard, but unseen, white skirts of the sea fluttered sweetly against its boundaries. Just as Nathan's kisses in the fog had warmed my sorrow to its bloom, and my love, though contiguous, had only served to enhance its somber colors, so the young physician's accidental exhumation of Boston had, immediately afterwards, caused me to see the loveliness of Chichester to which for several months I had been indifferent. And now, stopping to bury my face in a branch of lilac in a sudden infiltration of an unobjectified but passionate happiness, the purpose of my interview seemed to me to be but a tenth part of what had been accomplished, and the least important part, as if my fear that Mamma was insane had been only an excuse to know Dr. McAllister and had been, in a sense, almost as trumped up as my "message" from Miss Pride.

He had said, "We should not rush ahead to conclusions, but you should think this over. Let us say you keep her at home, protect her for the better part of your life so that you don't marry or don't realize whatever your ambition is. Would the martyrdom be worth all that? It's the question you must answer for yourself, for salvation for one soul is perdition for another and what might send me to hell would give you grace." His lofty terms, *martyrdom, salvation, perdition, grace,* were no longer the mere names of abstract states over which I had carelessly slid my eye on the printed page, but were the components of my own future, and I said "grace" aloud, my lips stopped by the dense purple trumpets of the flower I had pressed against them. My happiness confounded me. As though it were as perishable as the crisp lilac, I allowed no thought to come near it and refused to listen to the voices within the house behind the hedge which, organ of their owners' uncertainty, talked back and forth of the likelihood of rain. But the footsteps which I heard coming behind me, I did allow to intrude upon my mind, thinking perhaps they belonged to the doctor on his way home—his home? I questioned, but could see him only behind the desk in Dr. Galbraith's office where the white marquisette curtains were inflated by the breeze. The footsteps were quick and the heeltaps rang brashly on the sidewalk. Someone called my name, but there was no need to turn, for Nathan Kadish was beside me and had put his shoulder behind mine. When I saw his face, it was the good side at which I looked.

"What have you got there?" he asked me, although all I had, as he saw perfectly well, was the branch of lilac that I had bent down to smell, but love is a child at language, speaks nonsense, asks stupid questions, makes insipid replies—"Don't you know a lilac when you see one?"—and means to convey just the opposite of impertinence.

"You don't seem surprised to see me," he said. Rather he whispered, so close to my ear that his lips almost touched me, for the voices on the porch reminded us that we were not alone here as we had been in the fog. "I never can remember," said a woman, "whether it's feed a cold and starve a fever or the other way around just like I can't remember whether a ring around the moon means good weather or a storm."

"I guess I was thinking about you," I said, although this was not true. I had been thinking not of him, but of myself in whom the blood had defecated its black humors and had left only love but love as an envelope that was as yet empty.

"You're not sore, then?" He meant: Was I not angry, then, that my last glimpse of him until now had been when, shirttail out, he hotfooted it for the bus to Boston without a backward glance and had not written me a letter? No, I could tell him honestly, I had not been angry. I *had* been sore; my heart had been skinned by his silence. I had learned from his mother (who believed, for the simple reason that we were neighbors and about the same age, that Nathan and I were friends, but never dreamed that when she uttered his name my skin erupted into goose-flesh) that he would not be home again until the end of the term for he had got a job working in the Brookline Economy Store and all his leisure time was occupied. But I had not failed to call at the post-office once a day for two months in the hope of some word from him. The soreness had gradually disappeared, like a headache, and though I was not conscious of my relief, I was able now to pass the post-office with indifference. But just as the headache has not really gone but has been hidden under sleep and requires only a sharp noise to cast off its covering and meddle with our nerves again, so Nathan's appearance—weeks before I had expected him—reminded me of the shame of his neglect, renewed the sensation of his kisses, and

made me, as before, stretch upwards as if I stood on tiptoe to scrutinize his birthmark, sudden through the
lighted window. And I knew I had not ceased to love
him, that the wrappings in which I had laid away my
hopes were not winding sheets, were only masquerade,
out of which they came now with their sweet, young
faces.

The dense branch swung back to the bush from my relaxed hand as five o'clock rang out from the Catholic
church. "Golly, I'm late," I said.

Nathan stepped to one side and with a gallant gesture
offered me the outside of the walk. He said, "I know you
think it's impolite of me to walk on the inside. I do it intentionally because I do not believe in bourgeois etiquette. Probably you want to hurry because you are
afraid of the bawling-out you'll get from that bourgeois
ignoramus who has the egregious impudence to call
you her 'servant.' I have no doubt that if I invited you to
stop in at Red's café for a Budweiser draft, you would
refuse. I'm not reproaching you. You're merely victimized, a helpless cog in the machinery of social corruption."

"I would stop at Red's," I said, "but it's so late already
and I promised to be on time tonight. They're having
company."

Nathan's full lips curled in a sneer. "Don't go into detail, I can get the picture. I can just *see* their company.
Does that illiterate trollop, the daughter of the house,
still infect the atmosphere with her noisome presence?"

I told him that Betty was at school in New York. "As it
should be," he said, nodding gravely. "There she will
learn the elegant antics of the capitalistic prostitute. Oh,
lofty ideal!"

He was lagging, coming to a full stop occasionally to
convey his italics or exclamation marks by kicking a pal-
ing of the white fence, and if I quickened my pace, he
pulled me back by the elbow, saying, "Where's the fire?
Courage!"

I was nervous and bewildered by his talk, and although, when his fingers closed over my arm as he detained me, the contact softened my bones and caused me

to float without exertion, I could not help being disappointed that we dwelt in worlds so far apart. "Nathan are you a Communist again?" I asked him.

"Again? When was I not? Oh, wait a second. Do you mean am I a member of the Communist Party? Or do you mean am I a dialectical materialist? Am I a Marxist, is that what you're asking me?"

I could only shake my head at his terms.

"No, I belong to no party, faction, or school of thought. But I hate the bourgeoisie because they are the enemies of freedom. I am a revolutionist, yes; I am a nonconformist, yes. But no, I am not a Communist, I am a cosmopolitan. Sonie"—he turned to me with a serious stare—"I am going to Paris."

"When?" I asked.

"Typical," he said irritably. "Typical of an unimaginative woman to try to pin me down about *when*. Next you'll ask me where I propose to get the money and if I intend to live in the thirteenth *arrondissement*."

His irritation was transmitted to me. I was angry that from our conversation had been deleted any reference to ourselves except as we figured in the grim farce of existing Society, by the denunciation of which he made me cherish my desire to know what it was before it was annihilated utterly by the revolution. The word "society," even though I was sophisticated enough to realize that he used it in its larger sense, was reflected on my mind as "Boston Society." But while Nathan had no doubt that if, in his life-scheme, he decided to include me he could convince me of the truth of his cosmopolitanism, so I believed he would sacrifice his crotchets to my own. Each of us regarded the other as a child; each smiled inwardly and with indulgence at the other's self-deceptions. And when I said, partly to tease him, that I still admired Miss Pride, he patted my hand comfortingly as if to say all was not lost, that he himself would remove the scales from my eyes.

Now and again, I was exhilarated by what he said of Paris. "My genius will bloom in a shabby *bistro*," he said. "In the beginning, I will have only friends, rum, *bock*, and market girls. But later, having fame, I will, if I want her, have a bonafide Faubourg *duchesse*."

Without realizing that the source of my rage was jealousy of that imaginary duchess, I blurted out, "Oh, I'm *sick* of George Moore."

"Give me three reasons," he demanded.

"I'm not interested. But no one with that much conceit can be decent."

"Decent? What language they teach them in school nowadays! I suppose you think an artist ought to be a humble worm? Humble, like you? You, Sonia Marburgovna, are the most self-conceited baggage I have ever known."

"I?"

"Yes, you," he mocked me. "For example, on the night you made that melodramatic, also fraudulent, also imbecilic Lady-of-the-Lake voyage around the Point to deposit an imaginary corpse in the Atlantic Ocean, did you not later lap up for flattery what was intended as advice? Did you not, when I absentmindedly exaggerated your nature and called you deep, believe that you really were deep?"

I blushed and did not reply. We had turned into the street where the Brunsons lived, and Nathan stopped. "I won't go any farther. As it is, I'm close enough to smell the putrefaction. Since you won't—or as you are deluded into thinking, you *can't*—go to Red's now, would you like to after you have finished cleaning up their swill?"

I had not drunk beer since my father went away, and I was curious to know what it tasted like and what its effect would be. I was elated at the thought of the evening we might spend in the dark, disreputable saloon that advertised tables for ladies. Encouraged by the beer (and bock beer was in now), perhaps we would be able to revive the mood in the fog. But when Nathan added, "Shall I call for you here or at home?" the image of my home and its drugged occupant made me catch my breath as I realized with abject shame that I had not thought of my mother since the moment Dr. McAllister, changing the subject, had asked me why I had used Miss Pride's name.

"No, I'm sorry, I can't." Too late I saw I should have said, "I can't *tonight*," but the pressure of the immediate future when my mother should awaken made me unable to look further ahead into an evening when I might be free to drink beer. I think Nathan acted not out of embarrassment but at the command of a reflex when, before I had uttered the last word of my refusal, he put his hand to the left side of his face and leaned into the shade of the elm tree under which we stood. His unilateral smile of twisted lips and one bright, malicious eye measured the altitude of his anger whose heights he had instantaneously scaled. With his right hand he tipped an imaginary hat and said, "I *beg* your pardon, moddam. No offense intended, merely a case of mistaken identity."

I started to explain to him why I could not go with him, but he raised his hand for silence. "No, really, I'm not in the least interested. I was under the impression that we had a tacit understanding, commonly known as 'friendship,' but I see I was wrong. It is just as well. Momentarily, under the influence of certain romantic symbols, I forgot that I must burn the midnight oil tonight over the misguided but well-meaning Thomas More. Please overlook my brief collapse."

"Oh, Nathan!" I cried, hoping by the tender tone of my voice to convey my despair so that he would forgive me and I might then tell him about Mamma. But I did not achieve my aim. The long white fingers of his left hand stole downwards and revealed, bit by bit, his garish cheek. "It was all right in the fog where nobody could see you, wasn't it? But it's a horse of a different color—rather, to be more exact, a *freak* of a different color—in the clear public light of our respectable village *bistro*. Come off it, lovely, you call me Cranberry behind my back, don't you?"

I was possessed by the deliberate unveiling of the birthmark and in a voice that came not from my conscious self but from the fanatical rapture with which I had secretly stared at it when I was ten years old, I said, "No, I love your birthmark."

He had not expected me even to say the word, spoken perhaps for the first time in his presence since he was a child and was the target for his contemporaries' downright jokes. My beastly declaration, a maudlin lie as he believed, brought a flush to the uncolored side of his face. As if confronting me with the tool of my crime to watch as my guilt blanched and shook me, he slowly turned his head so that his right profile was concealed by the trunk of the tree and from the dull ember which ran from his hair to his chin, the diabolical eye winked its purple lid. His limber lips were drawn to this side and from them issued a laugh in which mirth was not even pretended but which was the distance-muted entreaty of a wounded animal.

"That's a hot one," he said. "*Very* funny. Your wit, if you must know, surpasses your beauty. Let me say, however, that I have always been attracted by your hair. I observed the redolence of its natural oils in the fog. It reminded me, I don't know why, of the interior of a water-logged tennis ball. I trust you will never cut its pristine grease with that decadent commodity manufactured by your Heroine of the Barstow, that is, soap. Well, I must go home. Hark! Do I hear my doting mother calling Cranberry! *Oh*, Cranberry!"

Jauntily, his arms swinging and his metal heel-taps clicking pertly on the sidewalk, he went back down the street, but at the corner turned and called, "I say, be an old dear and burn up those letters of mine, will you?"

"What letters?" I cried.

"Oh, curses on my absent-mindedness. Here I was thinking you were Josephine." And he was gone, around the corner, his footsteps audible for a few seconds.

I reasoned, as I lingered in a breathless sickness, that if he had loved me, he would have sensed that I was in trouble, would have reviewed my words and noticed that there had been an inexplicable change between the time we met and the time we parted, and that the love so obvious in my voice when I had spoken through the flowers could not have perished within the space of ten minutes. And yet, when I considered what our relations might be after he had begged my pardon (for I had gradually progressed from a state of dazed helplessness to one of indignation and desired not to make an apology but to be tendered one by him), I was not sure that my love had not begun to wane a little after all. I was almost certain of it later, at the Brunsons', when I heard Dr. Roberts remark. "We couldn't hope to get a prize like young McAllister for this town. He's cut out for a metroplitan practice. He'll be one of your fifty-dollar-a-house-call society doctors. He's got the style all right," I had just gone through the swinging door into the kitchen to bring more wine from the ice-chest. When I heard the young man's name mentioned, my cheeks warmed and I cooled them at the rush of frosty air from the opened door as I withdrew the bottle of sauterne.

In the following weeks, I did not become indifferent. The turbulence that stormed about my memories of Nathan did not subside but I moved, so to speak, out of range of its danger by promising that I would not make the first step towards our reconciliation. And in time the cool-headedness that I feigned became actual, and once more when I looked toward Boston, the city which I imagined stretching out behind the State House did not go beyond that part of the Charles visible from the top of Pinckney Street, did not include Boston Universtiy or the Brookline Economy Store.

2

Dr. McAllister, after he had seen my mother two or three times said that for the present she was well enough off at home. The first time he came, a few days after my talk with him, she was still in a state of total lethargy, but she had begun to speak English again. She was under the impression that the doctor had come to see her fancy-work and she exhibited it to him with the boredom and hauteur of a great lady who has at last summoned up the energy to pay a duty call on a dowdy friend and dispenses her good manners with an effort of will. "Thank you," she said when he complimented her on a set of table mats embroidered with yellow tulips. "It don't show up in this light but it's done well if you like tulips." Dr. McAllister said he was very fond of tulips and was surprised at my mother's indifference to them. She smiled with some lofty, secret knowledge of the flower's faults which she did not impart to us. Soon afterwards, in what I later recognized as a gauche breach of taste, I invited the doctor to drink a glass of brandy. My mother allowed her daft eyes to rove from one to the other of us. "Brandy?" she queried. "I don't know what you're talking about, Sonia. You must forgive my daughter, Mr. Whatyoumaycallit, she's always been a dreamy girl." I started to point to the shelf where the bottle stood, still half full, but the doctor shook his head at me, and my mother went on, "I had a little money here years ago and this silly child can't believe it's all used up. Mamma, where is the golden egg? she'll ask me and look in the Bible where we used to keep it. But she's a treasure all the same."

She would have gone on in an interminable eulogy of my abilities, my eyelashes, my character, had she not been silenced and rendered immobile by the returning torpor which immediately extinguished the light in her eyes and fixed her mouth. She sank to a chair and did not change her position for the half hour that the doctor lingered. Her hand, resting on the table covered with her fancy-work, could have been made of marble.

On his later visits, Dr. McAllister saw her alone, in the bedroom, and I could sometimes hear him interrupting her in the midst of what I knew, though I could not distinguish the words, was a tale of persecution. "Now, wait a minute, Mrs. Marburg, I haven't got the scene clear in my mind. Tell me what the place *looked* like." She would begin again, her voice sailing the calmed waters of her perpetual woe.

He told me that it was possible she was posing, that she was cleverer than I thought, but when I asked him what it was she could gain hereby, he could not answer to my satisfaction. "I don't know. Maybe she's afraid that now you are nearly grown you will leave her. But that mustn't alarm you, for I don't think she'd ever do anything drastic to keep you with her."

"Drastic? Why, she would never harm a hair of my head."

And he replied, "Certainly not," but his tone was so

225

positive that paradoxically it was suspicious and a week later, when I went to the hospital to see him, I said, "The other day when you said my mother would never do anything 'drastic' to me, did you mean it?"

"I knew you would be troubled by that and I regret I said it. But the fact is that insane people—and mind you, I'm not saying she's insane—can turn against anything if they feel they're driven to a wall. For instance, when your mother discovers that you lock her in, she may be furious. That's why we must decide about the asylum soon because you won't be able to deceive her indefinitely. And that's why—that and because even suicide is not an impossibility—you'd better get rid of anything she might use against you or against herself, knives and so on."

"I can't believe it," I said. "Why, now she's not much different from what she's been for years. Now that she's started to speak English again."

"I don't doubt that. But has it ever occurred to you that for years you have been in exactly the same danger that you are now? You don't think, do you, that this has come on her overnight,"

"Oh, no," I said. "I guess I've known it for a long time. I always just thought she was queer and never was afraid until that night Dr. Galbraith came."

I could hardly bear to be in the room with her, not because I was afraid of what she might do to me, for, despite the doctor's ominous warning I remained convinced that, as I had told him, she would not "harm a hair of my head," but because she trusted me and did not know that at any moment I might lock her up behind high walls whose corridors rang with maniacal laughter and groans of the hopeless damned souls of this hell on earth. And when Dr. McAllister one day gave the place, which hitherto had existed in my mind merely as the word "asylum," a name and said we would send her to Wolfburg, it seemed to me that evening that she must be able to read my mind, obsessed with its hypocrisy. For heretofore *the* asylum had been as remote in space as her admittance there had been in time. But the articulation of the name and, further, the articulation of one that was not unfamiliar to me, forced me to open my eyes to its masonry, its approach, its gates, for this was a tangible destination. Thus, we could no longer use the conventional formula, "If she is taken somewhere," but now must say, "if she is taken to Wolfburg." Moreover, Dr. McAllister had this time used the active rather than the passive voice, had said, "We will take her," not "She will be taken," making personal the escort which had formerly been an abstract force. The doctor said, "Wolfburg has beautiful gardens, kept by some of the inmates." I wondered that he, in his kindness, should have built me so cruelly real a picture, going even so far as to name a particular feature of the lunatics' industry, an herb garden rivaling the famous one in Concord. But his intention was not tactless; it was just because of his frequent references to Wolfburg in the weeks that followed that I was able, when I first saw it, to enter the gate with composure and to admire that very horticulture, the first mention of which had unnerved me.

Miss Pride, either through Dr. McAllister with whom I saw she was on very good terms (even though he was too "brainy" for her liking and though his liking of her had certain reservations which he had taken no pains to conceal from me) or through her sharp eyes, knew that something was troubling me, and from the first day of her return to the Hotel, I felt her observant gaze upon me, missing nothing, as I served in the dining-room. Forbearing to make any comment when I confessed that I had not read anything in *The Atlantic Monthly* but the stories and the poems, she gave me a look so discerning that I felt any explanation was unnecessary since she apparently already understood why I had not been able to study out the essays. I was careful to wear an imperturbable countenance whenever she was near-by. If it happened that during the night I had slept badly and had dreamed of Ivan and had wakened to my mother's presence beside me in the bed, then had been unable to burst from the infrangible circle of my anxiety over her, I was still not so forgetful in the morning as to

227

allow my face to relax into its natural weariness, but instead smiled and walked briskly as I took Miss Pride's dropped egg in from the kitchen. The effort that went into keeping myself upright and my eyes wide open perhaps imparted to my appearance the very rigidity I had strived for.

It was my misfortune, however, to be caught off guard several times by other guests. Mrs. Prather, for example, a woman of what are called "good intentions," had come to call on my mother at the very first of the season, for she had heard of Ivan's death through Gonzales. She was, as are all those with good intentions, democratic, as I had often heard her say. "I do not feel toward my servants as many people do," she would remark on the veranda. "I think of them as human beings, every bit as good as I am." In her humanitarian ardor, she called on us one Sunday on her way home from church, crept to the door with a soundlessness which may very likely have been calculated in spite of her charity. She caught me in tears, their cause being vague in my mind now, for I could have been brooding either over Nathan or over my mother. But I explained them to Mrs. Prather as being brought on by headaches from which I was never free. She refused to accept my reason and, offering me a handkerchief which she carried in a tatted pouch and smelled faintly of scent and, as if I were five years old, producing a lemon drop from a paper bag in her pocket, she begged me to tell her "all about it." I stuck to my guns and she asked then to see my mother, but I replied that she was in mourning and did not wish to speak with anyone.

After this visit, I sometimes overheard my name spoken on the veranda and I was said to be "looking badly." The voices were lowered as the ladies explained why I did. Some believed that I was anemic; others thought that my mother was ill and that my pallor came from staying up with her at night. No one suspected her of being mad, but they delighted in talking about Ivan, whose epilepsy had been reported to them in as much detail as he could recollect by Gonzales when he drove them from the station. A number of them said that the disease was hereditary and either through loyalty to their sex or through expostulation of my father whom they had never ceased to discuss, they designated him as its transmitter. They were opposed by the group who maintained that epilepsy was acquired after a blow on the head or an attack of scarlet fever.

Miss Pride, of course, took no part in these discussions, but possibly in the intention of showing the other guests that she had an interest in me far more generous than theirs, which was merely clinical, conversed with me as I served her. Far from elevating her in their estimation, her gesture was deprecated as bad taste and disservice to myself. "She won't go to heaven by bending over backwards to that child, pretending to be a Little Sister of the Poor, when she wouldn't part with a red cent of her precious money," it was said vindictively. "My word! You can't get credit for *talk!*" The old ladies were more displeased with Miss Pride this summer than ever, for the young Dr. McAllister was a frequent guest at her table and it was so arranged that it was never possible for anyone else to engage him in conversation. What if he *was* a personal friend of hers? Were not physicians, in a sense, public property? Consequently, since Dr. Galbraith, whose death was long and solemnly lamented, could not be consulted over the soup and since his successor never came to the Hotel for meals, Miss Pride's monopoly of the market was found intolerable. Finally someone hit upon the hypothesis that she had paid for his education and had offered to set him up in practice, the bribery being motivated by her desire to marry off her troublesome niece to him.

It was quite true that the chief interest in common between Miss Pride and Philip McAllister was Hopestill, proof of which required only the most casual eavesdropping. But it was also true that Miss Pride had known the young man's family for many years and had moved in the same feminine circles as his mother, who had gone that summer to London, and his grandmother. Dr. McAllister's father, a retired Unitarian minister, used sometimes to come to see his son and always made a point of lunching at the Hotel. I took pains to stay as near them as possible so that I might not miss any of their talk. The Reverend McAllister was withered and singed and clad from head to toe in decent black. All that relieved his funereal attire was a gold watch chain across his convex middle from which hung a Phi Beta Kappa key. He was a dabbler in oddities. He knew, for instance, that the armadillo always bore identical quadruplets; he offered this news with a brief, factual account of the duck-billed platypus, but he went no further, although Mrs. McKenzie, who overheard him, was enchanted and pressed him for details. Or he would trace at length the development of spiritism, but far from discussing it in the light of his religious tenets, he merely presented the case as though it had no bearing on anything else. Gravely he would imitate the Fox sisters, "Ho, Mr. Slipfoot, are you there?" Or, if he were invited to express his opinion of Christian Science, he would repeat an anecdote he had heard about Mrs. Eddy which was perhaps illustrative of his feeling but which suggested, to his discredit, that that was all he knew about Christian Science. He was, as his son remarked of him once, the kind of man who came out ahead in pen and pencil games.

Miss Pride did not particularly like "the Reverend" though she respected him, for she had been taught that it was improper not to respect the cloth. She said in a low voice to a friend who had come to dine with her, "He is a very good Christian, I grant you, but he's a frightful bore."

The friend, a woman with a broad, innocent face, said, "I can't believe he's a bore, Lucy, though I've only met him once or twice. Why, I was dumfounded, when I dined at his house once, at the size of his theological library. And the books were so worn, so obviously *studied*. No, indeed, a man who has read that much can't be a bore."

"I don't think Reverend McAllister *has* read them all," said Miss Pride with a malicious glint in her eyes. "As for their being worn, my dear, haven't you heard of second-hand shops? But I'm not singling him out. I think the clergy has fallen into the sere and yellow leaf where learning is concerned. Last New Year's Eve, I went to Estelle Hornblower's at home and was literally forced by Lincoln Nephews to go into the little white parlor where six ministers were sitting about like a plenary council. Lincoln had said, 'Lucy, I want to show you something straight out of Trollope.' Three of the creatures were Anglo-Catholics and were, I do believe, the poorest Latinists I have ever seen. They were talking about *On the Sublime and the Beautiful* by Theophrastus! Well, the Reverend was there. 'Hold on,' says he. 'Theophrastus isn't your man. He wrote those little vignettes you call *characters*.' 'Nonsense,' said one of the Anglicans, 'I'm not so rusty on my English as not to know those little things—sometimes I believe they're called hornbooks—were a seventeenth-century invention. But if Theophrastus didn't write *On the Sublime and the Beautiful*, who did, pray?' Do you know not one of them knew and Lincoln Nephews had to set them right?"

"Well, *I* wouldn't have known," said Miss Pride's friend. "I'm so ignorant I would never be able to criticize the clergy in that way. But in case I'm sometime asked, who *did* write it?"

There was an imperceptible pause. "Why, Lucretius," said Miss Pride. "I thought everyone took that in with his mother's milk." But a little later on, she interrupted an anecdote her friend was telling to say, "You'll tell me that people who live in glass houses shouldn't throw stones. Didn't I just say Lucretius wrote *On the Sublime and the Beautiful?* I must have been asleep, for as I perfectly well know it was Longinus."

However much she deprecated in private his want of education, she was so cordial to the minister when he took a meal with her that I began to wonder if the old ladies' conjecture had not been in part correct, that is, that she was anxious to make a match between her niece and his son. For it was only in the presence of these two men that she had nothing but good to say of the girl. Hopestill's defiance of convention was transformed at these luncheons into her "high spirits, her vigor." Her beauty, ordinarily spoken of as "something about her that her extreme clothes brings out which I find very strange," was alluded to with respect. She became "intelligent" instead of "foxy." But the Reverend was deaf to all these virtues of Miss Mather because he wanted to inform the company that some things had not changed with the times at all, that in reading Emerson's letters he had discovered that the train fare from Concord to Boston was exactly the same in 1860 as it was today. The young man, to whom Hope's graces were not news, as soon as possible effected a transition to another subject, less, I thought, out of embarrassment than annoyance because he knew Miss Pride spoke with shameless insincerity. Usually, he would inquire of her how she was progressing with her memoirs. "Hush!" she would say in real consternation. "You must not broadcast that. I'd be the laughing-stock of Boston if anyone knew. But since you ask, I'll tell you quite frankly that at times I despair. There is more to writing even of this sort than meets the eye. If I had a secretary, I feel that I could simply fly through them. The difficulty is that my sentences look so undistinguished when I see them in my own handwriting." She would glance at me as though to say that she had not forgotten our conversation in her library, and the young doctor, following her eyes, would briefly ponder me.

It was a midsummer night, cool after a sultry day. Gonzales had picked a bouquet of tea-roses and bridal wreath for my mother and I was taking them home, after work about nine o'clock. My mother, her face streaming with perspiration, was sitting beside the stove in which she had built up a raging fire that roared through the open damper. For further warmth she was wearing the old hooded wrapper and my sheep-lined slippers.

"Why, Mamma, why have you built a fire? It's like a furnace in here!"

I saw that despite her dripping face she was shivering and her teeth chattered between her words as she said, "Maybe you don't feel the cold if you're full of brandy. Not everybody has the good luck to have a little something to warm them up on the inside." The steady accusation in her eyes did not waver, and then I observed that the kitchen was in disorder. The shelves had been ransacked and half their useless objects had been thrown down so that broken glass and monkey wrenches and empty cans lay in a nondescript heap on the floor. Weeks before, at Dr. McAllister's injunction, I had taken the bottle of brandy to the shop. I said nothing.

"I suppose fairies drank it," said my mother. "I suppose the same little fairies that stole the golden egg so a person couldn't buy so much as a thimbleful of wine when they were dying of the cold. I guess they locked the door so a sick woman couldn't get a breath of fresh air if she needed it. It couldn't have been the invalid's daughter, oh, no."

I had often rehearsed my speech but as it issued, it sounded flat and false. My unsteady voice belied the words: "Yes, Mamma, I did lock the door. I didn't want to worry you and so I didn't tell you. A lot of houses have been robbed this last week and I didn't want the burglars to come here. You know how you lose yourself in your work and sometimes don't even hear me when I come in. I didn't want you to be taken by surprise."

She rolled her head crazily round and round, stopped, grinned at me, and rolled it again, repeating in what I suppose she thought was an imitation of my father, "*Ja, ja, ja, ja, ja, ja!*" Though the effort of moving in this inferno was exhausting, I started to clear the table, for usually at this hour we had a glass of lemonade and a sandwich of sardines or cheese. "Don't touch my belongings!" cried my mother. "Don't you dare!"

"Oh, Mamma!" I said, hoping to hide my alarm under impatience. "Don't be silly, Mamma. I'm not going to do anything to your lovely table runners. I'm only going to fix us a little supper."

"Come here a minute, Sonie," she wheedled. "Come over by my chair. I want to tell you a secret." I advanced with dread and knelt down when she touched my shoulder. "Closer, sweetheart. There." She pushed back my hair and pressed her lips to my ear. "I hate you!"

I tried to rise, but she had put her arm around my shoulders, holding me against her with prodigious strength and I felt that she had barely tapped her resources, that if she desired, she could crush my bones. And as she had used to do when my father was her victim, she repeated her words half a dozen times in a monotone but with a crescendo which was meant less to convince me than herself. Sweat poured from our close faces and I felt its tickling rivulets down my back inside my dress. I begged my mother to release me, but she was not sure that we both understood yet and she continued to reiterate her declaration until, like my father, I cried, "Then leave me alone! Let me go!"

She did let me go. She jerked me to my feet with her superhuman strength and, like a skilled wrestler, hurled me to the floor. My head struck the leg of the sink and dazed me for a minute as she stood looking down. I implored her to believe that I had not locked the door to torment her, that the brandy was all gone, that the golden egg had been spent years before. At each of my attempts at speech, she again rolled her eyes round and round and hooted, "*Ja, ja, ja, ja!*" She drew her chair to the sink and sat down, daring me to try to stir. I lay still. In a few minutes, I could feel the sweat spreading in a pool all about me. My mother leaned across to the table and turned down the lamp, but by the starlight from the window I could still see her glistening face, beatified in the repose that had settled for a time on her lips and in her eyes. If I rose up on my elbow or stretched my legs or rubbed my head which still ached, her crazy skull commenced its revolutions and the "*ja, ja!*" came forth like the rasping of an imperfect machine.

The heat made me drowsy and though I fought off sleep I surrendered to it for brief, troubled fractions of the hours my mother guarded me. Then I awoke, my head throbbing, my flesh swollen and drenched to see her shining eyes which, so far as I could tell, had not left me for a second. Each time, I heard a loud popping or dripping somewhere outside the house, like water falling drop by drop on metal or like a sheet of tin cracking with expansion. Confused, I imagined it to be hot outdoors and I dreaded the morning and the progress of the day towards noon, that debilitating hour of fire when the heat shimmered in visible undulations over the grass and the sun, the tyrant of the bright blue skies, roasted one like a sucking pig, unstuck the pores of the body so that the sweat poured forth like water from a tap, slackened the senses, and benumbed the mind. It was as if the streaming of my flesh was in anticipation of that hour. Then my mind cleared; I remembered that there was a fire in the stove. I heard the ocean and longed to bathe my scorched body in it; my throat was parched; I conceived the sound as the slow leak of an ice-cold spring. Once I murmured, "Mamma, can I have a glass of water?" but my plea evinced only her derisive grimace and her absurd "*ja, ja!*"

A little while after the church bells struck midnight, my mother fell asleep in her chair, her head resting against the corner of the sink. I sat up slowly lest I rouse her, took off my shoes and then I crept, inch by inch, backwards to the door. As I passed the stove, its dying but still ferocious fire made me feel faint and ill. I gained the door and stood up; I could see her still in the light from the window. She had not stirred. I slid back the bolt and went out, brought the outer key from my pocket and locked my mother in, and then, revived by the salt breeze, I ran in my bare feet over the sandy path to the shop. The shop was cool and damp and I shivered with the sweet change. I put a piece of smooth leather to my cheek, then pressed my forehead against the windowpane, then coiled the cold rosary into my hand. Coolest was the bottle of brandy which I held in the crook of my arm. I did not go to sleep again for fear my mother, waking up, would find some way out of the house. I remembered how Ivan had told me that if he ran to the shop to escape her, she came to the window and peered in at him. I sat at my desk playing Patience by candlelight. Maudie had taught me half a dozen variations and I played them all, winning often and easily. The dawn was an eternity in coming and yet it was not four o'clock when the gray impinged upon the black shadows and I could see the dim outlines of the Boston water front where lights still burned. In another hour the lobster men set forth; I saw their green dories and their small, white motor boats and heard their terse greetings to one another. But the signs of normal human activity and the faithful daylight did not, as they used to do when I was a little girl, rout my fear. My legs were bruised where I had fallen, and my head ached, no longer from its blow against the sink but from the beginning of a cold. I sneezed and wished for a handkerchief. I knew that I must leave the shop before it was any lighter, for I did not want my mother, waking, to see me through the window, but afraid that she was already awake, I lingered a little longer in indecision.

At the first flush of the sun I slipped out, stooped down low as I passed the house, then ran till the wind whistled in my ears, in the direction of the hospital. My bare feet stung and my temples throbbed, but now that I was actually escaping her I was conscious of nothing but my terror, and if I had paused, it would not have been to stop my little pains, but to look back to make sure that she was not coming. I flew down the street where Nathan and I had dallied by the lilac bushes and noticed that the dead flowers were rusty among the green leaves, but just beyond them on lattices or against the walls of the houses, morning glories had opened up their bright blue horns. Taking the short-cut, I ran past Mr. Greeley's mortuary where a green neon sign burned still in the front window: "Chichester Funeral Parlor." In a moment, when I had turned a corner, I saw the hospital at the end of its concrete driveway and to my relief, saw that the operating room on the top floor was illuminated with a livid blue light. I remembered that Dr. McAllister was the anesthetist. Uppermost in my mind then was my need for a handkerchief before I presented myself to him.

3

Dr. McAllister called for me every Sunday morning to drive me to Wolfburg. West and south of Boston, the asylum was not far from a farm where his aunt, with a large staff of gardeners and farmers, grew apples, roses, wheat, cows, and guinea hens. She, her nephew told me, would have liked to believe that she pitched hay, milked cows, churned butter, and cooked for the harvest men. Although the young man freely joked about her to me, almost a complete stranger, he was very fond of her and told me that he would not miss his Sunday luncheon with her for the world. I had not believed him at first, thinking that the aunt was apocryphal and manufactured to allow me to accept his charity. But Miss Pride, who knew of our expeditions, said, "I dare say Philip McAllister likes having company when he goes to see his aunt. You must ask him sometime to drive you past her place. Her roses are so splendid that I have often said she should go into the florist business."

While the drive to Wolfburg was either tedious (if I wished the visit to be over quickly) or too swift (if I particularly dreaded this day with my mother), the drive back was delightful. It was the late afternoon when the air was unburdening itself of the weighty heat and the tight sky was split with pink clouds. I could have liked to walk a little way into the groves we passed, where twisting avenues, flowery and humid, opened sometimes in a delta at the highway. But the desire was a lazy one and equal to it was the wish that I might go along this way hours longer, my obligations behind me, and all about me the embracing summer, most tranquil at this cooling hour, gentlest of this kind of road where the sheen upon the leaves proclaimed the heat and the shade between the tree-trunks proclaimed its compensation. The opulent overflow of verdure, berries, flowers, was arrested like the subject of a picture.

When we reached Chichester, it had been dark half an hour and Boston was alight. I stood on the steps of our house, watching the doctor drive away, and stood a little longer looking up at the Barstow where Miss Pride's three front windows were rosy with the light that came through her striped curtains. It was then, when I entered the house, that I realized more clearly than when I had been with her that my mother was no longer here, but in the vast, labyrinthine asylum where she was known by number and species. The mustard-yellow enameled walls of the main corridor were lined with hard benches where we, the visitors, sat bolt upright with cold, fixed faces as if we wished it clearly understood that we had no desire to sympathize or compare notes with one another. The blatant squawk of the girl at the address microphone came through ubiquitous concealed outlets: "Dr. Sho-ort." Or, in nasal ridicule, "Dr. *Fink*elstein." I could tell by the impatience with which they sometimes flung down their magazines that the other visitors detested the bodiless parrot as I did, and I wondered if they, too, desired to talk back to it, or, even better, to seek it out in its vociferous den and, if necessary, strangle it. One by one we were summoned to the gray cubicles where the jovial doctors in charge of our "case" glanced through a manila folder at typewritten sheets, the slowly accumulating history, the record of the arduous battle. As I passed down the corridor in the wake of a matron, silent with ill-nature or boredom or perhaps with the mere consciousness that she was sane, I peeped through the open doors of the offices and saw that all the other doctors looked like mine: their broad, red faces glowed with health; rimless spectacles sat on their neat tan noses; their grandiose condescension gave their voices a vast range of pitch, from a high amiability to a deep-toned expression of totally indifferent regret.

But it was neither the waiting nor the short visit with my mother that distressed me. It was the knowledge, after I had lighted the lamp in the house where she had always lived, that I had left her behind and that perhaps at this very moment she was imagining what I was doing. It was usually an hour before I was quieted, and then I began to read. Later, if the memory of her empty, staring eyes or her incoherent words came to me, I rationalized, said that she did not suffer as much as I since she was barely aware of her surroundings. I repeated to myself the doctor's exhortation that I must not feel guilty. His advice called him forth to replace my mother, and I searched the conversation we had just concluded for clues of how he felt towards me, if I were anything more to him than an element of a case that had been foisted upon him.

I had been nervous, on the first of these drives to

Wolfburg, recalling that Miss Pride had said the young man was "brainy," and I feared that he would discover that I was ignorant, that he would report his finding to Miss Pride, and that I would fall from favor. Consequently, I spent the Saturday evening before the trip poring over the several copies of *The Atlantic Monthly* which had come and memorized certain facts about Russia, about overproduction, about co-operatives. But my preparation was unnecessary. Dr. McAllister shaped the conversation to suit himself and I was relieved of any responsibility. He was principally interested, I found, in religion, but I was never sure whether he was religious or merely inquisitive. When he spoke of the survival of the churches in the Soviet Union and said he longed to go to Russia to see how religion accomplished its ends under official atheism, he spoke as someone might who wished to visit Heidelberg to hear medieval drinking songs in a country where only German was spoken, or to see pagan rites in Christian Mexico. I had told him once that my father was a Catholic and he questioned me in detail on fasting, confession, and holy days of obligation. Only occasionally could I give him an answer, and he marveled at my want of knowledge but marveled even more at my father's neglect of my spiritual education. He had heard (again his information was a tourist's) that no nation had bred a more devout species of Roman Catholics than Germany. And he observed, "If you had been brought up a Catholic, you'd know how to feel toward your mother, I dare say. You'd know so much better than I, a doctor, that you'd have no need of the advice I've given you." On another occasion, he asked me if I had ever heard my father speak of the Cistercians. "If I were a monk, that would be the order I would choose. I sometimes think there would be nothing pleasanter than a vow of silence."

I had noticed on my first visit to him in the hospital that his posture made one think his bones were of an unbending substance and when I observed over a period of time that he never relaxed, I inquired of Miss Pride if she did not admire his carriage. "Not at all," she returned, "but I do admire his fortitude." She told me then that, afflicted as a child with infantile paralysis, he had been able to assume only two positions, that one perfectly erect, the other bent nearly double at the waist. When he settled upon medicine as a career, he wished to be a surgeon and subjected himself to an operation of great delicacy which, if it were successful, would allow him to move freely. A surgeon could not be limited to a perpendicular position and a forty-five degree angle. The operation, involving the replacement of some of the atrophied spine, was followed by a period of twelve months in a cast from which he was released, totally unbenefited. He had had then to abandon his ambition. He did not reveal his disappointment to anyone, said Miss Pride, and refused to recognize his "handicap" or to refer in any way to what he might have been if his luck had been better. I think he endured a great deal of pain, at times, and I pictured him when he was alone, giving in to the agony that he had reined in all day just as I, on Sundays, delivered myself to the dejection that had been engrafted in me by the visit to the asylum earlier in the day. And as this gloom seemed to await me in my house, like a devilish creature that I had promised myself to on the condition that it would not come out into the light when I was still with my friend, so I thought that Dr. McAllister unleashed his tormentors in his room and permitted them to do as they liked with him for the season of his solitude.

Unlike Nathan whose disfigurement had given him a morbid appetite for abuse—turned either against himself or against those who he imagined laughed at him— Dr. McAllister had taken his much greater deformity almost as a gift of Providence, for, forced by the needs of his body into frequent hours of leisure, he had had the time to read extensively. But the leisure was work and if he relaxed his sickened muscles, he allowed his mind no rest. He slept no more than four hours, originally for the sake of discipline and later because his strict self-denial produced in him a habitual insomnia. He had told me, when I came to the hospital at five in the morning, that he had only just been preparing for bed when he was summoned to the operating room at four o'clock.

The evening, he said, he had spent in studying a Russian grammar, suggested to him by the inconsequential babbling of my mother.

It was perhaps because he knew the whole of my story and had even lived through a chapter of it himself that he took an interest in me which was disproportionate to any offering I was capable of making him. Or it might have been, instead, that the Sunday drives were a prolonged but unconscious apology for his unjustified rebuke on the occasion of my first visit to his office when he thought I was seeking an abortionist. No mention was made of his mistake again, not, I am sure, because a review of the incident would have caused him any embarrassment, but because he had forgotten it when I ceased in his mind to be the kind of young woman liable to the charge. He thought that the principle of my being was a fanatical filial piety, carried to a degree that necessarily excluded the sort of selfish attachment which could terminate in so sordid a dilemma as an illegitimate pregnancy. His misconstruction, his over-simplification of my relationship with Mamma made me suspect, sometimes, that he had not the insight into people which is, we are told, the prerequisite of the successful physician. Now neither had Dr. Galbraith understood our household but for a different reason. He had been a blind man leading the blind. But Philip McAllister, through an intellectual, an almost literary faith in the perfectability of human nature, believed that had I not been completely devoted to my mother, I should long ago have run away from home. Thus, assigning to me the sanguine humor in distinction to the bilious or the choleric, he neglected to take into account the fourth, that is, the phlegmatic, which made up at least half of my composition. But whatever his motive was, he succeeded in my gradual reformation. By respecting my loyalty to my mother, he unwittingly shamed me into a real loyalty whose articulation was my faithful weekly visit to the asylum which came, in time, to be essential to my life. Although nothing was accomplished and frequently I was not allowed to see her (for she had seasons of bitter hatred for me as the cruellest of all her persecutors.

These came when something sharpened her senses and she realized where she was), I was determined to regain her love just as the sometimes uncertain communicant is determined to learn faith through his reception of the holy water and his prayers.

Yet I sometimes confessed to myself that I was exactly the opposite of the altruist. The renascence of her love would gain more for me than for her; mine was a craven peace-making. I was further hypocritical in that I acted for the young doctor's applause. Just as I had concealed from Miss Pride the marks of sleepless, undisciplined nights, in the doctor's presence I feigned joy at seeing my mother again after seven days' separation, and, on the return, grief at her unhappiness. We can be over-scrupulous, beg our confessors to double our punishment since they, we declare, have been too innocent to grasp the magnitude of our sin. We can, in love, doubt that we really love and suspect that we have bluffed our lover into the passion which will at any moment perish when he sees we have won him with half lies; or, brooding over a slip of the tongue, a misstatement, we can convince ourselves that our minds are really stupid and that all our words are fraudulent. Our conscience is speaking to us in parables. Thus, my desire to become once more the center of my mother's life was earnest. What was contemptible was my publication of it to the doctor as if it could not stand alone, or as if since it could engender no reward for me I must seek his praise for compensation.

His education of me had its more practical specialties. Where I had heretofore read at Miss Pride's prescription and had felt false to her standards if I had chosen something not primarily useful, I now, at the doctor's advice, followed my own inclinations, and was even persuaded that the writers she most admired, that is, James Russell Lowell and Emerson, were by no means inviolable and that the mortar of her ivory tower was chauvinism, not knowledge or taste. For observe, Dr. Mc-Allister counseled me, she was uncritical of style and un-interested in a writer's conception of truth, but if he had been buried in the Sleepy Hollow Cemetery at Concord or lay in a less illustrious but still New England grave-yard, he was a great man. She believed neither in Emerson's oversoul nor in Thoreau's religion of blueberries and Walden Pond; she was unimpressed by Henry Adams' genius, had even remarked once that he was a little too long-winded for her liking. I was not disillusioned by this exposé, but on the contrary delighted in her consistency, deplored.by her demigod as the hobgoblin of little minds. But at the same time, I was liberated from the tyranny of *The Atlantic* and of Harriet Martineau's peregrinations.

It was towards the end of the summer that Dr. McAllister first asked me what I proposed to do after the Hotel had closed. I told him that Mrs. Brunson had invited me to be Maudie's successor. (Maudie had gone to Idaho as soon as the Brunsons left for Provincetown. She went by bus, taking with her a quart bottle of whiskey and parting from me with a hearty handclasp and the exclamation, "Idaho, here I come! It's round-up time for this here old bench.") The doctor said, "Is that what you want to do?" As if I were speaking to him in his professional capacity and telling him the symptoms of a disease which I knew to be incurable, I told him that since I could remember my goal had been Boston, that the only career I had imagined for myself was serving Miss Pride as her housemaid or her laundress or her lady-in-waiting.

"I dare say that could be arranged," he said. "She spoke to me the other day of getting a secretary and I'm under the impression that she had been thinking of you. She is very fond of you, you know."

I was not so pleased as I felt I should have been. It was as if she had sent the doctor as her ambassador for some obscure purpose of which even he did not know. And I was invaded by the same doubt of her that I had felt when she brought the cyclamen after Ivan's death and I had seen her in the winter sunlight for the briefest moment as an old, ugly woman inspired by a tenuous and urbane evil. But the doctor's blue eyes, in which were registered many thoughts in no way connected with me, were so ingenuous that I was convinced he spoke the truth and that she was, indeed, fond of me.

"That was good of her," I said. "But it doesn't help me, because I have no qualifications to be her secretary."

"But even that is of no importance. I've told you, I think, that she's thought to be one of the most generous women in Boston and there is no reason why she shouldn't send you to a business college."

On an impulse that I regretted and in which I heard myself speaking with Nathan's irascible and naïve resentment of wealth, I told the doctor how Miss Pride had conveniently arrived in Chichester the day after Ivan was buried in the potter's field, although I was certain she had got my letter sometime before. He answered with a laugh, "You don't understand the first article in the philanthropist's code which is that one never takes suggestions but always hunts on his own hook for the places where his money will do good. If it weren't for that, I would have suggested myself that she send you to a business school. As it is, we must simply wait and see if it occurs to her. And if it doesn't, that still won't mean you can't go to Boston. I'm a native of the place too and have ways of getting young ladies jobs. I might even hire you as my receptionist, though you wouldn't like that."

Our conversation took place on the last Sunday he drove me to Wolfburg. In the middle of the next week he was leaving Chichester for a vacation in Manchester where, as I knew, Hopestill Mather was spending the summer. Afterwards, he was going back to Boston to begin his practice in an office, outfitted by his doting mother with glass brick partitions, a costly imitation Kashmir, lucite magazine tables where would lie what she called "the leading periodicals" and the alumnus bulletins of Groton and Harvard. He had described the appointments of his office with what I felt was an unwarranted sarcasm and had told me that if I were ever ill, after I had come to Boston to live, I must allow him to examine me with his Shreve, Crump, and Low stethoscope kept in a Mark Cross case.

He shook my hand when he had stopped before my house and said, "Good luck. Perhaps we'll meet again in Boston." But I felt no promise in his words. I felt that he was already absorbed in the mainland while I was rededicated to my insularity and as, from the corner of my eye, I saw the lighted window at the Kadishes' and the shadow of Nathan's younger brother, I read the doctor's optimistic sentence as the epilogue to my long, feverish dream. A few hours later, reasoning that actually I had never been closer, that he was a more persuasive advocate than I could ever have been myself, I realized that I had not felt my isolation from the house on Pinckney Street confirmed forever, but that I had known I should never navigate the space between his planet and mine. The acceptance, without the least titillation, of the window which had once enshrined my first lover's birthmark, on reflection brought me, like a slow-working liquor, to a luxurious intoxication and I knew that for a second time I was in love.

My house was cool and it smelled of oranges that had faintly rotted in the window sill. I wished that I had asked Philip McAllister to come in to drink some brandy so that in the course of an hour I might feed upon his mobile face and his rich voice. I went no further in my demands, but I knew that so long as I remembered him, the light from the window next door would have no power to make me regret or desire or stew in anger.

On the Sunday after Dr. McAllister left, Miss Pride came to my house, catching me, to my consternation, reading the comic strips instead of, as we would have both preferred, finding me ensconced behind the last issue of *The Atlantic Monthly* or Mr. Emerson's *Self Reliance*. I had been lying on the floor, moreover, on my belly and had been breakfasting, as I read, on a banana and a jellied doughnut. When I sprang to my feet at the sight of her standing primly at my kitchen door, I put the inflated doughnut, oozing out its raspberry heart, on the shelf amongst the pipes and tools and empty jars. My guest had never been in the house before (or anything like it, I suspected) and as we talked, she examined everything, not overlooking the remains of my disgraceful meal, with extreme care as if she were trying to find one object less dreadful than the rest. With a candor that was both brutal and complimentary, since it assumed that my taste was akin to her own, she asked me if I did not find the two pictures above the table appalling. I agreed and she said, "I knew you wouldn't mind my speaking plainly. It is one of the privileges of age." Now I had some years before acquired an animadversion to the little girls and the springer spaniels and to the barnyard and, because I idealized him, I could not imagine what had possessed my father to buy them. But I concealed the identity of their purchaser by saying, "They were in the house when my father came. He always hated them but my mother was fond of them." She ignored this false and cowardly aspersion on my mother and stated the purpose of her visit.

"I thought, since Sunday is not one of my motoring days, that perhaps I could lend you Mac and my car for your trips. I told Dr. McAllister that he was rude not to warn me sooner that he was leaving. It only occurred to me this morning when I was served by the substitute waitress. I had forgotten it was Sunday."

I thanked her, not without noting privately that she herself was leaving Chichester a week from today. But she went on, "And something else came to my mind at the same time. Perhaps I mentioned the memoirs I hope to write this winter? And didn't I tell you I needed a secretary to do the 'dirty work'? I know you haven't the qualifications but after all you could go to a school of some sort to learn, couldn't you? The fact is that my niece who, as you know, has been living with me, is going to New York for the winter and I shall quite rattle about by myself in my house. I would like to offer you your lodgings as well as the trifling gift of your tuition. Would you be interested?"

She rose and drew on her gloves as if the matter had been settled and her question had only been rhetorical. I stammered, "Oh, Miss Pride, you are very kind to me!"

She glanced at the floor where my rainbow funny papers lay and I was not sure that she would not retract her invitation. But she said, looking up at me again, "Not at all. Now Mac is right outside and I'm going to walk back to the Hotel so you can start out to see your mother." She started to the door but turned. "My dear, you won't bring your pictures to my house, will you?"

Book Two

Pinckney Street

One

THE BACK BAY BUSINESS COLLEGE was a morose establishment in a once fine house on Dartmouth Street, now infested with tongue-tied girls who seemed always on the verge of tears under the persistent scoldings of the mistress, a vulpine woman in her forties who regarded herself as an educator. Had we been a little younger, I am sure Mrs. Hinkel would have rapped our bungling fingers with a ruler, for incompetence inspired in her the most ardent displeasure. At the very beginning, she had singled me out for especially lusty maledictions, insisting that I was wasting my money and her time, for I would never in a thousand years learn to operate a typewriter with any more skill than a dog. What aggrieved her the most in me was the "reach stroke" of my right fourth finger for which she held a marveling contempt: "Class, gather and observe! Observe the fantastic reach stroke Miss Marburg deludes herself into thinking is the *proper* reach stroke. Learn by this example if you ever hope to make an asterisk visible to the naked eye!" In other branches of my commercial education, I was somewhat abler, being at the top of the class in Business English (because I could immediately distinguish between the nominative and the objective cases and because the subjunctive mood did not baffle me) and being known as a "good worker" in the shorthand class.

The student body strikingly resembled the staff. They were all torpid and bird-like by turns and their humor consisted in such expressions as "I see, said the blind man," and "Well, laugh, I thought I'd die." I ate my lunch at a drug-store with five or six of my classmates who discussed silk stockings and serials in the *Ladies' Home Journal*. They could talk for three quarters of an hour, without any waning of interest, about the confections peculiar to the Boylston Street Schrafft's. The intimacy of the group (they referred to one another's sisters by their given names and inquired after mothers and fathers and aunts) made me suppose that they were old friends and had gone to school together and I felt, therefore, that my exclusion from their talk was not my own fault. I learned in time, however, that they had never met before the first day of classes at what they jokingly called "dear old Back Bay." The discovery made me feel immature and when I could, I avoided these womanly lunch hours, not through snobbery, but through a sense of maladjustment.

I detested the business college, but at the same time it afforded me a contrast to the rest of my life without which I might have come to regard as habitual those things which gave me keen pleasure. I enjoyed the retreat I made each day from the gray plaster walls, the methodical accent of the typewriters, and Mrs. Hinkel's dour face in which her acerbity was coagulated in a large, asymmetrical nose. I went slowly through the Public Gardens at the hour of the exodus of the nursemaids who wheeled out the infant Cabots and the recalcitrant Chandlers. I crossed Charles Street and in traversing the asphalt boundary, entered dissimilar territory: the Common where orators and their satellites and their hecklers yelped and gestured with impotent passion. My own latchkey, fitted to the burnished lock of the white door, admitted me to the silent vestibule, in the dim light of which the mahogany tables, identical and facing one another, gleamed smoothly. Not a sound greeted me. As I pushed open the door to the empty drawing-room, I heard the crackling fire that had just been started. In another hour and a half, this room would be the scene of the comings and goings of Miss Pride's callers whose voices were carried up the stairwell and into my room.

Some afternoons, I stepped across the threshold and wandered about the drawing-room for a quarter of an hour, musing on how it would be when it was occupied by Miss Pride's friends. At first I had thought of the room as altogether Victorian, but after a few investigations, I saw that its objects were disparate and that the only really Victorian part of the room was the bay window, furnished with an uncushioned love-seat of some stony black wood, the arms carved and embossed and curled; the feet of a stunted lion had been calcified and grafted on to the slender ankles of the seat's well-developed legs. On either side, stationed on the floor where presumably they got the morning light, were a variety of house-plants, no one of which laid claim to beauty. They were kept there and were replaced when they died (this happened rarely, their chief virtue being longevity) because they had been there forever just as a Pride or a tributary to the family had always lived in the house. Miss Pride detested them but would not have dreamed of having them removed; she was especially offended by one species which had large flat dusky leaves chased with pink striations. She did not know its name but called it after a kind of cookie it reminded her of, "Aunt Alice's Birthday Trifle," which had figured in her childhood. Evidently some former owner of the house had been a Francophile and another had fancied Oriental handi-work, for upon the ormolu top of a tulip-wood commode there sat a golden Buddha and above him on the white New England wall hung two Japanese prints of long ladies, long herons, and long sprays of wistaria. Yet at the Buddha's feet, as if to confirm the nationality of the commode, lay aimlessly an ivory-handled dagger of which the blade was inlaid with slate-blue *fleur-de-lis*. The sofas, high and stuffed with an inelastic substance, and the slipper chairs, low, velvety, resilient, had, like Aunt

Alice's Birthday Trifle, grown up with the house and their removal was unthinkable although even Miss Pride admitted that they were hideous. Cluttered and inarticulate as it was, I preferred this room to the library, for it was lighter, being at the front of the house and carpeted with a buff rug sprinkled with rich, blue flowers, and its anachronisms imparted to it an atmosphere of geniality as if each heir had accepted the vagaries of the one who preceded him with good will and added his own in the same spirit. The library, on the other hand, was a formidable, masculine province, dominated by Mr. Pride and by several umbrageous ancestral portraits. The furniture was plain, solid, useful. Miss Pride had told me that on Christmas Eve when the revelers and carolers thronged Beacon Hill and one's door-bell rang a hundred times whether or not one had intended to hold open house, her father had read aloud to the servants from the Gospel according to Saint Matthew while in the drawing-room his daring wife, trembling with fear at her own importunity, served sillabub and *lebkuchen* to the visitors. In the library, too, President Eliot had been in the habit of spending two or three evenings a month playing chess with Mr. Pride. His daughter described to me one such evening. "My mother sent me down to ask Papa if they would have some Brazil nuts with their sherry. She was never content to let well enough alone. She was a regular doter. The gentlemen were in the midst of their game and my father, very much annoyed at the disturbance, put his finger to his lips and motioned to me not to move a step nearer the table. President Eliot looked up and through me; my father finished a play and said, 'Sir, for your sake, I regret the brilliance of my rook's performance, for it has won the game for me.' 'You apologized too soon, sir,' said Mr. Eliot and bending forward with a smile like the Cheshire cat's, he captured the rook and checkmated Papa. Then, without any further talk, they set up the men again and to my question would they like some Brazil nuts with their sherry, Papa curtly replied, 'No.' But President Eliot, without looking at me though he glared at my father, said, 'Speak for yourself, Mr. Pride. I, for my part, would relish Brazil nuts as a reward for my triumph.'"

After I had heard this story, I never went into the library without being intimidated by the ghosts of the scholarly chess-players, for their sturdy square table and the board and men remained beside the fireplace, and a decanter of sherry with two glasses stood waiting on a cabinet. At first I thought the preparations were a memorial, as important in the history of the family as the silver christening cups and the yachting trophies on display behind the glass doors of the cabinet, and that in time, when the house became a museum, a copper plate, attached to the table, would inform tourists that President Eliot had played chess there. But I was quite wrong: the table was in readiness for Miss Pride who, with a manual of famous gambits, worked through game after game by herself every Sunday morning before church, and the sherry, too, was kept there for her when, having defeated the white men with Philidor's Defense, she took her own reward and, braced, went off to King's Chapel. Occasionally she would play a game with one of her friends, but these trifling conquests took place in the upstairs sitting-room, for the namby-pamby stratagems of the amateurs would have desecrated the ivory and ebony men of the library who had been in the service of brilliant generals.

The contrast between the drawing-room and the library was not, of course, accidental. Their distinct gender dated from the time the house was built and the drawing-room was still the "withdrawing room" to which the ladies repaired after dinner. The curious thing to me was that Miss Pride, being without a master for her parties, played both rôles. One morning she asked me to fetch her an aspirin tablet for she had a headache as the result of "combining spirits." The evening before she had been detained in the drawing-room by a boring nobody so long that when she finally arrived in the library to unlock the liquor cabinet for the gentlemen's brandy and whiskey (she would never in the world have allowed her servants to perform this duty), they were quite languishing and the delay made them drink twice as much as they would have ordinarily, to her appreciable financial loss. And she, although she had already had her Cointreau with the ladies, was so loath to go back to the tiresome guest (she was one of those creatures who late in life had become domestic and on Thursdays experimented in the kitchen with such material as junket and peanut butter, and on all the other days tired out her friends with forcing her barbarous receipts upon them) that she "took a breather" with the men.

Each day, I saw the first tea guests arriving, for when the sun began to set, I took up my post at the window of my bedroom and did not leave it until the momentary yellow light just preceding darkness had made all the leaves of Pinckney Street declamatory. I longed to see from the outside these windows through which I looked, but I could not relinquish the prospect I had of Louisburg Square, its dead grass and dumpy statues enlivened by the rich light while the iron palings reasserted their dead, absorbent blackness. At this hour, the letter-slots and knockers blazed; the marble lintels seemed as cool and old as something from an ancient palace. Long and lean, the houses deepened into purple with the decline of the sun. Far up the street, forming the background to a pattern of golden elm leaves, was a bright blue door. From time to time, a man in a derby and a black Chesterfield would briskly cross the square to our house, and in a moment I would hear the doorbell. Or a chauffeur would hand out a lady from a gleaming automobile. Talk and laughter presently surged up the stairs.

When the arc lights came on, I left the window and turned on the lamp beside my bed. My room sprang forth, enlarged, entirely changed by the light. The ceiling seemed immensely higher, the wide, polished doors as tall as a castle's portals. Even my single bed with its lace counterpane and folded puff was more luxurious. To the left of my double windows was a massive, flat-topped writing desk with deep drawers on either side which had been filled with watermarked paper, yellow second sheets, onion skin and carbon paper. Its surface was furnished with silver tools: letter openers, penknives, scissors, boxes of paper clips and rubber bands, and postage stamps. In a small upper drawer, there was pale green stationery with our address embossed in small white letters. The typewriter on which I practiced my home-work had its own stand at the right corner of the desk so that I had only to turn my chair to be facing it.

The joy my room gave me was, each day when I switched on the lamp, so intense that my being required its articulation and sometimes I could not see the deep mole-colored carpet and the silvery draperies at the windows for my tears. Again, the Breughel and the Vermeer and the Rembrandt prints, hanging on the ivory walls in double frames, could make me smile smugly. As large as a room, my clothes-closet was equipped with shelves for my expensive shoes, with padded hangers for my evening dresses, and with a ceiling light so that I could see to choose my costume. My bathroom was not ajoined but was down the hall a little way. Six thick, white towels, monogrammed "L P" hung about the gleaming tub. The medicine chest was filled with bottles of cologne, Miss Pride's soap, with a tooth-powder made up by a Dartmouth Street pharmacist, and with cans of faintly scented talcum powder.

On the left wall of my bedroom, near the fireplace, was a locked door leading to Hopestill Mather's sitting-room. And the windows above my bathtub gave on to a shaft across which I could see the windows that corresponded to mine above her bathtub. It was not until I had been in the house ten days or more that I saw her apartment. A maid was preparing it for her return from Manchester, and as I passed through the hall, I stopped to ask the girl some needless question about my laundry. I saw that it was true, just as I had imagined it, that the room and the one beyond it to which the door stood ajar was carpeted with green. In the generous bay window was a wine-colored *chaise-longue*. The fireplace was in the same position as the one in the drawing-room, and in Miss Pride's room directly below this. Over it hung a portrait of Hopestill as a child. She wore a full-skirted white dress, ballet slippers, and a green hair ribbon in her red hair. It was so striking a likeness that I could hear her voice calling across the dining-room, "Waitress!

255

Water, please." On either side of the hearth were wing chairs upholstered in green and wine-red stripes. Beside each was a table underneath whose glass top showed bright Italian tiles and upon which stood *cloisonné* cigarette boxes, match-holders and ash trays. Against the wall opposite the windows stood a delicate Victorian writing desk, flanked on either side by low shelves filled with books still wearing their glossy, gaudy jackets. Through the distant door, I caught sight of a mahogany highboy and the corner of a four-poster bed.

An hour after the tea guests had gone, I would join Miss Pride in the upstairs sitting-room where we had a glass of sherry and a light conversation, after which we went down to dinner. Sometimes she repeated an anecdote she had heard during the day or summarized a colloquy that had struck her fancy. Usually, though, she questioned me about my attitudes, interspersing her interrogation with pointers on conduct. One Friday night she requested me to come downstairs at tea time the following afternoon to be, as she said, "broken in," an unfortunate phrase since it was also the one she used in speaking of servants whom she had trained. I was never, she admonished me, to regard myself as a servant. But at this phase of my career, when I had learned little more at the commercial school than which were the "home keys" on the typewriter, she could not truthfully call me her secretary. Moreover, being a woman completely sufficent unto herself, she could not introduce me as her "companion" without discrediting herself or making her friends suspect that her eyesight was failing. Nor could she pretend that I was a distant relative or the daughter of an old friend who until now had been in boarding school in Switzerland, for it would take no more than one conversation for anyone to know that I had no connections with Boston and therefore none with herself. What I was, in point of fact, was her "case" or her "project" or whatever the word was that was then in fashion to describe the beneficiary of that allotment in a rich woman's budget called "Miscellany." But wishing to spare my feelings (and also because practicing charity under one's roof was seldom "done" unless the recipient was the orphan of a friend or relative who had been left with no money), she did not fancy my presentation in these terms. At first, it had been her intention to keep me imprisoned while she tutored me in etiquette and until I was able to operate a typewriter, but this plan soon appeared impracticable owing to the fact that my residence in the house had leaked out, presumably through the servants.

She had hit upon a solution at last. Until I should be qualified as a secretary and until she saw fit to admit publicly that she was going to write her memoirs, she gave me to understand that I was to offer no unsolicited information, but if I was pressed I was to say, quite truthfully, that I was studying to become the amanuensis of a writer whose name I was not at liberty to give, that she and I had met through Dr. McAllister and she had invited me to share her house which, in Hopestill's absence, would be too lonely even for her. I was permitted to say I was from Chichester but almost all the rest of my background was to be obliterated from my memory. Quite understandably she did not want it known that my mother was in an asylum. No more did I. There was little danger of the fact coming to light, for the summer residents of Chichester did not move in Miss Pride's circles nor anywhere near them and the only link presenting any danger was Dr. Barker, who not only had a bad memory for names but was also opposed to gossip and would certainly never dream of repeating anything so banal as his sister's report of Chichester's insane woman.

Having set the hour for my début in her drawing-room, Miss Pride went on frankly to clarify her plans for me. I say "frankly," but the word is inexact, for her confessions were so subtly put and she displayed so ambiguous a wit that it was only after I had left her and had gone to my own room after dinner that I realized how stark had been her projection of the future. She was mortally afraid of growing old; if she were to dodder into half-crazed and ludicrous senility, as both her father and her mother had done, she wanted a caretaker to silence her, to dissuade her from both the crabbed and the maudlin antics of old age. She feared blindness (she, whose eyes at seventy had never been fitted with glasses) and dreaded being deprived of reading and of walking. "I don't fancy taking up phonograph records to amuse me at my age," she said scornfully. She was not sure I was the right custodian for her; that, only time could tell, but she wished me to consider whether I should like to think of myself as permanently installed in her house, and she implied that I would not be forgotten in her will. I was grateful and happy at the prospect, even though it was impossible for me to imagine her so changed as to need the services of what amounted to a nursemaid. I told her that and she replied grimly, "My dear, we're all fools before we're fetched by the pale rider."

She dismissed me with that, but as I was passing through the door, she said, "Hope returns tomorrow. I fancy she'll come in about tea time."

"I am anxious to meet her."

Miss Pride looked directly into my eyes. "I am sure you are," she said. "I have the feeling that you have a preconceived notion of my niece."

"I saw her once, you know. She came to the Hotel some years ago. Perhaps you don't remember."

"My life has not been so helter-skelter that I do not remember its events, Sonie," she replied. "Nor have I forgotten Hopestill's dancing slippers."

A blush raced to the roots of my hair and my voice broke as I said, "My father didn't finish them."

She smiled wrily. "Hope refused to go to the party without them. I dare say if you had known that she spent that evening in her room, howling for her slippers, you would have sent them on." But while she twisted her dagger in me, her smile changed to one of great friendliness and she added, "The battle must begin early in our lives if we are to be victorious, isn't that right?"

2

I had dressed with care, but although I had been leisurely, I had a full hour before I could go down. Miss

Pride had told me that she had no intention of "presenting" me, that I was merely to appear and "take things as they came." It would be better, she told me, not to be too prompt. I moved impatiently about my room, sat at my desk awhile and read one sentence over and over in The Rise of Silas Lapham without ever comprehending its meaning. Moving to the window, I sat for a while on the ledge, shivering at the icy air that came through the cracks, and stared at a boy, dressed like a Harvard student, loping up Mount Vernon Street across the square. Something in his carriage reminded me of Nathan. Without any transitional thought, I turned back into my room and standing, one arm on the footrail of my bed, I opened The Confessions of a Young Man. When I had promised myself, on the night Nathan and I sat in the fog on the steps of the Hotel Barstow, that I would have the best, I had allowed destiny to choose the circumstances for me. I had at no time doubted that the choice of Boston by my guardian angel had been supreme wisdom, that this was the soil in which my gifts, whatever they were, would fructify. And thus, when I read George Moore, and I read him constantly, I did so out of the desire to prove to myself that the "best" Nathan had wanted for himself and for me was in reality only second best. My talents were not artistic, not creative. I felt that they were assimilative and analytical, that what I saw in Boston, what I had seen in Chichester I understood, but that I could not reassemble my impressions into something artful. I could not ennoble fact. It was experience of the most complex order that I desired, and while there were times when, exploring the narrow streets of the back side of the Hill, I wished my knowledge to include the cafés and *ateliers* and the quays of George Moore's Paris, the wish was diluted as I turned toward home and thought of my room, of Miss Pride, and of our conversation over the sherry glasses. She, I thought, was worth all the freedom and all the abandon, worth, indeed, all triumphs.

I closed the book. Opening the door, I heard many voices rising up, and I knew it was time.

A dozen people were already drinking tea when I went

into the drawing-room and were deep in conversation so that my entrance passed unnoticed save by an elderly gentleman, seated upon an ottoman though his years should have got him an easy chair. He rose at once and came toward me, fumbling in his coat pocket. "Hello, there!" he cried. When he had got midway and had put his eyeglasses on, he halted and said, "Oh, I thought you were Hope."

"No, sir, I'm Sonie Marburg."

He murmured something like "Well, that's nice," or "Well, I declare," but kindly offered me his hand anyhow, though he did not come nearer and I was obliged to go after it. I should have liked to prolong our handclasp since his plump fingers were warm, and I was chilled to the bone after this first day of cold weather in the Spartan temperature of Miss Pride's house. As I had come down the stairs just now where drafts blew out of the very walls, I had had to stop several times to rub my stiffening fingers together and to check the clatter of my teeth. But the weatherproof Bostonians, seated in the drawing-room which was not perceptibly warmer than the upper floors, were not only comfortable so that their bright cheeks glowed with excellent circulation, indeed, they had even suffered someone to "crack" a window through which came an unflagging blast of late fall air.

The old man's fingers abandoned mine too soon. He introduced himself as Admiral Nephews and then returned to his ottoman, leaving me where I had been intercepted, still faced with the problem of what to do with myself. I felt that I was undergoing a radical physical transformation and was sure that if I could look at my feet (I was prevented by the unshakeable rigidity of my neck) I would find them twice their normal size and that my hands, pendulous at my sides, had likewise doubled their proportions, while my neck and face were suffused with a rashy red. I was further certain that if I were called upon to speak, my voice would issue either croaking or inaudible. I was rescued by a sign from Miss Pride who, lifting neither a finger nor an eyebrow nor speaking my name, commanded me to come directly to the tea-table where she was officiating. So peremptory was her aspect which alone had beckoned me, as it had done in the dining-room of the Barstow, that had I been in the middle of a sentence or had someone been in the middle of one addressed to me, I should instantly have obeyed her.

"Take charge for a while," she said when I came to her. "I must speak to someone." Then, bending over as if to inspect the plate of lemon slices, she said in a much lower voice, "I think you should be more sparing of lip rouge." This was by no means the first reproof I had received since I had been in Boston. She had taken it upon herself to civilize me, or, as she called it, to "caulk" me, for, she said, not even the sturdiest vessel could weather such storms as I had without some damage. The "storms" were not so much the facts of my father's desertion, my brother's death, my mother's calamity, as they were the omissions in my upbringing. She had sent me out when I first arrived to buy my winter wardrobe and when I had returned with what had struck my fancy, she had at once sent for her car, taken me and all my purchases back to the shops and chosen my clothes herself. For, although I had bought four pairs of gloves, I had not bought a hat, and although the coat I had picked out was a formal Chesterfield, my shoes were all flat-heeled oxfords.

Out of sorts with the cold, terrified by the roomful of people, I might have risen at her criticism—not from resentment but from despair—and left the house had not Miss Pride immediately retired, placing in my hands the custody of the tea-table, and allowing me, by her quick departure, no time to worry my smart into a real state of mind. I was quite bewildered by the array of shining vessels before me and especially nonplussed at the sight of three pots of about the same size, any one of which might contain tea. Before I had time to lift up their lids to determine what was inside, the old man who had mistaken me for Hope Mather tottered up and extended his cup, winking so broadly that one whole side of his face was stitched up, and saying in a humorous

stage whisper, "It's my fourth! I thought I'd get my refill when Lucy wasn't here, what?" I chose the wrong
pot and filled his cup with hot water.

"Here, here!" he cried, laughing and turning away
from me. "I say, Lucy! Did you tell this young lady here
to give me water if I asked for any more tea? That's a
good one! It's like the orderly I had on the *California*.
He liked his gin, that chap. Well, ma'am, he drank so
much of it that towards the end of an evening, his
mates used to slip a bottle of water in front of him and
if he said it tasted queer, those rascals told him his taste
buds were paralyzed!"

By the sparse but indulgent laughter that followed
the mild little anecdote, recited loud enough for anyone
to hear, I judged that it was not a new one, and that the
interest which lighted up the eyes of all the guests was
not in the story-teller, but in myself who had been discovered, as if by accident, within the Admiral's orbit.
Miss Pride alone did not laugh. She stood by the door to
the dining-room, and it was only after she had transfixed me with a gaze of exasperation for my mistake, that
she attended to what she had gone for and rang the bell
for a servant. The others resumed their talk, but now
and then stole a tactful look at me, pretending to be
glancing at the portrait on the wall behind the sofa
where I sat or to be merely making sure that the Admiral was still there.

"I beg your pardon," I said to him. "I really didn't
intend to do it." I filled a new cup with tea and handed
it up but neglected to offer him any accessories. "Oh,
come, dear girl," he said, "you're treating me shabbily.
I take two of sugar and *copious* cream. You youngsters
these days don't believe much in tea, what? It's all cocktails for you, what? I remember, ma'am, that when I was
a boy I had carving lessons and my sisters had lessons
in the technique of the tea-table. Don't they teach that
any more?"

"I don't know, sir."

"Where did you go to school, mademoiselle?"

"In Chichester."

"I didn't know there was a school in Chichester.

I didn't know there was anything in Chichester except those humdinger cherry-stones and that scuttled hotel Miss Lucy Pride risks her life in every summer. Was it day or boarding?"

"It was a public school," I said apologetically.

"Oh!" said Admiral Nephews, drawing up a chair. "I dare say you wouldn't get anything fancy there. Perhaps it's just as well. Perhaps we all learned folderol, who knows? I expect you had practical things like manual training and geology, what?"

"Why, no, I think we had the usual things."

"Latin, I suppose. I guess *Arma virumque cano* isn't Greek to you!" He chuckled, wrinkling up his pleasant, rosy face. "And French. Everyone does a good deal of French. I did. It's a good thing. One goes to Paris after all and doesn't want to look like a booby. And English? You're up on your English, I wager. Let's test you. Now I'll give you a fleet of quotations and you tell me what they're from. Ready? First:

> Shall I compare thee to a Summer's day?
> Thou art more lovely and more temperate.

Well?"

"Shakespeare," I said, but in a voice that shook with dread of his more difficult questions. "It's the beginning of one of the sonnets."

"Good! Second:

> When in disgrace with fortune and men's eyes,
> I all alone beweep my outcast state."

"That's Shakespeare, too," I said.

"Where do the lines occur?"

"In a sonnet, sir!"

"Good! Good! Excellent! Once more:

> That time of year thou may'st in me behold
> When yellow leaves, or none, or few do hang."

"Shakespeare!" I cried, hoping he did not intend to go through the whole sequence.

"I'll give you E for excellence, young lady. But now I think I may be able to stump you. Try this one:

She shall be sportive as the fawn
That wild with glee across the lawn
Or up the mountain springs:
And hers shall be the breathing balm
And hers the silence and the calm
Of mute, insensate things."

My luck continued, for in the year past I had learned
my English from an effusive woman whose adoration of
Wordsworth had made her give all the rest of literature
nothing more than a lick and a promise while upon her
exegesis of *Ode on Intimations of Immortality* and *The
Prelude* she had spent six months.

"Bravo!" cried the Admiral, putting his hand on my
knee and continuing confidentially, "Do you know that
I committed every line of those Lucy poems to memory
in honor of Miss Pride? Perhaps she'll tell you sometime
how I recited them to her in this very room on the occasion of her twenty-fifth birthday. You may not see this
in her, but I still think of her as just what the poem
says, 'as sportive as the fawn.' "

The garrulous creature's eyes were dewy and I wondered if he had been a rejected suitor, for I was sure
that if he *had* been a suitor, Miss Pride would have rejected him straightaway after his recitation of the Lucy
poems. She must have been born hard-headed, I
thought, and at the substantial age of twenty-five would
have given anyone what-for who compared her to a
"sportive fawn." The fawn herself was moving in and out
amongst her guests and there was in her carriage such
a vigorous uprightness, and in her face, from which her
exasperation with me was not altogether obliterated, so
formidable an aloofness that I was on the point of laughing out loud at the old man's metaphor. As she halted
before each of the little groups, I observed that she
treated her friends with very little more warmth than
she did me or her chauffeur. She did not bend towards
them, but stood erect, looking down upon the interrupted talkers and perhaps rewarding them with a cool
smile. Her smile had about it the same economy that
had her speech and her eating habits and her apparel. I

do not mean that she lacked either cordiality or humor and no doubt she was genuinely fond of many of the people gathered here. But she was never, so to speak, surprised into a smile, and she allowed her smile to last only so long as it was justified by the nature of its provocation. I noticed, however, that she was not the only one who husbanded her responses, for often one of her guests cracked open and resealed his mouth as perfunctorily as she. I admired their abstention, regarding it as a kind of hallmark of the Puritans, like the haemophilia of the Bourbons. I had noticed, from the beginning, that Miss Pride was extremely frugal of her laughter. Now and again, she was amused enough to emit two muted barks of the same volume and duration, as if she were actually saying "Ha! ha!"

As Admiral Nephews followed her course with his nautical eyes, I warmed towards him for no other reason than that he admired her, and had not the very nature of my own admiration insisted upon discipline as its principal component, I would have exclaimed, "Isn't she wonderful!" in order to hear his corroboration. She was, in truth, more wonderful today than she had ever been. Although her guests were as pedigreed as she, and no doubt owned the famous names I had read on the calling cards, she outshone them all just as she had outshone Mrs. Prather and Mrs. McKenzie. Her preeminence came partly from the mere fact that she was the hostess and therefor the star performer, but even more from the *noblesse oblige* with which she had turned me loose in her drawing-room despite my over-painted lips. A lesser lady would have sent me back to my bedroom to remove the rouge lest my bad taste reflect upon herself.

The Admiral, having satisfied himself that I was tolerably educated, did not inquire further into my background but after congratulating both me and himself on our learning (for he found it as remarkable that he, an officer of the navy, was versed in poetry as that I, educated at a public school, was) said, "Hope Mather would have known them all, too. She's a clever one! I heard she was coming home today. Where is she?"

I told him she was riding horseback in Concord where she had spent the night, having only just come back from Manchester. Thus far, I had not seen her.

"Now there's a girl that can ride a horse. I suppose she's the best horsewoman I know barring Mrs. Nephews, who was perhaps a shade more prudent. I well recollect when Spencer Mather's daughter was no higher than a table, she managed a two-year-old that Mr. Apthorp had in Bedford. She was a caution! She had a way with the groom, that little spitfire had, and she got him to saddle the horse that wasn't really broken yet, and before a fellow could say Jack Robinson, milady was on the horse and out of the stable, riding him into the ring. We were just coming back to tea—I expect we had ridden to Carlisle that day—and what did we see but that redheaded baggage putting the colt through his paces. When he frisked too much for her taste, she gave him his comeuppance with a whack over the nose with her little crop no longer than my forearm. She sat like a lady! Well, ma'am, while Spencer Mather was giving the groom a piece of his mind, the governess was leading Hope away and I believe" (the Admiral, overcome with laughter, could not go on for a moment), "I believe she must have been *living* in the stables for the vocabulary she used on that poor little Parisian spinster. It was too funny, you know! Hope swearing to beat the band while the little mademoiselle was crossing herself. I dare say Hope doesn't remember those words now!"

After a few concluding chuckles, he sobered and went on to list Hope's further accomplishments. I gathered that she not only "sat a horse well" and "knew a good mount" when she saw one and had numerous other equestrian talents, but that she was an excellent swimmer (the statistics of the length of time she could stay under water, the distances she had swum, and the sensational dives she had executed, were quite lost to me who could not swim), could not be defeated on the tennis court, and was a girl who could jibe her boat into a sixty-mile-an-hour breeze with the skill of a veteran mariner. Indeed, what the girl could not do, he, for one, didn't know. "Why, she could milk a cow if she was asked to!"

Since he apparently knew her family well, I wanted to inquire of him whether Hopestill was descended from the famous Mathers, but I had no opportunity, for his praise of her athletic exploits led him to tell me about his grandson who was a lieutenant commander, stationed in Hawaii and who was also "no slouch" on a horse. It was the Admiral's dream that through this young man, Hope might be annexed to the Nephews family. "But neither party," he said with a sigh, "seems to want my will to be done."

I said, "Perhaps that's because they're so far separated?"

He replied, "No, no. It's a case of 'east is east and west is west and never the twain shall meet.' "

I was to learn that the Admiral could not get through a day without using at least one quotation and that because he had given up reading poetry some ten years before and now took his entire supply from Bartlett's, half the time his tags had nothing to do with the context of the conversation. But he was known in Miss Pride's circle as having a colorful and individual speech, the flavor of which derived partly from his literary allusions and partly from his use of polite address which, to ladies, included *"Fräulein," "Senora," "Madame,"* as well as "Ma'am," "Miss," and "Madam."

I thought Miss Pride must find his gabbling ludicrous and I was astonished when she came up to us and greeted him most affectionately: "Lincoln Nephews, you're too old to be flirting with this young lady. Now tell me what you've been up to. Evelyn Frothingham just told me you had been to a dance at the Country Club. What an old beau you are!"

"I was and I had a thumping good time. So often the Country Club is stodgy, but this time, ma'am, it was superb. Why, Lucy, I tripped the light fantastic until two o'clock in the morning."

I could not think what criterion of stodginess old Lincoln had set up, any better than I could imagine him "tripping the light fantastic," since all three words were so peculiarly inapplicable to his embonpoint. It gave me great pleasure to hear of "the Country Club," "the Chilton Club," and "St. Botolph," as though I were peeping through the windows of those chaste establishments where, in the libraries and the ballrooms and the parlors, the thoroughbreds of Back Bay and Beacon Hill were engaged in fashionable diversions, the nature of which was still unknown to me, though I pictured the Admiral nursing a breather of brandy in the company of his pink-faced and bald coevals, while Miss Pride and members of her "reading circle" traced genealogies over their tea. On the Saturday before this, when Miss Pride was lunching at the Chilton Club, I had received a telephone message from her which obliged me to go round there to deliver her calling cards which she had left behind. When the door had closed upon me and I was actually on the premises of this sanctum sanctorum, I could not have been more stirred if it had been the residence of queens and princesses, though I saw only the vestibule with its cloak booth, presided over by a matronly woman in spectacles and a starched white cap and apron who, with her cultivated speech and her remote manner, could have been a member of the club herself. Through the half-open door directly in front of me and at the end of the hall, I saw the edge of a dining-table and a thick gray rug and half a portrait of a lady. From the room issued talk and laughter so that I knew the ladies were still at lunch and I would not, therefore, be allowed to hand Miss Pride her cards, but must entrust them to the custodian of the wraps. A waiter, as distinguished in his swallowtails as an ambassador and having a foreign accent, said he would have someone remind Miss Pride in "Meesis Saltonstall's party" that a parcel was waiting for her, and he went off to elect a responsible member of his staff to bear these tidings to my mistress. Afterwards, as I walked home along Commonwealth Avenue where the bright early afternoon sun displayed to their advantage the genuine and the false violet windowpanes, I chose the houses where she might go that afternoon to drop her card when Mrs. Saltonstall's party, like a courtly banquet, had been adjourned. Until then she would be inaccessible to everyone but those whose lineage entitled them to push open the door in the Chilton Club and pass between the portals into the dining-room.

Miss Pride and Admiral Nephews briefly and malevolently discussed the Evelyn Frothingham who had informed Miss Pride of her friend's revels and was, I gathered, still in the room and possibly within earshot. Miss Pride said she was resembling a toad more closely each day and the Admiral agreed, adding that her model was an especially unsightly specimen. Having demolished the poor woman, they proceeded then to what I soon discovered was the favorite topic of their generation in Boston: namely, the Irish politicians who had "taken over" the city, and were an even greater menace in Cambridge. Today Miss Pride had the openers: she had heard that afternoon that a young lawyer, distinguished for his illustrious family connections, for his irreproachable court record, for his manners and his charm, had suddenly taken it into his head to campaign for the mayor of Cambridge, and had been seen, only the night before, at a roadhouse near Weston in the company of six Irish politicians. And the same unnamed source had informed her that far from being ill at ease in their midst, the renegade from the Republican party whose name was Carew or Carey, I could not tell which, was in his element, was actually the ring-leader and was so disheveled from drinking and shouting and lolling about that he was barely recognizable.

The Admiral had a counter: another man, of Mr. Carew's (or Carey's) generation and kidney had recently, to curry favor with these same Irish politicians of Cambridge, been overheard panegyrizing the Roman Catholic Church in the presence of certain notorious gossips who were sure to spread the word. "What would our great grandfathers have thought if they had known Boston was to become a Popish stronghold?" said Miss Pride, appalled at this "case."

"Well," replied the Admiral, "I don't know the answer to that one as I never had the pleasure of knowing my great grandfather. But I know that my grandfather would have said aplenty in strong words, ma'am, after the ladies had retired. My grandfather, you know, used to be acquainted with Matthew Arnold's mother, and when he learned that she turned all the pictures to the wall Sunday, when he came back from Oxford and had children of his own, he did the same thing. He was an exceedingly pious man and I dassen't imagine the way he would have scored the Catholics. In those days, of course, they hadn't become a problem. The old order changeth."

I stopped listening to the conversation, and while I was still digesting the fact that Admiral Nephews' grandfather had known Matthew Arnold's mother, I heard a sharp-faced, diminutive woman, who was sitting near-by, say to a young man, "Oh, a man and his books are quite separate things *I* think. I never knew anyone more charming and affectionate than Henry James and he was always one of my dearest friends, but I can't abide his books."

I could not evaluate accurately the aspects of this select world: whether the personal connection of these people with the immortals, or their poised arrogance in regard to such issues as the contemptible political machine of Boston, or their stylish language, or their blue-blooded ugliness was the more impressive. The roots of Miss Pride's guests were so deep and tough that I thought they were eternal, and the word "decadent" that Dr. McAllister, a traitor to his intended destiny, had used so often in speaking of Boston when he was trying to depress my expectations, was misleading. Decay must come from within and I could imagine nothing but an external calamity, a social revolution that could eradicate this solid society. Perhaps that was the aim of the ultra-montane newcomers. It was not, I concluded, that what they said and the judgments they passed were of any profundity or of any insight (on the contrary, they often sprang from a primitive and passionate ignorance of the opinions of the rest of the world but which, despite their egotism, contained a measure of self-distrust) but that the manner of these pilgrims' heirs was so fearless and direct that one was not struck with their fatuity. The woman who had been fond of Henry James spoke, a little later on, to the woman I identified as Mrs. Frothingham (she was, as her critics had described her, a reptilian, puckered, misshapen person), of her opinion of people who experimented with flowers. "Really, I do feel," she said, "that this craving for a *tulipe noire* is ridiculous. It debases nature." I believed her implicitly, though this was a subject I had never before pondered. Immediately thereafter I was won to the side of her adversary who, with as forthright a tone, rejoined, "I can't agree, of course. One might just as well say that formal gardens are a debasement of nature. Or that grapefruit is."

"I think grapefruit *is*. I don't care for it at all."

"But not formal gardens?" inquired Mrs. Frothingham drily.

"Ah, you have me there, you clever woman," laughed Henry James' friend, and I gathered that she had a formal garden. "I'll 'bone up' on that poser as my little Stephen says and tell you my answer Thursday at Sarah Cushman's."

"Shall you be there too?" said the other in surprise.

"Certainly. We have declared a most just armistice. I dare say it's in our blood, and no doubt we'll be far more battle-scarred than we are now before we die. But for the time being the white flag is up."

I was intrigued by this feud, so publicly alluded to, and was disappointed when later on I learned that the two warriors were sisters. Mrs. Frothingham and her friend, having shelved their differences on flowers and grapefruit, now exchanged views and reminiscences, having in their retinue a regiment of names as they traversed miles of drawing-rooms, summer residences, and the parks of foreign cities, dignifying the most trifling detail with a judicious and clear-voiced appraisal that made life and the world singularly leveled down and homogeneous. The small, sharp woman hated the new Pompeii for the same reasons (though these reasons were not stated, were, she said, "self-evident" so that I, who could not discover them, felt stupid) that she hated *tulipes noires* and grapefruit. Mrs. Frothingham maintained that these same mysterious reasons, which she readily apprehended and despised, were meaningless and that exactly the opposite was, in each case, true.

3

I rose, intending to make my way to the bay window and try covertly to close it for I was suffering acutely from the cold. Miss Pride detained me. "I want you to talk with Amy Brooks, who is over there by the fire. She's about your age and a very suitable person."

"She's literary, ain't she?" asked the Admiral.

"No, she paints. But she's about Miss Marburg's age."

She indicated a person whom I had noticed before and had taken to be about forty-five. Now I subtracted a few years, but could not believe she was any less than thirty-eight. She had been in conversation with a stout old woman who now got up and was about to leave. I heard her, in parting, say, "I wish I had been half so clever as you when I was your age, Amy. You must come to me soon and bring some of the thingumabobs you were telling me about." With this, refusing assistance though she was very lame, she began a labored journey with her cane towards Miss Pride, and as I observed her, waiting a moment out of respect for her age before I took her place beside Amy Brooks, I recollected a scene that each fall repeated itself in Chichester. In the afternoon, it had rained, but the air had cleared by evening. As I walked home from the Hotel after dark, ahead of me I heard the steady, three-legged walk of old ladies with sticks over the wet gravel road, and voices, strangely sweetened by the waves or by my distance from them, deliberating the further necessity for umbrellas, even though they did not stray far from the veranda and could immediately have got to shelter if the rain began again. Children of the village, playing Run-Sheep-Run, passed me and overtook the strollers, scampered through the weak circle that the flashlight of one cast on the ground, and ran on, giggling.

I stood aside to let the old lady, who was dressed in mourning, pass. She gazed at me with dreamy, half-blind eyes and gave me a smile, the sincerity and sweetness of which momentarily disrobed her of the concealments of age and revealed her as she once had been. "How d'you do?" she said. "I know all about you, my dear." But before I could reply, she had taken the Admiral's arm and was being eased into a chair beside Miss Pride.

My appointed interlocutor was ruinously plain, wanting both an adequate nose and chin, but having, for compensation, large square glossy teeth and hyperthyroid eyes. She was small and nervous and given to giggling as well as to sudden fits of seriousness when her whole organism tensed to apparently agonizing statements like, "I have been reading Eugene O'Neill!" or "Last week I went to T Wharf and spent an afternoon sketching!" Then for a few seconds she would stare at me with her high, blue, mammiform eyes.

I said, "Were you sketching boats?"

"Yes! All kinds. Even a dear little Chinese junk! Not from China, of course. It belongs to some arty people, I think, but that doesn't keep it from being cunning, does it? Do you sketch?" I regretted that I did not. "Oh, but you should! There's really nothing like the satisfaction it gives one. Don't you think one ought to have an outlet? I do! I think it's so important these days, especially. I don't pretend to be an artist, you know!" She was visited again, distractingly, by giggles which delayed her. She continued, "I mean, I think it's so necessary to be in touch with art, don't you?"

I supposed that it was, but I could not expatiate for I was tongue-tied before this ebullient spinster whose upbringing had taught her to say the most platitudinous things to a complete stranger but to say them so firmly and courteously that they sounded indisputable. Her zest—she said in a few minutes that the reason she sketched was that she wished people to know what she thought of life—was a consistent style, plagiarized and monotonous and eminently respectable.

Sorrowfully from Miss Pride and admiringly from Dr. McAllister, I had heard that Hopestill Mather filled her leisure time with none of the mild artistic enterprises commonly undertaken by young ladies who had been "out" for some time, the water colors, the humorous poetry, the informal essays, the sculpturing in plasticine, the rendition of Chopin. Yet, although she had repudiated the conventional patois and honestly acknowledging that she had not even the mildst of gifts, her opinions were by no means poles apart from those of Miss Brooks as I realized, recalling the doctor's further comments. For I had been told that Hope did not want to "lose touch" with art and desired to be one of its patronesses. Dr. McAllister's irony came to me only now, for I had not perceived that this innocently overbearing notion was not unique in the girl I had set out to dislike. Art, to the Misses Brooks and Mather, was a custom: one "kept up" with the newspapers and fashions, was on the alert for word of engagements, marriages, births, débuts, and similarly, one did not like to "lose touch" with art.

Miss Brooks informed me that her stepmother, the Countess von Happel, had done a great deal towards bringing good exhibits to Boston. "Don't you think Europeans have more *feeling* for art than we do?" she said. "My stepmother is Viennese. She may be here later on today." Nor had the Countess neglected contemporary artists, struggling in Boston and New York; she visited their studios and hung their paintings in her dining-room and very often sold one, for a small sum, to a guest who admired it. "It might be only fifteen dollars, but you know even fifteen dollars will give an artist a lift. Oh, I think it's wonderful the way they keep on in their horrid little studios!" "They," a grubby and deserving species, sounded like prisoners serving a term for a felony they had not committed, to whom a gift of cigarettes or chocolate bars meant a new lease on life. I said I had heard Hopestill Mather was another good Samaritan, interested in the artist's welfare, though no doubt not on such a grand scale.

"Well, with Hope, it's different," said Miss Brooks. "She's more *Bohemian* about it. I mean, Hope is almost more interested in the artists themselves than in their work. You know! She's interested in *people*. We call her the 'psychologist.' She wants to find out what makes an artist and not what an artist makes. It all depends on one's point of view. Now the Countess is a great admirer of Van Gogh, but she doesn't care a bit for all those scandalous stories about his ear and so on. But how Hope loves them! Art is my stepmother's life, art," she added, "*and* dinner parties." This last was offered with a freshet of giggles which I took to mean that the Countess' predilection for dinner parties was of notorious proportions.

This girl, so inferior to my ideal conception of a Bostonian, and yet, with all her cordiality, so aloof, unwilling even to inquire what my business might be in that drawing-room (For how could she have failed to sense immediately that I was an outsider?) had, when she began to speak of Hopestill Mather, changed her tone from nervousness to calm, as if she were held in check by a powerful emotion which had put a stop to the vertigo of her introspection and had made her temporarily critical. I said, "Do you know Miss Mather well?"

"Oh, of course," she replied. "She's my cousin."

In the course of that day, I discovered a Bostonian general principle: namely, that everyone was related to everyone else, or if blood kinship did not obtain, something else almost as binding did; people had gone to dancing school together or their fathers had been lawpartners or their mothers had been Red Cross nurses in the same village in France. But this kinship, even that of blood (perhaps actually it was true more of this than of the other kind) was so taken for granted that it was almost uninteresting. It was important to know who had married into what family and who were the forbears of the bride and groom and whether the bride's mother were the Martha Endicott who had gone to Winsor School with Priscilla Bradley but had married into Philadelphia. All of this was of vital concern, but half the time, the performers of that drama, coiled about itself innumerable times, were known most vaguely to their commentators. And the relation of twigs to the trees had become so complicated that no one could straighten it out immediately: the whole rigamarole must be gone through each time. Cousins were not appreciably more kindred than friends, and friends never knew when they would discover that they were really cousins, the fact being established only by an accidental remark dropped by a former Bostonian, who now lived in London, and relayed home in a casual letter by her visitor. Thus, Miss Pride had not told me that Amy Brooks was Hopestill Mather's cousin and Miss Brooks herself had supplied me with the information almost as an afterthought, really only to explain why she knew Hopestill as if their being cousins (since obviously they were not friends) was the only thing that would induce them to know one another.

Still, she had not spoken disloyally of Hopestill—perhaps, again, because her etiquette, the guardian angel of people in society, directed her, not her feeling—but she had spoken coolly and appraisingly as of a slight acquaintance and one whose "philosophy of life" was opposed to her own. But I suspected that there were other grounds, less intellectual, for the enmity, and that the divergence of their paths toward art was merely symbolic. It struck me that this poor ill-favored, twitching girl envied her cousin's good looks, or that she would really have liked to mingle with the Bohemians as Hopestill did but, being spurned by them, had to cloak her disappointment in an indifference to the "psychology" of the artist.

I said, "Perhaps Miss Mather spreads the word about her artists just as your stepmother does."

"Oh, certainly!" she cried vigorously. "You mustn't misunderstand me. Hope doesn't trifle with them. She *believes* in them, you know. It's her catering to them that I don't see."

"Her catering?"

"Yes! Literally! She takes them strong cheese and rye bread and marinated herring and beer. And don't think for a moment she does her shopping in any usual place like Pierce's! No, she must have the shabbiest delicatessen on Revere Street! Oh, Hope is all of a piece."

This time I joined in Amy Brooks' laughter and when

we had finished, I looked up to find that we were being approached by a pair of extraordinary young men, introduced to me as Mr. James and Mr. Pingrey. They appeared to have been turned out on the same wheel and in the same proportions and differed only in their decorations, like "basic" vases which may be painted appropriately for a particular décor. They were the tallest men I had ever seen and, though they must have been no less than twenty-five years old, were still unused to their height, as if they had shot up overnight and had not learned how to steer themselves. Their knees were in a perpetual state of semi-genuflection and they thrust their heads forward and afterwards tossed them back in an agony of clumsiness. One was dark and a little bald, sallow, thin, strained, but the other was blindingly fair, as shining as a Swede and having the color of new apples splashed recklessly about his broad, bony face. I had not witnessed their arrival and the shock of seeing them suddenly before us unnerved me: it was as if, like genii, they had vapored forth through the floor.

Miss Brooks, when she had presented her friends to me, travailed again in the mirth of her nervous system, and Mr. James and Mr. Pingrey were sympathetically infected, twisted and turned and bent their knees like two damaged snakes as between their giggles they all three reviewed some esoteric anecdote of their last meeting which, as nearly as I could make out, had been at a masquerade ball given by the Countess von Happel. I could not help thinking that the most elaborate costumes would fail to disguise any of these freaks in the slightest.

"And what have you been doing since?" said Mr. Pingrey, the fair young man.

"I was just telling Miss Marburg that I have been sketching. I was at T Wharf last week, Edward, and do you know there was actually a *Chinese junk* there?"

"I don't believe it! Truly I don't believe it! I must have proof! You must show me a picture of it!"

"*Do* come to see it. I value your criticism, you know. Come to tea soon, you will, won't you? And you tell me what *you've* been doing since that disgraceful party."

Edward Pingrey drew up a chair as Mr. James goggled uncertainly at me, not sure whether the *tête-à-tête* which was about to be launched between Miss Brooks and his companion would exclude us and necessitate a separate conversation. He also drew up a chair, to my side of the sofa, prepared for the worst. But Mr. Pingrey, though he bent toward Amy quite intimately and now and again emphasized a point by laying a huge, spatulate forefinger on the arm of the sofa within an inch of her hand, and addressed her solely, did not lower his voice and even glanced at us occasionally as he talked as though to make sure we were listening.

"Well, I've been doing something perfectly delicious, Amy. I have become intrigued with politics, of all things! You would never guess, would you, that a confirmed old ivory towerite like me would ever get involved in politics, but I have, my dear, up to the neck!"

"But what kind of politics, Edward?"

"By no means the usual kind! Not these tedious" (he pronounced "tedious" with a "j") "municipal squabbles. Don't misunderstand me: I realize the appalling state the city is in, of course, but there are so much bigger things! Such universal problems! I've joined an extraordinary group called '*Les Chevaliers de la legion de Lafayette*' which will eventually be *the* international party. We wear red shirts, and I just wish you could have seen us, sixteen of us, marching through the Mill Dam in Concord the day we were formally sworn in. Amy, they're bright red, really scarlet!"

Miss Brooks laughed. "I can't take you seriously, Edward. I don't believe for a minute you marched down the Mill Dam. They wouldn't *let* you in Concord!"

"Oh, wouldn't they though! You can never guess who is the leader of our group. Guess!"

"Someone proper? Someone I know?"

"No one but your esteemed Uncle Arthur Hornblower!"

I burst into laughter, an attack which came upon me quite unawares like a disease that strikes without preliminary symptoms. Until I heard Mr. Pingrey say "your esteemed Uncle Arthur Hornblower," as if "your esteemed Uncle Arthur" were his given name to match his absurd surname which came directly out of the *dramatis personae* of an Elizabethan comedy, I had not altogether been aware that Mr. Pingrey and his sallow shadow, Mr. James and Amy Brooks were three superb, natural clowns. Now I was shaken to the soul with the circus and felt that if I heard again a mention of its patron, Youresteemedunclearthurhornblower, I would roar uncontrollably. The three performers stared at me in amazement. I was silenced. At last I said, "I beg your pardon. I was only thinking I used to know a terribly peculiar person named Hornblower." But as I uttered the name again, I was overcome.

Mr. James bent a reproachful gaze upon me. "It's not at all a common name," he said.

At that moment I was saved, for I saw Dr. McAllister coming into the room. He paused on the threshold and surveyed the guests and when he saw me, smiled. He gestured toward Miss Pride to indicate that he would join me when he had spoken to her. I rose from the sofa. "I'm very sorry I interrupted you, Mr. Pingrey. I was ever so interested."

The two lengthy young men stood up and bowed gravely. Miss Brooks giggled and said, "I think Uncle Arthur *is* comic, for that matter. It's been so nice to talk with you, Miss Marburg. We must have another nice long chat about sketching." And she extended to me a smooth, dead hand.

4

In the earlier part of the afternoon when, each time the door opened, I thought Dr. McAllister would surely enter now, I believed that he would be distant, no longer interested in me since he was in the center of a web woven about him by metropolitan society. For while in Chichester he could combine the offices of friend and counselor, here, I thought, his science would be separate from his social manner and that still unable to see me in any rôle but that of factor in "the Marburg case" he would shun me, not uncharitably, but to spare me the repercussions of a chance remark that might be dropped by one of us and apprehended by some stranger who happened to be within earshot. But his smile, which was transmitted to me like a message in code, intended for only my perusal, assured me that his generosity had not been modified. On the heels of this sense of security, and at the moment when, deliberately turning his back toward me, he sat down beside Miss Pride and the Admiral, came a searing jealousy of the dozen people in the room who one by one broke from their conversations to cry out their delight at seeing him again or to go directly up to him with the request that they be allowed to "have" him next. For I had failed, in my portrait of him, to particularize the background, having painted it before I had studied him in all kinds of light and from all angles. I had been literal and knowing him out of his *milieu* had been blind to the fact that he belonged to a type from which he could never extricate himself though he might denounce it. As he himself had told me, among the idiosyncrasies of this type was a simultaneous craving for and aversion to society, so that a complete break could never be effected. These were not merely the habits of a lifetime, he had said, but were the habits of two and a half centuries. In the renegade who has extirpated his New England accent and has espoused the life of the new frontiers, there is still the Puritan within his unalterable bones: a forward young lady at a house party in Winnetka, Illinois, importunately makes eyes at him, and if he recovers from his surprise sufficiently to make love to her, his performance will be cold, utilitarian, and intemperate.

At the same time, I should have disliked it if, after his brief salutation to Miss Pride and the old lady in mourning, he had come at once to greet me, for I passionately desired to have evidence that he "belonged." Yet, because I believed myself to be in love with him, I was nettled to discover that he was a great favorite. Thus, at the same time that I admired him as an aristocrat (the critical "I" did this, the I who was not in love), I wanted him to be a superior plebeian, a sort of polished edition of Nathan Kadish. Now, on the other hand, I had no desire to emend Miss Pride; her text did not bewilder me, and I was confident that I could imitate her style. In order, however, to meet the demands the doctor would make upon me if that extra-professional friendship I so coveted were ever to mature, I would have either to add something original to my translation of the old woman (I knew that he privately deplored my choice of model) or practice a certain dishonesty in deleting the elements in her that especially annoyed him. I wished to do neither, and it was for this reason that I hoped he might shoulder the responsibility himself and discover to me a strain in himself which matched my own.

It was ten minutes before he glanced towards me again and even then he did not come to my isolated place in the bay window. Attentively and with a charming smile or as charming a look of commiseration, he listened to gossip, complaints and reminiscences, making no distinctions, as far as one could judge from his facial expressions, between youth and age or between old friends and slight acquaintances. As his tour (as impartial as his visits to ward patients) brought him closer to me, I could hear his replies to remarks addressed to him.

"Why, all I know of Germans is that in general their anatomy is similar to the American variety. That's all I'm required to know in my profession," he said to a woman who had just returned from a Bavarian watering place and confessed, with mock caution, that she had great faith in the Nazis (she pronounced the word with a scrupulous *tset*) as the liberators of the nation from her post-Versailles quandary. Now, in fact, I knew that the doctor had very strong opinions of the Nazis, but he refused to discuss the subject with this frivolous Germanophile who chose to esteem in the new system its most obvious, most spectacular, and most ambiguous virtues: the superbly trained Storm Troopers, the powerful health of the children in the youth movements, the touting of Wagner. He had deliberately made his reply as stupid as her observation, but if he hoped thereby to make her own words echo to her shame in her ears, he was disappointed, for she said, "Do you know I don't really believe you? I think there is some secret of strength in the German body that exists in no other. Why, half of them, I should say, eat oleomargarine and have for years, and yet they're the healthiest people in the world."

Not because he was in the least interested in the conversation, but because it was his moral duty, imposed upon him by his knowledge, to correct her, he replied, "Not only is margarine not unhealthful to anyone, but you would find if you cared to make a survey that an enormous percentage of the American people never use butter at all."

Vexed the woman dropped the subject of the German physique and said, by way of dismissal, "At any rate, I think we all must recognize eventually that they are the leaders of the world." Further infuriated by a remote, ironic smile on the young man's face, she abruptly turned to her neighbor and shouted venomously, "What is the shocking tale I hear about your nephew and the Communists in Cambridge?" Dr. McAllister made his escape and came to the love-seat.

"I've expected to see you here long before this," he said genially. "I thought you looked forward to tea-parties."

I explained that I had not stayed away by choice but that Miss Pride had been educating me up to this afternoon. I intended no disloyalty because, far from being indignant, I was grateful for my preparation: had I not had it, the discomfort I had felt when I first entered the drawing-room would have continued and my talk with the Admiral would have fared much worse. But the doctor was contemptuous. "She drives a hard bargain," he said. He inquired about my business training and he asked me if I had found Boston up to my expectations. I told him I could have asked for nothing better.

"And Miss Pride? She's teaching you the useful arts, I trust?"

"Oh, indeed!" I said. I told him of the early morning conferences at which I was present. We took our breakfast together in the dining-room (Miss Pride was never tempted to be served in bed, a practice almost universal amongst her friends who, she told me, took as much care in selecting their bed-jackets as they did in selecting their dinner dresses) and at the end of it, Mary, the cook, was summoned from the cellar. Miss Pride was like a general previewing, with his aide, the campaign about to be started, the ammunition being money aimed where it would do the most damage to the enemy, for the Messrs. Pierce, Anderson, Rhodes, and the anonymous gentlemen entrenched in Hood's Dairy, Lewandos' Cleaners, and the Megansett Fish Market were, to use her own expression, "to be watched untiringly." The flattering telephone voice of Mr. Campbell of Rhodes' might win someone off his guard to buy oranges at eighty cents a dozen by describing the properties of the fruit with such a wealth of mouth-watering adjectives that one might believe it was cheap at double the price.

Miss Pride had requested my presence at the meetings of the economists because she thought I should learn to run a house. If I proved to have any common sense, she might in time confer upon me the high honor of runing *her* house. She had long been desirous of some such assistance, for her other affairs kept her busy. These other "affairs" included not only her extensive social life (I had been agreeably surprised that she dined out so often and went to so many concerts and luncheon parties, for I had supposed that she was as ascetic in this department as in any other) but also with a great many negotiations with her lawyer over her real estate, with her affiliation with divers philanthropic organizations interested in women's prisons and in Christmas dinners for underprivileged children (whose fathers, no doubt, were those impassioned speech-makers in the Common who were after the blood of Miss Pride and her kind). She had recently, also, been in collaboration with the widow of a Harvard professor, preparing his correspondence and lectures for publication, and this took her to Cambridge for one full day each week.

When I mentioned the work in progress, Dr. McAllister interrupted me. "Have you heard that the correspondence has become a thorn in her side and she only does it now out of a sense of duty?"

"Why, no, you're quite wrong. It's exactly the sort of thing that suits her, she tells me."

"She tells you very little. But she tells me very much. She took umbrage last week when she found a reference to herself in one of the early letters. She copied it down and it was so priceless I learned it by heart. But I won't tell you."

"Why not?"

"Because you'd be furious."

My curiosity made me promise that I would keep my temper. But as he quoted the letter, my skin tingled with rage. It read, "Several of us dined two nights ago at Mr. Everett Pride's who, as you know has one of the most elegant houses on our fair Hill. His treasures include a superb Copley, an indifferent Badger, three Homers that they tell me are fine (you know I never get anything from him but *mal de mer!*) and an excruciating creation of his own, his daughter Lucy. Awful to look at, tormenting to hear, she reminds me of nothing so much as a curlew."

"What a fool he was," I said, "to write that down!"

"I will say for Miss Pride," said the doctor, "that her wit is always ready. She told me what she had said to the widow after she had run across the passage. She said, 'Bosworth was pretty damned gawky himself, Mildred.' "

He laughed at the sally which I found less amusing than I would have liked, and then asked me, "What do you think of Admiral Nephews? He says you're a pippin."

"I liked him. Is he . . . Nothing."

"Come, is he what?"

I flushed but plunged in. "I was going to say, is he fashionable?"

"The most fashionable you could find in his generation," returned the doctor with a smile. "Not in the one just after him, though—he's a Unitarian."

Because most of my information about Boston came from schoolbooks, I did not know, until Philip McAllister told me, that Unitarianism had been out of style for more than half a century. Most of its present-day supporters remained in the fold because that was the environment to which they had been, as the psychologists say, "conditioned." The Admiral, who was by nature a sensualist, would far rather have gone on Sunday to the Episcopal Church, the higher, the better. But an atavistic conscience held him in check and he made only a minor concession to his idiosyncrasy: he attended services at King's Chapel where, despite its dedication to that doctrine indigenous to Boston, retained still a Royalist flavor, and old Lincoln Nephews could listen without shame to the organ, choice of Handel for King George, and fancy himself in the presence of ecclesiastical pomp.

I was about to ask another question about the Admiral, but the doctor diverted my attention to a miniature which he had picked up from the table near us. Handing it to me, he said, "Boston *was* something in those days." The faded miniature in its napless, maroon velvet frame presented a solemn, forthright girl. The central part in her straight hair was as precise as a clean wound. It was a face that made no compromises and in which no rounded lines appeared save those essential to the cheeks; her eyebrows were straight, her lips were straight, her nose was like a blade. The painter's colors seemed artificial, for one thought that the original had been a study in black and white. The high, round collar was pinned with an oval brooch, and the invisible ears terminated in smaller matching ornaments. She was an Endicott, he told me, related distantly to Miss Mather's father. He meant that Boston was something in the days when hell was immediate, altruism was ruthless, and justice was Mosaic. Now, cured of its chills and fevers, its blood watered down, it was no longer exciting. Still puritanical, it tried to imitate Sodoms and Gomorrahs in their decenter fashions, but the result was only dowdiness. Consider the Admiral, my friend commanded me, who had sunk in his rosy obesity upon a sofa and was telling the old woman dressed in widow's weeds a joke at which neither laughed aloud although the exertion both of the telling and of the listening made all four wattles wag and the two heads nod. He was no cavalier! His cavorting at the Country Club was so respectable, so circumspect! His affectation of French phrases and his Latin, employed to give him a cosmopolitan piquancy, so marked him as a citizen of Boston!

"I find him charming," I said.

"So do I," replied the doctor. "But preposterous. That's my grandmother, by the way, whom he's regaling. She and Miss Pride are currently enemies."

I asked him why this was and he said, "Chiefly because my grandmother is a possessive old woman and next to her house in Concord, I am her favorite possession—her only grandchild, you see."

"But surely Miss Pride has no designs on you!"

"Oh, but she has. When you meet Hope, you'll see her aunt is barking up the wrong tree though. She wouldn't have a dozen of my kind."

At that moment, there appeared before us an anxious little man like a caricature of Terror, for his feline green eyes were immensely magnified by a pair of very thick lenses and his small mouth trembled beneath the insufficient ambush of a sandy mustache. He was a newcomer and said hastily that he intended to run right along as soon as he had spoken to the doctor whom he drew aside and talked with in a whisper for a few minutes.

The room was less densely crowded now for it was a quarter past six according to the delicate china clock on the mantel which, after it had made a sound like the last quiet purr of a cat before it goes to sleep, gave forth a single, bell-like chime, sustained and questioning. I had not noticed the clock before as it was dwarfed by the tremendous Copley incongruously placed above the narrow marble mantel. I discovered that I had not been conscious of the room at all until now, had not observed, as I had always intended to do, its transformation when it was occupied by guests. Now, at this late hour, dimly lighted, its walls pink from the fire in the hearth, it seemed surpassingly feminine and agreeable. I looked towards Miss Pride, handling her dainty Bavarian tea china and deftly replenishing the hot water in the silver teapot, conversing the while with her friends, so much the lady that both processes were carried on without any interference to each other. It came to me, so deli-

286

ciously that I wanted to clap my hands together and crow, that I had never seen Miss Pride in the library without her green beaver hat: thus she had given me my tea there on the first day I had been in her house and thus she was, ready for church, every Sunday morning when I went in to pay my respects as she was playing chess against herself. I recalled the way my father had always worn his hat in the shop but left it there when he went into the house. While I knew that Miss Pride had been bare-headed the night she joined the gentlemen in their brandy, I was sure some other appurtenance, conversational perhaps, had disguised her feminine nature so that the bequests of her male ancestors were more apparent than those handed down from the mothers of her line.

Dr. McAllister's alarmed little man scurried away, looking straight ahead as though he were afraid of being trapped. He was like a rabbit running through a clearing. He did not make it, for Miss Pride caught sight of him and cried, "There he is now! Stop, Otis Whitney!" Obediently and out of breath he trotted to her side. My friend sat down beside me on the love-seat and watched the scene: Mr. Otis Whitney had been pushed by a thin but powerful forefinger into a chair beside the tea-table and was undergoing an inquisition about the health of his son who was under Dr. McAllister's care.

Abstractedly the doctor said, "By the way, I told my grandmother a little about you. Nothing you wouldn't want known, but she's a kindly old soul and you might like to visit her sometime when you want country air."

Just as I glanced toward her, there came a lull in the conversation of the group that sat between us and the tea-table and I heard old Mrs. McAllister say to the Admiral, "The report from Manchester this year is the same as ever. Hope Mather had all the beaux. Isn't she a heart-breaker! But you know she comes by it honestly."

The Admiral, not only to flatter Miss Pride who had half turned away from Otis Whitney, but also because he believed it, replied, "Indeed she does that. Why, the only young lady who could hold a candle to Lucy Pride was her sister."

But the old lady, with the sure touch of malice, said, "I quite agree, but actually I was thinking of Spencer Mather at that moment more than of his wife."

I knew already the basis of the slanderous remark, and Dr. McAllister filled in some of the details for me. Hopestill's father had been a notorious libertine, had married Charity Pride for her money, had flaunted in her face his philanderings with common women, and had died most disgracefully at a house party when, drunk, he had been thrown by a spirited horse that he could barely have managed sober. His wife died shortly afterwards of humiliation, it was believed. The doctor pointed to the grand piano at the left of the love-seat. "Miss Pride keeps this, mind you, not in memory of her sister who was quite accomplished but in memory of Spencer Mather's brutality. It has a dummy keyboard. He was extremely sensitive to noises and could not bear to hear scales. After he got her this travesty—and she was so mild she didn't protest—he used to say, 'Look at poor Charity. She plays all day long and never gets anywhere.' "

In reply to my suggestion that the ill-will between Miss Pride and her niece stemmed from the former's dislike of Spencer Mather, Dr. McAllister said with a smile, "We don't speak of 'ill-will' between them, my dear. To use my grandmother's phrase, we say they are both 'strong characters,' But, yes, that is perhaps why they don't get on. That and the fact that Hope is said to resemble her aunt as she was at twenty—don't ask me why the similarity annoys her. One would think she'd feel the opposite when people say of Hope, 'She's the image of you, Lucy.' "

Miss Pride had leaned over the diminutive and still fidgeting form of Otis Whitney and was saying to Mrs. McAllister, "I heard you mention Manchester. I understand the summer was, as they say, a 'dud.' Hope wrote that if it hadn't been for your Philip's little visit the whole season would have been a total loss."

"Don't flatter me, Lucy," laughed the old lady and, turning to the Admiral, said, "Isn't she the purest Christian to compliment me on that no-account grandson of mine! There's nothing I'd rather believe. Why, I would be overjoyed if I could think that wild young rascal occupied the least place in Miss Hopestill Mather's heart! No, Lucy, my dear, *I* know and *you* know that she's a sensible girl. Look at him"—she pointed to my companion and at the same time sent him a conniving and adoring smile to indicate that she was merely playing a game, merely looking out for his interests—"he's barely civil! And I see he has already victimized the youngest lady in the room. I give you my word of honor, he has been boring her with some awful descriptions of his interminable 'cases.' Really now, Lucy, admit he's not nice."

Philip flushed and shook his head at his grandmother like a reproving parent. His gesture was unfortunate for she cried, "Now he's signaling me to hush! You see, he has a bad conscience. Admiral Nephews, what would you do with such a rogue?"

Miss Pride, who knew perfectly well that Philip was the apple of his grandmother's eye and who took as an insult to her intelligence this deprecation of him—so false that the voice with which she ran him down was brimming over with love—said, "I can't say I see eye to eye with you. What you say of Philip applies much more to Hope. Perhaps we're both right, though, and in that case . . . well, birds of a feather flock together."

The old lady was outwitted, for she could not admit that what Miss Pride said was precisely what she meant, that Hopestill was the unruly, fickle egotist that for the sake of her campaign against their marriage she had pretended her grandson was. She rose, fumbled for her stick, and said in a voice audible to everyone in the room, "Perly, Amy Brooks is coming to dinner with me next Tuesday. Can I expect you too? We can't get along without you if we play 'I am a famous man.'" And to Miss Pride, she added, "I dare say I couldn't engage Hope for that evening, could I?"

"On the contrary," rejoined Miss Pride, "she likes nothing better than to go to your house. Shall I give her a message?"

"I thought she was going to New York immediately," said the foiled grandmother.

"Not until next week." Then, with a slight sharpening of her expression, for evidently she had changed her tactics and had decided that it was better for the time being not to expose her niece to the determined old woman, she said, "But she will be occupied with packing. No, perhaps I'd better not mention it to her, for she would want to come and she really wouldn't have the time."

Mrs. McAllister sighed with relief, blew her grandson a kiss, and hobbled from the room on the Admiral's arm. Her place was filled at once by Mrs. Frothingham who asked for another cup of tea and said, "I'm lingering disgracefully long. I want to see Hope and hear all about what she's planning to do in New York. I do think she's too clever to go off all by herself. Can she really be serious about studying psychology?"

"You must ask her, Evelyn, for I'm too ignorant of the subject to know. Can anyone be serious about it? I must confess *I* can't. I have no more faith in dreams and the like than I have in Sally Hornblower's spirits. By the way, have you heard her latest? She swears that at a séance not long ago a Japanese girl was present and asked to be connected with some departed relative and, my dear, not only did the connection go through but the medium gave the message in colloquial Japanese!"

"Odd as that is," said Mrs. Frothingham in a lowered voice, "it's no worse than the way Arthur Hornblower has been cutting up. Have you heard . . ." But Miss Pride put her finger to her lips and motioned toward Mr. Pingrey who was still talking excitedly to Miss Brooks. "Is he . . . ?" queried Mrs. Frothingham. Miss Pride nodded and I caught the whispered words, "Berthe and I are campaigning in that sector."

Philip McAllister covered his smiling lips with his hand and then, on the pretext of examining a pot of philodendron, murmured to me, "My grandmother would like me to marry Amy Brooks. As you've probably deduced by now, our free will is purely relative. My mother had first say about where I was to go to school—

there was a great to-do about it, I've been told, when I was two hours old—and my grandmother agreed on Groton instead of St. George only on the condition that I marry Amy who was then sixteen months old."

"And you don't like her?" I asked.

He did not answer. In less time than it had taken for the sound of my voice to carry to him, he had moved into a world poles apart from mine. I knew by the eager light that suffused his pale face, until this moment drawn and mask-like with fatigue, and by the tensing of his fingers from which arose a hygienic odor, that what had galvanized him and was still invisible to my eyes was some private shock. I had heard the front door open and a feminine voice say, "Good afternoon, Ethel." The interval between the salutation and the appearance of the guest in the doorway—during which I identified the voice as the same one I had heard in this room when Miss Pride had left me in the vestibule—was an ordeal for both of us and in order to hide, on the one hand his impatience as a lover, and on the other, my curiosity, we began to exchange views on the probable success of Miss Pride's memoirs as if it were the subject we had wanted to bring up all along but had been prevented by the intrusion of gossip which we could not help overhearing. And when Hopestill entered, even though nothing could have torn his eyes away from her, my friend, in an untroubled voice, was telling me that he liked nothing so much for bedtime reading as personal reminiscences and hoped Miss Pride would take Saint-Simon as her model.

Hopestill Mather, whose autumnal hair I remembered from the day at the Hotel, paused at the door like an actress over-doing her entrance in the fear that the audience would not applaud. And then she pressed forward, leisurely, through the assembly of guests and bandy-legged slipper-chairs. Her eyes were astray as she murmured courtesies which marked her as a person of poise and breeding, as though she were ambling through an art gallery, untouched by what she saw but knowing, with a firm, sure, aristocratic knowledge, that what she saw was right: that the Rubensesque woman, who had been seated all afternoon beside the fireplace in conversation with a distinguished middle-aged man, was not to her esthetic taste, but that she recognized genius in the composition; that her cousin Amy Brooks belonged to an eminent school though she lacked the characteristic color that marked even the lesser works of Rembrandt. Though she might despise her aunt and her aunt's friends, she seemed not to question their essential mettle: they were the authors and the stewards of reality. For the time being, I had gathered, she had chosen to visit other worlds, both real and unreal, by which she had been remembered in the last will of a larger order than New England. Between these greetings (the uniform warmth and urbanity of which, exactly like that I had observed in Dr. McAllister, made me see, with a pang of envy, that to start with they had a fundamental fraternity), as she held up her manners like the emblem of a secret cult, she showed by a smile in our direction that she was sorry to be detained in her progress to us who were, she promised, to receive the whole heart of her vivacity and not merely these pulsations which she allowed to the others.

Even from this distance and unable to distinguish her voice from those chattering others, or to see, because of the dim light, what sort of body encased the person I had envied for so many years, even so I had a feeling of that allurement that had been hinted to me in various ways, for though she was not beautiful (there was enough light for me to see that) she emanated a terrible femininity, like a soporific perfume, so that the men, while they rose promptly to their feet, allowed her to speak first as if they needed time in which to collect their wits.

She bent down to kiss her aunt as Admiral Nephews stood up. "I'm next," he cried. "Hope, you outshine yourself. When are you going to have dinner with me?"

The girl turned up her smiling face to him and received his kiss. "You name the night, Admiral Nephews. For you, I'm always free, sir." She sat down beside her aunt and they began to talk so amiably that I doubted if, after all, they really were enemies. But they spoke formally as if, while they were good friends, they were not altogether intimate. Hopestill complimented her aunt on the sandwiches and Miss Pride congratulated her on her costume, even though she had once told me in disgust that the girl spent nine-tenths of her time and all of her money on clothes, an indulgence shocking to a woman whose wardrobe consisted of four identical black broadcloth suits and two dark red evening dresses, one made of velvet and the other of crêpe. Her niece had converted a simple yellow dress into a "costume" by the addition of an Indian belt made of great silver conches. Her arms were laden with bracelets and her fingers with turquoise rings. Her long hair hung as straight as rain, an angelic, down-burning fire that parted for her small, perfect face which disdained the pastes and pigments of the cosmeticians, but was pale where God intended it to be and shone where He had burnished it. She was tanned from the seashore sun and, from her ride this afternoon, retained the last glow of rosiness in her cheeks. She was tropical like the surcharged parrot; one felt that her flesh was hot to the touch and that her small feet, shod in white buckskin moccasins, were furnished with velvet pads like a cat's. When I first took her in, I did not recognize her belt as Indian or her yellow dress as being of a particular cut and fashion: it was rather as though she were clothed in some natural, unpurchased habiliments like a leopard or a Luna moth.

"Oh, please don't third-degree me," she said, laughing, to Mrs. Frothingham. "I don't know anything about psychology. I'm taking it up because I've soured on painters after this summer. It would shock Auntie if I told you why."

"Shock isn't the right word, my dear," said Miss Pride. "The nonsense of Wainright Lowe hasn't shocked me for years, but no one bores me more to hear about."

"Hope!" cried Mrs. Frothingham. "Don't tell me you picked *him* up!"

"How was I to know? Of course I *did* know the moment I stepped into his studio. But I simply couldn't shake him."

"He paints his pictures in half an hour," said Miss

Pride. "As a matter of fact, I think I could do them in fifteen minutes."

The Admiral said, "I must confess, Hope, that I'm glad you've gone in for something besides all this painting hanky-panky. Psychology is a little too new-fangled for me, but still . . ." He rose and kissed Miss Pride's proffered hand. "As always, I've enjoyed it, ma'am, and unless I'm dead before then I wager I'll show up again next week. I'm well pleased you've got yourself a companion for the winter since this intellectual young lady insists on going off to Babylon." The whole group at the tea-table glanced toward me and the Admiral said, "We talk the same language, Miss Marburg and I. I'm going to steal her some afternoon for a walk around Fresh Pond. Far from the madding crowd's ignoble strife, we'll revel in the English poets. Good-by Lucy, good-by, Hope, good-by, Evelyn. Good-by, you three graces!"

Mr. Otis Whitney, who for the past few moments had been invisible, being blocked out by the Admiral's bulk, stood up and implored, "Lincoln, if you've got your car, would you be so good as to drop me?" But Miss Pride pulled him by the coattails and said rather sharply, "You only just came, Otis. You haven't told me a thing about Frank. Now do begin from the beginning. Where did he get that disgusting disease?"

Hopestill excused herself from her aunt and Mrs. Frothingham and came to us. The doctor rose and, erect as he was because of his deformed back, gave the appearance of leaning forward. The hand he offered shook and the voice with which he greeted her was unnaturally high and diffident. He was not used to her yet, I thought, and his eyes had not accustomed themselves to her ferocious radiance. Oblivious to all save this ignited tulip, he raised his hand and touched her hair. I sighed without meaning to, as if the inhalation were the vehicle for this strange scene. The doctor introduced us and, sensible of my presence for the first time since he had heard the front door open, reinstated me as his friend. "Sonie will be glad you've arrived at last. She's been here a month and this is her first public appearance."

"How do you do?" said the girl, smiling warmly at me. "I'm sure it's been awfully dull for you, and I haven't a doubt that Philip hasn't lifted a finger to amuse you."

The doctor made the lame excuse that he had been busy, although, had he thought back, he would have known that I—who until this moment had not resented his neglect—could hardly swallow it since he had intimated that he had come to tea here several times when he expressed surprise that he had not seen me before. But I was more embarrassed by Hopestill's scolding than he, feeling that he found me a bore or that he had avoided me because he pitied my misfortunes or dreaded my complaints.

Hopestill looked restlessly about the room. "Five minutes of this sort of thing and I'm at the end of my tether. Don't you think we should have cocktails?"

There was a good deal of Miss Pride in her, I saw. Her eyes were similar, small and nacreous like painted ornaments. She had been allotted less than her share of flesh and it was as dry as paper, and so pale her mechananism seemed to run by something other than blood or else in her the blood was really blue. And her voice, which her cold spirit permitted to be merely tinged with cordiality, had the same metallic opacity, lacking resonance and melody but having instead a vast range of pitch.

"I would be delighted," said Philip. "But doesn't your aunt belong to the school of thought of my sainted grandmother which holds you mustn't drink for pleasure but for the sake of your appetite?"

Hopestill smiled vaguely. "If they're similar in that respect, they wouldn't admit it, would they? Why, if Auntie knew that, she'd either turn teetotaler or dipsomaniac."

"Or else tell everyone that Grandma got the idea from her and was secretly an old soak."

"I need a drink." She had been toying with the foliage as she sat on an ottoman. She was dismembering a spray of fern. "I hate this hair-like vegetation, don't you, Miss

295

Marburg? It fits though. My horse threw me twice today in the ring, in the mud. My trousers were ruined. I beat hell out of him. *That* I enjoyed."

A pained silence followed her confession of sadism. To consolidate our awkward triangle and to change the subject, I said, "I met your cousin and her two tall beaux this afternoon." And then, because she seemed to think I had something more to say, I told her of the predicament I had been entangled in by Your Esteemed Uncle Arthur Hornblower. Her face, instead of reflecting the amusement I had expected, hardened against me and anger brightened the flare of her eyes. I learned my lesson in the silence that followed my joke's collapse, but sick with humiliation, thought my experience would never benefit me, that this defender of her relatives whom she could not, nevertheless, abide, would refuse to have me any longer in the house. She looked away from me. "Have you heard the marvelous thing Uncle Arthur did? He changed his will last summer and left something like a hundred thousand to Vanzetti's sister. Isn't that really *good* of him?"

The doctor, perhaps not realizing that her chief purpose had been to reproach me, said, "Why, what a turncoat you are! I thought you were the most rabid supporter of the Committee's decision. Don't tell me you've got some inside information about their innocence!"

"On the contrary, I'm perfectly sure and always will be sure that they were guilty, but that doesn't mean Vanzetti's sister was. And Uncle Arthur, after all, could be prompted simply by generosity, couldn't he?"

"No," said the doctor with a smile. "But I say, about those drinks? Does she keep the makings in the library?"

"We'll have to have second best and that's in the pantry. Look, there comes the Happel. What a pity she has just missed seeing Amy flanked on each side by a tall beau!"

The scorn of her remark, far surpassing the acidity of mine, was deliberately aimed at me, and by it she gave me to understand that she was at liberty to say what she liked about her dowdy cousin, but that it would behoove any outsider to keep a civil tongue in his head. I was distressed when Dr. McAllister left us to confer with Miss Pride, for, since she had imposed upon my conversation a prohibition that applied to the only thing we had in common, that is, the guests, I had nothing to say to Hopestill. But she realized that it was her duty to select a subject for us and she gave me a sociable smile which only made me uncomfortable because it showed that she had now put me in my place and, confident that she would have no further trouble with me, could proceed.

"Aunt Lucy's house isn't the gayest in the world, is it? Has she sent up Mercy to keep you company?"

"Mercy?"

"She's my aunt's cat. Since her last accouchement, she's been rather peckish. Even so, I'm surprised Aunt Lucy hasn't introduced you. Do you like our house?"

I answered abstractedly, so overcome was I at the idea of Miss Pride's cat. There was something perplexing and a little unpleasant in her concealment of it. (When, on the following morning at breakfast, I confronted her with my knowledge, saying that I would like to see Mercy, she said, "She is nervous. Perhaps in time she'll be up to society again," quite matter-of-factly as if the person in question were a friend for whom a long sea voyage had been too much. I said it was strange that I had never heard the cat cry. "Oh, no," answered Miss Pride, "she's not much of a talker. She's well satisfied with her bedroom just off mine.")

"I'm sorry I must go on to New York so soon," said Hopestill. "Tell me, do you think you'll be able to stick it out?"

"Stick it out?"

"Yes, I mean it's rather a grim prospect, I should think, to be shut up in this gloomy old house where the ghost of my blue-nosed grandpa walks every night. Or perhaps you have friends in Boston?"

"A few," I replied warily.

"In that case, then, you won't be lonely. Where are you from, by the way? Auntie told me, but I have a rotten memory."

"Chichester," I said.

"Oh, of course. I know nothing about the place. I haven't been there since I was a very little girl." She paused and looked closely into my face, and then went on. "Chichester has produced a very objectionable person by the name of Betty Brunson."

"I know her."

"She turns up on Christmas Eve, at places she'd never be invited, with an entourage of horrible boys from New York. She's exactly like a guide and says, 'Now this is typical of Boston,' or 'You'd never find this outside Massachusetts,' and all in the world she's pointing out is someone's Cape Cod lighter or a Currier and Ives."

I was so panic-stricken at the thought that I might sometime encounter Betty Brunson in Boston that I could make no comment. Hopestill gave me a second of her searching looks.

"Have we met before?"

"No," I replied firmly.

"Your face is so familiar. Were you at the Porcellian dance last spring?"

"No. I'm sure we haven't met. I would remember you."

"I couldn't forget *you*. We *have* met, Miss Marburg. It was ages ago, wasn't it?"

Again I denied it. But she pursued. "Perhaps you were in Chichester one time, a hundred years ago, when I had a nasty meal with Aunt Lucy and Cousin Josie."

"Perhaps," I grudgingly allowed.

"Look here," she said, "I must get this straight. Auntie has been so damned mysterious about you. I know you're going to do the famous memoirs but what else? Are you somebody incognito? As they say, scratch a Russian waitress and you find an archduchess. I suppose it works the other way too, scratch an archduchess and you find an upstairs maid."

Taken off my guard by her unconsciously shrewd guess, I made a slip of the tongue which, had her attention not at that moment been diverted, would have let her know instantly all she needed to know about me, for I said, "No, ma'am, I'm not either of those."

"Look, Philip has seduced my aunt. What a perfect

butler posture! There—I've shocked you." She laid her hand on my arm. "*So* sorry."

The girl was aboriginal and had eaten the whole apple. A pagan priestess in her yellow vestments, she moved her supple arms and torso as if in an abortive dance, turning now to the infatuated doctor who was bringing the drinks like sacrificial libations, and now to me, her face a plastic substance that alternately showed derision or aggrieved boredom, or, if she had a moment before glanced at her aunt, a profound and muddled rebellion. In order to lower the tone of our conversation I said, "Do you sketch, Miss Mather?"

"No. Neither do I write nor take part in amateur theatricals. But I *am* literate. I'm what my long-suffering aunt calls 'advanced.'"

My question had been a happy one and she talked for some time, even after we had been interrupted by the arrival of the drinks, with a real enthusiasm which made me think she had, after all, some sort of inner life and that her interest in dress and horses was no more than a trifling avocation. She had recently "discovered" psychology and now felt she had wasted her whole life on trivialities. "The pious doctor calls me heathen because I believe in dreams and the *anima mundi*. You know, don't you, that identical twins have been known to have the exact same thought at the same moment even though they have been miles apart?"

The moment she had excitedly uttered the statement, her interest vanished. She sighed and said through a vapor of ennui, "Of course that sort of thing is trimming. What I'm interested in is the good of psychology, that is, the advertised good: no one, they tell me, needs to be neurotic."

"I quite agree. I wish you would tell that to your friend Pope," said the Countess von Happel who, with another woman, crowded into our little recess. Hopestill introduced me to the large, fragrant Viennese and to the other, Mrs. Choate. The Countess, speaking to her friend and to me, explained, "Pope is a surrealist, ladies, but I call him a fool. Hope, he brought me a gouache called 'When Lilacs Last in the Dooryard

Bloom'd' though it was just a great gray study of nothing at all. If you turned it upside down, you got a sort of feeling that a goose was squatting on a picket fence. I asked him why on earth he had picked the title and he said that the rhythm matched the 'color cadences' but, my dears, there was no color in it!" Fashionably dressed and set with colossal jewels, the Countess reached across to squeeze Hope's hand and with an equine laugh cried, "Admit it's a damned fraud."

"Oh, Berthe, *don't* let's have that all over again. You know I'm *quite* able to see the virtue of your Davids and Rembrandts and Bellinis. You just judge them and modern painting on different psychological levels."

"That's the fraud! Psychological levels indeed! But darling, let me tell you the rest of the story about Mr. Pope. He came to my last Friday wearing bathing trunks, galoshes, a figured waistcoat and an enormous tam-o'-shanter. Naturally we ignored him. We're not amused by such clowns, at least not in a small music room."

"He was pulling your leg," said Hope.

"Well, my soul, don't you suppose I knew that? But he got no satisfaction out of his performance and he's ruined himself so far as I'm concerned. I shouldn't dream of letting him come again. Annaliese Speyer was quite faint when she saw him. Really, she was! I had to send for aromatics."

The Countess resembled photographs I had seen of Empress Augusta Victoria. Blond bangs, arranged beneath a little green velvet hat, imperfectly concealed a high, wide forehead which, as the conventional sign of intelligence, was enhanced by a pair of large blue eyes, half-closed with a superciliousness which also infected the well-shaped, slightly curving mouth. Dominating the whole was a noble nose, too large, but soundly and handsomely built, and that this eminent organ, in which all the pomp of her history was centralized, might be displayed to its fullest advantage, she carried her head at a backward tilt. Less fine than the elevated nose but more commanding was the Germanic bosom of which the velvet covering was like the hull of some fictitious fruit. The voice, initiated in some other region, trav-

300

eled through the buried core and was flavored with a stout sweetness as though her words were sopped in rich, old wine. I should have guessed that she had been a singer from the massive bust, the voice, and the carriage. I did not, but she told me. She took the cocktail I handed to her and with her free arm encircled my waist so that I was gently drawn to her.

"You make me think of a pupil I once had in Vienna. Do you like Schubert?" I said I could not distinguish one composer from another and that I much regretted my bad ear. "Well, then, we'll train that ear. No one in Boston has a better gramophone or more gramophone records than I. You come to see me always."

The word "gramophone" misled me: I imagined a small box with a black enameled horn, shaped like a morning glory. Such an instrument had been kept in a far corner of the lobby at the Hotel Barstow, and occasionally in the afternoon when the guests had had their naps and had gone out for a brief "constitutional," I put on *Der Tannenbaum* or *Ich Liebe Dich* or "Drink to Me Only with Thine Eyes" sung in a sad, rippling tremulo which brought tears to my eyes. I told the Countess I was grateful, but this was a lie: her loving gesture, though it was only a part of her patronizing, impersonal manner, had made me think of my mother and had returned me directly, by no détours of specific memory, to the horror of womanly affection which I thought I had outgrown. As in a long moment when I rested against the firm pouch of her bust and inhaled the odor of lilac, as fresh and springlike as if it came from the living bloom, and my only thought was how best to disengage myself from her embrace, Dr. McAllister, from across the room where he had taken a cocktail to Miss Pride and Mr. Whitney, shot me a look of warning or disapproval and simultaneously I felt the Countess' strong arm tighten about my waist. Before my mind's eye, like the immobile tableau of a dream, she and I appeared in this fond attitude, alone, before the sorrowing tin morning-glory in a dim, overheated room. I said in haste, "But I'm not often free. I'm studying stenography and my classes last all day!"

She let me go and laughing on one rich, contralto note, chided me, "Go on then, dissembler! You don't regret a bit that you can't tell Bach from Offenbach."

Everyone laughed at her play on words. Miss Pride smiled and said to me, "You mustn't miss an opportunity like that, Sonia. Not everyone is admitted to that famous salon." Horribly embarrassed by my blunder as well as by my egotistical assumption that this resplendent personage had an ulterior motive in her cuddling, I protested, and the hearty woman, speeding me on with a resounding smack on my backside, forgave and engaged me to come two weeks hence to a *Kaffeeklatsch* where I would find other people "in the same boat" with myself.

Miss Pride at last released Mr. Whitney, who for the past half hour had been fussing on the very edge of the sofa, so anxious to return to the hospital bedside of his son to congratulate him on the good tidings he had received from Dr. McAllister. He had, being at the end of his patience and ready to scream with vexation, finally risen and squeaked like a schoolboy, "Lucy, I *have* to go!" Clutching his hat, which he had refused to give up when he came in, in the hope that he would be able to make a flying visit, he dashed from the room. Miss Pride left her post and came over to speak to the Countess.

"I hoped you would come in," she said. "I rang you up earlier to make sure, but you weren't home. I have a bit of news for you. You know what I mean. I had a telephone call from New York this morning."

"Indeed!" cried the Countess and a flush of excitement illuminated her already well-lighted face. "Well, darling, can't we step over there?"

They moved off arm in arm toward the tulip-wood commode and stood there talking gravely for some time. I thought it singular that these two should have a secret. Hopestill, perhaps sensing my curiosity, enlightened me. Both of them, being shrewd business women, were in the habit of exchanging tips on the stock market, but did so out of earshot of everyone else, partly because they knew their passion for finance (which they had managed to dissociate from "cash" and "money" and approached as a pure science) would be considered in bad taste, and partly because they were frankly unwilling to share with anyone else the precious information that their Wall Street brokers periodically hissed over the wires. They were subscribers to the daily forecast of the Dow-Jones averages and to Barrons, and when they met, if it were at a dinner party, in Stearn's department store, or in Mrs. Gardiner's palace, they instantly locked arms and conversed in whispers, comparing notes on the vagaries of the Greyhound Bus Company, like doctors consulting on a difficult case.

Mrs. Choate, stranded with the three young survivors of the tea-party, glanced from one to another of us and chose me to receive her first remark. "I know you must be a capable young woman. Just fancy learning stenography! Why, it's ever so much cleverer than my little avocation "

She studied me brightly. Hopestill and Philip, refusing to come to my aid, began a private conversation and I was obliged to inquire what Mrs. Choate's avocation was.

"I have taken up cookery. You know I'm a southerner and though I've been here for many years, I've never got used to Irish servants. I simply can't manage them! My cooks won't cook as I tell them to. And last year, I had gone without hoe-cake as long as I could bear it, so I simply went to the kitchen one Thursday and made myself hoe-cake. Ever since then, I've spent every Thursday experimenting. I'm always saying to Hopestill that she ought to take it up."

The woman gave Hope a humorous wink which missed fire and received no response. She went on, "Of course *no* one north of the Mason-Dixon Line knows how to cook."

Hopestill's voice was suddenly raised and I had the feeling that what she said had no part in her conversation with Philip but was merely thrown out as a bait. "It's a nuisance finding a restaurant when one's dining with a Negro."

The doctor, taking up her game, maliciously replied, "An awful nuisance. It's simpler just to dine at home."

Mrs. Choate paled. But though her face, a large and

youthful one, wore a hurt, quizzical look, she said determinedly to me, "Perhaps you'll come to me some Thursday for a meal of greens and spareribs. My soups and desserts are not strictly southern, for I invent things, but the main course is always authentic."

"I had a splendid time at his apartment in Harlem . . ." Hope was saying.

Rebuffed, Mrs. Choate rose. "I'm going to interrupt that conference of the experts over there. I want to tell Miss Pride my latest discovery. I have invented a divine egg, poached in thinned tomato paste."

Hope grimaced, composed her features, and said to the outsider, "Oh, Mrs. Choate, I hear you've turned cook. I'm fascinated. Do you really make corn-pone and all those amazing things?"

But the woman was on her guard. "It is nice to see you looking so well, Hope," she said. "Philip, how is your dear mother?"

"Mother is very well," he replied. "She has almost lost her British accent."

Mrs. Choate smiled sickly and took her leave.

"She isn't southern at all," explained Hopestill to me in a whisper. "She's just a terrible fake. You'd think she'd been born with a mint julep in her hand and a fine old southern grudge against the damned Yankees that did in her granddaddy's plantation. My Aunt Lucy, who can't stomach her and couldn't from the very first, found out that she lived in New Orleans for ten years before coming here but before that lived in California! But did we sound too beastly?"

They had, indeed, sounded beastly to me and I had suffered as much discomfiture as Mrs. Choate. I could not answer but instead inquired, "Is she the Countess' friend, then?"

"She's nobody's friend. She either just shows up at tea time and manages to walk in with someone else, or she makes everyone come to perfectly horrible parties— she uses marshmallows in her salads and starts off with hot wine and I'm sure none of *that* rot is southern—so that she has to be asked back."

Miss Pride had observed the approach of the bore

and quickly guided the Countess along to meet her, then seized Mrs. Choate and marched her back to us. "Of course I think," said Hopestill, "that the Negroes are the coming race."

The Countess leaned over and embraced Hopestill. "To use that word you're so fond of, Cousin Hope, you're too 'advanced' for me. So I'm going to leave before I hear why you think the Negroes are the coming race. You have frightened me enough already with your threat that Dali and Chirico will come into their own and reign forever. I couldn't bear to have the blackamoors reigning too! I love you! Good-by! Come along, Mrs. Choate, I'll drop you."

Miss Pride, to my astonishment, murmured to me, "From the top of a high building, I hope."

Our hostess went out with the ladies and from the vestibule, we heard her say, "Mrs. Choate, there is an article on New Orleans in a recent issue of *The Atlantic* that ought to interest you."

"Really? I never read *The Atlantic*. I just skim it the way I do the Bible." The Countess chuckled, but Miss Pride said coldly. "Some other day I must ask you to explain that provocative remark." There were brief adieux and afterwards Miss Pride went upstairs to dress.

The emptied room seemed smaller, for it was now quite dark at the windows and the pale lamps revealed only their immediate environs. We moved toward the fire. I knew that I should leave Hopestill and the doctor, but the cocktails had made me careless and drowsy. I did not want to lose my warmth by going up to my room where the fire had probably died.

"Sonia—that's all right, isn't it?—made a conquest of the Countess, Perly."

"That's only Berthe's way."

"You mean she loves *all* young girls?" said Hopestill with a laugh. "Tell me: How did you find us?"

"Oh, Hope!" protested the doctor.

"Don't be absurd, Philip! She didn't miss anything. Haven't I the right to know the total impression she's got?"

"I had a pleasant afternoon," I said. I could have

added that this termination of it was as disagreeable as anything I had ever encountered.

Hopestill extended me her small hand which, in my clasp, was as lifeless as the hand of a sawdust doll. "It's been so nice to meet you, Sonia. The best of luck."

I had not expected to be dismissed so soon and, clumsy in my surprise, I knocked over an ash tray on a small table by the hearth. I bent to pick up the cigarette stubs but Hopestill said, "Oh, for goodness' sake, don't bother about that."

Reddening furiously, I started to the door. The doctor walked across the room with me. "I wanted to ask you," he said, "if you still go every Sunday?"

"Of course," I replied.

"That's right. You're awfully good. By the way, don't think we're giving you the cold shoulder. The fact is I . . . we haven't seen one another for quite some time. We're *very* old friends, you know."

"Yes," I said, but my voice was unconvincing and he must have known that I was offended.

"Believe me," he said anxiously, "you *are* a good girl."

The door closed behind me. My goodness remained in the library with its advocate while I put my eye to the keyhole. The doctor was kissing Hopestill's neck. She paid no attention to him but poked the fire and at last, lifting up her head to address the Copley, "Great God, it's just like dancing school except that then you didn't have that ramrod down your back! Perly, Sonia is just the girl for you and the battle is half won because she's obviously mad about you." She flung back her head so that her hair reached to the middle of her back and laughed heartily.

"Hush!" said Dr. McAllister. "She may be in the hall."

I stood up quickly and went to the stairs, but I heard Hopestill pause in her laughter to say, "I meant absolutely no harm. I'm just a little giddy, and she was so *incredibly* solemn!" And then, as solemn as I had been, she added, "Imagine Aunt Lucy not telling her she had a cat! I swear I think the woman's mad."

Two

IN ORDER TO make my appearance at the Countess von Happel's *Kaffeeklatsch,* an attention to her I felt imperative since it was my first invitation in Boston, I had been obliged to negotiate with Mrs. Hinkel so that I could be excused from the last class, Business English. (The Countess kept European hours, serving her afternoon refreshments at four instead of five, a custom Miss Pride regarded as so novel that she was almost never went there to tea.) Mrs. Hinkel was furious at the presumption of her "laziest would-be professional woman" and said, "I suppose you think you know all about correct usage! I have not been headmistress of this college for fifteen years without observing, Miss Marburg, that the graduates of public schools, with the exception of those from the Latin schools, know next to nothing in regard to grammar. You may think now that dangling participles and 'due to' and prepositional phrases are the least of your worries, but the time will come when you will ask me for a recommendation and I will have to say, 'The candidate under consideration left much to be desired in her work in Business English.'

307

However, as the useless expenditure of my time and your money doesn't bother you, run, amuse yourself, go to the movies, go to the beauty parlor! Respecting your language, don't worry! Don't let business interfere with pleasure!" She dispatched me to my debauchery with a military salute and returned, secretly delighted with the rhetoric of her diatribe, to the book she had been reading called *Hints to Commercial School Teachers and Administrators.*

I would have liked to explain to her that the prospect of a musical afternoon afforded me no pleasure, that I could far better endure the boredom of the class in Business English (in which, as she perfectly well knew, I was the only literate pupil) than the snares I was bound to fall into at the Countess'. But I knew that I would only enrage her further, and I held my tongue. My hand was on the door knob when she burst forth again. "I may as well tell you, Miss, that I am so displeased with your work here, and feel so strongly that this expenditure of *my* time and *your* money is useless that unless I am informed of marked improvement in your attitude, I shall have to ask you to leave. My time is simply too valuable to be wasted." The threat was purest nonsense, for she would not have dreamed of parting with my money which came in regularly each week, but she was a great believer in intimidation as an academic principle, and having very soon discovered that I received her recriminations with just the degree of terror she needed to nourish her sense of power, she never let a day pass without summoning me to her office or cornering me in the corridor to remind me, exultantly, that my ignorance and lassitude were eating up her time.

I was on the point of tears, not so much from her scolding as from what was in store for me as I left the building and closed the outer door behind me, massive, black, embossed with a wreath. I was not only convinced that what Mrs. Hinkel had said was true, but also that the whole of my Boston enterprise was a fiasco. But just at the moment when I was wishing myself back in Chichester, I saw, mincing uncertainly down Dartmouth Street, a figure so familiar, so instantaneously reminiscent of the stuffed birds, the rocking chairs, and the chilled farina pudding at Friday luncheon, that its appearance was like an ominous symbol, and for a second or two I thought it had no substance or else belonged to a stranger and not, as I had at first thought, to Mrs. Prather. There was no turning back, for she walked quickly and was upon me before I could contrive an escape.

"Of all things," said Mrs. Prather, taking both my hands. "What on earth are you doing so far away from home? Do you and Mother live in Boston now? Around *here?*" I replied that I lived here, but by myself. Her weak eyes begot two tears and she squeezed my hands. "I'm the limit! Imagine not recalling that sad, sad story. Now, child, don't tell me a thing, I can read it in your face: you want work."

She opened her handbag which contained, I saw, an apple, a Hershey bar, and a great many loose lozenges, and withdrew a calling card on which she begged me to write my address so that when she heard of something she might get in touch with me.

"But I don't need work," I protested, making no move to take the proffered pencil.

She was surprised and, for the first time taking in my new, expensive clothes, she said forgivingly, "Dearie, it doesn't need to be all over for you. You write down the address and I won't hold it against you. We'll get you out of there just as quick as we can and no one will be the wiser. I would take you straight to Arlington this minute rather than have you spend another night in one of those places, but for the time being, I'm crowded for space."

Without mentioning Miss Pride, I made it clear to her that I was not living in a brothel. She was greatly relieved and said that in that case I might come to call on her some day and tell her "all about it." "Whenever you get tired of your present place, I know just the house for you. A dear friend of mine has never had a good second maid and I know she would take you in a minute if I recommended you to her. You would have a room to yourself, I happen to know, and two afternoons off not counting Sunday."

I was anxious to be off for I had just heard the bells at Trinity chiming a quarter past four, but Mrs. Prather held me another five minutes, describing the excellent treatment I would receive at the hands of her friend who, at last it appeared, was an invalid and in spite of suffering horribly from one of the digestive disturbances for which the Hotel guests had such an affection, had the "sweetest nature in the world." In parting, she tried to give me her Hershey bar which I refused, but not liking to seem rude, I asked if I might have one of the horehound lozenges. She then released me. "Good-by, good-by. I'm glad it's not what I thought. Now remember me and when you need me, come to Arlington. I'm in the phone book. I expect it's time for Cinderella to run home to her pots and pans. You know, the French people have an expression when they take leave of one another. Instead of saying 'good-by,' they say *au revoir* which means 'till we meet again.' So that's what I will say to my little Chichester friend, *au revoir*."

I did not stop running until I was two blocks from the Countess' house, and it was only then that I tasted the full flavor of the bitter, not unpleasant horehound. It was a taste that belonged exclusively to Chichester and the summertime, and it made me a little nostalgic. Although I realized that I had had a narrow escape and that I must henceforth be troubled by the knowledge that I might meet Mrs. Prather again round any corner and the next time might not be alone, this return of the past through the candy, despite my homesickness, restored my eagerness to continue the present time, and I was grateful for the old lady's errand that had carried her down Dartmouth Street in time to save me from a craven retreat.

The meeting had rendered me a service by taking my thoughts off the entrance I was about to make into a strange house, so that when I opened the street door, I rang the bell at once without having to wait for courage to lift my finger to the button. I was admitted by a manservant into a vast lobby lighted by three iron candelabra and a number of sconces placed at intervals like arc lights. I had heard of the Countess' prejudice against electricity, the effect of which, she claimed, was to destroy shadows, and shadows, like echoes and like the aftertaste of Moselle wine, were sources of inspiration to her. She had succeeded in creating with her candles a theatrical effect, and through some optical illusion made by the long shadows against the walls, which a highlight here and there revealed as lustrous and would have shone under electricity, the hall seemed much larger than it actually was and the ceilings loftier. I was guided over a Persian carpet and past "occasional" groups of high-backed chairs and console tables upon which stood vases of yellow rosebuds whose outer petals were ruffling into full maturity. Then, as though entering a bay from an estuary, we turned to the right into a wide, square room, dominated on the left by a staircase, illuminated like the entry with sconces, and on the opposite side by a portrait of the Countess in a double frame. She sat at a spinet in a pale blue Empire dress with her golden hair piled high, her head held well back to set off her nose. It was impossible to tell whether she were about to play or had just finished, for her musicianly hands rested in her lap, and the expression on her face gave no clue since all the other features were tyrannized over by the nose, sufficient unto itself. Just as the candlelight, perhaps intentionally, hinted that the owner conserved imported customs, older than the old Boston house, older than her own experience, dating from times before the fall of princes and the commercialization of palaces, and by its metamorphosis of the hall, otherwise so like all other halls on Beacon Hill, sharply designated the mistress as a member of a different species, so the portrait, pompous with the self-importance of the ruling class, gave those who viewed it to understand that an even further distinction was to be made between the Countess and her neighbors: that in that species she was a unique specimen, for she was not only aristocratic, but she was beautiful and talented as well, and, implied the station of the picture,

311

according to standards that were not local, the *most* beautiful and *most* talented woman in Boston.

As we reached the foot of the stairs, the manservant spoke for the first time. "The name, please?" When I had told him, he repeated my name, putting an interrogation mark after the "Miss?" not in contradistinction to "Mrs." but to "Princess" or "Baroness," as if he were not in the habit of announcing the untitled bourgeoisie. I took a dislike to him partly because of his tone and partly because of his impassive, coarse, cunning face in which I seemed to read condescension as if he had divined that until recently (or perhaps even now) I had been "in the service" like himself. I said sharply, "I am expected."

"Certainly," he said, a flicker of a smile adding, "Don't be so naïve as to think I will take your word for it," and he indicated a divan, wide as a bed and upholstered in yellow satin, where I might wait, and left me, sending his dignified shadow ahead of him between the misshapen parodies of the balustrades on the uncarpeted marble stairs.

The yellow sofa was so placed that from it one could look nowhere but at the portrait of the Countess; and so, in my enforced contemplation of it, I was amused to see that upon the spinet there stood a vase of yellow rosebuds, the duplicates of which were set in such fresh profusion upon the tables in the entry. But a second discovery was even more amusing: I had been struck by the radiance of the canvas because the nearest sconce to it was several feet away, and now I perceived that craftily concealed under the inner frame at the top was a long, fluorescent tube sending a smooth shower of light over the whole surface! This in a Puritan house! In the hall of a great lady so sensitive she could not abide electricity! It occurred to me that other people had not seen what I had but had simply taken for granted, or had not noticed at all, the extraordinary visibility of this one object in the shadowy lobby, for Miss Pride or Hopestill, when they had told me of the candelabra, would surely have told me of this inconsistency if they had ever observed it. For, although they were both fond of her as were their friends, they found Berthe von Happel irritating and would most likely have been delighted to learn that at least in one particular she was a fraud. "I don't mean to criticize Berthe's taste," Miss Pride had said, "because on one level it is superb taste, but I must say that there is something *malentendu* in the way she has turned poor Ralph Brooks' house into a museum. And not to put too fine a point on it, frankly, when I go there and the last thing I have seen is the Common, if I'm coming from Pierce's, or General Hooker, if I'm coming from Goodspeed's, I feel very much as if I were going into Loew's Orpheum."

The butler was gone so long that I began to think I had come on the wrong day or that the Countess was offended by my tardiness, or, worst of all, that she had not really meant her invitation, could not remember any Miss Marburg, and would instruct the servant to turn me out, a commission that would delight him. The the first time I reproduced the scene in Miss Pride's drawing-room, the date and the hour of the engagement were perfectly clear, "Friday week at four o'clock," but, as minutes passed and the porter of my banal name did not reappear and I again and again rehearsed the Countess' words in an effort to determine who was to blame for my mistake, I became so confused that had not the word *Kaffeeklatsch,* which I had never before heard spoken, been audible in each revision I made, I would have believed that the invitation was imaginary. Presently I heard the door-bell and stood up, thinking that the butler would come down to answer it and on his way would inform me of my verdict, and indeed, in a moment there came to me the sound of music as if a door had suddenly been opened on a floor above. Still, he did not appear. Yet I heard voices in the entry and immediately the treacherous butler, who had evidently come down another way in order to tease me, came into sight but vanished as soon as the visitor had turned toward the stairs. The visitor appeared tremendous, for he was magnified by the shadows: his pale hair, which might have been blond or white, lost and then regained its glow as he passed the first sconce. I stepped forward, still in the shadow, intending to ask him if this were the day for the *Kaffeeklatsch*. He wheeled, startled, and peered through the dimness.

"*Doch, ist's so spät?*" he said.

"*Nein, es ist früh, glaub' ich.*"

"*Warum denn . . . ?*" He came closer. "Oh," he said, "oh, forgive me. I thought you were my daughter, Annaliese. It's so dim here. I expect I'll find her upstairs. Excuse me!"

"*Ich bin auch Deutsche.*"

"*So?*" Impatient to be off, his eyes wandered up the stairs.

"I mean, sir," I said, "that for a moment I, too, was confused and I thought you were my father. But I see now that your dueling scar is not the same."

He gave a short, unamused laugh. "That's the way to tell, *nicht?*" And he ran up the stairs two at a time.

I had not, of course, mistaken him even though he did, in a general way, resemble my father, but I had been seized by a terrible longing to speak German and to be allowed to enter the upstairs room from which the music issued and which I conceived of as a world separate from Boston, the one to which I belonged and the only one in which I should ever be happy. But it was not only the man, apparitional and fugitive, that snatched me from the present time and Boston which I had hoped would be as familiar to me as a native habitat, it was, even more than him, the music. It was of a sort and played upon an instrument which I had never heard before: its academic precision was so intellectual, belonged so much to that altitude where mathematical progressions and retrogressions were animated by imaginative genius that, just as one cannot look directly at the sun, so I could not submit the part of the mind that hears without the protection of the part that sees. Thus, my pleasure came to me attended by memory of scenes or objects, my mother's face, the beach at Chichester, my father's rosary hanging in his shop, the summer drives to Wolfburg, so that the passage of the music to my heart was insulated, roundabout, enriched. And I saw, as though I stood upon it and not upon the costly

314

Persian rug, the sweating sand at Chichester, pawed by the surf on a glaring August day, where my father and I had stopped to watch a plover. The amber-clear, archaic notes, plucked from the siccative strings of the instrument I did not know, and the stranger's voice, and the somnolent waves cast out and entrapped my father's exclamation: *"Ein Regenpfeifer! Still!"* My longing to speak German was then elaborately if minutely satisfied by the redemption of *"Regenpfeifer,"* a word I had heard only that one time, twelve years before.

The cessation of the music reminded me that I had been waiting an unconscionable time and was no closer to the Countess von Happel than this romantic representation of her, larger than life size. I wondered if, by hanging it here, she had meant to tantalize as well as impress visitors who, unknown in the house, were not allowed to go at once into her presence. It was a mistake, if this had been her purpose, and an insulting one to prolong their suspense, for, like the magazines in the busy dentist's office, it became an unendurable bore, and one's temptation was to leave and come back on another day. The postponement of a disagreeable affair and the self-righteousness in which it has had its genesis afford as much relief as if the pain or the embarrassment has been undergone, is finished, and can be forgotten. But just as we throw down the magazine, so trashy it seems like a calculated insult to our intelligence, and prepare to announce cuttingly to the secretary that our time is precious, we had assumed, when we made the appointment for four, that we would be attended to at that time, the door opens and the dentist emerges smiling, disarming us with a genial apology and a word of sympathy about the suffering our wisdom tooth is causing us. I had reached the turn in the hallway and had just annexed a new feature to my grievance, for I was hungry and my vitals informed me that it was past the hour when it was my secret and shameful custom to eat two crullers and drink a cup of coffee in a small, steamy café at the top of Pinckney Street, an indulgence into which I had been forced by the meager fare at Miss Pride's tea-table. The butler, coming through a door at my right, which I had not noticed, stopped me, and said that I might go up now, that Madam had been playing and he had been unable to announce me at once. Then, by way of apologizing for his suspicions, he said flatteringly, like the dentist, "Madam is waiting for you."

2

"How d'ye do?" said the Countess who stood in the doorway and drew my arm through hers, the vegetative softness and fragrance of her person and the intense heat of the small room making me think of summertime. "It's a pity you had to wait. Tell me, how did you like that little likeness of me in the hall? Did you notice it?" She turned her profile to me, waiting for my answer, and when I gave it, saying that I had been charmed, she continued to pose a moment longer in imitation of the "little likeness" as if she were not in the least concerned with my opinion, the anticipation of which, in fact, had set every nerve in her body tingling. Then, pressing my arm against her, she said, "It's an excellent painting, even if you don't like the subject, isn't it? I debated with myself a long time before I hung it at all: Will people want to look at poor me? I said to myself. But what nonsense! The painting is the thing, you goose, people won't even recognize you, you're simply incidental to the composition." I agreed that the painting was excellent (for all I knew it was, but it had struck me as being remarkably dull), but that she was wrong in thinking people would not recognize her, for she, not the composition, was its *raison d'être*. She could not deny my praise, but brought up from her interior an exultant purr: "Did you look at the hands? They are divine!"

This toll was levied upon every newcomer; some, less green than myself, added a gratuity to the set fee. Twice during that afternoon and many times thereafter, I observed the transaction carried out on the part of the Countess with a sort of childlike poise which made one feel that she was not so much vain as honestly amazed

316

at her endowments. And when she had made her concluding remark, to one person about the hands, to another about the throat or the eyes, in a lowered voice as though she were praising someone within earshot, she became an amiable, solicitous hostess dedicated to the wants of her guests. Like the hypodermic injection of adrenalin that instantaneously relieves the asthmatic, the Countess' hospitality at once made me forget my annoyance and my hunger. She now allowed me to pass through into a small, bare room which in no way conformed to the speculations I had made about it when I was half submerged in the yellow satin sofa. It was an ascetic's cell on the top floor and at the back of the house, presenting a view from the uncurtained dormer windows of chimney pots and blind brick walls. Central in the room and, unlike the portrait, requiring no contingents to play up its merits, stood a rosewood harpsichord from which had been plucked the brilliant, incisive tones I had heard downstairs. The owner's seal, a silver pitcher full of yellow roses, had been placed on the wing directly in the player's line of vision. The other decorations of the room were testimonial: uncolored photographs of Mozart, Bach, Haydn, Handel, with perukes and lacy jabots, hung in a row upon one wall and opposite, between two bookcases, a deep square frame preserved a letter signed "Franz Liszt." Here and there stood high-backed, uninviting chairs without arms or cushions. The music, the wild log fire, and the table of refreshments were the only provisions for comfort. A few of the chairs were occupied, and several people stood around the table by the windows where they helped themselves to coffee and cakes.

The Countess, leading me to the table, said, "You must have been late, for I began sharp at four. There's no point in coming at all if you miss the music."

"I'm very sorry," I told her. "I met someone on the way. But there will be more, won't there?"

"More?" she repeated incredulously. "Well, you *are* a baby!" But she patted my hand kindly and chuckled. "No, after I've played one opus I'm through, for I won't mix composers and I won't overindulge in one. But you didn't know. All's forgiven. Next time you'll know better and not let yourself be waylaid."

"Then I may come again?"

"If you don't, I won't forgive you. Now let me get you started and I'll come back to you later on. Just now I must speak to *Herr* Speyer and his adorable daughter. I'm losing them. They're sailing for Germany, naughty deserters!"

The Countess plucked a boy by the sleeve. "I want you to meet this unfortunate young lady who got here late and 'sat out' the whole of the minuet."

The boy, a tall, frail Jew with a womanly grace in his long, supple fingers and a transparency of skin, turned eagerly at the sound of her voice, but not to meet me. "Oh, Berthe, you were wonderful today! When I closed my eyes, I could have sworn it was Landowska playing. I was overcome!" He was, in truth, dumfounded and gazed at her with famished, radiant eyes. The Countess puckered her brow in annoyance. "You're a trifler, Gerhardt, but you don't take me in. I'm improving, yes, but I'm still a greenhorn. Now be good and give Miss Marburg a cup of coffee." His eyes implored her retreating figure to come back, but simultaneously he said to me, "Will you have cream and sugar?"

I was surprised at the Countess' treatment of *Herr* Preis who was obviously head over heels in love with her. And being certain, from my own observation as well as from remarks dropped by Hopestill and Dr. McAllister, that vanity was the principle of her being, I could not understand why she had taken his compliment with so much displeasure. I thought perhaps he knew nothing of music and, being devoted to it almost as much as she was to herself, she could not accept homage to one and not to the other. But then I learned, in our ensuing conversation, that the unhappy boy had himself taught her how to play the harpsichord.

Because the room was small, it seemed crowded with people. There were, in fact, less than a dozen. They had not gathered into groups but wandered with their coffee cups to examine the letter from Liszt or the unrewarding view from the windows or to smell the roses on the harp-sichord. A hush prevailed like that in an art gallery. The Countess, engrossed in a whispered conversation with *Herr* and *Fräulein* Speyer, made no attempt to remedy her guests' unease. I had no choice but to remain with Gerhardt Preis who would have liked to leave me, like a wounded animal, to nurse his hurts in solitude. Feel-ing that for the time being at least, he was incapable of talk, I made the opening remark myself, expressing my surprise that the guests were not, as I had expected them to be, in the midst of a spirited discussion of music. I had supposed, I said, that the company would be made up of experts and of ambitious amateurs.

Preis gave me a pained smile. "Berthe does not allow us to talk music here. Why should she? What more can be said than she says when she plays?"

"But surely," I said, "she must like to talk shop. I thought all artists did."

He shook his head. "Not the Countess von Happel. She's above it."

"Well, then, I'm more comfortable. I thought, when I came, that the talk would be too intellectual for me to follow."

"Intellectual!" he exclaimed to himself and for a mo-ment drank in his own scorn. Then facing me with a civil smile, he changed the subject. "Your name is the name of my father's town. Do you know it?" I told him I had never been to Germany. "I shall never be in Ger-many again. No doubt you guessed that I am a Jew. I was born in Marburg, but I have no memory of it, for my mother took me to Paris when I was very small and we only visited Germany in the springtime. My father was a manufacturer of surgical instruments and as you Americans say, he 'made a fortune.' I'm therefore of that species Berthe finds so odd. She's completely above money, you know." I smiled, recalling her parleys with Miss Pride.

The young man continued. "Have you heard about the time she met the millionaire department store owner from Chicago? It's the most *Happelisch* story in the whole Berthe *Sammlung*. This Croesus was houseguest of someone she had invited to one of her Saturdays and he had to be brought along. As they were starting in to dinner, she said to him, 'You must go first, for I understand that you are a "merchant prince" and my only other noble guest this evening is nothing but a poor little Russian baron.' "

A pretty, dark-haired girl beside us took a step closer and frowned at Preis. "I was at the dinner party. It was appalling, because, you see, Mr. Bruce was my mother's guest and it was very trying to us. For he was no means a stupid man and he perfectly well knew he had been horribly insulted. You know, she ought to inquire into people's histories before she plays such a joke as that. We all think he is a fine man and not at all coarsened by his money. And anyhow, he came from Boston in the first place and went to Harvard. I think the Countess goes too far."

"I disagree," returned the young man sourly and his tone implied that the girl had taken far greater liberties than their hostess had done with Mr. Bruce. "It's of no use to criticize Berthe. She's unique."

"You forget that this is Boston," said his adversary. "To be quite blunt, Mr. Preis, what I mean is that we New Englanders were here a great many years before you refugees started arriving."

Immediately she regretted her tantrum since, though she had enjoyed it, it had been a breach of manners. But instead of apologizing, she simply left us and vanished from the room without telling the Countess goodby. I remarked to Mr. Preis that she seemed to have had enough of the salon.

"No, she hasn't had enough at all, and unless Berthe overhears her sometime, she'll be back every Friday all winter long. No one refuses invitations to this house. Berthe shouldn't live in Boston, of course, for it's very bad for her. She only does it because she's fond of the way she's done her house, though I've told her a thousand times she could have done a better one in New York. She's made for a Central Park penthouse. I hope you appreciate her, as I see you're not a native. If you have the good fortune to be asked often, I *beg* you to

see how adorable she is. I'm afraid this is my last afternoon here! I've offended her somehow. She's as sensitive as the princess who could feel the pea."

His misery was so acute that he clasped his head in
his hands and did not stir but sorrowed behind the
handsome façade of his Hebraic face, his eyes closed, his
full red lips parted as if in illness. I was deeply touched.
"Perhaps things will come all right in the end," I said.

"Oh, you don't know her at all or you wouldn't talk
about things coming all right in the end. No, when she's
through, she's through once and for all. I could no more
get her to forgive me than you could get her to play
again this afternoon."

"But what have you *done*, Mr. Preis?"

"I fell in love with her, and that's against the rules.
You can remember me as the first exile from Berthe
von Happel's Fridays you ever knew. It's no consolation
to me to know that you will see a good many more like
myself in the course of time."

The Countess had gone to the door with the Speyers
and allowed *Herr* Speyer to kiss her hand. Then, drawing Annaliese to her, she kissed the girl on the cheeks
and on the lips and cried, "Don't change a particle
while you are gone. I shall die of a broken heart if you
cut off that golden tail about your head! Good-by! I love
you!"

Above the heads of the embracing women, there appeared the face of a young man which, as the girl sub-
mitted to a final kiss upon her mouth, registered a virile
horror, a response that the scene did not elicit in my
companion who had not taken his eyes off the Countess
for a second. The Speyers left and the head which had
materialized out of the shadows in the hall acquired a
body. The Countess smiled radiantly and had already
forgotten her grief at the farewells. She told the young
man she was sorry he had been kept waiting, that she
supposed he had got sick and tired of her "little likeness"
in the lobby. I turned my head in embarrassment at the
repetition of her welcoming speech and told Mr. Preis
that I would like to look at the view from the windows.

"Well, I shan't go with you. As for myself, I find that

kind of view uninspiring. Do you really like to look at dirty chimney pots? Anyhow, I must speak to this low character."

The low character, having acquitted himself of his debt, hastened to greet his friend. "You're still here, then. I must talk to you. Can't we go now?" He started, seeing me. "Oh, I'm sorry. I didn't know I was interrupting."

"I was just leaving."

"Don't on my account, please." His bashful smile, as he blushed, so delighted me that although I should have left him at once to his confidences which he was perishing to impart to his friend, I did not move aside. He looked no older than a schoolboy and I could scarcely believe Preis when he introduced us, describing Mr. Garvin as a Harvard graduate student of philology, and went on, to the boy's discomfort, to tell me that his formal study of language was not enough, but that he was now about to tackle Japanese.

I said, "I am living now with the daughter of a Sinologist, or so I've been told he was. He had a large library of Japanese books too."

The two young men laughed and Gerhardt whispered to me, "He wants only a *speaking* knowledge of it, Miss Marburg."

"That's what I wanted to tell you about," said the other. "He's beat my time, just as we predicted."

"Who? Kadish?"

"Who else? He ran her down yesterday. And mind you, he had just left me five minutes before."

I could not help my outcry of surprise, but having no wish at that moment to acknowledge my acquaintance with Nathan, I turned abruptly and filled my cup from the large silver urn on the refreshment table. But I did not move out of earshot of the young men who, pausing for a moment after my ejaculation, continued their talk.

"And let me tell you what else he's done," said Garvin. "He is contracted to teach one Harry Morgan of Park Avenue, Long Island, Beverly Hills, and Sun Valley enough German to get him through the course he flunked last year. Where the hell did he get the German is what I want to know."

"Oh, he knows German," said Preis. "He speaks it like a native."

"Are you pulling my leg? I didn't know he knew a word of it."

"There's a lot you don't know about him. And a lot I don't know. But tell me how he got the *Japanerin*."

"Not here. Later."

"But how with that . . . Oh, all right. We'll go in a minute. Let me stay just that long since it's the last time I'll be here."

Gerhardt's face had lighted as he saw the Countess bearing down on us, sending her resonant laugh ahead of her. "Come along, Preis, you can't accomplish any more here than you can at Jacob Wirth's," whispered Garvin.

The Countess, without glancing at Gerhardt, took me by the arm and as she led me away, called over her shoulder to Garvin, "Come next Friday, won't you?" Then, in a lowered voice to me, "I didn't ask him to come for the music as I'm sure he hasn't got an ear. I'm trying to drop the other one, and I thought I might get his friend to take him away with him. I'm sure he won't show up again next week."

I said, "I'm sure I shouldn't want to 'drop' anyone who admired me so much as Mr. Preis does you."

The Countess shuddered. "Ugh! I can't bear it. Really, give a refugee an inch and he'll take an ell. You understand, I hope, that I am not a refugee?" I took her question as meaning, "You don't think for a moment that I have Jewish blood, do you?" or else as implying that she had come here of her own free will from a society that was not in the least threatened by the upstart revolutionists who had played the devil with people of Gerhardt's class, definitely inferior to her own.

I flattered her a little on her excellent English and asked her then how long she had been in America. I listened to her voluble reply with only half my mind while the other turned over the remarkable mention of

Nathan Kadish's name. I had been titillated at the sound of it, but without immediately being jealous of the Japanese girl whom he had "run down" I devoutly hoped I would not see him. With a coldness that startled and even alarmed me, I knew that at this juncture in my life, other things—indeed, *all* other things—were more important to me than being in love and, particularly, in love with Nathan.

The Countess was saying, "I have been here seven years and I've been a widow five, so you see I've had to make my own way like all the immigrants. How precious you are to praise my English! It's all right for ordinary chatter, but you'd never guess how it fails me when I'm confronted with a conversation about music: I can't understand a word. And consequently, much to my sorrow, I've had to avoid friendships with my fellow-artists. You can imagine how painful that has been."

The Countess puzzled me and from time to time the thought flashed across my mind that she was a fraud. Yet, I had it on what was probably good authority, that her talent was prodigious. Miss Pride had told me that before her divorce from Count von Happel and her marriage to Ralph Brooks, she had enjoyed a brilliant reputation in Vienna both as a singer and as a pianist. Hopestill Mather believed that her practice of filling her salon with people ignorant of music was sheerest snobbery, that she was the victim of the common European delusion that Americans had no taste and no artistic principles. And still, as Miss Pride pointed out, she had, with the sagacity of good breeding, made several concessions to Boston. True, she had remained aloof from its musical enterprises (tyros, asking her opinion of Koussevitsky, received the damning faint praise, "He's all right, though by continental standards, these conductors in America are a society of mountebanks.") but had gone in whole-heartedly for its art. Rather too effusively for her fellow-citizens who knew better, she declared that the Fine Arts Museum was superior to the Luxembourg. Miss Pride said that her concessions reminded her of the Greek who had set up the statue of Aristides in Louisburg Square and then to conciliate the rest of

324

the community had faced it with one of Christopher Columbus. "Two negatives don't, in that case, make a positive," she said. "If we *must* have Aristides, whoever he may be, why can't we at least have Daniel Webster?"

I was curious to know why the Countess had left her Viennese husband, but nothing she said enlightened me. Except for brief interruptions when she told her guests good-by, that she loved them (this was her unvarying epilogue as the reference to her portrait was her opening gambit), she would not let me go but for three-quarters of an hour interrogated me minutely. She appeared disposed to regard my candidacy to her salon with favor. To my relief, she was incurious about my background and when, in connection with something she said about a room at the Chilton Club, I told her that I had never been there for I did not belong to society, she laughed and squeezed me closer to her.

"American society! The nobility is made up of 'cattle kings' and 'wool barons' and 'merchant princes' and between you and me, you're just as good as the rest of 'em, whoever you may be. I must confess a great weakness for New England, but try as I may I cannot take any stock in its society. Why, my people, when they are calculating time reckon in centuries, not in decades. It so amuses me to see Lucy Pride (I love her dearly and I hope you do too) show off her tea service which belonged to some governor or other in the eighteenth century. I don't call it 'old,' though I do call it pretty. I brought very little with me from Austria, only a few knickknacks, among them a set of tankards that have been in my family since the thirteenth century. I think them fairly antique. I'm going to tell you a story on myself before you hear it from someone else who might make me sound brutal. I had only been in this country a few years and I had heard so much about the 'wool barons' and so on that I thought perhaps the government *had* established a peerage. You're laughing at my innocence and I don't blame you! Well, a man named Mr. Puce (I have to chuckle at the name because it reminds me of the gloves I have always had my chauffeurs wear) came to dinner here and the person who brought him introduced him as 'the Chicago merchant prince.' How should I know any better? American names are so exotic, you know, to a foreigner, that it's not a bit strange to think of a 'king of Wyoming' or a 'grand duke of Iowa' or 'prince of Chicago,' so poor me! I had him go in first to dinner. He was flattered half to death, and the only reason the Baron Kalenkoff didn't leave at once in a fury was that he thought I was playing a joke!"

I could make no counter to this, and instead went back to the beginning of her anecdote. "I would like to see your tankards, Countess."

She laughed richly. "I'm no collector, darling! I'm not interested in *things*. Art is *my* life. Make me happy and tell me that it's yours too!"

"But I'm very green," I told her. "I would like to make you happy, but I'm afraid all I can do is read."

"Oh, but that's marvelous! I hope you aren't so modern that you will find what I like *démodé*, as Hope Mather does. I can still cry at *Père Goriot*. As for modern novels, they don't touch me. Either they're cold or gross. And *need* they be so difficult?"

I could not resist the temptation to advance myself with the Countess. "Balzac is sublime," I said. "He has touched all passions and given the commonplace the stature of tragedy. I cannot feel that Shakespeare is any greater." I was quoting from George Moore, a passage which had at first captivated Nathan with its audacity and then had filled him with derision. Since I had read very little of Balzac and worshipped Shakespeare with the fine rapture of adolescence, I visualized inverted commas about my words, but my voice did not convey them to the Countess who cried, "Lucy said you were clever, but she didn't prepare me for this! What an addition to Boston you are!"

My voice shook with shame as I replied, "Oh, I have only a few tags."

"By the way, I don't understand your name, Sonie. Is it short for Euphrosyne?" Through a misreading of the word, she had metathesized the vowels and pronounced it "Euphrysone." I explained that Sonie was my own childish corruption of Sonia. "What a pity," she said.

"Not that I don't love Sonia for you, but it would have been so delightful if you *had* been named for the goddess of Mirth. Your eyes are so merry." She held me off at arm's length. With a supreme effort I obliged her by grinning, hoping to infect my eyes with the merriness I put into my lips. "There! Isn't it the image of Euphrysone!"

A woman and her daughter came up to us at that moment to say good-by. "Amelia and I have so enjoyed the afternoon, Berthe. I love your nest and your cunning little harpsichord. You're like a sirocco to warm our cold New England."

The Countess glowed. "You're a fibber," she said, rising and taking both hands of her guest. "But you must come and tell me the same sweet-sounding fibs every Friday you possibly can. Next week I'm going to play the Haydn Opus 21 in D Major."

"I don't believe I know it," said the woman who did not, in that sense, *know* any music. "But if you will let us, we will come, won't we, Amelia? Amelia is wild about music, aren't you, Amelia?"

Amelia, fourteen years old, a gawky girl with long legs and knobby knees who was, obviously, at this stage of her life, an enemy to music and to mankind, nodded in agreement and said in a high, rushing voice as if she had got it by heart, "Yes, I am, Countess von Happel. I don't know anything about it, but I know what I like."

The Countess took them to the door, kissed them and proclaimed her love to the furiously blushing and twitching Amelia. She returned and settled down beside me again to resume her inquisition. But at that moment, she perceived that Garvin was edging toward the door, leaving Gerhardt Preis still standing by the refreshment table. "Well," she said resolutely, "I may as well do it now, make it quite clear he can't come again. Lou," she called to a girl who was reading the titles in the collection of record-albums and turned at the sound of her name, "will you come meet Miss Sonia Marburg?"

Lou, who did not supply her surname, sat down beside me and laughed softly. "She's had to take steps at last, poor Berthe. You're new here, aren't you?" When I told

327

her that I was, she asked frankly, "May I ask how you met the Countess?"

"At Miss Pride's, at tea the other day. Do you know Miss Pride?"

"Oh, gracious yes, though I haven't seen her in a month of Sundays. Has Hope gone on to New York yet?"

"She left on Tuesday, but she'll be back tonight. She's going to spend week-ends here."

The girl laughed. "I dare say that was her Aunt Lucy's idea. Poor girl, she does hate Boston so. You didn't know she hated it? She has a perfect complex on the subject."

"I can't understand that. I've seen very little of it, but that has seemed charming."

"You mean you've never been to Boston before? But where . . ."

The Countess had dispatched Mr. Preis and returned to us. "I heard you tell Sonie that Hope has a complex. This child hasn't been here long enough to know all our complexes and reflexes and prefixes. Lou, and I don't want you to let our cat out of the bag. She'll detest us and run away."

"Berthe, you're priceless! Why, that's what makes us so interesting."

"Do you know what Amy and I think? We think Hope is going to change her tune and fall in love with Boston after all."

"Why that prediction?"

"Don't *you* think she'll marry Philip McAllister?"

"I'm sure I haven't the least idea," returned the girl coldly and rose. "Berthe, I've had a wonderful time. May I come again next week?"

"But, darling, don't go yet! I want your opinion. You know he went to Manchester for his holiday this year. Don't you think *that* indicates something?"

The girl merely smiled and drew on her gloves. "Will you ask Amy to ring me up? I want her to do Monadnock for me from the top of Prospect Hill. No, don't get up. Good-by."

When she had gone, the Countess put her arm about my waist. "Now I have you all to myself. Tell me, don't you think we're right about Cousin Hope and that nice young man?"

"I don't know Hope at all well. She seems a little . . ."

"A little highly seasoned for Philip? Of course we all think that, but that's precisely the reason we think he'll pursue her to the end. His mother and grandmother are so opposed, you know. Everyone talks about it *ad infinitum* so I'm not telling tales out of school. Haven't we got mean little minds?"

A hysterical laugh from the doorway announced Amy Brooks' breathless arrival. "Berthe, *darling!*" she cried and skipped across the room to kiss her stepmother. "I was so engrossed in doing the Oyster House that I completely forgot it was Friday. Mr. Pingrey was along and we've already had our tea. Do you forgive me?"

"I don't mind anything you do so long as Mr. Pingrey is your chaperon. We were just making a match between Hope and Dr. McAllister, and I was also on the very point of saying I'm betting on another marriage on a certain young lady not a thousand miles away to a young man whose name begins with P."

Amy Brooks collapsed in shaking laughter, her eyes brimming with tears, and I got up, unnerved by the spectacle and aware suddenly that we three were alone. The Countess permitted me to go only after she had got my solemn promise that I would come to her every Friday for the rest of my natural days. "And now, good-by, come back to me. I love you!"

3

Dinner was served punctually at seven, and nothing would have induced Miss Pride to delay it by a minute. She regarded tardiness at mealtime as the same sort of self-indulgence as illness. But as she insisted that I dress each night (she did not herself, but thought that I should "learn how to manage an evening frock against an evil day," the evil day presumably being the one on which I should be invited out somewhere) I could not help being late, and she had finished her soup when I entered the dining-room. "We dine at seven, Sonie," she said, laying down her spoon. "You shouldn't have changed."

"I thought you wouldn't like it if I didn't."

"When two rules conflict, the important one is the one that should be obeyed. It is commendable in you to remember to dress, but punctuality is infinitely more important. I understand that you were late to Berthe's today." She leaned forward so that her face was framed by the white candles as she confronted me with this astonishing information. Was I so simple that my very actions could be read in my face? I dared not question her and for some minutes she pursued the subject without hinting at the identity of the scout who had lurked about the doorway on Beacon Street to time me. But she was not angry. She smiled. "It was a mistake. Berthe is rather lax about everything except her Fridays. I suppose it meant you didn't hear the music and that never sets well with her. But she wasn't offended. She telephoned me the minute you left the house to say how pleased she had been with you. She referred to you by some foreign nickname that I did not catch. I was rather surprised you were already on such intimate terms."

I explained how she had come to call me Euphrosyne (rather, Euphyrsone) and while Miss Pride said nothing, I was sure she was taking in every word in order to repeat it the next time Berthe's name was brought up amongst her friends. I went on then to tell her that I had been delayed because I had encountered Mrs. Prather on Dartmouth Street.

"Who is Mrs. Prather?"

"Why, you must remember her. She has come to the Barstow every summer for years. At least as long as you have. She sits under the ptarmigan in the dining-room."

"Oh, yes, I remember. For a long time I thought her name was 'Mather' and I wondered if she were a relative of Hopestill's. I did not inquire. I don't understand why you should have been late on account of her, though. She's simply the kind of fright one stares through

330

if one's in a hurry, isn't she?" In a sense, she had forgotten who I was and that I could not possibly have cut Mrs. Prather. I went on to tell her of my conversation with the stupid but kindly old soul who believed I had become a prostitute. Miss Pride was vexed, not because of Mrs. Prather's delusion, but because I had spoken unguardedly in front of the maid. She rebuked me while the girl was still in the room. Upon her mischievous Irish face appeared a grin of malicious pleasure, so that I knew the scene would be reproduced in the cellar as soon as we had left the dining-room. "For a moment I couldn't place Mrs. Prather," she said. "But now I recall that she is a woman of great breeding, and if she thought you were pursuing the oldest profession as it were, she probably had good reason. I have often warned you, as you can't deny, that the excessive rouge you use on your lips is far from good taste. And I should remind you that in scorning Mrs. Prather's offer to recommend you as an upstairs maid may, in time, prove to be the greatest folly. If I were you, I would not be at all sure that I would not end up as an upstairs maid or even as a 'useful' servant."

She had never spoken so harshly before. In my agitation I took far more meat than I could use and it occupied so much space on my plate that when Emma came round with the vegetables I had to push it to one side and in doing so pushed it off onto the table altogether. Miss Pride, whose avian eyes had not rested for a moment in their barrage of killing looks on me, said, "Oh, my soul! Emma, bring a clean mat for Miss Marburg." The girl, nearly overcome, rushed to the pantry and banged the door shut, there, as I imagined, to giggle at my bungling. But when she returned with a clean napkin, the scolding was over and Miss Pride was genially telling me of her morning which she had spent with her Cambridge friend, the widow of the Harvard professor, in the Concord burying ground. "And that reminds me that Philip McAllister called this afternoon and said that his grandmother would like to have you and Hopestill come to tea tomorrow. He'll drive you up. If you have time, do take a stroll through Sleepy Hollow. But don't put it off until after tea. Laura McAllister is such a chatterbox you won't get away before dinner time." (Later that evening, she said, "When I spoke of Mrs. McAllister I didn't mean anything unfriendly by calling her a chatterbox. She's a charming woman, and it would displease me to hear that you had repeated what I said." With an antediluvian notion that marriages could still be made by families rather than by individuals, she was anxious to stay on the right side of Philip's grandmother.)

The account of her day amongst the graves alleviated only the suffering she had inflicted by humiliating me in the presence of a servant, but the other suffering that came from the fear that this was to be only the first of such occasions lingered as a dull but obtrusive ache. And because it was a symptom common to many diseases, there was no way immediately to identify it. It was inchoate fear, the first sign of all those irascible emotions that include hatred, contempt, despair, and so on. And after dinner, as we sat for an hour, according to our custom in the upstairs sitting-room and twice Miss Pride corrected my pronunciation of a word in the article I was reading to her from *Harper's Magazine,* the pain became acute for a moment and when it had gone I felt the vague nausea that accompanies shock.

We did not have our coffee until I had finished reading, at eight-thirty. It came up then on the dumb-waiter and Miss Pride established herself behind *The Boston Evening Transcript* while I filled the cups and brought a bottle of Benedictine from a closet in the "office." My mistress was proud of saying that she took no medicines but "vinous and spiritous liquors" which she called "the medicaments of Nature," and while she drank very little at a time, she had a glass of something at regular intervals throughout the day: at eleven in the mornings of week-days, she had a glass of port, but on Sundays, after her chess-game, she had dry sherry. Before luncheon and dinner, she had two glasses of sherry and in the evening with her coffee a liqueur or a meausre of rum which she took neat. The best of her liquor was kept in the den just off the upstairs sitting-room, and this was reserved for her own use. Less excellent whiskeys, brandies, liqueurs, and wines were kept in the library and given to guests when she entertained formally. The pantry and the cellar were stocked for the rank and file with domestic dry wines, low-priced Bourbon, and gallon jars of gin. I was not invited to pour myself a glass of Benedictine, but invariably she said, as she folded the newspaper but continued to read it and as I handed her the tiny green bowl on a thin gold stem, "Perhaps you'd like a glass of sherry. I won't offer you any of this, for I'm sure you wouldn't care for it, and it's so dear I can't allow it to be wasted."

Tonight, drowsy with the rich wine, out of touch with Miss Pride since she never spoke once she had begun to read the financial page, I felt simultaneously dissatisfied and proud. The dissatisfaction I erroneously (and perhaps intentionally) set down to the sherry, the effect of which had been to usher in a memory of the beer my father had used to pour into my soup. I conjured up his youthful face, so like that of *Herr* Speyer, and wondered at its incongruity in this rich woman's parlor, and felt that I betrayed him since my own presence here was no longer incongruous. It was as if I had supplied his attributes, plagiarizing those my creator had conferred upon me; or, conversely, that *I* was the chimera, the reflection in the flawed looking glass, the misquoted doctrine, and he the paradigm. His presence became as palpable as that of Miss Pride. The *du* of *Herr* Speyer's remark, that intimate address, lay like a ghostly hand upon my cheek. Like a pilgrim, used to sleeping out of doors and claustrophobic in a house, I inhaled jerkily as if the air within this silent, genteel room were poisonous to my lungs, as though, if I could, I would escape the carniverous flowers and come again among the harmless edelweiss my father's fancies had picked for me as I sat hearing his stories in the shop in Chichester.

I rose. "I believe I'll change and take a little walk, Miss Pride."

She did not look up. "I hurt your feelings at dinner,

did I not?" But there was nothing in her voice to indicate whether she were sorry or if she intended me to apologize for my milksop sensitiveness.

"No, ma'am."

"I've told you not to call me 'ma'am.' 'Sir' is all very well, but 'ma'am' I cannot tolerate. You mustn't take me seriously when I'm crotchety. I wouldn't let you be an upstairs maid for a dowager duchess, let alone for one of Mrs. Prather's hypochondriac friends. No, indeed, I don't intend to turn you out. Stick by me, Sonie, won't you, and put up with my flip tongue? My father used to tell me I wouldn't have a friend in the world by the time I was thirty. Perhaps he was right and the only reason people come to see me is that they're after the rum cakes on my tea-table."

"Really, Miss Pride," I protested, "I wasn't in the least offended. I thought perhaps you had been annoyed by something earlier and were just out of sorts a little."

"You guessed it perfectly. Now don't put a false construction on this, for on second thoughts I realized that I was quite wrong. I was annoyed by the way Philip McAllister asked for you on the telephone this afternoon. I had the disagreeable feeling that if you had answered, he would have asked you to meet him for tea, and I said to myself, 'Surely that child can't be having rendezvous with Philip who is virtually Hopestill's fiancé.'"

Until now she had been talking to me behind the rustling screen of the *Transcript*, but now she lowered it and as I earnestly denied that I had seen Philip at all except in her own drawing-room, I winced at the firm set of her jaw and the suspicious, narrowed eyes. Though what I said was true, I did not feel that I had been absolved of my guilt, but that she was reading my mind in which my sporadic infatuation with the doctor was trying in vain to flutter out of reach of her superhuman intuition. Her gaze was like a magnet that drew towards it my will-less secret. Five minutes before, I had not been conscious of my love which, at best, when I was not with him, was like the exhilaration the novice feels from drinking, not like the somnolent pleasure of the addict. But now I felt feverish and giddy. Thus, the innocent man on trial, under the skillful bombardment of the prosecution grows hot and quivers and finds his voice distant and shrill as if a subtler faculty than his conscious mind has been besieged and he is no longer sure that he did not commit the crime.

"Poor girl," said Miss Pride, "it's not easy for you. You're homesick, I expect, not lovesick. I'm not up on my psychology, as Hope would say. Tell me, did you meet any interesting young people at Berthe's today?"

I told her of Gerhardt Preis whom she had met and had not cared for. "When I was your age, I deplored race prejudice. To my dear, single-minded Papa's chagrin, I used to seek out your Israels and Rachels, the bigger the nose the better. But at last I admitted to myself that I was just like everyone else. I didn't get on with them . . . their aggressiveness distressed me in public and their money mania at last got the better of my idealism. Now, while I say 'live and let live' I must confess I sympathize with that particular of Hitler's program. Did you meet anyone else?"

With relief I spoke of Mr. Garvin—relief because I did not share Miss Pride's prejudice and while neither did I feel strongly partisan towards Jews, the subject always embarrassed me because, not being able to detect Hebraic blood at once except in a most obvious face, I was afraid that someone's toes were being trod on. And even here in Miss Pride's sitting-room where there was no one to be offended (unless I myself were partly Jewish, a not unlikely possibility), I disliked the openness of the attack because, by my ambiguous silence I was no doubt giving her the impression that I subscribed to her view, and later on, when a Jew was present, she might call upon me to confirm some anti-Semitic statement.

She was inordinately interested in what I told her of Mr. Garvin because, through my desire to hasten from the Jewish question, I exaggerated the scraps of information I had gathered about him through his conversation with Preis, and told her that he was a student of Japanese even though I had been corrected by the boy himself. "What a small world we have," said Miss

Pride, beaming with pleasure. "To think that one of your first acquaintances in Boston should have the same inspiration that my father had. Perhaps he would like to look over the books here. Is he a presentable young man or is he one of those brainy people, like Hope's artists, who don't wash very well?" On the contrary, I told her, Garvin was, if anything, overwashed. His tanned, freshly shaved face had been as clean as a baby's; his dark blue suit and his white shirt, his blue cashmere tie and matching socks were so fresh from the cleaner and the laundress that he could have posed, with no subsequent touching-up on the part of the photographer, for an advertisement of Miss Pride's White Cloud soap. "And what is his background?" she asked me next, but I could not satisfy her. "Berthe will know, I suppose. We might ask him to dine with us some evening. I don't want to deprive you of all society, you know, but at the same time I don't want you to drift away from me."

"Oh, I can assure you," I laughed, "that Mr. Garvin and I didn't strike up an acquaintance at all." Actually I did hope that I would see the young man again but only because I was inquisitive to know what sort of friends Nathan had.

"The Countess gave me a surprising piece of news. She says you're sharp as a tack on the subject of French literature. How in the world did you come by that?"

"She's quite mistaken. I know nothing about it . . . I . . ."

Miss Pride rolled her eyes in a way that was at once so omniscient and so repulsive that I had to look away from her. "You're quite right, my dear child, most of us are credulous geese. To be candid with you, I'd rather have you like this than have you be a real but bumptious intellectual."

"Like this?" I repeated, feeling that I ought to defend myself.

"I said *most* of us are credulous geese. But *I* know what you know. All I ask is that you don't take your game seriously."

I saw nothing for it but to confess that I had, indeed,

been bluffing at the Countess' and to my relief she dropped the subject.

"Am I right in assuming that this restlessness of yours —this wanting to go for a walk in the middle of the night —is just that same homesickness we were talking about earlier? And that you're not growing tired of your life here?"

I assured her that I had no different ambitions than to keep her company, but there flashed across my mind, set off by her uncertainty of me, a sense of power over her that allowed me to make a private reservation. I would stay with her *so long* as she upheld her part of the bargain and did not deprive me of my freedom in those hours which were not dedicated to her. For it had occurred to me that as she grew older she might become more demanding of my time. Indeed, she had prepared me for that in our conversation the night before my first tea-party when she had said, "I don't want you to make up your mind yet, for you may find me too exacting. It will not be my fault, for I pride myself on respecting other people's privacy in their leisure hours, but it will be the fault of senility, that wretched Mr. Hyde I shall become in my last days." I had then disbelieved her completely, even though a few days later, I heard Hopestill say to someone, "Auntie is so improvident in her choice of fixed ideas. She surely *will* dodder into crabbed old age if she keeps thinking of it."

Tonight, like a subterranean river, a senile complaint slipped through her words and it did not, at last, seem unlikely that in a while the undertone would become the minor key in which were played the jeremiads of those whose only future is eternity.

Laughing, when she spoke of the humiliating possibility of a wheel chair, I said, "Miss Pride, you should bone up on those Thibetans who claim they know how to live two centuries or so." I was recalling a photograph I had seen in a newspaper of a Hindu said to have been born in 1786, making him a century and a half old. The broad, bald skull had looked like a death's-head and the drooping eyes had been tenantless, mere vacant openings in round pits of black shadows. The long dark lips were stretched in a hideous grimace, not of scorn for the photographer but of a corrupt delight in the pyrrhic victory of flesh over time. The caption had read, "Says He Will Live Till 2000 or After."

"I should hope not!" she exclaimed. "Do you think I want to see Boston turned into a hive of Customs Houses and aeroplanes replacing automobiles? No, thank you. I don't fancy myself rocketing about in the air with Mac at the controls. A century is too long for anyone to live. To go beyond *that* is my idea of anticipating Judgment Day. Tomorrow afternoon at Mrs. McAllister's, you will possibly meet a Mr. Childreth who is the oldest living graduate of Harvard College. He was of the class of '67. Although he still has his own teeth—they're no beauties, however—he has quite lost his reason and reads books written for children. It always strikes me as ironical that on Commencement Day he marches at the head of the Harvard procession when he barely knows his A.B.C.'s."

"But *you* won't be like that, Miss Pride."

"I'm not at all sure. If I am, though, I hope you'll have the goodness to lock me up. Even my father, a most sensible man, got notions toward the end. He confused me with my sister Charity and believed that neither of us was his daughter but that our surname was Fleet. 'Charity Fleet,' he would say to me, 'I want you to take my green bag which is full of peanuts and go feed the squirrels in the Common.' He had never fed a squirrel in his life, and until he was in his dotage always referred to them as 'The Common rodents.' And of course his bag hadn't so much as a peanut shell in it, but only his rice-paper books."

She fell silent, thinking perhaps of her father, and I started toward the door to leave her to her reverie, but she looked up. "I don't know how I started on that digression. We were talking about your friends, or rather, your friends-to-be. I dare say it isn't my place to say this as it's the duty of one's mother, but since yours is not accessible, I must look upon myself as your guardian. To put it bluntly, Sonia, you don't consider marrying, do you?"

"I don't know. I suppose I've never thought much about it. Perhaps I shall want to after . . . that is, when I'm older."

"But, my dear child, don't you see? Hasn't Dr. McAllister ever discussed the matter with you? I think it's a pity he's your doctor. He's a perfect scamp in many ways and has *always* been a heart-breaker, but that's beside the point. He ought at least to guide you, knowing what he does."

"Do you mean that I shouldn't marry because of my bad heredity? Because, why, yes, he has talked to me about it and has told me I shouldn't think of such things." This was not quite true. He had one time compared me to himself and had said our misfortunes could be turned to good account if we looked upon them as symbols, perhaps of original sin or of mortality, like Dr. Galbraith's *memento mori*. However, this had been in one of his religious moods when he was gathering all manner of disparate elements into his train of thought. He had never actually spoken to me of marriage and I, who seldom thought of it, had not solicited his advice.

"Times change. Nowadays children aren't spanked, don't learn Latin, don't respect their elders. And I haven't a doubt it's thought old-fashoned to be wary of insanity in the family. But, Sonie, there have been *two* instances of it in your lifetime, very close to you. I must say it would give *me* pause."

Had Miss Pride been able at that moment to read my mind, she would have been convinced that my mother's idiosyncrasies were already cropping up in me, for as I listened to her, I lost my identity. I was invaded by the strange feeling that I was not myself, or rather, that this was a phantom of myself, projected into Boston by my real being, still in Chichester. I had had this sort of experience before: in the winter just past when the days were at their shortest, I had waked once at four o'clock but had had no way of knowing whether it was four in the morning or four in the afternoon. Even though my mother was still asleep beside me and though no sounds of life came from outdoors, I concluded that it was afternoon, that we had slept through the whole day, and

I rose in haste, ashamed of my sloth. As I shook down the stove, live coals fell into the ash box and I knew that it was morning or no fire would be left. Although I was wide awake, I had the sudden feeling that I was still in bed and that the person or the thing that held the cold stove shaker was not a dreamed-up aspect of myself but was a clever imitation. It was not so much Miss Pride's wounding, though perhaps sensible, counsel that made me take refuge in this fantasy—for I suppose the psychologists would say that my lapse was in effect an "escape from reality"—as it was that it did not seem to be the first time she had spoken thus. On one level, that of my conscious memory, I knew that this scene had not been played before, but on a secondary plane, her speech, down to the very syntax of her sentences, was so familiar that I knew, or thought I knew, exactly what was coming next. And for that short space, I believed that I was in my bed at home, enacting a daydream. The fact that restored me—in itself absurd, far from conclusive, but nevertheless as quick-acting as the cock's crow that hurtles ghosts and goblins back to hell—was the chiming of the clock on the mantelpiece marking ten. Or rather, I heard only the tenth stroke but knew that I had heard all the others as well and that Miss Pride's "Times change" had been uttered just as the first note sounded.

"I'm so glad to be here!" I cried.

"That's a *non sequitur*," smiled Miss Pride. "But I take it as a compliment, and also as a sly hint that you've had enough of my sermonizing. Very well, you win. I shan't mention it again. Let your conscience be your guide."

I ran up the stairs and locked the door to my bedroom. Standing in the pitch darkness, I imagined what I would see when I snapped on the light. For this was one of the moments, most delicious because they came so seldom, that I realized I was in Boston. My eyes grew accustomed to the darkness, and I could see across Louisburg Square to Mount Vernon Street where a house was lighted up for guests who came and went with singsong greetings and farewells. Amongst them, perhaps, were the Countess von Happel, the girl named Lou, Philip McAllister. Immediately above a chimney there shone a star so large that I thought at first it was a light. Automatically, I said, "Star light, star bright, first star I've seen tonight; wish I may, wish I might have the wish I wish tonight. I wish that:" But I had got my wish and could find no other. The room was here and my signature was on it: my own pajamas and dark blue wrapper would be lying on the turned-down bed.

I groped for the switch. The instantaneous flood of light broke my tension. But the order of things, deranged by two chance encounters, first with Mrs. Prather and then with *Herr* Speyer, and by Miss Pride's admonitions, was set right again. The mechanism would not be so tight for the repair, would henceforth be more liable to collapse, but for all practical purposes, it would serve. I was engulfed by a wave of love for Miss Pride, and gone with the dissatisfaction I had felt earlier was the spontaneous and perverse desire to marry that had not occurred to me until she had implored me not to.

Again, I so strongly disbelieved that she would grow old I wished to run downstairs to assure her. How could she? She who, the day before, had walked to Pinckney Street from Harvard Square and showing less fatigue than I who had strolled slowly home from Dartmouth Street, a tenth the distance, had taken me to King's Chapel where for an hour we had admired the shabby gravestones in the burying ground, smirched with the droppings of impartial pigeons. She had looked at her man's pocket-watch which she carried in her handbag and said, "Oh, we have half an hour before tea. I suggest we take a walk to Trinity and back." I had lagged behind sometimes, but she pressed on, her ruthless pace diminishing at no time, not even at street crossings. As she often said, she had been a pedestrian long before automobiles had been thought of, and she was not one to give them the right of way. The light on Arlington Street had just turned red and cars were commencing to move along against us, but Miss Pride did not stop. A truck-driver, halted by her formidable approach, leaned from the cab of his monstrous machine and said with certain

awe, "Look at that damned old bird." The old bird
gave vent to one of her rare laughs and said to me. "He's
only envious. The great thing has lost the use of his legs
from running that juggernaut. Come along, we must
work up an appetite for tea, you know."

Rejoicing in my success at the Countess' and in my
secure position in this house, I could not fix my attention on my shorthand exercises. I must have been day-
dreaming for some time when I became aware of voices
in the room below me, that is, an unoccupied guest room
where, as Miss Pride told me, she was sketching her
memoirs. I opened my door and stood in the hall listening. I could hear nothing but an unintelligible murmur
and was just returning to my room when a door downstairs was opened and Hopestill's voice came up to me.
"But how peculiar you are about it, Auntie! Why isn't
it possible that I saw her in Chichester?"

"She wasn't there that summer. But it's not of the
slightest consequence whether her face is familiar to
you, Hope. The important thing about Sonie is that she's
contracted to me."

I could fairly see the girl shrug her shoulders as she
replied, "I understand, dear. I shall keep my hands off."

"You do not become less vulgar. Good-night."

I slipped back into my room. Lying face downward on
my bed, I could hear the eccentric fury of my heart-beat.

Three

HOPESTILL MATHER, when she came home from New York for the week-ends, was so disarmingly attentive to me that I came to think of her as an ally though I would have preferred to look on her as an enemy. On certain evenings, usually Friday, when she stayed at home, she invited me to come to her room where she served me hot buttered rum which she prepared with water kept steaming in a silver pot under a cozy. Frankly impressed by the way the Countess had been struck with me (to my blushing delight she said once, "Aunt Lucy is going to give Berthe what-for one of these days if she doesn't stop telling everyone that *she* found you"), she was endeavoring, I thought, to discover for herself what it was that had so rapidly elevated me to a place of honor in the salon. It was not, she warned me, a very high distinction, for the Countess was a little too hyperbolical to be taken quite seriously. She was bound in conscience, more-over, to point out to me that I had arrived on the scene just at the moment that Annaliese Speyer's departure had, so to speak, left a vacancy. At the same time, she expressed her congratulations and told me that if I "handled" the Viennese properly I would find her a faithful friend. She had never been urged to entrench herself in the little society of the music room, possibly because, knowing too much about the Countess, she had never paid her the homage strictly required if one were to become a habitué.

Having gone this far, Hopestill decided to continue to the end and refilling my mustache cup with rum presented me with the bare and slightly scandalous facts about her cousin by marriage.

The Countess was a "natural," she said, having been blessed with a perfect ear and with perfect taste. But through an inertia, deeply hidden under nervous energy and physical tirelessness, she had never supplemented her native and very considerable gifts with any study, was and always had been totally ignorant of the science, the history, the criticism of music. And, although she had no intellect, she had the intelligence to realize that if she were to be happy in the kind of musical circles to membership in which she was entitled, she must learn to think about her art and how to talk about it. The task was too enormous and it did not occur to her guileless mind to bluff her way through, though she was not above setting herself up as an expert amongst people whom she knew to be worse informed than she. Thus, in Vienna, her peers and her admirers were never permitted to make her acquaintance. At the same time, because she had been born self-conceited, she craved to be spoiled by something more personal than the press and more objective than her husband the Count, her doting family, her aristocratic but inartistic friends. She was ambitious for a following of innocent people. Consequently, she had divorced the Count and married the New Englander (whose name, for obvious reasons, she did not take) and immediately on coming to America, instituted these little musical afternoons to which, as a rule, only young people ("preferable tone deaf," said Hopestill spitefully) were invited. And now, if she were threatened by one of her guests who was disobeying the rules and learning something about music, she could take refuge in her difficulty with the English language. The audacious guest was shortly dropped.

I asked Hopestill if this, then, accounted for her treatment of Gerhardt Preis. "In a way, yes," she replied. "But there's more to it than that. That part of Berthe is more complicated." She told me that the Countess had deliberately made the young man fall in love with her while he was teaching her the harpsichord, for, it was generally assumed, she far preferred his enraptured looks and his mash notes sent with the yellow roses he showered upon her to any formal discussions of the music she was studying, and because Preis spoke German she could not pretend not to understand him. Then, having extracted his usefulness from him and far outstripping him in her management of the instrument, she got rid of him. Here the second of her peculiarities entered in. Apparently it would have been simple enough to keep him on tenterhooks indefinitely, to make his lips always the vehicle of nothing more dangerous than professions of love. And it would have seemed that keeping him by her would be greatly to her advantage since everyone knew that his virtuosity promised him an eminent career. Why, not, then, since his sting was removed, save him as an ornament for her salon? The fact was that she disliked men.

I must have shown by my face how shocked I was at this revelation, for Hopestill hastened on to assure me that her cousin was not a Lesbian, was probably not even conscious that she preferred women to men. (It had not, of course, occurred to me that she might be perverted in this way. What alarmed me was the thought that she might prove similar to my mother.) She did not fear them, but she recoiled from them in a frigid, old-maidish way, and unlike Miss Pride who could join the gentlemen almost as a gentleman herself, she was ill at ease in their company, embarrassed, often rude, because her vanity warned her that they would make love to her. The third gift of her fairy godmother (the first two being talent and self-esteem) was a stern, intuitive moral nature which kept her so under control that none but the most astute observer suspected anything irregular about her, but which allowed her to surround herself with girls, to caress them chastely, to send them presents, and to write them affectionate letters, indulgences permissible since they could have no consequences. I asked how her second husband had figured in this intricate pattern.

"Oh, poor Cousin Ralph was baffled by her, but he was grateful because she was so sweet to Amy. Aside from that, the marriage was a dud. She treated him like a butler—always called him 'Brooks'—and wouldn't speak to him before four in the afternoon when she was certain of having callers."

"Do you think she's taken me up because she's certain I'll never know the first thing about music?"

"She's not *that* naïve," returned Hopestill with a laugh. "Why, the Countess is certain of nothing, but she has her high hopes."

"And did my predecessor keep her part of the bargain?"

"To the letter."

The Friday evening conversations became, after a few months, an established institution. Hopestill told me frankly that she far preferred to hear my bulletin on the afternoon in the music room to going to parties. I obliged her, partly because I would not have known how to refuse, and partly because it was flattering to have so eager a listener and so open an admirer of what she called my "faithful eye."

We who put in a regular appearance at the Fridays were all girls. Occasionally there turned up a pedigreed young man from Harvard or a European man engaged in some enterprise far afield from art. The girls were second- or third-year débutantes, girls in that interval between the coming out and the wedding. They waited charmingly and passively for the materialization of a husband. They made no effort to shorten the period of their retirement, concealing, as nuns conceal their bodies, the aspirations that fluttered in their hearts, but showed, by deferential questions and mild, general compliments to the correct young men that, as it was proper in society girls, they respected men as a superior breed in whose eyes they did, indeed, wish to find favor, but neither hastily nor through their own maneuverings. Perhaps it was their modesty that made them aloof, eclipsed their individual history, lined them up alongside one another like those rows of bathing beauties whose real names have been changed to place names such as "Miss Rhode Island" or "Miss Great Lakes." Perhaps the modesty was their strategic principle and the one whereby they were the most successful because its employment was so unselfconscious. I sometimes reflected that they were like their ancestresses whose names and probably whose noses and eyes they retained, of whom we know through historical, sociological, even psychological studies as "the New England woman," and whose personal style, whose distinctive behavior have been leavened by time so that we see as sisters and coevals and identical specimens Priscilla Alden and Mary Chilton and Margaret Winthrop, all dressed alike in blue-gray homespun dresses with white berthas, seated before a spinning wheel, all combining in equal proportions in their characters the virtues in whose names Pilgrim daughters were christened: charity, prudence, hope, faith, patience, from which admixture emanated dignity, loyalty, thrift. Now in these twentieth-century women, there remained all those traits but to no end (rather, to no end of which they themselves were aware) like the appendix in our bodies that no longer serves us. They were like ancient vessels the archaeologists disinter which have been revised by time and the earth's chemicals so that the luster has been obfuscated by a patina, a marine green-blue encrustation, here and there punctured, as by a star, by a minute gleam of the metal underneath.

I had no communication with them. They behaved towards me with a warmth, a sincere interest which for many months deceived and flattered me so that I was at a loss to explain why they not only did not invite me to their own houses, when they were so cordial—even to the point of seeking me out in the music room—but that also, when I met them on the street, as likely as not they cut me dead. It was the very lack of condescension, the tactful omission from their conversation of anything which might remind me, to my embarrassment, that I was not of the sisterhood that finally enraged me. It was no ordinary snobbishness which inspired them, on meeting me, to acquire a burning interest in an object across the street, and, indeed, it was perhaps not any kind of snobbishness but merely another aspect of prudence, resident in them all, that like a fog concealed the roads branching off from the one they traveled which, because they traveled it in homogeneous company and had been set upon it by their parents whom they had no reason to distrust was, they knew, the right one. Prudence lighted them and made the pitfalls solid; prudence, like a composition teacher, assigned them "topics" to beguile the tedium of the journey; and prudence, like a duenna, supervised their romances. A palmer like myself, straying by chance and for a brief season across their path, was not invited, as a rule, to travel onwards, for they had been warned, as children are warned against accepting candy from strangers, that appearances are deceptive and one can no more be sure of the probity of a slight acquaintance than one can be sure of the purity of the substance under the chocolate coating.

They dressed well and without taste as if the caution of their forebears lingered yet. They had let modern fashion shorten their skirts in the daytime and lower them again in the evening, but had stayed the hands that would cut too daringly, would drape them too caressingly. So, at the Countess' dinner parties (her "Saturdays," as they were known) they appeared in evening gowns which were not memorable; pleasing, they might be, or quaint, or festive (which boneless adjectives Hopestill, if she were present, employed in her compliments to them). Their tremulous chiffons and pale crêpes, enlivened but unrewarded by a locket or a brace of gardenias, passed muster and no one noticed them.

Similarly, their conversation was lacking in excitement, though it was grammatical and scrupulously took into account the interests and prejudices, so far as could be determined, of their interlocutors. They had no affectations, aired no scandals, and had no discoverable attitudes save those they had inherited, like their noses or their jewelry. Their differences of opinion gave rise to no choler when they found themselves beside the heir of a different type of estate. "Oh, I forgot you subscribed to the New Deal," would say the daughter of a laissez-faire liberal. "Don't tread on me and I won't tread on you." Or the devoted sister of a young man, who wrote abstruse poems, would reply blandly to the boy who had attacked the "cult of unintelligibility" in *The Harvard Advocate, "De gustibus.* I refuse to quarrel with you on that score."

I had acquired, through no endeavor of my own, the reputation of being "literary," and almost every Friday, I was approached by a Miss Hornblower or Coolidge (who the day before had failed to recognize me as we passed one another on the stairs of the Public Library) who would say, "I've been hearing the most interesting things about you. My mother, who is a dear friend of Miss Pride's, was telling me that you want to be a writer. Do tell me what you're writing, for I'm dying to hear." The notion, actually, was Miss Pride's own and was derived from an innocent statement I had once made to Admiral Nephews. He, because when I first met him I had recognized the passages of poetry he quoted, thought that I had the same taste in literature as his own, and he used to bring me, the moment he had finished with them, the novels he had borrowed from a lending library, and which I was obliged to read out of respect for his thoughtfulness. I had at last grown tired of pretending to share his enthusiasm for books that were barely plausible and were certainly not distinguished, and said of one I had just read, "No, sir, I do not think it is excellent. I could write a better one myself." This was not true, to be sure, and I did not say it with any intention of proving it, but the Admiral misconstrued my boast and acquired the conviction that I was secretly engaged in writing a book. He reported his suspicion to Miss Pride who did not bother to ascertain its truth and who henceforward told everyone that I was anxious to be a writer and even supported the fiction by such statements as, "But I know Sonie well enough to know that it won't go to her head. She's much too sensible to become one of your peculiar Bohemians." I felt like the person—the person we all are at some moment in our lives—who is asked to play the piano and who protests he does not know how, cannot tell one note from another, and who has never depressed a single key, but who is accused of false modesty and begged to run off just some simple piece. In vain the defendant repeats that he is ignorant, is let off with the threat: "Very well, but you won't get off so easily next time." To the girl who was dying to hear about my writing, I replied that she was mistaken, that I had no such lofty opinion of myself, and she would say, exactly like the hostess who swears she has often heard us play, "You writers are all alike. I suppose you won't even tell me where you publish your stories?"

The Countess, making the most of my imaginary calling, directed our conversation, during coffee, into literary channels and I sometimes found myself being posed a staggering question about French poetry, for example, on which I was said by our hostess to be an expert.

I was genuinely fond of the Countess and suffered considerable remorse after I had joined in Hopestill's laughter at her expense, just as I did when I listened, without protest, to trenchant comments on her aunt and on Philip McAllister. Nor had I any reason to suppose that I was not myself the object of that merciless judge of her peers, but on the contrary could fairly hear her say of me to Amy Brooks (as she had said of Amy Brooks to me), "She's such a *deliberate* fright." It was perhaps because of this sharp tongue that Hopestill did not get on well with other girls, like those, for instance, who came to the Countess'. She was not well liked and never had been. At school, she had broken rules, had been slovenly and disrespectful, and so lazy a student that she had failed to be graduated. At her début, one of the most lavish ever held at the Country Club (her grandfather had left twenty thousand dollars for this specific purpose), she had drunk so much champagne that she could remember no one's name, could barely dance in time to the music, and had been insufferably rude to several older people. She was, moreover, thought something of a slacker, because she had never sacrificed any of her time to "good works" and long after all the other girls, who had come out in the same season that she had, had dedicated themselves to nursing or visiting the poor or reading to blind old women, Hopestill continued to fritter away her time with all the indolent pleasures of the débutante. It had particularly annoyed her friends that she had steadfastly refused to take any part in canvassing for the Community Chest Fund but instead had "done her bit" by contributing a large check to the drive and putting the whole thing out of her mind.

Declaring that she found me a "relief" (I would have preferred to be a little more stimulating), she included me in most of her plans over the week-ends and shortly after our first meeting she proposed that she teach me how to ride. I had hesitated, fearful of the ludicrous figure I would cut on a horse, but she had been persistent and Miss Pride had welcomed the project with enthusiasm, for, as she said, "Anyone with your constitutional aversion to exercise must be *made* to exercise." And consequently we went to Concord each Saturday afternoon where I was slightly more competent than I had hoped. Philip had been as ardent a promoter of the lessons as Miss Pride to my slight resentment for I thought he regarded them as a therapeutic measure to distract me from thinking of my mother, something which I rarely did save on Sunday when I paid her my weekly visit. As a result of his interest, he arranged to have us change into our riding clothes at his grandmother's house and to have tea there when we came back from the stables. He nearly always joined us and drove us back to town.

The young man's gallantry was impartial even in Hopestill's presence and while I knew by the heightening of his color as he first caught sight of her that he was in love, he was no more attentive to her than he was to me. And I, having just come back from an expedition in which my performance had been at best tolerable and in which hers had been brilliant, was more nettled than if he had ignored me entirely. It was as if, on these occasions, he looked on me as an appendage to her. Curiously enough, I was conscious of being in love with him only when Hopestill came back to Boston. So long as she was in New York, I could hear his name spoken or even see him on the street or at tea without the slightest discomfort, but the moment Hopestill stepped into the house late Friday afternoon I was ignited with jealousy, made the more obstreperous because I knew she was not in the least in love with him. Particularly excruciating to me were some evenings when, Hopestill being otherwise engaged, he was asked to take me to the Countess' "Saturday" and while I had spent the whole afternoon in a state of tremulous anticipation, my pleasure ended as soon as he called for me. He was either too absent-minded to hear my answers to his questions or he assumed an avuncular manner, offering me the most banal and unwanted advice on how to converse with my mother. In either rôle, I sensed his dissatisfaction at not being with Hopestill.

On one clear February day, Hopestill persuaded the riding master to let us go alone. "I'll pay you double," she said. The man looked dubiously at me, one of his least accomplished customers, but Hopestill snapped, "What difference would it make if that wreck you foist off on my friend *did* break a leg? Besides, she doesn't go in for jumping." He reluctantly agreed and we set off. Ducking our heads, we cantered through the brushy bridle paths and then came out into the open russet fields. Hopestill ran her sorrel mare over a rise and down and out of sight; presently, far off, I saw her hair, sharp as a scream and sudden as a flame, fling up along the ridge and for a space it flew, bodiless and horseless like a burning bird. I sat on a flat rock under a wineglass elm tree watching her, while my horse stood near-by with a languidly drooping head, as disinclined for exercise as I. This was the first time we had ridden since early in December for it had been too cold. Today there was sun and air as gentle as spring. It was like the day the year before when Miss Pride had come to take me in to Boston. There was little essential difference, I thought, between that version of myself who, shabby and with grimy fingernails, had sat bewildered in the gloomy library and this one, pranked out in costly jodhpurs, waiting in a cramped and uncomfortable position for my skillful friend to ride back. There was a gross and disquieting discrepancy between my expensive clothes and my luxurious pastime and my little brother's unmarked grave.

As I thought of Ivan, there returned to me the mood that had followed immediately on his death. It was a recollection, rather than a memory, a poetic farsight, a distillation of a feeling which was not watered down by physical details but was the dense experience of comprehending death. I did not envisage myself standing beside his cot nor did I, as I usually did when I thought of the scene, redeem the odor of the benzoin. It can be said that memory is a sort of *entrepôt* serving the busy traffic of the unreflective mind, and that its stores, behind an unlocked door, may be rummaged through and plundered at any time; thus I had found the footsteps of the old ladies walking in the sand at Chichester to match the lameness of Philip's grandmother in Miss Pride's drawing-room, and thus, also, confused by the music and by the stranger in the Countess' lobby, had brushed off the dust from a forgotten incident and by a misapplication of the styles of sensation, compared the music to the sunlight of that past day, and remembered *Regenpfeifer* because I had been addressed in German. But recollection, on the other hand, is in more formal custody, can be seen only at certain hours and those being far apart, the time of day or month or season being rarely, or not at all, repeated. Thus we say of people who were once in love that they cannot "recapture" their joy and the words "I was in love with that person" are an historical statement which may be attended by illustrations: a café visited by the lovers when they were in love, a railway carriage where they sat with arms entwined, a shop where they met one day by chance. So also, when one says, "I was ill at that time," memory shows him the mercury of the thermometer at 104 degrees, but neither the rapture nor the fever is revived. The essential has been extirpated, whereas it is the essential and only the essential that recollection values.

Severe in its gleanings, it seeks to preserve our continuity: the old man recollects though his memory, we say, has failed.

With useless greed I tried to detain this temporary wisdom, this growing pain even when I heard the rush of Hopestill's horse's feet returning. But the sense of death was instantly annihilated by the sound. At the same time, the power that had generated the intense and total knowledge had not been all used up, and being unable, because the thing was finished, to repeat the process that had transported me to the past, I directed the residue towards an envious hatred of the girl who had now ridden into sight. It had occurred to me that if I were not obliged each week to compare myself to her, to my disadvantage in every particular, I would be appreciably more urbane than the chambermaid from the Barstow who had not known what to say when she was asked if she were an Anglophile. I could tell myself that Hopestill and I belonged to different species and should not, therefore, be judged by the same standards. But this was cold comfort. As she dismounted, I indulged myself in a feast of torment, taking in her green suède waistcoat under a silvery gabardine jacket, her slender legs in black breeches, her eloquent hair disordered by her ride to its benefit. I hated her the more for her good manners when she said, "I don't blame you for not coming. That bag of bones would drop dead of the shock if you made him run," because she perfectly well knew that I was afraid. We sat in silence for a few minutes. Hopestill lighted a cigarette and meditated the smoke.

"Are you going to Berthe's tonight?"

"Yes. Are you?"

She shook her head. "I'm going dancing."

I did not look forward to the evening. At the bottom of the Countess' invitation, a square of mellow vellum headed by a coat of arms instead of an address, the calligraphy of which was so elegant that the only decipherable symbols were the date and the hour (one could not possibly tell whether the guest of honor was to be a Belgian brain surgeon, an Italian poet, a Danish archi-

tect, or a Canadian bishop), she had written—this in
a legible hand—"Nicholas Doman, charming, from Budapest, will call for you." I was tired of the young for-
eigners she "dug up" for me. Their difficulty with the
language discouraged and then annoyed me as did the
Weltschmerz that was a property common to all their
eyes. Or, if they could speak well, I was irritated by another quality in them, one which I could not properly
define: it was a staleness or a frustrated sensuality or a
womanly tenderness, or perhaps all three that sounded
in their voices, as if they were visiting an invalid surrounded by flowers that had withered but had not yet
lost their fragrance. In the cushiony cocktail lounge of
the Lincolnshire, over the yellow, arid popcorn and the
dubonnet, rich, beautiful Gerhardt Preis, whom I had
met by chance in the Public Gardens, confided one afternoon in me that his ambitions were to live forever as a
celibate (because he could not have Berthe von Happel)
in a hotel in Paris and to write a book (he would give
up music, inseparable from her) which would be the
modern counterpart of Amiel's *Journal.* From his home-
less, continental Jewish face emanated the odor of po-
made. In the vestibule of Miss Pride's house, he kissed my
hand and then withdrew into the dusk, stealing on his
suave feet past Louisburg Square under the spiritless
rain that had begun to fall. I was certain that Nicholas
Doman from Budapest would not be as charming as the
Countess testified. He would very likely be addicted, as
most of her hangers-on were, to telling anecdotes in
French.

I told Hopestill my dilemma. "Oh, well," she said,
"you won't have to be stuck with him the whole evening.
That's the beautiful thing about Berthe's parties, you
can take your pick after dinner. Anyhow Philip will be
there."

"Will he? After dinner you mean?" I said.

"Yes. Why, Sonie, you're blushing!"

I was not blushing. I had been too taken up with a
plan to escape the Hungarian to care whether Philip
came, but her accusation immediately elevated the temperature of my skin and my eyes began to smart.

"If you say so, I suppose I am," I said.

She laughed. "Why don't you skip dinner and go afterwards with him and avoid the Hungarian altogether?"

"I couldn't do that. But I'm very glad he's coming. At least he speaks English."

"And he's very fond of you, too." It was a serious statement and I could detect no ridicule in her voice. She put out her cigarette on the trunk of the tree. "You know, somebody like you would be good for Philip McAllister. He's a monkish bloke."

"Well, I'm not," I replied testily.

"Of course you are. If you weren't, would you have chosen to be buried alive in my Aunt Lucy's house?" And after a moment, as if to herself, "Jesus Christ! How you could do it I shall never know!"

"I'm satisfied," I told her.

"Oh, I know. And so is my aunt. Poor creature, she deserves someone like you after me. Have you noticed, by the way, how much we would like to murder each other these days?"

I had, indeed, noticed that the girl and her aunt had found it difficult to be anything more than civil. Arguments arose at the dinner table over such trifling matters as the advisability of giving the Countess a set of artichoke plates for her birthday which Miss Pride thought would be welcome, or an onyx deer that had caught Hopestill's eye. Or they railed at each other over the season of some cousin's marriage or another's début. Or Hopestill would contend that her aunt's salad dressing was unpalatable because it was made with lemon instead of wine vinegar. Often I was called upon to settle a dispute. Invariably I agreed with Miss Pride out of cowardice, and while she readily used me as a court of appeal, she sometimes forgot, in her periodic scoldings, that I had settled an argument which otherwise might have gone on indefinitely, and she told me that she was by no means flattered at my constant agreement with her opinions. "I am an old woman," she said once, "and it has taken me many years to develop my prejudices and my affinities. It is nothing short of impertinence in you to adopt them without doing any of the work." Now

356

on the other hand, Hopestill frequently expressed her gratitude: "If you hadn't settled on the artichoke plates, we would have gone on quibbling for weeks."

"We've disliked each other more since you came," continued Hopestill. "But I suppose that's reasonable. Do you know what is making my aunt's blood boil now? She's afraid Philip is interested in you and she's perfectly wild that I'm not doing anything about it."

"Oh, drop it," I cried and got to my feet.

"As you say," she agreed, shrugging her shoulders. But she was not content to remain silent long and when we had got back to the bridle path, she said, "Really, I was quite serious when I said some one like you would be good for McAllister." Her use of his surname unaccountably put me at my ease and I asked her why. "Well, I'm sure I don't know if you're religious in the least, but you have a nice sort of tranquillity about you that might turn into piety. Philip's bound to get religion sooner or later and I'd be the worst kind of wet blanket. I'm like Aunt Lucy: I think of God as a great big man."

I laughed aloud for what she said was so absurdly precise. It was quite true that Miss Pride thought of God as a big man Who had, in misty times, drawn up the Ten Commandments, and about Whom it was in bad taste as well as half sacrilegious to talk. She had towards Him the same attitude as she had towards the figures of literature, save those who had died in her lifetime. They wore the same antediluvian halo which, if seen in the cold light of Boston, would have struck one as pretentious. And so, although it was fitting for one to have an acquaintance with God and with Milton, it was not proper to display more than the merest courtesy towards them. It was acceptable to discuss a literary person (or a religious one) to whose name could be affixed the title "Mr." Thus, Miss Pride spoke of "Mr. James" whom she had met several times and of "Mr. Emerson" and "Mr. Lowell" (she had caught a glimpse of these latter two when she was seven years old); but as no one knew anything about "Mr. Dryden" or "Mr. Goldsmith" it was best not to speak too cordially of them. God was no more adaptable. With no intention of disparaging her, I pre-

357

sented this observation to Hopestill and she agreed with an amiable laugh.

"Yes, God and Shakespeare frighten her half to death. I think that's why she's so bent on making you out a literary person. She can't ignore literature but wants it homemade and by someone she can eat dinner with. She tried very hard once to know Amy Lowell, but she never succeeded."

My disappointment at this statement was less than my surprise, for I had conceived Boston society as so closely knit that it was as strange that two members of it were not acquainted as it would have been if La Grande Mademoiselle had not known Madame de Maintenon.

By the time we had reached the elder Mrs. McAllister's house, I had recovered from my choleric attack and could look on Hopestill with equanimity. Fortified also with the knowledge that I could not possibly fare too ill at the Countess' that evening since Philip would be there by himself, I was almost buoyant.

The old lady always kept us waiting for at least a quarter of an hour in the libary after we had been announced. Then, the rustle of her black skirts and the tap of her cane apprised us of her arrival and we stood up as she, after a formal, "Good afternoon, young ladies. I hope you enjoyed your ride," sat down in a chintz wing chair under a portrait of her husband for whom she still wore mourning, though he had been dead for twenty years. She had no sooner put her feet on the chair's matching stool than she said, as if it had just occurred to her, "What do you say to a cup of tea? Perhaps they'll have something in the dining-room for us. My grandson promised to call on me this afternoon and I must have tea for him, you know."

Philip's grandfather had one time been headmaster of a school so imitative of Eton and Harrow that the whole house spoke with a British accent. It had been Mrs. McAllister's custom, in his lifetime, to have a "day" for chosen boys and because often as many as forty had dropped in, she had entertained them at an immensely long table in the dining-room. Although now there were never more than half a dozen people to be served, twenty chairs were in readiness and as many cups stood before the tea urn. We were fed the simple food the boys had been fed: gingerbread squares, small sweet buns, and English muffins. On the preposterous plea that she could not handle "them all" by herself, she always placed Hopestill at the opposite end of the table so that the poor exile's voice barely carried to us, while I was seated on her right ("I never have time to get really acquainted with this young lady") and Philip on her left ("so that he can fetch and carry for me").

Hopestill spoke of the old lady's "closed door" policy while the one employed by her daughter, Philip's mother, was the "open trap." The younger Mrs. McAllister joined us today a few minutes after we had taken our places. Her pretty, submissive face was framed with white hair, the overnight acquisition at the time her son fell ill of infantile paralysis. After kissing her mother and nodding politely to me, she went at once to Hopestill whose two hands she clasped as she cried, "How glad I am to see you! Here, let me feast on that exquisite frock. Who but Hope Mather would think of bottle-green velveteen this year when the rest of us are all in navy blue?"

Hope, complimenting her in turn on her hat, exchanged an amused glance with Philip while his grandmother said, "Bottle-green is very nice. Marian, would you look at this child's nautical costume. I swear she robbed Admiral Nephews for her buttons. Why, they're the real thing."

Her daughter nodded and turned again to Hopestill. "When are you going to let me have the honor of supplying you with a dressing room? I do think you're unkind to give my mother *all* the pleasure. I have three rooms that are never in use, and if you'd only consent I could have more than these five-minute glimpses of you. I'll tell you frankly that if I once got you, I'd kidnap you for a whole week-end."

Philip, knowing that his mother would make use of such an opportunity to satisfy so completely any curiosity the girl might have about him that she would never

359

want to hear his name mentioned again, hastily inter-
posed, "But, Mother, they would have to be driven
from the station then, for they couldn't possibly walk to
our house and the walk to Grandma's, as I understand
it, is part of the expedition." Both Hope and I confirmed
him, but his mother was stubborn.

"Does anyone have a more selfish son?" she cried.
"Really, Philip, one would think you were afraid I intended to blacken your character." This, of course, was
precisely what she would have done, by going into his
inconstancy, his hypersensitivity about his back, his egotism, his carelessness, by exhibiting his ugly baby pictures, by telling damning anecdotes, by resurrecting
instances of his devotion to herself and attempting, in
the light of the latter, to make Hopestill realize that she
must play second fiddle to her if the marriage ever came
off.

The conversation, passing beyond the skirmish of wits,
became general. Philip, casting a studious glance upon
me who did not participate, said, "You must have given
Sonie a run for her money today, Hope. She's got the
wind knocked out of her."

"Oh, on the contrary," she replied with a laugh, "she
gave me a run for mine." And she began to praise my
horsemanship and to deplore my horse, inventing a fantastically untrue account of my bold jumping and running which I was too dumfounded to deny. Old Mrs.
McAllister patted my hand, said she could tell by my
appearance that I could manage any horse, called upon
her grandson to agree that I was the very picture of a
healthy athlete, hoping to embarrass Hopestill who,
though she was sound as a dollar, looked frail, and had
chosen, instead of normal pleasures, the ugly affectation
of the bluestocking. "I think you're very wise, Sonia,"
she said. "Why on earth our Hopestill wants to waste her
youth and ruin her complexion investigating people's
nightmares I will never understand. And as for 'repres-
sions' and 'sublimations' and so on, I think the least said
about them the better. Goodness only knows we have
serpents enough in our gardens without importing any
more."

360

The iciness of Hopestill's smile was lost on her half blind hostess as she replied, "But, Mrs. McAllister, all of us are not so fortunate as you. My own garden was swarming with serpents when I first stepped into it."

Philip's mother, leaning toward her, cried, "You clever thing! You know how to get the better of my mother! Tell me, Hope, what sort of thing do you *do*?"

"Oh, I . . ." For the first time since I had known her, I saw Hopestill hesitate. Momentarily she averted her eyes as she jerkily returned her teacup to its saucer. Then, with a smile, she explained, "I'm not studying formally, you see, but with a psychiatrist. I see his patients and study their case histories and so on."

"What kind of patients are they, Hope?" pursued the woman. "I'm really ever so interested."

"Well, my man is rather fashionable and most of his patients are idle women who don't like their husbands for one reason or another or else don't have husbands and think they'll go off the deep end if they keep on living alone."

Old Mrs. McAllister snorted gustily. "And what's the cure, eh?"

"They're analyzed, of course, and Dr. Ragsdale gives them things to distract them. Ice-skating, knitting, growing herbs in the kitchen window."

Philip's grandmother was silent with disgust and then, in order to hear no more of Hopestill's nonsense which she was pouring out by request to her companion, she turned to Philip and said loudly, "I want you to give your father a talking-to, Perly. He's set on selling the Bedford Road house. I would as soon cut off my hand as see it taken over by a stranger."

"And so would I," said the young man in sincere alarm. "What gave him that idea?"

"I can't imagine," returned the old lady. "But between ourselves, I have never felt your father had much sense of history." Philip whispered, "You have never felt he had much sense of any kind, have you, Grandma?" But Mrs. McAllister was not going to agree to such a judgment of her son in my presence, and she went on. "I have always wanted *you* to have the house when you marry. Did you see the enchanting little water color Amy Brooks did of it for me last autumn?" Then, turning to me, "You must make Philip take you to see it some day this spring. You will not find a more charming place in all New England."

The conversation at the far end of the table was lagging. Hopestill, getting up, said, "We must go to see the house some afternoon. It's my aunt Lucy's favorite next to her own on Pinckney." She directed to me an ambiguous smile which I took to mean that she had not quite made up her mind to relinquish Philip altogether, but that she would let me know in good time if I might go alone with him to inspect the house.

"You three," said the young Mrs. McAllister, "you three are inseparable, aren't you?" I knew by her tone and by the look of injury on her turned-down lips that she liked me no better than she did Hopestill.

"We are separating now," said Hope. "But Philip and Sonie will meet again at the Countess'."

As I was taking leave of my hostesses, Philip and Hopestill went into the hallway to get our coats. When I started out to join them, lingering at the door a moment to receive a final compliment upon my robust health from the old lady, I heard Philip saying, "I don't need a procuress."

2

The Countess' "Saturday" was a formal dinner party for rarely more than ten, followed by a soirée at which one met chiefly Germans and Austrians who had had the foresight to leave (and in some instances, to leave with their money) in the early days of Hitler's regime. There were, in addition, titled personages from other parts of the world: a Korean prince, a Russian baron, a Polish count. The Bostonians who came were either charmed by the illustrious company or outraged, the latter group maintaining that "these refugees" were impertinent and arrogant because they had the crust to criticize the United States and even, with supreme bad manners, to imply that it was only through luck, not through wisdom, that we were not ourselves ruled by a Hitler or a Stalin.

The dinner, consisting of many courses, was served by two fat, frowning Alsatian matrons, while the wines were poured by a little Hawaiian houseboy, employed, the Countess acknowledged, because he was decorative. Otherwise, he had almost no qualifications and cried a good deal for a female monkey named Lilioukalani whom he had had to leave behind. Three bitches, a schnauzer, a Doberman, and a boxer, paced the floor beneath the table or stood between two chairs, gazing first at one guest until her wish was granted and he threw her a morsel from his plate, and then at the other until he likewise succumbed to the plea in the piteous eyes. Miss Pride who, characteristically enough, liked dogs "in their place" almost never accepted an invitation to dine with the Countess, but if she did, she overlooked the dogs as one would overlook a foreign object in the dessert. Unfortunately they were particularly attracted to her because she carried with her the odor of her cat, Mercy, and during the soup, when they had no pressing business in other quarters, the three of them clustered about her legs sniffing. Her aplomb was admirable: as she drank her soup, crumbled her bread, and listened to the man from the Rhineland who was interested in guilds, it was not apparent that a debate was going on within her, whether to kick the brutes once and for all or to endure.

As soon as the gentlemen joined us, the door-bell commenced to ring and rang at intervals until well past eleven o'clock, bringing to us fortunate ten a varied assortment of entertainers. Our hostess, immense and blazing in a diamond tiara and a cloth-of-gold gown which sheathed her ample flesh like hide and of which the central interest was a green orchid growing out of her mountainly bust, stirred her guests about, dispatching me to a Norwegian painter, Edward Pingrey to a cloth merchant from Berlin, Mrs. Hornblower to a young Puerto Rican of ambassadorial connections whom, unfortunately, it was easy to confuse with the

363

houseboy. We were not allowed to remain long on any assignment. The Norwegian woman and I would just be establishing a communication of sorts after several false beginnings, when the Countess would descend: "You two charmers mustn't monopolize each other! Sonie, go speak to that woman over there, the dark one, Frau Gross. She's perishing to meet you. You're much alike— imaginative, *spirituelle*. She's a little deaf." Frau Gross, more like her name than the Countess' description of her, had not wanted to meet me, did not know my name, had not, in fact, ever seen me before and could hear nothing of what I said. In this enforced rotation one could hear conversations on German airpower, on French food, on Roman relics in England, on American politics, on European and tropical diseases, on coin collections, on train travel in the interior of China.

If one flatly refused to talk, being stricken tonight with one of those moods of taciturnity that visit us all, the Countess suggested cards in the library. It was not too happy a substitute, for she forbade such banal games as bridge or hearts, allowed only recondite or obsolescent ones like omber, loo, piquet. It was nearly always my bad luck, if I were sent to "make up a table," to find Baron Kalenkoff and one other person preparing a deck for omber, the most bewildering of all the games. The Baron, a handsome, well-tailored man in his thirties, a cosmopolitan and sycophant of wealthy women, was, as someone said, a "rattlesnake" at cards. He had, in addition to that acumen known as "card sense," such perennial luck that his adversaries regarded him with suspicion, not as a shark, for he was clearly a gentleman, but as the darling of some prodigal goddess whose invisible fingers distributed the cards in such a way as to make him invariably win. Now the only two people who had mastered the rules of omber were the Baron and the Countess and of course the latter did not play on her Saturdays. Consequently, the two of us who were obliging the Russian floundered in terminology without having the slightest idea of the procedure and lost all our money, sometimes a very considerable amount as the Baron liked high stakes. I might learn the "basto" and the "spadille" and the "matadors" of one trump by the end of a hand, but my knowledge was useless in the next when a different trump was named. It did not bore the Baron at all to play with fuddled opponents. On one occasion the nightmare lasted three hours and a half and was only concluded because supper was announced.

After that calamitous evening (poor Mr. Pingrey and I each lost fifteen dollars and I had to borrow money from the Countess), I did not go any more to the library, no matter how indisposed I was to chat with the Korean prince who had acquired the remarkable notion that I was an ardent student of pre-dynastic Chinese bone inscriptions, on which he was an expert.

I remained in the large drawing-room, the setting for our ballet. It was furnished with the gleaming surfaces and floral furbelows of Louis Quinze, whimsically repeating the colors and the materials of the costume of the *première danseuse:* if she had chosen pale blue, it was to set off the chairs upholstered in azure satin or the skies in the murals inspired by Boucher and executed by a young relative whom she had sent home at once as soon as he had finished. Another night, as if the looped draperies at the wide bay window had not been admired enough, the Countess appeared in a dress of olive velvet and remarked, "I got the idea from my windows, as you see." There was a profusion of bare marble infants attached by their umbilica to the central support of gilt tables, or sprouting from the center of their curly heads bronze candelabra with a dozen sockets, or standing in pairs on the tops of cabinets bathing one another or posing as if for leap-frog or simply peeking at space with their stone eyes. It particularly irritated Miss Pride that two spurious Watteaus hung on either side of the fireplace where formerly, when the first Mrs. Brooks had been alive, there had been a genuine Trumbull on the right and on the left a stuffed twelve-pound trout from New Brunswick, caught by Ralph Brooks at the age of nine.

This evening, Baron Kalenkoff at once set about to recruit five gulls for loo, among them Nicholas Doman who offered me effusive apologies in several Continental tongues. Out of the corner of my eye, I observed the approach of the Korean prince and fearing that if I were cornered by him, I would miss Dr. McAllister, I cast about for an escape. To my relief, I saw Miss Pride entering with a young man whom I had seen here several times before, and I hastened to her.

"Your admirer is downcast," she said, nodding in the direction of the prince. (She had no use for any race but the Caucasian and she believed that no one these days was a prince and that no one would be until a son was born to the English king.) "Where Berthe finds them all one will never know."

The young Jew at her side gazed about the room with a supercilious detachment. "From an employment agency, no doubt," he said.

Miss Pride, regarding his witticism as inappropriate, gave him a lacerating stare. "And what is it you do, sir?" she inquired.

Several times I had been seated next to the boy at dinner and each time had experienced a pleasurable shock at the resemblance he bore to Nathan Kadish. He was intelligent and insolent, and his voice had in it the same overstimulated quickness that had my friend's. But I had always found in him something lacking but which I could not name. He seemed, despite his carefully composed effrontery, entirely innocent, like a hornet that has been disarmed. Tonight, a trifle not only showed me why I had never struck up more than the most formal acquaintance with him, but restored a scene in Chichester just as earlier in the day I had recovered Ivan's death. A girl passed by and a breath of her lilac scent loitered in the air. The fragrance brought to my mind the last time I had seen Nathan and what I had said to him: "I love your birthmark," but the words reverberated now with a new undertone and with the addition of two other words which had been elided, that is, "I love *you for* your birthmark." And I knew then that all that had fascinated me in Nathan was his disfigurement, solely that, for I had never felt protective of him, had desired more than anything else to touch, examine, and discuss what was taboo. This self-revelation

366

so appalled me that with a rudeness equivalent to that of Miss Pride's companion, I abruptly turned as he was in the middle of a sentence addressed to me, and offering no explanation, walked away to a deserted corner of the room, where I stood, faking a brown study so that I would not be disturbed, as horrified at my sinister nature as if I had found the marks of a vampire on my throat. (On the following day, Miss Pride, never dreaming of the reason why I had gone away, congratulated me on my resolute principles—for she assumed that I had been offended by his insolence which, in her fervor, she believed was incarnate in all Jews—saying, "I would have done the same. Courtesy to a discourteous Jew is beating one's head against a stone wall. And yet I, despite my strong feelings, could never have done what you did.") And I wondered if I would have coveted Philip McAllister if he had not been deformed. Dizzied by this symptom of an abnormal and somewhat repulsive nature in myself, I felt the need to be reassured, but paradoxically, the only person who could reassure me was Philip himself. The moment I had formulated the speech I would make to him when I asked his advice, I realized that I was really not in the least troubled by my perverse taste in men, that I had only been seeking an excuse to occupy his attention with my problems. I suppose that I was determined to be in love at whatever cost.

The Countess was surrounded by her guests who were pleading with her to play for them. The Korean prince had attached himself to Miss Pride and was no doubt lecturing her on bone inscriptions. No one noticed me as I left the room, picking up as I went out, a "fine" edition of Heine's poems, the sort of book to be found all over the house, expensive, delightful to the touch, kept pliable and burnished by a man who came to oil them twice a year. Reconnoitering at the foot of the stairs, I heard nothing save the voices above me, muffled into one, monotonous and fluid, and the occasional chime of metal from the subterranean kitchen. Then I sat primly down on the yellow sofa, letting the book fall open where a red ribbon marked a former reader's place. It was then that I was ashamed of coming down so frankly to waylay Philip, for, although I could not understand the poem, certain phrases, ironic, overharsh out of their context, stood out and served to dismantle me and the room of our reality, so that the lurching shadows, brandished by the candles, the histrionic portrait, the off-beat of my heart like a mis-set metronome became the properties of something third-rate and sentimental: I was like the hoydenish girl growing into womanhood who finds the foretaste of maturity cloying, drives back her unwilling body, partially relaxed in the bud of the bloom, to tomboy pranks. I wanted to get up from the sofa and go back to the drawing-room, but I did not move and told myself that it was absurd to regret what had not happened, that in all likelihood I would do nothing regrettable, but that it would be a test of my strength to remain.

The door-bell rang. I heard the butler pad out of the dining-room and his "Good evening, Dr. McAllister. You'll find them in the drawing-room." I had risen and could see, along the wall, his unaccompanied shadow advancing toward the turn in the lobby. My self-denial, in the half-second before we were face to face, held me poised, but when he had stepped around the corner, my resolve collapsed because the thought that came to me was not, "He has come at last," but "He has come alone for the first time," and I was less conscious of his presence than I was of Hopestill's absence. Thus, when I stepped forward, my gesture was annihilatory, was the action of jealousy so unreasonable and eyeless that neither love for him nor hate for her entered as items in its muddled contents. I stood, an awkward girl of nineteen, with one hand holding the book opened to "Enfant Perdu" and the other grasping the young man's shoulder, and I imprinted on his mouth a lightning-paced and pastoral kiss. There was not, as I wished, a pit of impenetrable darkness to receive me. I tottered back a step and let my hand fall from Philip's shoulder. As if to steady me, he took my hand and I was again propelled towards him while, by way of recognition, he spoke my name, or as by way of prelude, admonitory or consoling,

368

of the kiss with whose ruthless luxury he sought to shake the flesh from my bones. Its abrupt urgency was unmodified, but, like a sudden shaft of blinding light cast by a random luminary, it revealed to us both a principle, a basic form as simple, as abstract as the line between two points. We stepped apart, prepared to partition and bury the sheer serpent. He continued to hold my dry and bloodless hand.

Neither of us spoke, and I, glad that the incident was over and taking his silence as a token that what had just passed between us was not to be incorporated into our relationship (that, being an accident, it deserved neither apology nor analysis), started toward the stairs. But Philip detained me. "We'll go in together," he said.

"Oh, I think we shouldn't," I replied. "Miss Pride is here tonight."

"She doesn't own you. She certainly doesn't own me."

I was uneasy when we entered the drawing-room together, certain that the hubbub in my mind would be visible in my face. Miss Pride, still listening courteously to the Korean, missed nothing, but turned upon us those yellow and accomplished eyes which accused me of committing an outrage. I looked away but Philip returned her stare and said to me, "The effect was just what I wanted."

Miss Pride, scrupulously faithful to her word, did not deprive me of companionship. From time to time, she summoned to dinner a group of people near my own age who, although they were wellborn and well-educated, did not belong, and never would, to her sphere, but to a frustrated imitation of it. The young men, who showed by their faces and their manners that they came from good families, revealed by their clothes that they were not well off, while the girls, students for the most part from Radcliffe, had sublimated their natural longings for dress and parties into a defiant intellectuality, terrifying to someone like myself. The dinner parties were formal and while we were having our cocktails and elaborate canapés in the drawing-room, Miss Pride, grouping us together, attempted to break down the barriers between herself and them and between them and me. And if she succeeded at all and with the help of the Martinis we were talking with a minimum of restraint, our discomfort immediately returned when she, our only leaven, set down her glass and announced, "And now I'm going to leave you to yourselves. You won't want to be bored by an old woman. As my father used to say, no Utopia can destroy the aristocracy of years and the older one grows the more inferior one's caste. Good evening, I must hurry on to my fellow plebeians." She left us. A quarter of an hour elapsed before dinner was served and the cocktail shaker was empty. As she had not commissioned me to refill it, I dared not go back to the pantry in the fear that the vermouth and gin had already been put away and that I would return empty-handed, unable to explain my failure to my guests. A hush then fell upon us and continued through dinner. The young men joined us before half past nine and by ten everyone had gone home. Ashamed, disconcerted by the erudition of the college women who had been discussing Hegel's antinomies, the *Faerie Queen*, and *La Grande Jatte*, I went up to my room to drug myself with typewriter practice.

But because I did not wish to appear ungrateful or incapable of acting as a hostess, I said nothing when Miss Pride planned another of these exhausting fiascos. And since she was a friend of their families, her recruits rarely failed to accept her invitations, usually issued over the telephone to their mothers. Certain that she had pleased me and furthered my interests, she remarked once to the Admiral who had inquired how I put in my time, "Why, she keeps a regular salon to which only the cream of the intelligentsia is bidden. I don't stay among them, they're so formidable, so I always arrange to have other fish to fry. I wouldn't like them to find out what a dunce I am."

It was difficult to reconcile her selection of my friends with her antipathy to "braininess" for these young people had nothing if they had not that. And if she hoped to launch me on a social career which would not interfere with her other plans for me but would satisfy the natural demands of my youth, she was doomed to failure. They were all too busy, too ambitious, and too learned to seek me out, but it did not seem to occur to Miss Pride that it was strange I never received a return invitation.

I easily divined that the principal reason for her supervision of my social life was that she wished to distract me from thinking about Philip. She was not, of course, protecting me from disappointment but was looking out for Hopestill's interests, or rather, for the interests she devoutly desired the girl to have. I had heard from the Countess that the doctor had the reputation of being not only fickle but catholic in his love affairs, and just the year before had been all but engaged to a nurse from Nova Scotia in the Salem hospital whom he had boldly introduced in Boston even though she had, said the Countess, "the table manners of a Bavarian, the opinions of a barbarian, and the looks of a Paphian." It was true that she had been only a passing fancy and as soon as he had broken with her, Philip had fallen in love with Hope all over again as he had done each time he had strayed away. Just as he had often threatened to abandon medicine and become an astronomer or a carpenter or a Trappist monk but always returned to his profession with renewed enthusiasm, so he had invariably come back to Hope after an excursion in another quarter. While it was Miss Pride's belief (relayed to me by the Countess who did not dream, of course, that I had more than the merest interest in the doctor) that he would never marry unless he married her niece, she viewed with trepidation any symptoms in him of infatuation with another girl.

Although she did not mention his name to me and made no comment on the incident at the Countess', her campaign was perfectly apparent. She made a point of never inviting Philip to her house unless Hopestill was there, of always going to the Countess' when he was my partner and on such occasions of taking me home in her own car, of taking any telephone messages from him to me, even though I was at home, on the pretext that I was busy studying my bookkeeping or my shorthand.

He, on his part, was delighted to have a chance to tease her and all during the spring telephoned me almost every day, requesting her to tell me that he would meet me "as usual" at the Lincolnshire or that he would pick me up the following day at Mrs. Hinkel's. The messages were never delivered and he, of course, had not meant them seriously, but Miss Pride arranged to have me run an errand at the hour he had named and, in order to make sure that I was obeying her, telephoned my destination to give me a further commission.

I could have told her that her precautions were needless. We did meet surreptitiously but it was only their secrecy that made our evenings together more entertaining than those I spent with Miss Pride's academicians. We met once every two weeks in the Union Oyster House where, in an atmosphere of sawdust and the acrid rot of crustaceans' shells, Philip was by turns courtly and brusque, but neither the one nor the other to any degree that would have told me how he thought of me. Nor did I, indeed, know how I thought of him. It was as if both of us were engaged in a pursuit of phantoms. We parted formally at the door of Miss Pride's house, but in our short lingering there was a mutual inquiry as if we had seen for an instant that which we desired but which distrust immediately obliterated. We were like blind men who, through some somatic perspicacity, can accurately judge spatial relationships and sense the presence of someone in the room but cannot, without the assistance of their hearing or their touch, know who it is. So we were at once the blind men and were the coy creatures who would not speak and would not offer up their faces or their hands for the expert, identifying touch. Or we were amateurs after nightfall in a terrain we did not know, hearing the hounds bay their triumph; to our untrained ears the sound of these fanatics might come from any direction, and we stumbled, parting company, running this way and that, encouraged by the nearness of the sound which in the next moment was miles away. At last we were to find the captive in its dog-rimmed tree, the coon peering suddenly with its owlish eyes, the clever possum faking sleep; we had known this was the quarry, this quaint and useless beast, but we were disappointed, resented our fatigue and chill, wondered why hunters and dogs night after night returned to the woods for the absurd quest. But going back the way we came, we did not voice our foolish grief, merely commented on the sky and its omens for the next day's weather.

I would afterwards lie sleepless for hours in the double envelope of darkness and quiet. Sometimes my thoughts wandered to other things, but they returned to what most tantalized them, bringing back from the impersonal world, prosaic crusts by which to compare their banquet. I would consider Miss Pride, asleep on the floor below me, as stark as an effigy while Mercy, whom I had never seen, toured the room on considerately noiseless feet. Or I stared at the grove of sharp iron spikes outside my window to keep the pigeons away, like a full quiver in the arc light. Hearing the impatient whistle of a train about to depart, I thought of how, if it were leaving from the North Station, it would pass by Walden Pond and Concord. If it were leaving from the South Station, it would go towards New York, that unimaginable foreign country from which Hopestill dutifully returned each week-end. And I would ponder her in whom there was at work a ferment which neither Philip nor I could analyze. It was more, he said, than a love affair. She would not come back to Boston so faithfully every Friday afternoon if it were only that. Her whole life there was a secret she guarded so jealously that she had refused even to list her address in the *Social Register*. She gave no apparent signs of restlessness. We continued to go to Concord to ride and she as adroitly tortured the McAllister ladies as she had always done. The altercations between her and her aunt were a little more frequent but not much fiercer. But I knew, from our vague and slightly drunken conversations on Friday nights and from our sparse talk on the train back from Concord that she was on bad terms with herself. For there was no longer the camaraderie between us which had allowed us to gossip, to communicate on the same level. The Countess' musical afternoons did not amuse her, nor did she welcome any of my observations on her aunt's friends which heretofore she had relished, saying, "It takes an outlander to trap us alive." We talked now and again of a book, or in a desultory way Hope would tell me of an encounter in a Harlem night-club. There was thus apparently no more between us than between two people whiling away an hour in a train by means of a spotty conversation. At the same time, there was a bond of sorts between us which, although she did not know it, went back to the day when I, a little girl, had first learned that she lived in this house. Sometimes, against my will, my eyes were drawn to the portrait of her as a child. Once, seeing my contemplation of its delicate and sentimental color, she said, "I was really a nasty little proposition although I look so winsome there. But what child wouldn't be nasty who grew up in this place?"

I was infected both by Hopestill's furtive trouble and by Philip's capriciousness and had it not been for Miss Pride's reliably unchanging manner, would have probably given way to a dangerous dissatisfaction. She, I was sure, had no idea that my life did not satisfy me in every particular. She herself was so pleased with my progress that she invited me to live with her again the following year. Indeed, she declared, she hoped I would take up permanent residence on Pinckney Street. She regretted that she could not offer me her hospitality for the summer, but could instead provide me with a splen-did opportunity to put into practice my stenographic training. I was to work in her soap factory in Cam-bridge, an arrangement which everyone except myself regarded with the greatest enthusiasm. The plan was generally thought to be my own idea and Miss Pride would say to her friends, "Sonie is the cleverest person here. No summer stupor for her: she has got herself a job, mind you, and while the rest of us are loafing, she will be earning money." Only the Admiral expressed doubts. "Why, child," he said, "won't you be lonesome?"

I was extremely lonesome. Philip had gone back to Chichester, and all the people I had met at Miss Pride's or at the Countess' had left for the Cape or the North

Shore. It was too hot to read. My furnished bedroom on Kirkland Street was under the roof and the air was motionless all night. I lay naked on the bare floor, the sweat tickling my legs and back like flies' feet and, stupefied, I thought of nothing. It was, in this season, almost a pleasure to visit my mother. Although the trip was complicated, including three stages, by bus, by subway, and again by bus, I made it with a sort of martyred delight. As I sat in the crowded subway train, nudged by people carrying fading flowers and boxes of cake to their Sunday hostesses, or fanning their streaming faces with the Boston *Globe*, or swaying half asleep from the heat, I was more at ease than I had ever been in Miss Pride's house. At ease, even though at the end of the torpid journey there was neither rest nor entertainment, but the disinfected madhouse where I sat with Mamma, bored, sleepy but required to be on my guard each moment.

On the few unseasonable evenings when a languid breeze stirred the papers on my writing table and my pores stopped gushing, I wrote letters to Philip and to Hopestill and to Miss Pride, but only the last did I ever mail. On the way home from the letter box, I would stop and buy a bottle of sherry and once again in my characterless room would steep myself in the harsh, unpalatable wine and stare gloomily at the crabbed, complaining lines I had written to the people I could not fathom, yet could not ignore.

3

The second autumn in Boston differed from the first only in that we had begun the memoirs. We worked each morning except Sunday from the time our consultation with the servants ended until luncheon was announced, but for all our diligence we proceeded at such a snail's pace that I saw we had before us a labor of many years, and I wondered if the final product would be worth it. For Miss Pride, shrewd, witty, and fluent in conversation, was inarticulate when she began to write. The juvenility of her diction and the crudity of her syntax surprised me, for her few letters to me had been as elegant as her speech. After floundering for some months with no success, we at last hit upon a plan. She would write me a letter, very carefully in the style of Horace Walpole, of whom she was an assiduous student, which begged me to set down in "sound English" the anecdote which she then wrote out in her tumid language. As her calligraphy was obscure (not intentionally, as the Countess von Happel's was, but because she wrote in the heat of passion), it often took me a full morning to decipher a single sentence and in a short time my desk bore a formidable sheath of manuscript which I had not transcribed or edited. Thus, all morning we worked facing one another at two long desks which had been pushed together.

Hopestill came home less often than she had done the year before and when she did come, I rarely saw her. We discontinued our evenings in her room and our rides in Concord. She was apparently so uninterested in anyone in Boston that she preferred her own society and during her visits kept to her room, emerging only for meals. Gradually she became for me no more than a ghost, one belonging in a way to Chichester, and I was free at last of any envy of her. Her clothes, if they were more spectacular, were no more expensive than mine; if I did not have Philip McAllister's whole heart, as she had had it at various times in her life, I had his constant companionship which even Miss Pride had been forced to recognize and tolerate. In my good fortune, I could afford to pity her for her misanthropy, and for the solitude in which she inexplicably had immersed herself. It was therefore the more startling that we again came together without warning and with most savage intimacy.

Philip had not waited even long enough for a cup of tea, but had only come to arrange to call for me at dinner time. We were going later to the Countess'. The business had been transacted within earshot of Miss Pride intentionally, and while she made no alternative suggestion, she said with great displeasure, "I hoped you

would have dinner with me. Now I shall be all alone."
Philip gave her a smile. "She needs a change of air every
now and again, you know."

The younger Mrs. McAllister had been Christmas
shopping and declared when she came in that the only
thing which had relieved the tedium of the task was the
prospect of a "reviving chat with Lucy Pride." She had,
however, after a perfunctory, albeit effusive, salutation
to her hostess, immediately sought out Amy Brooks and
the two of them had sat, heads together, on the sofa
where Amy was in the habit of holding court for Mr.
James and Mr. Pingrey. Philip paid his brief compliments to his mother and left the room. I went to the
window and saw him for a moment hesitating before he
went down the street. I was surprised to see that he was
wearing a bowler today and that he carried a stick, for
usually his dress was of the most casual. I experienced a moment of peculiar distaste for him as I watched
his grotesquely military bearing in which, it seemed to
me, I had sensed a new element.

Half an hour after he had gone, Hopestill made an
entrance into the drawing-room, pausing as she had
done the first time I saw her, at the tulip-wood commode to reconnoiter and to determine which of the
guests after her aunt deserved her first greeting. She was
dressed in green moiré, the severity of which did not
check her flaming beauty but struggled with it in a magnificent combat, so that her sudden appearance in the
doorway, unexpected, was like a chivalric, plangent war
brought to our quiet gathering.

"Why, Hope!" cried Miss Pride. "I didn't expect you
for ten days."

"I know," laughed her niece. "It was to be a surprise,
Auntie. You're glad, I trust?"

Because she had never before "surprised" her aunt
with a visit, the old lady looked questioningly at her, but
smiled and said, "Delighted."

When she had kissed Miss Pride and the Admiral,
Hopestill crossed the room to Philip's mother who, on
seeing her, cried out, "Oh, how glad I am I dropped in
today! I never dreamed you'd be here. Philip will be

wild when he knows he missed you. He just this minute left."

"It's nice of you to say that he'll be 'wild,' Mrs. McAllister. But since Amy was here I imagine he had quite a full enough afternoon without me."

Mrs. McAllister bit her lip in vexation. Philip had only nodded to Amy. Moreover, Amy had dropped a few remarks that had intimated at a romantic attachment to Edward Pingrey. I had heard Mrs. McAllister say, "But, Amy, he's not really your sort of person, do you think so? I'm extremely taken with Edward, as we all are, but he has never really belonged to your set . . . to yours and Philip's, that is." Amy ingenuously replied, "Why, Philip and I don't belong to the same set at all. I believe he thinks I'm unconventional." Her giggles commenced and drowned out the older woman's next speech.

Now, unwittingly nettling Mrs. McAllister, she said to Hopestill, "He snubbed me completely. He only came to make a rendezvous with Sonie."

"Ah," said Hope, glancing in my direction. But she turned again to her cousin. "I like your dress, Amy." She could not suppress a smile for Amy, who had no judgment about clothes, was wearing bright red wool, most unbecoming to her colorless face to which she had clumsily applied orange lip rouge and excessive mascara.

"It's terribly red, isn't it?" cried Amy, beside herself with her strange nervousness. "Edward likes it! Hope! I have read Freud since I saw you last!"

Hopestill smiled condescendingly and turned to Philip's mother. "I hope your mother will still let me dress at her house."

"Will you ride in this weather?" cried Mrs. McAllister.

"It's just the kind I like. The colder, the better."

"Well, you know you're always welcome, my dear. You haven't changed your mind about coming to my house instead? But perhaps you wouldn't like to feel indebted to Philip for I should give you his old playroom and he's most sentimental about it. I don't blame you: I shouldn't like to owe that young man a thing. Tell me truthfully, Hope, don't you think he has a heartless nature?"

"Indeed I do," replied the girl. "And that's the reason we've always got on so famously, for I'm heartless too."

"What a fib! No one has a warmer heart than you." Hopestill, outraged because Mrs. McAllister had raised her voice so that everyone in the room could hear her, took her leave but not before she had said icily, "It's kind of you to compliment me so, but I'm bound to disappoint you if you really think I'm warm-hearted."

They embraced tenderly and the older woman said, "You could never disappoint me, Hopestill Mather."

I had been on the point of going upstairs for I had a few letters to type out for Miss Pride, but Hopestill intercepted me and taking me by the arm, led me back to the love-seat in the bay window. As we sat down, I saw that she was shockingly altered from the last time she had been here: the violet glades were deep beneath her glaring eyes and as deep were the new hollows in her pale cheeks which had lost their luster and had the gray opacity of fatigue. And as she talked, hysteria expanded her nostrils and shook her lips.

"Where did Philip go? To the hospital?"

I told her I thought he had gone home to dress for dinner.

"I'll telephone him then. I'm awfully anxious to see him. I don't suppose he told you what his plans were for the evening?"

"Why, yes. I'm having dinner with him and afterwards we're going to the Countess'."

She raised her eyebrows in a faked surprise. "Oh! I didn't know you actually dined with him."

"Yes. I often do."

She repeated, "I didn't know you actually dined with him. But it's of no importance. I dare say he didn't know I was coming on today. I wrote but perhaps the letter was delayed. I should have wired."

"You wrote?" My alarmed question was involuntary. Then, flustered by her lofty imperturbability, I said, "I've got some letters to go off. I'd better go up now."

"Will you look in on me when you've dressed, Sonie?"

I rose and started across the room as Hopestill went to sit beside Admiral Nephews. Miss Pride, who had left

379

the room just after her niece arrived, was returning and I confronted her in the hall. "I trust you're going back to the letters. They're urgent and must go off tonight by air." I promised that I would not fail to get them in the post and moved past her. "One thing more, Sonie," she said, laying her hand on my arm. "I cannot condone —and I certainly cannot overlook—your behavior with Dr. McAllister. Two people remarked to me today that you seemed to be flirting with him. For your sake, I denied the accusation though I regret to say that in doing so I was also denying the evidence my eyes furnished me. I speak only for your own good, believe me, Sonie. I don't blame *you*. What was more natural than for you to go to Berthe von Happel's little parties with him? But it shouldn't have gone beyond *that*, my dear. It's been imprudent of Philip to encourage you in this infatuation. If I had been he and saw what was coming over you, I would have left you strictly alone. Why, Sonie, you're too sensible a girl to hitch your wagon to a star like that. Surely you must have heard what sort of person he is—one can't count the girls he's trifled with."

"Oh, you needn't worry about me, Miss Pride," I told her. "I have my feet on the ground."

"That's the way to talk! I knew you had good sense. Well, we all must take our foolish holidays, mustn't we? But now, since you know people have talked—unjustly I do believe—you'll take care not to let them talk again, won't you? Run along now and don't forget the letters. Isn't it nice that Hopestill came back just in time?"

"In time for what?" I inquired dully.

"Why, in time for Berthe's party. This is her most elaborate one of the year."

It was still early when I went to Hopestill's room, but she was already dressed and was seated before her fire engaged in wrapping a Christmas present. Her small sitting-room was confused with suitcases and unopened parcels and in the window stood a locked wardrobe trunk. "As you see," she said, following my eyes, "I've come back for good. When I've tied this knot, let's have a glass of sherry. Can you believe it, I had the fortitude to take a bottle of Aunt Lucy's private stock." I said I would have none. "Oh, do!" She dropped her package and took hold of my wrist, digging her enameled talons into my skin, as if my abstention from the stolen sherry threatened a catastrophe. She filled two glasses and gave me one. "Here, take it. You've never tasted anything like it."

She took a sip from her glass and picking up the fallen ribbon and the shears, turned to her work again. "Sonie," she said, "would you mind awfully if I went to dinner tonight with Philip?"

I drank before I answered her. "Did your aunt tell you to ask me?"

"Auntie? Of course she didn't. What business would it be of hers?"

"I only wondered."

"Well, she didn't. It was my own idea. I knew you wouldn't mind and you don't, do you? Did he by any chance," she said, looking up from her package, "send you those camellias you're wearing?"

I said he had. "They're lovely on your dress and what a lovely dress it is, too." I could not return her smile. She went on matter-of-factly, "Look here, Sonie, you're not in love with him, are you? Because if you are, I'm devilishly sorry. I'm afraid I rather put ideas in your head."

"Oh, I assure you you didn't."

"Sonie, I simply couldn't stick New York any longer!" she burst out. "I don't think I'll ever leave Boston again. It's more than flesh can bear to be separated from the only thing in the world one gives a tinker's damn about."

"What do you mean? This house?"

"You know perfectly well I mean Philip." She gave me a quick, bright smile intended to tell me that I was the first to be let in on her secret. "By the way, would you rather have your Christmas present now or wait? You know this year, for the first time in my life, I'm actually looking forward to Aunt Lucy's Christmas tree even though there is something really revolting about

the way she hauls the servants up and gives them ridiculous presents. Do you know that once she gave Ethel
two decks of cards in a monogrammed leather case for
Whist parties?"

Wishing to have these pointless preliminaries finished,
I said, "I'd like to have my present now."

"Oh, darling! How impossible of me! I just remembered it won't be here until tomorrow. It's a phonograph
and several albums of records."

I was touched by her generosity and when I thanked
her, she said, "After all, it was the least I could do, wasn't
it?" The remark erased the kindness from her gift, told
me with its frank interrogation that it was even less than
solace but was the payment of a bribe the necessity of
which she had anticipated, even though she had declared
a little while before that she was not aware I dined with
Philip. Hearing then her condescending negotiations, I
was like a child who is told that he may not go to the
picnic but for his supper may have a cream-puff. In his
grief he believes he is offered a choice and cries, "But I
don't *want* a cream-puff!" and cannot believe that his
franchise is specious, nor can he persuade the governor
of the nursery that while he likes cream-puffs and any
other night would welcome them for supper, this is not
the night; he *wants* only the hard-boiled eggs and the
cold chicken that are to be on the menu of the picnic. I
did not want the phonograph although for several
months I had been wishing for one, and while I could
not say, like the disappointed child, that I did not, I
could, like him, point out certain drawbacks in the gift.
The child would say, "I don't want a cream-puff and it's
silly because nurse told me we were having steamed
pudding for supper and we can't have both and I think
they're horrid anyway," and I said, "But I wish you
hadn't bought me any records because our taste is probably not the same at all."

"Oh, Sonie, I'm sorry!" I had really distressed her and
thought I even saw signs of tears in her exhausted eyes.
She said, "I've tried so hard!" and thinking that she
meant she had tried so hard to please me and my ingratitude was more than she could bear, I quickly said,

"Oh, don't! I've really longed for a phonograph, and I've no doubt the records can be exchanged if I don't like them."

"I didn't mean that. I meant I had tried so hard in other ways. Well, it was all lost a long time ago and it's useless to try to regain it. I mean my balance was lost, my integrity, whatever it is in the name of God that keeps one together."

She poured herself another glass of sherry. "Do you want to hear an ugly yarn?" she said. "I haven't been 'studying' in New York at all, as Auntie knew and everyone must have suspected. I was going to a psycho-analyst and paying out fifteen dollars an hour for his nasty mumbo-jumbo. He had shaded lamps and old copies of the *New Yorker* and big divans in his waiting room where we all sat, so scornful of one another, pretending, every damned one of us, that we weren't there on business but had just come to pay a social call or had just dropped in to rest our feet. He had two Siamese cats that I grew to hate so violently that the doctor declared I had a cat complex, and he was beside himself with triumph when I volunteered, merely to pass the time, that Aunt Lucy had a cat that she kept locked up in her bedroom. He really said 'Eureka!' as though the whole problem were settled and it would only be a matter of minutes to find the cure. It's exactly like a dream and I can't really believe that he advised me that day to go out and buy a cat, *not*, mind you, a Siamese but a Persian tortoise shell like Mercy although I kept telling him that I had no objection to Mercy and it was his own wretched animals that I detested. He said I had come to substitute himself for my aunt! I kept going back because it quickly became a habit and at the same time I was doing just the same things I'd always done before because now I had confessed my sins they didn't seem very bad. He told me I wasn't co-operating and I got the notion that I was getting by with something because I was deceiving him the way I used to deceive the teachers at school and then Aunt Lucy and I enjoyed it all the more with him because he was powerless. I took the keenest pleasure in doing all the things I pretended I hated. His name was Dr. Ragsdale and I would tell him my dreams in which it was changed to 'Dr. Ratsbane.' He was pigeon-breasted and so evil I always knew he was homosexual and alcoholic as well as clinically insane."

"But why . . ." I began.

"Why, indeed? I kept thinking, I suppose, that I'd develop such a horror of my nature and the way he mauled it that I would at last be able to change. But I didn't. And so I have come back to Boston. *Here* maybe I can. There's probably a devil in me, one straight from hell like those in the Salem witches my ancestors used to burn."

She was sincere. A silence followed her words in which that evil she believed in and urged me to believe in was like a third person in the room; or it was like an innovation in the furnishings which was felt but not immediately perceived. I remembered, in that quiet, a series of small incidents which had puzzled me but which I had put out of my mind: once, the year before, when we were on our friendliest terms, she had brought me a present of a chartreuse evening gown which she had bought for herself and had afterwards discovered was too large. Chartreuse was a color I could not possibly wear as there were tints in my skin inimical to any variations of green or yellow, and since Hopestill and I had discussed this very misfortune sometime before when we had been shopping, I was naturally surprised at her gift. But in order to please her I put it on and went down to the sitting-room. Hopestill and her aunt were both there. "For heaven's sake!" cried Miss Pride. "Where did you get that frightful dress, child? You're the color of bile! Run back up this minute and change to that pretty blue of yours." "Yes, do, Sonie," agreed Hopestill, "it's awful." I was glad enough to change and went out, but stopping in the hall a minute to glance over a pile of letters I had put on the table to make sure they were all stamped, I chanced to hear Hopestill say, "I can't think what got into me when I bought it for her. I was so proud of myself to remember her size, but imagine my forgetting that she couldn't wear that color," so that I knew she had not bought it for herself as she had told me. Another time, she had told me that she wanted me to meet a very distinguished cousin of hers who had married an Oxford don and was visiting for a few weeks in Milton. She said she had arranged a small dinner party and particularly wanted me to come because she thought I would find Lady So and So very amusing. And yet, when the day arrived and I warned her that I might be a few minutes late as I had to run an errand for Miss Pride in Cambridge, she said, "As a matter of fact, Sonie, Aunt Lucy asked me to tell you to stay at the Cock Horse for dinner and she'll send Mac around for you at nine. We're having a little dinner party for a cousin of mine who's a great bore and a stickler for family and that kind of thing."

Her malice was conscious, but its genesis was abrupt and unplanned, or seemed to be, though actually it must have been calculated painstakingly in the craters of her subconscious mind, so that probably she had intended to buy the dress for herself but a sudden impulse had made her select my size rather than her own and she had forgotten, in her guilt, the story she had told me and had told her aunt quite another. Now, having discovered the diathesis predisposing her to these brutalities I looked upon her with detachment, and thinking that what she wanted tonight was not to be with Philip but to spoil my evening (a desire which came from the same mischief that had prompted her to give me the dress), I resolved to keep my appointment with him.

Her mood had changed from one of restive worry to a sort of mild elation. She stretched out full length before the fire, her hair like the beams of a monstrance as it lay gleaming on the green carpet. The arc of her wide turquoise velvet skirt was broken by her small feet shod in gold dancing slippers. About her throat she wore a tightly plaited gold chain from which depended a scarabaeus fluted with lapis lazuli. We were so still we heard Miss Pride moving about her room on the floor below us.

"It's late," I said. "I'm afraid I must go down."

"Go down? But I thought you had agreed."

I stood up. "You know I didn't. But if you insist on

it, take his flowers." As I unpinned them, I pricked my
finger and I thought how ruinous and beautiful this
jewel of blood would be if it were to drop and glisten
on her blue-green skirt.

She received the camellias, but as she pinned them to
her shoulder, a shudder streamed from her face to her
frivolous feet. "I wonder if he . . ."

"If he what?"

"If when he bought them he touched them with his
hands. Oh, God!" She covered her face with her fingers,
but her eyes were visible through the interstices. She
stared up at me with a plea which, being unable to
fathom, I could not grant. But as I turned to go, leaving
the issue constructed between us like a barrier with no
purpose, the girl's seemingly diverse moods which she
had addressed to me since our first words in the drawing-
room at tea time now appeared as an unbroken concatenation, and I was enlightened as I saw the uniform-
ity of her whims. I divined, through an intuition which
had never been exercised in me before, either because
of a physical immaturity or because of the want of
circumstances, that there was a sole exigency that could
drive her to this corner where, for all her insolence, she
was terrified. And as I realized that not the satanic par-
ticles but the organic chemistry of her composition had
led her to this replacement of myself for the evening
(a replacement she was determined, I now knew, to
make permanent), I was ready to withdraw any claims I
might have had since her need was so much greater than
my own. My delay at the door, occasioned by this certain
understanding, may have communicated its derivation
to her, although she said, to my surprise (for in this instant after I realized that my hand had been half a
minute on the door knob, I almost expected her to confirm my suspicions, to admit frankly that she was pregnant), "Take back the flowers and go to dinner with
him. I will see you all at Berthe's." I had not fully
turned around and I envisaged the flowers, their ma-
genta petals protecting the golden filaments of the core,
and as I went back to retrieve them (though I no longer
wanted them, for by their exchange of hands they had

386

been bruised and their significance had been polluted)
my eyes traversed the window where, by arc light from
Louisburg Square, the cold December snow was falling,
and I remembered, as we remember comfort when the
crisis of our pain descends and hints of our recovery
are given us, that Philip had told me once that camellias
bloomed in midwinter in New Orleans.

The single peal, three flights down, preceded a moment the six bells struck by the nautical clock on Hopestill's mantel. "It's Philip," I said, as I bent over to take
the flowers. My utterance of his Christian name, upon
the heels of my recollection of his report that camellias
bloomed this time of year in the south (for, unable to
visualize such a phenomenon, I had merely thought the
words, Philip said . . .) imparted to my flesh an inchoate, sensual delight, similar as I perceived to that I had
experienced when, identifying my own body with Hopestill's to make my diagnosis of her altered nature, my
comprehension had not been established by logic but
by the completion of my own ripening. Hopestill still
lay before the fire in her strategic immobility. It was
strategic because she appeared transfixed by an invisible
pinion to the floor as if, like the possum or the dung-
beetle playing dead, she would come to life at once upon
my departure. Her eyes, apparently shut, took in each
motion it was necessary for me to make to unpin the
flowers from her shoulder and, glancing at the bits of
shining eyeball, visible through her long, sparse auburn
lashes and seeing once in that brief space of my perusal,
the gold-flecked iris that enshrined the eye's soul, I knew
myself to be in the presence of desperation so rarefied
at this climax reared up by the signal at the outer door
that it resembled lethargy. And simultaneously, I knew
that no one else would see what I had seen and that she
would go scot-free. Although at this point in her there
was ambush and a cause for it, both would be obliterated; the sins would be exorcised not by the psycho-
analyst but by concealing custom.

When I had left her and had stepped into the corridor,
the sensation that summarized the scene in Hopestill's
sitting-room was not one of anger or indignation, had

nothing in it more unfavorable to her than my old and now enfeebled antipathy to the child in the Barstow dining-room. I directed the movement of my body to partake of the grace of my dinner dress, desiring, as though Miss Pride's dim hallway were lined with spectators, my organism to proclaim through its flattering draperies that the force inspiring me was one of fleshly love, akin to the passion that had undone Hopestill and with devoted obstinacy still clung to her in her dilemma. The love I felt, which like a rapid poison circulated throughout me, had no object, and until I was on the last flight of stairs from the top of which I saw Philip's hat and gloves on the vestibule table, my desire did not focus, for until then, the elusive lover I had tried to construct was that unnamed, unacknowledged man whose impregnation of Hopestill was also an exegesis of my own changing self. Then, attaching my attention to a well-known object, for the space of ten seconds, I was determined to finish with him what I had so indecisively begun. But the moment my desire materialized, it vanished; the shame that recalled me to my usual timidity was incommensurate with its cause: at the same time that I took in the doctor's bowler and the gray suède gloves. I heard Miss Pride's voice through the closed door of her bedroom: "You may go now, Ethel. I am ready to undress." The direction, which was probably superfluous to the well-trained maid who knew by heart her mistress's habits, fell upon my ear like an injunction repeated to herself by a nun, and I could no more imagine Miss Pride in the deshabille she painstakingly kept for the eyes only of her mirrors, than I could have imagined a Mother Superior in her nightdress. I took no pleasure now in the décolletage of my new frock, and thought it would be improved by the addition of a shawl thrown about my shoulders. But the atavistic reaction was not complete as it had been formerly, when I was a child and had loathed my mother for those qualities I had now discovered in myself. For I had gone too far, by becoming myself a protagonist, to believe blindly any longer that Miss Pride's was the ideal pattern: there was, in the tone of her voice, cold and neutral, a suggestion of ingrown, conceited lewdness which, having no sexuality to modify, advertised the secret nudity of the old, arid carcass.

The doctor had been shown into the library where he stood inaudibly conversing with a large young man, shaped like an athlete, but one whose muscles had relaxed already and beneath whose chin a soft second growth had begun. They turned to greet me and Dr. McAllister introduced me to his friend, Frank Whitney. The doctor was nervous and would not sit down. He said, "I've just lost my first patient and if there's anything here besides Grandfather Pride's port, I'd like to resort to the traditional sedative. Do you keep any whiskey here?" We did. I brought out a decanter of whiskey and a tumbler. Philip poured the glass three-quarters full. "I can blame only myself, although some kind-hearted person said the x-ray reading had been at fault. It was a skull-fracture and I advised against operating." He drank half the whiskey and then, pausing, with the glass still in his hand, he said, "How stupid! I poured out three times as much as I wanted," yet his hand remained suspended, clasping the tumbler and I knew that he wanted the rest of it, indeed, probably wanted another double portion, but that his will denied it to him.

"Hopestill is here," I said. The response on his face to my announcement was a compressed version of what I had seen on the first afternoon I met her when he raised his hand and touched her hair. But his look was not one of surprise and I wondered again what she had written him.

"That's convenient," he said. "Frank decided at the last minute to come along. We can all go together. By the way, some friends of Hope's rang me up a little while ago and said they were stopping by here . . . perhaps we can offer them a drink, what do you say?"

"Hope wasn't expecting to have dinner with us," I said.

"I'm sure we can persuade her," put in Frank Whitney.

"Oh, yes, I have no doubt we can," I replied. "She's very anxious to see you, Philip."

"That's good of her."

"She's come back to stay. Did you know?"

Hopestill entered the room. The animal that had matured in Philip's disciplined person, despite the herculean efforts of his Puritan will, strained towards its meeting with that other specimen of the same genus that I had seen rioting in the cold prison of the girl recumbent before her hearth. I turned away as he went to greet her and discovered Frank Whitney's dreamy brown eyes regarding me with wonder. I had picked up Philip's half-emptied glass and downed it. "Do you often do that?" inquired the young man. "I mean, drink that much whiskey neat?"

"No," I told him. "But it's a good idea."

Philip was telling Hopestill that her friends were coming here. "The person who telephoned me was named Morgan," he said.

"Oh, yes, of course. I know him," replied Hopestill. "He's from Long Island. From a branch of the family famous for its lack of fame. Quite a barbarian he is, but I'm rather fond of him."

"Morgan?" said Mr. Whitney as if it were a name he had heard in some unsavory connection. "I don't know any Morgans." He uttered it as an accusatory epithet, as if its etymology had vested the name with repectability but its root meaning glared forth in the pronunciation; it was as if he had said, "A rum runner? I don't know any rum runners."

The door-bell rang, bringing us, in a moment, Mr. Morgan and a couple who were introduced with a great deal of laughter as the Cabots, the reason for the hilarity being that their name was really Babbitt. Mr. Babbitt who, because of an unfortunate obtrusion of his mouth, resembled an animal that rhymed with both Cabot and Babbitt (I pointed this out to Frank Whitney later and he said gravely, "That's not our kind of joke."), came up to me as if we had known one another all our lives and said, "Where's the booze, honey?"

"The drinks are coming now," I said. Ethel had brought in glasses and ice at Hope's order.

"That's dandy. Are you going to Berthe von Happel's

shindig?" I replied that I was and remarked that I was sure it would be a very lavish party since the Countess had dispensed with the dinner party and had expended all her efforts on the midnight supper.

"Oh, she'll give us our money's worth tonight, bless her royal heart. I nipped in this afternoon for five minutes to see if I could lend a hand, and had a look into that gorgeous drawing-room of hers. Would you believe it, she has a Christmas tree—a *tannenbaum*, as she insists —reaching to the ceiling, an absolute smack in Louis Quinze's face. And she has poinsettias in green tubs all over the house, for all the world like a department store."

"She's really appalling," said his wife, "but it's impossible not to adore her."

This was a brazen untruth, but Hopestill, Philip, and Frank Whitney all enthusiastically seconded it. The irony of the expressions, "Isn't that absolutely the case!" "I love her parties, particularly her Christmas parties," and "She's a jewel, I'm head over heels in love with Berthe!" was so deeply embedded that had I not known that the authors of these praises actually despised the Countess, I should have thought them a cult convening to eulogize a high priestess. Thus, when they described her drawing-room to someone who had never seen it, they appeared to find it enchanting, and it was only the initiated who knew that some such statement as "She has two spurious Watteaus which are so charming one doesn't mind their being frauds," was actually inspired by the most savage spitefulness. The stranger, whose ear missed the note of contempt, at once admired the Bostonians for their defense of the Countess and felt little interest in the house itself, believing the word "charming" had been used out of simple generosity.

"Do you suppose Kalenkoff will be there?" asked Mr. Babbitt and the whole room laughed. Accustomed to their own habits of inbreeding and holding the common notion that royalty east of Austria was worthless because it was so abundant, these American aristocrats seemed to frequent the Louis Quinze salon chiefly for the purpose of snubbing its titled habitués. An obscure professor of physics from the University of Paris fared better at their hands than an archduke, and the dashing Baron Kalenkoff was invited nowhere while a wealthy British manufacturer of photographic equipment had a standing invitation to the best houses and clubs. They were so perversely American, so vehemently uninterested in any culture but that which their ancestors had found acceptable that they even went out of their way to offend the Countess' friends by their intentionally inaccurate pronunciations of German place names or their smug misconstruction of political philosophy or even, though this was regarded as *démodé,* by bragging of the excellence of the American sanitary system. On the one Saturday the year before when the Admiral had put in an appearance, he had said to Baron Kalenkoff, "Is it true, mate, that you Russian chaps sleep with dogs in your bunks?" The Baron flashed him a friendly smile. "It is customary," he said. "And when our guests are shown to their rooms they do not find detective novels and magazines on the night table to amuse them but they find the master's best dog in the bed. If the guest is any kind of a gentleman, he will refuse this extravagant kindness and will insist that he be given the *second* best dog. You may be sure, sir, that if he does not hesitate to climb into bed with his host's prize wolfhound, he will never be asked again." The Admiral was flabbergasted by this leg-pull and moved away, remarking gruffly to Mrs. Frothingham who quite agreed with him, "Those Russians have no sense of humor."

Mr. Morgan alone did not join in the laughter and I surmised that he did not know the Countess. He had said nothing after the introductions and I quite erroneously thought that he was ill at ease. But when the laughter had subsided, he stepped forward shakily and said, "Don't you know I'm to be congratulated?" Mr. Babbitt then informed us that Mr. Morgan was celebrating his coming into a vast fortune through the death of his grandmother. To my astonishment, I heard Philip propose a toast.

"Thank you, thank you," said the heir, bowing at his

stocky waist. "Somebody is missing from this conference, isn't somebody? It looks like a damned little conference, and what is this place we're holding it in? The Atheneum?"

"The missing person," said Mr. Babbitt, familiarly nudging me with his elbow, "beg pardon, the missing link is Miss Nanny Brewster whom you left in the ladies' retiring room at the Ritz bar."

"Nanny Brewster?" cried Hopestill shrilly. "What do you mean by bringing that street-walker to my house?"

Morgan patted her shoulder and said soothingly, "There, there, she isn't in the Atheneum. Didn't you hear John say she was in the W.C.?"

Frank Whitney abruptly presented his back to the company, whispering to me, "I remember him now," and began to read the titles of a section of books on Far Eastern studies. In a moment I joined him, preferring his pastime to the discussion of Miss Brewster's whereabouts, but not before Mr. Babbitt murmured to me with a moist laugh, "I don't know which one of them is getting the run-around." We were some distance from the others, Mr. Whitney and I, when he growled, "Bad blood is the rule with those Long Islanders. How can Hope stomach a buffoon like Harry Morgan?" And then, because Mr. Babbitt seemed to be approaching us again, he said, taking a book down, "Here's a funny thing, a Japanese novel translated into German. I call that too much of a good thing." Then when we saw that we were to be left alone since Mr. Babbitt was joining his friends, Frank Whitney told me about Morgan.

Mr. Harry Morgan was thirty years old. His equine face was being elongated year by year by the withdrawal of his black hair, and was being softened year by year by good living which the death of his grandmother, happily coinciding with Christmas, was evidently to make even better. We read in the newspapers that scions of famous families have gone to Hollywood to join, usually in a social capacity, the "film colony," and it is hard to tell, from the impartial journalists, whether the colonists or the immigrant are hereby benefited. Mr.

Morgan was such a person, although, if his credentials had been gone into, it would have been found that he was so distantly related to any of the celebrated tycoons whose name he bore that he was no more entitled to a share in their glory than is a person named Shakespeare entitled to the homage of literary people. But it happened that this Mr. Morgan was extremely wealthy and few knew that his money came from the maternal side of his family, named Schumacher, and had been made in a variety of enterprises, including brewing, the manufacture of artificial limbs, razor blades, hooks and eyes, and the breeding of longhorn cattle. But the fact of the money, not its history, was the important thing. It was likely that had his father's name been Schumacher and he had not used Morgan at all or had used it as a middle name, he would have been as readily accepted in California. However, "the wealthy young Morgan" was a title of more tone than "Schumacher, the artificial limb heir." At the same time that he maintained an establishment in New York near a café called the Lancelot Club which he owned, he not only frequently visited Sun Valley, Idaho, and while he was about it looked in at his Beverly Hills cottage, but he was also, and had been for years, a student at Harvard College. There was a rumor, Mr. Whitney told me, never confirmed, that he had once made application for a Rhodes scholarship.

"I won't go anywhere if that tart is going along," Hopestill was saying. "Really, Harry! And you're drunk."

"Let's not anybody quarrel," he replied amicably. "You had a last five or six drinks too many in the club car, sweetheart, you can't fool Harry. And how come you weren't on the train you told me to meet?"

"I got off at Back Bay," she said shortly.

It was as though we had come into a moving picture halfway through and because we did not know the beginning of the plot, could not adjust this scene to the foregoing action. Philip McAllister, standing witness to the intimate tiff, looked suddenly faint. "Excuse me," he murmured and backed away. For the second time, he

394

told Frank Whitney and me about the skull-fracture case, of whose fatal termination he had learned over the telephone just after he had left our house at tea time. "Let me show you," he said, taking a pencil and envelope out of his pocket, "what it was in the x-ray reading that deceived me," and he began to draw a skull, but his hand trembled so, either from his surprise at Hopestill's almost domestic shrewishness with Morgan whom she had pretended to know only casually, or from a relapse into his earlier shock, that the outline was pinked like a valentine. Above his insistent explanation, I could hear the others talking and I was so intent on their conversation that from the doctor I learned only that the skull might be likened to an egg, which, broken on one side, might break simultaneously on the other, that his patient, struck on the temple had "sustained" an occipital fracture which he had misread as merely the widening of a suture line.

The Babbitts and Mr. Morgan had grouped themselves about the chess-table and seeing the men set up on the board, in readiness for Miss Pride's Sunday maneuvers, remarked that this was the final touch which proved that they had strayed into a club. To create the illusion that it was a commercial club, they put the board and pieces on the floor and set up in their place the bottle of whiskey to which they freely helped themselves. Hopestill, who had been standing by the fire gazing abstractedly into the spurting logs, joined them when they treatened to put ice down her back if she didn't, and they sat, the four of them, round the little table, at play, as if they were in a night-club and had grown bored with their surroundings so that they had turned to their own private jokes and gossip for entertainment.

I interrupted the medical monologue. "Listen, Philip," I said, "this makes me nervous. What if Miss Pride should come in?"

"What if she should? Hope is her own mistress, isn't she?" he replied touchily.

"But such strange people," I said. Both young men stared coldly at me and I flushed.

"Helen Babbitt is Hope's cousin," said Mr. Whitney solemnly. "I must admit, though, that they *are* an unattractive lot."

Philip agreed with a laugh and turning to me forgivingly, he explained that Mrs. Babbitt had been a Miss Brooks and therefore related both to Hopestill and, by marriage, to the Countess, and while no one had ever liked her, for she was a fool and had not worn stockings to her wedding, people forgot this and came to believe that the interloper from New Jersey had made her into what she was. Admiral Nephews had remarked to her, "Madam, thou art mated to a clown," and ever afterwards it was the universal opinion that Mr. Babbitt had had the weight to drag her down. They came to Boston at Thanksgiving and Christmas to the great suffering of Mrs. Babbitt's family who were, ironically enough, related in several different ways to the Cabots.

"I suppose it's natural enough Hope's taken up with them," said Whitney. "She's probably lonely in New York."

"I would say the contrary," returned Philip drily. "I've concluded that Sonie is right: Miss Lucy would have epilepsy if she came in here now. I'll see what I can do." And he called across the room to the group at the chesstable, "Don't you think it's time we went on to dinner?"

"Why, doctor, what a childish idea," said Mr. Morgan, "we are just beginning our *apéritif.* It's my party and I name the hour. By the way, doesn't the Somerset Club serve meals?" He went back to his conversation, dismissing the interruption.

In spite of the objections one might make to his appearance or to his manner, whether one saw at once that he was crude or unscrupulous—for, although dissipation had obscured the sharpness of his face, a certain cunning remained in the eyes which did not look directly into other eyes—or whether he offended one's intellectual principles, there was about the young millionaire something so magnetic that exposure to the same air he breathed was similar in its effect to a love-philter. I had thought, in the first minutes of my admittedly enraptured regard of him, when my mind, operating simultaneously on two levels saw him on one as irresistible and on the other as repellent, that the sensuality manifest in his face was the forerunner of the corruption into which Dr. Galbraith had helplessly sunk. But presently I revised the prophecy that in twenty years he would be as damned a soul as the old doctor. For while he was sentimental—this was apparent from his slang, that badge by which we recognize the members of an egotistical and tenderly self-indulgent order—he was also shrewd, noncommittal, and even tonight when he was drunk, constantly on guard against involving himself with Hopestill, with Philip, in a sense, with this very room.

There are some people who we know at first glance will never marry. How we know, I cannot say, but we know as surely as we know that other people have taken a dislike to us at the moment of our presentation to them. Harry Morgan was such a man. What appealed then so strongly to me that it was only with an effort of will that I was able to look away from him was the challenge flung down by his self-sufficiency, which could not but rouse in any woman the desire to conquer him, and I felt a revival of that light-headedness—anticipatory, perhaps, it had been—in which I had descended the top two flights of stairs.

Hopestill, handing him a pair of ice-tongs, said something we could not hear and he replied, whispering in her ear as he put an assured arm about her shoulders. She lingered beside him the briefest time and then moved away. There was a look of outrage on her face, but not that he had been familiar amongst strangers, rather that he had with such facility, such untroubled certainty of where he stood with her, communicated to all of us: "I can take you or leave you alone," for his gesture had been at once possessive and indifferent.

I doubt if Philip or Frank Whitney discerned the agitation into which Morgan sent the three women in the room, for even Mrs. Babbitt, although she was obviously accustomed to him, looked at him worshipfully. Neither of the men could have sensed the source of his charm since it required the intuitive simplicity with which a woman perceives in a man the very embodiment of temptation. This is one of the mysteries of their sex by which men are infuriated for, being unable to solve it, they believe it to be a hoax: "Why, So and So is a perfect bounder. What can you see in him?" they ask of the women who can only reply, "I can't explain it."

"Listen, Harry," said Mr. Babbitt, "I want you to sing that song Miss Nanny Brewster taught you. You'll love it, Hope. It's funny as hell the way Harry does it."

"I'm not interested and I don't want to hear it. I think it's time we went on to dinner."

But Mr. Morgan had already risen to perform. He moved unsteadily across the room and stood before the Governor Winthrop and in a moment began to sing. Above his strange head, like a moon at half eclipse, Miss Pride's father stared at the trophy case. His loosely clenched hand rested on a table at his side as if he were about to make it into a fist and pound. The wavering Long Islander sang with a tuneless, distended insolence, rolling his eyes and suddenly closing them as, stopping dead in his song, he stroked imaginary female hips of extraordinary dimensions. The Babbitts, half in tears with laughter, kept filling his glass with straight whiskey, for at the end of each line, by way of punctuation, he drained off what he had. The lewdness came chiefly from his pantomime and his catarrhal voice, for the words that issued from his boneless face were only:

> I love to go swimmin'
> With bow-legged women
> And dive between their legs.

"Isn't he a scream?" shrieked Mrs. Babbitt.

Frank Whitney was pale. "Let's get him out, McAllister. He's drunk as a catfish." He started towards the offender, but Hopestill, who without trying to stop the song, had been gazing up at her grandfather as if supplicating him either to forgive this indignity or to put a stop to it, raised her hand in an apostolic gesture which said, "He has asylum here."

"He's perfectly all right, Frank," she said. "He's only

gay. He inherited two million dollars yesterday and he has every right to sing if he wants to."

"Repeat refrain!" cried Mr. Babbitt, covering his face with his hands while his thorax hopped convulsively like a jumping bean. Mr. Morgan obliged him and the words traveled slowly through his nose.

The door to the library flung open and crashed against the paneling. Miss Pride, dressed for dinner in garnets and black silk, stood on the threshold appraising the terrain. The first to speak was Harry Morgan who, going towards her with the sober countenance that appears in certain stages of drunkenness, said, "Miss Mather, I presume?" Miss Pride's enameled lenses suddenly could focus only on distant objects. She looked at me and said, "The letters, Sonie, which you promised to mail," and held them out. Mr. Morgan's rejected paw faltered uncertainly to his side.

"Good evening, Helen." She addressed Mrs. Babbitt frigidly.

"Good evening, Cousin Lucy," said Mr. Babbitt, bounding toward her, "I'm glad to see you." Miss Pride did not share his pleasure but glared straight through his head as if the gimlets of her eyes could puncture the optic nerve. She came to me with the letters. "Hello, Frank. Is Mary coming on for the holidays?" and as she took his hand, she gave me the bunch of envelopes and adroitly, so that no one could see, she pinched the fleshy part of my thumb between two fingernails so hard that I nearly cried out with pain.

For half a minute she stood there while Frank Whitney gave her news of his family. She did not release my thumb until he was finished and then she said, "I must go this minute. Hopestill, bring Frank when you and Philip come to the Countess'. I know Berthe will be delighted."

"We're all coming, Auntie," said Hopestill. "This is Mr. Morgan, Aunt Lucy."

"Good evening, sir," said Miss Pride and glanced up at the portrait of her father. "Papa looks *en prise*. Do set his men up again, Philip." And she left the room.

The only proof I had that she had been angry were the two white crescent marks on my thumb made, in her rage at something with which I had no connection, in the way one hurls a teacup to the floor because the contents of a letter have infuriated him.

"Waiter, bring me my bill," said Mr. Morgan with a foolish grin. "And cancel my membership in the Somerset. The bouncer gives me the creeps. Are you coming, baby?"

"No," said Hopestill. "Before you go, Harry, will you apologize to all of us?"

"Now I suggest," said Mrs. Babbitt in the voice of a peacemaker, "that Harry and John and I all go eat dinner by ourselves and let the ladies and gentlemen alone. Nobody's mad now but if we don't go right along everybody will be dreadfully mad except me."

"I won't be mad," pouted Mr. Babbitt. "And Olga won't be mad, will you, Olga?"

"Well, I'm damned," said Mr. Morgan, using his hands as binoculars and directing them towards me. "Is *that* Olga? Troika-ho, Olga!"

They left, Mrs. Babbitt's giggles leaving a wake behind. If I had been able to speak, I would have been profane, would have used every blasphemous and scatological oath I knew to tell Hopestill how I was affected by the knowledge that I had been the object of amused discussion. Olga! Her malice was so rich, so inventive that even now, exposed by the babblings of her drunken friends, she tried to hoodwink me. "I don't think Sonie looks all that Slavic, do you, Frank?"

The evening lay in ruins. My disappointments, my humiliation, and my scorn bustled through the branches of my nerves, created a tic here and a tingling there, an ache in my skull and fever in my eyeballs.

Mr. Whitney touched my arm. "Will you have dinner with me?" he asked.

Hopestill smiled. "Give the poor child a stout drink," she said. "She isn't used to the lower classes."

"Oh, I'll have a lot to drink," I said, and she and Philip laughed. They had forgotten us already before we had even reached the threshold. Hopestill was saying, "Well, darling, I've come home to stay. Aren't you glad?"

As soon as I could I left the Countess' salon and got my cape, but as I was starting down the hall towards the stairs someone laid his hand on my shoulder and I turned to find myself the captive of Mr. Pingrey. He said, "Sonia, Amy is in a tiz over your cutting her. You come straight along with me, you baggage. Mr. Hornblower is here and you have to meet him. He's just been telling the most delicious thing about Mr. Roosevelt. Did you know that the name is really Rosenfeld?" I was in no frame of mind to meet Your Esteemed Uncle Arthur Hornblower and told Mr. Pingrey that Miss Pride had asked me to run home to fetch something for her.

"Oh, stuff!" said Mr. Pingrey, flapping his hands limply in my face. "You're a perfect imp sometimes. Very well, but I will absolutely disown you if you don't meet him when you come back. Do you realize that he knows everyone of importance? Gandhi, Mussolini, Hitler, Trotsky, the Lord knows who. He's the most literate person here by far."

I felt this to be a slight exaggeration, but said I had not been aware that the Countess' parties were intended to be the meeting ground of minds.

"Well!" he gasped. "Frankly I don't know what you're talking about. Why on earth would one come otherwise?"

"Why, to drink," I said.

Mr. Pingrey did not drink or smoke, making his abstention from alcohol, tobacco, and highly seasoned food a fetish as obstinate as a vice. He put his hand to his heart as if he had been wounded there and might, after his valedictory, topple over dead at my feet. "I cannot, I simply cannot understand this transformation in you." His eyes, similar to Amy Brooks' (both of them were victims of excessive thyroid secretions, a bond which strengthened their friendship, I am sure, and played a strong part in their marriage and their subsequent production of two children with the same glandular vagary), bulged forth as he bent his ruddy face down towards mine to gaze upon the frog which, before the gods had been provoked to wrath, had been a charming maiden.

"Then go on to your . . . punch bowl!" he cried, and stepped aside to let me pass. Had I lingered a few minutes longer, he would have used such words as "wassail" and "negus" and "sack" to show that his acquaintance with alcohol was purely literary. Once, at an informal luncheon, he had inquired of his hostess if her servants made the mead themselves. "Mead? What is that?" she asked. He indicated the glasses of Chablis. "Oh," said the lady, who did not like him and was also vain of her learning, "no, my athelings have lost the receipt. This is a simple grape concoction made by the Christians in Gaul."

I was halfway down the stairs when he leaned over the bannister and implored, "*Do* meet Mr. Hornblower. He wants us all to come to tea at his house tomorrow. He's terribly anxious to meet you and says he will be ever so interested to hear your political conflicts—I told him, you see, that you were half Russian and half German."

As the next day was Sunday, I could not go. "I will be away tomorrow," I told him.

"Oh, but you must come," he protested urgently, "because Mrs. Hornblower will be there too!" as though, if it were a rare thing to meet Mr. Hornblower it was an ever rarer one to meet his wife. I repeated my refusal and Mr. Pingrey withdrew his head but not before he had stuck out his tongue at me like a peckish child and flung out, "Crosspatch!"

I had gained the outer hall when the door to the dining-room opened and the chauffeur shot past me like someone on a surf-board. He was carried along over the carpet by the leashed Doberman and the boxer to whom he applied, under his breath, the word "bitches" with venomous accuracy. Through the door I could see the supper table with its dishes arranged as tastefully as if they had been bouquets of flowers and were to serve no purpose other than ornament. The Countess had been planning this for months, ordering the strangest of the foods through importers, scouring Boston and New York for the finest Liebfraumilch and Niersteiner and champagne, herself supervising the decanting of the street wines and the liqueurs, and living through each step of the lengthy preparation of the *daube glacé* as if upon the proper contents of the bags of herbs depended her social success.

I had hoped to find the Countess here alone so that I could make my excuses to her, and I was annoyed to see that she was not in the room at all, but that wandering back and forth before the table were Baron Kalenkoff and a Jewish brain surgeon who were making hearty meals of the *daube,* the cucumbers in sour cream, the herring and salmon and caviar, the cheeses, olives, salads. Every now and again they abandoned the table only to repair to the sideboard where the wines were cooling. The two accommodators, hired for the evening, and the Alsatian waitresses stared stonily at the carnage, stood near-by the gormandizers waiting to pounce upon the empty dishes and bear them away to the dumb-waiter to be, if possible, replaced.

I entered the dining-room intending to seek the Countess in the pantry. This room alone had been left untouched by the new mistress of the house; its walls were hung with Audubon's eagle attacking the inflated white belly of a fish, his Iceland gulls and curlews, and interspersed amongst the birds were Currier and Ives Maine landscapes and paddle-wheel boats. Miss Pride said of it, "I could digest my food there as well as I did in Josie Brooks' day if only Berthe didn't let her livestock run free."

As I paused in the doorway, the Countess appreared, coming out of the pantry with the intention, probably, of having a last minute look before she allowed supper to be announced. It must have been shocking for her to come upon two guests who had gobbled up visible portions of the food and had destroyed the appearance of half the dishes by their wanton hunger and who greeted her with their mouths full, one hand holding a slice of bread piled high with a layer of pickled herring, a layer of jellied partridge, one of salt salmon, and topped by a round of marinated onion, the other hand clasping by its neck a liter of cold wine. But the Countess' hesitation was the briefest possible. Undismayed, she advanced and she said, as though she were delighted by what she saw, smiling, her large fair face aglow with hospitality, her diadem of sapphires forming for this perfect hostess an angelic halo, "Oh, you didn't find the Niersteiner. You're drinking that flat Moselle. Here, let me get you some real wine."

Then, having finished her ministrations to the vandals and having caught sight of me, she cried, "Ah, angel! I was just going to look for you. What are you doing with your cape? Going? But you've only been here five minutes!"

I told her I was feeling a little ill, I believed I was catching cold. "Oh, no! How shocking! I won't have you taking cold." She thrust a plate of lobster *en mayonnaise* in front of the Baron and said, "Try this, Alexy, and give me your honest opinion. Will you excuse me for a moment?" And taking me by the arm, she led me into the hall and towards the yellow sofa.

"Now!" she said, adjusting the camellias at my shoulder to her liking. "Now tell me why you're playing such a trick on me."

"But it's no trick, Countess. Really, I am all chills and fever."

"Oh, adorable monster! But I'll keep your secret. Is he gifted? Is he a gentleman? Darling, don't think I'm prying, but I love you! I could not bear it if my Euphrysone weren't treated well!"

Anxious to escape and afraid that if she kept me any longer I would blurt out the whole story of my wounded dignity, I put my cape around my shoulders and laughed, "He, Countess, is only Dostoievsky whom I shall read when I've taken an aspirin for my cold."

"Seriously," she said looking, indeed, very serious, "I am only thinking how Lucy Pride would feel about it. You know her anti-Semitism. But you do as you like, my dear pet! I will let you go *only* if you promise to be amused!"

"Oh, I do promise!" I assured her and I extended my

hand in farewell, wishing to end this baffling dialogue. The Countess got up, kissed me, and went to the stairs. "How stupid of me! I forgot to tell you that he's waiting in the library."

I had known, even before I opened the door, that I would find Nathan Kadish in the library. He was standing in the lamplight, his birthmark towards me.

"Well," he said, "aren't you surprised?"

"Hello, Nathan. I'm glad to see you."

"I should hope you might be, you poor girl! What you must have been through! Had I only known I would have come to solace you months ago."

"How did you get in?" I said, amused and pleased that he had not changed.

"It was a very neat coup. I saw you come in here with that St. Bernard—what a moron *he* looks like—and waited a minute and rang the bell myself. I must say I was ready to give up when I got a gander at that butler. He was tough sledding, but the lady was a pushover."

I saw that he was going over, with an admiring eye, the details of my attire, and I likewise allowed my look to travel upwards from his feet in muddied white shoes, over his immaculate gray suit and bright red bow tie to his face.

"Well, Sonie? Well, how would you like to get drunk? I very much regret that as I am currently in love with someone else, this is the only amusement I can offer you."

It was the only amusement I was capable of enjoying. Even the prospect was sedative. As we went into the hall, Nathan said, "I assume that you won't mind doing the boozing in my sort of saloon?" We met the soulless face of the butler who, opening the door for us, said to me, "Good evening, Miss Marburg. I hope you won't find it too wet underfoot."

"Want to come along?" said Nathan to him, but the man, ignoring him, said to me, "Of course you have a very short walk home."

"She's not going home, you buzzard," said Nathan, looking closely into the snobbish face. "Slave!"

Both the man and I were too shocked to speak. The white door slowly closed and I was certain that I looked for the last time upon the Countess von Happel's brass knocker.

Four

Now on the glossy Sunday after I had stayed until four o'clock in the morning with Nathan Kadish at a café in Scollay Square, I had as my traveling companions not only shame, jealousy, and despair, but in addition a headache that pounded and reverberated through each convolution of my brain and stretched to bursting each tunnel and cove of my skull, a tidal nausea, a chill as dry and plunging as a winter wind. Last night's snow was deep and glazed, played on by bright sun, and the pavement over which we drove was like a polished blade casting upward shimmering filaments of frosty light. The spruce, hibernal landscape, simplified like a conventional design in which the vitality and the heterogeneous shades of autumn had been discarded for a white and mortal rigor, gave to the condition of my body and the state of my mind an incisive accent, and I could neither see nor imagine a source of warmth (chilliest of any detail in this fixed scene was the dun tendril of smoke ascending from a white chimney), nor could I be reminded by anything presented here of the good, the gratifying, the ennobling, or the pleasing elements of life. For I could observe only contrast, and in personifying nature as one will sometimes do in illness or in melancholy or conversely in well-being or in joy, I saw myself rebuked by the immaculate, inflexible earth for having been the night before exactly the opposite, just as I had been rebuked earlier this morning by Miss Pride whose wintry eyes in her bone-clean face had extinguished my heart's heat so that I had stood like a stalagmite beside the chess-table receiving her terse lecture.

Nathan and I had revived and resealed our friendships with mixtures of rum and soda water, the number of which a persistent, unsolicited clerk in the back of my tortured head kept trying, this morning, to count from memory. And at some time these scorched, half-blinded eyes of mine had seen a chorus of footsore girls dancing on a platform to a rompish paraphrase of "O, Come All Ye Faithful." They had been dressed like Santa Claus, if Santa Claus had been a girl in red, fur-trimmed underdrawers and a brassière of gold stars and had worn, in place of the smile of a kind-hearted old innocent, a grin of the most workaday lewdness. Either before or after this travesty, which at the time I had taken for granted but which this morning possessed the impossible quality of a comic dream, a sailor in His Majesty's, the King of England's, employ had briefly joined us and in exchange for my wilted camellias which he requested, declaring that he would preserve them to the end of his days in his mother's prayer-book, he gave me a picture post card that we all regarded as irresistibly droll. It showed, in vivid colors, a small, libidinous, middle-aged man staring at a bathing beauty about to dive into the ocean, while his portly wife, surveying a group of new cottages, remarked: "Look at the seaside development, George." For some purpose, lost forever to memory, the sailor had laboriously printed his name, Sam Casserly, on the back with an obtuse blue pencil.

The iconoclastic antics of the dancing girls and the transaction with Sam Casserly together accounted for perhaps fifteen or twenty minutes out of the five hours we had spent in the crowded room where the green and

red lights, veiled by smoke, made the atmosphere cre-
puscular. But I remembered that we had not been idle
and that our intake of noteworthy amounts of rum had
been accompanied by unflagging talk which, although
its substance was irrevocable, seemed, on retrospect, to
have issued altogether from my lips. I could fairly see
Nathan's face patiently registering courteous sympathy
with my complaints, amusement at my mirthless anecdotes, respect for my moral and literary judgments.
And yet, gradually, as if I were reading a book which I
had forgotten I had read before, so much of my companion's current history came back that it seemed impossible, in view of the fact that I had learned all this
in just five hours, that I could have uttered a word, but
that the solo voice had been his, interlarding the calendar of his love-affairs and his scholastic enterprises with
expositions of his character, guesses about mine, and
childhood reminiscences common to both of us. He was
now, he told me, at Harvard and had been for two years,
studying literature with the support of a fellowship. He
was also tutor to Harry Morgan and was making so much
money (he lived very simply) that he had saved almost
enough to go to Paris after his graduation. Before the
flight from America, he thought he might marry a Japanese girl whom he described as superbly beautiful, or
else an elderly French fly-by-night who had no attractions
for him but who spoke both German and French and
could therefore act as his interpreter. And I believed,
though I could not be certain, that when I reminded
him that I was also bilingual (this exaggeration had
evinced no comment from him), he had accepted my
application, but had made it perfectly clear that he was
in love with the Japanese girl.

I could not, though I exerted a suprème effort, re-
trace the paths I had traveled in our conversation, but
I knew, if from nothing else than from the simple observation of human nature, that I had not been silent
this whole time. What troubled me, therefore, to the
point of tears which bubbled out of my red-hot eyes, was
that I had possibly so involved myself with Nathan
Kadish that I dared not cut myself off from him at once,

must see him immediately again to ascertain how much and from what irascible or sentimental viewpoint I had revealed. And yet, because I could not dissociate him from my malaise, I desired nothing so little as this second interview.

When we had traversed another mile, I remembered that we had made an engagement for that evening when, at eight o'clock, I was to call upon him at his apartment in Cambridge for the purpose of meeting the Japanese girl. Simultaneously, I recalled my astonishment at hearing him ask me, "Does Shura live by herself in Chichester now?" I had been in control of my wits sufficiently to tell him nothing but I had found, by careful questions, that he had not heard of my mother's commitment to the asylum, for he had been back to Chichester only twice in the past two years and by that time, I suppose, some new scandal was of more immediate interest.

I had no difficulty at all in calling to mind what had happened after we left the café in Scollay Square. Emboldened by my renewed friendship with this charming young man, this paragon, as I often told him as we ascended the back side of Beacon Hill, of sense and sensibility, I did not hesitate to adopt his suggestion, when we got to Pinckney Street and I found I did not have my door key, that I call out to Miss Pride while he bombarded her window with snowballs. For Nathan said that the procedure was more practical than rousing the whole house by ringing the door-bell.

"Hello, up there!" I cried. "Miss Pride! I'm locked out!"

"Hey!" shouted Nathan. "Hey, lady! Come down and let a person in! It's cold out here!" To our delight, one of the snowballs went in the window. I congratulated Nathan on his marksmanship and we shook hands, gazing at one another with deepest admiration. Presently Miss Pride's head appeared. "Hush! I'm coming." Nathan backed away and as he receded into the whirling snow, I had the impression that like the Cheshire cat, he was leaving his smile behind. He whispered, "So long, madam," and vanished as the outer door opened and Miss Pride stood shivering on the threshold in a brown wrapper. Her scanty hair was unpinned and it bristled about her collar. I was not in the least frightened. On the contrary I felt loquacious and was on the point of asking Miss Pride to join me in a drink of her whiskey as I was suddenly urged to tell her what I knew about Hopestill. But before I had opened my mouth to speak, she said sharply, "Come in at once and go upstairs, you wretched girl. If one whisper of this reaches anyone, I'll turn you out of the house." She said no more, or if she did, I did not understand her. But in the morning when I went to the library, she spoke at length.

The sight of the glass of sherry beside the chess-board made me gasp and lift my eyes to Mr. Pride, but the thought was at once in my mind that he and Dr. Eliot had one time eaten Brazil nuts with their wine. There was no corner of the room without its alcoholic associations: here Mr. Whitney and I had stood drinking whiskey, there Mr. Morgan had constantly refilled his glass, and Miss Pride, mercilessly smelling the bouquet of her wine between leisurely sips, reminded me that I had been drunk, had been drinking heavily, had had too much to drink, had reeked of alcohol, that I must learn to refuse the third glass of whatever it was, whiskey, rum, gin, brandy, wine. She had learned from the Countess that I had pled illness and had left the party (I could have wept with gratitude for the Countess' discretion), but she had also learned from Mr. Pingrey that I had said I must run an errand for her. The latter, comparing notes with his hostess, had been furious. Moreover, I had made no apologies to Mr. Whitney who had been kind enough to give up his evening for my sake, and I had refused point-blank to be introduced to Mr. Hornblower who was Miss Pride's cousin and who had had the generosity to show an interest in what he had heard about me.

In view of my egregious misdemeanor, I was to be punished by exclusion from a series of parties to some of which I might otherwise have been invited. These parties were to be in celebration of Hopestill's engagement to Philip which had been announced at the Countess' shortly after I left. The marriage was to take place in three weeks' time. On the day following this, a dressmaker was coming on from New York and Miss Pride had planned that she and I, for these pre-nuptial weeks, would dine together at an early hour, and the rest of the time, she implied, we were to make ourselves as scarce as possible except in those quarters dedicated to our work.

Just as one cannot be surprised at death when it has been prepared for by a long illness, as the liar cannot be surprised by the consequences of his lies, so I was not surprised by Miss Pride's news, for I had known from the moment Hopestill spoke Philip's name the afternoon before that it was her intention to marry him by fair means or foul. And yet, want of surprise does not cancel our grief over the death nor regret that the lies have been found out, and I did not hear Miss Pride without desolation. I mustered up what politeness I could, said I was sure she was happy over the turn of events, that it must have been something of a thunderclap since it was so sudden. Miss Pride assured me that on the contrary no one had been in the least taken unawares, but naturally everyone had been delighted.

What a revolting business appeared my sodden, sentimental interlude in the slums of Boston! While we had sat in dirty tumult, Hopestill in her turquoise dress with fresh camellias at her shoulder which Philip had bought her (probably at the same stall where earlier he had bought mine) was elegantly, forthrightly playing her game and playing it with an éclat which disguised her guile even to herself.

I was too absorbed with my diversified pains to determine, from Miss Pride's manner, whether the damage I had done myself in her eyes was irreparable. I recalled the pinch she had given me last night when she had discovered Mr. Morgan in the library. It had been a sort of gesture of fellowship, as though she had wanted me to know that she knew that I, her pupil, shared fully her revulsion. How appalling then must have been the sight

412

of my disheveled person, the sound of my thick voice as I stumbled into the vestibule!

No apology was forthcoming from my dry, swollen lips. I swayed, dumb and contrite, before the chess-table, awaiting my dismissal. She gave it finally and with a stingy smile, but one which made my heart leap for joy, she said, "I have been told that Bromo-Seltzer brings relief to your kind of suffering," so that I knew my exile would not be permanent.

If only the short space of three weeks would cure my other ill, my stifling and manacled envy of Hopestill! It was like a fretting child that having a limited experience of the mercy of time believes that the mumps and his imprisonment will last forever and that the time at playing he has lost can never be made up but must blight his whole life. Love, commingled with envy, confounds the mind like drink or fever and the world narrows to the size of one's own soul. Archimedes, if he could have got off the earth, could have moved it. The wretched person, if he could get outside himself, could find the proper physic. But one does not learn, believes with laic obstinacy that the efficacious remedy is the homeopathic one: the common cures, impotent as a broth of newts' eyes and bats' wool, are the escape from love into love, or into writing verses about one's love or reading other's verses, or into a recital to friends of one's love and its debacle. Our obfuscated faculties cannot comprehend that the addition of fuel to the fire will make the blaze brighter and the heat more intense. Thus, I desired to replace Philip with someone who looked exactly like him, who had the same sort of voice and the same kind of mind and had even the same stiff back.

2

Eleven o'clock each Sunday, when Mac and I started out for Wolfburg, was the hour at which the descendants of believers and a few believers gathered sociably before Emmanuel and Trinity, the furred issue of the limousines offering to each other hands in gloves, white even in the winter, or a caress that served as a kiss in these days of so many colds and "catching" coughs, but was rather the light pressure of cheek against cheek. Along Commonwealth Avenue, others briskly walked in typical pairs: the middle-sized man with a black mustache, a bowler, a Chesterfield, and gray suède gloves, was formally but devotedly protective of his wife or sister in a short mink coat, adorned with last night's gardenia for whose longevity the ice chest was reponsible, a dress of which the gentle-colored skirt showed beneath the coat, a small hat topped with a crinoline posy. Now and again, as we drove past, I saw someone I had met at Miss Pride's or at the Countess', and if my nod were acknowledged, even though its target showed by her thoughtful scrutiny that she could not "place" me ("That's Lucy Pride's chauffeur," said the perplexed eyes, "but who can the girl be?"), I felt mildly triumphant. But mildly, because the luxury which embraced me—the camel's hair lap-robe, the shining glass between myself and my impeccable driver, the thermos bottle of consommé provided me in case I should get cold, my own expensive coat imported from the woolen mills of New Hampshire —made these outward signs merely the superfluous confirmation of my good fortune. If my greeting to one of the Sunday promenaders was not received, I felt no disappointment for, if I needed them, I could summon any number of explanations for the slight, none of which reflected unfavorably on me: Mrs. Frothingham was without her spectacles, Mrs. Coolidge was flustered because she thought she would be late to church. Admiral Nephews did not fail to know me. "Hello!" he cried as he stopped before the red light on Exeter Street. "Where are you going on this day most calm, most bright?" He pointed me out to his frail wife who leaned upon a cane, and she nodded amiably but tugged at his arm to remind him that this was no time to dally.

On Commonwealth Avenue on fine Sunday mornings, there was an absence of children and of poor people, as if the territory were "restricted" like apartment buildings which will not let space to Jews or the owners of dogs. Down the mall towards the Public Gardens, there strolled the débutantes, airing their doe-eyed cocker spaniels, or laughing with their beaux whose cropped, uncovered heads and Cantabrigian costumes—long tweed coats with leather patches at the elbow, trousers that did not match, bow ties, cinereous summer shoes over the tops of which lazily cascaded woolen socks—were the badges of privileged youth who, having other things to do, did not go to church. A fair-haired, solitary girl in riding clothes, who was exercising a prancing black shepherd, called out a greeting to one of the older generation who kept to the sidewalk. "Good mahning, Mr. Pukins! I heah Billy's going to Chiner. I think it's mahvelous!"

Mr. Perkins, lifting his bowler, faced her across the engine of Miss Pride's car, his white teeth revealed in a smile that agreeably elevated his little mustache. "Good mahning, Susan! We're having a little dinnah pahty for him next week. You've been told to come, haven't you?"

"Indeed I have!"

They bowed and smiled again and as he replaced his hat, Mr. Perkins added jestingly, "I see you don't go to church."

The roar of traffic, commencing to move along again with the green light, drowned out her reply, but I had faith in her and knew she would not make a fool of herself with a serious counter. Probably at Billy Perkins' farewell party, when his parents made their appearance during cocktails, after which they would leave the "youngsters" to themselves, the sally would be repeated, and Susan would say something like, "I really enjoy church, you know! But Sunday is such a lovely time to exercise my dog!" making her neglect of religion rather endearing as well as temporary for, her gentle, wistful tone implied, she was prepared for the inevitable and would graciously assume her duties towards God as soon as she had settled down either as a matron or as a spinster. And Mr. Perkins, into whose glass was being poured a second cocktail while the girl extended her fingers over her glass to show that she had had enough, would say that he absolutely agreed with her and that when he was her age he probably would not have gone to church either if it had not been compulsory. "Things were so line and rule," he would say, making the staid girl's heart flutter at this testimony of her generation's liberty. "You wouldn't have had a cocktail, for instance," he would continue as she gazed proudly into her Martini in which the olive was still an inch from the surface of the liquid.

As one tenacious of sleep in the early morning, I hoarded the moments of the drive along the avenue against the time when we would turn off towards Boylston and then into the Fenway. For to me, as to those whom the Countess derided when she said, "Boston is a very small place," the city ended precisely at Massachusetts Avenue, and all the rest of it, the cold, uncrowded medical college, the spacious Brookline parkways, the large houses of new materials and derivative architecture, the wide modern drives, did not belong to Boston with its narrow houses and painted doors, and I felt that the expatriates dwelling in Jamaica Plain and Hyde Park and Milton were but wealthier versions of the bourgeois Brunsons. I admired the horseback riders along the bridle paths which bordered Jamaica Pond and the ice-skaters, but did so only because I thought they merely used the resources of these fertile outskirts but returned, at the end of their diversion, to Pinckney or Marlborough or Beacon Street. I felt altogether differently towards such towns as Concord, Lexington, Bedford, Lincoln, and these, together with certain parts of Cambridge and what I called "Boston proper" constituted in my mind "greater Boston" whereas everything in between, even though nearer to the State House, was clearly excluded. I could not revise my map even when I learned that eminent families lived, and had for generations, on Blue Hill Avenue in Milton, in Needham, in Newton.

In an hour's time, we had reached the country and drove between fog-filled woods. Fresh snow, still scathless, lay between the trees where only a few weeks before the stained leaves had lain; the natural paths, rejuvenated by the graduation of the landscape into winter, crept in their immaculate renascence back into the far blue shadows; and not too long from now they would waver forth in the marine spring. We had not gone more than two or three miles when to our left there rose up the high red walls of my mother's asylum; covered with woodbine that had caught the snow, they blended with the landscape. Presently they broke for an iron gate guarded by a fat, unpleasant man who let us in and said sardonically, "This way to the booby-hatch, folks." I had told Miss Pride of the gate-keeper's manner which no longer offended me but which I thought must horrify the relatives of other inmates, for I believed that Miss Pride, with the flourish of a pen, could have the man removed and a courteous one installed in his place. She did investigate and found that this greeting was only for our car, as Mac and the man had been companions in grammar school, though there was never the slightest sign of recognition on Mac's misanthropic face.

My mother came into the reception room, like a nun coming from the cloister, in her gray uniform, her eyes observing something beyond me or above my head. I nearly always took her flowers and as she sat down, her head bent to study them, she appeared to be waiting for the roses and the carnations to be given the gift of tongues. Then she lifted them to her ear. "Pretty *things*," she would say to them. She would turn towards me her lovely eyes that could see me only as a little child and drawing me to her she whispered so that no one could hear, "Darling, we're going visiting today. The flowers won't wilt if we wrap them in a wet newspaper." Then we rose and walked, arm in arm, down the long, gray hall, followed at some distance by an attendant, and entered the common room where the daffy, harmless women rocked and sang, nodding and smiling, their tender eyes roving private worlds which they sometimes found so amusing they had to laugh out loud. My mother's fancy-work and mine were brought to us; together we worked for an hour and my mother praised the tailless birds she had taught me how to make. "But, dearie," she would say, "there's something wrong with it, I don't know what. See mine, see how it goes?" And she held up the identical bird, bereft of its tail feathers, embroidered in green and yellow silk.

Sometimes my mother's affection (she would suddenly drop her work to kiss me) spread like an epidemic through the room and the demented creatures who that day had no visitors shouted and cooed and goggled their eyes and beckoned me with rapidly wagging fingers. One mild and motherly woman with white hair and dimpled cheeks would hold up a pink candy box that rattled when she shook it. "I'll show you what's inside, Ellen, if you'll just come to Granny," and when I shook my head, smiling politely, she would take a man's white handkerchief out of her bosom and cry a little and blow her nose. Once an attendant let her come sit beside us to show us her treasure, fifteen gallstones of varied sizes and shapes. My mother was charmed. "That's a fine one!" she cried as she picked one up, but the old lady snatched it out of her hand. "No you don't, my good woman," she said sharply. "Do you think they grow on trees?"

Most of the others had neither fancy-work nor gallstones to keep them occupied, and so they merely sat about, batting their eyes, grinning and purring like happy cats. The malcontents, arms crossed on their breasts, sat apart, muttering motley diatribes: "I called the police. No, couldn't make it, too busy they said. Busy, yes, no doubt of that, I said, busy taking the bread out of poor people's mouths, that's what you're busy doing. Called the newspaper. No, didn't handle such matters. Why not, I said. Do you mean to stand by and watch the people of your community suffer because dentists' brothers are politicians? Yes, ma'am, no, ma'am. Don't yes, ma'am, no, ma'am, *me,* I told them and hung up. It is a crying shame that you can't carry x-rays of your teeth in your pocketbook without gangsters, hired by dentists' brothers, following to steal them or substitute the real ones with other people's teeth or dog's teeth, for that matter. I merely walked into the restaurant and two men with revolvers were waiting. Merely stepped inside to have a cup of tea after the dentist's visit, and there they were waiting." The less articulate of the persecuted stared in silence at the attendants, their faces fixed in a monotonous sneer.

My mother no longer felt that she was victimized, for much had been deleted from her memory: if she ever spoke of a place other than the asylum garden or of the room we sat in, it was of Luibka's house or the officers' tavern, but not of Chichester. She did not forget me, although, because her sense of time had gone, she thought I was eight or nine years old, and the six days when she did not see me were like the six hours when formerly I had been at school; nor did she forget the cold, but she would rub my hands between hers in the old way and complain with sorrowful resignation that "they" put snow in the stoves instead of wood. "They" were unreal shadows, harmless, stupid, servile ghosts who required a good deal of pampering; because she did not wish to offend them, she always spoke in whispers. "A new one came this morning just after you left, darling," she would say, "and left the door wide open so the snow came in. That's why it's so cold."

She talked very little. For the most part we worked at our birds in silence. And so long as I was there, with the living proof before my eyes that she was not aware of her surroundings, I was not depressed but was even comforted by the soothing, aimless motion of my fingers as they plied the embroidery needle. I would wonder, watching her serene face, if I would ever achieve the degree of her beauty, for, if I still looked upon Miss Pride as my model for character, I was no longer deluded by that old hallucination in which I saw her as a beautiful person, and, at least on Sunday, I was as ambitious to look like my mother as on all the other days I was to be like Miss Pride. Unfortunately, I had a variable face so that my mirror showed me a different person half a dozen times a day, for I had inherited some features from both my parents and each set of genes struggled for pre-eminence: my hair was black like hers but my eyes were blue like his, and though my mouth was a facsimile of hers, its pure outlines were corrupted when I smiled and showed my father's crooked teeth.

Gliding, these hours, in brainless daydreams, fashioned from anonymous places and times, I would sometimes hear, like an echo, a voice of a familiar timbre. Like the person who, awakened by a scream, deduces from the cold sweat on his forehead and the trembling of his arms that the sound has come from his own throat, so I, recognizing the voice as my own, thought I had spoken. But in a moment, the words, which my nerves had retained though my mind had not yet comprehended them, were repeated: "Poor little blue cold hands," and I knew that it was my mother who had spoken, not I. Conversely, when I was not with her, when, for example, I was at the Countess' on Friday and everyone was chattering loudly, I was thinking of something far removed from the conversation of which I was a part and I heard my mother speaking; yet when the words returned they formed the banal, effortless answer to someone who had asked me if I had ever been to Ipswich.

The hours in the bright common room were like those a solitary traveler spends in a strange railway station, after a sleepless night, so that his weary eyes impose a glaze on colors; half-dozing, he wakes suddenly, thinking he has been asleep for an hour and sees that the old woman on the bench across from him who had taken out her handkerchief when he went to sleep has now begun to blow her nose, and that the man who sweeps up the burnt-out cigarettes on the floor has progressed at the most two feet. He sleeps again and wakes to see the old woman returning her handkerchief to her pocketbook, the cleaning man twelve inches farther along. Or they were like those moments when, succumbing to ether, the conscious mind suddenly revives, rises like the bobbing head of a drowning man, and hears the end of the sentence the anesthetist had begun as he attached the cone. The boredom of the traveler and the horror of the patient are unendurable when memory makes them so and pessimism complains that they may happen again. I never failed to dread Sundays nor to be distressed as we left the asylum; but at the time I was with my mother, I had no feelings save sensuous ones and nothing from the outer world accompanied me here. On the contrary, when shame or jealousy or despair had dogged me like a shadow all the way to Wolfburg, the moment the door to the common room was opened to us, I was beholden to no one and to nothing.

Each time, my mother was allowed to sit in the car for a little while before I left. An attendant sat in front with Mac, glancing often at us in the mirror over the wind shield. The meeting of my eyes with his trained ones, keen as a surgeon's (the medical effect was enhanced by the mirror in which he studied me, like the mirror of a nose specialist), produced in me a self-consciousness that warmed my cheeks and dried my tongue, and I blushed when I made some reply to my mother, although the glass was closed between us and my voice was inaudible to the men in front. What disturbed me —and marked the end of the hypnotic state that had enabled me to endure the visit—was that those watchful eyes included me as well as my mother in their vigilance. When my mother had been led away after a final sighing embrace from which it would have taken me hours to disentangle myself if I had been alone, and Mac had started down the drive, the embarrassment became a vague, irrational fear which was then followed, as the dénouement to Ivan's fits had been a coma, by a benumbing, anarchical depression which possessed me until finally, late that night, back in my room on Pinckney Street, I fell asleep.

3

It had never been so great a solace as it was today to sit in my accustomed place beside my mother in the unchanged common room, having no need to make explanations to anyone, not even to myself. Gradually the aspirin tablets which I had begged from a nurse (I had not liked to ask Mac to stop at a drug-store for Miss Pride's prescription for me) began to take effect and my nausea and headache were replaced by a sweet, feverish sleepiness. I had brought my mother some apples as well as the customary flowers, and their clean, wholesome smell was drawn from their satiny hide by the excessive warmth of the room. The last time, she had asked me to bring them. "Bring me some red apples, darling," she had said. "I know how smooth they are." But today when I opened the paper bag for her to see them, she had said, "What are these?" "Apples," I had replied. "You asked for them." She had put the bag on the floor and every now and again glanced at it. After a while she had said, "Sonie, tomorrow see if you can find me some apples. Bring me some little yellow apples. I've forgotten how they taste."

My mother was not well. For some Sundays past she had had a cold in the head and now today I saw that it had settled in her chest. She coughed considerably and her breath sometimes came with difficulty. An attendant had whispered to me that I must leave sooner than I usually did, for she had been in bed in the infirmary for several days, though she had been allowed to get up for a few hours each afternoon. Never talkative these days, she was more disinclined than ever to conversation, and we worked for a long time in silence. The lulling, soporific warmth, the wordless muttering of the woman persecuted by dentists' brothers, the odor of the apples, and the steady stitching of the birds so satisfied me as an opiate that I proposed to myself, with the seriousness that makes a dream of a five-inch man or a German-speaking dog or an encounter with a camel seem useful or irritating but not in the least strange, that I spend the next three weeks in this well-heated and peaceable place.

When I had finished inventing plausible lies for Miss Pride about where I should be and had imagined myself installed with a few books and my phonograph in one of the cells, something in the room, a voice or a falling object or the rattling of the gallstones, awakened me and I suddenly laughed. My mother looked up from her work and said, "You have caught my cold!" And when I assured her that I had not, she said, "But you just coughed. I heard you." She beckoned to an attendant who was sitting near-by reading the Sunday comic strips avariciously and without the slightest amusement and when he came she said, "Do you know where they keep the cough syrup? Sonie coughed and she'll be ill." I attempted to make a sign to the attendant but I was hampered by the fixed gaze of my mother as if she were waiting for the devil inside me to make me cough again so that she might pounce on him. He went back to his chair and from the table beside it, took a bottle from a box which seemed to contain first-aid equipment and returned to us, gravely offering it to me along with a spoon. My mother resumed her needlework and I said to the man, "But I didn't cough, I only laughed."

"Laughed?" he said, as if that were a kind of action unfamiliar to him. "Why did you laugh?"

"I don't know. But anyhow I don't need the cough syrup."

"Take it," he said, nodding in my mother's direction and he poured out a spoonful which he handed to me. It was strong and not unpleasant, tasting a little like Cointreau. I thanked him and he went back to his funny papers, but for the next hour he glanced at me from time to time over the top of Elmer Tuggle and Gasoline Alley (he read thoroughly and very slowly) as if he were trying to fathom my laughter.

For a long time there was no other interruption, and in this cataleptic tranquillity, my mind was blank, or, rather, was occupied by certain abstractions such as "warmth" or "absence of pain" or "motion." In demonstrating to myself the last of these, I felt myself sinking through boundless space; I was at once pressed down and pulled down, in the first place by a weightless force from above and in the second by gravity, of which the principle I experienced in a manner more entire than the simple, conscious observation of a falling object could ever induce, just as, at other times when I had been fatigued for some days together, I fancied I could sense in my tired muscles the slow vertigo of the earth. When I emerged from this ethereal baptism, I was more than ever at ease, and I was so freed of any anxieties, in this isolated place and in this parenthetical time, that

423

my mind could roam like an innocent child, at will, through grouped reflections and through favorite daydreams.

I had been following a string of associated memories which began with a clambake held about this time two years before by the senior class of the high-school. I had seen Ruby Beeler filing a boy's right-hand fingernails, and I proceeded from that to Mr. Henderson who all one winter had had a blue nail on his little finger. Abruptly the concatenation was unlinked by the obtrusion of a single, clear-cut image which could not be worried into any sort of relationship with what had gone before. Irrelevant, impulsively independent, there was before my eyes a room which I had never seen, but a room in which there was hardly an object that was unfamiliar. It was possible that I had briefly fallen asleep and had dreamed of such a place, and yet it did not fade upon my scrutiny of it, but, static, pictorial, it was present to me like a projection on a screen.

It was a dark and rather shabby room in which the solid, heavy draperies were threadbare, blotched and rotten in the folds. One of two casement windows was open, giving onto a court, and from it were visible frail balconies where mop-buckets and potted geraniums stood, and all the tattered, dirty overflow of kitchens, the rags and cans and empty cartons. On window sills were bottles, bowls, and sleeping cats. All the windows were red, reflecting a sunset; the light had an autumnal quality, discernible only through feeling since no other circumstance hinted at the season of the year. There were no trees in sight, yet had there been, they certainly would have been releasing their fissile yellow leaves. Probably if the room had been animated or if from its visible contours I had proceeded to list its likely attributes in other sensory perceptions, it would have included a coolness, a musty smell, and through the windows, the voices of boys loitering on the way home from school.

The furniture of the rectangular room was ponderous and dark and was crowded together, forming angles and recesses and deep shadows like hiding places. In the middle of the room, quite by itself, was a small round table covered with a white cloth which was clean but limp, as if in the ironing it had not dried properly. A bottle of red wine, bearing no label, stood in the center. The bookshelves which lined one wall and extended nearly to the ceiling were full and contained well-worn volumes largely, it seemed, in French and German. The titles were arranged in confusion. Among them was a bound medical manuscript dating from the fifteenth century. There was a book called *Der Traum den Rote Kammer*: its binding simulated rice-paper and there was a singular discrepancy between the design (a delicate torii and a path scattered with the petals of red flowers) and the curly German script of the title. Between the two windows stood a little Victorian writing desk, open, and revealing a portfolio of cheap Italian leather, dyed green; on it rested a horribly ingenious tortoise-shell letter-opener of which the handle was fashioned into a lobster's claw, cleverly grasping a solid sphere of agate.

It was like the room of some student of wonders and curiosities who had returned the books to their shelves for the afternoon and had got himself this bottle of red wine to enjoy as he looked upon himself in leisure, asking whether his study of prodigies had affected him in any way.

I reviewed rooms in which I had been, as far back as I could remember, but I could not place it, and while, as I have said, it was by no means unfamiliar and all the objects were as real as if I had owned them for many years, I could not, nevertheless, actually identify any of them. I cannot say how long the "vision" of this red room lasted, but while it did, I experienced a happiness, a removal from the world which was not an escape so much as it was a practiced unworldliness. And it was a removal which was also a return. The happiness was not unmixed: as I gazed at the red evening sunlight winnowed through the brick chimneys of the court, I was filled with a tranquil, mortal melancholy as if I were out of touch with the sources of experience so that I could receive but could not participate: that is, I could *assume* that boys were shouting on the street, but I could not hear them. The mitigation of the light seemed to sadden me even more, for it had a potential quality of "bursting" in upon me and yet upon my windows, it was a layer of rich opacity which did not, however, prevent me from seeing quite clearly the balconies and the sleeping cats.

From another world, from the streets of the anoymous city where the room had been in readiness for my return to it, a voice ascended and as the windows were blackened and the room disappeared in a darkness as complete as that immediately after the lights have gone off in a theater, I heard my mother say, "I'm in the crazy house!" Her eyes blazed with the anger of a terrified animal as she was forsaken by the merciful anesthesia which for these months had made her live burial tolerable to both of us. Those powerful eyes now saw the barred windows behind the coy, concealing blinds, saw the inimical, impassive strength of the attendants, saw the moonstruck women grinning and gurgling like babies and they saw, completing the circuit, wider with each new revelation, that I was not a little girl just home from school but was a grown woman whose fine tailored suit and costly shoes cried aloud my treachery. Her lips twitched with panic and vivid splashes, induced as much by fever as by her fright, appeared on her cheeks.

When she had spoken, it had been softly in a breathless voice, as though she must state her discovery but must do so quietly lest she not hear another noise, and she had not immediately looked for a door through which to escape but had surveyed cautiously her dangerous surroundings. But though I thought I alone had heard her, the vigilant attendant, trained to hear and see things that did not attract other people's attention, had laid aside his comic strips and sat poised on the edge of his chair, ready to spring forward. Thinking to adjust things quickly, lead her back to her world of tailless birds and little yellow apples, I put my hand on hers and said, "Mamma, will you rub my hands?" But she flung me off and seizing the flowers from their pitcher on the table beside us, she stripped the blossoms from the stems and hurled them like rocks into my face, spattering me

426

with drops of water as a shower of petals fell into my lap and obliterated the embroidered bird. As in the faithful dog that turns on his master, the stimulus for her assault was mysterious. She wanted to inflict pain on me, and in her rage she could not see that the soft rosebuds touched my face as tenderly as snow, and as if blood from wounds were pouring from me, she hissed, "Beast! Cheater!"

I could not remember what I had used to do with her in her exuberant furies, and with relief I saw the attendant approaching us, casually so as not to alarm the other patients, and knew that he would capably manage to quiet her. I had forgotten to be grateful that I was no longer responsible for her, but just as a woman whose children are grown recalls, on seeing a baby, the nuisance of infantile care, and as we are sometimes profoundly thankful as we witness the seething turmoil of adolescence that we are not and can never again be sixteen, so I counted my blessings as I watched the attendant draw my mother from her chair, and gently embracing her, move towards the door. Upon a signal from him, immediately after her first outcry—though it had been little louder than a whisper it had sounded like thunder in his alert ears—the other attendants had busied themselves with the patients, fussing with their clothing or asking after their wants, so that the crazy calm, the disruption of which had been threatened when my mother, pelting my face with the flowers, had become the cynosure of inquisitive simian eyes, continued as if there had been no hiatus.

I brushed the petals off my coat and finding no other place to put them, dropped them into the bag of apples which I picked up intending to take home with me. With the stubborn health of a strong animal despite what had just happened, I was hungry, for I had had neither breakfast nor lunch and the smell of the apples had so tempted me that it was all I could do to restrain myself from biting into one as I left the room. The rattle of the gallstones reached my ears as I crossed to the door and turning, I saw the white-haired old lady smiling beseechingly as she crooked her index finger at me. "Come here a minute, Ellen," she said. "Granny has a surprise

427

for you." But one of the wise and lifeless matrons sat down beside her, saying, "Mrs. Andrews, may I see what you have in your little box?" Delighted, the old lady opened it up and said in her kindly voice, "Ellen gets them all when I die."

As I went into the white-walled corridor down which my mother and her guard were strolling, like lovers, her head upon his shoulder, his arm about her waist, a doctor, who had been writing something in a notebook as he leaned against a radiator, stepped towards me. "Are you the daughter?" he asked. I replied that I was and I remarked that my mother seemed to be approaching one of those crises with which I was so familiar. The doctor, bluff, corpulent, with a large, limber face in which broken capillaries running in all directions made it look like crazed pink porcelain, shook his head and answered, "On the contrary. We think she is recovering."

Instinctively, as if to prove that he was wrong, I looked down the passage towards her and as I did so, she turned her head. "Sonia, Sonia!" she cried, sobbing like a child, but the attendant tenderly bent her head again into his shoulder and they disappeared into a doorway marked "Infirmary."

"Oh, no!" I said to the doctor. "She can't be getting well. Why, she's much worse today than she has ever been before!"

"No, you're wrong, my dear girl. Dr. Tudor and I have lately been much more hopeful about her. To a large extent, she has shaken off that intermittent amnesia, and a good part of the time she is at least semi-aware of where she is. We're now of the opinion that she will recover, perhaps not completely and not permanently. But it is possible and, indeed, very likely, that in another three months you can take her home."

I said nothing. My silence drew a smile of understanding to the florid face. "I've been over the case. I understand you had her brought here because you hadn't money enough to get someone to take care of her."

"Yes, I have no money."

He did not fail to scrutinize my clothes. "But you're well enough off now?"

"I am secretary to a wealthy woman," I told him, "but I have very little actual money."

"Mmm," he mused. "You're qualified to be secretary to someone else, I suppose? To someone who would pay cash for your work?"

"I can't!" My fingers tightened round the paper bag of apples as I imagined this future life he proposed for me: the rumpless birds gradually crowding us out of our house, the endless cups of tea before a fire so violent it threatened to burst from the stove, the incorrigible maudlin affection manufactured at top speed by the indestructible engine in her person, unvarying in its pattern. I could think only of my return after work in the afternoons: day after day and year after year of her pertinacious life, I would hear my name reiterated in different tones and in combination with a few simple phrases, falling from her lips like tears or like a molten substance used to solder one thing to another in obdurate unity.

"Why can't you?" inquired the doctor with interest.

"Because I am afraid," I confessed. Until I said the word, I had not been afraid. My feeling had been anger that I must give up my life in Boston as it was now for the lonesome, tedious sort the girls at the business college had been prepared for. And I was as defiant of my mother as if she had conspired against me with someone, perhaps with this optimistic doctor. But I knew, as soon as I had spoken, that I spoke the truth, that I was afraid, not of any harm that might come to my mother through my inexpert treatment nor of any physical harm that I might suffer at her hands. When the doctor asked me, I told him, "Because I think sometimes *I* might go insane."

Still, when he questioned me further, I could give him no reasons save that I could not bear to be alone in the room with the Countess because she reminded me of Mamma and each time, after she had kissed me, I ran through the Common to Boylston Street and then ran back again to Pinckney as though the whistling wind, my pounding heart, my smarting face, could efface the memory of that plastic bosom and those full, intemperate lips. Sometimes my distress was so acute that I was obliged to send down word that I could not eat dinner because of a headache, and all evening I was numb and visited from time to time by an abortive retching, a spasm of inexplicable terror. And I could tell the doctor how sometimes Miss Pride's eyes and sometimes Philip's were watchful and that the guard who sat with Mac in the car perused my face for signs of madness and that all these eyes, on certain nights, watched me from the corners of my darkened room.

The disclosure shocked me: it was as if I spoke of an absent person, sketched impersonally the strange behavior of a fictitious character. But I was not cheating. These things were true but until now I had not articulated them nor even recognized them. For months, though, I had felt presences in my room which came in that hazy interlude that foretokens sleep, and I had had the feeling that I was being watched, but like my mother I confused one sensation with another and said that the hallucination had come from the sound of the fire which, dying, soughed like a forest wind.

I did not convince the doctor. Even to myself my story did not sound like history but like an impromptu fabrication. I had neither the vocabulary nor the analytical gift to state my case in full, arguing from the past as well as from these present idiosyncrasies. But he was not unsympathetic, although he smiled with what may have been contempt.

"You must control yourself. If you want your mother to be well, you've got to help, you know."

"But *well*, sir?" I said. "I mean, how far will she be cured?"

"Why, I should think you'd be as good a judge of that as I. She'll be restored, we hope, to her original state of mind. From what we've seen here, we know that she is by nature an unstable woman and for that reason could never be thrown on her own. If she had no relatives and were completely alone in the world, I expect we would keep her here, give her some little occupation like helping in the kitchen. But you wouldn't want that, would you?"

"Oh, no," I hastened to assure him. Then, against my

430

better judgment I went on. "There was a time when I would have given up my whole life to her, but that was before I saw that nothing, no change of atmosphere, no improvement in our standard of living, could make her anything but what she has always been since I was a young child."

"And what is that?"

"A millstone," I whispered. "But I know I'm duty-bound. You needn't tell me."

"I had no such intention. I'm not a moralist."

I closed my eyes for a moment to shut out his professional smile and as I did so, I seemed to descend once more through the wide, moving air and then, purged, absolved, emptied of all that did not pertain to solitude, I saw the red room with its wedges of shadow, its prospect of eternally slumbering cats. When, with the opening of my eyes, the room disappeared, I thought of adding to my list of suspicions about myself which I had just given him, this phenomenal apparition. For whatever had been the emotions with which I had received the impression for the first time a few minutes ago in the common room, surprise was not one of them: the part of my mind, the spiritual optic apparatus, so to speak, had registered the details of the room so singularly tangible—down to the title of a book in German—when the details were some of them extraordinary, that the exercise could not be mistaken for a daydream or a dream and I knew (but how could I expect anyone to believe this subjective testimony?) that it was not a memory. But I concluded that this morning was *not* the first time I had seen it, but that something in the external world upon which I could not lay my finger had by accident dislodged it from the populous, diffuse, chimerical mazes of my subconscious mind. I had this second time, as before, felt safe and comforted. And it was because of this that I did not tell the doctor, out of the fear that if I told him, I would lose the room forever. Then as I looked again, straight into his eyes which regarded me with curiosity, I was visited briefly by a feeling of guilt and uneasiness like the thief who, having cached his plunder, feels that he has been observed though a second survey shows him that no one is near. When I spoke —and it seemed to me that a long time had elapsed since his last words—it was with a stammer: "I can't explain . . ., I . . . perhaps you don't believe me . . . that is, perhaps there's nothing to what you say. You say she has had fever. Well, often before, when she had fever, she seemed rational. It's nothing more than that, I can assure you." I cursed myself for this unsure speech, so insolent in its ambiguity, and as my eyes faltered and fell away from his astonished stare, the doctor said, "Why, you *are* at sea, aren't you? You must stop worrying. Go on back to town and see a movie and try to get a good night's sleep."

I thanked him and apologized for my hysteria. "Goodby," he told me and, as I retreated down the corridor, I could feel his eyes still on me.

As we drove back towards Boston, I ate one of the apples. My thorough enjoyment of its flavor and its frosty grain bitterly amused me: my perturbation was not of heroic enough proportions to kill my appetite; it was even likely, I thought, that I would sleep no worse than usual tonight. The satisfaction of my hunger urged me on to further practical action, and I proceeded to sound out for their utility the several impulses that came to me. My first and strongest was to go at once to Philip. It would be possible to tell him honestly why I could not live with my mother again, for he did not draw a sharp line between sanity and insanity but saw innumerable nuances between the two poles. But would a conversation with him now be as easy as in the old days, now that our incompleted gestures, their instigation unplumbed, were between us like a transgression that was not confessed because, having the appearance of accident, its premeditation on the part of either of us could not be proved? On the other hand, perhaps if I appealed to him now in my trouble and now that he had entered into a contract which precluded the maturation of that fumbling, dumb desire which had fled from the one of us as soon as it had made itself known to the other, perhaps now we could step backwards and, starting fresh,

432

proceed as before. *As before.* But could I, in this dark-ness, find my way back through the détour where shaggy shapes misled the eye: the shapes of *might have been* and *still might be?* And where, at such an hour, would I find him? Even if he were at home in his three large rooms on Beacon Street, would it not be highly im-proper for me to call upon him there even for advice? But he would not be at home. He would be somewhere with his fiancée. They were undoubtedly already being fêted. Someone would have arranged an impromptu cocktail party for them and they would be there now, receiving congratulations. Even if I went to him, even if he had nothing else to do but listen to me, he would not be able to keep his mind on what I said.

Would it be better to warn Miss Pride at once? Should I go directly to her bedroom where she would be resting until tea time and beg her for help, telling her that she alone in all the world could give it to me? She was angry with me; she had made it clear this morning that she did not want to be troubled with me for the next three weeks. Another time she might be sympathetic, might even suggest some way to preserve the separation from my mother, but the marriage of her niece was of more importance to her now than anything else; my life, beside it, was a project like the memoirs which must be set aside for the time being. I could not risk it. I would wait until the wedding was over, and then some evening, just before she picked up the *Boston Evening Tran-script,* I would say, "Miss Pride, may I ask your advice?"

Or should I now at this moment pick up the speaking tube and say, "Mac, turn around as soon as you can and drive me to New York." When I was alone in the car, Mac gave in to his temptations and drove both fast and recklessly. While sometimes I recalled with terror the talk of the old ladies who declared that he had heart disease and might suddenly die at the wheel, today his speed and his narrow escapes thrilled me as if he were already obeying my command to take me far away and swiftly to a new life. But the squat shops and movie the-aters of Mattapan were already huddled on either side of us and we slowed down with the thick traffic. Nudged on one side by an endless line of cars and on the other by the trolley that lurched slowly forward with loud ejaculations, at times we barely moved and I was gradually invaded by claustrophobia so insistent that the ligaments of my arms and legs began to ache as if I were actually cramped into a small space. How patiently our moral nature bides its time, how adroitly sets its stage, parting its curtains suddenly. As unprepared as Gertrude or her king, we willy-nilly witness our own villainy played out. It had not crossed my mind until I felt myself hampered, buried alive by the creeping machinery all about me that perhaps what the doctor had said was true and that my mother fully knew she was a prisoner whose release depended on me. Was it not the meanest beastliness even to think of flight? I caught a glimpse of myself in the mirror above the wind shield, and saw my black hair. What if I unpinned it sometime as she did always in her frenzies? What if my own passions became hopelessly entangled in a desperate disorder and what then if Miss Pride coldbloodedly, like me, disburdened herself by sending me off to an asylum and stopped her ears to my entreaties? For ours were not the kind of aberrations that Hopestill's fashionable psychiatrist could cure.

I suffered from my punishment. But I made a bargain with my sense of duty: I said that the red room would be my refuge, that when the time came I would resume the battle on the condition that I might always return to it, as a warrior pauses to pray. The milder, though not sovereign, wardens of my being, granted me permission, and a little comforted, I sank back on the cushions as we pushed on.

The house would be silent and my room would be cold. I did not want to go home. I remembered Nathan's invitation, and although it was not yet five o'clock, I directed Mac to drop me at the Copley Square subway station. My reason for going to him was no longer to find out how great a fool I had made of myself the night before. It was that I wanted company and I could think of no one more appropriate than my old friend whom I had used to watch reading on early winter nights.

434

4

The overwashed young man, his birthmark veiled in a shadow, was hard to establish in the surroundings of last evening and equally hard to establish in this cold, filthy, malodorous subterranean suite of two small rooms densely populated with furniture so shabby, fractured in so many places, that it seemed to be totally useless rubbish. I saw, as soon as I went in, that on his sick and sober awakening, Nathan had had no stomach for the visit he had suggested and that probably he had hoped I would not come. Not without irritation, he said, "Oh, it's you. It's only five. I thought I told you eight."

"I know," I replied. "I just had nothing else to do. I brought you some apples."

Perplexed, he took the paper bag from me; as he withdrew an apple, a shower of rose petals fell to the floor. "What the hell's going on?" he said.

I looked brightly about his place, ignoring the question, and said, "Well, you're cozy here." He was anything but cozy. The only light came from two small, high windows through which I saw a steady parade of legs marching briskly past as if they had been amputated but had retained their power of locomotion. There was no rug on the cement floor and this accounted, I supposed, for the galoshes that Nathan had neatly fastened over his trouser legs. There was a couch, covered with a foul green blanket, burned and stained; two overstuffed chairs with ruptured seats from which batting and horsehair indecently protruded; a desk, littered with papers, orange rinds, dirty cups, soiled handkerchiefs; a bookcase; a standing lamp with a paper shade decorated with a sailboat on a blue sea as flat as a table top. In the corners there were bundles, the wash or merely rags I could not tell, and stacks of magazines and pasteboard cartons full of trash. The air was damp and weighted with a strong odor comprised, I thought, of stale cigarette smoke and scorched coffee and fried meat. And yet the occupant of this squalid cell was cleaner than I had ever seen him. I thought at once of the young man, Mr. Garvin, whom I had met at the Countess' and who had impressed me because he gleamed so brightly with soap and water. I said, looking from Nathan to the unsightly blanket on the couch, "Do you sleep here?" and he turned down the cover to show me a pair of clean sheets.

"At present personal cleanliness is my principal fetish."

"Do you know a person named Garvin?" I asked.

"Certainly. And you knew I knew him. He reported to me at once that he had seen you at that fat German's house. And, yes, you're quite right, I got the washing habit from him."

"She's not German, she's Viennese," I said. "He did tell you he had met me? Why didn't you look me up?"

He shrugged his shoulders and with his old, still breathtaking gesture, drew his long fingers over his cheek. "Our last meeting—I mean in Chichester, not last night—didn't leave me with the feeling that you would want to see me again."

"But you misunderstood me!" I cried.

"I had hopes that that was the case, but since you never tried to explain, I assumed you didn't want to explain. And there's no use in your doing it now, because I have other fish to fry."

I was irritated that he thought I had come to resume our adolescent flirtation. "And what makes you think I haven't? You're as vain as ever, I see."

He did not reply. I sat down on the couch and for a time we were silent while he ate his apple. When he had finished he wiped his lips with the back of his hand and reaching down behind the desk brought out a gallon jug. "I suppose you want some of this? I haven't any glasses but I have some teacups. It is sherry, the poor dipsomaniac's drink. Well?" I thanked him, forgetting Miss Pride's admonition. He went on. "Yes, I am glad to see you. The past, that is, the past prior to that aforesaid encounter, comes back rather pleasantly. The fog, for instance. I hadn't thought of it for months."

His eyes narrowed dreamily to show that he was

thinking of it now with enjoyment. Likewise, to me, the past came back, for he had presented me with the brilliant cheek and my fingers tightened round the handle of the teacup, restraining themselves from reaching out to touch the skin.

"Oh, rest assured I didn't forget you. I merely set you aside as something completed, the way I did when I finally had to admit that your father wasn't coming back."

"You said last night you hadn't been in Chichester. Why not?"

"Why should I? Oh, I probably neglected to tell you my family moved to Lynn. But my family would never be a reason for my going back there anyhow. I did go back though, twice, just out of curiosity to know what the dump looked like. The first time it was in the summer and all I did was get a bottle of Moxie at Bennett's and get out as quick as I could. There was one of those Barstow hags in the store buying a stick of camphor ice. But the next time I went it was in the winter and it made me sort of nostalgic to walk past your house late in the afternoon. At first I thought I saw a light in the window but it was only a reflection of the sun. Does your mother live there by herself?"

"No," I said. "No, she isn't there any more."

He did not press me and while I longed to tell him where Mamma was, I checked myself and instead poured out to him the story of my meeting with Miss Pride last night and this morning, putting into my account all the feeling I had about my talk with the asylum doctor. Nathan, at first surprised that I had taken my scolding so seriously and then disturbed because he felt he was to blame, comforted me with sincere little speeches which I applied privately to my future with my mother rather than to the one with Miss Pride. He said such things as, "But it will all be over and forgotten," "No one in the world is that important," or "Things will be the same as ever in a little while."

"But you don't *know*," I said. "You don't know *her*."

"Why do you care so much? She sounds like a bitch. May I have another apple?"

"Certainly. I brought them to you."

"They're good apples."

As he ate, the fresh odor reached me through the other smells, and I said suddenly, almost without plan, "Look here, can I come to see you every Sunday?"

He looked at me over the apple in surprise. "That's a very peculiar request. How do you know you will want to come here or that I will want you to? Why Sunday? It's a very inconvenient night for me as I have an early class on Monday."

"I'm sorry," I said, blushing. "I don't know why I said it. Do forgive me."

"But what is there to forgive? You're very much odder than you used to be."

"Perhaps I am, but it's also odd of you to tell me so."

He smiled and filled our green teacups again. "I'll confess to you now—now that I don't feel the same way any longer—that I hoped you were so drunk last night you wouldn't remember that I asked you to come. I woke up thinking, Now I've done it again, got myself involved with the past again when it's all I can do to stomach the present. But I'm glad you did remember. And I'm touched by the apples. The rose petals mystify me, though."

I wanted to tell him how I happened to have the apples; I wanted to each Sunday night thereafter, through the winter and the long spring, but I was kept silent by indecision, for I did not know how my words would sound to him, whether they would elicit fear or sympathy, or how they would sound to me, whether I would be ashamed or comforted. Though the hours before I came to his apartment remained my secret, so that Nathan was still a stranger to one half of my life, nevertheless to me he became connected with it just as a landscape will seem to be inextricably involved with a remembered event although, at the time, it was hardly noticed. It was as if by giving him the apples that my mother had fingered and had not understood, I had joined them in an alliance which, for all its artificiality, consoled me. It was not that I had felt any disappointment in my mother's not welcoming the apples, nor that

438

I appreciated, by contrast, Nathan's enjoyment of them. It was not in my power to please my mother. It was more, also, than the comparison I naturally made in coming from a madhouse into the presence of a normal person. It was, in effect as a symbol, that I saw the execution of this kind of duty to be worthless both to the agent and to the recipient, for my mother derived no benefit from my gift and had I not brought it, she would not have been aware that I had failed to fulfill my promise. And I, being commissioned to bring the following week essentially what I had brought this week (smaller apples and yellow instead of red) was walking a treadmill. This was what I had wanted to convey to the doctor, but I had known that I would never be able to make him understand and therefore the only hope I had lay in the verdict handed down to myself by myself: whether the obligation, imposed upon us all by the Fifth Commandment, was to be taken literally or was to be interpreted. But since I knew of only one kind of action which could follow if my decision finally was that I owed my mother no more years of my life, that action being the flight I had thought of as we drove home, I could not tell anyone of my debate. For flight, no matter how it may be justified, no matter how necessary it may be to the maintenance of life, is an act of cowardice. One's alternative is protest; but to protest without fear, one must be convinced that right will win, and if it does not, must accept, at least temporarily, the triumph of wrong. The conscientious objector to war is generally regarded as a moral man, if too philosophical, and immune, through some strange means, to the infectious patriotism that sweeps his country in time of war; he may be criticized but only a few will call him a coward. But the man who kills himself, the man who hides himself away in the mountains or in the swamps to escape conscription, is abhorred by everyone. Yet it is possible that his refusal to fight is neither out of the fear of danger nor the dislike of regimentation, but that it stems from the same moral principles as those upheld by the objector.

I was not certain of this argument; yet, as I sat that afternoon with Nathan in his dirty room, I laid the foundation for the edifice that would please me, not the one that was sure to be the soundest. I was persuaded that when the time came, my decision would be impartial, that in the end I would not favor myself, but that in the meantime I was entitled to play with the idea of going away, as unconditionally as my father had done, as far, perhaps, as Nathan was going.

"What are you going to do in Paris?" I asked him. "Write?"

He laughed savagely. "I've got that nonsense knocked out of me. What a pipe-dream!"

"What are you going to do then?"

"You really want to know? It's not nice. It's a damned colossal bore."

"I do want to know."

"I'm going to study Old French and I'm not going in the fine, careless, romantic, high-spirited way I let on last night. I am going on a fellowship and it is my thrilling ambition to make a critical study of Bernard de Ventadour. On my return to America, one year later, I will present this study as a thesis for the degree Master of Arts. Then, oh, then, dear friend, I will be ready for that next step to glory, the Ph.D. And after that, if I am very well-behaved and keep my nose clean, I may get a job teaching beginning French to the boys and girls of the Chichester high-school."

But what had happened to his earlier plans, those he had made on the steps of the Barstow in the fog. "I just grew up," he said sorrowfully. "But this has its compensations. I get a certain sense of power making footnotes on my papers on various medieval subjects: 'Ysonde,' I write learnedly, 'is a rare Scottish form of the name, usually rendered Ysolt or Isolt, or sometimes Iseult.' You know I wanted to go in for Mittelhochdeutsch and work on Walter von der Vogelweide just as an excuse to go to Germany, but that's out now, of course. I'll show you what the University of Heidelberg sent me last year."

From an untidy drawer, he produced a prospectus containing photographs of the baroque Alte Gebäude half hidden by flowering lime trees, of the Castle in its massive decay, of the Old Bridge spanning the river, and of the Protestant cathedral with bookstalls stuffed between its buttresses.

"There are hills on either side of the river, you see," he said. "Garvin spent a summer there a couple of years ago. The first thing I would do would be buy a rucksack and take a long walk. Or maybe before I did that I'd buy a bicycle and go to Heilbronn. I know the map of South Germany by heart and just what the distances are and just where I'd stop overnight." He broke off and took the prospectus from my hand. "It makes me God-damned sore that I've got a name like mine. Do you think I look Jewish?"

"Not very," I said, thinking as I did so that I had never seen a more Hebraic face than this one.

"Well," he said dully, "let's change the subject."

I was surprised to find that Nathan was essentially un-changed but that my whole perception of him had al-tered. Where before I had seen formidable brashness, now I saw only a nervous arrogance which, at times headlong, was at other times so timorous that I had only to disagree in the mildest way to make him retract, apologize, abjectly humble himself. He began pontifi-cally to talk of books as if he had forgotten that I could read, had, indeed, been instructed by him, and when I took exception to his enthusiasm for a writer whose short stories were then much in vogue and which had, he asserted, revolutionized the art, Nathan's face ex-pressed his amazement that I had even heard the writ-er's name, then distrust of himself, and finally he said, "Of course! He's a charlatan! Why didn't I see that before?"

When, in our conversation, he hit upon a poet whom I also admired, he was overjoyed; he fairly frolicked with our kinship, treating me with a connubial warmth, congratulating both of us on this marriage of minds. Our enthusiasms were, indeed, so commonplace that he would have lived in limitless polygamy if he had courted further. His transports would be over Shakespeare's son-nets or Heine or Blake or Yeats whom he would come upon suddenly with as much surprise as a traveler who has been over a road many times will feel if, on one journey, he finds that a handsome new house has been built at the side of it since he last rode by. He told me that it was precisely because of his confusion that he had gone in for medieval studies. "Your taste doesn't matter much there. You don't have to commit yourself on whether you think *The Agenbite of Inwyt* is good or bad."

I asked him if he had ever gone back to the Communists. "No," he said, "but I hate the upper classes more than ever. Harvard College for Boys teems with them. I am employed by one of them, as I told you, a party named Morgan. I have tutored him in German for two years and I bleed him of a great deal of money and learn twice as much German as he does. But this is the kind of thing he'll do: we'll be translating along— he's a moron, of course—and he'll stop suddenly and say, 'Beg pardon, baby, I've got to make a phone call.' He *always* calls me 'baby.' He will call the air line and say, 'This is Morgan. I want a ticket on the five o'clock plane and I want to be booked through to Las Vegas. Put it on my charge account, will you?' His *charge account*, mind you. We go on with the translation—and you couldn't believe his illiteracy—and the telephone will ring. It will be a dame and Morgan will say, 'Honey, I love you, I love you, but right this minute I've got to hop a plane for the Golden West. I'll be back day after tomorrow. I've got ten drunks from Metro Goldwyn Mayer at my place and I've got to go out and police the joint.' We start out again and maybe do one, maybe two paragraphs of *Immensee* and his door-bell rings. His butler (butler, I said) comes in and says there is a little lady outside. 'Well, baby, let's let the Hun go for today. I've got to lay this little lady before I hop a plane. Come around next Tuesday. Tell my man to fix you a drink.' Need I assure you that I do not tell that fat, patronizing penguin that I want a drink?"

With some effort, I brought out, "Do you ever see any of the little ladies?"

"No. And I never want to. But I see their mink coats lying in the hall when I go out. And don't think for a minute I feel the least bit sorry for them. I would rather go to a whore-house myself. But why should he be successful with women? He's stupid and he subscribes to *Esquire*. Now I am extremely intelligent and once you get used to my face, I'm not really ugly. But do I have any success with women? Can I ever be sure of them? If I am sure of them, it's because they're too uninviting to be unfaithful and then they bore me to death. That middle-aged French baggage I told you about won't stir from my door-step and she annoys me so much I could strangle her without the least remorse. But on the other hand I never have been so in love as I am with Kakosan Yoshida and I can't trust her. She lies and deceives me and when I most want her she doesn't show up. And that was the way it was with you. When I specifically wanted to do nothing else in the world but drink Budweiser draft with you at Red's, you wouldn't do it."

We had been sitting in the dark for some time and now he turned on the lamp. He was as angry, I saw, as he had been on the way to the Brunsons' house, but I was equally angry and rose to go. As I reached for my coat, he grasped my hand. "Don't go," he pleaded.

"Oh, you make me sick," I said.

"I know it. I'm sorry. But please don't go."

"But your friend is coming. Your beautiful Japanese lotus flower."

"She won't come, and if she does, what good will it do me? I want to ask you a question, Sonie. Please sit down again and drink some more sherry or I'll make you coffee if you'd rather. The thing is this, do you think it will work, my going to France this way? I mean, if I don't marry Kakosan? I was joking when I said I might marry Andrée, she's impossible. Do you think it would work if I went by myself?"

I could not have answered his question even if I had had the time, for I did not know what it was he wanted except to live in Paris for a year and for that length of time to have a holiday from Mr. Morgan and his kind. At that moment there was a delicate triple knock on the door and Nathan rushed to unlock it and to admit his Japanese mistress, Kakosan Yoshida.

"I can't stay," she said, remaining on the threshold so

that, because the hall beyond her was dark, I could not tell what she looked like. I could see only that she was diminutive; the clear, dissonant notes of her voice were like a string of brilliant, hollow balls. "I cannot come in. I am sorry. You must not be angry, please. I promised to go to the séance. It can't be done without me."

"But you promised three days ago to come tonight," said Nathan.

She hesitated a moment. "Yes, that's true, I did. And I would rather stay with you. But they said they couldn't make the séance work without me and so I have to go. Please understand."

"Let me go with you, then."

"Oh, but you said you hated things like that. You hate me to go to them. I told them this would be the last time I would come. You wouldn't like to go."

"Yes, I would like to go," said Nathan firmly. "Is it cold out? Should I wear a coat?"

The high voice was desperate. "But you would hate it. It would be all right if just the *real* people were there. But riffraff is coming tonight. It's not by invitation tonight. Please!"

"That's all the better. If there are a lot of people I can leave if I want without offending anyone. Is it cold out or not?"

"Very well," said the girl angrily, "I won't go then. I told a lie. It's not for everybody. It is very exclusive. They wouldn't let you in. No, I won't go. I will sit here with you. But first I must call and tell them I'm not coming."

"All right," said Nathan. "You can use the janitor's telephone."

"No, I must go to the drug-store anyway. I must buy something. I will be back in a little while."

Nathan sighed. "Go on to the séance if there is a séance. But come in and meet an old friend of mine, an old, and up to a point, faithful, friend."

"I am too faithful!" she cried. Then, "Oh," she said as she saw me, "Why does he want me if he has company?"

She tipped her little saffron face up to him and smiled. He could not resist her, although he knew that there was no séance, that she was going to meet another lover, and taking her small, lovely hand, he kissed the lacquered fingertips. As she stepped into the full light, she seemed unreal, less human than animal material fashioned in the image of figures of painting and sculpture and the ladies of poetry so that it was almost necessary to understand the ideal in Oriental art before one could truly appreciate how authentic her beauty was. I would say of my mother's lips that they had the color of a rose, but of Kakosan I would have to say that her mouth was like a "mallow flower" for her loveliness was something so unfamiliar that the old words and metaphors would not do, and to say her lips were like a rose would be to say that they were beautiful but not to specify them as Oriental. She wore, under her incongruous American polo-coat, a dress of purple silk brocaded with gold. In the glowing blackness of her hair was pinned a white carnation, and on either hand she wore a jade ring. She was, with this costume, with her symmetrical, unblemished face, her tiny body as limber as a grass, something so conscious, so tastefully assembled that she was like a bejeweled ornament of incalculable worth. It was hard to imagine her in the arms of an Occidental man, harder still to imagine her as promiscuous as Nathan had implied she was and as I had gathered from her unskillful lie about the séance.

She sat down on the couch beside me and handed Nathan a parcel elaborately wrapped in white tissue paper and tied with pink ribbons. "It was to take my place," she said. "I found it in the store and thought you would read it tonight while I went to the séance. Do you know the spirits?" she asked, turning to me. I replied that I did not, and she informed me that I had missed half my life by not becoming acquainted with the supernatural. She told me that she had not only heard spirit voices imparting news of the other world, but had also been witness to the unaided peregrinations of chairs and tables and vases of flowers and, on one occasion, to the levitation by will alone of one of the sitters. "A year ago, my uncle, the tea-merchant, spoke to me. He died in Kobe three years before. He told

445

me I must not marry according to my father's choice. I am a Samurai daughter. How can I disobey my father?" She laughed. There was in her laugh something controlled and artful as if it were part of a song. "*He* should be happy at what my uncle said, shouldn't he?" and she pointed her finger at Nathan who was undoing the ridiculous pink bows on her present. "What would my father say," she whispered to me, "if he knew I had a beau like him? In a place like this? I call him *Gacho*. It means 'goose.'"

"And I call her *'hototogisu'* which means 'cuckoo.'" said Nathan bitterly. He had succeeded in removing the wrapper from the parcel and he withdrew a book. "Oh, thanks," he said. "I've wanted to read it." And he put it down on his desk.

"Now I must go," said Kakosan. "I am so obliged to meet you, Miss Marburg. Will you please go to the movies with me sometimes? Do you love the movies?" I said I had no burning passion for them, but I would be delighted to go to a matinée some day.

"Let's wait until the Garbo comes. I love the Garbo best of all. If I were not a Japanese girl, I would most like to be a Swedish girl."

As Nathan accompanied her to the outer door, I went to the desk, looking for the prospectus from Heidelberg. The book which Kakosan had brought was lying face down and I picked it up, curious to know what kind of writer she would choose to keep her lover company while she was deceiving him. The title was in German: *Der Traum der Roten Kammer.* The cream-colored binding was decorated with a black torii between whose posts lay several scarlet flowers; beyond the gate three cedar trees were visible. Although it had been in the shelves with all the others in my imaginary room, and I had only seen the back, I had known exactly how the front panel would look! When I heard Nathan's footsteps returning down the hall, I dropped the book suddenly as if I had done something shameful. But between the time I heard him and his entrance, the room appeared to me. This time, three positive things happened: I wondered if there were more rooms down the hall

446

from mine and if the buildings forming the court had a continuous passageway. Simultaneously a German word, *Gesäusel*, came into my mind and I seemed to stand in the doorway of the room, remarking the onomatopoeia of the word which meant "murmuring." Moreover, I recognized the writing desk as Louisa May Alcott's, on display in the Alcott house in Concord which old Mrs. McAllister had taken me one day to see. Upon this desk and under glass, I thought, had been Miss Alcott's diary, opened to pages of small, unreadable writing with the coppery look of aged ink. The town, from the windows of this room, eternally dead amongst its elegant trees, had seemed grandly harmless, and the glassed-in meditations of the gentlewoman were like a last testament begun at birth, like a happy, lifelong requiescat, and I remembered feeling as if I were in a different century. My lame and wattled companion, smelling of some faint, old-fashioned scent, had said to me, "Do you like the room? It is what I call a *gentle* place." But Louisa May Alcott's was not my room and we had not gone there at sunset, but in the early afternoon. Philip and Hopestill had driven to Walden Pond after luncheon to watch the skating, and Mrs. McAllister had said to me, "We mustn't stay in on this golden day. Let me take you to the Alcott House. It is closed for the winter, but the caretaker will let me in." And we had gone out in the pure yellow light of the winter afternoon.

Nathan touched my arm. "A trance?" he asked me. "Isn't it revolting the way I let her lie to me? I should have told her never to come back again or else I should have beaten her to death. And that book! Do you see what it is? A Japanese novel translated into German. Can you tie that for a pure waste of time?"

But for me, it was not a pure waste of time. His words were but a slightly altered version of what Mr. Whitney had said as we stood last night in Miss Pride's library and he had taken down a book from the shelves. I did not remember having looked at it at all. I was weak with relief that I had seen another copy like Nathan's, and I began to laugh. It was a deep, interior, physical laughter, as beyond my control as hiccoughs, the kind that afflicts children in grammar school who bend their little shaking bodies forward and hide their heads in their folded arms and want to stop but cannot even when the teacher reprimands them.

"But it's not funny!" cried Nathan.

I could only splutter a reply, and after a time when I was quiet, I explained to him that I had not been amused by anything, that I was only nervous, probably from all our drinking the night before and the dressing-down I had got from Miss Pride. He looked down at me contemptuously. "Nervous, is it? You're more fashionable even than I thought. I suppose you are being psychoanalyzed."

"Certainly not," I rejoined with some annoyance. "You want to know too much."

"I assure you that I have not the slightest interest in knowing why you laughed. If you are a giggler, more's the pity. It is particularly offensive when it comes late in life."

I wrapped my muffler about my neck, resolving not to come back again. Although a little earlier I had wished to explain why I had not drunk beer with him at Red's, I now wished only to expunge him and the memory of him from my mind. But, as often in the past, he disarmed me. He sat at his desk, his birthmark hidden by his hand and regarded me with a piteous entreaty. "Did you really mean it when you said you would go to the movies with her?"

"Oh, I don't know. Probably not. It seems very unimportant."

"You could help me if you only would. If you could convince me that she's a bitch, possibly I could eventually break off."

"I'm not interested, and now I've got to go home."

"I'll be lonely if you go. Will you come back again next Sunday?"

"No," I told him. "You're too rude."

"You can't hate a cat for killing a bird because it's the cat's nature, and you can't get sore at me for being rude because that's *my* nature. Please, Sonia!"

"All right," I said. "I'll try once more. It will be a little later next Sunday, I expect." We shook hands and said good-by with an exaggerated warmth.

I walked quickly between the banks of snow which lighted the streets like moonlight. A few doors from Nathan's building, I heard someone playing a recorder and I paused for a minute to listen. It was a tender, doleful tune like some Irish lamentation. The bold blood rushed to my face and fingertips. I passed on and peered into the uncurtained ground-floor rooms of students, for no other purpose than to see that they were all clean and comfortable, all unlike Nathan's and unlike my red room.

The room had been a little random daydream which I could have again, or it was like a lengthened *déjà vue,* that evasive quasi-memory which is a sort of unlearned knowledge of the soul. I could, I knew, in time, name in its real place each object in the room, and I felt confident that even after my vivisection, the room would accomplish again its impeccable synthesis, a fused and incomprehensible entity. It was a sanctuary and its tenant was my spirit, changing my hot blood to cool ichor and my pain to ease. Under my own merciful auspices, I had made for myself a tamed-down sitting-room in a dead, a voiceless, city where no one could trespass, for I was the founder, the governor, the only citizen.

Five

THE DRESSMAKER who had been imported from New York to make Hopestill's trousseau was known by her trade name, Mamselle Thérèse, which she herself always substituted for the nominative case of the first person singular pronoun, as though she were her own interpreter. "Mamselle Thérèse does not touch the potatoes," she said on her first evening to Ethel who frankly tittered. She said to me, "Mamselle Thérèse goes to a night-club twice a week in New York," by which I understood she wanted me to supply her with the Boston equivalent of this diversion, but I did not respond as she had hoped and thereafter she made no more such overtures but amused herself (and presumably me) in designing costumes which she said would "bring out" my personality. She spoke of Chanel, Lily Daché, Mainbocher as if they were Brahms, Bach, Mozart, or Plato, Descartes, and Hegel. "Daché composed a superb number for an archduchess last month, a really revolutionary turban. People were simply swept off their feet." Like the bald barber recommending a hair restorer, like the dentist whose teeth are false, Mamselle Thérèse dressed most frumpishly. She wore a strange assemblage of seedy garments, too large for her spare, nimble frame, out-of-date, soiled, frayed, reminding me of the hand-me-downs that two or three times a year the Brunsons' Boston relatives sent them to be given to me. And it was not only that the little modiste had clothed herself out of a rag bag, but that she had very bad taste, burdening herself like a fancy-woman with gimcracks from the five and ten cent stores: wooden brooches in the unreasonable shape of a Scotty dog or of an ice-skate or of a Dutch shoe or of a football; enameled beetles or dragonflies or cobras made of tin, with blinding rhinestone eyes; earrings in the shape of oak leaves or candlesticks; and with any costume, upon her right arm, she wore nine thin silver bracelets which she clanked interminably. Her shabbiness could not be explained by poverty, for she had a flourishing business, and the expensive dresses of her two assistants who had been lodged in a house on Joy Street, suggested that she could afford to be generous in their salaries. She was charging Miss Pride a shocking price for this assignment, as I knew from the estimate she had handed in on the day she arrived. She spoke quite openly of this as "a good thing."

"Now for you, angel," she said, "Mamselle Thérèse would sew for next to nothing, but for them, the price is in the hundreds, sometimes in the thousands. It is an art, *n'est-ce pas?* Wouldn't they pay ten thousand for a picture by Rousseau? Then why shouldn't they pay ten thousand for a dress by Chanel? Mainbocher? Mamselle Thérèse don't kid herself. She knows she isn't in that class yet, but she works slow and sure like a mole. Five years from now Mamselle Thérèse will be in the movies like Adrian."

Her ruling passion was business, and she could see nothing except in terms of its commercial value. Thus, when she learned that I had gone to a secretarial school, she said, "You must keep your eyes open and when the time comes, rush in and nab yourself a plum. Mamselle Thérèse's advice to a young girl like you that has a good head on her shoulders is: be a secretary to a big-time lawyer. There's the money! There's the prestige! I'm telling you. What good are you doing yourself fooling around up here with that *vieille furie* when you could be on Fifth Avenue, New York? Mamselle Thérèse has a girl-friend working at Number One, Wall Street, on the thirty-fourth floor and she makes fifty dollars a week. I'm telling you."

She talked ceaselessly in a hoarse whisper as if we were two business men making a slightly shady deal. Often she worked arithmetic problems with the tip of her finger on the polished table, so obsessed with the imposing figures of her last year's state and federal income taxes that she did not leave off even when I warned her that her nails would scratch the finish. It was of no matter to her that I contributed nothing to the conversation but answered only with a monosyllable or a forced smile when she put such a rhetorical question to me as "Does Mamselle Thérèse know all the answers in the business world?" Her chief ambition was to receive a commission from visiting royalty; it deeply thrilled her to imagine some queen or princess finding, after she disembarked, that she had not brought enough evening gowns: " 'I must run right to Mamselle Thérèse. She will make me a *chose merveilleuse* for the White House ball.' Wouldn't Mamselle Thérèse be knocked off the Christmas tree?" Sometimes, impassioned by the memory of a gown that Mainbocher had executed for some foreign personage or by the contemplation of vast sums of money owed her by her "élite clientele" she would pursue me to my room, having given a peremptory order to Ethel as we left the dining-room, to bring our coffee to the third floor.

Occasionally, out of self-defense, I would deliver her a little lecture, on how much I liked the town of Concord and its environs or on the splendor of the Countess' Saturdays, but Mamselle could attend nothing of what I said and the moment I paused, she burst in with a raging river of facts and figures to obliterate completely my little trickle of talk.

But she was not, as she seemed, out of touch with human affairs. She was not especially interested in them, but nothing escaped her shrewd French eye. Believing

452

me to be Miss Pride's secretary and nothing more, she spoke unguardedly of the household. *"Mon dieu,* that bridegroom! Angel, he is a fool, I'm telling you. Mamselle Thérèse don't need to make his acquaintance to know that like she knows the palm of her own hand. She only has to contact the fiancée, *n'est-ce pas?* That rich *renarde."*

"Why do you say she is a *renarde?"* I asked.

"You can tell by the eyes. They are sub-zero. You know? It is on her part a *mariage de convenance."*

"And how do you know that?"

"Because they haven't slept together. And how does Mamselle Thérèse know that?" She tapped her forehead. *"Par intuition."*

"But perhaps it is a *mariage de convenance* on his part too?" I suggested.

"Maybe. Yes, maybe. It is a cold place, this Boston. He marries her because she is rich, beautiful, what-not. Because a doctor should have a wife. She marries him because she is *enceinte, n'est-ce pas?"*

I should have laughed and denied the charge, but I was so astounded at the woman's wizardry that I could not gather my wits together for a moment and when I did, knowing that her conviction was not only right but that I could in no way shake her from it, I said, "You may be right, but I beg you to say nothing to anyone. It would kill Miss Pride."

Mamselle Thérèse was offended. "Why should Mamselle Thérèse gossip? She is here for the money. She don't care a damn about the *mariage.* Angel, it is a dirty business and not for me. This little up-and-coming *couturière* stays single, I'm telling you. Plenty of boy-friends and not a husband. Don't mix business with pleasure, angel. So why should she interfere with someone else's *mariage?* Mamselle Thérèse won't talk to the interested parties. She is interested only in the money from the interested parties."

We were sitting in my room at the time of this conversation and it was rather late, perhaps eleven o'clock. Both Miss Pride and Hopestill had gone out for the evening. Presently we heard light footsteps coming up the last flight of stairs and Hopestill's door was opened. Evidently she had come back to get something for in ten minutes, she went out again and back down the stairs. Mamselle Thérèse, not so much through the fear of being overheard as through boredom with the subject, dropped it instantly on hearing the footsteps and began telling me about a new costume she had designed for nuns which would be at once more sanitary and more beautiful than their present ones. She had interviewed innumerable Mother Superiors and had written to various bishops and to the secretary of the Archbishop of New York. As she had what is aptly known as "total recall," she repeated verbatim each conversation, each letter, and each reply, all of which seemed, on the part of the ecclesiastical authorities, to be stubbornly hostile to her proposition.

But the soliloquy, which lasted for half an hour after Hope left the house, did not prevent me from hearing through the wall which separated our rooms, the soft collapse of the girl's body on the *chaise longue* and a sob, stifled at once as though she had pressed her face into a pillow. The sound would probably have escaped me if I had not heard it before and had not come to expect it as the expression, in a sense, of the reason for her visit to her room during the evening. Almost every night when there were dinner guests, she came up two or three times, and usually I heard that secret, frustrated outburst like a checked curse. On such evenings, she might stay as long as a quarter of an hour and hearing her footsteps back and forth across the carpet, muted so that I could not be sure if I really heard them or only felt the vibrations of the floor, I sat at my typewriter unable to strike a key, embarrassed because she must have heard the clatter of the machine which stopped as her door knob turned.

I could not immunize myself to her misery and pitied her for whatever punishment her conscience was meting out to her. I was impelled to go in to her in the way one may start, hearing a human cry in the night and think it is someone lost or hurt and in need of help. Beside a warm fire in a light room, an impression of the night's

454

cold and darkness superimposes itself upon the altruistic impulse, and one rationalizes, says the cry comes from the throat of a drunk or of a cat that can sound like a woman or even that it is the lure of a thief. I would wait until I heard her going down the stairs again and then I would shrug my shoulders with a resolute indifference and say aloud, "It's her affair, not mine."

Before my brother was born, I could not bear to have my mother speak of miscarriages and of "the pains" because I was sure that pain must be much more terrible to other people than to myself. And when Miss Pride reproved the Gonzales boy for stealing her soap to carve his little Virgin, I would have been glad to exchange places with him in order not to see the shame in his downcast face and the limp arms hanging at his sides, the palms of his hands turned out in broken-hearted supplication. And now while I did not minimize the discomfiture of my own position and spent a good part of every day in sorrowing over my unjust luck and even thought that in the end, my lot was much the worse, I felt that I was somehow better equipped to endure than Hopestill. She, the frail sheep lost from the herd, could not find her way back nor could she make her way alone. She knew already, as these flights to the privacy of her room showed, that she could not carry it off, for even if the discovery of her deception were long postponed or never made at all or made only by a few people who would not blame her or, if they did, would keep silent, she had nevertheless ruined herself in the only *milieu* for which she was trained. She had ruined herself even though there might never be suspicions or rumors, for she would never be *sure* that she was not suspected: she would hear the most innocent remark as a *double entendre,* the most amiable question as put with an ulterior design. It was possible, too, I thought, that after the secret gratitude to Philip for unknowingly saving her from disgrace had expired, she would commence to hate him, as the impoverished libertine, her father, had hated his martyred wife whose rich dowry had provided him with the means for his philanderings.

Long before this, Hopestill had damaged herself,

though not irremediably, by her connections with "the Bohemians." She had occasionally brought young men, who let their beards grow and who dressed most unusually, to the houses of her friends and her aunt's friends, exhibiting them like trained poodles. Unconventional and explosive, they alarmed the hostesses whose disapproval could not find its exact target and fired nervously upon all sides. The poverty of these barbarians was thought to be an intentional and Communistic affront; they were believed to be practitioners of free love, companionate marriage, and atheism; their painting or their writing was eyed with distrust as revolutionary or satirical. The Boston hostess, finding herself at the mercy of a novelist (she had not heard of him and therefore could not tell if he was a satirist or not) guarded her words against the escape of a stupid or a typical remark, yet most typically, most stupidly, said, "I hope you won't put *me* in one of your novels."

It would have been tolerable, everyone thought (according to the Countess, my faithful informant), if Hope had been content merely to bring her friends to parties for, despite their appearance, they behaved usually quite well. It was that Hope had given herself such insufferable airs, sprinkling her talk with the cryptograms of literary critics, explaining, unbidden, the meanings of abstruse poems. She had painstakingly studied out an erudite essay on "physical distance" the year before and for several months judged thereby every book, painting, play, or movie that came up. But as someone remarked—someone who probably had never heard of the esthetic principle she used so boldly—she shot only at sitting birds, and she was openly laughed at when she was heard to say to Amy Brooks, "The trouble with your Oyster House pastel is the figure in the foreground, which is under-distanced. He is simply too much the pitiable bum. He actually brings tears to one's eyes, and that won't do."

To be sure, she was over her "intellectual" phase and no longer carried marinated herring to the obscure studios. But she had not become any more manageable. Exactly what she was doing in New York no one knew.

456

Indeed, no one knew her address beyond the vague fact that it was "in the fifties." When someone said to her, "I wish you'd look up my friend so and so. She has a charming place on the Park and I know you'd find her amusing," Hope replied with a warm smile, "It's terribly sweet of you. Of course one *never* does anything one wants in New York, but do give me her address anyhow." Only once had anyone seen her and that only by chance. A Miss Bradley, an elderly spinster, idling away an hour between appointments in Central Park, had come on Hopestill staring raptly at the sea lions who were being fed. "Oh, aren't they beautiful?" the girl had cried. "Oh, aren't they wondrous! Oh, if only I had seen them when I was a child. You know, Miss Bradley, that Aunt Lucy never let me go to the zoo." Miss Bradley, reporting this uninhibited speech to Amy Brooks, said, "I expected her to give me a lecture on child psychology, but she spared me and we had a very pleasant little chat."

Now that she had made the full circuit and had 'returned to the starting point, she was generally forgiven all her past peculiarities, and there was universal rejoicing in Miss Pride's circle that the marriage, prophesied for so long, was at last to come off. In my exile, I was obliged to rely entirely on the Countess for my information, and she assured me that both Philip and Hopestill were ecstatic, that it made her quite giddy herself just to be in the same room with them. Hope, she said, had never looked so well or so handsome.

I would have been glad to believe the Countess, but I could not because of that testimony of Hopestill's misery that I heard nearly every night. As soon as her footsteps had died away, I would give in to a vicarious fear that set me trembling and, suddenly cold, would go to the fire to warm myself. I would muse into the brilliant coals and shut my eyes. The inner wall of my lids retained the clarified red of the flames like the surface of one of those freakish hot pools in certain places where minerals behave in a fanciful way. Willfully I would force myself downward through a red wind until the door to my imagined room was opened and I stood upon its threshold. Recently I had identified the lobster-claw letter opener as belonging to a very aged woman who lived in Chichester and had rendered some service to my mother when I was about five years old, so that we went to call on her one afternoon at tea time. I had been given the letter opener to play with and I was horrified by it, but I was bashful and did not want to be rude to the kind old lady, and so I had twirled the agate sphere and stroked the reptilian claws until I was nearly sick and had to refuse the hot cocoa which had been made especially for me. Still, the aged woman's room was not my room. I remembered distinctly that she received us in her bedroom because there were no fires in the rest of the house and that the spool bed had been covered with a blue and white quilt with a design of five-pointed stars and crescent moons, and that I had sat on an ottoman covered with scarlet oilcloth and that the tea things had been on an old-fashioned washstand through the half open door of which had been visible a chamber-pot with pale roses painted on the side.

My memories of rooms where I had been were delineated with the perfection of detail of truthful photographs. I saw Miss Pride's room at the Hotel as it had been one day after a windy rainstorm. A cherub pillow had been by the open window and one of the castles was dark with dampness; an elm leaf was flattened against the screen, and a letter which had been on the sill had been blown to the floor. One day I recognized the unlabeled bottle of red wine. It had been in the Countess' music room one afternoon, late, when I had gone there to listen to some records and had been alone. I had tasted the wine, but it had gone sour and I concluded that it had been removed from the cabinet to be taken downstairs but had been forgotten.

My visits to the red room were infrequent. Though I was convinced that there was no harm in it, that it was, if anything, an achievement of will that should be envied and applauded by other people who had not so sure a refuge, I was, at the same time, loath to make my seclusion there a habit. I entered it only (rather, I stood upon the threshold, for I was never actually in the room and could not visualize myself taking a book out of the shelves or sitting at the desk) when I felt that I could not withstand the onslaught of worry or of loneliness. Whenever I realized that Sunday was approaching and I must go again to see my mother and probably to have another conversation with the doctor, whenever Miss Pride reminded me that I was in disgrace, and whenever I came to think of Hopestill, then I would turn to my ghost of a sanctuary as I might turn to a drug.

When there were no guests but Hopestill and Miss Pride had gone out and Mamselle Thérèse was in her own room working at her sketches of a renovated nun, the stillness of the house unnerved me and if by chance there was a wind lamenting in the trees of Louisburg Square, my heart was plucked quickly like a taut gut. It was not that I feared sneak-thieves or murderers or Kakosan's spirits, nor did I feel, at this particular time, the watchful eyes of people who thought I might repeat my mother's pattern. It was a fear I could describe only approximately as a fear of *myself*. It was not a new experience. Sometimes in Chichester, I had taken care of children in the evenings at a lonely house almost at the Point. An old, one-eyed Airedale kept me company, snoozing on the sofa. Abruptly he would waken and lift his head, pointing his nose toward the door, and then, assured that there was nothing outside after all, he would look at me with his one intelligent eye. This look, so companionable and preternaturally wise, frightened me more than his attention to the door, beyond which he had sensed the lurking of some unknown thing: I was afraid the dog would speak. This droll idea, of brief duration, was but the envelope for another fear: the fear of my own mind which had conceived so awful a possibility. Like the motorist through dense fog at night who has proof of only himself, his automobile, and the road, and must accept *a priori* the fact that the rest of the world has not been dematerialized, I could not demonstrate the external authorship of myself and the dog nor our independence of one another. What proof had I that the dog was not the creation of my own mind and being such might, if I willed it, speak to me; conversely, what proof was there that I was not the dog's

459

idea, evolved in those mysterious, perhaps Olympian, brains behind the obtuse snout? What broke my ghastly reverie was the registration of sound on my mind, the footsteps of some later walker, or the rustle of a bed above me as one of the children turned in his sleep. I argued that since my mind had been altogether on the dog, it could not have produced a noise in the distance. My hearing re-established my spatial relation to the outer world's complexities and immediately thereafter my judgments were restored.

Similarly at Miss Pride's on silent nights, what unbalanced the poise of quintessential self (a play on words would come to me: the eye was the proof of I, not only of my own eye or my mind's eye, but the Cyclopean eye of the Airedale) was the protesting, bewildered cry of Miss Pride's cat shut up in her bedroom. It would come toward the middle of the evening and was no more than one prolonged off-key yet musical howl which petered out on a descending scale.

I had seen Mercy only once or twice in all the time I had lived with Miss Pride. When I first came, I had been told that she was jumpy and unfriendly because her kittens, begot by an unauthorized tomcat during the summer when she had been entrusted to the care of the Hornblowers in Concord, had been chloroformed as soon as they were born, and the mother, her instincts baffled, hunted them with piteous persistence, crying and snooping through the closets, the bedroom, the bath, and her own apartment, a storeroom no longer in use. Until her mesalliance and its results, she had been allowed to roam at will throughout the house, but Miss Pride, attributing a high degree of intelligence to her, thought that by way of revenge, she might now defile upholstery and rugs, in her search might overturn vases and clocks, might in her despair and anger scratch visitors and claw their stockings. By this time, she had surely forgotten her kittens, but Miss Pride had decided to make this limited arena permanent, for what reason I do not know. Each morning, I saw Ethel putting Mercy's sand-box (called by Miss Pride "the kitty-cat's water-closet" but by the embarrassed servants "the cat's carton") shrouded with last night's *Transcript* on the dumb-waiter to be emptied and filled with fresh sand. This and the lonely cry at night were the only evidence I had that there was an animal in the house.

One night I thought that it would do no harm if I let the prisoner out for an hour or so, bringing her up to my room which was not a spacious place to romp in but would at least be a change of scene. I went down. Miss Pride's room was dark except for the fire that had burned down to a rich glow and at first I could not see the cat. When I was accustomed to the shadows, I perceived a pair of sulphurous eyes which, seeming to be suspended in the air four feet from the floor, regarded me with the unflinching stare of the hypnotist. I switched on the night-lamp beside the bed and in its weak light saw the animal perched on a chest of drawers beside the fireplace. For a moment she did not move but only looked at me. She had a short, square face and silver whiskers that curved downward from her tawny cheeks, marked on each side with two black stripes. She sat with her front legs straight and her luxurious tail curled about her feet. I moved toward her and she started, thrusting her head suddenly forward so that I could see the pure white fur under her chin. "Kitty, kitty," I said. She leapt from the chest with a chirrup of fear and ran to her room, a streak of fur that blended shades of red and yellow and blue, all overlaid and softened with a cloudy silver and striped with black. As she ran, her tail dragged on the floor like a train. I did not pursue her, for there had been in her face as she saw me coming toward her a look of primitive terror that could, I thought, easily become the rage of a wild beast. I ran back up the stairs two at a time to my cheerful room where all the lights were burning. Three or four nights later, again hearing the cry and again wishing to bring her upstairs, I went down to try a second time. I found the door to Miss Pride's bedroom locked.

It was easy enough to explain the locked door. I remembered that in my haste the first time to get away from the cat and to end our mutual fear, I had neglected to turn out the night-lamp, and Miss Pride, finding it and realizing that someone—probably a servant, she would think—had been in her room, henceforth took precautions against Mercy's escape. She preferred to do that, I reasoned, rather than to shut the door to the storeroom. But ever after that, when I passed through the hall on the second floor, the fact struck me as potentially sinister that I had never heard Mercy's call until these last weeks when I, too, was virtually a prisoner, heard it only at night when I was alone except for Mamselle Thérèse and the servants who were all on the floor above me. As I went on and ascended the flight of stairs to the third story, my common sense returned and told me that heretofore I had been reading aloud to Miss Pride at this hour, and that on the nights when she was at home, I used my typewriter, the racket of which shut out all but loud noises or very near ones. But there is a side in us that courts and would like to believe in the fanciful. "Of course it was no more than coincidence," we say, but we would like our audience to share our wonder and reply, "Coincidence, certainly, and yet . . ."

2

By day our house was the scene of what Miss Pride crossly called "a needless hullabaloo" for which, as a matter of fact, she was largely responsible, for while Hopestill and Philip had wanted a small wedding, she had insisted that a step of this kind be taken with public pomp. It was typical of her to speak of it as "a step of this kind," as if it were some sort of sensible negotiation which had been undertaken after several other "kinds" had been discarded. It was she who had wired Mamselle Thérèse (recommended by the Countess and deplored by Hopestill who had her own modiste) and she who had sent out invitations to three hundred guests for the wedding breakfast, and she who had persuaded a notable clergyman who had left Boston several years before to perform the ceremony. There had been some argument about this last detail. Both Miss Pride and Dr. McAllister's father were Unitarians and did their best to dissuade Hopestill from being married in the Episcopal church in which, adopting her father's rather than her mother's sect, she had been confirmed. She was adamant and requested, moreover, that the minister from whom she had received the Eucharist at her first communion be brought back for the occasion. In only one other particular had she insisted on having her own way. She refused to be given away by her uncle Arthur Hornblower or any other relative and before even consulting her aunt, conferred the honor upon Admiral Nephews.

I thought that she wanted to be married in the Episcopal church out of a nostalgic attachment to her childhood, as it had been a better and happier time. I could find no other reason, for she was altogether without religious conviction and never went to any services. I divined, too, that in denying any member of her family the right to participate actively in the ritual, she was relieving them, symbolically, of any accessory responsibility.

In the week before the wedding, my duties were many and complex. I acted as the intermediary between Miss Pride and the representatives of florists, liquor dealers, caterers, and took great pleasure in ordering such things as twelve cases of champagne and thirty pounds of filet of sole. Miss Pride would have preferred to attend to these matters herself because all tradespeople were scoundrels and I was both gullible and extravagant, but she was occupied with other things, among them with ridding the house of kinsfolk who came in droves beginning at nine o'clock in the morning, expecting to be asked to luncheon and then tea and even dinner. They infuriated her by telling her that she looked "worn-out" and that they were going to make her go to bed while they themselves took over, lock, stock, and barrel. To such a suggestion, Miss Pride would say, turning her eyes like pistols on the offender, "If I want crutches, I'll *buy* them, Sally Hornblower." They were full of plans for what she would wear to the wedding (I knew what she would wear: a new black broadcloth suit and a green beaver hat) and for the most decorative way of arranging the display of gifts. She would nod her head and say, "I dare say that would be nice. But I shall just muddle on

463

in my old way. You can't teach an old dog new tricks." Once, after this cliché, she gave a mirthless "Ha! ha!" and sounded, indeed, like the dog that could not be taught but had learned in his youth the trick of biting trespassers.

The continual stir of the house was intoxicating. On my way out of the house to run some important errand, I would glance into the upstairs sitting-room where the presents gradually were accumulating. Hopestill might, as I passed, be unwrapping something that had just come. She would hold up for me to see a blue plum-blossom jar or a silver pitcher. We could hear the bee-like flurry of the sewing machine and the animated conversation of Mamselle Thérèse and her two assistants. The door-bell and the telephone reiterated their clamorous demands until the servants were beside themselves. Leaving Hopestill surrounded by her treasure, I would go downstairs to receive a final instruction from Miss Pride. Nearly always, on one of the tables in the hall, there was a silver bowl half filled with water on whose surface floated the disintegrating but still fragrant flowers that Hopestill had worn the night before. I was curiously moved at the sight of them, and imagined her coming in late, the dangers of another day behind her, Philip's car already pulling away from the curb. I wondered if she would not ponder her face in the mirror above the table as she unpinned the orchid or the gardenias just as I pondered mine a moment before I left the house. Which face would she see? The one with which everyone was familiar or the one I had seen on the day she had come home when in her distress she had seemed old and plain?

The churchly odor of old wood and stone was sweetened with the perfume and boutonnières of the wedding guests assembled twenty minutes early. A beam of sunshine came through the open door and extended the length of the central aisle until, at the sanctuary, it joined in a pool of opaline light with another laden shaft sifted through the stained glass windows, of which the three segments were so detailed that I could read in

464

them no narrative but saw only brilliant colors throwing off the glitter of jewels. Then, through the gilded haze the altar was visible, furnished with a massive cross, two golden urns of white azaleas, and pale candles still unlit. The sun and the flowers and the open door made me think of spring, though I had only to look at the fur coats to remember that it was not yet midwinter and that the cool of the church was withal warmer than the outside temperature. The freshness of the bath I had just taken and the clean, acrid odor of my new clothes combined with this pleasure to give me a general sense of well-being and excellent health, as if I had shaken off the aches and miseries of one season and had entered upon the next under favorable omens, like the day on which we realize that our blood has expunged the last particle of disease. Two incidents the day before, which was Sunday, had lightened my heart. When I went to the library in the morning, I found Miss Pride more cordial than she had been since the night of my defection ("the night," she called it, "when you came home in such an informal state of mind."), and by way of showing that I was being recalled from exile, she gave me a glass of her fine personal sherry and told me that I must not fail to be at the wedding and the wedding breakfast the following day. Then, at the asylum, I was told that I could see my mother for only a few minutes as she was very ill and was confined to her bed in the infirmary. The doctor, the same one I had talked with before, admitted that he was not so confident of her cure as he had been. He was positive, he told me, of her ultimate recovery but thought she could not be moved for at least six months instead of three as he had told me before. The extension of time seemed like an act of benevolence performed by the doctor himself out of the goodness of his heart and I so ill concealed my gratitude that I drew from him a smile and a companionable pat on the shoulder as he wished me a Merry Christmas. I was, moreover, in good spirits today because the end of my suspense was at last in sight and henceforth I would not hear Hopestill weeping into her pillow nor catch in her face an occasional look of alarm.

465

From where I sat at the back of the chapel, I could see Miss Pride in the front pew sitting between the Reverend McAllister and his wife. She was wearing a new suit, but as it was made in the same pattern as all her others and cut from the same wool, perhaps I alone knew that it was new, for I had seen the tailor's bill. She had made one concession to her relatives, and in place of her green beaver wore a small hat planted with red posies which caused her so much consternation, because she thought it would fall off, that during the ceremony, as she told everyone later, she could think of nothing but the moment when she might take it off.

She and the clergyman, in their sober black, whose forebears had not taken passage on the same boat with the Tory Almighty who had lodged in this chapel since pre-Revolutionary times, sat rigidly, staring straight ahead with disapproval at the Popish paraphernalia of the altar which, as Miss Pride said, was "tantamount to a repudiation of the Declaration of Independence." Distrust of the high-church folderol as well as of her headgear gave her face the dour immobility of a Protestant martyr and she did not smile once or look either to the right or to the left from the moment Frank Whitney ushered her to her seat of honor until she left it. The Reverend McAllister, on the contrary, sent his eyes meddling into the nooks and crannies of the "temple," as he spoke of it, and glowered upon the kneeling attitudes of some of these first cousins to the Roman Catholics, into whose ranks he was heartily disinclined to release his son. The Reverend was a man of extraordinary obtuseness and had he ever taken the trouble—as his wife and mother did—to observe his future daughter-in-law even to form an impression of her external appearance, he would have been freed at once of his suspicions that she was leading Philip to the Pope, would have been far more worried that she would lead him to atheism. I had heard that at the time Al Smith was running for president, Reverend McAllister had been the victim of a recurrent nightmare in which a company of dwarfs (presumably Catholic dwarfs) attempted to stuff him into a confessional box, and he remarked to several people that if Smith were elected, he would die. Very likely he would have. He had presented himself at the house this morning to pay his respects to Miss Pride and as she was then engaged, I went down to entertain him until she would be free. He was a teetotaler and refused the port I had been commissioned to offer him. For five minutes he listed some facts to me which he had gleaned from his reading the night before, among which was the sagacious custom of polar bears who, when stalking seals, covered their black noses with their paws so that there was nothing about them to show that they were anything but mounds of snow.

Philip's mother who, although she would have preferred to wear black as a sign of mourning for her son, had finally decided that it would be too much of a good thing if all four of the chief relatives were attired as for a funeral, and was dressed in pale blue, becoming to her rosy cheeks and her white hair and her blue eyes, which had not been reddened but made only prettily clouded by the incessant stream of tears they had released ever since the engagement was announced. She had lost her appetite, had been unable to sleep a night through, and had not appeared at any of the pre-nuptial parties. It was said by her husband that her heart was temporarily "out of kilter." She had several times written Hopestill begging her to come to Concord: "We have so much to talk about," she wrote. "I feel there are many things you must know about Philip which only I can tell you. The hastiness of your wedding has prevented us from getting really well acquainted, but perhaps we can make up for lost time if only you will agree to spend two or three days with me." Hopestill, either because she was harassed by the business which the wedding involved or because she could think of no way to refuse the invitation graciously, did not answer, a breach of manners that had already had serious consequences. The elder Mrs. McAllister had told the story everywhere and, making use of her daughter's unwittingly accurate phrase, repeated often, "The wedding is too hasty for me. Marian and I both wish they'd wait until June. It is breaking Philip's mother's heart that she can't have a garden party for them. And since the poor thing's ill now, she can't even have an indoor party for them. I do think it's inconsiderate." The heart-sufferer, through a supreme sacrifice of her health, had managed to come to the wedding, though she would not be able to come to the breakfast. Her excuses, "doctor's orders," had been made through her husband this morning, as if she could not bear even to speak to Miss Pride.

The Countess, resplendent in a gray suit and a fox scarf, was sitting with Amy Brooks some pews ahead of me but she had spied me and was mouthing something which I could not catch and so mouthed back, "I can't understand what you're saying." It came out later that she had been telling me to be sure to look at Mrs. Hornblower, who had oddly enough come in evening clothes. I had, as a matter of fact, been on the lookout for Mrs. Hornblower who had heretofore seemed mythical, for I had learned on asking someone why it was that the tea-party to which I had been invited was such a remarkable event because the host's wife was to be there, that while she was on the friendliest terms with her husband, she did not share his house or his servants but lived in her own establishment fifty yards from his, a path leading from one door to the other. I asked my interlocutor—it was, as I remember, one of the girls at the Countess' Friday—to explain this. "They're just cranks," she said, shrugging her shoulders. "Mrs. Hornblower used to come to tea with my grandmother now and again when she was in town and she was at that time wrapped up in spiritism. It made poor Grandma have bad dreams about Mrs. Hornblower's astral body, and once when she said, 'Mary, I can simply walk through that wall if you only have faith in me,' Grandma shrieked, 'Nellie!' at the top of her lungs and it made Mrs. Hornblower furious although Grandma passed it off very nicely by saying that she just wanted Nellie to bring some more muffins. After that she took up the cause of Sacco and Vanzetti, but she didn't come to call any more for, as she told someone who of course repeated it to us, she didn't think my grandmother was interested in ideas." She had given up the occult for more pressing matters, but every now and again she would put in an appearance at a séance for old-time's sake, and at one of them, Kakosan had met her. Mrs. Hornblower had been a tremendous success and Kakosan, who assumed that because I lived opposite Louisburg Square I was intimately acquainted with everyone of consequence, had begged me to arrange an introduction. Mrs. Hornblower was a person of fine bearing, a large woman of whose face one immediately said, "She must have been lovely when she was young," and now, pitifully palsied, her white hair stained with yellow, she was still handsome. Much larger than her chubby husband who, although he was her senior, was better preserved and still wore black hair in which there was not a trace of gray, she bent toward him the loving and respectful looks of the obedient young wife.

Sitting at the aisle in the middle of the church, casually dressed in tweeds, Mr. Morgan slouched against the side of the pew, his chin in his hand, his eyes closed. He had not been invited, as I well enough knew because I had checked over the list of guests. But I was not in the least surprised to see him although I could not be certain of his motive, whether he had come to tease Hopestill or if he was in love with her and wished to torment himself, or if it was that desiring to escape suspicion he had thought it the better policy not to hide himself away. He had, if this last was his intention, made a serious mistake in his costume and continued, throughout the ceremony, to make an even graver error in his indolent attitude and his drowsy grin, for he was most conspicuous in that church full of people whose dress (with the exception of Mrs. Hornblower) was all so similar it was virtually a uniform, and thus he was set down by everyone who saw him—and he escaped the notice of very few—as vain and impudent, for in gainsaying the decrees of custom, he was usurping custom's power. His presence relieved me on one point and troubled me on another. Evidently Hopestill had not been seeing him, as I had suspected from time to time, for if she had she would have told him not to come. I had suspected meetings between them because I had learned from Nathan that

Morgan was in town all the time now and there was no falling off of his visits and telephone calls from young women. What disturbed me—vaguely because this morning I felt detached from the whole business—was that since he apparently thought there was nothing odd in his coming this morning and coming with so blatant an air of indifference, there was no reason to suppose that Hopestill and Philip and their friends would be deprived of his company in the future.

Nathan, after two years of anatomizing his pupil, had come to the conclusion that he was not really selfish nor cold-blooded but that he was one of those unfortunate people in whom is missing the talent for falling in love. Such people do not give up but suppose that love will come at last in the person of some now unknown woman, just as other people do not relinquish their hope that belief in God will at last batter down the impregnable battlements of the soul. He carried on two or three affairs concurrently and was equally tenacious of each of his women because it was possible that *she* was the one who would, under an abrupt and accidental change of circumstances, become his solitary objective. This being the case and if Morgan's need for the centralization of his life about one woman was as urgent as Nathan would have me believe, would not Hopestill's marriage be an obstacle of slight consequence to him? I could only conjecture what had taken place in New York, but I was sure that if Morgan offered to marry her (and I imagined that he did, for he was the kind of person who could, with the left hand, dispense a sort of sentimental honorableness at the same time that the right hand was composing a love-letter to another woman) Hopestill had refused, not because she did not love him, not even because she was unwilling to support his infidelities, but because her pride had been mortally wounded and its resuscitation could be effected only if the accessory to the crime were out of sight and, eventually, out of mind. The refusal (I continued my hypothesis) impressed her lover who had not reckoned on so easy an acquittal and after his first sweet sensation of relief, he became tantalized with the possibility that he might have fallen in love with her on the revelation of her stern character which, in spite of her yearning, had firmly dismissed him. Perhaps he had come today, then, for the simple reason that he wanted to see her, to refresh his memory of her beauty and to determine, from the expression on her face and the way she walked, whether his siege of her would be rewarding.

In the hush that forewarned the wedding march, a hush that fell upon the flesh as well as on the ears so that the guests froze briefly in their postures of kneeling or leaning towards their neighbors, a faintness passed over me, obliterating the vigor of a few minutes before. And as from its rich reservoir, the organ's voice ascended, translating the march from *Lohengrin* into its ecclesiastical language, I was apprised of the crisis of my complex feeling about this wedding, so similar to the sickness of the flesh that it was as if the very guardians of my body's fluids had told me of my disequilibrium. My dizziness had no cause more serious than excitement, was but another and more acute version of that agitation which caused the women in the church to apply handkerchiefs to their eyes. And yet, the anguish, that one moment inched like a cold worm through the tunnels of my flesh and the next kindled a fire that spread from branch to branch until I was all aflame, was so much fiercer than any emotional distress I had had before that for a time I believed I was really "coming down" with some disease. Tears boiled over my eyelids and half screened the four bridesmaids in their green tulle dresses, preceding the maid of honor whose medieval velvet gown, a deeper shade than theirs, was like the outer leaf and theirs the paler inside ones. As I was on the verge, I thought, of toppling forward over the back of the pew ahead of me, my mind, like a rapid finger flicking through a book to find a special passage, went over possible diseases and diagnosed my weakness by presenting to me Hopestill's face, shrouded in shadows, as I imagined it might look in the mirror above the table in the vestibule. Certain then that my symptoms were not physical, I sought to efface them by an effort of will. My eyesight, still somewhat deformed by the tears, cleared enough so that the maid of honor was less nebulous than her vanguard. With a smile directed towards nothing but an abstract point of the compass, she addressed to her gait as much science and regard for the rhythms of the music as if she were executing a step in a difficult dance. But although I saw her thus and followed her slender body and the head whose black hair was caught in a cap of gold and perceived that in her hands she carried a bouquet of yellow roses, I saw her also through the hot vapor of my tears as a mobile stain upon the undulating curtain that obscured the church and the wedding-guests. Similarly, while the music advanced from chord to chord, it clung, at the same time, in my ears, to one deep, roaring note everlastingly renewed by its infinite vibrations. Closing my eyes, I saw repeated on the black waves of my blindness, the same green smear which my sightless pupils pursued until it swam out of their ken, yet entered again at once when the ball rolled back to its central position.

With the passing of the maid of honor, I felt a temporary return of strength. The vertigo ceased and my mind cleared. Across the heads of the audience, who were turning to behold the bride, I saw Philip entering from the chancel, and through some unstudied sophistication, I saw him separate from the person I had known but instead, as a total stranger who, in a few minutes, could no longer lend himself in my imagination to romantic equations of which I was the other magnitude. He underwent a second metamorphosis and became "the physician." It was under the auspices and according to the rules of this genus that I should henceforth govern my relationship with him. In the service of my own interests, I was then able to transmute the smile of a young man about to be married, who at this moment had caught sight of his bride as she entered the chapel, into the smile of the understanding healer who by his attentiveness seemed to exist for me alone. And taking this clean-boned Yankee together with his opulent and august setting, I was, despite my frustration, glad that our flirting had come to nothing, that he would be unchanged when throughout the years I sought his advice.

The dazzled guests watched the proud flower for whose protection and enhancement the leaves had been created: a chaste and perfect column draped in satin as pure as the wax of the tapers on the altar and out-doing their flame with the hair that blazed through a calotte of pearls. Her face, white as her finery and her lilies, wore an expression of solemnity befitting the occasion, although, as I heard someone whisper, there should have been something of a smile in her countenance, if not upon her lips, then at least within her eyes, for joy should be in proportion equal to the other feelings of the partaker of this particular sacrament. Her look, to me, was one instinct with death, yet death less chill than that which now like a layer beneath her skin gave off a waxen luminosity and imparted to her movement a brittleness as if the soft integuments of skin and cloth concealed a metal mechanism. Her thin fingers were tightly curled on the Admiral's arm. Harry Morgan had turned, with all the others, and while I could not see her face, I knew by his, when she had passed by, that a sign had passed between them, for his mouth curved into a serene smile as if he had half won his battle.

It seemed to me, as they joined before the minister, that Hopestill shuddered as she had done when she took the camellias from my hand. If this was seen by anyone else—indeed, if it occurred at all—it was attributed to her nervousness, the understandable and appropriate reluctance of a girl about to relinquish her virginity by so public a ritual. With a tidal rustling, the audience sat down, arranged their hands in their laps and adjusted their spectacles like people anticipating a well-known and beloved piece of music. It was, to be sure, an artistic performance, for the minister, wreathed in benign smiles, posed his literary questions and offered up his prayers with the intonations of a Shakespearean actor, which grace of pitch and diction was afterwards to evoke from Reverend McAllister the remark that the service had been "nothing but rhetoric." I was astonished at the brevity of the cross-examination, and before I had accustomed myself to the idea that something of great importance was going on, the whole thing was over and the man and wife were coming back down the aisle, arm in arm, smiling to their well-wishers, their faces illuminated by the sunlight into which they were walking. Hopestill did not fail to include her husband in her dispensation of impartial smiles, but her hand that clutched the bouquet of flowers was clenched like stone.

The drawing-room, the library, the dining-room overflowed with cawing guests and the stairs were packed with two lanes, one ascending to view the wedding presents, the other coming down. As soon as I had offered my congratulations (the bride and groom were stationed before the bay window. Both of them had protested against this lavishness and were so harried that they seemed not to recognize me at all), I pushed my way through the throngs who, because they blocked the way between myself and my room for which I longed, offended me as if they were being intentionally hardhearted. Outside the drawing-room door, I met Miss Pride who had got rid of her hat and looked refreshed. I told her that I thought I was ill and wanted to go to my room.

"Nonsense," she said. "I've never seen you look better. There are two or three things I want you to attend to in the pantry. Come along with me and I'll show you."

I said, "I thought that if I went to bed now the cold wouldn't have a chance to develop."

"Oh, I know your kind of cold, you vixen. I'm not as easily taken in as Berthe, though, and won't let you off. What I think is that you're just concerned too much with yourself. After this is over, we must have a long talk and straighten things out."

I followed her docilely down the hall to the door of the pantry where she instructed me to post myself in order to see that the dirty dishes were immediately sent down on the dumbwaiter to be washed and sent up again so that everyone might be served. The waiters, who were perfectly capable of managing by themselves, regarded me with such wounded displeasure that for the half hour I stood on guard I did not utter a word, but leaned against the window where the sunlight was warm, drinking the remains of the champagne in the glasses that came out from the other rooms. Once I closed my eyes to feel the sun on my lids and when I opened them again saw Harry Morgan lounging up against the door giving me what I could only call "a once-over." Fearing that if Miss Pride chanced to come into the pantry and saw us there together she might surmise that I was responsible for this intrusion, and being, moreover, greatly perturbed by his prowling eyes, I exclaimed, "My God!" and he, straightening up, extended his hand as he said, "May I share your quiet inglenook, dear, just we two?" One of the accommodators, a portly middle-aged man with a bald head and a frowning face, turned on him a look of avuncular disapproval as he pushed past with a tray of glasses and I said, "It's very crowded in here."

"Well, then, let's find a place that isn't crowded. I can't go back into that crush."

"Nobody asked you to," I said, so nervous that I was obliged to put down the glass I was holding for fear of dropping it. "Nobody asked you to come in the first place."

"What kind of talk is that? I am guest Number One. I came at the urgent invitation of the doctor himself. No one asked me, indeed!" He laughed openly at my perplexity. "Well, in that case," I said, "you ought to join the party."

I myself, feeling that my services in the pantry were dispensable, went out, taking up a place between the long buffet table and the doors to the drawing-room which had been slid back all the way there to examine the implications of the conversation I had just had. I was prevented from a long study by the Admiral who, with old Mrs. McAllister, appeared slowly making his way toward the refreshment table. "Ah," he cried, spotting me, "here we have an ally. Sonie, what could you do in the way of a hot bird and a cold bottle for two old fellows? I'm hungry as a bear. I tell you, giving away a young lady is hard work. It's a strain on the heart! Particularly if you wanted her for your granddaughter-in-law." He winked at his companion. "Well, all's well that ends well, as they say. And while I'm about consoling myself, ma'am, let me congratulate you on getting a pippin for the boy."

"Much obliged," said Mrs. McAllister coldly. "I think Hope looks ill."

"Ill? Why, ma'am, though you're a woman, you don't know women. What female creature ever looked well on her wedding day? I always say the expression shouldn't be 'white as a ghost' but 'white as a bride.' And the whiter they are, the prettier, what?"

Mrs. McAllister received a plate of sole and salad and a glass of champagne from me. Refusing from that moment forward to discuss the wedding, the wedding breakfast, or the bride and groom, she commenced on an analysis of Amy Brooks' water colors in which she displayed more affection than intelligence. "The sweet thing, knowing that I don't get about, brought a whole portfolio full of them to me yesterday and I was perfectly charmed. She has real talent." She went on to describe in particular a little scene Amy had done of the hemlocks in the Arboretum. While I nodded with interest and even volunteered a few comments ("How much I should like to see the picture. No, I have never been to the Arboretum, but I hope to go on Lilac Sunday," etc.), I was actually engrossed in staring at Harry Morgan who had belatedly followed me out of the pantry and was in conversation with the Countess who, from her smiles and laughter, appeared to find him delightful. A surge of people presently obliterated them and I turned my mind again to what Mrs. McAllister and the Admiral were saying. The Arboretum had led her to her own garden in Concord, and Concord had led her to the bitter announcement, corroborated by her son, Reverend McAllister, who edged his way up to us, that "I suppose you've heard Philip Senior has given the young couple a handsome wedding present? That house on the Bedford Road left to him by my husband."

"I declare!" cried the Admiral. "That *is* handsome of you, Phil. Why, that's a humdinger of a house. Up on a hill, ain't it?"

Mrs. McAllister sighed deeply. "The loveliest house in Middlesex County, Lincoln. One of the loveliest in New

England. I have always said we ought to turn it over to a historical society."

"No, Mother, not in my lifetime. I hope the children will get some pleasure out of it. I've never cared much for the house myself. Would have sold it long ago, Lincoln, but Mother here didn't like it's being in the hands of a stranger."

The old lady pursed her lips, said nothing, but obviously was thinking that the house *was* in the hands of a stranger.

Her son asked me then, "How much champagne would you say Lucy Pride ordered for this collation?" I told him exactly: twelve cases. He raised his eyebrows, appalled. "If all the money spent on drink were handed over to the missionaries, we would have a Christian world."

Mrs. McAllister, who had wanted her son to go into the navy, had often been heard to speak like a pagan. She snapped at him, "I hope that time never comes, son, for I feel that there are times when one *needs* alcohol. Now, for example. At weddings and at funerals." Her voice had risen to an impassioned shriek and her son put his finger to his solemn lips. "Hush, Mother, they say it takes very little to go to one's head when one is advanced in years."

The Admiral snorted, "Your mother can take care of herself, old man. She hasn't had enough to drink, that's her trouble. Hand me your glass, ma'am, and let me refill it."

"Good afternoon," said Miss Pride crisply from behind us. "Ah, Sonie, I see you're taking over out here. I don't know what I would do without you. Well, and have you seen our poor lambs, Sarah? They're complaining that their arms ache from shaking hands and their faces hurt from smiling. They groaned when I told them they must stay another hour at least."

"At least," rejoined the old lady, staring hard at Miss Pride. "Why, I dare say that less than half of Boston has had a chance to congratulate them. My dear Lucy, you have outdone yourself!"

Miss Pride smiled pleasantly and turned to the Admiral. "I haven't even thanked you, Lincoln, for contributing to the occasion, but I'm angry with you for not wearing your decorations."

"Not with mufti, ma'am. Not me, thank you!" returned her friend, beaming all over his pink face in gratitude for her mention of his medals.

Old Mrs. McAllister, determined to find one barb at least to pierce Miss Pride's composure, at this said, "How did Arthur Hornblower feel about it?"

But she did not fell Miss Pride who retorted, "I expect he breathed a sigh of relief when he knew he wouldn't have to perform in that church. You know his objection is not to the Romish atmosphere but to the English. He's a great Anglophobe."

"Oh, I'm quite aware of *that*," said Mrs. McAllister with considerable asperity. "We've had several disputes. I tell him he's provincial, he tells me I'm a snob and we get nowhere."

"You would have quarreled with Papa, Sarah. I have always been glad that he died before war was declared because, since he liked neither France nor England, I have no doubt he would have made himself talked about in Boston. Oh, I don't mean to imply that he would not have supported the Allies wholeheartedly as far as the United States was concerned, but he would have turned a cold shoulder on England, I'm sure. His sister, my aunt Josephine, had what Papa called 'the hebetude' to marry a baronet and to be called henceforth 'Lady Fulke.' It was the name, even more than her large and totally inconvenient country establishment, that struck Papa so ridiculous. And I recollect that at the time I was presented at court and we were perforce staying with my aunt and my uncle Geoffrey, Papa consistently introduced her as 'Mrs. Faneuil' or 'Mrs. Fuller,' being unable to bring himself to say 'Lady' or to utter a name so peculiar as 'Fulke.' But I remember, also, that my sainted father was worsted on one such occasion by Mr. Henry James who turned to an English woman and said, 'One may forget other names, but Faneuil Hall is always on the tip of the tongue.' Papa was no backwoodsman: he blushed to the roots of his hair and never returned to England again or permitted the names of Mr. James and Sir and Lady Fulke to be spoken in his presence."

"Ha! Ha!" laughed the Admiral who was well-known himself as an Anglophile. "Lucy, you're a real raconteur!" But old Mrs. McAllister, pretending that she had not heard the story, groped for my hand which she pressed as she said, "My dear, do find Amy Brooks for me!"

As I went in search of Hope's cousin, the Countess, fragrant as a whole garden, came towards me with outspread arms, bumping everyone who stood in her way, among them the easily terrified Mr. Otis Whitney who immediately fled through the drawing-room in the direction of the door and was not seen again. She had nothing to tell me of any more consequence than that she loved me and that I was not to wear anything ever again but that same shade of green that I had on today and that if I did not come to hear the "Scarlatti I've dismembered, dismembered, my angel," at her next Friday, her heart would be broken into a thousand pieces. As she embraced me at our leavetaking—she had of course given me a welcoming hug and had let me go for only about a minute—she dropped her effusive tone and spoke as if we were contemporaries: "I'm not pleased, Sonie! I'm much distraught. I've been talking with a young man who has given me a real fright. You . . ."

But she could not finish for, to my great vexation, we were interrupted by one of the girls who came to the Fridays. Martha Dole was a large, plain bluestocking whose embonpoint was apportioned helterskelter so that the thin, rectilinear legs did not harmonize with the bossy torso and likewise the long, willowy neck was inadequate support for the full-blown Norman face. She, like the other young ladies, had always shown me great cordiality in the Countess' presence, and had two or three times sent me tickets to the theater or to concerts with which, to be sure, she had parted because she could not use them herself but which were accompanied by a flattering note which told me I was more deserving than she to hear the music or to see the play. Only three nights before, I had gone, thanks to her generosity, to see *Hamlet*, but this had not prevented her, on the following day, from becoming suddenly so engrossed in her companions that she did not see me, even though I passed directly in front of her, when I entered the cocktail lounge of the Parker House to keep an appointment with Nathan and Kakosan. Yet, her first remark to me this afternoon was, "Who was that lovely girl, Japanese, Chinese, whatever she was, that I saw you with the other day?"

"At the Parker House, do you mean?" I asked experimentally, watching her face to see what degree of confusion would be recorded there. If there was any, it was too infinitesimal to be measured, and she said, "Was it at the Parker House? Yes, of course, that's right. She was exquisite! We were all quite enchanted and I was greatly set up to be able to say that even though I didn't know her, I did at least know her companion. She looked as though she had stepped out of a fairy tale. You would have fallen in love with her, Berthe!"

The Countess gave me an indulgent spanking. "What do you mean, you wicked creature, keeping all of this from me? No, no evasions! I want to know all about her. Oh, such a betrayal!"

I explained that Kakosan was a stenographer in some firm, the exact nature of which I had never determined, for she always referred mysteriously to "the commodity" which might have been anything from ink to corsets. I told them also that she was the daughter of a nobleman in exile, a cultivated patriarchal gentleman who preserved all the customs of his country and his class, writing *hokku*, painting water colors of the Yanagawa from his faithful memory of it, sitting beside his pool in the American duplicate of his garden in Kyushu, in contemplation of the Zen-Buddha to whom, each day, he paid his ceremonial respects in the tea-house. As I observed the mounting interest in the Countess' face, I regretted I had made Nathan's mistress sound so interesting for I had no wish to bring her to the salon. My reason was that I could not trust her to exercise any restraint in her conversation. The several times that I had seen her (in my exile, I had welcomed her invitations to the movies), she had been naïve enough to tell me, when we had stopped at Schrafft's for raspberry frappés, about her lovers previous to Nathan whose attentions she described with a thoroughness that made me blush. I had no reason to suppose that she would be less candid with the Countess and the Boston girls.

"But she sounds charming!" cried the Countess. "Just imagine a real Samurai daughter simply at large in Boston! I've never heard anything so exotic! I command you to bring her to hear the Scarlatti on Friday, and if you do not, Euphrysone, I'll think up some really humiliating punishment for you. I'll make you spend a whole evening with Kalenkoff playing omber!"

I agreed, with misgivings, to bring Kakosan, and started to take leave of the Countess to go in search of Amy when Mrs. Hornblower approached us and halted me with an upraised and trembling hand. Gently with a dreamy, timid smile on her face—entirely out of keeping with her reputation of being a firebrand in political discussions, of being a sly one, and possibly engaged in subversive activities on the behalf of the Third Reich and Mussolini, having long since lost her interest in Sacco and Vanzetti—she said, "Lucy Pride told me where I'd find you. Someone told me you were acquainted with a young lady whose address I'm very anxious to get hold of. I mean the little Japanese girl, Miss Yoshida, or, rather, I should say, Yoshidasan without the 'Miss,' shouldn't I?"

"Ah, it's an epidemic!" cried Miss Martha Dole. "Imagine Sonie being in the key position!"

I told Mrs. Hornblower that I did not know Kakosan's address but that I should be glad to give her a message as I often saw her in Cambridge. "I'm getting up a benefit party for the Rebels in Spain, and I want her to come, partly for decoration, partly because I suspect that she's a sympathizer. Wouldn't you like to come too? Or don't you believe in Franco?" I had no strong feelings for either party in the Spanish Revolution and agreed with Miss Pride who said, "When the pot calls the kettle black, I shan't back either one."

"No, I can't say that I do think Franco's right," I said, and the Countess, a rabid Loyalist supporter, squeezed my arm and said to Miss Pride's cousin, "Sonie and I would be driving ambulances if we could, wouldn't we, darling?" This was not in the least true. The Countess supported "causes" solely in her drawing-room and the drawing-rooms of her friends, and I, for my part, was too ignorant of world affairs to be anything but apathetic towards them.

"What a pity," said Mrs. Hornblower. "I have not found many recruits here. Countess, have you stolen everyone for yourself?" And turning to me, she said, "I had thought that you . . . your name, you know, such *echt deutsch* . . . might be of our persuasion. *De gustibus non est disputandum.*" She moved off murmuring half to herself, "So few people are willing to take the long view, the *Weltanschauung.* But the time will come." These words, proceeding from a face so venerable and harmless, gave me such an unaccountable fright that for a moment I stood looking after her, and what occurred to me as she was swallowed up by a crowd of people in the doorway was that perhaps my father, if he had gone back to Würzburg, had become a Nazi.

Martha Dole, espying an old friend, left us and the moment she was gone, I said to the Countess, "You were telling me about Harry Morgan."

"But he told me something extraordinary! Something too really strange! Don't misunderstand: I like him although he's rather racy in his language. I'm only wondering how everyone will take it."

"Take what, my dear Countess?" I cried with impatience.

"Oh, it's probably nothing at all. It's only that he told me that Philip has asked him to take charge of doing over the Concord house, and it only struck me odd because of the way Mrs. McAllister feels about the place. And of course, no one *knows* him. D'you understand me, Sonie?"

"Yes, yes," I said. "But what I *don't* understand is why Philip asked him. He hasn't known him for longer than a month."

"Precisely!" said the Countess with a wink and then, perceiving that her stepdaughter was at her side, added, "It is precisely as you say: a 'four-square' sonata, as tedious as a wooden block."

Having delivered to Amy the message from Mrs. McAllister, I made my way into the drawing-room where the crowd was beginning to thin. Hopestill beckoned to me. "Go up with me, will you, Sonie?" she whispered. I glanced towards her maid-of-honor and she said impatiently, "I've arranged that, don't worry." Philip's face was fixed in a smile that revealed his teeth which were so regular and white they looked almost false. The adjective "sanitary" flashed across my mind as I took in his clear, intellectual eyes, his fair hair, his meticulously cared-for person, and in that moment, I preferred his bride upon whose cheek there was a light streak of dirt and who was frankly exhausted and was making no attempts to conceal the fact. I told her that I would meet her in her room and she left when she had said something to Philip who, looking at me as if he had never seen me before, formally shook my hand, not altering his grin in the least. I laughed uneasily and said, "I've already congratulated you once, don't you remember?" and he replied, "How stingy you are! Can't you congratulate a man twice on the happiest day of his life?" But there was in his voice a note of such staggering unhappiness, so taut an irony that I could make only a feeble rejoinder, told him I must hurry up to Hopestill, that I wished him all the happiness, that I . . .

Hopestill had flung her bouquet down the stairwell, but one flower, limp and ragged at the edges, was caught in the pointed cuff of her wedding dress. She was waiting in her sitting-room for me and she could have been waiting ten years, she had changed so much. The structure of her face was loose, as if the sagging muscles had weakened the mortised bones. There was a starched pallor on her thin lips, a narrow canniness in her eyes, and the skin, in the brief time since I had seen her in the church, had lost that shimmer which had seemed to be touched by the moon rather than the sun, to have been

483

inoculated by the spring rather than the summer, was ashen now, darkening to a bruised blue beneath her eyes. She had had a drink and when I came in, put down her glass. There was a newly opened bottle of whiskey on the table near where she stood.

"By God, he can wait for me!" she cried. "I'll go down when I'm Goddamned good and ready." And she sank into one of the wingchairs and poured herself another drink.

"It was a very nice wedding," I said.

"Lock the door, Sonie. I won't have any of them coming in here! I won't! I wish I were dead!"

I locked the door as she ordered me and reluctantly returned. She directed me to sit down opposite her and she said, "I really mean it: I wish I were dead. Now if I were you, I wouldn't wish that, but strictly *sotto voce*, strictly *entre nous* I wouldn't predict what you'll be feeling if you go on living with Aunt Lucy for another two years."

"Well," I said, "it's not quite the same thing. It's not the same at all, Hope."

"Listen to me, you child, you baby, you innocent little girl: the time will come when you see through that woman and know her for the bitch she is. It's that she's got to have power. All of us do here: we are obsessed by it. Philip is. I am. As soon as Aunt Lucy saw she couldn't control me—up to a point she could because she was my guardian and doled out my money nickel by nickel—she got a cat! That's the vile perverted thing she did! And kept the cat locked up in a storeroom deodorized by pine-scent! Oh, she fed Mercy well: the best tinned salmon, the finest kidneys, the richest milk, and every now and again the 'Persian fat lady,' as she was revoltingly referred to, was allowed to come down and purr for Aunt Sarah and Uncle Arthur and Admiral Nephews. Until, mind you, she had a chance to perpetuate her species and have four hybrid kittens and then she was permanently incarcerated."

"Oh, that's not the reason," I said, determined to defend Miss Pride.

"Hush! Let me finish. But a pussy-cat wasn't enough,

and now she's got *you*, and she intends to have the time
of her life with you because you're helpless. You're de-
pendent on her. No matter what *gaffe* you make, if you
get drunk and use obscene words in front of Mrs. Frothingham, Aunt Lucy will find some way to keep you."

"I am not property!" I cried, angry with Hopestill
and at the same time perturbed.

"Well, dear, that's beside the point. All of this is beside the point. I'll have a drink if you'll pour it for me,
please, and tell you what *isn't* beside the point." I filled
our two glasses. I was muzzy and out-of-sorts with this
oblique diatribe. "What isn't beside the point," she continued, "is that all I've accomplished today, all I've accomplished in my whole life, is that I've transferred
myself from one martinet to another."

"You didn't have to marry him."

She got to her feet and glared at me. "I'm sure I don't
know why I've taken you into my confidence, and you
can jolly well forget this. Now I'm going to dress."

The crowd had thinned considerably when I went
down. In the vestibule, I heard a woman remark, "I
wouldn't mind if my income were cut to fifteen thousand. I'd just go out to my farm for the whole year."
And another voice replied, "Of course it wouldn't go
hard with you, Augusta. Why, you have a fortune in
your roses if you'd only do something about it." Augusta,
whom I immediately knew to be the aunt Philip had
visited when he drove me to Wolfburg from Chichester,
laughed heartily. "That's what my nephew tells me, but
he's a pipe-dreamer. I'm so glad that at least one of his
pipe-dreams has come true. Hope is the sweetest girl in
Boston, I've always felt."

"Wasn't it strange," said the Countess to Miss Pride,
"that Mrs. Hornblower brought her present with her?"

"I didn't know she did," said Miss Pride. "It was peculiar enough of her to come in an evening dress."

"That's not all. She unwrapped it herself as well, and
what do you suppose it was? A dozen perfectly horrid
souvenir coffee spoons."

"My dear!"

Hopestill was coming down the stairs and in her carefully composed face there was no sign of the fright and anger that had made her burst out to me in her room. She joined Philip at the door and they went out, sped on by the uproar of the guests who had lingered.

"At any rate," Miss Pride was saying at my elbow, "I haven't lost this one," and she slipped her arm through mine. Through the sleeve of her black suit, I felt her bone on my flesh like a steel wand or, as she bent it into a hook, like a thin, inflexible staple. "And now," she went on to the Admiral, "now I'm going back to my memoirs."

The Admiral smiled radiantly. "When is this celebrated volume to be finished?"

Miss Pride returned his smile. "I dare say it will be years. At least that's what I intend, for I want something to occupy me so that I won't get foolish, and to occupy Sonie so she won't forsake me. Am I selfish?"

"No, ma'am. You're the most generous woman in Boston." He bowed deeply and then said to me, "And you, Mademoiselle, are the luckiest."

It was with a sort of sudden desperation that I saw that the drawing-room was empty and that the accommodators were taking down the extra tables in the dining-room and that through the open door to the library only Reverend McAllister was visible, holding open in his hands a large dark green book which I knew was a volume of the *Encyclopaedia Britannica*. Voices still came from the upstairs sitting-room, but presently a little group of people appeared at the head of the stairs and as they came down in a gust of talk, I could tell that even that room was empty now for Ethel, who had evidently been waiting for her chance, crossed the hall and went in with a tray to pick up the glasses that had been carelessly left there by the sightseers. I wished to detain these last few guests but they were saying good-by. Gratuitously they told their hostess where they were going: to the matinee of *Richard II*, to the Country Club for ice-skating, to Brookline to shop at Best's. Amy Brooks and Mr. Pingrey, shy with one another because Amy had caught Hopestill's bouquet which she clutched tightly against her quivering breast, shaken with silent giggles,

486

passed by me without a word because they could not see me or hear me though I called out to them, "Oh, don't go yet!" Their only thought was to get through the door and away, by themselves. They hastily told Miss Pride good-by and Amy screamed, "It was lovely! I caught the bouquet, Cousin Lucy! Edward and I are going to Agassiz! I am going to do the glass flowers in pastels for Mrs. McAllister!"

They were gone then, the last. Miss Pride, still holding my arm, linked her other in the Admiral's, and three abreast we went down the hall towards the library. "We'll quickly get rid of Ichabod," whispered Miss Pride, nodding in the direction of Reverend McAllister who was still absorbed in his book, "and then we three can have a nice talk."

"Right-o," said the Admiral. "Ain't it a pity my wife had to miss this! Why, Lucy, I haven't had such a good time since I went dancing at the Country Club, unless it was a month ago when Rose Park gave the cocktail party for her Community Chest people. I'm gay as a lark. Aren't you, Sonie?"

"Oh, yes, sir!" I cried. Miss Pride released us both and after she had gently closed the door behind us, switched off the ceiling light. The sun had gone behind a cloud and the library was shadowy and cold. "There now," she said. "It's cozy. It's just right to have this sort of *dämmerung* follow a wedding. It is the anti-climax to these affairs that I like most."

Six

PHILIP MCALLISTER, I was thinking, was one of those men in whom there lingers the perfectionism of childhood, who, when his stature was Lilliputian, saw the world as titanic, saw love centered in a goddess as a principle of salvation, as the meaning of that large, floating life, seeming so shapeless and so wonderful, like the shifting clouds of summer which veil and unveil the sun, that life he thought might vanish before he had sprung forth from his dwarfish body. We say of such people erroneously that they have never "grown up." We should say instead that they grew up too quickly, skipping certain years and finding themselves flowering alone, and in the snow, months before the spring. The phantom he had been pursuing all his life, and which he believed was at last entrapped in this girl whom he had loved intermittently for many years, had escaped him and the love with which he thought to imprison her had dematerialized, leaving him without love and without an object to try to love.

I was coming from the Countess' and was on my way to the young McAllisters' house where they were having a cocktail party and I was going over, with distaste, the conversation I had just had with my earlier hostess. Having summoned me over the phone that morning to have luncheon with her, she began, the moment we had left the dining-room for the library, to state her object. It was nothing more than simply to satisfy her curiosity. For some months past, indeed, ever since Philip and Hopestill had come back from a wedding trip to Canada, everyone had been slightly or greatly (depending on the extent of his prejudices) shocked by the almost constant presence in their house of Harry Morgan. The Countess von Happel wanted to know what I thought of it. Had I any idea why such otherwise attractive people set loose upon their guests a person of such execrable manners, such unrelenting buffoonery? He was addicted to imitations and in the course of a single evening recently, the Countess declared, had "done" President Roosevelt at a cocktail party, Katharine Hepburn at a psychiatrist's, a Negro on trial for murder, a priest confronted by Mae West. There was little to distinguish one from another and no one could understand how he could delude himself into thinking he had the least gift for mimicry. "If he's as inexpert at architecture as he is at imitations," remarked the Countess, "the Concord house will be a scandal." The Concord house was already in a sense a scandal, for Hopestill and Morgan spent a great deal of time there, often without Philip and without any more chaperonage than that of the carpenter or the gardener.

Did I believe, as some people did, that Philip was perhaps endeavoring to show Hopestill how detestable his predecessor was by forcing the man upon her, much in the way some mothers allow their children to eat their way into an indifference for candy? And was this newly announced pregnancy part of Philip's plan to tame the wild creature who had lived amongst wolves so long that she had come to howl like them?

I was disinclined to confide in the Countess my own opinion for she was a notorious gossip and was not above naming the sources of her tidbits, and so, to all her queries, I only replied, "Oh, I suppose he amuses them," or "He's not such a bad sort when he isn't clowning."

But I was not to be let off so easily. The Countess,

489

who enjoyed nothing so much as contemplating people's motives, continued her anatomizing.

"I cannot accept the attachment between Philip and Mr. Morgan as altogether genuine. And if he is trying to teach Hope a lesson, isn't he a bit innocent? I mean, my dear Euphrysone, one can't help hearing things. One hears of Mr. Morgan's reputation."

We are instantly put on our guard by the effeminate man who, as if to dispel our suspicions, says, "You know, homosexuals interest me very much psychologically and I must confess I have a number of good friends among them whom I would like to have you meet," or takes an even bolder stand and says, "I am so amused by the rumors I have heard about myself that I have been tempted to give people really something to talk about by having my hair curled and my fingernails painted" (so that we know, in the first instance, that if the homosexuals have admitted him to their minds which he is investigating in the interest of his hobby, they have as well admitted him to their arms, and in the second that curling his hair and painting his nails are probably what he will shortly do, but not for the reason that he has prepared us). Just so, the confidence that Philip placed in Harry Morgan made the astute Countess suspect that he did not trust him at all, that he was jealous of those New York days and New York evenings to which the young millionaire so casually referred, calling upon Hopestill to confirm the name of a restaurant or of a mutual friend.

"Pretend you're a European, darling! I love you! Don't be shocked! Tell me, dear angel, if you don't agree with this evil-minded old woman that Philip McAllister has some reason—don't interrupt, Sonia—for being disappointed in that lovely bride of his? And . . . Come sit beside me. I don't know where that Filipino child of mine is. And that he does not really adore her so much as he appears?"

"I don't follow you, Countess," I said nervously.

My friend pouted and then laughed. "Of course you don't *follow* me, precious scamp, you're a mile ahead of me."

I was by no means averse to gossip but I did not enjoy it with the Countess who, for some reason unknown to me, was reined in by no inhibitions when she spoke to me although I was certain that she was discreet with others. She seemed to be under the impression that my moral view had the same generous, continental latitude as hers. My disquietude, as I fumblingly put down my coffee cup, was transmitted to her and a small silence came between us, as precise as a picture hanging on a wall.

The Countess went on, more gently. "Oh, I have not been nice at all! But you and I, Sonia, observe things other people don't. Don't we now? Wouldn't you agree with me that probably you and I are the only people, besides the principals, of course, who know that Mr. Morgan was Hope's friend before her marriage?"

"Friend?" I repeated. "But of course they were friends."

"I use the word in its European sense, darling, as you perfectly well know." She crossed the room to the bell-pull, and stood poised a moment, the light from the window enlivening her fair hair with brilliant undulations, her nose aloft. There was something at once so childish and so wise about her pose as well as about what she had just been saying that I smiled. She caught my smile, returned it, and said, "Don't try to pretend any longer that you're not a spy. You were spying on me just then. We will have some more coffee and something very special, a beautiful brandy."

Bit by bit, in the course of the afternoon, my hostess' conjectures came out. Some she revised, others she left intact; I proffered nothing new, but I was forced, by the sheer weight of her intuition which had synthesized random elements into a composition as clear as a case history written in a book, to agree with her. I did not, however, know any ease even with the assistance of the crystal-clear brandy, for I felt somehow that simply by listening I was letting Hopestill's cat out of the bag.

Berthe von Happel, through the same sort of almost physical insight that Mamselle Thérèse had employed, had known from the beginning why Hopestill had suddenly decided to marry Philip. In another sort of society, her guess would probably have immediately occurred to anyone who did not believe that the girl was in love. But it would never have crossed the mind of, for example, Amy Brooks. Hopestill might be disliked, might be criticized for her inability to get on with her relatives-in-law, for her sharp and often cruel treatment of servants, for her bland disregard of charitable works, but no one would have dreamed of accusing her of so great a crime as the one she actually had committed and the one the Countess took matter-of-factly. For whatever else she was, Hopestill was a member of a society which did not countenance illegitimate children, which, in a sense, did not believe in them, just as the prim Victorian who is told for the first time of sodomy says with a firm scoff, "I never heard of it before. I don't believe it. It's merely a bit of obscene nonsense." To be sure, shop-girls and servants frequently ruined their lives through such misdemeanors, but the people one lunched with and invited to dinner chose other means: dipsomania or betting on the horses. Bastardry was not acknowledged as a possible function of the upper classes. (I recalled, in a momentary flare of anger, how the first time I had met Philip McAllister, he had accused me of coming to him for an abortion.) But there had been a time, the Countess declared, when New England had not been so naïve, when sin was looked for in every stratum and duly punished.

Had I never seen in Philip McAllister's eyes the fanaticism of a Puritan? Had I never noticed how, at a dinner party, his flushed face did not turn when he spoke to someone but was kept tensely in an attitude that allowed him to keep a constant vigil on his wife, as if he were trying to read the thoughts in her deceitful head, or as if he wished to convey to her some message that would inform her he knew everything and forgave her nothing? Oh, to be sure, most people took this as a look of love. Indeed, the sole criticism of him was that he prolonged beyond the point of decency, his look of nuptial rapture and the vagueness which rendered him, in conversation, slightly stupid.

It was true, as the Countess said, that in public his eyes, across the cerulean azure of which there passed a flare of hotter blue like the quick, staggering stab of sun to the heart of a diamond, never left his wife but studied her as the rapt jeweler studies a rare stone through the little magnifying glass enfolded in his eye. And while he watched her, he praised her to everyone within earshot: no one had her genius for dress, or her hair, or her enchanting voice in a high minor key, or had that pearly shining flesh in which only the mouth, the palest pink or, in some lights, faint lilac, broke the lily-like monotony. In these first months of her pregnancy when it had not yet made itself cumbersome, she had reached the pinnacle of her loveliness, like the forced flower, blossoming under glass and out of reach of the distractions of other flowers and the alteration of its color by the sun or by the shade. No less embarrassed than her guests was Hopestill whose protests only made her husband the more extravagant, the more hysterically flattering: "And her greatest charm of all is that she doesn't know how charming she is!" he would cry.

I told the Countess that I did not quite see the logic of her argument: if Philip was aware that he had been tricked, and if, as she maintained, he was a throw-back to early Puritanism, why did he not divorce her or punish her by depriving her of all society, or, at the very least, refuse to have Morgan in his house?

"Oh, don't think he wants anyone to know. He wants them to suspect, probably. But he can't punish her openly, can't divorce her—for I have no doubt he feels strongly about divorce—can't burn a scarlet letter in her forehead. Darling, unconsciously he's imitating Dante: Don't you remember that the lovers' punishment is to embrace forever?"

I could not bear to listen to any more and got up. "I'm due at Hope's house now," I said, "though I'm sure I don't know how I'll face her."

And she replied, "Why, be that same inscrutable Euphrysone we know so well. You cannot fool me! You have known all along! I love you! Give Hope a kiss for me!" And she deposited a kiss on either cheek, one for myself and one for Hopestill which I did not propose to deliver.

The Countess' house, like her person, was overheated and over-fragrant, and it was a relief to be on the street. I idled, taking the longest way to Hopestill's house, and finding an organ-grinder on Marlborough Street, I stopped to watch his monkey. I did not really attend the sad little dressed-up animal, but I put penny after penny into his leather hand and dreamily looked at him and at his soiled old master who could easily have been his father. The trees had been out for some time and although now, in the twilight, it was cold, there was a quality of spring in the air. I wished that I were in the country or that, at least, I might stay out of doors until it was quite dark, doing no more perhaps than paying the monkey for the windy tunes.

I moved on. Undoubtedly the Countess was right. Philip's disappointment had made him hate Hopestill. And his hatred, coupled with his atavistic, vindictive morality, prompted him to torture her, to batten himself upon the love of the two sated and now unwilling people. But simultaneously, as he caused them to remain at their revolting banquet, though they were gorged, caused them, like Paolo and Francesca, to embrace forever and be embraced by hell, he, as overseer, must also be in hell, must see to it that they rendered him the true accounts, and did not embezzle from eternity one instant of relief.

Only for Harry Morgan did I have no pity at all. The Countess, while she had deplored him, had seemed to accord him a measure of sympathy as the victim of Philip's persecution, although she could not deny my charge that he was in no way bound to accept invitations to Hopestill's house. There was one reason and I suspected two why he continued to come. The first was simply that he was a snob and had no intention of cutting himself off from the one house where he was welcome; he was a climber and would have given a good deal to be "in" as he was in other parts of the country. A fortune, he had discovered, was not the open sesame in Boston that it was elsewhere and he had once observed to me with a sort of bitter wonder that he could count on the fin-

494

gers of one hand the débuts he had been invited to in this "city of the dead, this town where human life is at a premium." But there was, I thought, another reason why he did not refuse to come to the McAllisters' dinner parties and that was the new addition to Hopestill's gatherings (and the Countess', too, for that matter), that is, Kakosan Yoshida. Whether they saw one another anywhere save on Commonwealth Avenue, I could not tell, nor did I know if their friendship had progressed beyond the raillery they engaged in over cocktails, but I had perceived that they nearly always separated themselves from the rest of us before dinner and, by the time the highballs were served, had drifted to the sofa at the end of the drawing-room farthest from the fireplace. What they talked of, I could not dream, for I was sure that Kakosan had not told her new friend that she was acquainted with his tutor. Certainly, I had not told Nathan of any of this. He would have been maddened with jealousy if he had known that they were ever in the same room.

Kakosan had been an immediate success on the first Friday she had gone to the Countess'. Her conduct, of which I had been uncharitably dubious, was exemplary and her beauty, set off by a yellow satin dress embroidered with white flowers and a white carnation in her hair, distracted everyone so much from the music that the Countess was a little reserved in her conversation afterwards and we left rather earlier than usual. But Berthe von Happel bore no one a grudge and in a very short time she appeared at the Fridays and the Saturdays as often as I did. Likewise, she was taken up by Hopestill, and even Miss Pride, on one occasion, invited her to tea, though she confessed afterwards to me that she "found it a very pretty head but uncommonly empty."

If I had not let it be known that Kakosan was a typist, no one would have suspected that she had any other occupation than that of arranging flowers in a bowl or playing jackstones in a garden complete with torii and tea-house. For she was one of those people who have the enviable knack of keeping their addresses a dark secret without appearing to hide anything, of answering ambiguously or not at all questions about activities, backgrounds, preferences, antipathies. If someone said to her, "Where did you live before you came here?" she would reply, "My father, you see, has copied his villa on the Yanagawa. You should see it! He is a great gardener. And how sorry he is he cannot have the tsubaki in this country he loved so much in his beautiful homeland. Do you know what it is? It is red like fire and sometimes it blooms in the snow. But he has some of the Japanese flowers, you know, wistaria and cherry trees and iris. He has to have flowers, of course, for he is a Zen-Buddhist and must decorate his tea-house. And do you know that even though it never snows where his villa is, just as soon as winter comes, he covers the lanterns with straw mats as he used to do in Kyushu?" A persistent busybody, charmed with this information but nevertheless determined to know whether the villa was in California or Florida or Louisiana, might say, "Where did you say he has his villa?" As if she had not heard the inquiry, she would go on, "Oh, yes, and he has two red pines which he sprays twice a year, for it is the custom to remove every single dead needle." This was a side of Kakosan that I never saw when she was with Nathan or when she and I made our expeditions to the movies. With us, she talked only of her chief interests which were the "spirits," film stars, and some disreputable young men with whom she often conversed in the Common on her way home from work on a subject she called "nationals" and which we translated roughly as "politics." Or she would tell us the little adventures that took place in her office which sounded so remarkably like those I had heard from my classmates at the Back Bay Business College that I automatically envisaged Mrs. Hinkel as I listened to her.

But in the Boston houses, she was remote from anything worldly or anything Occidental, and I, along with everyone else, was captivated afresh each time my eyes came to rest on her dexterously wrought face as, when a conversation was in progress into which she could not enter, her golden mask became immovable and the eyes showed her to be humble before her intellectual su-

496

periors while the proud arch of her neck showed that the nobility of her blood forebade her too free participation in the meaningless talk of people who were "without tea." She was apparently the "real thing" and seeing her thus, I longed for Nathan to possess her forever as the reward for his generous overlooking of her faults. But the moment she dropped her "company manners" and exchanged a few words with me in private, I hoped that the affair would be swiftly over. The repugnance I sometimes felt for her (when she revealed herself as being so far from the "real thing") was the kind one feels toward anything that is not true to its origin if its origin is admirable or attractive: the book that begins well and peters out in mawkishness, the picture which at first seems profound until, on further study, we find that it has only the virtue of brilliant draftsmanship. She used only as ornaments the Samurai code, her father's gentlemanly pursuits of religion and art, and they were as removable as the flowers in her hair.

Nathan, feeling that he was required to justify his love of her to me (rather, to himself, for he was sometimes agonized by the discrepancy between his vast love and its mean, elusive object) often denied that she was unchaste and stupid, not stating his denial with a negative but offering me instead instances of her talents which opposed and triumphed over her defects. He did not say, "She is not stupid," but he said, "In some ways, she is very intelligent," and as an illustration of her insight, he told me that she had once observed something in him he believed he had perfectly concealed. "No, really," he said, "since I'm so generous with her, how could she know that I'm a miser?" I did not point out that the very energy of his generosity gave him away. Nor did he say that she was not promiscuous, but that she had been "misled." At one time, he would declare that she was not a harlot because she had been in love with each of her bedfellows. At another time, in a fit of jealousy of all those unknown possessors of her, he said, "She has never been affected by any of it. I am quite sure this is the first time she has been in love."

In the past month, she had been required to go to so

many séances (some of which I knew to be imaginary, to be, actually, the Countess' Saturday. For some reason, probably a clever one, she had never told Nathan that she had been "taken up" by Boston) and had broken so many appointments with him that he had become hollow-eyed with anxiety, unstrung with the suspicion that she had another lover. It was this, combined with their very evident enjoyment of one another, that made me think Kakosan and Morgan had at least entered upon the preliminaries of a love affair.

2

I had no more than let myself in at Hopestill's unlocked door than I was confronted with the proof of my suspicion, and it resulted from an incident which, by one of those almost supernatural timings of chance, occurred within the same hour that Nathan, two miles away and across the river in Cambridge, made the same discovery, his evidence being but slightly different from mine. The hall, through the carelessness of a servant, was not lighted yet, although it was quite dark, so that I could not distinguish the two people standing at one side of the door, possibly in an embrace, possibly helping one another with their wraps, but I heard Kakosan's high-pitched voice, suffused with childish laughter, cry, "Gacho, don't!", the name by which, it will be remembered, she called Nathan. And Harry Morgan said, "Okay, baby, but wait till I get you home." I was shocked, not only by the frank implications of these elided remarks, and the foretokening in them of Nathan's heartbreak, but also by the boldness of this love-play, a dozen feet from the drawing-room door. I concluded that they had already been to the party and had been relaxed by the cocktails. This, at any rate, was an advantage, for I should not now be obliged to talk with either of them. It would have been too much, I felt, if I had had to be omniscient witness to the antics of these two as well as of the McAllisters'. I hurried past them and as I went up the stairs, caught Kakosan's terrified murmur. "That was Sonie Marburg!"

Hopestill's drawing-room was so spacious that despite her many guests, it did not seem crowded. As Miss Pride said of the room, "It's not the temperature but the color that makes one think of an ice-chest. The fire in that pallid hearth gives no more warmth than the ones in the theater made with flashlights and red tissue paper." It was called the "blue room" in contradistinction to an even chillier chamber, "the white parlor." The floor was carpeted in silvery blue; the graceful chairs and sofas were upholstered in gray satin and heavy blue curtains hid the violet panes in the bay window at the far end of the room. Bare of pictures ("I can't afford originals and one doesn't have prints," she had said), the white walls were striated with gray shadows, for the room was dimly lit by a single bulb under the blue-green shade of a Chinese lamp. There was, as the Countess complained, nothing to look at in the room, for Hopestill detested bric-a-brac, having had her fill of it in her life at her aunt's and, influenced perhaps by her prejudice against the maidenhair ferns and Aunt Alice's Birthday Trifle, did not even put flowers on the tables.

"Oh, it's California, very likely," Miss Pride was saying to a youngish woman I had met before. "Most of them settle in the west, you know."

When Miss Pride spoke of "the west," it was as if she said "somewhere." It was not quite a void, but it was something stretching interminably behind one's back. Yes, she replied to her friend, she had been "out" once, and had not the least desire to go again.

"I dare say their rugged life and bad climate make the people hardy. But I must confess I find the Rocky Mountains quite hideous, quite lacking in style. They're too much of a good thing, so to speak. Even if the landscape didn't offend me, though, I couldn't endure the place more than ten days at a time. There is a crackly feel in western speech that sets my teeth on edge."

Her friend had spent three months in Saint Louis and countered, "But you should go to the middle west if you want to hear really peculiar speech. Of course Saint Louis is neither fish nor fowl nor good red herring. I could not get the key to the city. Is it southern? Is it midwestern? Is it an imitation of a German industrial town? I don't know. But I do know that their accent makes it almost impossible for an easterner to understand what they say. If someone told you, 'I lived tin yars in Versales, Mazura,' would you have the least idea that he meant, 'I lived ten years in Versailles, Missouri'? By the way, isn't Versailles an amusing name?" The woman, whose home was in New Canaan, pronounced "idea" with a clear final consonant.

I was curiously soothed by this colloquy which was the first thing that came to my ears, for Miss Pride, no matter what scandals and disasters were perpetrated under her very nose, would never change. I assumed that she and her companion had been wondering where Kakosan's father lived. Miss Pride's announcement, "Most of them settle in the west, you know," made the Japanese immigrants as remote and unconnected with the world in which she lived as if they had never left their native shores, and Kakosan Yoshida herself went up in thin air. So long as Miss Pride was here, I thought, I could face anything. I was comforted to see that while she disdained the tray of canapés held before her by a maid, she exchanged her empty glass for a full one when the butler came round, so that I knew she would stay a little longer at least.

Feigning great interest in someone's proposed walking tour through Britanny, and someone else's plan to present Hopestill with a set of lawn bowls for her Concord house, and Edward Pingrey's recent attack of bronchitis, I actually only heard Philip's voice, superimposed upon all the others. He was not yet drunk, but he had reached a stage of animation which often just precedes almost hysterical excitement.

"What so amuses Hope and Harry about my father," I heard him say to Mr. Otis Whitney, a life-long friend of the Reverend McAllister, "is the titles of his books." And he went off into a spasm of pointless laughter in which Mr. Whitney joined with only a pained smile. His father was well-known as a mountain climber and had written three small volumes called *To the Jungfrau and Other Adventures, The Challenge of the Medicine Bow Range of the Rocky Mountains,* and *A Hymn to the Himalayas.* The titles, of course, amused everyone. But what variety of madness was making Philip's tongue wag on in so embarrassing a *gaffe?* One immediately pictured his wife and Morgan poking fun at his father while he indulgently looked on. It was no secret that Philip had no respect for him, but he had never expressed his contempt, had been friendly and even affectionate in his occasional little jokes about him. It sounded now as if his wife, through some obscure wile, had so corrupted him that neither taste nor common decency was left in this erstwhile dignified young man.

Evidently they had been discussing the renovations of the Concord house and the Reverend McAllister's name had come up in this connection, for Mr. Whitney, putting his glass on the mantel and murmuring that he must be going on, said, "I shall want to see the place when it's done."

"Oh, it will be a gem, I can tell you, Mr. Whitney!" cried Philip. "You should see the fireplace Morgan has designed. It doesn't look any more like a fireplace than you do."

I hoped that others were not, like myself, concentrating on the over-pattern of our host's voice. When Mr. Whitney had excused himself, Philip moved on to another group and repeated the reason why Hopestill and Harry Morgan were so amused by his father. Alcohol flings back, almost illimitably, the boundaries of humor so that we can find uproarious things which our poor sober friends miss altogether. It is necessary, if the joke is really good and really should be shared, to repeat it time and again until finally it penetrates those solemn skulls. Philip had for the third time cried out the names of his father's books. "I had never realized how terribly funny they were until Harry Morgan and Hopestill pointed it out!" Hopestill, detaching herself from Amy Brooks and two other earnest girls, came swiftly to her husband's side and slipping her arm through his, said,

"Darling, Admiral Nephews wants to talk to you. Do rescue the poor old lamb. He's over there, you see, with Mr. James who's boring him to death." Perhaps, in one of those flashes of sobriety that intermittently punctuate the state of drunkenness, he realized that he had gone far enough and he obediently followed his wife, pausing to speak to me and to say, in an undertone, "Is there something up between Morgan and your Japanese friend? I shouldn't like that at all. I'll talk to you about it later."

I could keep my mind on nothing that was said to me and I moved with my cocktail to the fireplace where Hopestill's powerful dog, a Doberman, lay on the hearth, lifting his muzzle to me as I approached. Kurt had once belonged to *Herr* Speyer, the German who had mistaken me for his daughter as I waited in the lobby on my first musical Friday. When he left the country, he gave Kurt to the Countess who, having three dogs already, had handed him over to Hopestill. Despite his savage appearance, he was gentle and welcomed the advances of strangers who could not fail to be impressed by his gleaming black coat and his sharp, intelligent face. I never saw him without being reminded of his owner and the encounter with him that had given me so keen and so long-echoing a pleasure.

I sat down to contemplate the play of the flames on the short black hair and in the wise eyes that were now amber and now jet, and to restore the Nordic face that I had seen that day through the flittering shadows from the sconces and the voice, overlaid as by a filigree, by the music that descended to us from the room above. "Here, boy," I said, patting my knee. The dog wagged the stump from which his tail had been amputated, lifted his head to me, but did not get up. I wheedled a moment longer, then said, "Kurt! *Kommst du!*" and he bounded to me to put his forepaws on my lap, his shorn hind-end prancing. I was deeply attached to the affable animal who, though he bore only this resemblance to them, that is, that he could not talk, inspired me with the same joy—best known in memory—that certain things in nature did, and, in particular, through association with *Herr* Speyer, the August day when my father and I had seen the plover. Frequently Hopestill, who knew I was fond of Kurt, asked me to take him walking. We would hurtle down Clarendon Street to the Esplanade and race along the river bank. His strength and grace were communicated to me through the leash by which I restrained him and I was exhilarated with the swimming speed he demanded of me. Suddenly he would stop, listening. A growl would purr in his throat, but the bark it heralded did not come and instead, he would turn his head towards me, his companionable eyes informing me that he would not desert me after all for the excitement he had heard or smelled, far off, and we would resume our run.

Now Nathan and I, dreaming of Germany, had borrowed from libraries innumerable of those travel books which are written with a missionary's zeal, quick to report slighting comments on their darlings in order to refute them. Amongst these enraptured Valentines to Baden towns, we had found one that was full of photographs from long study of which we had come to feel familiar with the walks, the bridges, the castle gardens, the cafés, the parks, the University of Heidelberg. As I walked with Kurt (born in Garmisch-Partenkirchen and intended, with his siblings, for a career on the Munich police force), I imagined that I was on the north bank of the Neckar River, proceeding towards the suburb of Handschusheim, the hills rising to my right, while to my left, across the river, I could see the mansard roofs of the old University and the spire of the Cathedral of the Holy Ghost. Just as in Chichester, I used to fancy Miss Pride's house in the shadow of the State House dome, so, taking the cathedral spire (the *locum tenens* being Eliot House across the Charles) as my landmark, I placed my red room somewhere to the left of it. Unless he was too impatient, I persuaded Kurt to stop awhile and I sat down on a stone bench. I ran my hand along the space between his pointed ears and like a child speaking to a doll, I told him about the room which had now acquired a locality, which was Heidelberg, a town plucked at random, and a temporal dimension which, owing to the peculiar light that stained the windows, was specified as autumn. At some change in the tone of my voice, the dog, hoping that we would move on again, would part his jaws in a grin, and I would say, *"Ja, Kurt, Ja, Kurt!"* and then take pity on the imploring tilt of his head and the little whine that sounded like a puppy's.

"Doch, ist's so spät?" I said to Kurt who was nuzzling my hand with his busy nose. I repeated the sentence in imitation of his former master and as I did so, tried to hear my accent which Nathan declared was more Russian than German. Experimenting a third time, I heard my mother's voice and experienced the now familiar sensation that it was actually she who was speaking. Instantaneously, upon my image of her which accompanied the sound of her voice through my lips, she vanished like the will-o'-the-wisp and what stood before me was the red room. The apparition had never been quite like this before: through the windows, instead of merely other windows and sleeping cats upon the sills, I saw, framed by soiled and motionless curtains, in a flat opposite me, a real face but one which I could not see clearly since it appeared to be obscured by a sort of mist. It was an old woman's face whose eyes seemed to be urged from their sockets a little, staring at me with malevolent fixity. The mistiness evaporated: Miss Pride was there, in the flat across the courtyard and the sunset had changed the color of her olive hat.

When I vainly tried to see not the room but Hopestill's bare white walls and gray chairs, when I strained to hear the voices of her guests and could not, I knew that my game had got out of control and that Miss Pride had found me out in my retreat and was judging me a lunatic. It occurred to me with a terror that elevated me to an unimaginable height, that the only remedy for my obsession was a desperate one: that I must find the room in the real world before the real world intruded, as Miss Pride's face was doing now and confused me to the point of madness. For at this moment—and it was only a moment that I was conscious of her scrutiny—I was seized with a madness that was like an intense pain and was something outside myself, a violent force which urged my footsteps for the first time across the threshold onto the threadbare carpet with its faint green design. The knowledge that something external had precipitated my entrance was confused by a vertiginous and inarticulate emotion and for the present, I could not name the frenzy that had threatened but had not yet gained entrance. Despite the agitation into which the watchful eyes had flung me, I thought I sat serenely at the writing desk and sometimes smiled and other times rubbed my forehead with the tips of my fingers and then turned in my chair to examine the books on the nearest shelves. I noticed that the chair was exactly the right height, made so by a cushion. I was proud of my medical manuscript so beautifully preserved. The voice of my remembering self, roused from its sleep, said, "It was on Dr. Galbraith's desk the day you went to get him for Ivan." But my peace did not last. As Miss Pride's face moved closer, leaning out the window, her eyes pursued me and I whirled like a spinning top, whisking from corner to corner, fleeing them. I was strung out long like a bright wire that ended in brittle rays of copper, shining and pointed and raw. The eyes, like a surgeon's knives, were urged into my brain. The edges of the knives screamed like sirens; their sound curled in thin circles round my hot, pink brains. I crouched in a corner of the room, down behind the bookcases, safe, I thought. But I was plucked up by the burning yellow flares that went in a direct path like a sure blade. Miss Pride blinked her eyes. The room vanished. I had not moved but I felt an overwhelming tranquillity as if my brain were healed again, was sealed and rounded and impervious, was like a loaded, seamless ball, my hidden and wonderfully perfect pearl.

"Well!" said Miss Pride jocularly. "What a profound slumber you've just had."

Her niece stood beside her and both of them looked at me so curiously that I quickly said, "I was trying to remember a name." I was still trembling from my shock and I wondered if my voice had betrayed me. What shall I do? my eyes inquired of Kurt. His elongated face was up-pointed, immobile, and alert. I answered myself, "I must find the room or I will be like Mamma and then Miss Pride will find out and lock me up!"

Miss Pride said, "Hope tells me she wants you to stay here for dinner. I must be going on now."

"Oh, don't go just yet, Auntie," said Hopestill, her eyes wandering away from us as she sought her husband.

"I must," said her aunt. "I am behind in my political articles. Do you follow Mr. Roosevelt, Hopestill?"

Hopestill, who prided herself on not reading the news-papers and who, at the moment, was too distracted to comprehend what Miss Pride was saying, replied, "I haven't seen him in ages. I had dinner with him two years ago in a very muggy place in Cambridge. Surely he isn't *still* at Harvard!"

"Oh, no," answered Miss Pride, winking at me. "He's in Washington now."

"Really? As I recall, he was driving a banana-wagon that evening."

Disliking the prospect of having dinner alone with the McAllisters, I said to Miss Pride, "You said this morn-ing, you know, that you wanted to do a little work this evening. Perhaps I should come along with you now."

"Oh, work is out of the question. Hopestill has made me quite tipsy. You stay here and enjoy yourself."

She turned away and Hopestill, leaning towards me, said in a whisper, "Why don't you want to stay, Sonie?"

"I didn't say that," I told her. "But the fact is that I wanted to make a telephone call. I . . ."

"Go into Philips study if you like. You won't be dis-turbed there. I especially want you to stay. That is, I'm afraid if you don't, I'll have to eat alone because Philip will obviously pass out before dinner."

I relished no better the thought of being alone with Hopestill. The Countess' conversation, my knowledge of Kakosan and Morgan, and the visitation of the red room had combined to put me into an unsettled state which I knew only a normal evening with Miss Pride on Pinckney Street could cure. And, still, recollecting how her eyes had tracked me down, I was not sure of myself, felt I might suddenly cry out as she opened the

Boston Evening Transcript or, more dreadful yet, the room might take me unawares again as it had done this afternoon and I would be obliged to explain my trance to her. Abruptly, I was stormed by a claustrophobia so violent that every element of the scene before me assumed the proportions of destroying force: there was no reason for this gathering, no reason for this elaborate amity amongst people whose civilization had pruned down their impulses to a set of manners which imperfectly concealed a dead indifference, no reason why I should be sitting here in this wealthy drawing-room when I, so far from being embourgeoised, could find pleasure only in the society of the dog, Kurt. I was alarmed by Philip who, damaged, loud, unrecognizable, was repeating anecdotes he had heard from Morgan and, to the even greater horror of his guests, was telling professional secrets about his own colleagues. Under what influence, wifely, personal, friendly, it was not known, he had, for some time past, seemed discontented with his profession. But he had not discussed it; people had only had a "feeling" that he was going through some crisis which would undoubtedly be happily resolved. Equally alarmed was I by Hopestill in whose eyes, strikingly like her aunt's today, there was an insistent plea that I remain. She had selected me, I reasoned, because she was perhaps actually afraid to be alone with Philip and because I, of all the guests at the cocktail party, could be trusted not to carry my observations to the fastnesses of the Vincent and the Chilton Clubs.

If anyone was in need, I thought, it was myself. It had been true, as I told Hopestill, that I wanted to make a telephone call. It was, though I did not specify this, to Nathan, or rather, to the janitor of his building who would occasionally understand (he was quite deaf) what I wanted and call my friend to the telephone. For I felt that I must see him at once, must make him understand fully where the apples came from, must impress upon him the necessity of my finding the red room. Moreover, I wanted to see, simply by looking at him, that he did not know who his rival was.

And I did not want to telephone from Philip's study. I had thought of a booth in a drug-store on a certain corner from which, and only from which, I had always put through my calls to Nathan, so that I had come to associate with his distant, often blurred voice, the wooden counter visible to me through the glass door of my little cell, where a pharmacist of Hellenic beauty stood as if guarding his rows of amber glass jars full of pills, his curly golden hair occupying the place of greatest light under the neon legend: "Prescriptions." It was nearly always necessary, since several minutes elapsed from the time I got the janitor until I heard Nathan's dazed "Hello"—these calls were even now a surprise to him—for me to deposit a second or third nickel in the slot. The young god, pushing aside a ciborium of nux-vomica, called, as I hurtled out of the box, "Here, I'll change it for you," having two nickels in exchange for my dime already waiting in his outspread hand. I had not time to thank him, for I was afraid my connection would be cut off, but when I had hung up and was leaving, expressed my gratitude and made a vague promise that it would not happen again. His large, heavily-lidded hazel eyes twinkled, either because he felt he was in on a secret (perhaps he thought that my parents would not allow me to see the person I was telephoning and that I was arranging a secret rendezvous) or else because he was amused by my absent-mindedness or by the loquacity which made all my calls cost double. He said: "I always have change back here any time you need it," as if he had no wish to be deprived of the spectacle of my flurry. Once I had got Nathan immediately, for he was passing by the janitor's door as the telephone rang, and the original coin I had deposited sufficed, my message being short. The pharmacist, who had been slowly doing up a package, glanced at me through the glass door from time to time and when I came out, rapidly produced two nickels from a box at the end of the counter. I thanked him but said I had finished and he exclaimed, "You didn't get your party, then!" in a tone something like disappointment.

It was in that place where, creature of habit that I

was, I wanted to make my engagement with Nathan. Superstitiously, I felt that if I telephoned from this house, its owners would be drawn into my maelstrom whereas the pharmacist could not since he knew nothing of me and I knew of him only his youth, his beauty, and his deep voice containing the vestiges of a Nova Scotian accent. I was afraid, moreover, that if I did not make the call and see Nathan tonight, my determination would wane and by morning would have perished altogether so that the day to which I opened my eyes would be identical to all other days save that the danger was nearer, but not near enough, in the bright sunlight streaming through my familiar windows, to make me remember clearly enough how terrified I had been by Miss Pride's eyes.

When Hopestill motioned toward my untouched glass and asked me if I did not like the cocktails, I realized with a start that I had been here only a few minutes. I drank quickly and guiltily, gave Kurt a parting caress and, at Hopestill's injunction, set out to find the Admiral.

Throughout the half hour that I exchanged quotations with Admiral Nephews and soberly discussed, with Frank Whitney, the horrors of Communism, listened attentively to a drunken middle-aged man whom I had never seen before who was writing a book on a subject which he did not divulge, one part of my mind was busily casting about for an excuse to leave before dinner. Why did I not now slip upstairs, get my coat, and leave without saying good-by, then go to the drug-store or directly to Cambridge? In reflecting on one's own or in considering another's frustrations, one sees them as unnecessary, forgetting that the amenities of society, arbitrary and often absurd, beset us at every turn and it is only in larger things that one's will is really free. Thus we cannot, unless we have expert tact, or unless we are resigned to being called rude or erratic, turn from our door an unexpected visitor who arrives in the midst of a quarrel or an intimate conversation which we are loath to break off, or when we are at work. Yet, by suffering the intrusion, we accomplish nothing but ill, for our visitor senses that he is unwanted and does not understand why and we, on the other hand, are so displeased with him for not understanding that we fill our stilted, sporadic talk with little barbs, deeply offensive, so that when he leaves he may be resolving never to see us again. For there is, in the patois peculiar to the guest-host relationship, an ambiguity that penetrates to the very roots. Thus, the hostess who for the past hour has been grimacing with swallowed yawns, has, almost unconsciously, been emptying the ash trays and collecting the glasses, begs us, when we get up to leave, not to go yet, that it is still early, that she wants another drink and cannot have it unless we stay. If we do remain there eventually comes back to us, percolated through our mutual acquaintances, the remark she has made over the telephone the next morning, "So and So is very nice but someone should explain to him that there is a time beyond which one does not prolong a visit," or, "Like all great talkers, he's quite unaware of time. I was simply nodding in my chair and he didn't notice at all for he was only conscious of the sound of his own voice."

Philip was studiously avoiding me, and while the last thing I wanted was to talk with him, I was disturbed by the way in which, whenever our eyes met, he seemed not to see me at all and, if he found himself by accident standing near me, he immediately moved away, sometimes in the midst of a conversation. Hopestill, on the contrary, was almost constantly at my side. Her voice became progressively louder, as if she were trying to drown out Philip.

Guests were beginning to leave and there were only a dozen or so left in the drawing-room, loitering over a last cocktail. There came a general lull which was broken by Philip's clear voice saying to a young woman, the wife of a colleague of his, "I can't persuade Hope to go to Dr. Masters. She goes to a New York doctor just as she goes to a New York modiste. Fortunately our good friend Harry Morgan is decent enough to drive her down for her appointments."

As everyone knew, Hopestill was under the care of an obstetrician who served all the matrons of her circle, whose office was a few blocks from her house on Dartmouth Street. This very afternoon, she had been comparing notes with someone who had recently had a child and who declared that the process, under the supervision of Dr. Masters, was actually a pleasure. Hopestill had agreed warmly that she was devoted to him. Moreover, it was known that she had been only once to New York since her marriage and that time in the company of the Countess and Amy Brooks for the purpose of shopping and going to a Picasso exhibit. Yet, if she denied what her husband said, it would appear to the guests that she was in the habit of making trips either to New York or to some trysting place with Harry Morgan (Concord! thought the guests. Would she have the *nerve?*), using to her husband the excuse that she was visiting a doctor. Consequently, although the young woman with whom she had discussed Dr. Masters was still in the room, she said, laughing, "Oh, I only go to Dr. Ragsdale for good measure. I am quite loyal to Dr. Masters." Dr. Ragsdale, evidently the first name that came to her, had been her psychiatrist.

Philip smiled innocently across the room at her and said, "Why didn't you tell me you were seeing Dr. Masters, darling? I would have been greatly relieved to know that the product was not to be labeled 'made in New York.' "

The guests stared in hopeless embarrassment, full of pity for this naïve cuckold and regretful that he was so trusting of his wife that he had all but published her shocking subterfuges, and full of indignation that he had reached such a state of mind that his social sensitivity had been completely dulled. Specific pregnancies were not and never had been openly discussed in so loud a voice.

I waited for no more but left the room and went directly upstairs. As I picked up my coat from Hopestill's bed, I heard women talking in the dressing room adjoining. "Isn't there something in the Hippocratic oath he's disobeying?" said one. "He has the taste, thank fortune, to mention no names, but, for example, there's only one person he could have meant when he was ridiculing

511

plastic surgery. It's frightening to see how high and mighty he is." "I've never particularly cared for him," said another, "but I find him quite impossible now. And of course Hope has such strange notions. I dare say she picked them up in New York." "New York won't hurt a flea if it's a good flea," returned the first. "Mother says it's a question of blood. 'By their fruits shall ye know them,' says Mother." "Everyone was devoted to Mrs. Mather, you know, although I've heard she was a neurasthenic. And of course her father! No wonder Hope is what she is."

I was surprised by this comment on Miss Pride's dead sister for it was like the statement of the anti-Semitic, "To be sure I have known Jews whom I've liked. I was very fond of So and So, for instance, though even in him, you must admit, the objectionable characteristics of his race were not completely obliterated." Summary pronouncements upon personalities are common to people in society who, looking upon families as units almost as disjunct as nations, acquire a prejudice against or an affection for one member, make a declaration of war against or an alliance with the whole but make certain reservations in either case, in order to appear fair. In a moment, I overheard the first voice remark, "Miss Pride has always been rather underhanded, Mother says. It's perfectly absurd, at her age, to continue to regard Admiral Nephews as her beau especially when poor Mrs. Nephews is confined to her bed most of the time."

My departure, observed by no one, gave me a feeling of security, and painful as it might be to try to explain my dilemma to Nathan, I looked forward with pleasure to this evening which I would spend in his grubby rooms. On the way out, I bought a bottle of Liebfraumilch which came, green and dripping, out of an icechest, and, to take home later to Miss Pride, a bunch of mountain laurel which came, I was told by the vendor, from West Virginia. The jade-green leaves and the pink flowers like little bonbon cups made me think of Kakosan and her father's garden and the garden that Nathan had promised, in the delirium of his rapture, to build for her in some distant time and space, a castle in Spain, a vine-covered cottage, that shrine which varies according to the experience of the lovers, but is an essential of love's culture.

He had been trying for the last hour to telephone me and as I came through the murky basement, ducking under the obese pipes of the furnace that stretched out like the arms of an octopus, I found him emerging from the janitor's flat where he had been making one last attempt to reach me. I knew that he was in severe distress for it had been agreed at the beginning that he was never to call me at Miss Pride's. He told me tonelessly as his baffled eyes roved my face as if he half hoped to find there what he had lost, that two hours before, he had gone, by appointment, to Morgan's apartment to give him a lesson and had found that he was not there. But there was a note for him which the butler went to fetch. As he waited in the hall, he saw lying on the table a copy of the book, *Der Traum der Roten Kammer,* identical to the one Kakosan had given him. He could not decide whether to go away at once, leaving it untouched, maddened with uncertainty, or to probe its pages for evidence of her guilt, for marks, inscriptions, a chance slip of paper. He concluded that he must know, once and for all. First he opened it and smelled the pages which gave off, just as his did, a fragrance of her favorite scent (he had given her a flagon of it only a short time before), for it was her romantic habit to spray her letters and gifts. And then, upon the flyleaf, written with the curlicues of penmanship she affected only in notes to intimate friends, was the same girlish, warmhearted endorsement that appeared in his—and both in red ink—"For dearest Gacho from his Hototogisu." He had then torn a page from his notebook and written to Morgan that the pressure of examinations would prevent him from giving any more lessons.

Somewhere the block-flute which we often heard gave out a waggish excerpt from *The Well-Tempered Clavichord.* The surface of our cool, golden wine was marred by floating bits of cork. Nathan's face was three-quarters turned towards me and his birthmark looked like a shadow. I was conscious of these things in terms of a painting. They were a flat surface with only a representation of dimensions and I projected them into Paris, pretending that we were there and presently would go out for a *pernod* at the café Nathan had always said he would visit first, the Closerie des Lilas. Or I imagined us wandering through the crooked streets and over the bridges of Würzburg where, at any moment, we might pass my father or jostle the elbow of my cousin Peter. Or I was in Heidelberg and the block-flute became the song of a foreign bird entering through the windows of my ruby room.

If Nathan had been listening to me as I told him what I had come for, if he had heard me taking off, layer by layer, the wrappings of my jewel, I might have lost it forever. To my own ears, my revelation sounded banal, my terror was flaccid, unimportant, trumped-up. And I was surprised that I could not make him see what I so clearly saw myself: this churchly, peaceable hallucination. I had reached the end of my account and said, "I want to find the room, you see." But I was not really conscious of this need which, until now, had seemed so urgent, and when Nathan said, "I'm sorry. I haven't been listening. What did you say?" I was comforted that I had not, after all, admitted a trespasser. I returned to his immediate and frenzied world, feeling wise, mature, and safe.

3

In the spring, the young McAllisters opened their Concord house where they spent week-ends. Frequently they entertained and their country parties were more successful than those they had had in town, not only because there were more things to do—Hopestill, although she could not participate herself, organized horseback parties by moonlight, fitted up a badminton court with lights, arranged half a dozen other diversions that appealed to her guests, and gained for her the reputation of being a highly resourceful hostess—but also because Harry Morgan was no longer in evidence and Philip had for all practical purposes become once more the person everyone had liked and admired.

Guests, approaching the house at night, were deceived by its size. Under the influence of the darkness, out of which the ell loomed suddenly, incandescent between the blooming apple trees, it seemed of manorial proportions. The impression, actually false, was strengthened by the landscape. On two sides, there was a wide sweep of lawn bounded by low stone walls in the shadows of which grew violets and lilies-of-the-valley. At the back was a grove of pines, the entrance to which had been cleared into a precise avenue where I sometimes took a walk in the early morning, relishing the blackened trunks of the pruned trees and the rich brown of the resilient needles out of which, here and there, a shell-pink mushroom thrust its tender cap.

It was not the house itself that had been renovated in Harry Morgan's startling manner, but a smaller building which had formerly been Philip's grandfather's study. No one, not even the older McAllisters, could complain that there was anything amiss in the main house. The room into which one entered was ancient, stiff, yet withal charming. The wide, thickly knotted boards of the original floors were darkened to a rich red-brown. The dresses of some of the ladies and the hides of some of the hounds in the narrative wallpaper had faded from red to the color of a wine stain and from yellow to a sandy pallor. At one end of the room was a long fireplace whose white mantel was laden with pewter plates and tankards and, at either end, ivy cascading from amber bottles. It was not a room for casual lounging. The hostility to comfort seemed to have been intentional and every article of furniture had been designed to punish the flesh: the high-backed, cane-bottomed chairs, the cruel, three-cornered "roundabouts," the cherry settle, as harsh as a pew. But the eye was pleased by the pure white doors and by two corner cupboards facing one another at the far end of the room which showed, through leaded panes, old red china, silver goblets and a flurry of bibelots.

It had been a shock, on the night of the housewarming, to go from this eighteenth century parlor to the "studio." It was like the transition from one extreme of temperature to its opposite. The studio was a box in two stories, the lower one being given over to one large room, at the end of which was a completely outfitted bar, curved and equipped with a chromium foot-rail and high maple stools upholstered in red leather. On either side, French doors opened out, on one side to a path leading to the open slope between the main part of the house and the ell, on the other, to the pine grove. The new, waxed floor was bare. Here and there, scattered about its long expanse, were massive leather chairs of an obtuse structure, but one which afforded great bodily comfort. For tables, slabs of flawed plate glass with a greenish tinge lay on iron frames. Sofas, chairs, tables, bookshelves were low as if the people meant to use them had shrunk from a normal stature but had, at the same time, become uncommonly wide. The tall, thin guests, engulfed in the cavernous chairs, had seemed fragile and undernourished, no match for the thick, pint-sized and blood-red glasses out of which they drank.

A pair of pyramidal green vases stood on the mantelpiece and, with their insistent geometry, influenced the tulips springing from them to resemble also a "new idea" so that they did not belong to the world of nature but to that of mathematical design. There was a card table in whose four legs were inserted wedge-shaped shelves to hold the drinks of the players; a pair of crystal andirons for the remodeled fireplace which, as Philip had once said, looked no more like a fireplace than did Mr. Otis Whitney, and which he referred to as "the antrum." It was a low, square hole overhung by a vast rectangular marble shelf. A fire there could be tended, Miss Pride said, only by a dwarf and even he would be in danger of dashing his brains out. On the hearth stood a sandstone carving which represented three plump women in a happy embrace and was entitled "Breadline."

The Reverend McAllister, leading his mother about the room, had been less distressed by the bar than he had been by three pen and ink drawings which hung over a bookshelf and which produced an optical illusion: from one point of view they seemed to be illustrations of the myths of Venus and Adonis, Orpheus and Eurydice, and Narcissus, but by a slight change of focus, one saw that their subject was phallic, an assemblage of genitalia in coy half-ambush behind fronds, lotus flowers, and broad leaves of palmettos. The pictures had been a present from one of Hopestill's former friends on Joy Street, and although she was quite aware of their intention, if someone gasped and whispered in an appalled hiss that she evidently did not know what they were, she replied, "You're not the first person to tell me that, and I'm beginning to think there really *is* something ambiguous about them, though for the life of me I can't see it." It was quite true: she had seen the symbols in her first glance but had thereafter refused to let her eyes see anything but Orpheus holding his lute and Adonis lying in Venus' arms. As the latter, they were wholly without distinction, so that people thought either Hopestill's taste had gone terribly downhill or else that she was lying. As the clergyman stood before them, a dark blush stole upward from his stiff collar and he exclaimed to his mother, "I seem to be seeing things!" The old lady fetched her lorgnette from her handbag and moved up close to the pictures, although her son made an abortive attempt to stop her. She turned away, ferreting Hopestill out to kill her with a look, made particularly baleful by its filtration through her haughty instrument. Afterwards she was heard to say, "I shall never go into poor Edward's renovated library again. It gives me the same feeling of distress that I would have if the Old Manse were turned into a Howard Johnson." Miss Pride, refusing to acknowledge Harry Morgan's authorship of the changes, said of it, "Berthe von Happel, for all her eccentric notions about decorating an interior in Massachusetts, could not have produced that monstrosity. I do believe that children are born with a mental disease these days." And the Countess, looking with frank horror upon a kidney-shaped writing desk with a bakelite top and two chromium legs, one obese, the other as thin as a rail, murmured to me, "I dream! There has

517

not yet been devised a machine to make anything so out of the question as this."

It struck me that the studio was a rarefied extension of that state of mind which had sent Hopestill to Dr. Ragsdale's consulting room. It was the demonstration, in meaningless shapes, in dislocated structure, of the rebellion to which she had become addicted without volition. Rather, the volition had existed in the beginning as a defense against her aunt, but it had now evaporated. What had taken place between her and Philip after their cocktail party, I never guessed, but none of us saw Harry Morgan again, and from that time forward, Hopestill was altered. It was difficult to say exactly what was changed in her except her appearance. She seemed to have gone beyond fear and beyond rebellion, beyond, indeed, all feeling and to exist automatically. Perhaps she had surrendered completely to Philip's hatred and had allowed her physical being to share in her moral disintegration. The demolition of her beauty was, everyone thought, merely temporary. After her child was born, her skin would regain its luster and her eyes their animation; she would be as brilliantly organized as she had been before. I wondered, though, if she would ever again be beautiful, and I thought that perhaps what we had seen as beauty had not been beauty at all but another quality, an emotional or intellectual force so powerful that it actually appeared in her person.

It will be remembered that when I was a little girl, I thought Miss Pride was beautiful. Later on, I did not call her that, but neither did I call her ugly. It was that my feeling had changed: from admiration of her carriage and her clothes, I had progressed to love of her. If by saying "she is beautiful," we mean something more (as I must have meant even as a child), we mean this as a commentary on our relationship with her, we have actually said, "my gaze is freighted with feeling and my love has urged this face to resemble my sweet memory of it." And that "feeling," like the catalyst which remains stable, must remedy, through its unchanging agency, the imperfections of what we see. Conversely, when we hate, our hearts can deceive our senses so that we find hideous what has beauty inseparably in it. In this way I, at the time I had said Miss Pride was beautiful, had simultaneously said that my mother was ugly or else that her beauty was something gone bad.

Now it was not only Hopestill's illness that made me think she had always been ugly. There was a force at play in my altered perceptions that was subtler and stronger than that which had come from my expanding knowledge of beauty, or that gradual repudiation of childhood criteria, or that vision, enriched by maturity which allows one to speak of "types of beauty." Rather, it was that I had slowly come of age in knowledge of her and of her *milieu* into which I had willed myself. What marked the advent of my adulthood was a moment when I, standing in the doorway of the studio, saw her lying barefooted on the couch. She was alone and Kurt lay on the floor beside her. Her small, bony feet were busily prehensile, spryly fiddling with the cushions, the toes opening and shutting like a cat's claws, the arch bowed tightly. I thought of her green slippers and how I had longed to be Hopestill or a girl just like her. Now, receiving her greeting, hearing her barren voice, I thought, "Why, it is her life that is ugly and has been from the beginning."

"What shall I do, Miss Pride?" I asked.

She deliberated the chess-board, not my question, and replied, "And how do you feel about it? Do you think she will be cured?"

I told her my opinion and then I waited, my heart palpitating at the sight of her as in her green beaver hat and black suit, whose nocturnal sobriety was relieved only by the white collar of her mannish shirt, she moved the men across the board. I knew that today after church, she was to have luncheon at the house of a Coolidge and that the guest of honor was to be a Mrs. Roosevelt, née Cabot. "Thunder!" she said suddenly. "I've made a mistake. You've rattled me and it's all spoiled. Well, Sonia, I would regret parting company with you, my dear girl, for I find your services useful and your manners steadily improve. I suppose there are other establishments besides the one your mother is in now? Of a different character where one would pay her keep. At any rate, I shall investigate."

She had set the men up to begin again and was referring to her manual, holding it at arm's length in the far-sightedness of age which she would admit to no one but me. I believed I was dismissed and turned to go, but she said, without taking her eyes from the diagram she was following, "Sonia, let us say for the sake of argument that I *do* agree to set your mother up in a private sanitarium: What returns will you make to me?"

Thinking that she wanted to know how I would repay the money, I replied, "I don't know what I *can* do for many years, Miss Pride. But perhaps I could set her up myself. I don't spend what you give me, you know."

She squinted in my direction. "My dear child, the pin money I give you wouldn't go very far in one of those places. Mind you, I know all about them. They're run by bloodsuckers and don't be told anything different. Mrs. Eppington's oldest daughter, who is named something remarkable like Margarine, though of course it isn't that, married a Russian who went quite mad and was sent off to one of those fashionable bedlams at a ruinous cost that led her eventually to opening a little tea-room in Newport, where all you could get for love or money was some horrid red soup and salads made of Bartlett pears. Not that the marriage wouldn't have been absurd anyway. They had an apartment facing Washington Square, furnished as we don't furnish apartments in Boston, with couches that became beds and a bar in a closet, and I believe he had an icon, though he wasn't that sort of Russian. But I wander. No, Sonie, returns of that sort are not what I have in mind."

I started to speak, to assure her that I would not leave her. But she held up her hand for silence.

"If I undertake to support your mother as well as yourself, I shall be doing it with no thought of being paid back. I must repeat—although I am sure you return my devotion—that this is, I know, not much of a life for a girl your age. You have your moods, as we all do in our youth, our sentimental dreams of adventure, our fancied love affairs. Here, I've moved the rook too far." She changed the man's position. "You're unusually steady to be sure. I have only had inklings of a certain restiveness at times. I had it, for example, one evening not long ago, when you brought me that charming mountain laurel." She paused and glanced up at me. "Sonia, my father, a blunt man, but one who husbanded his words, brought me up in the belief that silence was the ideal policy, that honesty was next best, and that falsehood should be reserved for state occasions. For example, the only lie I ever heard him tell was to Mr. Charles Francis Adams' secretary who, under the impression that Papa was Mr. *Stanley* Pride, Consul General of Madrid, asked him to renew his acquaintance with the Secretary of the Navy at a dinner party at the Yacht Club. Papa said, 'I shall be delighted to renew my acquaintance with Mr. Adams.' He claimed that this was an equivocation rather than a direct lie, for he did not say Mr. *Charles Francis* Adams, and he could have meant Mr. Richard Chilton Adams or Mr. Archibald Revere Adams, two perfectly bona fide Adamses with whom he lunched every day at the Harvard Club. But silence, silence was what Papa chiefly counseled, and while I have so far as possible followed his precept, I must confess that there are times when you are a little *too* silent. Sometimes I cannot compass you. You become a cipher. I am afraid you will disappear altogether, vanish utterly. On that evening, for example, that you brought me the mountain laurel, I had the feeling while we talked that you were paying no attention to what you said. I did not ask you where you had been, though I had heard from Hopestill that you had not stayed for dinner, and I do not ask you now. But, my dear child, I cannot live with an image of you! If you are troubled by something, I implore you to let me know."

"That night," I said, "I had had too many cocktails at Hopestill's."

"I'm not entirely satisfied with that, but we shall let it go. You will keep me company, help me with my little book in the twilight of my life? You will not go away from Boston?"

"But I have no intention of going away from Boston!"
I cried.

She drew her game to a close and glancing up at the
clock which indicated twenty minutes before eleven, she
waved her hand toward the cabinet where I went to
pour out her sherry, I noticed that her hand shook; she
seemed to shrink as I watched and her hand, curled into
a trembling, beseeching cup, was like a beggar's, asking
for alms. It was not the sherry that she reached out to
seize, but it was myself. Putting the glass down beside
the chess-board, she extended her old claw to me.
"Agree!" she cried. "Agree never to leave me until I die!"
She smiled, but the terror of death was in her yellow eyes
and in her voice, and although I took the proffered hand
and smiled back at her, my whole soul retreated from
her in the appalled vision of her awful dependence, her
hideous cowardice. "Agree!" she was crying.

"I agree," I said, but my voice was unnatural and I
could feel perspiration collecting on my upper lip.

"I thought you wouldn't fail me. Poor Hope failed
me but I dare say it was partly my fault. Lord, I must
get to church! I wish you could hear our new Reverend
Jackson, from New Jersey, oddly enough, but he
preaches admirably. Good-by." And she went from the
room, her martial tread echoing with a decreasing resonance down the corridor until the diminuendo ceased
with the opening and closing of the outer door. Ethel
peered into the library to announce that Mac was ready.

On the way to Wolfburg, I was fretful, then scolded
myself for my directionless discontent. My problem had
been solved, and I could ask for nothing more. It was
perhaps only the spring air that made me suddenly *wan-
derlustig*. Perhaps it was Nathan's preparations to leave
for Paris that inspired me with thoughts of leaving Boston. He had often told me that he had money enough to
pay my passage. I envied him his mobility; my double
servitude, that to my mother and to Miss Pride, lay heavy
on me, and now, since our conversation in the library
this morning, the die was cast. I could not, morally, disappear. Just before we reached the asylum, I regained
control of myself, said I loved my mother and I loved

Miss Pride and Boston and that nothing could ever shake me from my resolve to live the rest of my life exactly as I was living it now.

My mother had been over her illness for some time, and as I waited in the corridor, I determined to outdo myself in tenderness and to tell her, if she was in despair, that she was to be moved soon to a house that she would like. One by one the visitors were summoned to the doctors' cells and I saw them then going off to the reception room, their hands full of flowers or fruit or magazines. And presently I was quite alone save for the tireless, ethereal voice warbling for Dr. Finkelstein and Dr. Short. A doctor crossed the hall and seeing me, said, "You aren't Miss Marburg, are you? Well, then, will you just step this way a moment?" We went into "my" doctor's office and my escort put his arm about my shoulder in a paternal affability. Another doctor besides mine was sitting on the window-ledge.

"Miss Marburg," said Dr. Tudor, "Dr. Burns, who spoke to you last winter about your mother, has presented his findings to us and we have been going over the case." He cleared his throat and said something in an undertone to his colleague at the window who then went to a filing case and brought back a bulging manila folder. "As you know, psychiatry is not a definitive science any more than medicine is. And diseased minds are as liable to relapse as are diseased bodies. And, if anything, they are more difficult to dignose accurately. Now let us say we have concluded that a man with pulmonary trouble has fibrosis. His symptoms, blood-tests, x-rays corroborate our opinion. He is kept in bed sufficiently long to remedy the trouble and we let him get up. But his fever rises, he begins to cough blood. We put him through another examination and find that he has tuberculosis of the lungs. We were probably not wrong in the first place. He *did* have fibrosis, but the tubercula bacilli, present in everyone, were working under our very noses, so slyly that none of our tests registered their progress. And now we must change our offensive, go back to a point near the starting line and begin again. Sometimes this happens in diseases of the mind. Originally we called your mother a 'manic depressive' and we had hopes of her complete recovery by simple treatment. But recently, particularly since her last attack of bronchitis, she has at times revealed symptoms of another disease, that is, catatonia."

The doctors all were watching me, and I had the feeling that they were taking note of everything, that they saw, and afterwards would discuss, the slight tic that began at the corner of my right eye.

Dr. Tudor continued, "I must tell you frankly that what we have concluded is not hopeful. No treatment we know of can certainly arrest the course of catatonia. Two days ago, your mother, who is now in a room by herself, was seized with a violent attack of vomiting, after which a muscular rigidity set in which has continued with rare intervals of relaxation. Sleep is possible only if we give her opiates. Her hallucinations have increased and have become so diverse that they appear entirely unrelated to anything we know of in her history. It is bad news, Miss Marburg, but like all bad news, it is better to know it at once."

"Do you mean, sir," I said, "that my mother will never be well again?"

"We can't talk in positive terms like that, as I have said. Patients have recovered. Many have made partial recoveries. Your mother may be one of those fortunate people who do regain their health. But it will take a long time and we can promise you nothing."

"Does she know? I mean, is she . . ."

"You mean, is she unhappy. Subjectively, that is. Let me assure you that she is in a world of her own. She is frightened, yes, but nothing we can do, nothing anyone can do, can remove the cause of her fright."

"Perhaps I could! Perhaps if I took her away, back to Chichester, she would be better."

The doctor rose and came around his desk, standing over me with a benevolent smile that was yet somehow hasty as if he wished to draw our interview to a close. "Believe me, there is nothing you can do. For the time being, your visits will be of no use. She is very sick."

"Poor Mamma," I murmured.

"You go on home now. When we have anything to report, we'll drop you a line. Some day you can see her again."

"Some day? But when?"

"That, I can't say."

"Will you give her my flowers?" I asked him, holding out the waxy Easter lilies I had bought that morning at Mr. Quince's. Dr. Tudor laid them on his desk and, finished with my case, led me to the door. The corridor was silent, for all the other visitors had gone to their melancholy meetings. My footsteps on the hard, rubbery floor sounded wet and loud, and the sunshine which stopped halfway from the door seemed remote, a golden bay. The indefatigable voice pursued me to the door, calling after me, "Doctor *Fink*-ull-stein! Doctor Shor-ort! Doctor Baaxter!" I was conscious of the terrible permanence of the asylum: forever, in the same inflections, the voice would chant and bleat the names of the same doctors, would echo through the glistening halls where every surface and every shadow was rounded, where even the doctors, at their most precise, smoothed down the sharp edges of what they said. Only the shafts of sunlight were sharp, but they were laden with round motes.

Poor Mamma! The red room, now that I needed it, would not come. Instead, there came to me the kitchen in Chichester and the hot night I had lain on the floor at my mother's feet. Suddenly, with the same kind of uneasiness I had felt when I thought Father Mulcahy said "God's warning," rather than "Good morning," I believed that her change had come about through my own treachery. For several days my conscience did not allow my thoughts to stray from my crime, and it tormented me, saying, "You must not believe them when they tell you she isn't conscious of her misery." But at last I conquered the moral voice, and when I told Miss Pride that henceforth I should be free on Sundays to accompany her to church, and she did not ask me for any explanation, the recrudescence of the pain and remorse was momentary. For the time being, I had walled up my mother into the farthest recess of my mind, knowing that the time would come when I must let her out again.

4

I had only just learned to smoke. Like most tyros, mistaking the habit for an exciting vice, I had elaborate equipment: holders, lighters, cases, and expensive, unusual cigarettes with which I sometimes vapored through a whole evening without requiring any other entertainment than that of watching the smoke I expelled ascending in lively indirection, the thin columns expanding or splitting, and of feeling an occasional pain in my diaphragm when I inhaled deeply as if a weight had plummeted downward through my esophagus and simultaneously had delivered to my skull a faintly dizzying blow. My imagination, consigning insidious properties to the cigarettes as if tobacco were cousin to opium, through its perhaps intentional error, rendered to my thoughts a dreamy quality, the reality of their objects being interrupted just as my vision of the walls, the windows, the furniture was interrupted by the smoke. I experienced, as in illness, an imperviousness to time, feeling that I was an inviolable bystander before whose serene eyes the raging world catapulted through arbitrary, mechanized hours.

I was sitting one afternoon in the Concord cemetery, leaning against a mossy tree. Below me was a green, stagnant pool into which now and again fell a twig or pebble but it made no sound for the surface of the water was velvety with mold. From behind me came the sound of the gardener's lawn-mower and the occasional click of a trowel on stone. The faintest wind soughed in the branches and brought me the smell of pine-needles and lilies-of-the-valley which grew in profusion there amongst the graves. As I had come up the slope called "Authors' Ridge," I had seen tourists gazing respectfully at Emerson's clumsy pink quartz gravestone and at the slabs marked "Alcott." I had known by their pronunciation that they were outlanders, for they accented Thoreau on the last syllable and pronounced Alcott with a short "a." Miss Pride detested sight-seers who visited the cemeteries. One day she had seen a man set up a tripod and produce a great lot of photographer's contraptions to make a snapshot of Longfellow's sarcophagus in the Mount Auburn graveyard. Taking the law into her own hands, she accosted him and said, "Look here, sir, this is not permitted." A rude man, he asked for her authority, and she replied, "I just stepped out of my house, Elmwood. My name is Mamie Lowell." No longer interested in Longfellow, he turned his camera on her and before she could collect her wits, he had taken her picture, saying, "This is even better. I'd rather bring 'em back alive than dead."

I knew that I should go on to Hopestill's house where I was to meet Miss Pride, but I was too languorous to move and repeatedly said to myself as I fitted a new cigarette into my carved holder, a present from Kakosan, that this would be the last. Between puffs, I held the holder horizontal and mused on its giver. It had been a token of her gratitude for my introduction of her to the Countess and had been sent, fantastically enough, by messenger who, in the employ of the telegraph company, had appeared vexed to be the porter of a parcel wrapped in pale blue tissue paper through whose silver ribbons three dark violets had been passed. "It ain't a telegram," he said, not by way of information since there could be no doubt on that point, but to show me that the absurd kickshaw he handed to me was in no way comparable to the important yellow envelopes which it was his proper function to deliver and several of which now conspicuously protruded from his breast pocket.

Kakosan, along with the present, had sent a note in her characteristically inconsistent style: upon a calling card giving her name in Japanese characters which ran like red bacteria down one side, she had written in a neat commerical school hand, "For a swell pal."

She, like Morgan, had disappeared from the blue drawing-room after the cocktail party, although, as I knew from Hopestill, she still received invitations. I concluded that she did not want to see me, remembering her frightened whisper, "That's Sonie Marburg," as I went up the stairs. She had made several futile attempts to see Nathan who steadfastly refused to consider a reconciliation. I had seen her only once, by accident. We met at dusk one day as I was going home along Commonwealth Avenue and we stopped beside a false magnolia shrub that had just come into flower. The white petals were smudged with pink and a lilac color; the thick, broad leaves were stiff and glossy as if they had been varnished. We talked only of the flowers and of Ginger Rogers. But on the following day, she sent me a set of brushes in an ivory box which she asked me to give to Nathan in memory of her. She had promised, long before, to teach him to write Japanese.

Nathan was torn between the desire to keep the brushes and the desire to wound Kakosan by returning them. I persuaded him to keep them since they would be a souvenir of that aspect of her he had loved. It was sometime before he ever used them, but when he did, practicing the few brush strokes he had learned from her, there came to the good side of his face a look of tenderness and longing, not for the person he no longer loved nor could love, but for the girl he had known in the beginning, had pursued like a bloodhound down the streets of Boston, hiding behind the subway kiosks as she, this still unknown beauty, stopped to buy fresh posies for her hair. Finally, after months of this delightful chase, he had accosted her at a street corner as they waited for the traffic to pass and had asked her if she knew of anyone who could give him lessons in Japanese. He would put down the brushes, pass his fingers over his marked cheek, and then would pour each of us a teacup of his violent sherry and tell me, for the thousandth time, that he would never love anyone but an Oriental woman again with the same kind of wonder that he had loved Yoshidasan in the first of those days.

I looked at my watch: at this very moment, Nathan's train for New York was leaving from the South Station. At midnight tomorrow, he would sail for France. I felt no particular sense of loss. This morning when I had told him good-by in his basement room, stripped of his personal gear, his books and trash and the photographs of Dostoievsky and Heine which had hung over his desk, I had, on an impulse, taken between my hands

528

his mutilated face and kissed him on the lips, and my kiss was not only a farewell to him but a resolute farewell to the temptations he had put in my path which had attempted to make my staid feet nomadic.

I flung my cigarette into the slimy pond and got up. If there were time, before we went back to Boston, I would take Kurt for a run through the woods behind Hopestill's house. I hoped that I would be offered one of the rum cocktails which had been invented by Harry Morgan, the household's former *arbiter bibendi*. Miss Pride had been making a tour of the Concord gardens in the company of several people whom she did not like, including the Mesdames McAllister, and I was confident that she would find herself in need of a restorative and would suggest to her niece that she "concoct a little something for us."

The old lady, all alone, was sitting on the lawn in a cane-bottomed chair. She was reading and did not hear my footsteps on the driveway. I was struck by the singular composition of the picture before my eyes: the spare black figure central in the expanse of shining grass and behind her the white house with its pedimented windows flanked by green shutters and its paneled door which was slightly ajar; burnishing the whole scene, giving to it that final fillip which distinguishes art from nature, was the clear light of early summer as skillfully executed as Vermeer's sunshine. She looked up with a smile as I approached.

"I hope you have enjoyed Hawthorne's grave better than I have done the gardens. I have no horticultural principles, yet had the great misfortune of being taken in tow by Mrs. Bigelow who feels very strongly about *tulipes noires*. I could not comfort her at Charity Brewster's, where she was confronted by several specimens."

I laughed and asked if Hopestill had accompanied her and she replied, "No. I don't know where she is. There isn't a sign of life about the place. Not even her animal is here."

Turning her eyes once again to her book, she indicated that she had spent enough time on me and I left her, making my way round the house to the studio. I helped myself generously to whiskey from the bar and put a Brahms piano concerto on the automatic phonograph. There was a sweet flamboyance to the music; it was like a plump and tender hug into which I burrowed luxuriously. Whiskey and music, I reflected, especially when taken together, made time fly incredibly fast. When the long concerto was finished, it was growing dark. A little wind had come up, threatening a storm. The air itself, more than the dark clouds, presaged the arrival of the thunder and the rain. I went back to the house to see if Hopestill had returned. Miss Pride had gone inside and the lawn was bare again save for the deepening shadows of the apple trees along the drive. There was a note for me thrust into the knocker which read: "Undone by the gardens I have gone upstairs to rest. When our tardy hostess arrives, tell her that since we have been given no tea, we shall expect dinner. Lucy Pride."

An hour later, just after the storm broke, Hopestill, wild-eyed, tousled, burst into the studio. She did not take off her wet raincoat but sprawled in a vermilion chair and the legs she stretched out before her were clad in jodhpurs, a fact that did not strike me as odd probably because her whiskey had rendered me impervious to surprise. Nor was I taken aback when she asked for the decanter of whiskey and took three large drinks neat and with a masculine rapidity.

"Do you believe in supernatural things?" she said quickly in a shrill voice and leaned forward with an eager look in her harried face.

"Some, I suppose." I regretted that I had drunk so much. I felt that there was something amiss and could not capture it.

"I mean, do you think hate can kill? There is a story about a woman who makes a doll in the image of another woman and burns it and the woman comes to some dire end, I think. It's been so long ago that I can't remember, but lately it's been haunting me."

"I don't believe in *that*," I said.

"Where's Aunt Lucy?" she asked, sitting up. "I want to ask her something. I want her to give me Mercy."

530

"What about Kurt? He'd kill her."

"Kurt? Oh . . ." Although she had poured herself a fourth glass of whiskey, she put it down before it had reached her lips and her face became instantly as pale as moonlight. "Kurt is dead," she said.

"Dead?"

"He was killed this afternoon . . . run over on the Bedford road."

"Was he off his leash? Weren't you with him?"

"No. He had been with me. I was riding. I had been running my horse and he was keeping up with me. Something frightened Chiquita—you know that little palomino mare?—and she stopped suddenly and reared. Kurt went tearing back, here I thought, but just now, as I was coming up the road, I found him."

"I wish you hadn't let him go with you," I cried. "Why didn't you follow him? Why were you a whole afternoon going after him, Hopestill? Didn't you care?"

"I had had a little accident and couldn't get back. Chiquita threw me."

Now I saw the riding trousers for the first time, wondered even in my alarm when she had got them to fit her now misshapen body, and my voice issued as a scream. "You are ill, then!"

"Yes, I suppose that I shall be very ill."

"I must call Philip." I stumbled to the door.

"Don't! He'll think I did it intentionally." She slipped off her short boots and her damp socks. "And of course I did. I made Chiquita do it. Once, I remembered, she threw me because I was wearing some Indian bracelets which rattled and the sound made her wild. I wore them today." And she pulled up the sleeve of her raincoat to show me three thin silver bands.

"You hadn't any right!" I said furiously and ran out and round to the house where, without disturbing Miss Pride, I telephoned Philip in Boston. As I waited for the sound of his voice, I could think of nothing but Hopestill's nimble feet as they had looked just now on the bare floor. They were somehow aged, for the skin was stretched and blanched and over the sharply knuckled bones, the tracery of veins stood out, blue and vermicular.

When I had got Philip and he promised to come at once, I went outside and stood in the drenching rain under an apple tree and over and over again hummed the phrase from *The Well-Tempered Clavichord,* the favorite of the anonymous block-flute player. And I did not leave my dripping sanctuary until, three-quarters of an hour later, the lights of Philip's car came bobbing through the trees.

When I went back to the cemetery in October, half a year after her death, I could not remember at once where Hopestill was buried. At the time of her funeral, I had not heeded any landmarks, and all I could see, in my mind's eye, was her grave as it was yawning for her casket and, a few minutes afterward, as it became a fresh mound and pile of flowers. Built on a hill, this graveyard of a small New Hampshire town was cut by a spiraling road into four or five sloping tiers, all similar in appearance. Identical paths ran parallel to each other and every tree, spruce, or cedar, or elm, was mimicked by a twin. Hopestill was at the very top, beside her father. They were farther up even than the graveyard's only mausoleum which, in a splendor of marble and genuflecting angels, housed the bones of a distinguished bishop, native of the town, who had returned from the wide world to settle in the dust of his last vestments under his boyhood's earth. Miss Pride, the connossieur of graves, had remarked as we drove away, "I'd *walk* if I were buried there. From what you can tell of his Grace's taste from that outrageous excrescence, he must have been a trying party when he was alive. I dare say he went in for parlor statuary."

It had begun to snow long before the bus that brought me had bumbled into the little town, and by the time I had found her stone, it was covered over by a deep layer of white which was replaced by another as soon as I had brushed it off. Indeed, there was no need for me to see it, for I clearly remembered the bare factual legend engraved on the plain granite oblong: that she had been born sometime and given the name Hopestill Pride Mather, and, being married, had taken McAllister, and that she had died a little more than twenty-one years after her birth. Nor was I, uncovering it and shielding it from the snowfall by my hunched-up body, urged by this physical symbol into recalling her better. I could not, as I crouched there, gazing, feel any harmony with her soul as it existed now or with her soul as it was arrested when her breathing stopped. I had not the faith as had her loving old friend the Admiral that her "spirit" still lived, though what he meant, approximately, was, "I have faith that Hopestill's soul continues its existence. What I *know* exists is my faith." But I granted the possibility that a soul might continue to operate in some imponderable place. There was, though, no affective coloring to the hypothesis: the grave could not become to me more than a little elevation of the soil and a flat stone and the skeleton which I visualized could not be hers but merely "skeleton," merely "heap of bones," and it was almost an accident that these bones had been the framework of someone I had known. I wondered when, in her grave, her hair had stopped growing and when its gloss was gone and if its dust were gray or red. I could see it yet, blandished by every change of light, the only remnant of her loveliness left when she lay in the fern-fingered casket. I shivered with the cold and with the memory of my mother's obsession over Ivan's hair which she thought had grown long in the water and was tangled with seaweed.

I had come this long way in the cold to finish her history, in a sense. I thought that if I saw her simple, conventional grave, like all the others, I would be able to efface from my memory the unhappiness of her last days. Although passion was withheld from me as I knelt and I was conscious of the cold which, chilling the dramatic core of my errand, made it folly, tears fell from my eyes, as tame as the windless snow. But they were tears almost of ennui because the death for which she had made so wild a preparation, no longer shocked me but seemed a languid petering out, like the expiring fire from which there comes a final flare and hiss of resin and then is ash. My weeping did not last and when I stood up, I saw that for a moment the snow had stopped and the air was clear enough for me to see the village's green roofs and white church spires.

The snow returned, colder than before, and obliterated the hill opposite the one on which the graveyard was built. A wind came down from the north, swift and soundless. As clearly as though it were borne by the rushing air, I heard the block-flute piping *The Well-Tempered Clavichord*, and trembled, recollecting how, all during her illness I had sat in my room on Pinckney Street humming it over and over again so that I would not hear the telephone which at any moment might bring us word that she had died. That revenant, whose single tune had joined my very blood so that its floating through the canals of my body depended for the tranquillity of its progress upon the cadences of that passage of music, purling in my ungifted throat, brought back, as the sight of her grave had been powerless to do, the person of Hopestill, not as the shrunken creature in the casket nor as the handsome girl of Boston, but of the little girl with the long red hair in the dining-room at the Hotel Barstow. All the time she had lain in the hospital dying, I had been able to think only of her bare feet and of the green slippers which I had defaced and slashed and of her recollection, that night in the studio, of the effigy-burning in *The Return of the Native*. Reason told me I was laughable and self-important in feeling myself an element in her death, but superstition rebuked me, made me deafen myself to the telephone with Bach.

She had been unrecognizable in her casket: her hair had been curled when half its beauty had been its straightness. A little rouge had been put on her lips which had never before been so treated. She was dressed in her wedding gown; she looked pinked and cooked like a frivolous cake. Mrs. Frothingham whispered in someone's ear, "Such a pretty girl to make such a plain corpse!"

I sat behind the straight, black backs of Philip and Miss Pride. Once Philip's shoulders lifted with a sigh. The Countess and Amy Brooks, the Hornblowers, the

Admiral, all the cousins, and the friends wept. The Mc-
Allisters were rigid like Miss Pride and Philip. The organ music seared me as it had done the day Hopestill
married, and the bright, hot sunlight on the wooden
floor of the little church stole into my very brain, burning it like liquid gold.

The minister said: "One thing have I desired of the
Lord, which I will require; even that I may dwell in
the house of the Lord all the days of my life, to behold
the fair beauty of the Lord and to visit his temple. For
in the time of trouble he shall hide me in his tabernacle; yea, in the secret place of his dwelling shall he
hide me, and set me up upon a rock of stone." The even
voice and the words were cooling and when we knelt to
pray, I mouthed the word "tabernacle" against the
smooth wood of the pew ahead of me.

Outside, in the merciless sunlight, the guests, with
their faces streaming, were grouped about on the lawn.
The white spire of the church pointed up to a sky where
shiny cumulus clouds were approached by gray rain
clouds. It was impossible to tell which went behind; the
rain was coming, we all knew, and we waited impatiently
for the signal to move on to the cemetery. It had been
quite a nuisance for some people to drive all the way up
on such an uncomfortable day. Of course, it was understandable that Hopestill should want to be buried by
her father. Even so . . . Little conversations, far removed from the dead girl, had started up everywhere,
and I heard a woman say to her companion, "He is very
interesting, I suppose, but he is so alien to anything I
have ever known. He has the word 'success' written all
over him like the measles and his children have come
down with it, too. The boy is very fat and was unmer-
cifully teased at St. Marks, but somehow or other he
has got in with Alexander Hornblower's son and they're
as thick as thieves. So he gets on, you see."

The Countess, more moved, I felt, than anyone except
perhaps myself and Philip, pressed a point-lace handkerchief to her eyes and said to Miss Pride, "Ah! Let
us pretend we are children again and are being escorted

by our mammas for the first time through the Tuileries. Wasn't it wonderful! Wasn't it bliss to be ignorant then and not . . ."

But now the casket was borne out and she did not finish. As we got into the automobiles, the merging of the clouds was completed; no blue sky was visible. A heavy rain fell, but in five minutes, by the time we had reached the gate of the cemetery, the storm was over.

Soon after the funeral, Miss Pride and I left Boston to spend the summer in Mattapoisett. She had not liked, she said, to leave me alone in Cambridge again and although it might seem strange, at her age, to begin going to a new place, she had been rejuvenated, she said, by our work on the memoirs. We had not spoken of Hopestill at any time.

I started down the graveyard hill. When I reached the road, my depression lifted and I was reassured that what I had just left *was* a tabernacle. I felt strangely energetic and as if I had completed a difficult task. It had not snowed here, but there was the bluish fog of autumn between the trees; there was the smell, acrid and like the moist hull of a walnut, of maple leaves that had begun to fall. From a second rise, the last little hill between the graveyard and the town, I saw that the mist was vanishing as I watched, and the sun was coming out. Snug and rubicund, splattered with scarlet and golden leaves, the earth lay at its meridian.

It was late afternoon when I got off the bus on Tremont Street and I hurried. Miss Pride was giving a little dinner party, in honor of the engagement of Amy Brooks to Edward Pingrey. She had invited the Countess and the Admiral, Baron Kalenkoff, Mr. James, the Arthur Hornblowers, and the Norwegian water-color painter. We were to start with cocktails made with the second best gin, but during dinner were to have the best champagne. "Champagne, you know, shouldn't be kept too long," she had said. "I have had this two years and I really must have it drunk up."

As I crossed the Common, where the leaves were curly underfoot and the squirrels were lively in their heyday, I glanced up at the State House dome still shining brightly in the last rays of the descending sun. I used it now as a sort of register for the light. My glance told me that if I made haste, that same glow burnishing the golden sphere would still be on my windows. I hurried on across Beacon Street, down Mount Vernon, then turned into Louisburg Square. For a few minutes I stood at the farthest corner, looking at Miss Pride's house through the high black iron palings with their tops shaped alternately like sword points and sword hilts. Every seventeenth bloomed with a flower on a stalk like Grecian drapery. Frost had made the beds of myrtle droop, but the stunted evergreens were bright. Small Aristides and Christopher Columbus regarded one another across the expanse of dead grass.

The sun had left the lower windows of our house, but mine and Hopestill's on the third floor, and the servants' above were red. I knew that within, the Cape Cod lighter on my hearth would cast forth blinding spears of light. For a moment, the scene seemed remembered, not perceived; it was as if some intelligence in my eyes themselves believed that they would take in the house with its green shutters, its brass letter-slot on the pure white door for the last time now and therefore saw all the details overlaid by a film, by an impalpable smoke like the twilight which presently would absorb the sun. Perhaps the time had passed and I could not, save in imagination, traverse the short cobblestoned space between my vantage point and the door to which I owned a key. But then, immediately upon the full development of my feeling that Boston was a part of the past for me just as it was so completely for Hopestill, I was brought back to the present time and knew again that these realities had not diminished in size and in distinctness. Years hence they would perhaps, after Miss Pride was dead, and they would be like the trees of an avenue which perspective reduces and shrouds.

Through the doorway of the building on which an inscription read: *Per Angusta ad Augusta,* a man and woman emerged. The man put on his bowler, then drew on his gray suède gloves. Their voices carried across the quiet square.

"Is it too late to look in at Lucy Pride's?" asked the woman.

Her companion took his watch out of his pocket. "It's six. Wouldn't that rush us? I dare say it wouldn't, but even so I'd rather not at this hour. Lincoln Nephews is usually the only one left by this time, the old loiterer."

The woman laughed. "You're only angry because he gave you your comeuppance in charades."

"*Ulalume!*" cried the man with bitter scorn. "Who but the most egotistical pedant would act out such a thing as that!"

They moved on down Pinckney Street and I ran across to Miss Pride's house. As I fitted my key to the lock, I noticed that the last of the rosy light had gone and that over the steep street lay a topaz patina. Far below, the fragment of the Charles was pure, cold, blue, and across it, a single sail, like a perfect iceberg, moved slowly. From within the house came the Admiral's voice, so close to me I knew he was about to open the door and I withdrew my key to wait for him. "Good-by Lucy. I'll be back in an hour. Back to Lucy's cot where she dwells in untrodden ways. Ma'am, that was a bang-up tea you gave me. I'm so stimulated I could go waltzing and not peter out till morning."

"Nonsense," came Miss Pride's voice. "My rum cakes have gone to your head, Lincoln. Run along now, do." The Admiral laughed and with him laughed his friend. "Ha! Ha!" her rare bark burst upon me and when the old man opened the door, he found me on the step laughing too, for what reason I was not sure. She was there, behind him. Under the lamplight, she appeared vigorous and even youthful, as if her age which she had passed on to her niece were buried along with Hopestill in New Hampshire. She looked again as she had done when I was five years old in Chichester; her flat, omniscient eyes seized mine, grappled with my brain, extracted what was there, and her meager lips said, "Sonie, my dear, come out of the cold. You'll never get to be an old lady if you don't take care of yourself."